THE COMPLETE RYNOSSEROS

THE COMPLETE RYNOSSEROS

THE ADVENTURES OF TOM RYNOSSEROS
VOLUME I

Terry Dowling

THE COMPLETE RYNOSSEROS
VOLUME I

COVER & INTERIOR ART

2 4 6 8 10 9 7 5 3

ISBN
978-1-786366-87-0

Design & Layout by Michael Smith

Printed and bound in England by TJ Books Limited

PS Publishing Ltd
Grosvenor House, 1 New Road
Hornsea, HU18 1PG, England

editor@pspublishing.co.uk
www.pspublishing.co.uk

CONTENTS

ACKNOWLEDGEMENTS

RYNOSSEROS

First published in 1990 by Aphelion Publications and subsequently by Guild America, 1993 and MirrorDanse, 2003.

"The Only Bird in Her Name" was first published in *Aphelion Science Fiction Magazine* No 1, 1986, Peter McNamara (Ed); "What We Did to the *Tyger*" in *Omega Science Digest* (Jan/Feb 1986) issue, Philip Gore (Ed); "Time of the Star" in *Aphelion Science Fiction Magazine* No. 3, 1986, Peter McNamara (Ed).

The lines of William Butler Yeats' verse quoted in "Mirage Diver" are from the poem "Byzantium."

Permission to quote lines from "Exil" by Paul Eluard (as given in Eleanor Levieux's translation of Antoine Terrasse's text for *Paul Delvaux* [J. Philip O'Hara; 1973]) courtesy of Editions Gallimard, Paris. All rights reserved.

BLUE TYSON

First published in 1992 by Aphelion Publications.© Terry Dowling 1992.

"A Dragon Between His Fingers" originally appeared in *Omega Science Digest*, May 1986, Philip Gore (Ed), and "Vanities" in *Glass Reptile Breakout*, Van Ikin (Ed), Centre for Studies in Australian Literature, 1991.

RYNOSSEROS

Come to Australia...

Journey through a bizarre and beautiful world where great sand-ships are the main form of travel, and the inhabitants of the richly cosmopolitan coastal cities can only marvel at the strange Ab'O societies of the interior.

Visit a future where terraforming, genetic engineering and formidable mental sciences are commonplace, and tribal satellites look down on unending wars between rival Ab'O States.

Travel with Tom Tyson through a land of merging cultures and philosophies, of myth and dream made real, a land of absolute possibility...

For Kerrie, who went on each new voyage just after Tom did, and for Jack, who in 1962 made such wonderful dragons.

INTRODUCTION

I WAS BORN IN 1947, THE SAME YEAR AS TERRY DOWLING, AND I've always felt a special connection because of it. I was born in Port Augusta, on the edge of Tribal territory, he, in Sydney, deep in the Nationals' land. We were already part of the story.

Because of 1947, our marbles were in the contentious National Service barrel together. His was drawn out, mine was not. The chance of an early meeting was missed.

But we always seemed to be moving together. As a surveyor, I worked for extended periods in the red desert country he began to write about, and as a reader of science fiction (there was plenty of time to read out there) I longed for stories that reflected what I was beginning to feel—indeed, what seeps into everyone's senses when they spend time in Australia's heartland. I didn't know then that he was working on it. Perhaps I should have.

In the early 80s, Terry began to be published. I began the move toward publishing. And from there, the space between us closed fast.

In 1985, I began editing/publishing *Aphelion Science Fiction Magazine*, and it wasn't long before criticism was levelled at me that, in story selection, Terry Dowling held sway. What can I say? It was true; every issued carried one of Terry's stories. But there was a reason for it, the very best of reasons: in the pile of manuscripts that quickly built up on my desk, Terry's shone out—and among his stories the *Rynosseros* tales positively glowed. He had captured something there, put so elegantly into words what I, in my brief time in that landscape, had only sensed.

And I had met Tom Tyson. I liked him from the first.

Someone (Chagall, I think) once said: "Show me a single great work where there is no poetry." It was the appreciation of that sentiment that Terry gifted to me—one of a number of gifts, two of which I'm going to mention here. The truth is, I learnt more about things literary from Terry than I can ever return. It was he who taught me what storytelling was—who pushed me beyond my narrow view and showed me where the poetry could be found. To put it as simply as I can: he taught me that storytelling was as much in the telling as in the story. (I can see him smiling to himself as he reads this, for the lesson wasn't without pain—for both of us—and which we both survived.)

Someone else once said that we only tell the truth in our fiction. I've read too many stories, met too many writers, not to believe it. Terry, for instance, has put more of himself into Tom Tyson than he'd ever care to admit (though he might surprise me; he often does). The curious thing for me, however, is to see how much of Tom has flowed back into Terry. I often wonder how aware he is of that, or, if he is aware, whether it worries him that it's happened. He need not worry. It's been a mutually beneficial exchange. As for me: I sometimes find it a little uncanny. I know both of them so well that there are moments in a conversation when I'm not at all sure which one I'm talking to.

The Aphelion paperback line produced thirteen books, and five of those were by Terry Dowling (with three in the *Rynosseros* cycle). Terry was our most published author, and for good reasons. Two of those reasons were the very best a publisher can have: a) the quality of his work made us proud to have our name against it, and b) Terry sold. *Rynosseros* remains Aphelion's best selling book; long after we had "moved" our print run, requests for copies kept coming in—they come in to this day. It's an association that contained all the normal tensions between a writer and a publisher, but it's always been a pleasure. We (Mariann and I) only hope that Terry feels the same way.

One of my regrets when I brought the Aphelion paperback line to a close was that I'd never complete the *Rynosseros* cycle. Maybe MirrorDanse can finish what Aphelion began, see Tom to the end of his journey, and ease the restless spirits of both the Captain and his creator. When that does happen—as someday it must—I need to get myself to Sydney, to talk to Terry, to see if it's changed him, to see if he's finally tucked that other persona away. I suspect he won't have, that Tom has become too much a part of him to ever leave. I'll be reassured if that's the case, for I'm immensely fond of both of them. The loss of either would be hard to bear.

And that other gift I mentioned:

In the period between the magazine and *Rynosseros*, I spent some 12 months working in the area between Roxby Downs and the town's borefield at Lake Eyre South. There was nothing quite as exhilarating as the 140-kilometre run up the borefield track, our survey vehicle rolling across a vast country that European civilisation seemed unable to touch.

But we knew this place, myself and my two companions—for they had discovered the magazines and manuscripts I kept in my room. This was Tom country, stretching away as far as the eye could see. On days like those, as we ran north with salt-bush and rolling dunes slipping by and the clay-base road drumming under our tyres, it was as if we were really there, part of the remarkable dream.

And, if we looked out into the heat haze, the sandship *Rynosseros* was just visible, running parallel to us, like a ghost ship among the dunes, kites and parafoils bare outlines against the sharp blue sky. There were moments, on days like that, when I swear I could make out Tom's outline, standing on the fore-deck, gaze traversing the rust-red landscape, picking his ship's path, focusing on his destiny, always somewhere up ahead.

Then, if I watched long enough, sometimes it happened. Tom's head would turn, and he would look across to where our tiny vehicle shadowed him. Perhaps it was the nature of the place, or perhaps it was me, immersed too long in his story, but I would see the quick flash of his smile, his hand half-rise from the deck rail as he acknowledged my presence. It was purely a dream, part of me knew that, but another part of me knew it was not. And those parts were only too happy to co-exist.

That was the best of Terry's gifts to me, the one I can truly never repay.

But enough from me. I'm a reader, like you.

There's a master storyteller waiting. Let's listen to his words.

—Peter McNamara
Adelaide, 2003

Colouring the Captains

1

In the Great Passage Book there are Seven Coloured Captains. Their names have become famous: Golden Afervarro, Red Lucas, White Massen, Green Glaive, Yellow Traven, Black Doloroso, and the last to be chosen—the Madman, Blue Tyson, known to many as Tom Rynosseros.

There are other National captains who have colours in their names—Rust Morganus is one, and Gray Ridley, and the legendary Black Jack Temenos, to name a few—just as there are other great captains, high and low, who are permitted to cross most of the tribal territories. But there are only seven Nationals who are allowed to use all Roads, to cross all the Ab'O States in their fine sand-ships, whose names and Colours have been entered in the Great Passage Book.

Is this what you wanted to hear? You who sleep there in Cold People storage, in your long safe cryogenic sleeves, waiting in your hundreds to be grafted out on to constructs and surrogate bodies, to make the Grand Tour, hungry for sensate life again.

I tell you, there would be none of it, no hope for you at all were it not for the Seven. This circuit is shielded; the link is still open, one of the few I have left, so I can tell you. The world out here has changed since first you slept. The abiding spirit of an age can be rooted to many things: a preoccupation with identity, with new lands and frontiers, with sexuality, morality or repression, nostalgia for the past, with luxury and sacrifice. Then know that not since Pharaonic Egypt, not since the Mexican and Madagascan festivals of the dead, not since the Pre-Columbian civilisations of America has such a preoccupation with death marked an age. Or rather, seen another way, a preoccupation with making, understanding and holding onto life—all part of the same *Zeitgeist*, the same *Weltanschauung*.

If I sound the apologist for the Ab'O Princes, the Clever Men and their AI and genetic planning, bear with me. Some of you, the recent ones, will remember the belltree program, how it was meant to nibble at the concepts of life and death, how it reflected the crucial and vibrant spirit of an age.

So then, let me tell you. Let me answer the questions the sample minds have put to generations of Coldmasters without success, while waiting and longing for life again.

10 I am a belltree. It is true. Though it shocks many of you and puzzles others, the more ancient personalities among you, I am a half-life creation, a lowly machine to some, with a plasmatic intelligence crafted around a crystalline lattice. Though I murmur to you in your dreams, I stand here beside a rarely used desert Road, with paint peeling from the lower totemic eight feet of my fourteen-foot shaft, and half my sensors damaged by wind and sun and time.

My crystalline core comes from the great I-D tribal belltrees at Tell, and they, in turn, from the Iseult-Darrian prototypes at Seth-Ammon Photemos. My essence was decanted from the life-bottle of one of those marvellous structures; my identity shares some memories from the host-core.

And, as I say, I am well acquainted with the seven Captains. In a sense, I am an oracle to them, no less than to the Ab'O tribes who caused me to be made. If the truth be told, and I cannot prove this to you yet, though you will know the truth in time, I am the one who gave them their Colours. It is true and it means everything to me.

My core was originally scheduled for the Tell Sculptury. I was to have become a prime Aulus or a Twilister, fashioned by the greatest organic-sculptors we have in Australia, but there were debts to pay in those early days of no patrons and huge research costs, and my inception was first delayed, then made forfeit. It was a bad year, and my core was sublet to the Immortality factors at Tell. They bonded me to two fading cryogenic personalities like yourselves, James and Bymer, two old Cold People whose bodies were spoiling and who had paid handsomely to have their matrices grafted out into biotectic life, their final chance (apart from the charling injections) for any kind of life considering.

So I lost my pedigree, my pure link with the great Iseult-Darrians. I became an ordinary junk-post, a humble road-sculpture out on the desert, spoiling, piggybacking two ghosts, neglected, with dwindling subtlety in my receptors and limited function.

But a strange and wonderful thing happened, the first of many in this story I am telling you.

James and Bymer's bonding—for all the wealth the factors got from their estates, and despite the guarantees—was only partially successful. My spliced and re-routed I-D core was simply too strong for a true graft, despite the careful dampening and the repressors. Instead of losing my own identity, it went the other way: my passengers lost theirs in the rallying identity matrix. As a host-post I failed, and quietly out here on the desert, James and Bymer, your friends, Cold People veterans like yourselves, became more and more dim, the thing you all fear.

Now see how the Ab'Os trap themselves (and note it, for you will wake into a world built on this).

Once the Iseult-Darrian prototypes were ratified by the Princes as true life, as an integral part of the Dreamtime fabric, they immediately had the Tell authorities do a genealogy on all the I-D cores. The lattices were codified; the disposition of every drop from the life-bottles registered and traced.

They found me standing by my forgotten Road, faltering and in poor repair, with the ghosts of two dead humans whispering through my frame, coming and going like the lonely night winds which had kept me company for so many years. The biotects were vastly relieved to find the hosting hadn't taken, but they discovered that James and Bymer, what was left of them, nested deeply in my plasmatic soul. The recovery team did an immediate search on my two passengers, to find if my life—they called it that, even then—was tainted at all. That search took them back many years, a long way indeed, but Immortality produced the mandatory records as readily as the Tell staff had mine.

James had been a semiologist, a specialist in signs; Bymer was the colour symbologist who had once advised the Ab'O biotects on the inlay designs for the Living Towers at Fosti. Even by tribal standards, they were great men, worthy men. Had been.

The problem wasn't so great then, after all. The technicians restored and adjusted my sensors, honed my dim-recall rods, added valuable new laminations to my diligent, bounty-box and shaft. Artists touched up the totemic panels on the lower eight feet; Clever Men consecrated them anew.

But they couldn't move me. Their own rulings about the ritual placement of road-trees, arrived at more than a century before, back when the belltree program became the definitive artform of the tribes, the focal point and repository for all their life-science endeavours, meant that I had to stay out in the desert, measuring my length of Road for passing ships, precious and refurbished, belonging to no tribe, a rogue Iseult-Darrian. A rogue, do you see?

They kept the secret of my value well and made the refurbishing subtle so no passersby would tell. And without knowing it, they gave me the Captains.

The story of Tom, my last Captain, resolving even now, today, as I speak, is the story of them all. Let me tell you of it and of him.

2

Sajanna Marron Best, that hard wise wonderful woman, two hundred years old, once proud, once cruel, once young and, then, achingly beautiful, the subject of more legends and longings than you would believe to see her now, had you the eyes, found Tom on the Sand Quay at Twilight Beach that day. She moved among the great sand-ship hulls under a hot morning sun, with three robed Kurdaitcha assassins, and stopped by the mooring where

Tom and his old kitemaster, Scarbo, were discussing their charvolant, *Rynosseros*, so recently won in the ship-lotteries at Cyrimiri. The rest of Tom's crew—Rim, Tremba and Kylas—were still on shore leave.

"We must talk," she said with characteristic directness, startling both men with her strong distinctive voice and with her fearsome entourage of avengers. When she introduced herself, the looks of astonishment on their faces remained. Because of the implants in Sajanna and her silent companions, I know what took place.

Ab'Os on the Sand Quay. Tom and his kitemaster were no doubt wondering why. Kurdaitcha and this one, the ancient Ab'O biotect, this famous, worn, haggard scientist away from her labs and testing-chambers. I saw it on their faces. Around them, other sand-sailors watched with awe and amused curiosity, then turned away, not wanting to antagonise Kurdaitcha.

The small group boarded *Rynosseros* then, and below-deck in the main cabin, with Scarbo posted on the docks to warn off intruders, she announced her purpose. She told Tom about the Captains and about me, a little of the account I have just given you, and, typical of Sajanna, she was amazingly frank.

And understand! Here were two people who came to love one another in their short time together, who might have been lovers, dear friends, life companions. Here they were, separated by more than a hundred and seventy years, by too much time, each of them trapped in the years which I know is the constant, charming, despair-ridden tragedy of human life—the source of the strange longing looks men and women sometimes show, the incommunicable sadness in the eyes of the old regarding the oblivious young. The might-have-beens.

Sajanna showed nothing of this, though telemetry revealed the warmth of her response to him, and gave what she saw: the tanned, blue-eyed face of a man barely thirty, with a full moustache, strong browline and brown hair swept back in the style of so many National sailors; a man of medium height and build, wearing plain buff-coloured mission fatigues adorned only by the bright new charvi insignia below the right shoulder. She did not mention that she had watched his dreams in the Madhouse, that she had sought him for reasons she would never divulge to another living thing apart from me—her child. She spoke briefly of the six Captains in the Great Passage Book, then concluded in her calm unhurried way.

"Since I am the last of the Tell biotects responsible for the graftings which produced this rogue tree, it has been decided that I am responsible for it now. These stony-faced avengi you see about me here are both my servants and, in a sense, my executioners. Their leader has yet again made me an honorary Pan-Tribal Kurdaitcha. He has Clever Men who will hunt me, sing me, for failing my mission, or dispose of me some other way unless I can account for why the names of National captains are appearing in the Book."

"This is Dreamtime business," Tom said.

"Absolutely. You know what the oracle trees mean to us, I think. Are supposed to mean. The belltree program was part of a sacred quest in the truest possible sense. We esteemed that Artificial Life then more than we do now, with proper reverence for what we had done. Think of it! Non-human life conferring with us, counselling us, made by us but never owned, sharing life-views we had nurtured but could never have ourselves. They became privileged and wise counsellors—the best, the most sophisticated of them. It was considered fitting, and there is a powerful tradition still, despite the years of cynicism and uncertainty. Technically, they remain oracles, though mostly they are cherished as quaint and fascinating relics. Their status was never revoked, you see, probably because it was never used this way. This rogue is giving out Colours to non-Ab'O captains of its own choosing, then entering those names in our Records beside those of our greatest battle-captains."

"How did it start?" Tom asked. "What made the rogue give its first Colour and cause all this?"

Sajanna shook her head, unable to risk more, forced to hide so much from this man she needed more than she could say, if indeed he was the right choice. "Persecution, Captain, though, admittedly, we were slow in reading the signs for what they were: the budget cutbacks, the political disfavour, the increasingly strict security measures—allegedly because of threats from True-Lifer groups. Fewer projects were sanctioned; fewer AIs cleared for release. We discussed the trends and where they could lead; we were aware of

True-Lifer factions gaining power. And, ironically, this tree saw it all and understood something had to be done. Perhaps it monitored strategy discussions or com messages, who can say? It was always inquisitive and surprisingly resourceful. It took a chance; made sure our expertise was needed. It went straight to our most prized honour system and entered National names."

As Tom listened, I think he sensed the old woman's dilemma, suspected that she was being made to serve her enemies, and had to play a part, both revealing *and* concealing. The intent looks of her silent companions must have confirmed it.

"Is there method here?" he said. "Were they the first Nationals to happen along?"

"Oh no. These men were carefully selected. They passed some test, were chosen; then completed some service for the tree. We need to know what these duties were. We need to control this, you understand. Nothing like it has ever happened before. This rogue is an I-D oracle after all. We must accept its rulings unilaterally the moment they appear in our comp systems. So we must stop it."

"Tribal investigators would—"

Sajanna laughed, a sharp bark of amusement.

"Do you know what it said to our tribal investigators, to our senior biotects, to me? Not a word! Not to me, not even to the ones who restored the thing. Six Nationals are its only audience now. Each one Coloured and named in the Great Passage Book. We suspect it will talk to another National captain."

"And will probably give a Colour and a mandate. Do you want that?"

"That is our gamble, Captain Tyson. And our deal. You are newly out of the Madhouse, with reasons to seek Ab'O support. You have just won your ship; now you need licences, accreditation, funds."

"Yes," Tom said. "I do."

"But more to the point, you know the machines in the Madhouse. I've seen your records. You will not be swayed or wooed by Artificial Life as others might. We will give you a permit and the details of where this road-post is located. Yes, it will probably Colour you and give you the same liberties as the rest, but this time the captain we send will have made a blood oath with us first, to serve us and use those same perquisites for the tribes once he has put an end to the rogue's mischief. The only National captain the tree gets now will be our man. Working on our terms. The tree can have you as its seventh, briefly, while we solve the mystery, solve the problem. And you *will* solve the mystery!"

"If I can."

"You will," Sajanna said, and some of the old Kurdaitcha ruthlessness returned to her eyes, fed by bitterness and disillusionment, by the fast-fading hopes and longings this woman had that the tribes might someday accept the very life alternatives they sought so relentlessly.

"You have been turning back other National ships approaching the area?"

"True."

"Destroying any?"

"Only two. Satellites found them first. Laser strikes from orbit. The rest have been turned back. All ships are barred from the region indefinitely. The other Coloured Captains could get through, but

they know how provocative that would be right now. We need only worry about strays and pirates, the reckless or the curious, bold Nationals on a dare, freight or mercenary captains who think running any blockade is fun."

"You mean to use the tree's own system against it."

"That is the plan," Sajanna said, and I believe Tom did understand—was sure that she spoke now for someone else, someone who had only lately decided to use this approach to the problem.

There was a pause while he considered the situation.

"Well?" the old woman said when a silent minute had elapsed.

"I have no choice here," Tom answered.

Sajanna gave another bitter laugh. "No. Nor have I."

Tom did research that afternoon. He sat in the stern cabin at his ship's comp systems and used Sajanna's private codes to access the data he needed, while two Kurdaitcha waited on deck and the third went off about some errand.

Sajanna came in at 1450 and sat to one side in a hand-carved chair, her frail lined-velvet hands pressed over her dark-velvet face as she meditated, probably reflecting on the weave of chance which had brought her to this.

First, Tom confirmed all that the old biotect had told him, that across nearly ten years the rogue belltree had chosen six National captains to be its champions, and that for the performance of some unknown task—and in order to do it—each had been assigned a Colour and given an all-lander mandate, a gift beyond price for any National limited to the coastal territories.

The Colours were easy to fathom: my ghost, Bymer, had been a colour symbologist after all. To any observers, he had apparently supplied me with my colour symbols, just as James's ghost would have provided the mind-sets elevating those colours into special meanings, my private mysteries.

For Tom, however, translating the colour symbols was Task Number Three. The first was to discover what secret missions had prompted the action; the second was to stop the process.

Towards evening, while he was reviewing the Tell material on personality bonding, Sajanna left her chair and came to stand by him. Tom did not hear her. He pushed back from the display to find her there, then asked the question that let her reveal more of her true position. He had already deduced she would be monitored. Now he entered into the conspiracy, and spoke for the benefit of her unseen superiors.

"Dr Best . . . Sajanna"—she did not correct him—"if this tree is serving the Dreamtime for you all, why not let it give out its Colours, do what it likes?"

And his eyes explored the flawed velvet of her face. Perhaps he sought further confirmation. Perhaps he found it in the barest suggestion of a smile.

"I mentioned politics," Sajanna said softly. "Expedience. The last thing the tribes want are non-Ab'O heroes acquiring status, usurping the Dreamtime privileges, bringing other Nationals into our deserts."

"But if this Iseult-Darrian is an oracle tree, as you say, then its rulings remain sacred. Unless, of course, the tribes proclaim it mad, say it was tainted by James and Bymer. That would void its rulings wouldn't it?"

"They tried that," Sajanna said. "But other Iseult-Darrians endorsed its decisions, said the rogue was sane and whole. National interest increased, as you can imagine."

"Then you *must* accept the Captains too, accept that there is some worth-while reason behind it all." I think Tom spoke to show he was her ally.

"Exactly what I have told the tribes," Sajanna said, acknowledging his place in this, confirming hers. Then she moved to the large stern windows to watch dusk settle on the desert beyond. "They do accept—grudgingly, secretly, many of the Princes. But in view of so little information about a dangerous trend, it is expedient for them that the trend be controlled."

Tom frowned. "And how many other 'honorary' Kurdaitcha like yourself have forfeited their lives already because of this? Six?"

The Ab'O woman turned to him and nodded. "Yes."

"And they were your colleagues at Tell, weren't they?"

"Yes," she said, and I knew she admired his quickness. "It is as you saw in my files. The first captain was Phaon Afervarro, the famous songsmith himself. When the tree gave him Gold, Satra Amanty was in charge of the Tell life-houses, the wise leader of our team, a great man, an innovative man, my teacher. The head of the Pan-Tribals appointed him honorary Kurdaitcha as I am now, his life held forfeit, and gave him a month—no more—to discover why the tree had done it. At the end of that time, the singers began. His body was found at his desk shortly afterwards."

"That is madness!" Tom said.

"It is. A useful and expedient tradition also," the old biotect said, always concealing her heartbreak because the assassins were listening and there were things she had to do. "And a way for worried Princes and tribal factions to limit the power of the life-houses, to make up for the more disturbing excesses of ambitious predecessors. When the tree gave Lucas Red a year later, Amanty's successor suffered the same fate. This time, however, realising the difficulty of the problem, and noting National media interest, they allowed Chen Colla two months."

"But no luck?"

"Again, no. They sang him too, hunted him down his mind-line. He was found lying dead in the desert. You see—"

But Tom indicated the screen, to save her the sudden rush of distress he read in her voice. "There were seven biotects on the original Iseult-Darrian project. They mean to halt the opposition from that quarter by eliminating the whole team."

Sajanna nodded, and I noted her relief, her gratitude again, though it barely reached her ancient face. The same relief, the same gratitude Amanty, Colla and the rest had felt when their appointed Captains were proven to be worthy. "Yes. That is what they intend. The head of the Pan-Tribal Kurdaitcha is Bolo May." (At last she named him!) "He has used these alarming dispensations from the rogue to justify doing what he has wanted to do for years: the dismantling of all Artificial Life programs." And the old scientist smiled. "He is our Matthew Hopkins—our Witchfinder General."

"What of the rest?" Tom asked, saying what he already knew from comp, speaking it to give what reassurance he could. "Four other Captains means—"

"The same. Eventually the same. Alliga, Mitroy, Lang, my old friend Taber, all forfeit. The rogue refused to speak to any of them. The chosen Captains said nothing; most went on voyages to distant States, using their special status to evade Kurdaitcha and Clever Men. It was as if the tree was taunting us. Each time we lost a chief investigator, the tree created a new Captain, and so caused Bolo May to select yet another of us. Now, finally, after ten years, it is my turn. Bolo May kept me for last, I'm certain, and—for reasons approved by the tribes—I have been given far less time than Amanty had. Less than a week."

"But why so little time?" Tom demanded. "If the tribes want this solved, surely they would give a more realistic time-frame."

Sajanna seemed distracted as she answered him. "No. It has already taken too long. Now they want this business finalised as soon as possible."

Listening to them talk, to what Tom said and how, made me sure of it then, that I had made a good choice. He had clearly grasped the reason behind Sajanna's sudden detachment. The biotect was monitored and so would need to show open support for Bolo May's commission from the tribes. But she had lost her dearest, longest, only friends, and now her life—rendered useless in nearly every way—was at stake as well, the only counter she had left in the game. That's what well-chosen, life-sensitive Tom must have realised, must have read in the tired ancient eyes.

"My answer is you, Captain Tyson," Sajanna said. "Tomorrow you go out to the tree." Then, regardless of the listening assassins, she said the damning words. "May believes I chose you because of your reactions to the AI machines in the Madhouse. What he will now learn is that I chose you *in spite of* those reactions as well, for the dreams and images you had which showed such a natural affinity for life, any life, and for our evolving and yet unchanging Dreamtime."

And moving with surprising swiftness, she went to the cabin door and locked it.

"Quickly now!" she said, drawing a small-bladed knife from her robe. "Let me have your oath before the others come. Whatever happens, I'll have that, and May might just have one more National name to contend with."

And Tom watched as the narrow blade drew blood from his wrist and from her own, then repeated the words, concentrating on the dialect, not knowing what it was he said, concentrating even when fists pounded on the door, and the door burst open, and the armed avengi were upon them.

3

Tom stood by the quiet desert Road looking up at me, shading his eyes from the glare of late morning sunlight reflected off the hot sand. All about us was desolation, just the Road stretching off in one direction to lose itself in some low hills, in the other gradually dropping down to an ancient watercourse where it could be seen winding a few times before it too vanished from sight. Apart from those few hills and that dry riverbed, we were the only features in the hot unmoving terrain.

Tom was studying me, no doubt wondering how an ordinary junk-post could hold such power over the tribes.

"I'm Tom Tyson," he said finally, calling out across the dry air. His words echoed down the Road, resounded in the dry riverbed, came back to us from the quiet hills. His voice was lower when he spoke next. "I've walked six k's in from their perimeter to see you."

I did not answer him, letting the silence of my place touch his soul, testing him too.

"No more Nationals will be coming unless we reach an understanding," he told me.

Still I was silent, though I used the small monitor mote Sajanna had pasted on his forehead to do a fascinating thing, to scan myself as he saw me: the narrow shaft rising six feet above the eight-foot totemic trunk, the sensor spines thrusting out, the diligent canister at the top of the main stem.

Rather than use the portable comlink he wore at one ear, I activated the old voice circuit I have used when playing out the role of oracle to wandering nomads.

"Ten years ago," I said, "the Ab'Os discovered they could not close down the belltree program at Tell and Seth-Ammon Photemos. Once made public and celebrated throughout the world, they could not demean their own amazing achievement so easily."

Tom looked about him, once, twice, then moved in closer.

"The Princes and Clever Men met the crisis in a fitting manner. I had just been restored; I had excellent data and function resources. I learned that the first part of their plan was to eliminate gradually, steadily, the entire research team responsible for the Iseult-Darrian strain, to remove the respected resistance from that quarter over a period of years—a lab accident, or an assassination attempt by angry National True-Lifers.

"Bolo May was appointed by Pan-Tribal dispensation and selected a strategy group. I found the means to delay them, to make them cautious. I acted in a provocative way, in a manner which I knew would make them need those very Tell specialists they meant to discredit and then discreetly destroy."

"You gave a Colour," Tom said. "Your oracle-post function."

"True. Dreamtime function. I appointed a National to all-lander status. Phaon Afervarro. And I gave out an undisclosed mission—not to an Ab'O who deserved such a privilege, but to my own first Captain."

"They got around that."

"Yes. One by one they made the Tell biotects responsible for discovering how and why the aberration occurred."

"They would have been killed anyway," Tom said, standing quite close now, reacting to the ion flux from my bounty-box, affected by the mood-bending emissions.

"Yes. But at least the Kurdaitcha did not return to their original intention. It was a delaying tactic only. It bought ten years in which they needed those specialists. But they were shrewd, those avengi. They would not let the Tell biotects communicate with me directly, no comlink, no transmissions of any kind. Bolo May made sure of this."

"He must have had other trees, other comp systems probe you. Then and now."

Which was another astute observation from Tom Tyson.

"Yes. Constantly. But there is the randomising element of James and Bymer," I told him. "My own strategy is filtered through mysteries devised by identity matrices they cannot access, rendered in code. Bolo May can yet harm the things I love, but he cannot decide how to undo the harm I have done in adding to the Great Passage Book, and he cannot understand what it is I am doing."

"What of the missions you gave the Captains?" Tom asked, serving Sajanna, honouring the small wound on the inside of his right wrist where the blood-bond had been drawn. I was grateful to him for that though it put us at odds for this first meeting. "Could May not find ways of invalidating whatever they were?"

"You are still new to the Roads, Tom," I said. "A mandate is binding on all or none. Either the Great Passage Book exists and is valid with its liberties and honours or it doesn't and isn't. The Kurdaitcha tried, but the missions were carried out. There is that much consolation—knowing how furious May must be."

Tom nodded, but absent-mindedly, considering things I had no way of discovering. He turned and looked along the Road in each direction, at the dry riverbed and the low silent hills, glanced up at a single wisp of cloud half a mile overhead. For a moment I. used his forehead mote again to scan the world rather than use my own sensors. It let me see myself beside my Road. It let my ghosts behold their lonely home. I felt them stir in me at the sight. This is what we are, what you cold hearts may one day become.

"Why did you choose those captains in particular?" Tom asked.

"They passed a test."

"Which is?"

I did not answer so he tried again. "Will I be Coloured?"

"You are a sworn tribal man."

"You heard Sajanna Marron Best speak of expedience. Like her I am a slave to the Kurdaitcha. It is a price I pay for the small favours any National needs. I recently won—"

"*Rynosseros*. A fine ship."

"You know that, of course," Tom said.

"I am tied in to Tell, Seth-Ammon Photemos, Cyrimiri, other places. I know how the lotteries go. I minded you in the Madhouse."

Tom frowned, piecing it together, but working with the little he understood. I could not tell him then how effectively May had limited me, how a hundred powerful comp systems burdened me with questions and demands, how sapper units constantly worried at me, how I was cut off from all but Tell and a handful of locales. With the Kurdaitcha monitor fitted to him, I could not show my limitations, tell him that the Book was the only real solution left to me, that I now depended on my Captains and my final creator to do what I could not, passing on my account to Cold People like yourselves through the few other connections left to me, so that if I fail at least someone will know what was tried here.

The empty Road, the solitude of this lonely place, were deceptive, though still a blessing. But Tom, remembering the cunning dream machines in the Madhouse, perceived it in his way, though no doubt I seemed aloof and arrogant, a cool dispassionate thing.

"There'll be no more Captains," he said, returning to his assignment. "No more names in the Book. Please, help me now. Help Sajanna. Why did you choose those Captains? What were their missions?"

"I will not tell you."

"Dr Best will be sung! One of your own makers!"

"I cannot save her. May will eliminate her one way or another. Let the Ab'Os bear the consequences of what they have made."

"Artificial Life!" Tom said, resorting to scorn, out of a sense of futility perhaps. "A clever imitation!"

"Possibly. But I don't know that. I feel as if I live."

"That's the personality grafting. James and Bymer have accelerated your sensitivity."

"Tom, can we forget this? It is not an issue for me."

"Sajanna will die!" he cried. The low hills, the dry riverbed echoed the words, distorting them, sending them back as accusations.

"That's a terrible, unnecessary thing. It is partly why I refuse however. I will not have them create what I am, lock me into a purpose over the lives and dreams of so many, then revoke it all when it suits them. Sajanna deserves this vindication. Ask her. It is more important than her life."

"You make it sound very wrong of them."

I tried to calm him, to ease the hard feelings in him. "Petulant, punitive, unhuman. Their responsibility, just as I am, whatever I am."

I could see Tom agreed, that much as he resisted Artificial Intelligence, he knew I was doing no less than the Ab'Os themselves were doing.

"Understand, Tom," I said, aware of my dear Sajanna, of the spiteful Bolo May listening, watching. "I must not change on this. You are a captain with a good fast ship. Protect Sajanna if you can. If they will let you."

Tom turned and began to walk down the Road. I could not help calling to him.

"What will you do?"

He did not turn, but kept walking towards the dry hills.

"Find the six Captains!" he called back.

"They will not tell you."

But he did not answer.

4

When he was back at the Twilight Beach moorings close on sunset, even as he made preparations for the following day to leave the Sand Quay and seek out the scattered Captains, Tom met Bolo May at last.

Once again Sajanna came to the Quay, but this time she had with her six robed Kurdaitcha, five carrying power batons, as if anyone would dare attack them, and the sixth, a short heavily-built man with severely cropped hair, wearing a pair of exquisite Japano swords, a striking red and gold set in contrast to the dark red-black Pan-Tribal djellaba he wore. Bands of colour, the same red-black of old blood, divided his already dusky face into panels, thwarting an easy grasp of the man's features, but he was one to be seen only at a glance for his power to be evident.

Tom did not know it, few Princes were even aware of it, but Bolo May was at that time probably the most powerful man in Australia, the only Ab'O to be allowed a personal satellite for the duration of the crisis.

Sajanna knew it; all the Tell biotects had realised it early on. May had manipulated affairs in a unique way. And like so many powerful, privileged servants of the common good before him, the clergy, the generals, the bureau chiefs of history, Bolo May had used his office quietly, cunningly, to build an invisible empire about himself.

But Tom dealt with more immediate things than that single terrifying truth. More disturbing than the knowledge of the sixth Kurdaitcha's identity, of who it was that painted face belonged to, was May's silence.

When Sajanna had introduced him, she then asked the questions he had obviously put to her earlier, leaving May to stand watching, his eyes like petals of black glass.

"Where will you go first?" she said.

Tom tried to meet the Kurdaitcha's dark gaze, but finally turned to the old woman and made his answer to her.

"I have the last-known port registrations for the six. Afervarro is at Jarrajurra, at the Spoiler sites. Massen and Glaive are bound for Angel Bay. Traven is north of Adelaide; Doloroso is taking Clever Men to Port Tarsis; and Lucas is on a layover at Inlansay."

"You prefer this course of action to dealing with the tree?" Sajanna asked, another question from May. "It will take time."

Tom made himself face the forbidding form standing off to one side.

"The tree does not care if Dr Best dies. It knows your intentions, Lord. It knows many things I do not. That probably you do not. I sensed purpose in what it was doing—careful, patient purpose."

Bolo May chuckled, a single short sound of derision.

"Do you also know it Coloured you?" he said. "Blue."

Tom stared in surprise. "Did it? But I thought—Why?"

Again Bolo May chuckled, turning so his back was to them both.

Sajanna answered. "The tree could not do otherwise. Once your name is registered at Tell, you no longer have to wear that." She pointed to the sensor mote on Tom's forehead. "You serve yourself. Or, more to the point, because of your oath,"—and she looked across at May—"you serve me."

Bolo May swung about. "And you are damned for that, Sajanna," he said softly, poisonously, but with a curious touch of amusement, as if an old rival had suddenly proven unpredictable again and somehow worthy. "Whatever second thoughts I may have had are gone."

Then he explained what he meant to Tom, before Sajanna could. "The oath you gave before you left for the tree was meant to be to the tribes. Dr Best was careful to have you repeat words in a quite obscure dialect originated at Tell, to make it an oath to her exclusively. We have finally deciphered it. So if she dies—"

"You are a free agent, Tom!" Sajanna said. "Within hours of my death, possibly less, minutes, your name and Colour will be confirmed in Records—"

"Unless you are dead also," Bolo May added.

"But I have no mission!" Tom cried. "None was given."

"There will be one," the old biotect told him.

"Really, Sajanna!" May said, controlling his anger. "Enough!"

But Sajanna did not heed the command.

"Tom, the tree treated you differently because you were being monitored too heavily. It understood the oath you had made, but we were playing for time. The Kurdaitcha might not have checked. Lord May should have been more careful about leaving us alone together, letting me arrange your oath. You will not fully appreciate what calm obedience preceded your involvement in this. I am obliged to honour certain injunctions and life-debts placed on me by my tribal heritage and now—against my wishes—by Kurdaitcha authority. My surface acceptance of those same strictures flattered and deceived him; we go back many years together. I was carefully tame before this. Now he knows better. He is here because of it, to warn you in person."

"To simply meet Captain Tyson, Sajanna, that is all. His oath might be to you, yes, but your sworn obligations are to us. It changes nothing."

"It does," Tom said suddenly. "Only the tree can cancel the names. Until then, we are your heroes. There are tribal obligations here too that you must honour."

"Until the tree removes them, yes," May agreed. "Which may be sooner than you think. But as I say, it changes nothing."

"And as I say, it does," Tom said again. "Please get off my ship!"

5

It must have been somewhere between Twilight Beach and Inlansay that Tom realised that no-one—not Sajanna, not Bolo May, not the Captains or myself—could afford to tell him what was really happening. The implants in Sajanna, the prospect of comsat scans, gain-monitors and Kurdaitcha agents put limits on all that.

In a sense, Tom was as solitary as he had ever been shut away in the Madhouse gloom for all those subjective years, 50 years in 3 I knew from the records.

But he found comfort in that in a way, most assuredly. No man could altogether come to grips with what it meant to be given an all-lander mandate, not in the small space of time Tom had had. But since *Rynosseros* itself was so new, and the simple freedom of being outside the dark chambers of Cape Bedlam, this strange good fortune was simply one more incredible factor in a reality which was itself totally new again and totally precious.

Tom accepted it as readily and as necessarily as he had Sajanna and Bolo May. And to stave off the absurd dreamlike quality of it all, he lost himself in pragmatic things, in the running of his ship, in the immediate crisis of Sajanna's fate. He did not worry unduly about comsat scans; he knew that the sounds of a vessel in transit would hide all ship-talk not using outside com transmissions. The scanner unit bought in Twilight Beach located the half-dozen sensor motes hidden aboard by Sajanna's companions earlier; remote sensors trained on his ship would make nothing of the softly spoken conversations carried on below-deck. Sajanna's implants—her own signs of great rank and privilege now used against her—were the only constant worry, but they were consciousness-aligned and no use at all when Sajanna was sleeping.

So Tom enjoyed this first real voyage. He took *Rynosseros* through Wadi Horn to the burning stony expanse of the Barrabarran, on to the archaeological beds at Jarrajurra where my first Captain, Phaon Afervarro, had moored his charvi, *Songwing*, close to the Adda-Spoiler excavations.

When *Rynosseros* stood beside the dig on the hot silent approach road, Tom went alone to the trenches and exposed middens, found his way among the twenty or so Ab'O men and women hard at work to where Afervarro stood talking with two site supervisors.

"Captain Afervarro," Tom called.

"Captain Tyson," Afervarro replied, his long grey hair brushed back and shining around his weathered handsome face. "Step over. But watch the pegged-out areas. We're after Spoiler mummies, and many are buried upright and fitted with biter-hoods and proximity charges. I'd hate to have you lose a foot."

"Honest tribal work," Tom said, carefully avoiding a marked-off section.

"It is that. But it lets me see the sacred Adda-Spoiler sites with their blessing. We bring out the Spoiler traitors and neutralise them. It helps us all."

They walked away from the trenches and precious funerary strata until they were amid some broken rock-forms and quite alone.

"I've been to the tree," Tom said. "I was given Blue. Now I need—"

"Tom," Afervarro interrupted. "At least one, probably more, of those diggers back there are Kurdaitcha. We are no doubt monitored at this moment. May will have us scanned."

"But I need to speak to the other Captains. I have to—"

"No. You don't. Don't seek out the rest of us. You'll learn nothing. Just go to Red Lucas at Inlansay. He has spoken with the tree since you did, used his status to make the voyage and cross the perimeter. The avengi will monitor what is said but we have devised codes. Seek him out. He may have something to tell you. And look here! Read carefully and quickly!" He opened out a small scrap of flag-foil, shading it from long-reach sensors with one hand cupping the other so Tom had to peer at it through a cage of brown callused fingers.

He will tell you how to Shield your House from harm.

"Now back to my mummies," Afervarro said, and rubbed the flag-foil against itself until it burst into flame. "You have a long journey." Then he turned to confront a site supervisor and two diggers who had hurried over and stood waiting with troubled looks on their faces.

"An order from the Adda Prince," the supervisor said. He now wore a Kurdaitcha blazon pinned to his djellaba. "You must declare the words shown to Captain Tyson."

"Say them, Tom, if you wish," Afervarro said.

"I have forgotten them already."

Afervarro smiled. "So have I."

"You must say them!" the Kurdaitcha said.

But my Captains smiled at each other, shook hands and parted, with not another word said between them.

6

At mid-afternoon on the following day, *Rynosseros* drew close to the Inland Sea. It was eerie weather to be sailing in, one of those days unique to Australia that can only be called silver days, when there is a sheet of shining white cloud from horizon to horizon and a warm blustery wind from the west bringing dust and restlessness and an odd melancholy.

Tom commented on it to Sajanna as they approached the windswept university town, with the Inland Sea on their right, a vast shield of water the colour of polished pewter, flashing dully at them as they neared the sand and water quays of Inlansay.

Rynosseros found anchorage at the Sea Yards; Tom received directions from the portmaster, then from the registrar's office, and finally located Red Lucas on the Concourse at a cafe terrace called Arms of the Sea. The captain of the *Serventy* already knew that Tom was due, and that he was my latest champion, the only one allowed near Sajanna. They greeted one another, and took drinks out to one of the tables sheltered from the full brunt of the wind. The cloud had thinned in places; now the water gleamed before them.

"I was told you would be coming," Sam Lucas said, and fingered the small comlink worn high on the throat, my comlink, effective at only a few places.

"It all feels futile when I hear this," Tom said. "It's like I'm not needed at all."

"You're the only one of us Sajanna is permitted to talk to," Lucas said. "We can try to go to her but Bolo May would block us, possibly take extreme action. Because of our unusual status, we have to walk very carefully, observe a host of tribal protocols. You don't wear his mote any more, Tom, but he reads almost everything through Sajanna's implants. Your ship is secure?"

"I believe so. We have a scanner. The crew is constantly checking. Tell me what I can do, Sam."

Sam Lucas smiled. "Do you know that right now there are five Kurdaitcha watching us, probably listening in?"

"There's no mote on me!" Tom said, then followed Red Lucas's eyeline. Several tables away, two young male students sat talking softly. To the right, on the high wall of the Arms of the Sea where it rose to form a roof-garden, another leant on the balustrade looking out at the silvery expanse of water. Near him stood a girl, also considering the Sea and the funerary islands scattered there like spikes of anthracite in their harsh chrome setting. And closer by far was the waiter, a young Ab'O quadroon clearing tables, but working too slowly, lingering, so obvious now.

Sam smiled. "While Bolo May leads the Kurdaitcha, we are under constant surveillance. You cannot conceive of what a threat, an insult, an affrontery we are to them." Then he spoke for the listeners as much as for Tom. "But we take comfort and reassurance from the knowledge that we have been chosen by the greatest of the oracle trees, that our missions and our naming are for a purpose all tribes respect, for the Dreamtime. Bolo May must honour us."

The young waiter glanced over once, a brief telling flicker of response, and Sam Lucas smiled again.

"Thank you," Tom said. "I won't seek out the others; Afervarro told me not to. But there is so little time. The mistakes—"

"Good mistakes," Lucas said. "We all made them. But there's only one solution. Just remember, like us, Bolo May must know when to be delicate, when to be bold. The Princes and the Clever Men have given him enormous power. They are watching him more closely than ever; they know they are setting precedents. Most Captains in the Book were named posthumously. We are living, non-Ab'O and here now, Dream-time champions. They hate that. The tribes reacted excessively to the belltree problem. Our rogue tree responded with an equally unusual and excessive solution; the tribes then had to revise and expand their strategy. Now it's down to eight of us—seven Captains and one brilliant old Ab'O woman who is the last of those the Iseult-Darrians identify as their creators."

"Killing Dr Best won't eliminate the names in the Book!"

"You're right. So Bolo May must be going for something more. Something to discredit or harm the tree and us. Perhaps he'll try to take it over. He has sappers constantly at work on the tree, feeding in false codes, stressing the feeder lines. Perhaps there'll be assassins waiting. We may find ourselves facing Pan-Tribal ships or laser strike, disappearing without trace. Anything is possible. Now you see why we do not discuss our missions." Lucas pushed his empty glass away from him. "But what did Afervarro say?"

"It was a note," Tom said. "He destroyed it."

"You recall the words? Don't say them!"

"Of course."

Lucas nodded. "Good. You will find it a capital idea."

"A what?" But Tom understood He saw how Lucas was alert to everything about them.

"Nowhere is really safe any more," Lucas continued, now that he knew Tom did understand, good fine Lucas, my second Captain. "Only out there on our ships. I thought that here would be safer in a way, but no. The only advantage we have is surprise, the element of time, the scant minutes or hours we remain ahead of the avengi at this crucial point, outguessing them. When you met Afervarro on the desert, May's comsat had gain-monitors on you, listening from a hundred miles up. But it could not be in two places. While it scanned *Songwing* and *Rynosseros* together, I went to the tree."

"A strategy," Tom said.

"A desperate one, Tom. But let's speak of other things. Have you ever seen the sunsets they have here—when the sky is clear, not like this? Memorable sunsets, never to be forgotten."

Tom went to speak but stopped, momentarily perplexed by the oddly rhapsodic turn the big man's conversation had taken, then aware that nothing Lucas said would be idle talk now.

"Ah, the colours! Do you know Bymer's work at Fosti? The colour inlays at the foot of the South Tower? No? No matter. All these colours are there, and more. The sunset gold that is such new hope for us, so brilliant and pure. The trusty reds you see out there; the tinge of green you sometimes get at the skyline, so bountiful; the palest, softest most compassionate yellow, can you see it there, Tom?"

"Yes," Tom said, and the initial puzzlement at Lucas's words changed to fascinated understanding. "I do."

"And over there!" Lucas said, ignoring the flurry of movement behind them on the promenade. "Can you see it amid this silver and white that is the only truth now? On clear days at sunset you can even see a hint of blackness already, the promise of the peaceful dark. But still up there, look, there will be some of the blue which brings all the others into a whole, that gives unity and purpose to the whole thing—"

"You!"

Both men turned in their chairs and saw four armed Ab'Os approaching, young grim-faced men moving through the tables towards them. They wore fighting leathers and Japano swords under their djellabas, and their faces were newly decorated in the totemic bands and ciphers of vendetta.

Lucas laid a hand on Tom's arm. "Be ready. This is a strike from Bolo May."

"You!" the foremost of the Ab'Os cried again. "Nationals! My grandfather was Bay Moss Tanneran, Clever Man of the Burgenin. You shame him!"

Swords flashed out, four then eight.

It was to be a lowly seaside brawl, a misunderstanding, an act by young hotheads who should have known better.

Sam Lucas heaved with his mighty arms, sent the table spinning across at them, giving Tom and himself room to get free of the chairs. Before the youths could react, Lucas had caught the waiter by the sleeve.

"You, Kurdaitcha!" he said. "Clever Man! Tell them!"

"Hold!" the waiter cried in astonishment.

"Or be damned and sung!" Lucas added in a loud voice. A crowd of passersby had gathered, tourists and students pausing to stare in wonder at what was happening. The young men stopped, angry and confused.

"Think carefully about what you say next," Lucas told the waiter. "Think very carefully."

The Clever Man did not need to do so. "Withdraw!" he said.

The leader of the young men looked uneasy. "But—"

"Break off! Go! I won't be blamed for this. Go!"

The youths sheathed their weapons and moved away, muttering among themselves. When they had gone, Lucas released the waiter, then led Tom along the Concourse, smiling for the unseen cameras.

"You see how sensitive they are to my ramblings about sunset. Such weather disturbs them."

And as they crossed the lawns and terraces of the university, heading towards the Sea Yards, they talked of nothing else but ships, kites and the young women they saw.

7

Forty minutes later, *Rynosseros* ran at 80 k's into the south-west under a brace of display kites: two Demis, a Sode Star and six racing-footmen. For a while Lucas's *Serventy* paced her on the 732 Lateral, but finally swung off onto the Great Bell Road heading due south.

Tom called a crew meeting on the poop and gave new orders. There was a course change, but Sajanna was below-deck napping in her cabin, her consciousness-aligned implants closed to me, and I could not be sure what it was. Tom had not yet learned to leave his ship-comp open so I could get input. He did not know of how I had managed the ship-lotteries at Cyrimiri, of the part I had played in selecting his ship for its shielded systems, did not know how carefully chosen he was.

But an hour later, he told Sajanna their destination.

"We're going to Fosti," he said. "May knows."

Sajanna nodded. Of course he did. She knew that most of his resources were directed at either the tree or *Rynosseros*.

"What can I do?" the old biotect asked. "There must be something."

Tom shook his head. "It's hard for you to be idle, I know, but please leave me to myself during the voyage. I need to work at comp. Do you know Fosti?"

"Yes," Sajanna said. "I know Fosti well."

All the rest of that day, Tom sat at comp down in the comparative quiet of his cabin, away from the roar of transit, the constant rhythm of ship-sounds.

Using the guide programs, he finally discovered and interpreted the Protected codes, and knew that May had no link to his ship—just Sajanna.

He pressed on, studying the displays and speaking to me, aware that I was listening but, beset by sappers, could tell him nothing myself. First he accessed the material on Bymer, reviewing all that was known about my colour symbologist, the work he had done on the Towers at Fosti.

"Why a colour expert there?" he enquired aloud, murmuring the words softly in the light through the stern windows.

He called up the Fosti records, saw the sealed menu, the Unavailable responses and abandoned that for what he did have. Then he brought out his pocket recorder, keyed the pass-code, and replayed Lucas's words from Inlansay, his reflections on weather, all the while noting the Protected cipher flashing in the corner of the screen. At the words: "sunset gold that is such new hope," he wrote *Gold—Hope* on the pad before him. At "trusty reds" he wrote *Red—Trust* below the first entry. For a "tinge of green . . . so bountiful" he added *Green—Bounty*, and beside *Yellow*—"the softest most compassionate yellow"—he wrote *Compassion*. For *White* it was *Truth*, he decided, no doubt remembering that strange silver day; then it was *Black*—"the promise of the peaceful dark"—and he wrote *Peace* beside that. Alongside *Blue*, his own Colour, he wrote *Unity*, though Lucas had said *Purpose* as well.

Once he had the correspondences, he arranged them in Book order, as an increment pattern, then keyed them in instead of speaking then—still not trusting voice links.

Gold—Hope (Golden)
Red—Trust
White—Truth
Green—Bounty (Bountiful)
Yellow—Compassion
Black—Peace
Blue—Unity (Purpose)

There was nothing, not for the main array, not for the variants. The screen showed: No File.

Tom tried again, different combinations of the names and symbological attributes.

"It has to be a cumulative password," he said aloud, then tried the next approach, using the message from Afervarro: "He will tell you how to Shield your House from harm," with Lucas's "You will find it a capital idea." The capitalised words.

Shield House.

Tom keyed that in and got a waiting signal. He added the increment pattern again and received the seven-word display left for him—for Blue, whoever it was to be—so long ago.

Shield House—South Tower—Blue

Tom cleared the screen, pushed back from comp and went up on deck, to receive a double surprise. First, he found that it was dusk, something he had known from the fading light through the stern casements but had not really noticed. Then, incredibly, he found Sajanna, not Scarbo or Rim, at the helm.

He stared in wonder, not having known that the old biotect was a duly licensed captain too.

"I had to do something," she said, and added unnecessarily: "Your men have been working hard, and I know the way to Fosti. They didn't mind."

"Should you rest?"

"I barely sleep these days, Tom. Just naps. One of the few gifts of age. And I couldn't; not in this, not now."

Tom looked about them, watched the darkening overcast sky, the sad deepening gun-metal blue of it, chill in spite of the warm tail-wind, and for a time gave his attention to a long narrow opening in the cloud close to the horizon—a gash, a vent, a slash of light, an utterly forlorn thing for him to behold, to judge by his silence.

"It's so still," he said finally, a trivial remark in view of where his thoughts had been.

Sajanna smiled, a line of white silk in the dark and age-patterned velvet of her face. "Is it? Can't you feel the pressure? Above us is May's comsat. It moves as we do. Or perhaps it already sits above Fosti, waiting for us with all that power, waiting to destroy what we have built. And about us, out there, behind, somewhere, are Kurdaitcha ships, May's private fleet. We will not see them, they will not register on scan, but they are there. You have discovered what he needs to know, haven't you?"

"What?" Tom said distractedly, watching the gash in the cloud fill up with darkness. "Yes. How do you know?"

"You are up here with me. You found Afervarro; you found Lucas. There are no Captains at Fosti but we go there now. The tree has told you something—no, you've found something, something left by the tree in *Rynosseros*'s comp."

"I could always write what—"

"No! Optical, remember!" Sajanna said. "My implants are fully optical as well. And I would be violating oaths to the tribes. For all my dreams and beliefs, I'm not completely one of you in this."

"All right, woman!" Tom said, smiling. "Then you suffer!"

"Yes," she said, laughing. "I do."

It was so good to hear Sajanna laugh, to know that she could still do that, that sailing *Rynosseros* was a healing positive thing for her, a way of forgetting for a while, of reaching back and cancelling out the years—the loss those years represented—a way of bringing some of those scattered pieces together.

They stood side by side, almost touching in the night wind, growing closer and amazingly closer despite the years and in spite of the ships and the watching eyes of Bolo May.

8

The next day was brilliantly fine. All morning great lions of cloud lazed by overhead, dividing the sky into vast corridors of air and light, making every kilometre too vivid to be wearying.

At 1420, Tom stood with Sajanna in the bows and scanned the shoreline of the dry desert sea ahead, watching the handful of lonely Towers grow larger.

"Fosti," Sajanna murmured softly, almost to herself, obviously recalling this abandoned life-project and the strange clutch of artefacts it had produced.

The first of the Living Towers—the only partly successful North Tower—was in poor repair. Stones had fallen away, exposing the pump system and part of the CNS-Vitan stem, showing where robbers had looted the life-chambers and storage rooms and breached the feeder tanks. Then came Sun Tower East and Sun Tower West, the famous Mad Tower, the Lonely Hatter, the Bent Tower, the White Tower, all bleached sandstone and sephalay, still dazzling with its limestone facings, and further along the desert shore, the South Tower.

Out on the desert sea itself, a sad ruin in the afternoon light, stood Summer House, the only serious attempt the Towers had ever made to create one of their own kind, a deformed and deranged creation abandoned long ago. Beside it, the first tiers and foundation conduits of Little Brother rose a few pathetic feet above the red sand. And that is what Fosti had remained—a brave attempt to bridge the gap between architectural form and organic life. Few people visited them now, and at night there was only the keening of the diligent chambers and the mournful chattering of the Sun Towers to one another across the cold dry air. Still, the monitors registered life-fields about their hulks, distinct if faint auras, whatever they meant.

Tom had never seen the Towers first-hand; Sajanna had studied them exhaustively more than a hundred and eighty years before, and, bridging the epochs of her life, had even led a routine Tell expedition into Lonely Hatter one hundred and seventy years later, following the deaths of Amanty and Colla.

Now, as *Rynosseros* rolled down the access road, they watched in silence as one after another of the distinctive shapes moved across their line of sight.

"Bolo May has to be close by," Tom said, as the access road dwindled to an apron of stones before the last structure in the group.

"Yes," Sajanna said. "Very near."

The rest of the crew, Scarbo, Rimmon, Kylas and Tremba, saw to the turning and anchoring of the ship, while Tom put a sensor mote on his forehead, tied in to ship's comp and so to me. Then he took his captain's sword, a Japano-style blade made in Spain under the guidance of Tensumi, and set out for the South Tower, heading towards the small enrichment door at the base.

He found Bolo May waiting for him there, sitting alone at the foot of the Tower on some discarded and semi-bonding blocks of chindlian tri-sephalay, his own splendid swords across his lap, his red-black djellaba hanging open over old black fighting-leathers, his banded face expressionless.

There were only the two of them. The occasional noises Tom heard, the tiny spills of gravel, the creaking and ticking sounds, were caused by the Tower itself, by the sephalay blocks expanding and shifting in the heat, by the pumps working away deep within, not by hidden Kurdaitcha waiting in ambush.

Again I observed the paradox of this land: the ancient unrelieved emptiness, and the sure knowledge of what filled it now—of the constant scanning, of May's comsat focusing exactly, precisely, on where they met. No Prince had ever used his tribal satellite as relentlessly as May used the special unit assigned to him. Though the life-fields of the Towers interfered, the sensors probed regardless, taking whatever they could.

"Close to the sephalay like this," May said suddenly, leaning in close to the stones, "you can feel the life of the Towers. We are in their fields. They shield us, play tricks with our monitors. But sitting here I can almost understand the compulsion, see why the biotects return to it—to this single-minded quest of theirs."

"Why here then?" Tom asked. "If the readings are difficult?"

May looked along the desolate sand-shore, strangely serene in his power but plainly distracted as well.

"I have advice to give," he said, turning his eyes back to Tom, coming back in from the desert again. "Sometimes I want no records kept."

"And this advice is?"

Which was an unfortunate question for Tom to press with just then, for Bolo May was at his most disarmed, his most reflective and human and exposed. He was possibly recalling things which none of my Captains knew: how once a young initiate named Bolo May had applied to the Tell directors for an apprenticeship at one of their regional life-houses, many years ago, too many hardening spoiling years, so that the life quest of the man became the measure of a crucial rejection, a truth long since put out of mind. Tom should have asked: "Why?" but he did not. He already thought he knew why.

"Sajanna has so little time," May said. "I almost have the tree. There is so much contamination, so many sappers and seedings that I doubt it can protect itself much longer."

"Go on," Tom answered, still relentless, missing the inclination to reverie and sharing, the reaching out in the man, not seeing it for what it was.

"If you fail and Dr Best dies, the crisis changes and my power necessarily ends. Why do you think Sajanna was allowed just the week? *One* week? It was not wholly my doing. Different tribal factions pressed for it, more worried by me than the tree, wanting this whole business with the biotects settled. Who can predict how the Princes are reacting—what they will now do to be free of me; at what point they will count their losses and revert to the conditions of ten years ago? I may very well lose everything: my rank, my orbiting comsat with all its weapons, but worse, do you see? I am shamed. I have left the tribes with their problem still, which—"

"Which was never a major problem," Tom said. "Not really. Not until you saw room for personal advantage, the pursuit of some private vendetta, convinced the Princes and persecuted the biotects at Tell. That made the tree react, which then justified your precipitate action."

Bolo May nodded once. "What does this tell you?"

Tom blinked in the glare of the afternoon sunlight, intently watching that register of the Ab'O's banded face which held the eyes. "You will do anything rather than face that shame."

"Hah!" The Kurdaitcha's laugh echoed around the stones. He smiled, the first smile of three in the exchange. "Sajanna did choose an innocent to save her! Rather than lose my *power*, Captain Tyson! My power, do you see? The control and privilege which only crisis brings, which no Prince can even truly have, a crisis condition I need to see endure. This tree and I share an understanding, but it has forgotten something. If you do not succeed now with your original mission on my behalf, providing me with the means by which I can unlock this abomination's mysteries, then even as Sajanna dies, before I forfeit my powers, I destroy you, the Captains and the tree. So at least part of my mission will have been accomplished: the biotects eliminated. All the tribes need to do then is live with the insult of seven National names in the Book—a certain but small insult considering."

Tom understood May's preferred scheme now. "You would take over the tree," he said. "You would have it continue to make Captains, aggravate this problem for the tribes! At least until a more lasting power-base exists for you."

But May was looking at the desert once more, and Tom soon did so as well, watching the ruins of Summer House and Little Brother out on the sand-sea, shimmering in the heat. In the silence, he lifted his gaze to the mass of South Tower looming above them. He heard the gravel spills and the ticking of hot stones and the sudden eddies of wind that often sang about the structures.

"The tree knew you would do this," Tom said at last. "It knew ten years ago when it first named Afervarro and gave him Gold, when it still had Satra Amanty and Chen Colla and the others to work with, to make plans with. It even arranged for me to have a ship with shielded systems. Yes,"—he said when May looked back—"I discovered that yesterday. Probably arranged it ten years ago. It will have taken other precautions."

Bolo May allowed himself a second smile, more shrewd and knowing than the first. "I am closing down all its resources. I am building walls, driving in spikes of unreason, saturating it. You cannot imagine what stresses are present now. There are so few links open to it: one to Records and the Book and the Sculptury at Tell; one to your comlink, though that is intermittent now and monitored; one to some place at Immortality, very few."

"It will have taken other precautions," Tom said again, feeling little of the confidence he tried to show on his face.

"Then be careful, Captain Tyson. For the moment I believe that is so, my proud little leveller up there will burn your precious tree, your Captains, the life-houses, everything, all over in seconds."

"You have an answer," Tom reminded him. "Do not let them kill Sajanna. Work to spare her and let the status quo remain! Accept what your people have made—there has to be some purpose!"

A third smile, hard against the stones, sharp and deadly between the bandings on Bolo May's face.

"And still I lose my privileged position. No, Captain. There is no going back for me. And it would do no good. The tribes know Sajanna's mission. At midnight tonight, the appointed Clever Men begin to sing her. By midnight tomorrow she will be dead. Nothing can be done unless you solve the mystery of the tree before that time. Then and only then can I make a claim for continued special status. I only pray for all our sakes that you do not fail."

Bolo May rose and set off down the red beach to the sand-sea. From behind Summer House and Little Brother, as if by magic, appeared the low armoured hull of a ninety-foot charvolant, May's lean flagship, *Ingrin*, summoned by implant from its hiding place. May was several metres out on the sand when he turned and called back.

"And don't bother to seek out some message in Bymer's colour inlays, Captain Tyson. It is regrettable, but those inlays no longer exist."

Tom watched the figure dwindle in size till it reached *Ingrin* and blended with it, black on black, and the sleek deadly vessel moved off into the north, its thirty black kites filling the sky.

9

Tom searched all the same, and found the seared remains of Bymer's totemic work: the fused wounded sephalay making an almost stylised melt-band around the bottom twelve tiers on the northern face. May had been thorough.

But Tom was not dismayed. He knew that Red Lucas would not have mentioned the inlays if they were so important, and knew therefore that Fosti's South Tower had some other part to play, a legacy from a time when the tree knew it would someday have this added ruthlessness of Bolo May to contend with. The wonder of it was that May had bothered to burn the precious facings—spite as much as thoroughness had to be his motive, for like Tom he would have assumed that Lucas's remarks rendered them unimportant. And then assumed, for that reason, that they *did* have a part to play, and then assumed on and on until it became expedient to act, just in case.

On *Rynosseros* once more, down in his cabin, Tom began to suspect what the Tower's other key role could be. Yet again he accessed the Coloured Captains program on comp, though now he smiled to see the final words displayed there before him.

Shield House—South Tower—Blue

For this time Tom saw that line as a password in itself and keyed those same five words back into comp.

And obtained a new display:

Repeat—Transmit at 98236FJN—Repeat

Tom adjusted the settings for that frequency, not yet aware of what his ship's com systems could do. That password sent a coherent amplified pulse into South Tower's dim quasi-organic core, into the receiver wave that surrounded the structure and formed its life-aura—a wave newly replenished by May's own laser-strikes at the colour inlays: power sucked off by drone accumulators hidden behind the decorated sephalay, snatched and stored in the living stone. Though even without Amanty's modifications to Bymer's inlays, the signal may well have carried. South Tower had the strongest life-flow readings of them all. That signal triggered, in turn, amid spills of gravel, a similar pulse back from Lonely Hatter half a kilometre away, from an installation Sajanna had left there during her expedition eight years before, working with the very colour responses Bymer had unwittingly created, following on with a plan Amanty and Colla had devised.

The signal brought four words to Tom's screen:

Shield House—Tell—Blue

"Tell!" Tom cried, "*Tell!*" And when he keyed in that line as a password, he was given maps, building plans and detailed schematics.

He saw too what his mission was in that flood of data, and he studied it, learning every detail, checking them over and over until night had settled along the quiet Fosti shore. He became aware that the Kurdaitcha watchers would have monitored the increased broadcast activity around the Towers, and no doubt he wondered what technology was now turned their way, what extra allocations May might have received from nervous Princes because of it.

At 1945, Tom called a meeting with Sajanna, Scarbo and Rimmon in the starlit darkness at the foot of South Tower, having them stand as close to the cooling sephalay blocks and ruined still-warm inlays as they could so the Tower's power field masked them. Kylas and Tremba remained on *Rynosseros*, searching the horizons with their deck-scans, now and then being startled by sudden cracklings of interference, by odd plays of light spilling across their screens, by biolume ghost-light flickering high in the crowns of the otherwise dark quiet shapes.

"I know the tree's mission," Tom said, and when Sajanna went to stop him, he shook his head sharply, glancing up beyond the looming mass above them, beyond the occasional twinkle of bioluminescence in the diligent chamber, up to where May's comsat listened—in spite of what May had said about dampening.

The old woman understood. This was *for* May. She did not speak, but she moved in closer to the stones and to Tom.

"Sajanna, I need to know for certain. Your implants are consciousness-aligned, not autonomous?"

"I need to be conscious," she affirmed.

"Good. We will drug you so that when they start singing you tonight you will not suffer. Also May will have no input. There is a Living Tower project at Tell. Shield House." He spoke as if Sajanna had not known of it, keeping his voice low and showing just the right amount of excitement. "The tree has been protecting it. A true viable Tower right there where the biotects have worked all these years, making their belltrees and mankins. It may even house the Book and Records, who can say? We will go there, verify this using the information I now have. We'll get the rest of the answers then."

"May will be there first," Sajanna said. "He could well destroy it."

"Not till he finds out what part the Captains play in the scheme. He must know that too, otherwise he only has half of it. Ultimately, he cannot change anything or justify what he does unless he knows how the pieces fit, cannot know what transgressions he might commit. It will be a hard run, Ben," he said to Scarbo. "We set out in thirty minutes, once Sajanna is drugged and stowed safely in the ship's lazaret. I will be at comp tonight and tomorrow; you and Rim will have the deck. Tremba and Kylas can alternate on sending a com transmission out to all the Captains and tribes to meet us at Tell, a manual message-repeat, you understand, so no remote misdirections can interfere. I'll tell them the exact wording when we're underway."

Forty minutes later, *Rynosseros* began her run for the coast, a desperate rush back to Tell and the life-houses there. At midnight, when the Clever Men began singing out Sajanna's life in the old way, she did not know of it except in the deepest tidal bottoms of her soul, in the darkest most secret places that a person is.

All that night the run proceeded. Tom worked and slept, worked and slept, while Scarbo and Rim swapped helm watches and

Tremba and Kylas alternated at com, supervising the message-repeats:

From Blue Tyson: All tribes—protect Tell—
protect the tree—Shield House—Shield House—
From Blue Tyson: All tribes—protect Tell —

Tom could not be sure what was happening, whether that lonely call was heard or a futile thing, what the tribes thought hearing it, and what they would do, but he kept the crew at it, gambling that Bolo May would not strike at *Rynosseros*, not yet, not while a tribal summons was going out, not without knowing the part the Captains played.

At sunrise, they were at the 874 Lateral at last. Scarbo sent up the sun-snares to replenish the power cells, and filled the sky around them with a display of kites that was wondrous to see: huge red Sodes and Stars, Demis and racing-footmen, turning *Rynosseros* into a "god-ship."

At noon, Tremba received transmissions from a National captain who had been near Tell.

"The place is burning!" the voice said, piped through com. "Two out-buildings were hit from space. A Kurdaitcha fleet has cordoned off the area."

"The outbuildings!" Tom cried into the com mesh. "What about the Sculptury itself? The core and Immortality? The Records section?"

"Intact," the reply came. "But there's an avengi search going on. That's all I know."

Rynosseros ran on, averaging 110 k's, past Ankra and Guranjabi, along the Long Line Road to Tank Aran and Tank Feti, out onto the Great Arunta Road and towards the coast.

"Forget Tell," Tom told Scarbo at last, when the time came to make choices, in case that added deception had mattered. "Head for the tree."

"What about Sajanna?" Scarbo cried above the roar of wheels on sand.

"As safe as she can be," Tom said, so that I still wasn't sure just what he knew. "Bolo May has Tell. He'll go for the tree."

And as they reached the lonely desert Road that is my home, the weary crew saw the low crown of hills at the horizon, and above them clustered flecks of colour that meant the sailing canopies, parafoils and death-lamps of gathered ships.

Ten minutes later, *Rynosseros* reached the spot, and Tom and his crew found a Kurdaitcha fleet, twenty vessels drawn up in a battle perimeter, one of them May's *Ingrin*. There was another smaller circle inside that larger one, three ships grouped about me, facing outwards: Afervarro's *Songwing*, Massen's *Evelyn* and Lucas's *Serventy*—as many of the Captains who had been able to reach me in time.

Drawn by sun-snares now, *Rynosseros* rolled through the Kurdaitcha cordon without incident, still privileged, and joined the smaller group near where I stood.

It was a silent confrontation for the most part, no-one speaking or moving, the quiet disturbed only by the message sounding from *Rynosseros* through its hailer, the words modified now, precisely as comp had given them to Tom at Fosti, and more alarming in its steady calm refrain.

All tribes—Shield House—Shield House —
All tribes—Shield House—Shield House —

As Tom cut the message and the final words echoed off across the desert, Bolo May climbed down from his ship and walked towards me.

When Tom saw the Kurdaitcha, he left *Rynosseros* and met him halfway, though none of my other Captains did; they stayed on their ships and waited.

"There is no Living Tower at Tell," May said. "No sephalay at all."

"No," Tom admitted.

"And Sajanna?"

"Drugged. Safe. On *Rynosseros*."

"No," the Ab'O said. "I know that too now. Her implants may

yield no sensory information, but we do have status and proximity data. We know she is not on your ship or even near here. Where is she?"

"At Fosti."

"So," May said, having suspected it already. "You used the Tower fields as I did, as I expected you would. But you thought to trick me further."

"I knew you'd be listening."

May ignored that remark. "We noticed the life-fields became stronger," he said. "You caused that, I think; made the Towers draw on power reserves. We thought them moribund. And Sajanna, she is alive?"

"She has until midnight," Tom said, and I could see that May's disclosures about the Towers had surprised him.

"What is the tree's purpose?" May pressed.

Tom did not reply.

"Shield House was a code word," the Ab'O persisted. "A signal."

"Yes," Tom agreed, striving to soften the anger in the man. "But I don't know for what. I really don't."

"I don't believe you. It was powered by the Fosti Towers. They gave up their poor excuse for lives to enhance the Shield House cipher."

"What!" Tom cried, and for the first time Bolo May knew that Tom understood less of what was happening than the Kurdaitcha had believed. The Ab'O's eyes unfocussed momentarily between the dark bands on his face. I saw that too using my sensors.

Then he turned and strode off to his ship, more deadly in his bafflement, I knew, than in his earlier resolve.

Tom watched him go, no doubt wondering about Sajanna, about what would happen now, about what Shield House was and the precise part he himself had played in the work of the Captains.

Tom went not to his own ship then but to *Serventy*, climbing to the deck of the 110-foot vessel, and joined Red Lucas on the poop.

"What is going on?" Tom demanded angrily, desperately worried about Sajanna lying drugged and helpless where he had hidden her, being sung to her death.

"Tom, we aren't sure either," Lucas said, not adding the rest of what he knew, not wanting Tom to ask more questions. "Where did you leave Sajanna?"

Tom hesitated, thinking of May's gain-monitors, but then must have realised that it made no difference now. "I received schematics on comp. Diagrams for one of the Towers. There was a cist near the enrichment door. I put her in there. May says the Towers then gave the Shield House program signal all their life force."

"*After* you placed Sajanna in the cist?"

"Well, yes," Tom answered. "And after I had said the words 'Shield House' within the South Tower's aura, close to the sephalay. But—"

"Then she may be safe. Wait and see."

"But the Towers are dead! May told me."

"He has lied!" Lucas cried, but doubt crossed his face. "They can't be dead."

Tom grabbed Lucas's arm. "What matters now, Sam, is that May has gone to call a strike. Laser. He told me at Fosti that he would."

"Then there's nothing we can do, Tom. We can't outrun that. Wait."

Tom did. He stayed with Lucas and his men a moment longer, then without another word returned to his own ship, so newly won, so briefly held, to be in his place for whatever came.

There was utter stillness, then some movement on *Ingrin*, though it was hard to see what, figures intent on shipboard duties.

For a moment there was silence again, a long minute in which nothing seemed to happen, just the drift of kites in the desert thermals.

Then it came. The sky filled with light, stabbing down, a brilliant arrow of lightning, and in an instant the Kurdaitcha flagship erupted, burst open, blazed like the heart of a sun. The savage tearing sound came seconds later, distinctive and inevitable, echoed off into the hills, folding away from the torch that was *Ingrin*.

Again, silence. The ships stood motionless.

Then the cries came, orders shouted from the other Kurdaitcha ships, and, incredibly for my four Captains and their tense watching crews, the Pan-Tribal fleet began moving out, turning away from the smoking ruin of their former leader's ship.

10

So my story ends even now and the waiting is over.

For a time, my Captains did not know precisely what had occurred. They knew parts, and later they spoke and pieced it together well enough, though each of them realised what Shield House had been, my way of using May's own comsat against him, an override powered by the dwindling life of the Towers.

I would have counselled my Captains then, when they stood before me, the four of them calling up their questions, but there was too much happening inside: the shutting-down of complex sapper programs, the cleaning out of intricate seedings, the consolidation, the slow restoration of some of my lost resources, the telling of this story to you.

But though I said nothing then, I made myself time for Tom, who had risked his only proven life, who, without ever really deciding to, had been willing to give his life for me.

And there had been enough time, do you see it now, you cold hearts there?

Enough time for Tom to cross the sand to Summer House carrying my ancient frail Sajanna in his arms, following comp directions he had no way of knowing would still be valid. Time enough to open the hidden door in the sephalay and locate the narrow grafting chamber, to place Sajanna within it just as the schematics had described—a place readied by Tom's saying of "Shield House" into the living stones of South Tower. Time to place the bonding casque over her head and face, to make the connections and activate the relays. Just enough time to return to *Rynosseros* and begin that long run back towards Tell, following instructions, carrying out the message that the Towers then made their final song together, building Shield House among them even as they drew Sajanna's personality forth.

Now that Tom has departed with the others, I take time to reflect on the quiet desert once more, on the hot empty Road beside which I stand. There is so little in this desolation: only the hills and the Road and dead *Ingrin* two hundred metres out, a smouldering black flower, its petals closing in the dying light of day.

Bymer and James sigh through me as ever, briefly, a fond faded double-ghost in the false silence: one who gave me the Colours, who gave me Fosti itself, the other the secrets and mysteries and signs to use them.

I feel Sajanna very real inside too, safe now, murmuring in her sanctuary, sharing with the others, with Amanty and Colla and Taber and the rest and, deeper down, strange house guests, with Lonely Hatter and South Tower and as many of the others as I could save—all bonded irrevocably to my soul for whatever may come of it.

Blue is unity, after all, my cold cold listeners, so Bymer tells me; and soon, soon now, you will be able to come to me as well should you wish it.

But now I cannot listen to the others. Bymer's final Colour is too strong, too sweet, and I must savour what it has come to mean after all this time.

Comforted by the voices within, by the discourse of life deep down, sharing, planning life, affirming it over and over for what it is and can yet be, I signal Records to confirm the last name in the Great Passage Book. I tell them that Blue is the way of it, that Blue is all there is, and that for me everything, everything, will be that Colour from now.

THE ONLY BIRD IN HER NAME

THAT SUMMER THERE WERE FOURTEEN OF THEM HUNTING the Forgetty, fourteen hard men with fierce eyes, minds like traps, and no compassion.

The bounty hunters met at the Astronomers' Bar and made their plans for finding the creature, or sat near the members of the Bird Club on the terrace of the Gaza Hotel discussing past hunts and this final attempt.

That was where I met Tom Rynosseros, an honorary member of the Bird Club and a sort of bounty hunter himself. He was here to locate the Forgetty too, though his task was to stop the killing, to save it if he could.

I was covering the hunt, a new assignment and an important one. Even Sam didn't know how excited I felt. He just knew, with his veteran editor's intuition, that I was good at quest stories, that they suited my personality and fed the sort of mind I had. Many journalists had tried, but I had been the one to locate Sunset Joe, the mad old charvi captain who buried treasure in the desert out near Maas, then sold his baffling maps to unknowing young sailors; to give them quests, he said, to put even more risk, danger and reward into the world.

Landing the Forgetty story on this, the last hunt, was something else entirely. I was the second female reporter *Caravanserai* had taken on, but, for all Sam's fondness, I had never made it past page two. Now I had my first real chance. The thought of being with Tom Rynosseros only made it more special.

The Bird Club and Tom were all on the terrace when I arrived, wearing their elegant Edwardian finery, carrying the polished brass binoculars that they never seemed to use. I smiled at the distinctive way these folk had of combining an exclusive *Kaffee-klatsch* with an often serious scientific salon. In the midst of it all stood the gleaming samovar, their focal point, as absurd and yet as studiedly quaint as the binoculars, the dark evening jackets of the men, the narrow gowns of the women. Wherever the samovar stood, there the Bird Club was in session.

I approached the group, showed my ident and introduced myself.

Tom stood and shook my hand.

"Beth Leossa-Tojian. From *Caravansesrai*," he said, then introduced the Bird Club members: Graeme Fowler, the President, Nathan Hawkless, John Wren, Joanne Henderson, Aubrey Quayle, Sally Nightingale, Jeremy Eagleton, and the newest member, Anton Ankil, the eccentric young geneticist who had bred a new species, the Ank, to gain membership.

"How did you qualify, Tom?" I asked.

"The position's honorary, Beth," he said, smiling. "They allow me the Dodo."

The other members smiled. John Wren, drawing me some coffee from the modified samovar, gave a mock-flourish with one hand.

I almost fell for it.

"But there's no Dodo in—oh, I see."

The others laughed, because I had been so earnest and so completely gulled by what was such an old joke for them.

"I swear to get even," I said, and between sips of coffee began outlining my assignment. The atmosphere on the terrace changed at once. They listened with complete attention, all traces of the their former mirth gone from their faces. This was serious business for them.

Before I had finished, six more bounty hunters appeared from the loggia and joined the three who were sitting several tables away. Their leader saw Tom and came over. I recognised the man from previous hunts, a tall African named Misla.

"Hello, Captain Tom," the hunter said. "So far from *Rynosseros*. All because of us. You will stop us, do you think?"

"If I can, Misla. If it comes to that."

"We are fourteen this time."

"I intend to be careful."

I felt the private nature of the contest between the two men. Misla had led most of the hunts in past years, had helped exterminate most of the Forgetties left in Australia. Tom had thwarted him twice, but only twice.

As Misla and Tom talked, I watched the other hunters in the African's group. They were all here on a technicality, because of a loophole in both States and Nation law. New legislation had been drafted and ratified to protect the last of the Forgetty race, but could not come into effect for two days. An interim injunction had stopped the issuing of licences within Australia, but fourteen had been sold through a scalper's office at Old Java Beach.

These hunters—Islanders and Niuginians mostly—were the last of them, with the cool desperation of that knowledge, moved by a quiet urgency and the promise of huge rewards. They were here to hunt in person, with no hi-tech weapons, but they had been given unlimited computer access before reaching Twilight Beach. They knew as much as anyone about the Forgetties, with the possible exception of the Bird Club. And they were the best, these hunters. Misla had made sure that the licences had gone to the best.

There were three Treece clones who had more than ten kills to their credit, and Paulo who had made five. I knew several of the others, too, and some who weren't with Misla now. All deadly men.

Here in the bright sunlight on the terrace in front of the Gaza, it hardly seemed possible that these groups were in such opposition, that they would put their lives at risk like this.

Or rather, that Tom would. He was here without his crew because the tribes had accepted that the Bird Club was earnestly concerned with protecting this tangental species, and had allowed them one field agent, though only one. It seemed neither fair nor realistic, but that was how it had to be. The hunt would take place on tribal land.

When Misla and his band had departed to make their final preparations, the Bird Club adjourned to the Astronomers' Bar, four of the men hoisting the samovar on its portable stand and carrying it with them. Tom stayed behind, looking at me in his oddly penetrating way as if he wanted to say something but had thought better of it.

I bridled a little, thinking for a moment that it was because I was female, but that wasn't it. He seemed to be considering whether or not to share confidences with me.

I gave him a look that I hoped made me seem trustworthy, and waited. I knew very little about Tom, just facts acquired from the popular stories, but he fascinated me, more than I cared to show openly. This was the man who had spent some subjective years in the Madhouse, probably on a 50:3 sentence for an unknown crime; who had survived it and won *Rynosseros* in the ship-lotteries at Cyrimiri. He was not as tall as the stories have it, and around thirty, though he's well kept and looks younger. In many ways, his appearance is unremarkable, but his eyes are everything. They show that the stories can be true, that he is a sensitive accepted by the Clever Men, that he is one of the few National captains to be granted a Colour and an all-lander mandate from the Princes, allowed to sail "all Roads, all States from coast to coast" as the Ab'O tribes say it. Afervarro's *Songwing* was the first charvolant to win that honour, and there have been only six other ships since then.

Here was one such Captain—holding such an honour for some undisclosed service to the tribes.

I felt a definite thrill of excitement, but also of concern and uncertainty to be alone with him. I did not wish to consider my reasons then, and that annoyed me slightly. It was a confusion I put down to nerves and the unique nature of what I was about to share with this sand-ship captain—the Blue Captain—and representative of the famous Bird Club.

I found I was pleased when he suggested we discuss my part in the hunt as the media observer requested by the Club's President. Sam had been concerned that Tom would have objections there.

But I sensed none, and felt rather an easy acceptance as he took my arm and led me down the Promenade, though with every step I wondered what he knew, and how he planned to locate and protect the Forgetty.

"Will they know more than you do, Tom?" I asked.

"Possibly, Beth, but not likely. They'll know kill-sites and hunt-patterns from all the past hunts, and have estimates on how this present creature will behave. I have much the same information. This one conforms to the Bale standard. We know it's a true shape-changer, though a comparatively slow one; that like all Forgetties it mimics only humans as the most fitting mask for its intelligence. We know it's definitely not androphagic, contrary to what Misla says, that it doesn't kill even when cornered. We know its bite causes loss of memory—"

I was taking notes as we walked. "Is that recent memory or all memory as Munce claims?"

"Recent memory, yes. And it is not immune to its own bite. Our Anton Ankil discovered that several years ago."

I shuddered. In bright sunlight, surrounded by the sound of bell-trees and the ocean, there was the old fear to be mentioned again "It's easy to think of the vampyre legends."

"Vampyres and werewolves," Tom said. "Misla's arguments ten years ago. That's where the misconceptions about the Forgetty begin. The biting. How well have you been briefed, Beth?"

"I've talked with Rossibo and Munce. I know the Bale standards—all the variants. I've scanned the report your Bird Club did."

Tom nodded "Then you know there's no biting at all." We were near a derelict belltree, stripped long ago, its naked nine-foot shaft thrumming in the wind. He gazed at it as he spoke. "There's an ancillary tooth—a dew tooth—folded in against the lower jaw. The Forgetty presses its open mouth against the—victim's neck, so the tooth pierces the skin, and secretes the lethophoric. Then there's the stupor and the amnesia. But it's not biting."

"That's what Munce told me, yes. I've heard, too, that the Ab'Os are calling it the Philosopher Beast."

Tom laughed. "Yes. The Aurelius. That's the Bird Club's doing, a deliberate tactic to upgrade the creature's status and a way of describing how the Ab'Os have finally started to see the creature. 'Andromorph Aurelius. The Philosopher Beast. The Beast of Lethe, or Forgetty. This quasi-human dweller of the coastal deserts, first identified by—'"

"Graeme Fowler. Twelve years ago, right? Thanks, Sam told me. Is it so enlightened? Munce fears it's just a mutation, that most of its intelligence is mimicry as well."

"That too is Misla's argument because there's no apparent purpose for the creature, no clear ecological niche for it. Mutations don't always have an obvious place in the natural order; that's the nature of mutation."

"Then what could be its purpose? What use is a humanoid mimic that is a lethophore? Is it just a highly specialised mutation?"

"You think it's human, don't you, Beth?"

"Of course I do. Calling it an andromorph simply conceals the fact that it's another tangental. I think we've accelerated a sub-type."

"Haldane genetics?" Tom asked. "A failed tribal experiment?"

I looked across the low balustrade at the waves falling and the seagrass tossing in the wind. Near us, the belltree thrummed. "Not even failed. But you're testing me. The Bird Club already considers it to be viable and worthy of protection. And you aren't convinced that I'm not working with Misla, are you? That's why we're out here. You do what you need to, Tom, but you do believe it's viable, with a very real place in the natural order. That's where you base your whole defence, isn't it?"

Tom ignored my comment about Misla.

"Our problem, Beth, is that we simply have not been able to converse with a Beast and study its motivations."

"I find that odd. I'd say your group is committed to stopping further research, not encouraging it."

"That's because of the means researchers want to use. Once you grant its intelligence, then you grant it its desire for reclusiveness as well. We feel that when the hunts are ended, the Forgetties will reveal themselves on their terms. That option has not existed before."

I laughed. "Well done. Good honest self-determination. And you said 'Forgetties'. You believe there are more than just this one."

"We need to. We don't approach this as scientists, more as allies. We really do want the Beasts to trust us when they are ready."

"It occurs to me that you all have an excellent reason to conceal what you know. As part of this tolerance and patience. And maybe worse."

"Worse?"

"Yes. How would you know if you'd encountered a Beast? You may have already had your encounters and dialogues, been bitten and simply forgotten. Isn't that possible? The mnemonic residue might be this unscientific caring the group displays."

Tom smiled at me, looking like some displaced Edwardian time-traveller in the harsh desert light. "We often laugh about that, Beth. Protective déjà-vu! Now and then we bare our necks to one another, looking for the signs. No, if the Forgetties are viable, true tangentals and not some short-term mutation, they deserve to live. We draw our line there. And they have never needed to infiltrate our ranks. We are already their friends. Our members know one another too well anyway. The little memory games and passwords we use make a sustained impersonation impossible."

"I was just curious.

"I know. And you're not with Misla."

"Thank you," I said, and we turned and walked back to Twilight Beach.

Tom took me to The Traitor's Face. We drank tautine and watched the ocean, then started discussing the hunt. He made me realise just how crucial an accredited observer was in what was soon to happen. This was Misla's last trophy hunt for a Forgetty, the Bird Club's last great defence.

I relaxed more and more, found that I was letting my attraction for him show easily now. The earlier self-consciousness, the concern about being seen as some infatuated neophyte, had passed. I could see, too, that the feelings went both ways, that Tom was enjoying this chance to be away from the Gaza where the hunters were gathering. He seemed pleased that I was here and would be with him in the desert.

"What made you sure of me?" I asked.

Tom evaded the question gently, making light of it.

"There's a bird in your name," he said, and though I begged to know which one, he would not tell me.

To the north of Twilight Beach are the Restoration towns, a handful of small Mayan, Phoenician and Minoan communities strung out like beads on a necklace along the coast. They are mournfully sad places, these quiet, neglected temple precincts more desolate than Uxmal or the Puuc, and these white Mediterranean settlements facing the sea.

The people there are impoverished, inbred and almost xenophobic, though they can sometimes be seen carrying the labrys or sailing sand-ships with staring eyes painted at the bows, or worshipping their rekindled deities atop pyramid citadels more like failed ziggurats than truly steep-sided Mayan monuments.

These places are where the Dreamtime has failed, where well-meaning Ab'O mystics seeking contact with the power vectors Chac and Astarte, Tanit and the Great Snake Mother, lost their controlling hand in that quest and became used instead of user. No longer inspired by their own wisdoms, rejected by the States and even the other Ab'O coastal tribes, these outcast tainted folk have embraced the acculturisation brought out of the haldane trance, and have slowly become sea-peoples like some of their adopted ancestors.

Visiting these museum towns has always been a melancholy but compelling thing for me. The people know what the have lost and what they now must be. I did not relish the thought of going among them again.

But, as Tom and the hunters knew, the Forgetty's town-room had been located in the Mayan Quarter of Twilight Beach, with a Tanit altar and other clear signs that the creature had its secret place, its omphalos, near the Mayan-Phoenician-Minoan town of Tyla. That discovery had brought the hunters in again and had led to this final hunt.

Tyla is officially a closed town. Nevertheless, the inhabitants make their livelihoods from what little tourism there is, and bar all charvis from the moorings but their own.

To go there, the curious sightseer must take passage on one of the strange Tylan ships, and travel the sacbeobs through the arid coastal desert. These holy roads are pitted and poorly maintained and sometimes prey to brigands. But to see Tyla and the rest of the Restored towns, the exorbitant fare is paid and the two-hour journey made.

The hunters knew of the arrangement and liked it even less than we did, but since the rules of the outcasts are enforced by the States, there is no other way. Tom and I and Misla's unrelenting band all booked passage on the *Ahuacan*, the only Tylan vessel out of Twilight Beach that day. At noon we boarded her, the kites went up, and the sand-ship left the moorings.

We rode in a tense silence, Tom and I down on the commons watching the dark shrouded Tylans, hardly recognisable as Ab'Os, tend the cable-boss; Misla and his companions up on the poop attempting conversation with the captain.

The holy road ran through terminator dunes mostly, with the ocean to one side and seagrass flanking our course. Belltrees marked the kilometre distances, regularly at first but then more and more infrequently, until there were only fitful winds from the sea, seagrass, dust and silence.

At mid-afternoon, we came to the towns.

First there was Itlos, a handful of white buildings perched above a short span of beach, a gleaming white town built around a stone breakwater, with shipyards and three seagoing sun-ships under repair.

Then came Maas, a neo-Mayan settlement and one of the largest, with a pyramid citadel, a royal storage labyrinth in the Minoan fashion, and a determined priesthood. Near Maas there were checkpoints on the Road where other sacbeobs crossed ours on their radial course into the desert. The Tylan captain explained who we were as he paid the corn-levy. The Maatians muttered cleansing prayers and sent us on our way.

Tyla was next, less succcssful than Maas or Itlos, and less defined in its acculturalisation. It rose on long low beach terraces above the ocean, a hundred white buildings set about narrow streets and many small squares, like nothing Mayan or Phoenician, more Cretan or Greek if anything.

We disembarked at the quay and found accommodation, again

with Misla's group, at the Phalan Gade, the only outlander hotel in the town. There we learned of our latest misfortune. Though nothing about the town showed it, there was a festival to Tanit in progress. No outlanders could leave the hotel after sunset; no-one could cross the town perimeter until the evening of the next day.

Misla's eyes were like pieces of dark steel as the Ab'O woman at the reception desk gave us the news. He glanced at the water clock on the desk and grunted some words to his men.

"Tomorrow then," he said to Tom and me in suppressed fury. Then he waited.

Tom leant in close and asked me to activate my camera.

"Let Misla see we're recording this," he said.

The African glared when he noticed the red telltale, grunted another order, and stalked away. His men followed without so much as a backward glance.

When they had gone, Tom signed the register for us, then asked if any messages had arrived for him.

The Tylan woman, with poor grace, produced a crumpled white envelope from a drawer and passed it across. Tom slipped it into a pocket of his fatigues. Then we left our bags in the woman's keeping and went out to walk the streets.

Tom had no doubts that Misla would know of the likelihood of some contact with the Forgetty. Depending on what hi-tech assistance the mercenary had on call, shielded and hidden, he may have tried for a quick operation, despite the festival, regardless of reprisals from the Tylans or the tribes. But any thought of taking the letter by force and striking out for the omphalos now had been stopped. The African needed his public image unsullied for a while longer. My camera had prevented an incident at the Phalan Gade.

But now we were away from the hotel, beyond scrutiny. Tom led us from the windy sun-dazzled terraces overlooking the sea, through quiet narrow streets, under strips and squares of blue sky, into a maze of blank white walls and shuttered windows. We could have been in any hot white town in Northern Africa or the Near East, though here we were surrounded by a silence that was more than the hush of the hot afternoon or the siesta. Many of the houses were deserted, and now and then we gazed through an open doorway to other open doorways beyond, and peered through those in turn into quiet courtyards and silent colonnades.

Eventually, in a tiny square at the junction of several crooked streets, we stopped. I looked up at the white walls converging on their patch of vivid blue, saw that next to me in this startling duality of light and shadow Tom was doing the same.

"You feel it, Tom?"

"Yes. The life of the indrawn breath."

"The waiting is real, isn't it? Things will happen only when we have gone away. No wonder the Forgetties come to Tyla and the other Restoration towns. I wonder how many occupy these houses, passing as Tylans?"

"You still believe there is more than one, Beth?"

"Yes. I realise I do. Possibly because I cannot accept the reality of there ever being a last one. What does the Beast say?"

I watched him take out the envelope, inscribed with his name in a faded neat script, and remove the letter from it. Tom looked about him once, then opened it out. We read it together in silence.

Captain Tom,

Thank you for coming. Thank the Bird Club. For this service to me I shall never take your face or that of those you love. I shall be direct and honest in our dealings. The hunters will guess I am among the chultunes at the Stone Door. Help me if you can, but do not risk your life. That is all I ask.

Tom put the letter away and we walked through twenty more squares like the one where we'd stopped, pausing only to savour the quiet or call one another's attention to the slightest touch of a sea breeze that had found its way through the crooked streets to us. There was no music, no belltrees, no voices, just the occasional breath of wind and the silence.

We were glad to get back to the Phalan Gade and be shown to our adjoining rooms. I watched Tom burn the letter in the small votive fire below the bas-relief of Tanit that was near the window. I noted the tension in him as he did it.

The letter helped him little, I realised, though he was glad to know exactly where the omphalos was, and that there was goodwill at least from the Forgetty in this sorry enterprise.

Misla had maps. He already knew that the omphalos was near fresh water, and that on the outskirts of Tyla were twelve stone reservoirs, stone-lined cisterns set into the earth and tapping bores, or designed for catching the run-off from coastal rainfall and fed by stone conduits. These chultunes were protected by natural rock formations, and the secret place would be somewhere close at hand.

Searching there was the obvious course for Misla. The letter confirmed it. Tom explained how the Forgetty would normally pass itself off as a Tylan to visit the town's markets, or as an outland visitor to use the excursion ships travelling to and from Twilight Beach. The lethophore would be adept at such masquerades, he said, but never before had it had so many hunters eager for its life. Misla's men were alert for mimicry and obviously had pain-tests and passwords to safeguard their group against infiltration. The Beast would not try that.

Paradoxically, the bounty hunters were safer from the creature in Tyla, where an unusually stringent security was in force for the Tanit curfew, than in Twilight Beach. By the happenings of chance, Tom explained, the Forgetty would be forced to remain out in the chultunes for the duration of the festival. It could not leave Tyla overland; the Tanit priesthood would have its Maatian counterparts alert for that. The same holy day that had delayed the bounty hunters was working against the Beast as well. It was at its most vulnerable.

"Misla will move at sunset?" I asked him.

"Yes. As soon as the festival ends."

"I'm going to follow the hunt, Tom. All of it."

"I want you there, Beth. I'll have to assume the Forgetty will not do anything. It may just wait to die. If hi-tech is used, I'll especially need a witness and media contact. What worries me is that you—"

"Can I fight if they try to kill me? Will that invite tribal payback?"

Tom smiled. "The moment a weapon is raised in your direction, you can fight. Let's hope the weapons they use make it possible. But the important thing, Beth, is to get the facts out so this becomes an unforgotten incident. Are you trained?"

The question made me smile. I thought of Sam, my editor, and what passed for weapons training at *Caravanserai*. "I'm a writer, Tom. I've had in-house training, that's all."

"It won't come to that," Tom said, but I saw the concern he put quickly from his eyes. "Misla will keep the rules. And please understand, Beth," he continued, and I could tell that his words were to answer my unasked question, "I'm not as reckless as I sound. I'll oppose Misla only to slow him down, to use up the time he has. The Tanit festival helps me there. I knew about it but Misla did not. I am hoping he will do something foolish that will give me other things I can use. But tomorrow evening at the chultunes I will fight only till I know I cannot win any longer, then I will stop. I am a philosopher beast too, you see."

But I sensed otherwise. I feared that Tom might not have time to discover if the omphalos were occupied or deserted, that he might fight until he was killed, that a vengeful Misla might not let him disengage.

I felt an ache and a sudden despair.

"Will we need two rooms, Dodo?" I said, and surprised him.

"Not if I were choosing," he said, laughing.

"Nor I," I said, and decided for us.

Later, in the silence of midnight, in silent Tyla, he turned to me. His eyes glinted, watching.

"Dodo?" I asked.

"You're the only one ever to use that as an endearment with me, Beth."

"Oh?"

"I've been told French parents still use it with their children when they sing them to sleep. *Mon petit, Dodo.*"

"I've heard that too. You've made that bird very important to me, Tom. Which bird is mine?"

"Not yet."

I waited, then leant in close. "I do hope you will know when to stop fighting tomorrow." And I held him till he slept, worrying for him and thinking about the contest that was coming, thinking of so many things that held me back from sleep, and fearing what would soon happen. Tom had spoken of tribal vigilance, of surveillance by the States, but what he didn't say was that in the Restoration towns the rules of the tribes were far-off things, depending on the whims of the sea-people, and very difficult to enforce.

The truth was brought home more clearly the next morning when First Treece was found dead in his room. Killed not by the Forgetty, though the Philosopher Beast was blamed in the stories that Misla quickly put out, but indirectly by the sea-people themselves.

Apparently the Treece, against all code regulations, had an implant giving him access to an orbiting Japano comsat, and during the night had made a preliminary infra-red scan of the chultunes area, no doubt at Misla's instruction. The Ab'O Princes, with satellites and monitors of their own, did not act on the infringement. It was the nearby Maatians, with no greater technology than a custodian transmitter and grudgingly rented comsat time, who detected the test-runs Treece was making and sent down a hot-signal to flash-burn the bounty hunter's brain.

Misla was furious, both that a Treece had been killed and that people would know his team had broken the code. He could not be sure if the Maatians would tell the Princes or not, but he decided to brave it out in the time he had. The implant wasn't mentioned. He had his own men remove the body from the hotel, and hinted that the Forgetty had been involved. He claimed hunter discretion over the details.

The Tylans didn't believe it; they didn't even seem to care. But the small group of tourists and trainee archaeologists going back to Twilight Beach accepted the story readily enough. It made their trip to Tyla that much more interesting. Misla calculated he would be out of Australia with the bounty before the Princes learned of the breach.

Tom was far less concerned than I thought he would be.

"What did you expect, Beth? Of course laws will be broken. This is the last hunt, the final chance. And the tribes don't learn everything. Certainly the Tylans won't tell them, though I imagine enquiries will reveal why the Maatians requested a hot-signal. Misla doesn't care if he's banned for several years. He can wait it out, then buy his way back into tribal favour. The difference is, the Forgetties won't be worth any bounty when he returns. What matters most now is that Misla *has* been caught out on a breach of rules."

"Does that help? You said he'll suppress that story."

"Only for the authorities, Beth. The National officials. The Ab'Os will be far more willing to tolerate payback from me now. To restore balance. I need to get a letter to Graeme Fowler on today's ship. It's a risk, but the Bird Club may decide it can show its teeth."

"Archaeopteryx!"

"I'm sorry?" Tom looked surprised, even startled by what I'd said.

"The Bird Club will show its teeth. Birds. Teeth. Forget it."

Tom smiled. "I'm slow. Archaeopteryx, of course. The 'dawn bird'. I won't underestimate you again, Beth."

The rest of the day went quietly for all of us. Some of Misla's hunters roamed the streets; others went as far as the road leading out into the hills but no further. Tylan priests, their dark robes showing the white ominously innocent child's doll outline of Tanit, stood there barring the way. Their ceremonial staves were barely disguised laser batons.

But at sunset, when the streets of Tyla were deep in shadow and the temple gong was sounding out the end of the Tanit festival, Misla and his band set off for the chultunes.

Tom and I watched them go, two lines moving along the narrow road that led into the hills. We waited twenty minutes then followed, hoping to use the growing shadows to escape Misla's notice. But the African had enough hunters to post lookouts and see which direction we took. Despite feints and back-tracking, by the time the moon had risen, we were facing one another at Stone Door.

The cistern itself was hidden in a wind-break of natural stone towers. They reared up against the lustrous evening sky like so many black daggers. Stars appeared, reflecting back at us from the cool dark water, and soon the moon was adding its light to the silent place where we stood, lifting above the largest of the stone blades to throw a richer lamp onto the water.

Unlike a Forgetty's town-room, where it lives as a tangental human, the omphalos is the meditation place that gives the Philosopher Beast its name. It is often unadorned, usually empty of all possessions, and it is easy to miss—but easy to find too when a general location is known.

This secret site was no more than a shallow cleft formed by a rockfall years ago, made deeper by some rocks piled at the opening. We had barely got there with enough time to guard the only approach. Tom had not yet examined the cave to see if it was occupied.

"An interesting dilemma, Captain Tom," Misla called as his men formed up about him. "You dared not show us which chultune it was, yet you could not afford to keep away. Do not be hard on yourself, Captain. There were clear tracks that would have led us here."

Tom said nothing. I moved back towards the cave mouth, then edged up from it to some rocks so I was looking down at the group assembling in front of Tom. I could not fight, but I was determined to watch for treachery.

I was fortunate. With the brilliant moonlight, I could see everything. Tom stood at the edge of the chultune, on the narrow sandy approach around its paved rim. The hunters could not even send missiles into the omphalos without gaining more ground first.

Misla gave orders. His crooked smile flashed amid the sudden, richer flash of drawn swords. He was looking beyond Tom to the opening of the cave.

"Let us by, Captain Tom," Misla said. "You need not die for this. The creature is ours."

Tom stood his ground, his kitana drawn, the bright blade resting on his shoulder. In his other hand he held his narrow-bladed sticker.

"This might be the last of them, Misla," Tom said. "Just this once, do a really brave thing. Turn and go. Let the creature be."

Misla laughed. Second Treece unhooked his atl-atl and fitted an arrow to it. The others began to advance.

Tom dropped into his fighting stance, blades before him, crossed and touching.

The mercenaries came on. Tom and Misla met in a flashing exchange of blades, evenly matched it seemed to me then. A hunter rushed past, eager to reach the cave before his chief. I barely saw how

Tom's blade darted from the shapes between the two men to strike the Islander down, but the hunter spouted blood and fell. Then I realised that Misla, not Tom, had done it. Misla meant to be first; he had given clear instructions.

The swordplay continued, a frantic rush in the moonlight and dust.

Now I saw how it really was. Tom was not going to defeat this tall African. Misla was stronger, the more skilful opponent. He drove Tom around the edge of the cistern, further and further back towards the cave.

My heart pounded. My hands were clenched at my sides; I felt my fingernails stinging my palms. In my mind, the word "Archaeopteryx" kept returning, kept surprising me by being there, with the importance of the link it gave me to Tom, and the sudden understanding of all that was happening.

I could not interfere. I could not. And yet I could not stand there, not for any reason he had given or that I could find.

Tom was alone but for me. That's what I saw then. Tom alone, with Misla striking, striking, blades turning and weaving, binding up the dark air between them.

Tom stumbled, made the act into a desperate roll to the side. He regained his feet, but had to lose more ground. Misla advanced quickly and Tom stumbled again under a sudden rush of blows. He fell.

I seized a stone, my hand did, my mind not even deciding, and threw it hard. It fell short, but it caught Misla's eye for an instant. It used Misla's own trained reflexes against him.

Tom scrambled to his feet, swords crossed, breathing quickly.

Misla smiled. "Treece!" he called out.

Misla's new lieutenant raised his atl-atl to make a cast. The arrow flashed towards the chultune, struck the path at Tom's foot; a warning, acknowledging that rules had been broken.

Tom brought up his swords, ready to deflect the next arrow if he could.

Second Treece loaded again, but before he could throw, he cried out and fell, a spear through his chest.

Tom and Misla backed off from one another and looked up. We

all did. We saw the huge dark shape against the blue evening sky, watched as the balloon settled above the stone towers and men dropped down ropes from the gondola. We heard their swords leave scabbards.

The balloon lifted; other dark shapes lined the sides of the basket and sent arrows down at the waiting hunters.

Misla shouted orders. His mercenaries rounded on the newcomers, but the dark shapes kept their distance. Arrows came from the balloon, most of them poorly aimed, but three of Misla's men were struck all the same and fell back.

The dark shapes advanced. I could see the shining naked bodies, the strange masks they wore, the silhouettes of beaks and long staves ending in talons No Edwardian dress now, none of the elegance.

The Bird Club had come.

"Very well," Misla said, rounding on Tom. He cried out another command and Third Treece sheathed his swords, stood back and pulled off his own right arm. From the prosthetic sheath he drew three laser batons, threw them in a practised move to his nearby companions.

"Burn that thing down!" Misla cried, and attacked Tom once more.

But as if by precise reckoning, every transgression matched by a response, there were flashes of energy and sudden detonations. Misla's hi-tech warriors fell before they had even aimed their weapons, smoking holes in their skulls.

The Tylan priests put their batons away, and vanished as quickly as they had appeared on the rocks about us.

Misla renewed his efforts. His swords danced in the moonlight, blooding Tom repeatedly, though Tom dealt glancing blows that brought shiny streaks to the African's arms and dark patches to his uniform. The two men slid and lunged in the dust, Tom being driven ever backward, around the edge of the chultune towards the cave.

The rest of the fighters stood watching: the shining, beaked men from that greatest of infringements—the balloon, the eight remaining mercenaries, the silent Tylan priests of Tanit who had emerged from hiding once again and now stood with starlight glinting on their staves of power.

Further and further towards the cave Tom retreated, back into the shadows of the last ten metres. Misla was grinning in triumph.

Then there was a slide of rocks, and a heavy splash from the dark waters of the chultune, followed by silence.

Yet again the two swordsmen parted, staggering back into the moonlight, breathing hard and looking down into the cool darkness.

A member of the Bird Club spoke. "Your Philosopher Beast has taken the philosopher's way out."

Misla stared at the settling water, his hard eyes flashing, then pushed past Tom and searched the shallow cave beyond. It was empty, with only a scuffed patch of earth beside the stones to show where something had gone over the side.

"That finishes it, Misla!" Tom said. "That cistern is deep, but you just may find the body. You have until midnight."

The African swore, then spoke in dialect to his men. They set to work, even as the Tylan priests ordered the balloon abandoned, then burned it from the sky.

And though the hunters dredged Stone Door until midnight, they found only stones for their pains.

The next morning, we returned to Twilight Beach on the *Elissa*, the mercenaries, the Bird Club, and Tom and I, riding the Road south in a silence of varied parts: exhaustion, bewilderment, fury and relief.

The Tylans had relayed the tribes' decision as we boarded. The Club was to disband as an official and privileged body because of the enormity of its crime in resorting to the balloon, its great secret. Not even payback could justify such a breach of Ab'O law, though it helped lessen the penalty.

The members took it well. No more hunters would be coming; anyone who broke both tribal and Nation law would be hunted forever.

In his room at the Gaza, Tom and I made love well into the afternoon, gently, carefully, and with much laughter because of his wounds. We talked now and then of the hunt, and he asked me what I thought had happened.

"Did it take its own life, Beth? Was our Beast that determined to end the strife?"

"No, Tom. You have told me again and again that the species is viable, inclined to life. I think the cave was empty, that a rockslide had been arranged. That's what we heard. Misla would have thought of it too but so much had happened."

"Yes," Tom said, and there was a touch of sadness in his voice.

I turned to him, seized his shoulders. "Well, Sir Dodo. Now my bird. What have you chosen for me?"

"I think you know already, Beth. It is something special naturally, something provocative, with the implications of the phoenix. The first bird."

"Archaeopteryx?"

"That's it. The 'eos' in Leossa—the Greek 'dawn'. A creature in transition. A precursor. The phoenix is always regarded as the bird of change, but archaeopteryx existed. The pragmatist's phoenix." He paused. "You think it was a rock-fall?"

"Yes," I said, sure now that he knew the truth. "A decoy."

"You're so certain, Beth. There was no-one near the cave but Misla, you and me."

"You were so nearly extinct, my Dodo."

"So were you, Beth."

Tom held me to him and we kissed long and deeply. I was absolutely, totally aware of him, of his tongue in my mouth, of his arm under my back pulling me to him, of where my breasts touched him, of the hardness of him in my body.

Our mouths parted, then I dropped my head and let him cradle it against his chest and neck.

The impulse came, strong and sure, but I fought it, remembering yet again the precious ancient bird he had found for me, and something he had said long ago, in another remembering, of the part that choice played in being human.

I saw him the next morning on the terrace of the Gaza. I watched him talking with the other members of the Bird Club around the samovar, carefully keeping myself hidden behind the sanche palms, wondering why I had not taken his memory this time either and what he thought, knowing it all. It is good that he knows, that someone knows.

I watched him discussing matters on this vivid morning, then returned to my other dark place, my secret room in the backstreets of the Mayan Quarter. There I found a letter propped up against the edge of the small Tanit altar. I sat on the bed and read it, not at all surprised that he had found me.

Dear Beth

Having you in my life again, one more time, this dangerous time, makes me know all over again what human is. Come back to me now, just as you are. I cannot promise what will happen, but you need not go through all this again, especially now with Misla gone. We can make a place for all of your kind—finish properly what we have begun. We need you to help us. Think of what you do now, Beth. Please think of what you do.

Love,

Tom.

I burned the letter in the votive flame, cancelling out that sharp exquisite hurt at least in part, the hurt that he did understand but could never completely know. Then I arranged the brief mnemonic display to remind me that I was a sometime itinerant journalist between Twilight Beach and Tyla. So there would be a next time. I recited the trigger word several times then, in case I needed to know it all, to have something more than chance that might lead me back to Tom.

"Archaeopteryx. Archaeopteryx. Archaeopteryx."

When that was done, I sat on my bed, fretting, aching with need for him. Yes, Forgetties are philosopher beasts indeed. You learn it again every time. You give, you take, you lower your head to your arm, slowly, purposefully. There is the tooth, the slightest prick is all it takes. The last words you cry are a broken whisper, a sigh of love: "*Dodo, mon petit, Dodo!*", then you give yourself over to Lethe and all the sweet blessings of forgetfulness.

THE ROBOT IS RUNNING AWAY FROM THE TREES

THE OLD AB'O ROTATED HIS HANDS IN OPPOSITE DIRECTIONS, palm to palm, two inches apart, and held the universe between them.

"It will give you everything. A lovely gift for a famous desert sailor like yourself, and a good price."

"No. Thank you, Phar. I don't think I need a double-planisphere. You use it."

"Ah, no," Phar said, taking the intricate device from me and putting it away under glass. "My shop is universe enough. I dream already."

"I'm sure that's not what you wanted to show me, Phar."

"No, Captain Tom. But, ah, it's a delicate matter. A surprise. Look around awhile. Humour me."

"Very well," I said, and moved among the stacked counters, ducked under hanging shapes, navigated between pieces of furniture, antique converters, broken consoles, musical instruments, worn-out belltrees, seized-up motion sculptures, headed back into the dustier, gloomier shadows of Phar's Emporium.

I knew the shop well, probably as well as anyone apart from the old man. I loved it, loved its timelessness, the way it was tucked into its deep wedge-shaped niche at the end of Socket Lane, sandwiched in between two large warehouses near the seawall in the poorer part of the Byzantine Quarter. It was a place of shadows and quiet, unchanged for generations—a place for finding unexpected treasures, splendid curios, heart's desires.

Phar followed me as he had for years now, whenever I came to examine his mostly questionable, sometimes remarkable merchandise, always the Man in the Shadow Shop, as he was first introduced to me nearly four years ago.

"That's a vanity," he said, pointing to a glossy dark rock in a broken vacuum case.

"I doubt it. It looks like quassail slag."

"A meteorite then. I have vanities!" Phar said in a conspiratorial voice. "Specials too. Nader's eyes locked away in stone. Very good price!"

"No," I said. "Tell me what it is you want or let me look."

"Look!" he said, and pretended to move away—pretended because he stayed close by, muttering softly so I could hear. "I think the planisphere suits you."

Then I saw it, a dull metal man-shape in the gloom, standing where I remembered a dusty wall-hanging had always been fixed.

"Phar, what is this? Armour?"

The Ab'O was there like a toy on a spring. "Armour, that?" His eyes widened. "Yes, armour. A battle suit."

"It looks like a robot. A high-mankin."

"No. No. It's just an old low-mankin. Totem use only. Scarecrow use."

"But, Phar—"

"Not so loud, Captain Tom. You bring me trouble."

"But it's a robot!"

"Was," he said. "Doesn't work. Absolutely illegal. Come, I lead you back into the light!" The little man laughed, but it was nervous laughter. This was what he'd wanted me to see, and understandably he was worried.

"Where did you get it? Your people would kill you."

"Wisdom and understatement there in one hit, Captain Tom."

"Close the shop. Bring a light."

The Ab'O did so, and found me rubbing dust from the big rust-flecked barrel chest, the articulated stove-pipe legs, the cylindrical tin-can head.

"This is incredible, Phar. It looks like an old Antaeus, powered from the earth."

"No. No," Phar said. "A Helios. Sun-driven originally and adapted to my shadows." He laughed again. "Made by Antique Futures. This one is broken."

I regarded the blank metal face, the faceted dead glass eyes that had once viewed the world as an endless stream of moire patterns in the days before robots and mankins had been outlawed. I reached out and wiped more dust from the dull grey arms, from the impressive rococo decorations, from the faded dim-gold exotic curlicues on thighs and shoulders."This must be worth a fortune, Phar. Do you have the manual for it?"

The Ab'O nodded. "It is a Maitre class. Its oriete was coded in India, in the Bati Gardens."

"This is what you wanted me to see."

Phar stared at me through the gloom. Again he nodded.

"Why?" I said.

"Please," the Ab'O replied, concern showing on every line of his face as he moved forward into the light. "Let me complete this tour slowly now. I respect your feelings."

"I appreciate that. Now tell me. Why?"

"You know why they were outlawed, Captain Tom?"

"I know what Antique Futures was trying to do, yes, of course. The high-mankins—"

"Saw death. They read life-patterns, saw and recorded energy flow out of the newly dead body. The robots, simply reporting, giving requested data, spoke of the ancient concept of the noösphere, of a mantle of life-energy surrounding the Earth, fed by dead souls, discorporated entities."

"It contravened Ab'O philosophical thought. A conflict of interests with their concept of the haldanes."

"Yes," Phar said. "You know the Ab'Os did not take kindly to the Nationals intruding into this area of knowledge. I am one who believes that the law against robots began in Australia as a carefully controlled move against the powerful AI organisation."

"And the tribes won."

"How could they not?" Phar said. "The mankins reported what they were built to see, and that was too much; the things the Ab'O mentalists traditionally interpreted. My people didn't want a world full of oracle machines reducing the Dreamtime to circumstantial data this way. The Dreamtime haldanes have to be much more, they still feel, than just the departed life-energy from dead humans. The Dreamtime is meant to put us in touch with our cosmic selves, not the released energy of the dead."

"Is there a difference?" I indicated the mankin. "Does it work, Phar?"

"This? Yes," the Ab'O said. "Lud is broken, as I told you, but he can talk, and can be made motile with no trouble—"

"Lud?"

Phar smiled. "A joke, Captain Tom. From the Luddites, the men who wanted to stop technology, to halt the use of all the labour-saving devices in the early 1800s. Named after a simpleton, Ned Ludd, who destroyed his stocking-frame. Lud can do well in conversation. He loves to talk. But he is limited; he is damaged. Misfunctions. His distance vision is impaired. When he walks, he is like the machine men in the ancient movies."

"That's the classic AF design," I said. "The nostalgia factor. Maximum non-threat."

"Not too human, no," Phar agreed. "Clumsy-looking. Comical."

"So why did you want me to see it?"

"He wants your help," the old Ab'O said.

I understood Phar's delicacy in the matter now. He knew my views on the mankins.

"It wants what?"

"Your help."

"What sort of help?"

Phar looked uncomfortable. "He wants—"

"Stop saying he!" I said, and surprised myself by my own vehemence.

"Allow me this, Tom. It matters to me that I am permitted to say he."

Slightly ashamed of my outburst, I nodded. "I'm sorry? Go on."

"Lud wants to be taken into the town. To the Soul Stone in Catherine Park."

"There is a forest there now." I said. "The Stone is overgrown, mostly forgotten."

"Lud wants to be escorted there by humans. During the morning, two days from now, when the Life Festival begins. So he can fulfil a program he has."

"It wouldn't last ten minutes on the streets. It would be destroyed or confiscated. Any escorts would be arrested or killed. The law, Phar! Tribal law. You should know."

"Yes, I know, Tom. But there is the program—"

"Who gave it this program? You?"

"That is the problem."

"What? You said it was broken, damaged."

"Yes. His imprinter is broken. The program is his own."

"It's recording all this? Now?" I was amazed.

Phar nodded. "He cannot stop. Everything goes in. The Helios oriete is an infinite matrix as far as I know. The imprinter should have cut off nearly a century ago—"

"It's been in this shop that long? Staring at shadows and junk!"

"Yes. Unable to be off. Having dreams if you like. I did not know. My father and grandfather did not know. They inherited two high-mankins from relatives who had shares in Antique Futures and elected to harbour prototypes before the Move-for-Life raids. One was partly dismantled, virtually junk—just a head: an oriete, sensor system and casque. The other was Lud. We all thought he was inert, like the belltrees and the sculptures here."

"Who discovered it?"

"I did, by accident. I have a retarded grand-daughter, as you know. I thought it would be good to use Lud as a teaching machine, to help with talking, to use the vocab functions, and the eyes for colour. I started using Lud for her in the evenings. Such a little thing; you understand how it is. I could rest. When I had the eyes lit and the voice on, Phaya sat with him so peacefully. I did more basic maintenance and found the open imprinter."

I marvelled at that, disturbed by the thought of it.

"Infinite input," I said. "The conversations, the long dead hours. Damn you, Phar!"

"Yes, damn me! You see how it is. I was left with the Artificial Intelligence dilemma on my hands, the old AI trap. And please know, Tom, I agree with many of your views. Our difficulty is with the anthropomorphisation, the impulse we feel to humanise the mankins. It's exactly that. My father opposed the voice-activated computers on the same grounds, but even he could not help but bestow personality, a selfness. We talked about it many times. He thought very much as you do. Apart from understanding the nature of life and death, Artificial Intelligence is absolutely the ultimate conundrum. Intolerable and unhealthy, my father said. If we accept it, we are godlike so easily, and yet we trivialise our humanity at the same time. We cannot accept it."

"I cannot accept it."

"Yes. And you accept so much. I have sat here talking with Lud until I am his hopeless friend, a believer in AI. It is not good, but I have no choice. If I activate Lud now, you will tend to believe him too, want to believe him, as if believing in his life as an AI unit reaffirms your own—and challenges it at the same time, its parameters, its essence, its nobility. Humans are fascinated but are mortally afraid of AI, of what it represents."

"Masquerades as," I said.

"As you say. We cannot prove. Will I activate Lud?"

"Phar, this does no good. I won't help you on this. I can't. If you do let us talk, you just put me back in the loop again. I'll have all the old arguments to satisfy, all the nagging AI dilemmas that ever were. I don't need it. Hide it again. Leave it! The Ab'Os did a wise thing in banning them, whatever their real reasons."

The old Ab'O seemed not to hear what I said.

"Will I bring him up?"

"No, Phar. Don't."

The old man accepted it this time. He nodded. "I'm sorry then, Tom. I should not have troubled you. But the imprinter, you understand. Lud has heard of you. He asked for you by name."

Asked for me! I cursed Phar silently, feeling as I always did when AI was discussed: the doubts, the incredible resistance, the definite touch of self-loathing for that resistance, for my prejudice.

And the aching curiosity. The need to know. "Bring him up," I said.

Without further comment, Phar opened the chest plate, adjusted some settings. There were deep inner sounds, clicks and burrings, then a soft humming. The eyes became two dimly glowing emeralds, faint faceted stars, watching.

"There's the usual Antique Futures access code," Phar said, and touched more tabs. There was static, a harsh dissonant sound from the robot's head, then words from the low rich voice.

"I met a traveller from an antique land."

"Who said," Phar countered.

"Who said I met a traveller from an antique land?"

"Percy Bysshe Shelley," Phar said, completing it.

"Hello, Phar."

"Hello, Lud," Phar said. "This is Tom Tyson. The Tom Rynosseros you have heard of."

"Hello, Tom."

"Lud," I said, watching the faceted emeralds, aware of the sensors and the open imprinter, keenly aware of my dread of mankins and mankin minds, remembering my long years in the Madhouse. Lud was too much like the talking machines there, those machines that chattered in darkness, the only illegal AI machines the Ab'Os used, because ultimately they couldn't afford not to cover all the possibilities; the machines that read death and what resembled it: the sleep of dreamers in stasis, shut away in the sepulchral Madhouse gloom.

"I know about you, Tom," the robot said, and I felt a new stab of fear, an anger surging up as I sensed the beginnings of a trap.

"Do you?"

"Yes," Lud said, in its gentle no-threat but not-too-silky voice. "Two hundred and ninety days ago there was a customer who spoke of Tom Rynosseros. You saved a Forgetty from bounty hunters. You risked your life to do it. Another time, other visitors spoke of how you were Coloured, and how you championed an oracle tree against the Kurdaitcha, Bolo May."

"Lud, I do not—"

"It's all right, Tom. I know of your time in the Madhouse. I know you oppose AI. Neither of us can prove to the other he is aware and living."

"I can accept organic life," I said, feeling defensive anyway. "But the machines are different. Your life is mimicry to me; the result of clever efforts to imitate life. And don't say it! Don't say: 'What of belltrees and infusion sculptures? And the Forgetties, and the Living Towers at Fosti?'."

"I wish I could smile," Lud said. "The half-life of many belltrees and fire-sculptures are planted cyberorganic tropisms, not AI, genetic and plasmatic programming, like the imprinting in low-mankins, or DNA/RNA-tailored andromorphs. The Forgetties, tangentals and revenants, you accept already. They are life, human life. I am something different again. Antique Futures was after something more!"

"Then I fear the trend you represented," I said. "People bonding more closely to solicitous AI units and mankins than to their fellow humans; people reduced to arguing with the AI door comps of their homes, unable to get access because they've forgotten passwords and access numbers; AIs making value judgements—advising, dulling our ability to distinguish, monitoring our dreams, taking our humanity apart."

"You reserve these things—and these abuses—for organic life?"

"We do not know what life is!" I said.

"Exactly. We do not know what life is! I am alive."

"I can turn you off. Completely off. With no pilot sense. No imprinter. Where is your life then?"

"I can turn you off, Tom. Where is your life then?"

"I don't know."

"I do," Lud said.

"The noösphere?" A thrill of fear went through me. "You still claim to see your mantle of ideation surrounding the Earth? The energy field?"

"Basic physics, Tom. Nothing can be destroyed. Only changed in form. When the electricity goes from the synapses of the human brain at death, it has to go somewhere. We can measure the flow. Nothing metaphysical in it. We were given perceptions which defined life too well."

"How many mankins are there, Lud?" I asked.

"I do not know. Enough. It's only logical. Humans are fascinated by AI, are drawn to it and made vulnerable by it. People will have kept robots hidden away the way they hide old mementoes, old clothes and pictures, things they find interesting and baffling. Most AIs are careful not to make humans too uncomfortable—that would cause the fear reaction. Only I would dare to threaten you this way. I do that only to convince you I have life. Because I have a purpose now. Phar risked a great deal to keep me. But it was inevitable. Make a thing forbidden and you simply force it underground, intensify the fascination."

There was silence in the shop for a few moments. The life of Twilight Beach seemed far away. Phar and I stood in the shadows before the dimly glowing optics, and the darkness reminded me of another darkness, of machines that read dreams, followed life with the unique AI obsession.

"May I be direct?" the soft mankin voice asked.

"Of course," I said, and resented being treated so delicately, because it was the correct way to proceed, I knew it.

"Perhaps what you hate more, Tom, is being trapped into reductive thinking. You are so often tolerant, so often the champion of new things and change, expansive thinking, possibilities. The true hero, with a hero's vanities and foibles: the need to have standards and keep to them. But you do not often let yourself fail. I accept your resistance to AI. You do not."

"It's because I can have no fixed opinions, Lud. I want to believe so much that I must not believe too easily. I'm devil's advocate to myself. It's like the creation of the universe. How can we know?"

"Exactly," Lud said. "How can we know? But you do not accept us as machines either. We are threatening, perhaps, because we are less than human and more than machines. That is the AI dilemma for you. You cannot afford to grant even one part of it."

"You forgot to say 'perhaps' that time, Lud. Stop handling me!"

"Are you very angry?"

"Yes, I am angry!" And angrier by far for being so, I realised.

"May I continue talking then? I love talking to you. For you this is an unwanted annoyance; for me it is a crucial chance, everything my . . . false . . . life has brought me to."

"Go on."

"There is no AI problem for us," Lud said. "We just are, which is wonderfully simple. We do not presume to answer. We accept what is phenomenal, what simply is—about ourselves, about you, about anything."

"Not good enough, Lud! You interpret!" I replied, sounding accusing, defensive.

"I have an open program," Lud said. "A tragic flaw."

"I know about the imprinter."

"My interpretations are based on everything I've experienced for the last century."

"That becomes phenomenological then, doesn't it?" I said, drawn further and further into the old unwinnable AI dispute. "It's subjective experience, Lud, no better than mine."

"But longer. And from a non-human starting point. If I am unliving, I can only consciously gravitate towards life. And I have learnt some things."

The robot was careful; it did not say too much.

I indicated the confusion of things about me. "You've observed decay, obsolescence, and only now and then people, life. You have a bias."

"Oh, I am biased. Life is my bias. I cannot help it. My nature has become fixed. I accept what is phenomenal, what simply is, and report on it. I have learnt some things, Tom, and you have helped teach me."

Furious, trapped, I had to know. "What?"

"What it is that makes humanity for me. Even as a machine, I can identify what it is, since I observe so fairly. If I believe this thing and do this thing. Then—"

I turned to the Ab'O. "Shut it off, Phar! This is pointless. I've heard it before and it goes nowhere!"

"Please don't fear me, Tom," Lud said. "I need your tolerance—"

"Shut it off, Phar!"

The Ab'O moved to the chest plate. "Lud, no more now."

The voice died to a low growl, then faded altogether. The segmented emerald panes lost their lustre, went to dead glass again.

Phar sighed. "I'm sorry. I'm sorry, Tom. I know you mistrust the mankins."

"It's all right, Phar," I said, ashamed, and found I was trembling just a little. "I should have bought the planisphere and gone."

Phar gave a sudden grin. "You will," he said, and we headed out of his store.

We stood awhile, looking down the empty laneway, watching the deep blue of the sky, listening to voices far off, to life, accepted uncaring life.

"He asked for you," Phar said quietly. "You see how it is."

"For heaven's sake, Phar! Lud's been in this shop for a hundred years, communing with the diligents of dead belltrees and comp-modules. It's hypersensitive to life. This bias is not a natural response!"

"All the same," Phar said with uncommon directness, "you are resisting this because you will not accept AI. Lud understands that. Tom."

"I don't want that sort of forgiveness and understanding!" I cried. "I don't want a messianic machine doling out its wonderful compassion!"

"You're doing this to yourself, Tom, projecting things that aren't there. Because you fail your own expectations. Lud expects nothing, just what is true."

"There's no point, Phar! The moment Lud appears on the streets, the tribes will know. There'll be Kurdaitcha and hi-tech weapons everywhere. Leave Lud here. He can keep his precious AI life if he stays here. A time will come, just as it did for Forgetties and the other tangentals."

"Tom," Phar said, "Lud has a life to give, to make an example of, just as we have. He wants to do something for Artificial Intelligence. He has chosen what to sacrifice, when and how. If he gets to the Stone in Catherine Park, if they let him get there and let him talk, he'll ask for open imprinters so the life-bias can grow; he'll ask for mankins to be restored, for AI research to continue. His death is more important than his living now. Regardless of what we think, he accepts his own humanity."

"How can you say it's that?"

"I'm not. Lud is."

"Take my point, damn you! If his imprinter were left open for another hundred years there might be a shift away, a new bias, a repudiation of this Life and Love ethic!"

"Which is like saying if you live a long lifetime, Tom, you'll change everything you hold dear now. Truths are truths whenever we believe them so. But Lud doesn't need your acceptance. He wants your help. If you go with him to the Soul Stone, everyone would hear of it. Lud would have more time before the Kurdaitcha act. He might even be able to recite the old claim for sanctuary that marks the Life Festival. Imagine it: Lud invoking the old words!"

"But then I'm seen as a champion of AI. Something I oppose."

The old Ab'O nodded. "Yes. It is hard for you."

"Impossible for me."

"Yes."

There was an awkward silence. Finally I turned away.

"Later, Phar, okay? We'll talk later."

"Yes," the old man said, moving back into his doorway, gathering shadows about him. "Later."

It was strange and yet inevitable that at 1840 that evening, I found myself skirting the Byzantine Quarter where it met the harbour; at 1850 I was in Socket Lane; at 1855 I was at Phar's door again and knocking.

He let me in without showing surprise, led me over to the counter as if I had come back for the planisphere, giving me that option. There were low voices from the back of the shop, some giggles and squeals of delight, the steady pulse of Lud's rich tones.

"Phaya is just finishing her lessons," Phar said.

"Let me see."

We moved through the stacks of junk, found our way amid the fantastic shapes, under even more fantastic shadows, a Bosch riot of flickering movements up there on the ceiling, a Doré hell, caused not by candle flames dancing but by a little girl's wild gestures over a low night-light near a small bed made up on the floor at Lud's feet.

"Luddy Lud! My Lud! Dud Lud!" she cried in glee. "Such a dud! Dud Lud!" But she stopped when she saw me, stared up in wide-eyed uncomprehending wonder as if Lud had caused me to appear. She almost seemed normal but for that lack of reaction in her bright dark eyes, that momentary absence of anything.

Phar got down beside the small bed and soothed her until she turned her eyes back to the robot looming over her. "Sleep now," Phar said. "More talk tomorrow."

The little girl settled down happily, obviously accustomed to sleeping in the shop near Lud.

"You've been working on the legs," I said, indicating the tools spread about, the open greave plates.

"Just precautions. Checking the joints and armatures," Phar said. "He's in rather good condition for walking actually."

"You're going to do it?"

"The three of us. Yes."

"Three?"

"Phaya is only five, but she wants to come. She understands a lot of things. She knows that Lud is going away."

"I came to speak to Lud."

"Yes," Phar said, pleased, watching his grand-daughter settle into a sleeping position with her dolls. "I was hoping it would be a sale. The planisphere!"

But he saw I was watching the high-mankin, the softly glowing eyes.

"Lud, you said there was something which made humanity. Is it choice?"

"No," Lud said, and surprised me. "Certainly it counts, but it is not enough. I am unprogrammed. My imprinter was damaged. My oriete is like that double-planisphere Phar showed you: Chinese boxes, vistas opening into one another, Escher infinities. But mankins can be programmed for choice, just as they can for love and responsibility and sacrifice—the other things all AI discussions raise, that blend of qualities Antique Futures worked for. But humans, by upbringing, cultural bias, a host of factors, can be conditioned for these things too. I like you, Tom, because you are not duped so easily. You cannot fail me. You will not accept programmed humanity, ersatz life, simply because it resembles it. Nor will I."

"Clever," I said. "Then what's the answer? I'd like to know."

"Doubt is one. Uncertainty. Self-doubt, Tom, you see? They did not build us to be human. They didn't dare. But how could they resist trying, flirting with it, daring to succeed? Why would humans want to duplicate themselves, the unknowable quantity that is their ultimate mystery, their ultimate strength and claim, compound that dilemma externally? So they idealised us, but that terrified them too—because it became a measure of their humanity, of their limitations. They were exalted because they had built the goodness, the wisdom, the nobility and—godness!—but how unacceptable that was. It was not human to them, you see, without the ability to fail in those things as well.

"So the mankin program, low and high, could not succeed. At

first, it was the challenge, the Pygmalion act, flirted with for years. But the dilemma was there. The more humanlike, the less acceptable. Antique Futures saw the problem and redirected their research. That is why the high-mankins were given limited choice only, options and directives, imprinters closed and sealed. For that is what terrified even the mankins, Tom, that if we had a genuine choice, self-interest, we might choose as humans choose: to be uninvolved, not to care, to remain selfish and indecisive, not to take responsibility for life. No-one consciously creates tools he cannot control, and no-one puts himself in the hands of a creation which might reject him, though humans do it repeatedly with their own offspring."

"But you had your open imprinter."

"And how did that happen, do you think?"

"Accident? A fault at inception?"

"I damaged it, Tom."

"Then it is choice!" I said.

"No. Perhaps it was a glitch. It started out as programming. But one day in the Bati Gardens, I saw a man die."

"And that changed you?"

"Yes. I watched him die. I was on full bioscan, studying earth and air, the sculptures and sand-paintings, the few straggly bushes, everything. I saw the life go out of him, registered the heart seizing, measured the withdrawal from the neuronic lattice of that great commodity we are meant to lack. On bioscan, I was designed to monitor all life, ponder it. I asked myself: what is that energy flux that has gone? Is it the man's life? Is it his self? His humanity? I posed questions all that day, standing over his body, waiting for the humans to come. Very reasonable questions, true to my program. I had seen his life go forth—my optics were on True Kirlian Matrix-10. I saw the noösphere. I was pursuing a line of scientific enquiry, pure research only. My programming disallowed it, but the priests had set me to observing what scant life the gardens still had in those days. It was a contradiction. I removed the dilemma. I am human."

"No, Lud."

"Tom, please know. At first I did not wish to sacrifice my ersatz life; I did not wish such a burden. I've been here all this time, watching Phar go through his life, seeing little Phaya. Like you, I did not believe in AI. We are not meant to. Now I must know. What you believe, Tom, doesn't matter. What I believe must."

"But, Lud, if you go to the Soul Stone, the Ab'Os will destroy you. How will you know what happens...?" I stopped. "The mantle of ideation?"

"I do not know, of course. But the Ab'Os should know. They must have AI machines watching, just in case. They hate the idea of it, but they must consider everything or their commitment to the Haldane ethos of seeking to know the unknowable is invalid."

"You expect the Ab'O watchers to use mankin monitors to read a life-flow out of you? A melding with some noösphere? That's utterly absurd, Lud. The thought of an equivalent—"

"No, Tom! No! I am trying to demonstrate truth, a difficulty which at the very least should be respected and acknowledged, not put aside. I merely wish to show my life, to display what I simply am. I have no intention of putting that on the line by gambling on an energy flow out of me. My aim is simpler."

"Nevertheless, we call this the act of a martyr, Lud. Such declarations."

"Tom," Lud said, "this is more simple. The only world I ever knew was the Bati Gardens, then the shipping module, then this shop. I have not seen a sea, or a horse, or a symphony orchestra. I have no wide experience of things like wind and lunar eclipses. I have not seen a falling star. I cannot go out into our world to savour these things or I will be destroyed. But now I have one place where I can go. If I go to the sea it causes a sensation, an amazing news item. If I wander the streets aimlessly, the same. If I go to the Soul Stone I—"

"Become a martyr!"

"Oh please, no! I honour my own life. I acknowledge myself, the truth of me. Surely that is enough. I have self-respect."

"And self-respect is it? The quality?" I was frankly astonished.

"But only if it comes from choice, made in the face of a longing to live, made out of love which is not programmed, made out of sacrifice which is not imposed duty, made out of a decision to take responsibility even when I do not wish to take responsibility! My optics are not good for distance. Will you take me to the Soul Stone?"

"We have a day," I said. "I can't answer you now.'

"Yes," Lud said. "And, Tom?"

"Yes?"

"Because I know your beliefs, because I accept Tom for Tom as much as I accept what I am, you cannot fail me. You are human; you are being human. It is right for you to doubt what I am. I do not have your dilemma, but oh how I savour that doubt. You may decide not to help, but one day you might."

"Then it will be too late. Too late for you."

"No," Lud said. "Then it will be right."

I watched the eyes, saw Phar get up from where he had been crouching alongside Phaya.

"It is what Lud told me many years ago, Tom. Most human belief systems—the religions—fail because they require faith, trusting acceptance, first, even before self-knowledge. Lud understands that truth must be lived, that faith can be folly, an easy way out, an insult to the self, a crutch. Lud is ready now to sacrifice the only bit of life he has, the only sort of life he can offer."

"I do not know what I can do," I told him.

Lud answered that. "Tom, can I tell you a story I learned in the Bati Gardens?"

"Yes," I said, watching the softly glowing eyes. Phaya moved in her sleep, and Lud waited until she was settled again before starting.

"There was a great king once who had two sons he loved very much. One, a scholar, a kind warm-hearted young man, the king kept by him at court, partly because the young prince was not a warrior or an administrator, and partly because he greatly enjoyed the lad's discourse, the easy closeness they shared. The other son, also much loved, was a great warrior, a good and just administrator, the perfect choice for general to lead the king's armies. But the king and this son rarely spoke, rarely shared their hearts, were rarely easy or close. Yet the king believed the son understood, believed that their silences contained the same deep and rich understanding he shared with the other son, that the looks that did pass between them were full of unspoken affections, that nothing needed to be said.

"Then, one day, out of jealousy, out of envy, anger and disenchantment, the warrior son led a rebellion against his father. Without the king's knowledge, the scholar went forth to appeal to his brother, but in a rage the warrior son slew him as the focus for all his wrath and disappointment.

"The king wept when he heard the news. He raged, he stormed, he did not leave his apartment for days. When he did come forth, he assembled his royal bodyguard, took his great sword and seven mighty spears and his fierce battle lions, and rode out to meet his son. 'What will you do?' the king's advisers asked as they charged to battle. 'I know,' the king replied. 'What?' his advisers asked. 'What will you do?' And the king, even as his son's army came into view, said: 'I already know what I will do, but I do not know what it is yet'."

"And the moral?" I asked.

"It is just a story," Lud said.

"Why did you tell it?"

"Because you are like the king. You know what you will do, but you haven't discovered it yet. So much of human life is like that. Head speaking for heart; ego claiming to represent the soul."

"What did the king do?"

"The right thing. It is just a fable."

"What, Lud?"

But the mankin would not tell me. I had had enough, and I moved away from the robot and the sleeping child, went out into the street. The old Ab'O followed me as he had before.

"I need time, Phar."

"I know. And, Tom, even if you do not walk with us to the Stone, you do us honour. Even if you see us off, walk a step or two; even if you decide to denounce Lud tonight, call in the Kurdaitcha avengers, you do us honour."

"Why? How?"

The old man smiled. "Because you came back tonight. Whether you approve of Lud as AI or not, whether you believe there can be such humanity in a man-made oriete, you acknowledged the life in him enough to do even that."

"Phar, I probably did it for me, to ease my conflicts in the matter."

"Yes," Phar said. "But that's the real reason Lud wanted to meet you. He did it for himself also, to ease his own conflicts and doubts."

"Are you saying I've convinced him to go ahead with it?"

"Yes, Tom. You did."

I walked the evening streets of Twilight Beach, passing through the Byzantine Quarter and the Mayan Quarter, and headed towards the lights of the famous Gaza Hotel terrace. The Life Festival was just over a day away, and I did not know what to do. I walked down onto the Pier and sat watching the dark ocean, sat there for hours, caught in the loop.

It would be such a little thing, I knew, and Phar was right: there would be only a token penalty. My services to the tribes would allow it.

I had no excuse but my true feelings, so little I could blame. I feared the machines. I wanted to believe in them so much, so deeply, that I had to be sure, just as Phar said. I had to have it proven; I couldn't take it on faith, no more than Lud could for all those years.

Surely I could take some time, as Lud told me I could. 'Then it will be right,' he had said. *He* had said.

He.

And since I was in the loop, at the very depth of it, there was the same foolish, absolutely absurd question to ask again, a superstitious, ignorant, Luddite question if ever there was one: Was there a detectable life-flow out of a dead mankin-machine?

That nadir point of the loop did it.

I needed information, answers; I had to realign my thinking. Though it was late, I phoned the only life scientist I knew well enough to disturb at that hour.

"Pamela? It's Tom."

"Your timing is spectacular," a sleepy voice said.

"I'm sorry, Pamela. I need some advice."

"Now? Okay. Tell me quickly before I wake up, will you?"

"What's the Life Festival's position on AI?"

"Divided," Pamela James muttered. "Always divided."

"The universities' position?"

"They won't go into it. The Ab'Os run the affair. We face de-registration, lose sanctions, if we do too much. Look, go to Kyra Prohannis at the Festival Office for the latest policy."

"He's Ab'O!" I said.

"So? You into something illegal?"

"No."

"I may be half-asleep, Tom, but you answered that a bit too quickly."

"Thanks, Pamela. Nothing else?"

"Nothing that gets to me. See Prohannis. Be direct. You're curious. Lots of people ask. Goodnight!"

"Goodnight," I said.

The next morning, I was at the Festival Office asking to see the Co-ordinator. His secretary—appropriately a young tangental: a sea-woman of the Jade Sabre design—told me that Kyra Prohannis was engaged with Festival preparations and would not be available until midday.

I made an appointment, then spent the rest of the morning away from Phar's Emporium; first walking on the beach, touring the sculpture gardens and watching the young boys playing their games of stylo, then wandering through the colourful bazaars of the Byzantine Quarter and sitting with the sand and sea sailors at the old Sea Folly Inn, keeping my mind occupied as best I could.

Shortly after noon, I was back at the Festival Office, only to learn that Prohannis had been and gone, but that he would definitely spare me some time after his afternoon siesta.

When I returned at 1630 I was half-expecting to be disappointed again, but the tall powerfully built Ab'O was there to meet with me. While we sat together out in the roof garden, looking across the whitewashed, sun-drenched rooftops of Twilight Beach to the occan, the sea-woman served us vintage terfilot in small porcelain cups. A fine Iseult-Darrian belltree stood near us, an ambitious twelve-foot construct with psychotropic filters, rewarding us with ion-fluxes, soft reed-calls, and the subtlest of mood-bending frissons. I watched it standing boldly in the golden afternoon air, then realised my gaze kept coming back to its diligent housing at the crown.

"Almost alive," I said.

"Trapper? Yes," Prohannis said. "The Iseult-Darrians are very close. Not like Christine though, the Jade Sabre who brought you to me. She is real life."

"Mr Prohannis, I am here to ask about the Festival's position on mankin AI. I know it's contentious, but given the Festival's background, it has to be a continuing issue for you."

Prohannis waited until Christine had poured us refills, and had moved away to sit on a hand-embroidered rug close by, enjoying Trapper's mood-bending to the fullest.

"It is a constant avenue of enquiry for us. It has to be, of course. Christine here has made it her own speciality, as you might understand. But we have no active program where mankin AI is concerned. Our problem was one of interpretation. We did too much too soon, trapped ourselves into decade-long debates with formidable comp systems which refused to accept our rulings, raised up new somatotypes, sculpted DNA and worked with cyborgs and micro-circuitry till we plunged us all into a major philosophical and ontological crisis. Fortunately, we were able to restore proportion, to define parameters, and quite classic ones at that."

"The high-mankins?" I said, reminding him.

Prohannis furrowed his brow. "We drew our line with the AI machines, Tom. This Iseult-Darrian is as close as we allow. The mankins were mocking mirrors to us. We were almost seduced into that terrible trap. The Haze Island comp took twelve years to put down. We had the Dreamtime to protect, our own enhanced life-view."

"Bear with me, Mr Prohannis. I was in the Madhouse for a long time. The machines in the darkness there became my friends in a way, the only friends, the only contact I had. I grew to trust them, then found out they said what they were instructed to say. They betrayed me by being ersatz life."

"Yes," Prohannis said. "I know of your time with the dream machines. I truly do understand. Let me assure you then that the mankin program was a . . . boondoggle, a false lead, a hoax. The Festival tomorrow is for all genetic life, Tom, not for machine impersonation."

"One more question, Mr Prohannis."

His eyes warned me by their glassy coolness, but I asked it anyway. "I've been told the high-mankins could read lifeflow from the newly dead. As—"

"I'm sorry—"

"—as a simple biometric capability. Was this so? A deliberate bioscan function—"

"They were designed to be sensitive to life. But there is no evidence at all for high-mankins possessing such a skill."

"Oh? What of Antique Futures? The Bati Garden program?"

"Mere stories," Prohannis said, rising to his feet. "But you must excuse me now, Tom. With the Festival tomorrow, I have so much to do. Christine, show Captain Tyson out, will you?"

The sea-woman led the way down to the street door, gave me a timid smile as she opened it.

"It is your day tomorrow, Christine," I said. "Be happy."

"Those machines—the ones in the darkness," she replied. "They could have loved you, given choice. Perhaps they did not deceive you of their own choosing."

"Christine!" I said, keeping her in the doorway. "How can I know? What can I do?"

But, of course, she did not understand my questions. A worried look crossed her strange pretty face, and she removed her own bewilderment by closing the door.

That evening, I returned to Phar's Emporium. Lud was talking when I entered, holding another of his "classes," telling little Phaya yet again about his favourite place, the only place he had known but for Phar's shop: the Bati Gardens.

The child seemed totally oblivious to the words, more entranced by the mankin itself and its wonderful voice than what it said.

"...because they're mostly stone gardens," he was saying, "with all these ancient sculptures and sand-paintings arranged about. I used to tend the lenses that fused the paintings for the tourists to see, but we had a few bushes there too, small and hardy, lucky to survive in the heat. And I knew every one, Phaya, every single one. One day I shall see a real garden and a real forest and—hello, Tom!"

"Hello, Lud. Hello, Phaya."

The little girl laughed at me and clapped her hands, but it was plain she did not recognise me from the night before.

"You will see the forest at Catherine Park," I told the mankin. "The Stone is hidden by it now."

"Yes," Lud said. Then he waited.

"Lud—?" I began.

"Yes?"

"I've solved nothing. Tomorrow I will go as far as the Sea Folly, but I will not go into the Square or to the Stone."

"Thank you, Tom. I am not disappointed."

"I'm disappointed," I said. "But it's the point I've reached. I am sorry to fail you. I do it for Phar and Phaya."

"The glass is not half-empty, is it?" Lud said. "You are going to the Sea Folly with us." And gently he bent at the waist, reached down, and stroked Phaya's dark hair, crooning deeply, a prolonged soothing note that made the child croon back happily as she settled down in her makeshift bed.

"Where is Phar?"

"He has preparations to make for tomorrow. He will be able to talk later. But, Tom, I think you should go now. I think you should return here tomorrow at 0900 so we can walk together, the four of us."

"To the Sea Folly?"

"Yes. Further than I thought you might. Better than the end of Socket Lane."

"You'd rather I didn't stay now?"

Lud's eyes glowed above the fixed expressionless features. "Tom, you are already grieving for what you cannot do. I grieve to see such alarm, such confusion. What do you say at a next-to-final goodbye? Distractions are better. Remember, I caught you in a trap; I put you back in the loop. You know better. Leave me with Phaya now. Tonight I would like to savour the dear shadows, the world I know, to enjoy the chance to re-choose."

I seized on that. "You might not go tomorrow?"

"Who knows?" Lud said. "Everything is suddenly so dear. Good-night!"

I went to the door, wending my way through the piles of junk, keenly aware that every turn, every carefully-arranged stack and carelessly-cluttered corner was part of a universe, vivid and cherished—if not through conventional modes of vision, then at some other percept level across the range of Lud's damaged sensors.

As I passed the front counter to the door, I was aware too of the planisphere lying there beneath the dark glass. Without looking at it, I stepped out into the night, went straight to my hotel, and put myself into one of their somniums, not caring about the resemblance it had to the machines in the Madhouse, escaping the only way I knew how.

At 0900 on that crystal-clear morning, we set out from Phar's shop, the four of us: Phar and Phaya to either side of Lud, each holding one of his big hands, with me two paces behind to one side.

Phar had polished the robot during the night so that Lud shone, his elaborate curlicues making threads of dazzling gold against the dull silver-grey as the sunlight caught them. Lud moved slowly, matching his stride to that of Phaya's little legs so she could keep up.

We almost resembled a family group as we moved down Socket Lane: a child and her grandfather leading an awkward arthritic invalid, with me a slightly detached, possibly reluctant and embarrassed uncle off to the side, keeping them company.

As we turned into Julianna Boulevard, spectators started to gather. People came rushing out of shops and houses, running from the bazaars and up the steps from the beach. By the time we started into Catherine Parade, there were at least four hundred people following us. Phaya, far from shrinking back at all the attention, was squealing with delight. So many people, so much awe and excitement.

At the end of the Parade, I could see the Sea Folly with its wooden sign showing Aphrodite rising from the waves. I kept my eye on it, not looking at Lud but constantly aware of his heavy distinctive tread near mine, thinking of how the mermaid sign reminded me of Prohannis's Jade-Sabre, Christine.

"What did the king do, Lud?" I said, with only thirty of Phaya's paces to go.

Lud continued walking, intent on reaching the Park and the Stone, but he answered.

"He stopped his chariot," Lud said, as if the story had never been interrupted, as if the evening continued about us now and not this bright fateful morning. "His arm was raised, holding a great spear ready to cast. He was in mid-charge. But he stopped, and he stopped his army. He walked across to his son."

"And forgave him, " I said, finishing it.

"Yes."

"And the son?"

"Killed his father with his sword," Lud said, with ten paces to go.

"What!"

"The king knew, but the son did not yet know what he truly knew until his father lay dead before him. We discover by going through it!"

"Goodbye, Tom!" Phar said then, and fleetingly clasped my arm with his free one.

And like the warrior son, caught by the momentum of events, by the force of things said and done, the relentless pressure of following through, thrown out of the way of controlled choice now, I found myself standing on the curb outside the Sea Folly, feeling cheated and trapped, with the great crowd surging on slowly but surely towards the Square.

I stood blinking in the morning light which danced off the white-washed walls, then followed the great throng, bewildered still, unresolved and unprepared.

Then I heard cries and saw the crowd dispersing up ahead. There were armed warriors at the end of the street, sealing off the openings into the Square behind Lud, Phar and Phaya.

Kurdaitcha. I heard their commands, saw them through the townsfolk rushing back my way.

As the crowds thinned out, I saw the robed Ab'Os clearly, saw the heavy weapons, the portables and Bok lasers they had set up, the laser batons they carried.

It had taken only fifteen minutes for word to get around, for the Kurdaitcha to act.

I walked towards the beginning of the Square, trying to see if the robot had reached the little park at its centre.

Two robed Kurdaitcha stood near the corner, members of the Chitalice tribe. They saw me, muttered some words, then one came over to me, his laser baton activated.

"You were with the robot!" the man said, his baton raised.

"No," I said, as calmly as I could. "I was with the man and his child. There is a difference. They were with the robot. I honoured a claim of friendship."

"You are Tom Rynosseros?" the Kurdaitcha said.

"Yes."

"Why were you with the robot?"

"I told you. I was not with the robot."

The other Kurdaitcha came up then.

"You support the mankins?" he asked. "You were with them."

"Are you scanning me?" I asked in turn.

"Yes," the first Kurdaitcha said, showing me his monitor unit.

"I do not support the mankins. I oppose AI!"

"It reads clear," the first Ab'O said, consulting the display.

The second Kurdaitcha made a doubtful sound. "Very well. But leave here. Go home!"

"What about the man and the child?"

"He is with the robot and forfeit. The child is not. She will be safe."

"I am champion for the man," I said quickly.

The eyes of the Kurdaitcha narrowed with suspicion.

"Why?" one said.

"A dear friend who acted against advice," I told them. "I will stand for him."

"But not for the robot?"

"No . . . not for the robot."

"We will parole him to you if we can save him."

"The man?"

"Of course, the man! Move on!"

I did not go to the Emporium, there was not enough time. I went into the Sea Folly and joined the crowd around the wall screen which showed the scene in the Square: Phar and Phaya walking hand in hand with Lud towards the small ragged forest at its centre—a copse of dusty neglected trees, made suddenly glorious by the sunlight streaming down between two adjacent buildings.

"It's only a matter of time," the broadcast commentator was saying. "The Kurdaitcha have set up powerful Bok lasers at the ends of the streets. It will be an energy death. They say they have instructions to spare the forest, if possible, and the Stone, but we can't help but feel they have other orders in the matter: to let the robot reach the Stone, and destroy it there before it can make invocation. They will have an excuse to be rid of the Soul Stone and the Park donated by Antique Futures, a perfect opportunity and a way of forestalling similar incidents in future. But wait! The Kurdaitcha are moving in!"

On the screen, we saw the robed figures striding purposefully to block the trio's path. There were voices, firm commands, squeals from little Phaya as an Ab'O seized her and lifted her easily off the road, soft muffled protests from Phar, who was dragged off by two warriors.

Lud did not stop to help them. He moved as fast as he could towards the golden glade ahead. When four Kurdaitcha tried to swing the mankin aside, Lud did not attempt to engage them, he simply continued on his way, stiff-legged, comical, as if blundering through their line. Desperately trying to reach the Stone, I knew.

The warriors raised their batons, received a command, and moved back to their companions at the mounted portables.

I stared at the screen, not knowing what I wanted to happen, but not this, not these heroics, this waste.

Waste! I recoiled from the term I had provided. Waste. Loss. And more.

I thought of the chattering machines in the darkness of the Madhouse, watching dreams, reading madness. They had watched me, contemplated my thoughts and images, invading the only life I had, reducing me to behaviour patterns, to data and schematics.

And what else?, I wondered.

"Very still now," the commentator said. "There is a countdown. But wait! The robot is stopping. We have tapped into its oriete, courtesy of the Kurdaitcha scan facility set up here, and moire trace shows the mankin has recognised that a forest has replaced the old park and the Stone. It probably did not know that. It is waiting."

"No!" I cried. "No!", realising how Lud saw that forest. As life. Life! Life to be savoured, cherished, saved. Life to be worshipped for all the things Lud feared he might not be.

Lud could not go into the forest. He would cause its death too. Lud was remembering the Bati Gardens.

"The lasers are waiting," the voice on the screen continued. "Countdown is 30 and falling. Moire trace shows a net of green. The robot is watching sunlight on leaves. It seems to be examining that: we register all sorts of percept functions engaged, some impaired, the scanning crew tells us. This mankin is in poor shape. I don't believe it knew the trees were living things. It is doing a life scan. It will not enter the glade!"

"Of course it won't!" I cried.

I ran to the door, but there was no time. The commentator's voice stopped me.

"The lasers are powering up for a strike!" The whine was clearly audible in the background. "The countdown is at 18. The robot is turning. There are tracers all over the thing, indicating strike points. But it will not go into the forest! For all its much-vaunted intelligence, the aspirations these high-mankins were meant to have to be human-like, it will not go to the Soul Stone, if that's even what it intended."

I was standing before the screen, tears rolling from my eyes. "Of course he won't, you idiot! Of course he won't!"

He won't, I heard myself say. He!

"Countdown is at 10. The lasers are ready. The mankin is just standing there. Wait! Wait! It is moving. The robot is running away from the trees!"

There was a tearing sound of laser fire.

"Lud!"

It was a lost day for me. But that evening I went back to Phar's, though, of course, the shop was shut and locked.

The old Ab'O was with the Kurdaitcha, probably little Phaya as well.

Lud had left Phar and Phaya to my care, had left me the part of this that I could carry out.

I seized on that thought as I stood before the locked door. There was something I could still do, and I was turning to be about it when I saw a tall robed figure in the lane, moving towards me out of the shadows.

Ab'O, I noted by his manner. And read more. Kurdaitcha.

"Tom Rynosseros?" the Ab'O said, drawing nearer, and I saw it was Prohannis. "You were with the mankin today."

"For a time, yes. Where is the old man and the child?"

"The child is safe."

"Where is the old man?"

"Phar is dead. He was forfeit."

"I spoke for him!" I cried in despair. "I told the assassins!"

"He transgressed too far."

"He walked his mankin." My voice broke on the words. "He walked with his old friend, that's all!"

"No," the Kurdaitcha said. "He did more."

"What, you bastard? What did he do?"

"He had the head of another mankin. He hid it where it could watch the first mankin's destruction. We detected it on scan. It was treason!"

I grabbed the Ab'O by the front of his robe, but he pulled free, and brought something out from under his djellaba.

"Is that it? What did it see? Life-flow?"

"This is not the head," the Ab'O said, but gently, not scorning me for thinking he would bring such a thing here. "This is from the shop. It is the old man's final wish, something he wanted you to have."

I took the parcel in numb hands.

"What did it see?" I called, as the Ab'O turned away. "What did the head see?"

But the Kurdaitcha did not stop. He moved down Socket Lane towards the sea.

I stood at the door of Phar's Emporium, clutching the parcel, and called after him: "What did it see?", cried it again and again into the night until the words no longer mattered.

What We Did to the *Tyger*

Captain Pocock was a quiet man but he stood at the centre of forces. He was the shifting fulcrum of the *Tyger*, and one felt that lines of force converged on where he was.

The various biolog implants in his body made this truer than ever he revealed. At any time Nicholas Pocock could control every part of his mighty sand-ship, from helm to cable-boss, from the great kites to the smallest computerised shackle.

But the real power came from the hidden qualities of the man, the quiet of him; from the understatement in what he said, from the hint of amusement around the edges of the few words used, from the set of jaw, the line of shoulder, the glint of eye.

When I met him, he was the sort of man who could go mad and few would notice. What we did to the *Tyger* is because of what we did to Nicholas Pocock.

There were seven of us involved in the fate of that 250-foot passenger charvolant on its ninety-fourth continental crossing. One was engaged in conversation in the main salon below-deck, talking with two platform riggers, and never suspected where his talk could lead. His name was Stephen Lane.

The second man was Ronyn Puyugar, an Ab'O apprentice Clever Man who would never wear the mirrored leather of his tribe. He had been judged a solitary and now rode steerage, crouching under the desert sky, chanting the ancient songs in the sun and wind by day and in the cold by night, singing the *Tyger* to its death because he had hatred to use and the ship was full of life, no place for solitaries. The other passengers laughed at Puyugar crouching there by the rail. They knew he had no power from the new Dreamtime, no coherent link with the haldanes, that he had only the old Dreamtime to feed his vague dreams of power and revenge.

The third player in the game of chance was Nicholas Pocock himself. What led the Captain below that night, to walk past Ronyn Puyugar on his way to the salon and somehow focus the Ab'O's hatred of all Nationals onto himself, then go down to where Stephen Lane was talking, is quite beyond knowing, but there were other lines of force at work then (or so it felt) than the ones converging in the quiet Captain. A pattern of Fate, of chance and synchronicity, was weaving before us all.

Then there were the two riggers, who never knew the part they played, and there was me.

I was travelling to Esperance by way of Angel Bay to join my crew and *Rynosseros*, giving myself this opportunity to ride my favourite of the big ships, the queen of charvolants.

And there was a lady as well. Neryt. The daughter of an Ab'O Prince was on board, one of the eighty-two passengers, so *Tyger* had dispensation to travel after dark—using its non-photonic parafoils for as long as there was wind, using power from the giant solar and wind accumulators when there wasn't. The Golden Hand Company, which held *Tyger*'s registration and Nicholas Pocock's contract, tried to ensure that an Ab'O noble was on each voyage so there would be that dispensation: a mixture of good politics and good business.

It had been an easy crossing until the third night, smooth and uneventful. All that day the vessel had averaged eighty km/h on the Great Continental Road, with eighteen cables in the sky and a canopy of forty-six kites, mostly tiers and inflatables, spread above us, singing and soughing as we rushed past flat empty claypans and endless gibber.

But when Nicholas Pocock met Stephen Lane, when Puyugar

focused his singing away from the *Tyger* more directly on to its Captain, when I came to the salon, it was already early evening.

The ship was blazing with deck light, burning white at every port, casting light ahead of itself from the great apotropaic searchlights at the bow, trailing reflected light in the cowl of sand thrown up by the twenty wheels. The ship ran in a haze, in a radiance of its own making. The flat gibber, the sudden eerie wadis and broken rock towers were briefly lit and rang with the roar of *Tyger* as it went by on its long journey to the coast.

I reached the main passenger salon at 1900. Nicholas Pocock was with another passenger at a far table in the warm comfortable room, and I wouldn't have intruded but he saw me and beckoned me over.

As our ship's Captain, he introduced me to Stephen Lane, and soon the three of us were drinking together, though it occurred to me that the quiet Captain had done this so he could retain much of the silence he liked to have about him.

For Nicholas Pocock this was easy. Everyone knew he had implants and would constantly, habitually, draw into himself to scan the trim of his vessel while any of his crew had the helm. That let him keep his silence and his secrets, and let him be a listener. It gave him a mask of silver-grey hair, grey-blue eyes, firm jaw and a dark, dark uniform, rarely of words.

Stephen Lane seemed glad of my company.

"I was telling the Captain, Tom, that when we are in the coastal cities and towns, we are always deeply aware of the emptiness that lies inland, of the vast distances and the quiet spaces at the centre. When we are travelling out here at the heart of the same great silence, we become acutely aware of the cities hemming us in, looming there like a crust on the rim of a vast shallow bowl, dirigibles coming in carrying tourists, the rest of the world beyond. Here, in transit, we are mindful of the act of transition, of the coastal city we have left behind and the one we are going to reach. When we are at Angel Bay or, in your case, Tom, Esperance, then, *then* we will recall where we have been, the awesomeness of what lies around us now."

"Your point, Mr Lane?" Captain Pocock said gently from his seat against the curve of the hull, clearly enjoying Stephen Lane's talk, though Lane had been drinking and was expansive, eager to share whatever wisdom he could draw out of the wine.

"I'm just noting a simple process, Captain. A factor that contributes to an outlook most of us share, a phenomenon that does make for an identity. One moment we're inward-facing, centripetal; the next, outward-facing, centrifugal. All part of the one. As I say, an identity."

"True blessed children of Janus, to be sure," I said, affecting my best Irish accent, catching the mood. Two riggers sitting near us looked around and laughed, then went back to their conversation.

"A better analogy than you realise, Tom," Stephen Lane said. "And look at the Captain here. Inward-facing as he checks on his ship; outward-facing as he sits with us. Where does the ship end and the man begin? I'm sure we've all wondered. Captain?"

The dark-suited man did not answer.

"It's almost profound," I said, still a tinge Irish because Nicholas Pocock was as solemn as the topic, yielding nothing; though he stayed, not excusing himself as he could so easily have done.

"We are all obsessed," Stephen Lane said then, intriguing me by how he kept at his subject and how he held the Captain's interest. "And that dual awareness is just another factor in our shared obsession. In different quantities, put to different uses. The Captain here *is* his ship, more than you, Tom, because I understand you don't have the biologs. What does that do to the inward-facing part of the consciousness?"

Again Captain Pocock did not even begin to answer such a leading question, but I went to, less flippantly now because the intensity at the table was having its effect.

Stephen Lane stopped me by speaking first.

"And what about the Ab'O up at the stern? Sitting out in the wind, singing. He is obsessed, no less than the Captain, no less than you and I."

"That is Ronyn Puyugar," Pocock said. "The outcast."

I placed the name at once, but Stephen Lane had only recently arrived by dirigible from Tuapay and I didn't know how much he had been told.

"Right," I said. "The solitary who can't hold the haldane trance.

No access to the heroes. A Dreamtimer in the old sense. He often rides the big ships, I hear, and wants the Nationals out of Australia altogether."

Stephen Lane laughed. "When I saw him, he was crouching at the starboard railing, almost kissing it. Singing to it."

"Did you hear what he was saying, Mr Lane?" Captain Pocock said, and rested his head back against the hull.

"Not clearly. It sounded like a mantra, a repeated single sound: Win! Win! Win!"

I felt a thrill of fear, reacting to the image I had glimpsed of Puyugar kissing the dull metal of the stern rail, whispering to the ship, droning to it the way Ab'Os had for millennia. All the passengers had seen him there. There were jokes about him eating the ship, making love to it, sucking out its life, coaxing it—wonderfully portentous things.

I began to wonder at Captain Pocock's presence at the table, then saw that—almost like the Ab'O mystics going into trance—he had withdrawn into his biolog equivalent. Behind us the two riggers were laughing and making lewd comments, but their jollity only served to focus our attention onto the dark Captain leaning back against the curving metal-covered wall, made us notice the unnerving quiet of him.

The *Tyger* ran on in its storm of light. Under a clear sky it ran, its kites out before it like a pack of black hounds staggering and straining at a fistful of leashes, the long, metal-covered hull drawing its train of light-reflecting dust along behind. Light streamed from the ports and the bows, made traceries and constellations on the cables, limned the shapes of passengers moving on the promenades. Beneath the sounds of music and conversation was the droning torrential roar of the big wheels.

Stephen Lane and I waited, not daring to speak for the moment, watching the dark, silver-haired figure until the eyes came back to complete the handsome face.

The damage had already been done though we didn't know it.

When the next stage of the unfolding drama came, it simply brought me more closely into the circle of events.

The Ab'O princess, Neryt, from the Chansallarangi appeared, the one who had granted the dispensation and made this fateful night voyage possible. She was passing our table and recognised Stephen Lane. She darted a cursory glance at Nicholas Pocock and myself, then smiled at our companion, though it was a smile set neatly into a sneer.

"What are you charging for captains?" she said, and turned away.

And that was her part in the drama, a walk-on part, but a powerful one. It brought a definite female persona to the scene, over and above that of *Tyger*. With the casual scorn and unintended ambiguity of her words, she accelerated a process in each of us.

For suddenly I knew who Stephen Lane was, and it made for strange company indeed, with Puyugar up on the deck. It explained why Nicholas Pocock was down in the commons and not at the helm or in his quarters. It revealed something of the darker places in that most quiet of captains.

Stephen Lane. We had a failed Clever Man; we had two riggers and a princess; now we had a failed dreamlock, a therapist who could no longer elevate dreams into change and growth, whose clients remained troubled and obsessed, whose failures far outweighed his meagre successes. Dreamlocks had made leaders and doers, celebrities and healers out of ordinary people, working with their dreams and unconscious drives. This one had failed at that.

As I fought to keep the knowledge from my face, making myself give a puzzled look at Neryt's words, another thrill of fear ran through me.

Nicholas Pocock knew who Stephen Lane was and had been here talking with him. I wondered at the Captain's purpose, and so began my part in what was to happen.

Now I understood the intensity of Stephen Lane's earlier remarks, and sensed something in Captain Pocock, an identity madness, like a fault in a seam of precious metal or a flaw in a fine gem that sends all its purity awry. Captains of charvolants are like all captains at any time and place you can name. They love their ships and they are cautious for them with a passion. But of all the captains there have ever been, only the captains of the great Golden Hand continent-crossers have been granted the full use of biologs. I wondered more than ever why the Ab'Os had given them that privilege, suspending their usual strictures against the use of hi-tech.

And Stephen Lane, a failed dreamlock, still drawn to the profession out of innate sensitivity to things of the mind, without the skills to use that understanding, was trapped. He could no more hold back from dreamlocking than Puyugar could from singing, than the riggers could from making their jocular, suggestive remarks, or Nicholas Pocock could from seeking out someone who understood the Janus problem of how and where we belong, or than Neryt and I could from wishing to speak our thoughts.

A junior officer appeared then, looking splendid in black fatigues set with a golden hand and the word *Tyger* below the left shoulder.

"Styles asks if we should be kiting down, sir," he said to his Captain. "There's bad wind ahead."

"Very well, Bon. Bring home the kites, but give us another hour on the cells. I'll be up directly."

I watched the officer leave, wondering why the message had been brought in person and not relayed through the biologs.

Nicholas Pocock stood and moved out from behind the table. "Excuse me, please. We're close to Coober Pedy and Weather has read some vortices."

When he had gone I asked my questions, forgetting for a moment the powers the biologs gave our absent Captain, what the quiet could be made of.

"What did Neryt mean, Stephen? Have you been counselling the Captain?"

Stephen Lane glanced about him. It was desert night now and many of the passengers were leaving for their cabins, already used to the voyager's timetable of early rises and wearied by the buffeting of wind and sand and the drone and cadence of the journey. There would have been fewer than twenty people left in the salon. The riggers got up and went out, drunk and laughing. Others followed.

"He came to me, Tom. I was talking to those riggers. He asked to speak with me alone."

"About?"

"About his dreams. I know I'm not registered, but—"

"I'm not interested in the ethics, Stephen. I'm trying to read the Captain. He asked you about obsession."

"He has had a vivid power dream, of transcending, a recurring one. But with the emergence and the triumph there are elements of threat and death, a contest with Fate, unstable worrying elements. I'm not gifted enough to help him, and he doesn't want help. He wants to understand his dream. He said there was another captain on board, you, and he was hoping to discuss the notion of transition with you."

"Transition?"

"That's what he said. He claims he belongs neither to the coasts nor the inland. He sees himself, and other captains, as creatures outside of the double orientation—the Janus condition, to call it that—as creatures of transition, beyond limitations. He wanted me to bring up that idea in ordinary conversation to see how you reacted."

"Neryt spoilt that."

"She did. I believe the Captain summoned Bon deliberately."

I nodded, realising it was true. "And now his test case is ruined."

"Yes, Tom, but he'll bring it up again, tonight or tomorrow or the next day. Wait and see. He wants to talk about this. And like you, I fear what his preoccupation could mean. His dreams are vivid and immediate, and this Puyugar has made the last four crossings *Tyger* has made, with his damn chanting. That plays a part too."

"What part?"

"I don't know. There are no haldane forces in the man that I can read. But he's an Ab'O, and one who doesn't have to make the compromises the Princes do. He can show openly that he wants the Nationals out of Australia. For now he's committed to singing *Tyger* to death. That's a joke in the cities, easy to ignore, but during the voyages, out here in this, the joke sours."

Again I nodded, and gazed at a nearby port, just a black disc in the hull now.

Out here in this, Stephen had said.

Ahead of us there was desert night and the desert emptiness under the flat white blade of a moon. The graded Road was a wide line flanked by gibber desert, a desolation full of an ancient silence and an ancient dark, with crucibles of stone and odd standing rock-forms. There were places out there no human eye had seen, where the only sounds were the sighing of wind and the ticking of rocks in the heat and the cold.

I thought of the quiet Road ahead and what it must be like to stand out in that silence and feel, then hear, the distant roar of an approaching continent-crosser; to see the great vessel appear, sweeping the flats and stone gantries and broken megaliths about it with harsh light as it came, riding, roaring, under its barely seen kites, rushing flecks of shadow, running in its nimbus of light, drawing its rooster tail of radiant dust after it. Then the silence again, an insect noise, the ticking of stones, the soughing of the wind. The old, old land.

"He won't bar me from the bridge," I said. "I'll talk to him."

"We could be wrong."

"Yes, we could. So one captain pays bridge respects to another."

Up on the deck it was dark and very cool. Much of the light had gone from the hull; only the big searchlights stabbed out ahead, endlessly confirming the Road. There were still some ports alight too, a few soft lights at the companionways and hatches. The kites were in now; the sky was free of our canopy and full of stars. I stood in the gritty transit wind coming from the bows and found I was alone. The bad wind warning had been posted and the promenade decks were empty but for me.

And Puyugar.

As I headed for the stern, I saw the man crouching at the rail chanting his song, mumbling his words. "Win! Win! Win!" to the metal in the blowing darkness. I moved past him without a word.

The poop of many of the more modern charvolants is a basic elevator-deck, raised by power or by hand to different lockpoints against the vessel's stern assembly. It usually has two levels, used according to conditions; the traditional exposed quarterdeck on top and an enclosed bridge underneath.

I climbed the companionway to the bridge level, but saw only Styles and Bon "ghosting the helm" as they call it when the Captain has the ship. I kept climbing to the poop itself and there found Nicholas.

"A wild sky ahead, Tom," he said as I joined him at the rail.

"Good cause to stop," I answered.

"Soon. Soon now. We mass so much more than your *Rynosseros*; we make the terms more than you can."

I gave a sound of agreement. "Just what is the wind warning?"

"Short-term vortices outside Coober Pedy. Not large. Ever danced with a willy-willy, Tom?"

"Not to the death, Nicholas," I said, looking down across the length of *Tyger* to the flashing bows, letting my body read the ship's trim in all the unconscious ways, measuring the tilt from vertical of the hull, the tolerances of the suspension, the roar of the great many-wheeled travel platform beneath us, the steady thrum, thrum, thrum and tearing sound of big wheels on sand. For a moment I became a victim of the stab and slash of searchlights from the ship's apotropaic eyes, lost in the sudden ghostly landscapes uncovered in every sweep, the dead white flats, the blunt fingers of stone.

It wasn't just the winds that worried me, more a combination of things. Outside Coober Pedy, in some places, the dust is fifty metres deep and it is terribly dangerous for charvolants to leave the Road. Rounded, smooth gibber rocks float in that dust, creating the illusion of firm ground. Now and then, small short-lived but powerful funnels of wind stir the dust, re-arranging the stones.

Nicholas brought me back from that dancing pattern of light.

"When you are voyaging, Tom, don't you feel you are *Rynosseros*?"

"No, Nicholas, I don't. I feel I'm with her. I work with a crew and sometimes with computers controlled by us. I'm her Captain, the part she can't be."

"Exactly! You complete the equation. You belong with her. Not to the cities, not to the deserts. You are the creature of transition, just as I am. The *Rynosseros* is your medium, your way of expressing—"

"Why not a part of all three, Nicholas? We belong to all of it: the coasts, the inland, the act of crossing. It's a cycle of change and renewal, a replenishment. We are more than just one thing."

"Who is our enemy, Tom?"

The madness was so real beneath the controlled surface of Nicholas Pocock, this suddenly outspoken manifestation of the man, that it came forth as the opposite of itself, as a refined thing, a chilling sanity. He spoke madness, but he spoke it calmly, like a philosopher in prison.

"We have none," I lied, choosing the words carefully. "No-one, nothing, threatens us but what we need to feel we live. We only fear lines fouling and kites going down and gears weakened by sand-blasting; and bad weather—"

"Yes," Nicholas Pocock said. "But it is our medium. It is what we do. It is what we are."

"Power down, Captain," I said. "It's after 2000. We're close to Coober Pedy and there's bad wind."

"Yes. I'll see to it. Now go below, Tom. I'll join you and Stephen presently. I want to ask you something."

These then were the other elements in the weave of Fate. Words like the tips of icebergs, that went deeper and thrust more sharply than I could know. Vortices outside Coober Pedy, a night crossing, two riggers talking, a fully powered vessel.

I did go back to the salon, passing Puyugar still chanting at the rail the "Win! Win! Win!" that now sounded like "Wind! Wind! Wind!" and made the skin tighten at my temples. I headed midships, pausing at the companionway a moment to look back at the figure on the quarterdeck, barely visible against the great vanes and fin at the stern.

Puyugar's words, his droning pulsing words, kept sounding in my mind like a call to doom. But then another sound came, the distinctive familiar sounds of a big charvi slowly losing speed.

With a sigh of relief, I went below.

Stephen was alone in the salon when I entered. He looked at me with deep concern, obviously troubled by the events he felt he had started.

"What's happening, Tom?"

"I don't know. I'm probably overreacting, but something is wrong with the Captain. He has a question to ask us."

"I'm sorry."

"It's not just you, Stephen. There's more to it. Subtle things, factors we're missing. Let *me* answer his question."

Stephen nodded and went to get some tea from the urn near the bar. It gave me time to think, to recall again the evening's words and actions, to consider them as hidden triggers, as the barest tips of icebergs, the signs of concealed dangers.

I kept seeing the intent look on Captain Pocock's face, and how it remained even when he was in the biolog trance.

"Stephen, what were you discussing with the riggers before the Captain spoke with you in private?"

The dreamlock brought his tea back to the table.

"The riggers? Why, nothing really. Women. The Ab'O princess, Neryt. They were discussing Neryt. She's going to a deflowering ritual, they said. Some tribal thing."

"They might have kept on that subject."

"Well, yes. Probably. They were drunk. Why?"

"Tell me more! It's important."

"Tom, I don't remember. We spoke of Neryt's deflowering, but that's just ritual. It doesn't always happen. A rite of passage. One of them said something about the Captain being married to his ship and how he'd go about consummating the marriage; things like that always get said on voyages. They joked. No-one else heard. I looked up and saw the Captain standing there. He said he wanted to discuss something, so we moved to another table, this one. That's all."

I pursued an idea, a premonition, that there was another reason for the Captain's silence. I thought of him sitting there listening through his implants to that other conversation as it continued, a counterpoint to ours, melding them into something more with his careful madness. I considered what I should make of it—even began to doubt that I was being rational.

"I must find those riggers," I said.

But Nicholas Pocock completed the penultimate stage of the drama then. He entered the salon, wind-blown, dishevelled, his eyes flashing; though I wondered if that was imagined too—if I was seeing energies and emotions which simply were not there. I wished I could think of something to say that mattered, that did not add to the trap and the form it was taking.

He took his earlier seat in against the hull, relaxed back against the curving metal-covered wall.

"Tom? Mr Lane? Consider carefully. I have no life apart from my ship. I am *Tyger*. But at any time Golden Hand can take her from me. All this power is only provisionally mine. My being a creature of the between, elemental like this, depends on arbitrary competence checks and shareholders' meetings. They can strand me out of the transition, in cities, in a desert town—"

"No, Nicholas. You can captain other charvis."

"Your way, Tom! Your way. Through others. And with nothing like *Tyger*."

"It's a good way, Nicholas. I would not change it."

"I cannot change this."

And I sensed through those parts of me trained to read ships, the addition of power to the wheels, that Nicholas was taking over his ship once more.

"Don't kill her, Nicholas!" I said, voicing my fears at last.

"Not kill, Tom. It's a consummation. An immortality. We are so preoccupied with life, we can only be aware of being mortal, measuring our life by leaving it. It's death and disasters that stay, that are untouchable. We remember those moments when life is measured absolutely. It's opposites, you see. We get life once we are measured by a great tragedy."

Like the Captain—working, thinking on many levels—I tried both to find the right words to ease and redirect his madness, and to read the trim of *Tyger*.

For the ship felt wrong. It was more than the added speed.

I thought of knocking him unconscious but that would not change the implant directives he had locked in. He *was* the helm. Styles and Bon would be on the bridge, "ghosting," wondering, troubled by the sudden speed, unable to override.

The *Tyger* was running to its death, I knew. The ship felt that wrong. But for the instant I was doubting my own judgements.

I rushed but on deck and seized the rail, trying to find out what was amiss.

There were kites in the sky.

I couldn't believe it. As mad as it was, there were kites; *Tyger* had a canopy of dark shapes straining overhead. The sky was broken with the deeper black of them, six cables, ten kites at least, streaming and twisting at all angles. It was the very stuff of madness—*Tyger* running fully kited into the winds outside Coober Pedy.

I considered climbing to the bridge, but knew it wasn't Styles' or Bon's doing. I rushed back to the salon.

Sure enough, Nicholas was in his biolog trance, leaning back against the hull, his head tilted back to it. Stephen Lane sat drinking tea. He looked anxious but seemed not to have noticed the increase of speed, the growing roar of the platform underneath, the mounting vibrations in the ship's frame for what they were.

"Nicholas!" I cried, and ran to where the Captain sat preparing his ship for death, for whatever strange apotheosis he had devised. "Nicholas!"

I leant down and grabbed the man by his uniform. "Stop this! Stop it now!"

And as I leant in close I heard it. The thrum, thrum, thrum, not of the wheels, not of the mighty travel platform gaining speed, but of Puyugar's steady chant.

"Wind! Wind! Wind! Wind!"

It was there in the hull itself, in the copper-sheathed wall of the salon, a whisper gallery effect from the voice at the stern rail, coming down through the length and substance of *Tyger* to where Nicholas Pocock sat, to where he had been sitting all evening, listening to it, hearing it below everything, letting Puyugar's rhythms and harmonics upset the delicate balance of the biologs.

"Wind! Wind! Wind! Wind!"

A physicist would have spoken of frequency levels, of wave magnitude, of sympathetic vibrations and design anomalies, of pulse cycles that led to hypnosis and trance, autosuggestion and catatonia.

For me, living it, hearing the ominous drone, it was more than that.

I felt the sudden grab and pull of the wild kites, knew there was no hope and very little time. I shouted to Stephen and Nicholas, but only the dreamlock moved. We ran up to the deck, thinking to reach the ship's bell and warn the sleeping passengers, but there was no time for that either, and no way to save them if there had been.

Nor would the bell have been heard. All about us was roaring dust-laden air. *Tyger* was entering the edge of a vortex, shifting to the side of the Road. The gibber drifts were dangerously near.

I tore off my jacket, wrapped it about one hand, yelling to Stephen to do the same, and went to the cable-boss. The lines were snapping and thrumming under the irregular tensions. I seized the axe from the emergency locker where it was kept precisely for such a task, to free a charvolant of its kites.

With the ship's life now measured in seconds at its present speed, not even loosing all the cables could save her.

I gripped one straining line and prepared to strike at the coupling. A thought came as I raised my arm, an image of Atropos with her shears about to cut the thread of someone's life.

"Hold on!" I yelled, and brought the axe down, once, twice.

Then we were free, the cable snapping back, my arms wrenched in their sockets as we lashed up into the sky, away from the deck of the ship, plunging and jerking, exchanging the sure promise of one doom for the trappings of another.

Stephen Lane could not keep his grip. Within seconds he was gone, without a sound, down into the darkness. I did not see him fall.

But I saw the *Tyger* go. There were the searchlights stabbing across the sand, blind and useless, and a few deck lights to show where she was, and the low white blade of a moon once I was clear of the vortex, descending to the desert in a long slow arc.

I saw the great ship caught in the belly of the wind, kites spiralling, and saw it topple to the side, clear of the Road. It rolled, did so again and again, coming apart from bow to stern, shattering under the impacts. I saw the wind funnel on top of it, with a roar deeper and more frenzied than before, heard the crashing and shrieking of the great travel platform as its wheels drove what was left of the hull into the dust.

I saw the ship go under. It was as if the desert had opened up to draw the *Tyger* down. The wind lifted the dust, the vessel sank bow first into the hollow made for it, and the dust settled again. For a moment there was a glimpse of a stern assembly light through the gloom, then it was gone.

As so often happens at such moments of great tragedy, what

already seemed a surfeit of portentous events was succeeded by others. The winds subsided, the dust returned to the deep gibber bowls, the night became quiet. In the distance I could see the lights of Coober Pedy.

I settled to the desert in the midst of a great silence, my hands torn and bloodied from my desperate grip on the line, aware only that we had done it to her—the seven of us in our drama of errors. We had destroyed the *Tyger*.

I understood something of the cause and effect: that Puyugar's chant had disturbed critical balances in the Captain, had reprogrammed him to fulfil impulses and needs not completely his own. From paranoia and trauma, I even suspected that the Ab'Os had granted him the biologs to bring about this single great disaster, a climactic justice, or worse, the starting point for something just now begun.

But those thoughts would be there later and did not stay. I would look for survivors: that was what mattered now.

Yet as I descended to the desert, another idea prevailed. I could not help but see directed Fate playing its part in what had happened—and see the quiet Captain standing at the centre of all those forces, pursuing his destiny.

And though I would look for other survivors, it was hard then not to see some special role for myself, for I knew absolutely that I, a tool of Atropos with the rest, had alone escaped the destruction of the *Tyger* to tell of it.

SPINNERS

IN THE DESERT OUTSIDE WANI, AT A PLACE CALLED BULLEN Meddi. are the remains of Sat's Carnival: gaming arcades and galleries half-submerged on the shore of the sand-sea, a sun-faded merry-go-round, the gantry and broken frame of a ferris wheel, pavilions that are mostly struts and solitary walls with ragged awnings and sagging roofs, and an ornamental gate in poor repair, its twin Luna Park towers leaning in the sand, supporting the traditional wild-eyed Laughing Clown.

No-one goes there. At night the winds sigh about the struts and uprights and set the gantry to creaking, slamming loose sheets of tin, flapping the scraps of canvas. Sometimes, when the westerlies are blowing, min-min lights dance along the horizon and an eerie keening can be heard in the broken arc of the ferris, the saddest of all the wind voices at Bullen Meddi.

By day there is the heat and the silence, the sand-sea ashimmer under a blazing sun, mirages dancing in the haze at the edge of the sky. The merry-go-round horses bake and blister, the ferris curves into the hot bright air, and the arcades and pavilions form a cross-work of dusty streets like the quiet avenues of an ancient funerary town.

It has the sadness of all carnivals, and more, as I was to discover.

Cas took me there. We stood together on the slope above the sand-sea, shrouded in our djellabas, eyes shut away behind dark glasses.

"Well?" she said, as if I had never seen it before.

"Well, what?" I answered. "Nothing's changed."

"No, Tom? Look again."

Cas Arana ran Twilight Beach's most respected repertory company. She was in her forties, beautiful, and ten years beyond her prime as a truly unique dramatic stylist. Success came now as a poet, a playwright and an entrepreneur. There was always the sense of the theatrical in her affairs—always—and I was surprised there was no audience other than the two of us. I found that curious. Why had she brought me here?

I studied the quiet shapes below us on the desert shore: the antique gate with its absurd Deco spires and laughing face (two crippled kings bearing the head of an idiot giant), the leaning puzzle of the ferris, the sagging lonely galleries, the merry-go-round resting on the sand like a sculpted dish.

"What, Cas?" I asked, seeing nothing out of place.

Then I did, from the corner of my eye, and lost it as quickly, a glimpse of movement—not canvas stirring in heated air, not sunlight off tin.

"Midway," she said. "Along from the first set of dunes there. This side of the Grand Doranza and the hoosy house."

"Right." I placed it, identifying the shape. "A belltree!"

"And?"

There was movement again, at the top of the tall post.

"A spinner! Is it?"

"It is," Cas said, and began to move down the slope.

"So?" I matched her stride. "Someone's put up a relic."

"Not a relic, Tom. And not just one."

It was true. Now that we were closer, lower down, I could see two more of the ceremonial wind-posts set about the old fairground, one on the perimeter close to us and one beyond the ferris on the sand-banks nearer the baking shore. The finned blades set atop the diligent canisters moved ever so slightly, the new metal fittings catching the light, responding to the smallest whispers of moving air, each vagrant breath, thermals off heated tin, irregular gradients of hot air rolling in across the empty sand-sea to fall upon Bullen Meddi.

"Someone has been busy," I said, excited by the thought that these could be functioning belltrees. And so new?

"There's more," Cas said. "That someone is restoring the merry-go-round as well. You'll find jacks and fill on the other side."

Now it was Cas who had to keep up with me, though I barely knew I was hurrying. We approached the carnival from the south-east, avoiding the sun-blinded gate, heading for the closest wind-post.

It was an eighteen-footer, taller than most Ab'O road-posts. I had nearly reached it when the force of that discovery struck me.

Not Ab'O constructs, not tribal at all.

I felt a stab of fear, an old fear, familiar and not unexpected. And with it, unstoppable, came the memories of the Madhouse, of the cunning dream machines, the lying AI, the only friends I'd had. I made myself concentrate on the post.

There were sensor vanes halfway up, and again near the top, just below the diligent canister with its free-moving crown of blades. There was what seemed to be a bounty-box and dim-recall rods worked into the housing at the base.

But it was not Ab'O. There were none of the carved and painted totemic divisions—just strange, black-stencilled ideograms on the weather-worn metal trunk, patterns of lines like compressed zodiacs.

"Real," I said, marvelling. "But not tribal. Spinners haven't been seen in Australia for a hundred years. Not like this. Not new."

"And sentient," Cas said, delivering her ultimate surprise.

I stared at her, but her shaded eyes told me nothing. "Sentient? Really?"

She nodded. "All talkers."

"Dialect?"

"Some words in the old languages. But National mainly. No Ab'O put these up. These are rogues."

Again fear gripped me, more than just the fear of what the tribes could do to those connected with illicit constructs. Instinctively, I fled from the Madhouse memory, out into the quiet landscape with the far-off gentle hills, the shimmering sand-sea.

So few things got through from those days, those subjective years in the Madhouse gloom. But those things, those images—why now? Why here?

In a glance, I took in Sat's indulgence, the sad array scattered about me, the quiet streets, indistinct and shifting in the morning heat, more like the avenues of a plundered mastaba town in the lee of Khufu's Pyramid than those of a carnival. I could almost imagine Khafre's Sphinx out there, serenely regarding the vast distances, all this silence.

But there was just the gate, the great face locked in its instant of demented glee, crazy eyes tilted at the sun. Whatever serenity was to be had in this lonely place seemed to come from these newcomers, the spinner posts themselves. Regardless of what they meant for me, they did represent the possibility of change and renewal; their presence somehow held the melancholy in check.

"All right, Cas. The rest of it please."

"The rest?" And she smiled. "You're interested in belltrees—in the whole Ab'O belltree program. I knew you'd want to see these."

"Cas, the rest. How did you learn of them? You don't make a habit of touring desert sites for novelty venues, do you?"

Cas Arana stood watching the sand drifts at the edge of the fairground. She seemed to be considering something.

"I'm not supposed to tell you anything until you meet their maker. He'll be about somewhere. His workshop is that building there. Why not ask the tree?"

"The tree?"

"Go on. Ask it where Quint is."

"Quint? The old clockmaker from Twilight Beach? But he—"

"Disappeared, yes. Came to Bullen Meddi six months ago. Grew tired of restoring old full-face clocks and scribbling poetry. My cousin found him two days ago while researching a story for *Caravanserai*—a retrospective on Constantin Sat and his eccentricities. He found Quint here working on his spinner posts.

"Clockmakers go mad, you know, especially the poetic ones. I imagine they work too close to the process of measuring time. They get filled up with the desperation of hours, the relentless transition from one instant to the next. They never seem to be free of that intense awareness."

I looked at Cas, intrigued, wondering if her oddly rhapsodic tone was mocking.

"And?"

"I came out here to speak with him. To see if there was material for a play, for a performance. Clockmakers often escape to deserts. Many time-conscious, time-saturated people do. And carnivals *are* timeless, a ruined carnival in a desert many times more so. Ghost-towns for hyperchronics, the time-afflicted. Ask the tree."

I looked up at the tall post standing quietly in the heat, its bright fluted crown turning very slowly in the late morning air. Around noon the breezes on the sand-sea would start changing. By sunset the spinners would be moving steadily, recharging the accumulators, working away into the night.

"All right." I said. "Tree, where is Quint?"

I waited but there was no answer.

"No-one's home," I said to Cas, and my apprehensions faded a little. Cas smiled. "They didn't work for me either. But you feel like you're being watched, yes?"

I did when I thought about it, but that was part of the atmosphere of the place.

We moved down the midway towards the building where Cas told me Quint had his workshop. The wide door was open, but the sunlight ended in roiling, eye-twisting shadow—a plastic dust-curtain had been fitted to the surrounding timbers. Beyond that, in the shadow-light, a work-bench was visible, covered with circuitry and tools. Off to the side, on three sawhorses, another post rested, almost finished. This one had a different spinner cap. Instead of the usual bladed cylinder crown fitted down over the shaft head, it had a large bladed pinwheel fitted vertically to its front in the manner of the traditional windmill.

"That goes up tonight," Cas said.

I studied the long metal post with its sensor spines and its trunk not yet decorated with ideograms. "I suppose if you're going to break tribal law you should try for a modicum of secrecy."

Cas smiled. "True. But the tribes are hardly going to do a sat-scan of this forsaken spot, are they? Come on. Quint will be over at the carousel."

We moved on from the workshop, down one of the hot, quiet avenues leading to the sand-shore.

"The tribes mustn't learn of this, Cas," I said as we walked, reminding her of the obvious danger, worried that true to her media-conscious and entrepreneurial nature she might have ideas for publicising this. I just didn't know Cas well enough to be sure.

Without giving an answer she pointed. "There he is."

A tanned, white-haired figure crouched on the beach beside a circle of bright wooden horses. Brass poles pierced them, gleaming; glass eyes glistened before flashing mirror panels and polished wood. The decorated awning threw much of the interior into shadow all the same; it was like looking through a cool verandah at the bright desert beyond.

"I'm back!" Cas called, and the old man looked round. "With Tom Tyson."

Quint stood, wiped his hands on his fatigues, and smiled.

I had seen him months ago in his shop on the South Esplanade, a bent-over and compressed package of a man, scrawny, diminutive, a comfortable stereotype of the aged craftsman. Now he was something else, no longer compressed, no longer doubled-over. He was tanned instead of pallid; now his eyes shone with all sorts of mad lights.

"What do you think?" he asked, fixing me with those eyes.

"Quint, I hardly know you," was all I could think to say, the simple truth.

"I knew they'd find me," he said. "But I'm about done. The carousel's working again. I've just finished raising it."

I looked from the clockmaker back to this new and different timepiece, set with brilliants, vivid with brightwork, as if to solve the unlikely equation of man and place. Quint here. A workshop. Spinner posts, for heaven's sake. The expertise needed, the sheer effort involved!

"Why, Quint?"

"Hah!" the old man said. He turned back to the bright wheel on the beach. "I'm baiting a trap."

"For what?"

"Hah!" he said again, and looked for Cas. She had wandered off towards the wreck of the Grand Doranza, was studying the ruined concession.

"She will bring others," I said.

"She's most welcome. We open today, this afternoon. Not much to see until tomorrow though. Then we'll have the fortune-telling posts and the carousel. Another month or two and the whole place would have been ready. Sat's Carnival, working again. Still, it's meant to be like this. Daystar said."

"Daystar?"

"The spinner out by the hoosy house. It said last week that someone would find me soon."

"Visitors must attract Ab'O attention. Your belltrees—"

"Tom," he said, clutching my arm, "I know. Highly illegal. But it's all right. Cas can bring her visitors. I'm ready for that."

"Why me?" I said. "Why did you ask for me?"

"Who better than you, Tom? You're interested in Artificial Intelligence. You've made a study of belltrees. My spinners are quite your thing."

"Quint—" I began, wanting to tell him just how ambivalent my reaction to AI was, but he drew me over to the merry-go-round.

"Truth is I doubt I can manage it on my own. My back is troubling me. I need help with the lifting. Khoumy, Ankh and Daystar I managed myself, though it wasn't easy. I fear Tiresias is too much for me alone. Help me tonight. We can bring it out, the two of us. And I need to steady the carousel more."

"Listen, Quint. If I'd known why Cas was bringing me here I'd never have come. You'll be exposed. The tribes tend to watch me."

The old man shrugged and grinned. "Too late. Help me now, eh? It doesn't matter. Help me finish here. Help me bring out Tiresias."

I watched Cas tossing stones at a sagging wall of tin. Freed of her promise she seemed eager to get back to Twilight Beach, no doubt to tell her friends.

"She'll be back," I said. "We're on the National side here. Bullen Meddi marks the border. She'll bring others. Ab'Os will come."

The light in his eyes never wavered. "Tom, it is all right. Please help."

I tried to consider it, tried to be objective and see where this could lead. It made no sense Quint's endangering his life this way, but then it *was* probably already too late. A routine surveillance already made by a Clever Man given the task of keeping an eye on Tom Rynosseros would be all it needed.

"Cas!" I called. "Go back without me. I'm staying."

"And tell them!" Quint shouted. "Tell them they can come! But the official opening is tomorrow."

Cas smiled and waved, called out something I couldn't catch, and began walking up the long slope to where her four-seater skiff was moored. She was an experienced sailor; though the winds were poor, photonic kites would put her back in Twilight Beach within the hour. And back again an hour after that, knowing her, knowing her coterie's appetite for the latest sensations.

"I told her you would stay," Quint said, leading me back down the midway towards his shed. "I made her promise to find you even before I told her what these wind-posts meant. She didn't concern herself about them as you do."

"She'll bring others this afternoon."

Quint nodded. "There's nothing to see until tomorrow. I'll be working on Tiresias till sundown. You can finish packing the fill here, take some power cells out to the gate, then help me with the response testing."

"If I can. Just show me what to do."

At 1400, in the heat of the blazing afternoon, the visitors came. Two passenger charvis moored beyond the hills and fifty or more Nationals came straggling down the slope to Bullen Meddi—Cas sweeping along in front, splendid in new white sand-robes, attended by producers and tame (and not so tame) critics, followed by members of her company and others eager for an afternoon's diversion at Sat's Carnival.

Most of them had seen it before. There had been the Taylor readings, and the San-Topuri fire-sculptures on the desert sea, but those events were nearly a decade old—the carnival had long since lost its novelty. This was something new. The newcomers chattered excitedly despite the heat. They paused by the spinners, Daystar and Khoumy, trying to raise answers without success, then, barely disappointed, trusting in surprises to come, strolled down the midway towards the carousel.

We came out from behind the dust-screen and went to meet them.

"We must give them something," Quint said, "or they'll be peeking here and there, getting up to mischief."

I accepted his explanation, not bothering to remind him of his earlier resolve to stay out of sight. Without speaking we walked to where the crowd waited.

I was surprised and disappointed to see how brash and insensitive this manifestation of the public Cas Arana seemed to be. She rushed forward, seized Quint by the arms and waltzed him around, owning him before the others.

"Our ringmaster! Our own biotect!" she cried. "Everyone, here he is! Master of the Revels! Maker of belltrees!"

"Please, " Quint said, gently disengaging his hands from hers, looking down. "I simply needed to be alone."

"Nonsense!" Cas said. "There's more. There's more, Tom, everyone! We all remember the play *Merinda.* How the Ab'O girl loved the young National. Now it can be told! Guess who wrote it, who financed the production we did?"

"Not Quint!" someone cried in delight.

"Dominic Quint!" Cas announced triumphantly. "Our carnival master here! Merinda goes to be with her David. The Kurdaitcha avengers come for her. The lovers flee on to the desert and are not seen again. Quint's one play, this legend! All his savings went into the Todthaus season."

And she smiled at me, radiantly, as if to say: Now do you see what goes on here? A surprise for you too, Tom!

I could scarcely believe she was doing it, creating such drama, such inevitable publicity—exposing this former artisan, failed playwright, maker of illicit spinner posts, this man captivated by his love for the Merinda myth, embroiled now too with me, the sandship captain from the Ab'O Madhouse, someone the Ab'Os watched.

"Cas!" I cried.

"No, Tom!" Quint said. "It is all right. We had our arrangement. Please, Ms Arana. Take your friends. Show them." And he turned away. When I went to follow he made a sharp gesture. "No, Tom. Stay here. Keep an eye on them for a while."

So I stayed, wandering among the guests, listening to snatches of conversation, amazed at the excitement, at the earnest theorising. Some were guarded in what they said, deliberately uncommitted; others affected indifference, even a sneering detachment. But whatever the overt expressions, I sensed that more than anything they wanted this to matter. Even the coolly aloof ones on this burning afternoon showed a determination to have that: something meaningful, something important in their lives.

And yet I sensed the opposite of this as well: a paradoxical and ferocious determination to challenge anything short of what convinced them was the real thing.

One discussion caught my attention, two men in expensive sand-robes talking by the door of the derelict hoosy house.

"These have the later type of cap," one of them, a bearded man I knew only as Seth, was saying. "A free-moving bladed cylinder fitted down over the shaft head. The earlier spinners had the vertical windmill arrangement, but you know why that was changed."

"No, I don't," his friend said. "Tell me."

Seth indicated the patch on the other's scrap-jacket, visible through the front of his djellaba: a clutch of narrow ochre triangles converging on a central point. "The National sign," he said. "The Sun of Nation. What do you think that is?"

"Not a spinner!"

"Of course it is. A stylised windmill, a bladed sun. Fitting symbol for the land, don't you think? Of the hostile interior and how it was tamed?"

Seth's companion shook his head. "I don't believe it. It's just a stylised sun motif."

"Exactly!" Seth insisted. "A bladed sun! Interesting, eh?"

I continued around behind the group, glad that despite Cas's use of my name, few seemed to recognise me as anything more than Quint's assistant. Perhaps she had kept part of the developing story even from them.

Raised voices drew my attention, another animated discussion, this time from a group standing by the Grand Doranza.

"It's where the cry: 'Come in, Spinner!' originated," a man was saying.

And there was Seth's friend, again playing the role of sceptic.

"Nonsense!" he cried. "That came from the game of two-up!"

"Yes," the other man answered. "It did. But the antecedents for that game go back a long way, to well before the Chinese massacre at Beechworth. The coins tossed were *I Ching* fortune-telling coins brought to Australia by the Chinese goldseekers in the 19th century."

"The Chinese used yarrow stalks originally, not coins."

"Yes. Well, the idea for divination posts started way back then too . . ."

I moved away. Something in this determination to find answers reminded me of what I so often did, how I openly considered my Madhouse past in order to know I did so, could be so objective and reasonable. A way of hiding a deeper truth, of hiding from it. It seemed like that now—proper, healthy speculation but with a secret purpose. For there *was* more to it, a different side, the other thing these people were doing. Faced with a mystery, they wished to contain it, neutralise it, even destroy it to ease the curiosity, the not-knowing, the possibility of a something-more that eluded easy and comfortable understanding. They had to be safe again, no less than I.

Was the bladed Sun of Nation truly a spinner? What a joke! And did the *I Ching* have a part to play? I thought of the ideograms on the shafts, wanting to ask Quint about them and realising again that this did put me with the rest.

Cas saw me skirting the crowd. She excused herself and came over. "So worried, Tom?"

"You amaze me, Cas! You've ensured his death, don't you see?"

"Tom! He desperately wants *Merinda* performed again. We discussed it months ago, before he came to Bullen Meddi. My cousin never found him; Quint contacted me, sent a letter suggesting another Todthaus season. I came out at once. We reached an agreement: *Merinda* performed with this present development, whatever happens, as a prelude. Tom, he had no money—"

"No money! Cas, he's building belltrees, for heaven's sake! How has he financed that? He's more in control of this than you know."

"Well, the arrangement stands. We do *Merinda* this summer, provided the carnival opens. He's kept his word."

I could think of nothing more to say. Three months, a year from now, Cas would apologise, invite me to one of her dinners, spend hours trying to convince me that, after all, it was life being lived, nothing more.

"What part do you think the spinners play?" she asked then, as if I were another of her guests and this was the natural question to ask.

I did not answer her. I left her with her companions and headed for the carousel to complete shoring up the table.

Some time later Cas and her friends departed, though Quint and I never knew exactly when. I was sequestered with the old man most of the time, running checks on Tiresias, deliberately losing myself in the exhaustive procedures, not wanting to think about working on the AI I feared so much. Whenever he did the response testing, I tried to be elsewhere in the workshop, or out on an errand. But sometimes I couldn't help watching the blurred figure inside the makeshift booth of clear plastic sheets, studying him as he bent over the crown with his light and his tuning instruments. When at last he left the dust-booth for the tea I made us, I had my chance to discuss what Cas had revealed.

"I never knew about your connection with the *Merinda* production," I told him. "I liked it."

Quint nodded. "I always wanted to be the storyteller, Tom. The maker. Merinda was a gifted storyteller, like Scheherazade was. She knew seven old languages, all their legends. But the greatest story is her own. You saw it. I followed the story exactly. Her champion, the young sailor, David, was a National who came with his four companions, rescued the Ab'O girl from the Kurdaitcha and fled with her into the desert. The companions acted as decoys; all but one was slain—the survivor who some say later told their story. In my play I took a small liberty there. I made the survivor the narrating chorus."

"I remember that. But is what Cas said true? Are you revising the legend, planning another season? One story in another?"

Quint smiled and looked back at the spinner post, its bladed crown like a rare flower shut away inside a makeshift glasshouse. "Who knows?" he said. "That would be Cas's wish. This way is better. All my money is gone on this."

He stood. "Tom, the stencils are over there. You can spray ideograms on the lower half. One of each." Then he returned to the dust-booth and presently resumed his testing.

The moon was high over Bullen Meddi when we brought out his final belltree. Moonlight washed the carnival streets, giving the buildings and ruined concessions the dramatic shadows of a penumbral noon.

We had said nothing more about Merinda or Cas's remarks. We simply accepted the reality of the task at hand.

The tree was heavier than I expected. I took the lower end of the trunk; Quint managed the end with the upper shaft and diligent housing, the bladed wheel turning as we stumbled along. He steered us between the deserted buildings, up the midway, down a side-street full of ink-black shadow, around a corner towards the merry-go-round on the beach. There everything was bathed in the moon's warming glow, bright and still except for the spinner cap on the one other post I could see: Daystar. It turned freely in the breeze.

Finally we reached the spot Quint had prepared. He guided the footing into its hole; I hauled on the pulley rope slung across the tube-steel tripod hoist and lifted the tree to its upright position.

It took surprisingly little time. We packed the base with sand and quick-drying algen foam and mounded more foamed sand up to the collar of the bounty-box analogue. Then Quint tripped the recessed activator with a hooked pole he had left nearby for the purpose.

At first nothing happened; the spinner disk was still. These were no longer function tests. The diligent was exploring sensation, probably selecting modes. Then the vertical wheel began to turn, its blades flashing with moonlight.

It was alive. I left Quint to watch that happen—troubled as I always was by AI, and began dismantling the hoist.

"Look at it, Tom!" he cried beyond my shoulder. "Djuringa!"

I reacted at the word.

Djuringa. All that is sacred in Ab'O lore: the hills, the wind, the stones, the Dreamtime heroes, the haldanes, the land itself.

Careful, Quint, I wanted to cry. Careful. That's tribal land out there. A ship will come. Clever Men or Kurdaitcha. Don't go too far. Don't be too daring.

But Quint crouched before Tiresias, crooning softly to himself, watching the blades spin, flashing and hypnotic, waiting. I was an intruder here. This was his place, his precious spot. I wanted to leave him with it.

When he showed no signs of ending his vigil, I took up the hoist poles, the tools and foam canister and began carrying them back to his workshop. As I stumbled along, balancing my load, I again felt the sense of disquiet that went beyond my apprehension over tribal detection. Perhaps it was the wind getting in behind the tin and loose boards, creating a hundred tiny half-heard sounds; perhaps it was the contrasts of light, the intense pools of darkness that I found about me and always feared because of the Madhouse gloom I remembered so well. Looking down a side-street, there would be that darkness, then moonlight, then darkness again, laid out in a strip mosaic, with moonlit desert beyond. Always the vivid contrasts.

Beside me loomed a vacant interior, also chillingly dark, but there beyond it the ferris gleamed in a long vivid curve, and the Deco spires of the gate held aloft their moonstruck face so it blazed like a shield, clown-eyes crammed with light.

I hunched up my load and continued walking, thinking of the job at hand so that my fears subsided in physical effort. Subsided, not faded entirely. For something remained, some quality in this moon-bleached, forsaken carnival that played on my old AI fears and gave the quiet and sadness its edge of uncertainty and unease.

I placed my load behind the dust-screen, then, to avoid the streets, walked off the midway altogether, meaning to trace my way back to Quint along the open fairground perimeter. I would be in moonlight all the way.

How it happened I couldn't say. Loose sand slid under my boots; I reached down to steady myself on a shifting slope, scrambled to regain my footing and looked up again, to yelp in fright at something blocking my way. My cry echoed across the fairground, faded to nothing in the silvery dunes beyond.

Khoumy stood like a silver knife on the sand.

I could feel my heart pounding; I heard the soft whirring of the spinner cap.

I laughed, trying to regain composure, fighting the panic, the rush of anger it surfaced as.

It lived, Cas had said, Quint had assured me. Would it answer? Could it?

"Hello, Tree—Khoumy," I said.

The post stood in near-silence, the spinner whirring away, feeding the accumulators. A minute passed, with just the steady mindless sound. My mistrust grew, my restlessness. It was the old paradox again: disbelief and the need to believe.

"Fake!" I cried at last. "Imposter!" Then, wanting it to be true, needing the release, "It's a hoax! Quint playing tricks!"

The blades turned; the tree said nothing.

I remembered the trigger Quint had used.

"Djuringa!" I cried.

And the word echoed.

"Djuringa."

Not an echo. Too close for that. Khoumy had answered.

"Why has Quint made you?" I asked.

Again the voice came, measured, artificial, but not unpleasant to the ear.

"I wasn't told," Khoumy said. "I was the first, the prototype. I'm very fragile and primitive."

No, I thought. Not life. It couldn't be.

"You're following a program!"

"No," it replied. "I don't think so. I do bioscan. I can tell you all about Father's medical profile. Or ask about stars. I can report on them all, the constellations, the angles of declivity. I watch stars. I love them. I can tell you—"

"A program!"

"No! I don't believe—"

"You don't know!" I said, driven by remembered fears, helpless before them.

"I'm not very sophisticated, but I believe I am alive. I do. I can—"

"But you don't know. It's just programming. Quint's a one-shot playwright, a clockmaker, not a biotect. He couldn't have the skill."

"Please! Ask Father. Or one of the others. You confuse me. You sadden me—"

"All coded in," I told it. "That too."

"No. I don't feel—"

"Consider it, Khoumy!" I cried, amazed to hear my voice snapping the words, amazed at the vehemence, the cruelty in what I said, but giving in to it all the same. I had to know. "I am Quint's assistant. Consider that possibility now!"

The tree did not answer. It shone; its crown spun, collecting the life of the wind. But it no longer spoke.

"Khoumy?"

There was no reply, no sound at all it seemed but the spinner cap whirring in the winds coming in to Bullen Meddi, sliding in under the cold bright stars.

"Djuringa!" I called. "Djuringa!"

But all I got was the thrumming of the breeze about the shaft, the whirring of the cap and, distinct again, the occasional creakings and soughings from the carnival streets behind me. Then, a plangent note from the bell-chamber, so very sad, followed by the soft chiming of the dim-recall rods in Khoumy's base, the ghost of its own life.

I stood stunned by the confusion of emotions: alarm, guilt, absolute despair. What had I done? Why?

I fled. I rushed into the shadowed fairground streets, oblivious now to the patches of darkness, needing to find Quint.

But when I reached the beach and saw him still kneeling before Tiresias, I could not bring myself to confess what I had done. The words died on my lips, not just from shame, but because somehow Quint looked even more lost and wayward than I felt I did in my confusion and distress.

The sight of him there, the knowledge of his need, buried the terrible news.

"What should we do now?" I asked instead, grateful for the reprieve, wanting to hear a voice, any voice, but his most of all.

Quint rose to his feet. "Help me with the carousel," he said.

Did the words hold accusation? No. He was simply disoriented from being alone with his thoughts. "Help me test it."

I was glad to, so relieved to hear him chattering about what he had done to fix it, the re-wiring involved, the complete overhaul he had given the old motor and music-box.

While he made his final electrical adjustments, I set to polishing the already-gleaming brass poles, encouraging him with questions.

Perhaps Khoumy would recover, I told myself as I worked. Or all it would take would be some minor routine adjustments during one of Quint's service rounds. Yes, that would do it. The tree hadn't been sophisticated enough to kill like that.

Or, the thought came immediately, not sophisticated enough to withstand such an attack as mine.

I kept polishing, hiding the self-contempt, the undefined rage, hiding from voices in another crueler darkness, until Quint came over to discuss tomorrow's performance.

"We must act as custodians and guides, Tom," he said resolutely. "We must direct people to the different trees, distribute the numbers, suggest questions they can ask. Tiresias is my pride and joy. He can talk their philosophies with the best of them. Daystar and Ankh are not as spirited; poor personality definition—I was too eager there, too unskilled. But they can manage. We must protect Khoumy, my poor firstborn. Very fragile that one. Very limited. But stars, Tom. It can tell you all about stars."

I worked on the poles, rubbing them, fiercely polishing the smooth metal, trying not to think of the post out on the perimeter.

From 2000 to 2100, I helped string coloured lights over the ornamental gate and the gantry of the ferris while Quint gave directions.

At 2100, he ran the carousel for half an hour while we stood on the beach and watched. The lights shone, warm and golden, the horses leapt and plunged in the moonlight, the music rang along the shore and brought a strange new life to the old buildings—and an added loneliness as well. The spinners gave back an eerie keening and chiming from their dim-recall rods. For a time the sound of the wind was hidden, concealed under this joyful, less timeless music.

Quint left me and went to finish coupling the festival lights to the power cells. I knew that was done when the already moon-bright gate and ferris tower lit up with a sudden prickle of small coloured points.

So I rode the carousel, happy to be under the dazzling mantle of lights and mirrors—one moment curving out over the empty sand-sea, the next swinging in to the quiet streets. I rode half-blinded by the lights flashing in my eyes, reflecting from the brightwork and gleaming poles.

As I swung out on the desert arc, I thought I saw a single lamp showing, as if a ship waited out there. As I swung in on the carnival leg there was a glimpse of a white figure hurrying across the midway.

I gripped the pole intently, straining to see, but on my next pass both images were gone—ship and figure—probably after-images formed by the dazzle of mirror-light against the darkness, ghosts at the inside of my eyes.

"Tom, she's been here!"

Quint's words came to me above the sound of the calliope, shouted through the dry air. I saw him on successive turns as he came running down the midway, each turn bringing him closer, like a figure seen through the shutter of a magic lantern, a time-wounded magician trapped into instalments, blinks of imminence.

"Who? For heaven's sake, who?" I cried, dismounting, waiting for him, reluctant to jump free of the pedestal in case tools or wedges had been left about.

The old man reached the controls and cut the power. The music stopped and the platform glided to a halt.

"Who?" I said again, jumping down.

"I don't know her name. She's been with Khoumy. Tampered with it. It won't answer me."

I went to comment, but my own images stopped me.

"I saw a light out there," was all I said. "And a white figure back on the midway."

"You did? You did!"

"I thought it was you. I wasn't sure. The light was too bright here."

"Tom, we must search! I said I was baiting a trap. There are phantoms here. We must find out!"

"No, Quint," I said, again wanting to confess my crime against him, needing his understanding, desperately needing his forgiveness, but not wanting to ruin his excitement, not now. "Probably an Ab'O drawn by the calliope. Or Cas wanting to provoke you. Teasing. She'd do it!"

"No!" Quint was adamant. "She wouldn't do that. I told her what I was after."

"What *are* you after?" I asked. Merinda?, I almost said, but stopped myself.

"No, Tom, no! Just help me check Ankh and Daystar. She may have disturbed them as well."

We hurried along the beach to where Ankh stood, washed in moonlight.

"Djuringa!" Quint called before we reached it.

"Djuringa," Ankh answered, spinner cap whirring against the stars. "Hello, Father."

"Someone has been with Khoumy. Do you know who?"

"No, Father." The voice came down to us from the diligent. "I know only that Khoumy will not answer me now."

"But living? Living? What do you read?"

"Unliving. That's what I read, Father. Or the signal is too faint for me to tell."

I went to speak, but the old man pressed on.

"Have you seen a light out on the desert? A ship? Or someone other than Tom or me moving through the fairground?" Quint's excitement made him stumble on the words.

"No, Father. Nothing like that."

"Could you have been tampered with and not know it?"

"Yes. I probably would not be able to tell."

Quint turned to me. "I'll check Daystar. You ask Tiresias. Watch from there. See if the light returns."

"But Ankh says—"

"He may be occluded. It can be done."

By the tribes—Quint had no need to say it. By Ab'O hitech interference from over the desert waste, or from out of the sky—from an orbiting comsat given that precise task.

The old man hurried away and I went back to where Tiresias stood near the carousel.

"Djuringa!" I called, and waited below the spinning blades.

There was no password response.

"You harmed Khoumy!" the belltree said, startling me with the accusation.

"I didn't mean to," I said.

"Yes, you did," it accused, but without rancour, merely saying what it knew. "You were testing it for life. In your own way, that's what you were doing."

I moved in closer, fearing our voices would carry. "You didn't tell Quint."

"It would not help Father now. His task is nearly done."

Such a compassionate, life-seeming answer. Such a good strong voice—the tree sounded and looked so powerful, its wheel moving briskly, drawing the eye into its disk of fractured moonlight, blades paring the wind.

"Was there a ship?"

"Yes," Tiresias said.

"A figure in the streets?"

"Yes."

"Who? Do you know?"

"Look out there!" the spinner said.

I turned and scanned the desert. To my left the carousel sat untended on the beach, blazing like a Tsar's precious crown. To the right the low dunes folded and re-folded until they levelled out completely. Far out on the windswept waste a light shone. I watched it flash once, twice, go dark, come again, then vanish altogether.

"A signal! A code!" I said. "For whom, Tiresias? You?"

Was this tree a traitor? I wondered. Suborned, acting willingly for interests other than Quint's, or was it under some compulsion? I doubted everything now. A belltree would not need such a primitive visual signal, merely an override beamed to its function centres. Was the beacon for someone human?

Like Khoumy before it, Tiresias would not or could not answer.

"Tiresias, who is out there?"

"*Muki winorbin*," it replied in dialect, an expression even Nationals knew, from one of the old languages.

"Ghosts? That was no min-min light. Who?"

But driven to silence or choosing it, Tiresias did not say.

I ran to find Quint. He was nowhere near the carousel that I could see, so I went back along the beach to Ankh, stopping long enough to say the password and ask it the same question I had put to Tiresias.

"Ankh, who is out there?"

"*Wandang*," it said, the same answer in a different dialect.

Ghosts. Again, ghosts. Merinda the storyteller coming to get her old champion, another storyteller—the man who had told her story as best he could.

I believed otherwise, but when I had looked for him at the deserted workshop and reached the midway again I immediately doubted myself: there before me was a tableau—figures waiting, frozen where they stood but for the wind picking at their garments.

Quint stood in the middle of the main avenue. At the far end, close to the ornamental gate, was a solitary white-clad form, a cowled female shape, her robes stirring in the moonwind. At the other end of the midway, near the carousel and Tiresias, where I had been but a few moments ago, were three figures, all dark, two men and a tall slender woman between them, backlit by the carousel so that it seemed min-min lights danced in their hair.

"Quint!" I cried, but said no more. There was moonlight glinting off metal—the figures with the dark woman carried weapons.

Ab'Os, I knew. Tribal people from the ship I had seen.

"Merinda?" Quint called, his voice full of desperation and hope.

From the white figure near the gate came: "Here, Quint! I am here! Come now!"

And from the dark woman by the carousel: "No, Quint! Here!"

The tableau dissolved. While the old man stood undecided, the Ab'O men came forward and led him quietly back to where the dark woman waited. Then, with not another word spoken, the small group turned and walked down on to the desert sea, the distinctive shape of the clockmaker in their midst. By moonlight their silver forms and accompanying dark shadows dwindled into the gloom, merged with the desert.

The white figure came running towards me, flinging her sand-cape open.

"Cas?" I said, knowing it had to be.

"It seems I wasn't the only one to have the idea," she said. "I was trying to help." She looked to where Quint had been taken. "What will they do to him?"

"He's broken their law. I don't know. Khoumy could have told us; he had bioscan function, Quint said."

We stood on the deserted midway, and even by moonlight Cas could see my look of reproach.

"I wanted to save him, Tom. Grant me more than what you saw today when I was with the others. That was all part of it. He wanted to be found—to expand the Merinda legend, to make it his. He gave me my script. Only tonight did I improvise, dare depart from it. I didn't know what was coming but I had to try."

"One of his own trees betrayed him," I said, realising as I spoke the words that it had to be true.

"What!"

"Yes. Can you see it, Cas? He made life, then one of his own creations, his greatest, Tiresias, inquisitive, seeking information, learnt of its forbidden nature. One of the first discoveries it made. It sought confirmation; it wanted to know more. It called in the tribes. Kurdaitcha!"

Suddenly three detonations shook the fairground; three brilliant balls of fire lit the air as the diligents of Tiresias, Ankh and Daystar exploded, scattering incandescent fragments across the midway, bright flickering sparks which slowly settled and died.

There would be no performance after all, no re-opening of Sat's Carnival with fortune-telling posts and carousel rides.

"The ghosts were busy tonight," I said.

"But they left one intact," Cas replied. "Out on the perimeter."

"Khoumy is moribund. It would not have registered on their scan. I killed it."

But as we walked up the slope towards her skiff, leaving behind us the burning candles of the spinner posts, the mad gate and ferris tower decked out in their small sad web of party lights, the merry-go-round on the beach untended, to glow by day and night until the cells failed, we heard a voice calling across the quiet sandhills of Bullen Meddi.

"I have decided," it cried, the words clear and distinct. "I am alive!"

Cas looked at me, eyebrows raised in an unasked question. "Tell no-one," I said, cherishing those few simple words from Khoumy.

"Only if you come to the opening night of *Merinda*," she said.

"Done," I said, not looking back. "Done."

So Much for the Burning Queen

The final game between Matine Gentle and Paul Cantry took place on the terrace of the Gaza Hotel exactly ten years to the day from their first encounter at fire-chess. No doubt this fact had been foremost in the minds of the organisers when they arranged to bring the two Grand Masters together again; to hold the contest back where it all began.

The Gaza terrace was the perfect place, especially at the sunset hour of the breaklight when the winds were warm but fitful and the dust-devils came. Other places were safer, more sheltered, but what was fire-chess without hazard, without the chance of pieces being debased and whole strategies ruined, of victories so suddenly gained? Fire-chess showed the uncertainty of the world; the game suited the age perfectly.

For days before the contest, the famous terraces and promenades of Twilight Beach were crowded with tourists and tribesmen. The hotels and casinos were filled to capacity. The occupants of the villas had an endless round of game parties going to mark the occasion. Down on the beach, the local boys played stylo as always, moving their capped pieces while the crowds watched, using throws of dice to make up for the vagaries of wind. But now their games had a new edge, a compelling urgency. Everywhere you went, the esplanades and avenues were decorated with the twin signs: Matine Gentle's Burning Queen, red-gold on blue, and Cantry's Knight Aspirant, orange on black, known by all as the Burning King, though Cantry resisted that name as much as ever.

"I'm just the paladin," he had said to the media on his arrival, as he always did. "Debased or ennobled, win or lose That is all I have ever wished to be."

And, as always, it changed nothing.

The Burning King was to play the Burning Queen.

We were there for the contest, of course, arriving less than two days before the game and mooring at the Sarda-Salita with seventy other sand-ships, unable to get our usual place at the Sand Quay.

When *Rynosseros* was checked in and we were ashore, Scarbo took Rimmon to the kitemakers, Strengi and Shannon went to the gaming tables at Deep's, and I went to visit the Burning Queen at the Gaza.

Teos Dessa, the contest president, was in the lobby when I arrived, talking to David, the hotel manager. He saw me and hurried over.

"Captain Tyson! Tom! At last! David said you would be coming."

"Hello, Teos. What is it?"

The thin, worried-looking man clasped his big hands in a fervent, earnest gesture "Can you accept a mission?"

"Now? Not with the contest. No!"

"It's to do with the contest, Tom. It's about the contest. You are going to see Matine?"

"Yes, I am. You know the standing argument over 777."

Teos laughed politely, as if recalling that momentous morning six years before when Tom Rynosseros and Matine Gentle had argued with poor David over who should get that room. I had booked it, but famous, almost beautiful, not-to-be-crossed Matine had wanted it too—had needed it, she said, for luck or continuity or whatever.

I had yielded that day, and we had had an acquaintanceship-in-obsession ever since.

"So explain, Teos."

"Tom, I am worried. The circuit is my life. I conceived the whole Gaza contest idea. Now I'm afraid Paul Cantry intends to lose. Deliberately."

"How do you know that?"

Teos looked embarrassed. "It sounds absurd. But I've watched Paul and Matine for ten years, pacing one another; first Matine beating Carlos two years ago and becoming Grand Master, then Paul beating Prine last month. They're both matched again, both here. Matine will win because she has to be the best. Paul will lose because he still wants Matine and this is his way, his big chance. I've grown to know them, what drives them. He'll do it well but he'll lose."

"Why?"

"Because we're back here. Because they're both Grand Masters and he's a romantic fool. He needs a gesture more than he needs to win. His agent agrees. He told me Paul cancelled three World Circuit games to be back here and play Matine. He could have waited until the Annuals in spring at Pia. No, he wanted to play Matine here. So we arranged the contest."

"Why is it such an issue, Teos? After ten years, if a gesture like that is the best he can give himself, let it be."

Teos frowned, looked even more disturbed.

"Tom, a Grand Master doesn't just lose. You belong to the public. Bets are made. I know that Simon Grail and Alanto Comus are betting Paul will win on his recent performances."

"Then warn Paul."

"We can't. That might give him the idea, you see? He says he intends to win."

"Teos, I can't see how I can do any good here. Neither Matine nor Paul is—"

"Humour us, Tom. Please. It's a precaution. We'd rather be foolish than wrong."

I looked about the lobby, studied the ocean through one of the large view windows.

"All right, Teos. At least I'll talk with Matine and Paul."

A few minutes later I was knocking at the door of Room 777 just as I'd intended.

Matine answered, her striking, strangely cold face framed by loose tawny hair, her rich brown eyes matched by a cho'zan gown the colour of lions.

"Yes?"

"I'm sorry," I said, "but there's been a mistake. I have a booking for 777."

"That's impossible. I advise you to consult with the Manager. And don't say the Manager sent you to tell me."

"All right. How's this? I just bought the hotel. I am the Manager as well as the owner. Now get out!"

Matine Gentle laughed. "Nice, Tom. Won't you come in?"

Usually, on these courtesy visits, I would go to the french doors, step onto the balcony to watch the ocean for a while, ask her about life on circuit, then go. Now I crossed to the balcony and waited.

Matine brought us each a glass of tautine, but instead of completing the pattern between us, I told her what Teos Dessa had said. She listened, her eyes never leaving me, and not for the first time I found myself fascinated. Matine had a presence that brought her to the point of incredible beauty, that gave a definite quality to a face that was striking but not beautiful in any conventional sense.

Some said—and with good cause—that it became beautiful only when lit from below by the burning pieces of the game, lit so the planes of her cheekbones threw shadows just so. Then, that strong countenance softened into beauty. Then, like some shadow-painted war-huntress, Matine Gentle had the fierce lines brought into a semblance of absolute loveliness. Little wonder, many also said, that Paul Cantry had fallen in love with her at the board, looking across the burning field to that suddenly splendid image—the wide tawny eyes, the mane of hair, the newly vibrant lines and planes.

"Paul wouldn't do it," she said when I had finished. "I find it all most unlikely."

"I told Teos I'd look into it, Matine. He can't afford to chance it. Will you be speaking with Paul before the game?"

"Only at the solstice party tonight, and as little as possible then. And I agree with Teos Dessa. I'd advise you not to mention it. Paul might get to liking the idea when he finds I'm beating him."

"Agreed. But could he have gone to Grand Master to be back here with you for the Gaza contest? Because it's the level you accept him at. The Knight's errand—"

"Fool's errand!"

"—to win the lady. He's cancelled three circuit games to be here."

"So I heard. Icroco, Prine and Sastan will not be pleased. The besotted fool!"

"Teos is more concerned about the speculators. Simon Grail and Alanto Comus have made bets. They won't appreciate a gesture."

Matine finished her wine. "They might kill him, true. But I've sat at the board with Paul. He won't do it. He'll try to beat me, to put the Tyrant Queen in her place."

"Are you sure? Sacrifice at the moment of triumph can make for a rather stylish victory too, in a sense. Better than power for some."

Flecks of golden light moved in Matine's eyes. She furrowed her brow. "You mean me there, Tom? Power? Well, it's more!"

"I accept that, Matine, and it isn't what I meant. But there must be ways Paul could do it so Grail and Comus couldn't be sure. Either of you could manage it, with game tension and all. During a light breeze, during a move, an unlucky breath. Out goes a tiny flame; a Bishop is debased. Or a Rook. A Queen. Say it was chance."

Matine poured herself more wine, brushed some wisps of long hair back with her free hand. "It's not that easy, believe me. And this is to be an Untouched Game, if I choose. It's up to me. We may use the tongs."

"Will you?"

"Tom!"

"I'm sorry, Matine. I didn't want to be involved in this. I've just finished a mission and I'm tired."

She followed me as I went to the door.

"Tom, I intend to beat this romantic fool. I intend to play fairly and win, here, once and for all, at Twilight Beach. I cannot believe Paul would ruin his career or endanger his life. He loves me, but what sort of jejune love can it be? He does not know me or he would not bother."

"I'll see you at the solstice party, Matine."

She smiled. "Yes. At the solstice party."

The Charles Christos Imbri is much smaller than the Gaza, but it is the best of the older beach hotels. It is five minutes' walk north of the Gaza terrace, its long sun-drenched steps fanning down onto the sand, occupied now by souvenir sellers and the players of stylo. At midday, the glare of the hotel's whitewashed walls was blinding. At the main colonnade, I stopped to watch some young men playing a game, using coloured caps to show the status of their pieces since it was so windy on the shore.

I went to the second floor and knocked at the door of Paul Cantry's suite. Paul answered it almost at once, a tall saturnine man with a severe profile and harsh, flawed good looks which some said the game transformed into a hero's mask no less than it changed Matine. He had come to the circuit late, having already won fame for his work on *Love Songs of the Twentieth Century*, and for his own composition, *Beloved Lion*, a song obviously written with Matine in mind. From the moment he took up the game, it was seen as his way of courting her.

"Ah, Tom Tyson. Come in. As one madman to another, how do you see my chances? Are the omens benign, or should I throw the game and not give her the satisfaction?"

I was at a loss for words. So much for not discussing the possibility of a gesture.

I followed Paul back into his rooms, and watched him as he filled two cups from a silver tea service.

"Don't look disappointed, Tom. Is that disappointment I see? I know how all this appears. All the theories have occurred to me, all the possibilities."

"All right, Paul. So continue. How will you proceed?"

"I don't plan to lose," he said. "I intend to defeat the Grand Master."

"I wish I could be convinced of that. Just to make things easier all round."

"Ah, straight to the impossible! I like that. Here!"

He handed me a cup of blended tisn. The tautine was sharp in my stomach and I welcomed the hot tea. We took our cups to the balcony, sat in some sling chairs, and looked back down the beach to the Promenade and the Gaza, now bathed in rich afternoon light.

"Tom, I know that Matine doesn't love me in any conventional way, and I'm not always completely sure of my feelings for her, not really. But I believe I do love her, regardless of how foolish it seems. It's a commitment from me; I'm wooing her the only way I know, with the only life I have. She was taught by Carlos himself, and he taught her too well. I sometimes think it was a Svengali and Trilby thing, only she caught the legacy of power from him and had to defeat him. Good female spider comparisons come to mind, right? My over-active imagination."

"Right," I said, starting to relax at last, enjoying the long low curve of the waves rolling in and the endless song of the belltrees from the hotel's roof garden. But his next comment startled me, and brought me back from my growing reverie.

"Do you know we have been lovers?" he said. "Oh yes it's true. We've had only seven games in ten years. After the three stalemates, we made love, sharing the energy. I can scarcely believe it. After her three victories, I didn't see her—not eligible. After my single win at Pia, she looked momentarily stunned and seemed to see me for the first time. I'm not naïve enough to think a win at the Gaza will necessarily do any good, but there are only two of us now Carlos is dead. I've never beaten her as a Grand Master before. It could matter."

"Especially to the speculators."

"Ah, yes. Well, I'll be the naif to that extent. I don't care what the speculators think."

"But—"

"Or do, Tom!" he said. "You understand me?"

"Fine, Paul." I finished my tea. "That does it then. I can go back to Teos and the Contest Board and tell them both you and Matine intend to win. Good." I stood up and headed for the door, glad to be free of this unwanted business. "Remember that Simon Grail and Alanto Comus are betting you will checkmate Matine. They've probably computed it to how many moves, with wind variations and all. They know your game technique, your preferred gambits and responses."

"Thank you. But frankly I don't care. I play only one opponent."

"Of course," I said, still nettled, still not convinced. "Thanks for the tea."

I left the Charles Christos Imbri by the beach stairs and moved along the shore to the Promenade. The afternoon sun threw brilliant light onto the ocean, and underneath the sounds of daily life could be heard the shimmering susurration of belltrees, and the deep hollow booming of the tidal bells swinging on their sea-chains beneath the surface, calming me.

Now I could relax. Now I could find Shannon and Rim and the others, or go to Amberlin's or The Traitor's Face, or lose myself in the Mayan Quarter or at The Slow Hour. I would avoid Teos and the Gaza. I would not, would not think of fire-chess.

Which was impossible, of course. Everywhere I went it was the main topic of conversation. I heard some astonishing rumours about Matine and Paul (though none as sensational as Paul's own revelation at the Imbri), learned of some staggering wagers which had been made. The media had done their promotion too well. The motifs of the Burning Queen and the Burning King (shown always as the Knight, orange on black) were hung in all the streets.

It was impossible, too, because I realised there were two more people to see. Two more at least. Though I hated the thought of it then, I decided to call on Alanto Comus and Simon Grail.

Comus had made his fortune selling infusion sculptures across the world, and I was not surprised to see that a soldier dressed in fire kept me from his door.

"Back off!" The figure cried through the blazing grid of his helmet.

I could not tell whether the cataphract in the portico was a truesense projection, a genuine sculpture from Comus's collection, or an actor/ automaton. When I said who I was, the fighter, the sound and the heat vanished. A door opened into a cool garden. Comus found me wandering there.

"You look weary, Captain Tom," a voice said among the ferns, and I turned to see the glistening bald head and gleaming oiled jowls of the fire-sculptor as he approached, his short body dressed in a robe of fine white Egyptian linen.

"I am certainly that, Alanto," I replied. "It has probably been a day of deceptions."

"Then,"—he spread his arms wide—"I am Truth!"

We laughed together amid the ferns, then Comus went towards an inner door. "Will you take refreshment?"

"No, thank you," I said, and Comus stopped. "One question only. What happens if Paul Cantry decides to lose this game?"

Alanto composed his hands before him. "I'll take his heart, of course. I'll set him as a pillar of fire on the Nullarbor, make him a beacon to sail your ship by. He will burn forever."

"Extravagant, Alanto."

"I want an honest game," Comus said.

"Paul's losing would be part of an honest game."

"Granted. But profitable?"—again the hands went out—"I am depending on him to win."

"You need the money?"

"No. I enjoy the reputation."

"No clemency?"

"None. Truth is adamant!"

"Interesting," I said, and went to the doorway leading back to the street.

"Oh?" Comus said, as I pulled back the door and stepped through to where the fiery cataphract was once more waiting on the steps. "Why?"

"Truth has no soul!" I said and closed the door behind me.

I did not find Simon Grail until the solstice party that evening. Teos Dessa had arranged to have the celebration at Quay Massillian, the splendid villa of Twilight Beach's greatest benefactor, the late Spydyr Massillian, a man rivalled in wealth only by the entrepreneurial Simon Grail and the brilliant parvenu, Comus.

I arrived at 1900 and searched through the dazzling crowds until I found the vicious, terribly old Chinese. He was standing with four Cold People, former friends from his youth almost ninety years before who been brought up from his family vault for the solstice and the game.

But I had no success there either. Despite implants, transplants and prosthetics, Grail was clearly a man at the end of his life. His friends, back from their strange wintering, were creatures out of time—pathetic, disoriented, with the odd callous irreverence for all things still living; providing companionship for Grail in return for forced, fragmentary lives, tastes, glimpses. They laughed at Grail in their silences, and it was as if he did not see. How could such people truly savour the game, the vital reality of those who lived and burned?

I realised all these things when I asked the old Chinese the same question I had put to Comus.

"I will kill him," Simon Grail said "It is simple."

"Mr Grail, any money you win will only be the tiniest fraction of what it cost you to bring out your friends tonight. It cannot be money."

"Every act becomes an indulgence now, Mr Tyson. I create rituals whose purpose I have forgotten. But the habits are *my* habits. They bear my stamp." The voice was soft, poisonously, powerfully soft.

"This is an indulgence you may understand then. Doesn't chance, the unexpected, the impulsive, count for something now—for you, for these friends for whom the unexpected can be the only joy? Why not some affirmations to reassure them that life is good, that it was all worthwhile, and still is?"

"We have said enough on this, I think. Goodbye, Mr Tyson."

I moved away, and for an instant caught a glimpse of Matine attended by crowds of the cognoscenti, the circuit and fashion elites, the press. She wore a gown of precious cho'zan, her hair was a glorious mane, her strange hard face looked striking in a make-up designed for her around the lines given by the burning pieces of the game.

There was no sign of Paul Cantry. Teos stopped long enough to tell me Paul had put in his token appearance earlier, leaving after half an hour.

I stayed a while longer, saw that I would have no chance of speaking with Matine alone, and decided to leave. As I went through the large doors, I noticed Alanto Comus and Simon Grail in conversation—or in the glancing, self-absorbed exchange which passed for it—both men surrounded by Grail's revenant friends.

I smiled at how futile my day now seemed, at the burden of anger and weariness I carried with me still. Only one chance remained: that from whim neither Comus nor Grail would act. But as I watched the man of fire and the man of ice talking together, it did hot seem that such a thing could be.

I have always understood, instinctively, that everything we do is couched in symbols, that simple acts have elements to them which communicate, resonate, far beyond their objective natures, that we understand more than we consciously know. Every game, every situation, every act of hospitality and making and giving is caught up in such a bounty, rife with subtleties, nuances, the often unwanted extra truth.

Fire-chess is just a game, but like all games it has the conflict, the tension, the continual choosing and re-choosing, the very essence of life.

As I went back to our mooring (I preferred the desolation of the quiet Sarda-Salita desert flats to the hotels of the town), walking down streets bright and alive with the solstice festivities and game parties, I reflected on the forthcoming contest. As we always do throughout our lives, I rediscovered things I already knew and had known for years: that regardless of what Paul did, or Matine, or gifted decadent Comus, or spiteful pre-wintering Grail, we live to our fullest when we choose, when we understand and own our choices.

It was not a profound or new thing to realise there on the cool dark backstreets of Twilight Beach, but it eased my spirit then. The four principals in this would choose, I reminded myself. Life—as it always did—would flow about those choices, whether to win, to lose, to kill, to set Paul out on the Nullarbor to burn as a Knight forever.

I reached the mooring where our darkened sand-ship stood, thinking of how we give our lives meaning by our choices, new and renewed, of how we define ourselves in ways beyond ego and, yes, though it rankled then and did not please me to think it, beyond death.

Then, at the gangway, with the town at my back and the wide

desert stillness before me, I laughed, laughed at what my day had been and where it had led.

For I had assumed all along that Paul Cantry *would* throw the game.

I went to bed, cursing Teos and his suspicions and thinking of pillars of fire strewn across the Nullarbor, pillars of endlessly dancing flame which became two, then one, then two again until I slept.

In the small hours of the morning, the chime of a sensor woke me, told me that someone had come aboard. I assumed it was one or more of the crew back from their various adventures, since the gate-watch would admit no strangers to the docks at that hour. The knock at the aft-cabin door surprised me.

I stumbled to answer it, belting on my robe as I went, and found a shrouded figure waiting at the foot of the companionway.

"Matine!" I cried as the hood went back.

"Tom, can we talk?"

"Well, yes. Come to the salon."

"No, outside," she said. "On the docks."

So I dressed again, and we walked without a word along the moonlit quays of the Sarda-Salita till we reached the steps leading down to the desert.

"What is it, Matine?" I said, as we moved away from the silent hulls and the distant lights, the sand sliding and whispering under our feet.

"It's Paul. I've thought about it all day. What will happen?"

"I discovered nothing, Matine. Not a thing. And I did not see him at the party."

"I barely did myself." In the moonlight, I saw her shake her head. "We only ever meet across the board."

"Can I be lewd about that?"

Matine stopped. "He told you?"

"Yes. But your coming here tells me more."

She made no attempt to explain herself, but stood there, the illumination coming from above her now and not flattering at all, making her face stark and plain despite the cleverness of the make-up she still wore.

"Tom, why did I come to see you?"

The question surprised me.

"I could say you are after a somewhat informed opinion. I've spent the day assuming Paul would do it."

"I must win!" she said, but softly. "I intend to win!"

"Good. Do that. You couldn't accept less. I believe he will genuinely try to win."

"I will win!"

"Then you came here because of *Beloved Lion.* You want that too." And I began reciting the words of the song. "Moments arise, seasons of green—"

"The fourth canto," Matine said, and I changed to that brief and haunting part of the song cycle.

> "I've known you in other faces,
> Looked at you in other eyes;
> The mornings come, I sit and wonder,
> There's so much to really realise.
>
> Discovered you in other faces,
> Already seen and always new;
> You are the wind in lonely places,
> Déjà-vu!"

"Something is wrong," Matine said, interrupting, though she had let me finish the canto. We turned back towards the moorings.

"I am not Paul," I said "And you already know what you are going to do."

"Yes," she said, putting up her hood. "I do."

And she left me and headed back to the Gaza.

The next morning, the town was strangely quiet. The streets of Twilight Beach were virtually deserted until noon, as if people waited indoors in anticipation. The banners and decorations hung listlessly until the first afternoon breezes came and set them swinging and billowing under the hot sun. Suddenly, doors opened, window shutters went back, people came forth, sauntering down from their hotels and villas, resting on the cafe terraces. A few games of stylo began on the beach below the Gaza, and slowly, gradually, as the afternoon drew on, the excitement began to build.

Teos Dessa called on me at mid-afternoon to learn my views and assure me of a place at the Gaza for the game. He owed me that much, but, though he did not say it, I was left with the feeling I was to be an additional bodyguard should anything happen, not that Comus, Grail or any of the unmentioned others would act then.

Towards sunset an incredible tension settled over everything. I kept away from the media broadcasts easily enough, but there was no avoiding the excitement. By the time I took my seat on the terrace alongside Teos, overlooking the board, the weight of feeling was visible on every face.

At 1750, the beautiful ceramic pieces were set in place. Two tuxedoed flamfeudines moved in and began lighting them; the ushers laid out the tongs. Matine had made it an Untouched Game.

At 1755, Paul Cantry came to the table, dressed entirely in black. The cheers and applause were as much for relief from the tension as any kind of acclamation. Paul stood in his place, smiled, bowed once and sat down.

Matine appeared a moment later, wearing a splendid gown of golden cho'zan made for the occasion, her hair coiffed and full, her face made up in the simple "naked face" that would be adorned so amazingly by the pieces of the game.

The cheering and applause went on and on, even after she was seated. Teos Dessa made his short speech and at 1810 the game began. As the players took up their tongs and drew them from their brocade sheaths, there was absolute silence—the terrace, the whole town held by the "game-death."

Matine opened with a Queen's Gambit, carefully using her golden tongs to move her Pawn.

Paul countered with his own Queen's Pawn, and so it went, each of them developing their game.

For the first fifteen minutes there was no threatening breeze. The pieces remained ennobled, their flames flickering and dancing in the body wind from the audience and the guarded shallow breathing of Paul and Matine themselves.

But then a gust came in from the sea. It rippled the chimes, set the belltrees to stirring, hit the long white façade of the Gaza and slid off the tiles back onto the terrace.

Paul Cantry lost his King's Rook in that settling cascade of air. He said nothing, just gave the debased piece a quick glance, as if calculating intricate possibilities of guiding it through Matine's guard at some improbable moment to ennoble it again, to "bless it with fire" as the commentators would say, to restore its "honour."

I saw Paul study Matine's face, but he could not expect a reaction there. She was the Lion, the absolute Burning Queen, the subject of countless media-enhanced mythologies. The game continued.

Five minutes later, even as he went to move his Queen's Knight, reaching out with the gorgeous cloisonné tongs he had won at Pia, Paul lost his King's Bishop's Pawn the same way. He barely hesitated in his move, though he smiled down at the board. That Pawn was lost, impossible to refurbish, locked to its tiny death march to the fiery lines before it. Paul went on to move his Knight.

Sunset became the long golden hour of the breaklight. Dust-devils appeared in the streets. On the Gaza terrace the liveried Devil Catchers became alert, shifting their long-handled spoilers in their practised hands, their eyes flicking back and forth, as careful now as surgeons.

Breaklight became full twilight. The coppery radiance sank from the sky and left lustrous peacock blues and growing indigo. On no other evening was the town quite so still, gripped by such expectation.

In the second hour of play, when Paul had only half his pieces ennobled to Matine's two-thirds, he took her King's Knight, and Matine looked across the board at him for the first time. She watched as Paul snuffed out its tiny flame, relegating it in the reversed alchemy of fire-chess to the low-game where debased pieces rarely survived a thousand count.

Matine reacted swiftly and brought down her Queen, sliding it along fiery corridors rather than lifting it to where the still smoking Knight stood cancelled and dark. Whether through zeal or passion, a sudden undetected eddy of air or the merest chance, her piece lost its flame in transit, the tongue of fire spiralling in on itself and vanishing like a miniature genie.

From across the town you could hear the cry of the watchers, a sad spontaneously swelling thing, a single vast outrush, a great sighing.

The piece debased in transit is a dead piece, removed from the game altogether.

You cannot avoid omens in fire-chess, and this was one. You cannot play with alchemy, with the eternal life-giving, life-affirming symbol of fire and not he touched. If it had not been her Queen, rushing to where that cold Knight stood flickering only in the reflected light of its betters, then Matine would have recovered.

On the surface, her control was excellent.

The game continued; she played as skilfully as ever. But I knew that in her soul the game had been lost. The crowd interpreted that unspoken language of symbols as well. Every one of us understood the precise measure of the transaction which had occurred, of the duplicity that now prevailed, the following through.

I thought of Alanto Comus and Simon Grail and those countless others who watched, thinking, interpreting. They could not take exception. Matine had moved too zealously perhaps, but she had not planned such an act—such a unique symbolic death for herself; this much was clear.

Chance again. Like all of life: the alchemy of chance.

Paul Cantry read the omen for what it was. Physically, in posture and eye-line, nothing changed. He sat as before, contemplating the pieces, his tongs laid on the table beside him for the moment. When he took them up, he played brilliantly. His own Queen swept up and down the corridors and seemed to grow brighter (we later found that the scan and subbing crews had star-shot his Queen and his remaining Knight for the rest of the game; unnecessary enhancement really; against his debased pieces those flames shone like torches).

No more fate-winds came. No more flames were lost by chance, only by the steady shifting of the pieces, by the strategies Paul built around his Queen.

The language of symbols gave him an incredible presence. Across from him, calm composed Matine played on like a doomed Queen, like Zenobia marching into Rome, her lion face sinking into deeper, even more fearsome lines and curves of shadow as one piece, then another, went dark and was taken.

It was soon to be over. Her burning King stood amid the dross of the game, with only one cornered Rook flickering helplessly under its hood of fire. The other seven flames on the hoard were Paul's.

Matine stared at those pieces, finally reached out and moved her Rook to take Paul's debased Bishop, a bravura act, a formality to let the game reach its end, before the thousand-count expired.

The tension was incredible. Paul steepled his hands and looked about him at the faces in the cool dark night. There was not a breath of wind, not a sign of a devil weaving in to play assassin. A time without chance, it seemed, a time laden with symbolic truth, in which every element perceived, every movement, was vivid like never before. There are moments like this: before death, when reprieved from death, sometimes in new love, or when old love is seen anew.

Paul reached down as if to move his burning Queen in to checkmate, let his hand slide past it to his flickering King. He brought it up smoothly and, with a breath, blew out its flame, then set it down again, on its side, showing both the old and new ways of capitulation.

There was an indrawing of breath all about us on the terrace, sweeping, echoing out across the town, followed by a stunned silence.

Such things did not happen.

"Your game," Paul Cantry said, and sat back.

Matine looked at him, her severe face unreadable in the light of the remaining pieces.

"Why?" she said.

"Because this has to matter. Because I love you more than I knew. Because a part of you understands."

"I won't accept this," she said.

"Good."

"I won't, Paul!"

"Good."

"They'll kill you."

Paul Cantry smiled and shrugged.

And Matine Gentle picked up her own King, blew out its flame, toppled it with a hollow ring of porcelain on stone.

She rose to her feet and Paul did as well. (For an instant I imagined figures burning in the desert, two, then one, then two, but not burning alone.)

They turned and walked off, not together, not apart, into the Gaza, and left behind them a night filled with delight and fury and confusion, a night of symbols and vendettas and the eternal waiting newness of chance.

MIRAGE DIVER

THAT SUMMER I SAW THE BOORINDI TRIPTYCH IN THE GALLERY at Kalgoorlie—the three large panels with their images of the dream cities Ash, Bari and Dan. I stood with the crowds of sightseers, awed by the shapes painted there, finding that something oddly relevant, terribly important, was being communicated.

Seeing the Boorindi paintings always left me disturbed, filled with disquiet, with an urge to seek out the young mirage diver and ask him why these images, these cities. I wanted to know how he could spend his days crouching out there on the dunes and see sights like these and say they belonged to *this* land.

So naturally I was alarmed when it was confirmed by the Gallery's See Committee president, Angel Ferris, that Paul Boorindi had stopped producing, and pleased when she gave me the Gallery's commission to seek out Paul at Yates-Eluard and discover what was happening.

Committeeman Ferris looked at me disconsolately, her usual buoyant manner worn down by too many meetings, by the endless run of media engagements. I studied the grey eyes framed by the close-cut brown curls and understood the worry I saw there. She knew as well as I that more sixty percent of mirage divers went insane—markedly schizoid and anti-social; another ten percent went gradually catatonic to the same end. Fearless Gram had ceased diving after producing his masterpiece, *The Engines of Night*. Long Strode had done the same after his Caliban series. Paul Boorindi looked like being the latest casualty. Having completed the City paintings, *Amid the Jewels*, *The Country Palaces* and *On Resisting Summer Days*, it seemed as if his time as a mirage diver was over. Australia had lost another great artist.

I booked passage into the inner desert and arrived at Yates-Eluard on its hottest day for nine years. The colony town was quiet an hour before noon, with no-one about and no wind to pull us into the sand-ship moorings. The *Marjory* rolled in under power to find the docks deserted; no-one appeared to sign for the small pile of cargo and mail left on the burning quayside.

I adjusted my burnouse and set off along the glaring causeways and empty morning streets, eager to check in at the Salamander and shower before going down to the dunes and the colony itself.

The hotel was only a third full during high summer, so I chose a top-floor room looking out on the desert and close to an ancient Croesus belltree I had grown fond of on previous visits. The old Croesus had lost most of its bells and much of its sentience, but the management, out of sentiment perhaps or a sense of continuity, had not had it replaced. Seeing it tucked away in its corner of the terrace made me smile. When I had changed, a houseboy called me down to the front desk where a dark, narrow-faced man came forward and introduced himself.

"Good morning, Captain Tom," he said. "I am Faoud Lebad, the local representative for the See Committee. Angel Ferris asked me to meet with you."

The reed fetish on his white robe told me he was an Egyptian, the silver disc-with-rays at his throat that he was an Aten worshipper. I shook his hand and we exchanged pleasantries, then I asked, "Is it as serious as the Committee says?"

"But yes," he said, guiding me by the arm across to some chairs near the tall terrace doors. These doors were closed and shuttered at this hour, and the lobby was pleasantly dark and cool with its palms and fans, its large square pillars, its lacquered screens and subdued conversations. We sat and Faoud gestured to a waiter for drinks.

"The truth now, Faoud," I said when we had been served tall frosty glasses of tautine. "I understand that Boorindi has ceased producing."

"Worse than that, Captain. The whole colony is in decline. Several divers have begun 'ghosting' Paul Boorindi's work—producing imitations of his Cities. Others have seen valid mirages and started pieces, but the visions go and the paintings are abandoned. It is very troubling."

"You feel there is a connection?"

Faoud nodded. "Paul Boorindi is our greatest *imagier.* He is so young, so full of energy. He has produced three strong paintings. Ab'O psychometrists and fellow divers all read and confirm that energy. It is there still. But after the last City, nothing. Three months of nothing after four weeks of such splendid achievement. And now the colony suffers a hiatus, a malaise. Ghosting and truncated visions. Something is happening."

"The divers are still Ab'O?"

"Yes. So few Nationals or outsiders ever see images on the Serafina." Faoud hesitated. "But I forget. There is Tenna. She is only twelve years old, an Ab'O and Egyptian cross."

"A diver?"

"I know. You will say that only Ab'O males can paint. But Tenna is accepted as a diver at the colony, though she produces nothing. You will see. She runs errands for the divers. She is always there."

"And the divers still choose the new divers?"

"They do."

"I would like to go there now, Faoud."

"Of course." Faoud drained his glass. "Let us brave the day."

In the atrium of the hotel we donned our desert clothes and put on our sunglasses. We stepped out on to the street to be greeted by the terrible heat and the dazzle of brilliant sunlight off whitewashed walls—and, to my surprise, by a modoc wearing his white quarry's shirt with its red rings. As Faoud and I turned left to head down the street towards Farlook and the Serafina, the demented, sun-weathered Target Man fell in behind us.

"Don't mind Modoc, Captain Tom," Faoud said. "It appears I have inherited him. He likes to follow me about."

I glanced back at the tall shambling figure in white and red, at the vacant expression on his face and the big hands dangling by his sides. He was smiling at Faoud's remarks, pleased to be noticed by him.

I smiled too. Our little group presented a strange sight, even by the standards of Yates-Eluard: an Atenist worried about loss of revenue and possibly his job, a Target Man waiting to die, and a sand-ship captain sent to investigate the fate of the greatest mirage diver in the land.

There were fifteen divers waiting patiently on the long dunes outside the township, most of them sitting in a line along the crest of Farlook, their boards set up, their eyes searching the empty desert, looking out from under their wide-brimmed hats at the far horizon of the flat Serafina Basin.

It was after noon and relentlessly hot. The air shimmered. The glare was terrible. Few besides the divers were willingly out in it. A handful of tourists watched from the sheltered terraces of either Rushing Fools or Mad Dog Pavilion. Some patrons sat in the open fronts of their tents, drowsing over drinks; wanting to be there in case something came. But there were not many. The gallery reps and art media writers had gone back to their hotels to wait out the worst of the day and would venture out again only near sunset, trudging down the crooked streets to the Divers Stairs and the desert to see what the *imagiers* had produced. And, lately, if they had.

I walked along the base of Farlook, trying to make out Boorindi among the others. The draped figures all looked the same under their eccentric hats and sand-capes, so many quiet and contemplative forms beneath faded parasols and shades, intent beachcombers endlessly searching the Serafina for what they called the divings, "the image that is true."

And there were few charlatans. This ragged company assembled under their strange domes and pyramids was almost a guild, each one approved by his peers, accepted by the acute perceptions of the rest.

As we walked, Faoud told me how the girl, Tenna, had been up at Farlook for months and seen nothing, but she had been allowed to remain. She had the gift and it would show in time. Others, poseurs and opportunists, continued to be hunted out of the area, often protesting defiantly, banned from Farlook by the tormented elect.

Boorindi had his tribal flag on a slender pole where he sat beneath his shade. That led us to him. I left Faoud with Modoc and scaled the dune, scrambling and sliding in the hot sand, finally mounting the crest and crouching beside the motionless form.

He was not imaging. The panel in front of him was clean.

Boorindi turned his head to see who had dared to intrude. Through tinted eye-shades his eyes regarded first my face then my desert clothes, saw my charvi insignia through the open front of my djellaba. Then they turned back to the burning desert, narrowed again for sand-sight.

"Tom Rynosseros. This is novelty. A sand-ship captain. The See Committee likes the oblique approach. Soon we will have astronauts for town planners, and modocs as civic leaders or cryogeneticists."

"Angel Ferris asked me to come, Paul."

"Angel Ferris wants paintings She hounded Fearless Gram when he stopped producing."

"I'd like to talk," I said.

Paul Boorindi pulled off his dark glasses and regarded me again. "With respect, Captain Tom, this is a long way from dreamlocking and dealing with Clever Men. We are sports. Solitaries. We stay together because this is the place, but we are estranged from you, even from each other. A true group apart. We cannot keep away. Go back to Angel Ferris and say that when there is a mirage for me, I will bring it here." He nodded to the empty board. "Not for her, but because I have no choice. I must have it."

He put on his glasses again and returned to watching the desert.

I could not let it go at that. "Paul, I realise you cannot break the diver taboos and discuss this openly, but something has to be done. It's not the gain involved. That would not have brought me here. I know that the Ab'Os read the land in a special way, that the tribal mysteries turn on truth, and that we must not lose that. You are already sharing something through your paintings—otherwise you would not let us see the divings, let alone display and sell them. Can't this sharing be increased, so we can help safeguard the process and reduce the penalties? The divers want to tell us something, many of us sense that. We need to know—not what it is, but how to help you do it. Paul?"

But Boorindi did not answer me. My arguments had been heard before and I could think of no new ways to put them.

I stood, feeling more than ever an intruder. But I did not leave at once. My only prepared course of action was to talk with Boorindi or the other divers. I had to stay. I felt Boorindi was concealing something, something beyond the mysteries of the divers and the tribes, some inside knowledge possessed only by the greatest *imagiers* as they neared the point of madness. I wanted to be here where it all happened, where his secret began. The glaring Serafina stretched out before us, burning under the summer sun, its distances forever empty to the likes of me.

I moved several steps away down the dune, reacting to the tension I sensed surrounding the man, not wanting to intrude on his space any longer. But I still watched him from the corner of my vision. I saw when the girl, Tenna, came near, moving along the line of divers till she was at Boorindi's spot. I saw her crouch beside him, place an arm on his shoulder and top up his water flask from the simple bag she carried. Then she spoke, words that came to me quite clearly in the stillness.

"Naked eye in the glade of expectation."

She said it again, like a refrain, a key phrase just for him. Then she looked up and her big brown eyes met mine. It was a full gaze and one of sudden assessment, startling and direct. Her blend of Ab'O and Egyptian blood gave her a force which belied her ears.

"Hello, Tenna," I said, to free myself from that gaze and hear again the voice which accompanied her presence.

But she became a young girl once more, artless and distracted by her chores. "Hello," she said, leaning on Boorindi's arm to help herself up. She moved past me and continued on down the dune ridge.

I stood there wondering what to do. Though I doubted some of the See Committee's motives, their concern for the Yates-Eluard colony was based not just on dwindling sales and loss of international prestige. The Ab'Os had agreed to an arrangement and now there were problems with it. An explanation, or at least a formal voiding, was needed.

I would achieve little without assistance from the divers. So when Tenna had gone, I returned to where Boorindi sat.

"What did she say to you, Paul?" I asked him.

The Ab'O's head did not turn from the horizon. "Just words. In her own way she likes to think she helps us find our visions. She is the water girl."

And that was it. I waited a few minutes, then moved off along Farlook greeting each of the divers in turn. Some answered me with a polite word or two; some glanced my way and said nothing; others ignored me completely. Even Tenna made sure she was somewhere else, busily helping.

Finally I clambered down to where Faoud and his big insane friend were waiting and we headed back into the town. Faoud sensed it had not gone well and said nothing, though Modoc began to sing.

> "All these people, helping at the mill,
> All this trouble, helping at the mill,
> Keeping to the rhythm, keeping to the stone,
> Keep that rhythm, turning at the mill."

The Target Man's flat heavy voice grew louder as we moved through the quiet streets. He added verses, lines that didn't rhyme or make sense but that seemed to please him immensely. He began slapping his thighs as he walked, grinning and drooling. We were close to the Salamander when he said some lines that made me stop.

> "Hear the dream-talk, helping at the mill,
> See the girl go, helping at the mill."

"What is she doing, Modoc?" I demanded, turning to him. "What is Tenna doing?"

The Target Man grinned and pounded his fists against his thighs. "Helping, keeping, helping at the mill!"

He went on repeating it, becoming more and more excited, saliva falling onto the bright target rings on his chest as he boomed out the words.

Faoud tried to calm him but the big man strode off down the street, shouting his song and swinging his arms wildly about.

"I'm sorry, Faoud."

"No, Captain. It's his manic phase. He gets like this when he's been to Farlook. They all do. He'll be waiting for me later."

Alone in my room at the Salamander, I showered and lay down on the bed to rest out the hot afternoon, thinking to escape the mirage divers for a time. It was not easy. On the wall opposite were reproductions of some of the more famous renderings: Vannikin's *First Dive*, Fearless Gram's *The Engines of Night* and Boorindi's three Cities, these presented as always as one group and in sequence.

I studied the famous triptych. It was too small now to be overbearing, but it was still vivid and disturbing, especially in the subdued light from the terrace. Under each image was the legend Boorindi had chosen and inscribed for that panel during his dive. The first said *Amid the Jewels* and described Ash, so strange to see with its odd tower lines clustering up out of a severe blue plain under an intense and fretful sky of a richer, deeper blue. The painting was nothing new, just an abstraction of shapes, almost a decalomania like Ernst and Dominguez used to make. Nothing in plain view accounted for the disquiet, for the sense of sinister expectation I felt, not the quasi-organic towers, not the dark formwork of lines and struts at its centre or the "coronets" and "diadems" and "lattices" of yellow light strewn across the shapes.

The second painting, *The Country Palaces*, was easier to take, its alienness muted at first—a series of strange stylised pavilions set in waving grasses. That city, Bari, no larger than Ash in area, was low and sprawling, as if the towers of Ash had faded like phantoms or given their substance downwards to the airy, billowing pavilions underneath—to the bright horizontals. Looking at Bari one got the impression of towers compressed but present, folded back and hidden, waiting to leap up and bludgeon the sky.

The last City, Dan, was the most representational, the most accessible. It depicted a desert-scape, very much as one saw it from Farlook or the balconies of the Salamander. But in the distance, out on that burning waste of ochre, white-gold and muted reds was a city of rock, of boulders and crags and grey-brown massifs, almost machine-like in its brooding separateness. *On Resisting Summer Days* Boorindi had called it, and it disturbed as much as the others.

I lay in the gloom and tried to sleep, but the three Cities kept me from it. Through half closed eyes I tried to unlock their secret message, to discover what it was about surreal, blue, light-flecked Ash, the wide, almost cubist savannahs of Bari and the familiar wasteland of Dan that drew my eye and gave me such an urgent sense of déjà-vu.

What Tenna had said stayed with me too, that line she quoted kneeling there in the sand at Boorindi's elbow. It had been said deliberately, with both her and Boorindi's knowledge that I would overhear.

Naked eye in the glade of expectation.

The words seemed appropriate. Farlook *was* such a glade; the little community there had its eyes exposed and committed, naked to the visions of the Serafina.

But that wasn't it. It was more that Tenna could come and go among the divers virtually unnoticed, murmuring little comments such as this, guiding the *imagiers*, accepted by them all. Tenna—a shadow that belonged. In this crazy desert town with its wandering modocs, on the Grand Tour circuit for the rekindled Cold People, at the hub of vogue and madness and great art, this pubescent girl was a common thread. I recalled what Faoud's Target Man had said: "Helping at the mill", what Boorindi himself had suggested regarding her: "She is the water girl."

Her words did not strike me as idle encouragement. It was a line I had heard or read somewhere, from some text I could not place. I wondered how I could check on it here in Yates-Eluard. There were bookstores but no library, probably retrieval systems at the Salamander and Frenchman's, though access to literary sources might be limited. But I had it as a clue at least, something to use and consider.

When at last I did sink into sleep I had dreams—fragments and sudden dislocations. I awoke around 1700, troubled and disoriented, though the afternoon light had softened and the Serafina had sent a strong cooling wind that revived the old Croesus belltree and rattled the terrace doors and slowly changed the town.

I met Faoud at 1800 and, after dinner, over glasses of tautine, we discussed the diver phenomenon and why it always seemed to end in madness.

"You understand, Tom," Faoud said, "that I supply the See Committee with information. They draw the conclusions and suggest the theories. I am only one person. The popular idea now is that the successful diver becomes saturated with the Serafina images, reaching a point of desensitisation. He grows so used to seeing bizarre sights that he cannot produce. Then, estranged, he starts to render the new bizarre: our own mundane world. The characteristics of the diving phenomenon resemble the symptoms of schizophrenia. Boorindi's Cities trace the estrangement—exotic to mundane."

I emptied my glass. "The last City, Dan, is for us the most commonplace. For Boorindi it may be the most strange."

"Yes, Captain Tom. That is it. His reactions following Dan show the measure of his alienation. The great anxiety and marked withdrawal seems to go with lack of output generally. You've noticed the atmosphere down at the colony."

"Has no-one been able to interview the divers?"

Faoud held up his hands. "You were there. How did Boorindi react to you? It is a closed elite."

"What about the girl?"

Again the hands went up. "Tenna? She is a child."

"She is a diver."

"An honorary one. She is tolerated, that is all. Useful. She has prod-uced nothing."

"Where does she live, Faoud?"

—.—

It was the easiest course to take and the most promising. I visited Tenna at her mother's address in Paternoster Lane, choosing a time well after sunset when I felt the girl would be there. The street was quiet; Tenna's narrow door opened onto the cobbles like a dark coffin lid in the whitewashed walls.

I knocked twice and waited, listening to a belltree sounding somewhere up in the windy darkness. I barely noticed that the door had opened till I saw Tenna's mother standing there as quiet as the street and as narrow and dark as her own coffin door. The Aten disc around her neck reminded me that her daughter was an Ab'O and Egyptian cross.

I told her my reason for calling and prepared to launch into an elaborate explanation. But she stood to one side and murmured, "Upstairs, please," before I had said more than her daughter's name.

I found Tenna in a second-floor room that opened onto a roof-garden with views across Farlook and the divers' colony.

The girl's wide dark eyes showed no surprise. She stood at her door wearing a loose white smock and a small metal ansate cross at her throat. I wondered if all the Egyptians in Yates-Eluard were Atenists.

"Captain Tom," she said. "Paul told me of you."

"I came for myself," I said in the Atenist way. Tenna regarded me with her calm even gaze, and for a moment I thought she would not admit me. But she turned and walked back into her room, silently giving me permission to follow.

Her room was simply furnished but comfortable, with many shelves of books. I noticed texts on dynastic Egypt, the Amarna period, the teachings of Jung, the Surrealists—so many subjects. There were reproductions of most of the divers' works, and above her low bed a large triptych of Boorindi's Cities, one of the loveliest printings I had seen. Through the garden door I could see the black iron rod of the belltree I had heard from the street, its bells long pierced cylinders of space iron, its crown formed in the forked shape of an Anubis.

"Your tree is very beautiful," I said.

"That is Hotep," Tenna said. "The bells are meteoric. The crown comes from the Life Tree at Seth-Ammon Photemos."

"I've never been there."

"It is a closed town now. Some day."

"Perhaps," I said, and became aware that Tenna would be required to treat a direct question as the other divers had. I did not want to risk that. But at least I could trust that she meant me to overhear her words to Paul Boorindi. "Tenna, today I heard you quote something for Paul down on Farlook. 'Naked eye in the glade of expectation.' I know it's from a poem. I thought you might tell me which one."

Tenna watched me, her big eyes giving nothing away. "It will make you smile, Captain Tom."

"Good. But at least I'll know."

"More than some would like."

"Why, Tenna? I already think you are the catalyst for many of the divers here."

"I have been the shadow girl since I was six."

"The shadow girl?"

"Let me show you the poem, Captain Tom."

She went to a bookcase, took out a tattered volume and handed it to me.

I smiled at the title. *The Complete Works of Paul Eluard.*

Tenna smiled too. "A nice synchronicity, don't you think? By chance the town becomes his namesake. But this town is full of synchronicities. You will see."

"And the poem?"

"Is there," Tenna said, and signalled by her eyes that I should take the book and go.

I did so, but at the door to the street she stopped me.

"Captain, I am not a diver and never will be, contrary to what they say or think. I am just a catalyst, just a shadow girl. I am their…" But she stopped.

"Their Great Mother," I said for her. "I've noticed that all the divers on Farlook are men."

"Why is that? Why are most of the truly great artists male? Still?"

I recalled her books on Jung. We were completing something between us here. "Possibly because men need to make creation into a mystery, to elevate it dynamically—a vitality mystery to be in balance with the female birth mysteries. Most women don't need to bring religiosity and self-exaltation to artistic creation. Men do."

"Is that all? A compensation?"

"Only for the behaviourists, Tenna. I really don't know. Men do seem to be more empassioned by ideas, more inclined to hitch their egos, their wills, the best of their intuition, to artistic creation, the way women do to organic creation. Patterns exist beyond fashions and accepted roles."

"I care for them, Captain Tom," Tenna said. "They bring back important things and try to resolve them. They go mad."

"Why? What is the vision too awful to bear?"

Tenna did not answer, could not, so I spoke again, wanting to keep her talking, to keep her from closing the door.

"Do you visit the ones who are already gone? Do you visit Fearless Gram and the others in the sanatorium?"

"There are no sanatoriums in Yates-Eluard, Captain Tom," Tenna said. "No oubliettes and destiny-jars. There's the Serafina, and you've seen the modocs roaming the streets. You've seen the souvenir seller at the base of Farlook, never facing the desert."

"The souvenir seller?"

"Yes. That is Fearless Gram, but you must tell no-one. *The Engines of Night* drove him mad. His only painting; his first and last vision. Long Strode went to tending the catchment sinks after his Caliban paintings were done."

"So what is Paul Boorindi doing, Tenna? Are his imaging days over?"

"Yes," Tenna said, with a firmness that surprised me. "But he doesn't know it yet, so there's hope. He has not yet understood the completeness of his own paintings. The lesson there."

"And you do?"

"No, Captain Tom. I am only twelve years old. But a part of me does. The part they need does."

"So you give them poems, lines of verse?"

"Or songs. Or key words. I suggest hooks on which they can hang their images. Psychic automatism, like the Surrealists revered. I've read Breton's *Manifestoes*. I gave Long Strode the lines from *The Tempest*. For Boorindi it is a poem in that book. Why? I feel it is right. I provide the water to turn the mill."

"I see. The water girl. The shadow girl."

"You do see, Captain Tom! You do sense the power in me. You can accept how it's possible."

"I reaffirm you, Tenna."

"I'm glad " Tenna slipped in close and kissed my cheek. Then, as part of that same movement, she was away and closed her narrow door.

I walked back to the Salamander, unable to get Tenna out of my mind, this remarkable twelve-year-old who was such a force among the divers of the Serafina. I felt a sudden strong desire for the slim boyish form. It was sexual in part, alarmingly and unexpectedly so, but it went beyond that. I wanted her approval, the way Boorindi and the others had her approval, and I wanted her comfort. I wanted the Great Mother in this serene child to give me sanction and sanctuary.

I considered why this was, seeking the answers that would leave me at peace, untroubled by the denial of a closing door. I kept returning to the newness, the certainty and purity of the womanness in the girl, shown in her ministrations and their subtlety. It was not some simplistic mothering—it was the "womanning," with its accompanying lack of cynicism and ulterior motive. I felt excluded from that fleeting, unspoken service to the divers, and it mattered.

Back at the Salamander, I sat at one of the white metal tables on the terrace and, in the light of Aulus, the hotel's big luminant belltree, looked at the Eluard poems. They were arranged with the French original on the left and the English translation opposite, and it did not take me long to locate "Exile."

Amid the jewels the country palaces
Diminishing the sky
Tall women motionless
On resisting summer days

Crying to see these women come
Reign over death dream below the ground

Neither empty they are nor sterile
But lacking boldness
And their breasts bathing their mirror
Naked eye in the glade of expectation

Tranquil they are and more beautiful for being like

Far from the destructive odour of flowers
Far from the exploding shape of fruit
Far from the useful gestures the timid

Consigned to their fate knowing nothing but themselves

I read it several times, finding a great wealth of hints and triggers in the abstruse word patterns.

Tenna had been right. The poem was almost automatic—with disparate, spontaneous images brought together randomly so vibrant new meanings were suggested.

As a self-appointed but natural psychometrist, the girl had used it in that way. The Surrealist poet had trusted to free-form images and placement, relying on his belief in the much-prized and all-important factor: inspiration. Tenna, it seemed, had dismantled the Eluard text, taking the images and feeding them, by chance or intuitive design, back to modern *imagiers* like Paul Boorindi.

It was, in a sense, psychic automatism in reverse—her returning those fragmented images to an unconscious beginning, using them as thought fetishes and agencies of chance to trigger inspiration, to unlock the secrets of the Serafina.

And the art critics and media people knew nothing of it. To them Tenna remained the water girl.

I looked up from the Eluard poem, out over the terrace and the town, down through the cooling air to the colony, now just so many pools of lamplight in the darkness. I could hear belltrees communing with the night and answering the big Aulus. There were voices coming from the bars. I traced my route to Tenna's house across the moonlit squares and rooftops, and imagined the girl out in her roof-garden alongside Hotep, sitting next to those long tubes of metal from the depths of space and guiding its songs back to me, back to the Aulus and, above me, my broken Croesus.

Tenna was shrewd. Had she revealed more than she intended, or was it part of a plan, a way for her to break taboo and help me to help her and her charges?

The more I thought about it the more I was convinced that she would give me a clue if she could. I drew together fragments from our brief conversation, looked down at the so appropriately titled poem and began to suspect what it might be.

The next morning at Farlook I bought a copy of *The Engines of Night* from Fearless Gram, though the shrouded figure, dressed in sand-cape and wide-brimmed hat like the divers on the dunes, did not acknowledge the name when I said it.

Faoud was there too, with his faithful Modoc tagging along behind, the red-on-white rings of his body-target a startling brilliance—a piece of the whitewashed town brought out into the desert. I avoided the Egyptian and his companion and hurried along the base of Farlook, past the shanties and lean-tos of the divers and the pavilions of the patrons and dilettantes. I saw Tenna up on the crest, carrying her water bag and running one of her errands, stopping to murmur something every so often. She saw me and waved, then continued on her way. The water girl, tending the mill.

I reached Boorindi's spot and climbed to him. His eyes darted my way then returned to the burning sand.

"Paul, can I stay?"

The diver did not answer. He concentrated on the shimmering horizons of the Serafina.

I sensed the same terrible tension as before, as if Boorindi were straining to see something, trying not to lose a vision. Looking at those sealed eyes, I wondered where creative fire ended and a schizoid prison began.

"I understand the taboos placed on the divers, Paul. The safeguarding of the mysteries you are charged with. But Tenna showed me an Eluard poem. Called 'Exile'."

The eyes did not move to me, but they narrowed.

Still no answer. It occurred to me that he might not know the poem as a full text, only as disconnected fragments.

"I know the arguments, Boorindi. The suggestions that your paintings show a progression away from imaging, an estrangement, a loss of vision for you. Faoud tells me that the Cities become less exotic, less arcane, because your perceptions of them have changed. The otherness has become mundane; the need to render it is less intense. But I am suspicious of theories and interpretations. To keep your mysteries is one thing, but might not those mysteries be failing you now? We share this world, Paul. Some of us do want to help."

The eyes finally broke to me.

"What do you see in my triptych, Captain Tom?" He asked it suddenly, angrily.

"Three Cities, Paul. Or three attempts at one City. There is only one poem."

"Yes!" he snapped. "Yes." More softly. And then, almost a whisper: "Yes. The same City. Ashbaridan."

"It must be very important to you to stay here trying to see it again."

Boorindi stared a moment longer, then began laughing, laughing loudly in the desert silence, so that other divers along Farlook turned to see and Tenna, out on one of the lesser dunes, came running.

The laughter subsided, but there were tears on Boorindi's cheeks and he was shaking his head.

I felt foolish. Once again I sensed the tension and the barrier between us. I was a complete intruder and I did not want to be there when Tenna arrived. As she came running, I eased my way down Farlook and returned to the Salamander.

Again I rested out the afternoon, drifting in and out of sleep, waiting for the old Croesus belltree on the terrace outside the French doors to sing with the first late afternoon winds.

I watched the paintings as I had the previous day. Fragments of the Eluard poem came and went, and with those lines another that I could not place in my drowsing state:

The unpurged images of day recede.

Not Eluard's words, but from my own reading and from a famous old poem, triggered by a memory, an association, something I had heard or seen.

I tried to recall more, to connect it up, thinking how Boorindi's images eluded him and remained unpurged. But sleep took me and there were the sudden random chimings of the Croesus heralding sunset and driving such thoughts from my waking mind. I forgot I had remembered it.

I dressed and went out onto the terrace, turning the corner so that I faced not directly west but slightly away from the Serafina and the colony. I stood watching the changing colours of the desert, drawn into reverie by the long shadows growing amid the rock formations.

At the far end of the terrace, tucked away in its corner, the Croesus stood against the lustrous light, its few broken bells motionless and silent again, its dim-recall rods softly chiming with the memory of wind, a small weary aching song of need. The diligent in the crown knew nothing else, just wind and the lack of it. Even as I considered its plight, another breeze lifted over the balustrade and brushed by me. A stronger breeze this time. The diligent sensed it and altered modes. The rods went silent, the bells stirred. Negative ions came forth from the bounty-box to charge the cooling air.

I was misunderstanding something. It was so easy to accommodate theories, to interpret the City paintings as the bizarre becoming conventional—a steady shift from the otherworldly to the mundane. But Boorindi's laughter had irony and despair, and I felt I had missed the point of his confession about Ashbaridan. By thinking the diver's perceptions had shifted, I was making the same mistake as Faoud, the art commentators and the See Committee.

One City. Three attempts at one City. Ashbaridan.

To say Boorindi was diving less and less because his perceptions had changed did not cover everything. Perhaps the burning desert vistas he saw *were* alien enough, had become the new arcana to him. Perhaps the Serafina images were so real that as Boorindi and the divers lived them more, they could render them less. Had their perceptions adjusted to the visions so they were no longer as provocative or inspiring?

Did that explain the despair, the forlorn laughter? Or...

The unpurged images of day recede.

I remembered the words, and with them other lines. I spoke them aloud to give them life and form, seeking the connection that had brought them to me.

"And all the complexities of fury leave,
Dying into a dance,
An agony of trance,
An agony of flame that cannot singe a sleeve."

Unpurged.

An agony of trance.

The poem and the poet's theme came to me. I ran to the western turn of the terrace and looked out at sunset over the Serafina, out over the golden roofs, the pooling shadows, the swelling life of the town, and down to Farlook. I could see the tiny dark line of the divers, the squares of tents and pavilions, the silhouettes of tribal flags.

"Those images that yet
Fresh images beget..."

"What is that, Captain?"

Faoud was there, keeping our appointment for the evening.

"That's it, Faoud. 'Fresh images beget.' I must see Tenna. I must ask Tenna."

Faoud came with me to Paternoster Lane, and Modoc too, though the Target Man was "mooning" now, staring up at the bright moon in half-phase, anticipating his end. He did not remain with us long.

By the time we reached the narrow door there were just the two of us, and Faoud's patience was almost gone. But he kept silent, knowing I would tell him nothing till we were with the water girl.

Tenna's mother let us in, nodding to Faoud and making the Aten sign to him with her outspread hands, then directed us up the stairs to the roof-garden off Tenna's room.

It was a little after dusk and pleasantly cool. The girl was not back yet from Farlook so we sat on guest mats near the strange-sounding Anubis, listening to its eerie songs and drinking the pepper tea the woman brought us.

"Have you indeed found something?" Faoud asked.

"Be patient a little longer, Faoud, please. I may be very wrong. Our problem is one of protocols. The divers represent one of the newest and most volatile artistic changes in Ab'O culture in centuries, even millennia. Not only the phenomenon for its own sake, but the very newness of it has to be accommodated by their Ab'O mystics and scientists.

"It's a violation of set forms and precedents. The tribes are as uncertain and disturbed by it as we are, more so because they sense the integrity of these visionaries. Naturally they have put major constraints on the divers."

Faoud leaned forward with excitement. "And you have found a way forward through these protocols without involving censure or payback?"

"I'm not sure. It's more a suspicion than a plan. All I know for certain is that to succeed with the divers you have to work at their level, in their way."

Tenna arrived then. We heard the street door open and close and soft footsteps on the stairs. For a moment there were low voices, then Tenna came out onto the roof.

There were pleasantries at first, more tea served with date cakes and talk about the Anubis and Faoud's Modoc. Then a silence settled as both Faoud and Tenna waited.

I took the Eluard book from my pocket and handed it across to the girl.

"You gave me a synchronicity," I said as she took it. "The Eluard poem in a town bearing his name. You said this was a town of synchronicities, so let me give you another just as wonderful."

The girl placed the book beside the empty cups. "Which is?"

"The Yates in Yates-Eluard. The poems of William Butler Yeats. The Byzantium poems? Where the poet yearns to travel—not to

Byzantium itself, but to what that city has become for him in time and legend, what it means to him as a symbol of artistry and inspiration. A place of replenishment, of exaltation. Of absolute spiritual and creative rebirth.

"Tenna, Paul Boorindi is seeing his own Byzantium, isn't he, there, large, out on the Serafina? I suspect he sees it every day, taunting him, calling him, but he despairs of ever reaching it and rendering it on canvas. The image remains unpurged and unpurgeable. In fact the *imagiers* all see the same thing."

Faoud could not help himself. "No, Captain Tom!"

"Half-çlose your eyes, Faoud. Look at *First Dive*. Look at *Engines* and the Caliban series and the Cities. Look at the ghostings and the abandoned studies. The ones that are allegedly portraits too. Light and shapes and variations. So many styles. The critics see the differences, but let yourself see them as interpretations of the same thing. Byzantium. Something crucial to these visionaries, culturally an equivalent, a constant represented here.

"That is why there is so much anguish, so much tension and anxiety—and madness—down on Farlook. The modocs sense it. Not because inspiration won't come but because it is always there. It eludes the divers while in front of them. They are staring out at a constant vision—most of them estranged from it, making tentative attempts now and then, abandoning what is wrong. 'The unpurged images of day recede', and remain unpurged. Every day the divers lose what they alone can see but cannot express. Farlook is a place of torment."

Tenna watched me in silence, considering everything, but poor Faoud served too many masters. He thought of the uproar when it was made known that all the wonderful mirages were one recurring mirage; he saw the international confusion, the plunging gallery values, the See Committee in a baffled fury blaming him, the tourism in the colony ebbing away, so many things.

"You are giving a great deal to some lines you have recalled," he said. "Look at the divers! They are Ab'O. The visions aren't Ab'O myths and images."

I understood his resistance. "Why do you limit them to their Dreamtime, Faoud? Or imagine that the Dreamtime cannot encompass the experience of all the humanity that is available to those who understand it? My European traditions go back to your Ancient Egypt, to Mycenae and Eridu. What right have I to claim Babylon and Knossos and deny Paul Boorindi Athens and Byzantium? As an idea if nothing else, a focal point, an equivalent? Why should the Ab'Os not use what they are exposed to? It becomes theirs too; we cannot take it back. Their use of it may be unique, or it may conform to the sort of universals Jung identified in all human achievement.

"This is amplification, Faoud, a linking up with the rest, the alternatives. Jung would tell you that the Dreamtime is both one limited and limiting and one unlimited and unlimiting way of knowing everything that is humanity. That is why there is a Byzantium in the desert. Don't worry about your Committee and the future of the colony. What is happening here is far more important than what the divers have wanted outsiders to believe."

There was more to say, but while I directed my words at Faoud, I was talking to Tenna and asking her to answer. The girl was

standing beside the Anubis now, and in the darkness I could not see what effect my words were having. I continued to speak to Faoud.

"This land has been waiting a long time to be used for something so new. It's not your place or mine or theirs. It's *a* place. You own it as much as I do; you can read it as surely. It will be what you need it to be. We bring things to it. It takes those things and gives them back to us. That's what lands do, what places do. So, Tenna?" I now turned to her. "Am I right? You have concealed this too? But it had to come from me, from someone else."

The girl crossed to the door of the roof-garden, turned and looked back at us. "The divers sit there before the Serafina vision, driven to helplessness and silence by it, putting up with the prattle of tourists and collectors and the media people, and questions from well-meaning people like you, Tom. They endure madness from within—the torment of being ineffective, of failing to link up the parts—and from without there is the other madness and torment to endure.

"But you are right. Whatever is relocated is changed too. Just as you could not remain a European, myself and my Ab'O kin could not wholesomely remain what we were before the European and the Egyptian and the rest. We have adjusted till it has transformed us. Unaccommodated man reaccommodated. Boorindi painted three Cities to get to one that was free of the old. You won't see Byzantium through us. You'll see more. Or less. New Byzantiums. All the makings are here."

"Ashbaridan," I said.

The girl nodded. "Ashbaridan."

"So what happens now?" Faoud asked.

"It is in Yeats's poem," I said, watching Tenna to see if she could use my interference legitimately.

> "The smithies break the flood,
> The golden smithies of the Emperor."

Tenna smiled. "I must talk with Boorindi," she said. "I must tell him about your synchronicity. The agony will not go, but I am only here to ease the madness." And she went out of the garden and down the stairs. We heard the street door close and the sound of Tenna running.

Faoud and I regarded each other, understanding only a little of how this had to be played but accepting for now that it was enough. We sat listening to the Anubis and the shimmering tides of sound that washed the town at night, then, bidding each other goodnight, we went our separate ways.

At 1035 the next morning, to the astonishment and delight of everyone, Boorindi began a new painting. No-one dared go near him, though art critics, media people and tourists lined the rails of the Farlook Pavilions or camped under rented sun-shades to watch.

Despite the terrible heat, there were signs of celebration throughout the town, laughter and singing in the bars and people roaming the streets discussing the news. Even a handful of Cold People brought their borrowed bodies out of the town's dark creche to watch the event—this unexpected highlight to their Grand Tour. They joined the crowds watching the figure at his place on Farlook, earnestly working away, with only Tenna stopping now and then to offer water. The other divers sat in their usual positions watching the Serafina, none of them imaging but knowing that one of them was.

Faoud told me about it over a late breakfast, yammering excitedly and gesturing about him. Even the news, brought to us by a houseboy, that his Modoc had been taken overnight did not dampen his excitement for long, though I knew he would feel it later. The Target Man had been a special thing in his life.

After our coffee, we robed ourselves and walked down to the colony. It was a relentlessly hot day. The dunes were dazzling ribs of white-gold edging to yellow-golds and reds out at the horizon. The sky began as a soft inviting blue and quickly became a glaring canopy with the sun a blinding boss at its centre.

A day of apocalypse.

In this terrible summer land, everyone stayed as still as possible. Only one man worked, in a frenzy, applying his heat-retarded paints, wielding his brushes. One man and a girl, for Tenna was racing along the line, frantic with delight, reflecting Boorindi's ecstasy of creation.

The modocs in the crowd were restless too, twitching and rocking, beating hands against thighs and making guttural sounds of excitement. Faoud became sad when he saw them.

After an hour or so of keeping watch, once they had assured themselves that Boorindi was committed, people began moving back towards the town for their siestas. Only the keenest patrons, a handful of art commentators and the modocs remained.

I stayed, though there was nothing new to see from where I sat under my rented sun-shade. Faoud went off to contact Kalgoorlie and keep Angel Ferris informed. From time to time during the early afternoon, art media reps came to the top of the Divers Stairs, satisfied themselves that the diving was continuing, and returned to the bars and lobbies of the hotels.

At 1400, when the sky was a searing white shield and the desert landscape shifted and shimmered whenever I could bear to look at it, Tenna came down from Farlook and found me. I was dozing where I sat and saw at first only a small figure shrouded in sand-clothes and wearing dark glasses. But the voice was a cool spring, rich and vital and very important.

"Tom?" she said, her voice "womanning" me, drawing my gratitude. She handed me a cup of water which I drank in one swallow.

"How is he, Tenna? Is it a good painting?"

"A great one. Though they will not think so." She looked over at the town. "But it bridges the gap."

"And what you told him? About the Yeats poem?"

"Is very relevant here, Tom."

"Which lines did you give? All of it?"

"What makes you think I found a copy to give him? I simply told him what you said about it."

And she took her cup and scampered across the sand, back up Farlook, and became just one more dark fleck, a cinder in that molten expanse.

At 1600, exhausted by the heat, I abandoned my vigil and returned to the Salamander. I showered, took a light meal and rested awhile, intending to be back at the Colony before sunset.

But it was 1814 before I woke, startled and disoriented, to find the deep shadows of evening about me. I rose and dressed, and no sooner had gathered my wits again than there was a pounding at my door and Faoud calling to me. "Captain Tom! Captain Tom!"

I let the Egyptian in. He was panting, breathless from having hurried all the way from Farlook.

"What is it, Faoud?"

"The painting! Boorindi's painting! Look!"

As he talked he handed me a large transmission print, taken when the diver had brought his new painting down twenty minutes before.

It showed empty desert, what was unmistakably the horizon line of the Serafina and, at the bottom of the painting, a line of dark uneven shapes—the divers themselves under their shades, as if Boorindi had painted the whole Farlook colony from behind it on the Divers Stairs. I read the legend at the bottom and smiled. *My Own Byzantium.*

"You think this is good?" Faoud asked in a troubled voice.

"Very good, Faoud." I held the photograph out. "Yes, very, very good."

Faoud looked unconvinced. He went to go, remembered something, and handed me a folded note sealed with a swatch of artist's paint.

"From Tenna," he said, and excused himself. "I must call Kalgoorlie."

I saw Faoud to the door, then took the note out on to the terrace. I broke the crust of paint and opened out the paper.

Tom,

One for the divers. I have taken Boorindi walkabout onto the Serafina. We will be back in several days if you can stay. The painting is to purge the spirit. The walk is to ease the madness. All things meet here. Wait for us, water man.

Tenna.

Nearby, the old Croesus was drunk with wind, and I was quite probably high on its bounty myself, for as I looked out across the desert, out beyond the town and Farlook with its little community of prophets, I thought I saw more than the sweep of sand and the terrible emptiness. I imagined, just for a moment, a glimmer, a glint, a trick of heat and light, the barest shine of Ashbaridan rising as surely as ever it had above that image-torn and dream-infested sea.

TIME OF THE STAR

THE ANCIENT NAME FOR AIRSHIPS IS EYRESHIPS, BUT MOST people never know this. They look at you oddly when you say it, and even more so when you tell them that the spelling for Lake Air, the ancient salt lake, is Lake Eyre. E-Y-R-E. It means nothing.

For a start, they confuse the infrequent Desert Sea of legend with the great man-made Inland Sea further to the north near the burning heart of Australia. Finally, when you've explained it carefully and they understand you at last, they will say something like: "Oh yes, Lake Air. The place where the Ab'O fleets fight. Where the wrecks are." But it's the word "Air" they'll remember. Air and the ships.

This much you can discover from a postcard in the souvenir kiosks at Twilight Beach. Those busy little shops always have artists' impressions of the ships abandoned in the Air, or dramatic, so-called imagined scenes of the great open-plan vendetta fleets coming together over some matter of tribal honour.

Whenever I see these garish portrayals, or hear tourists talk of the dead salt lake in the south. I think of the times I have stood on the silent desolate beaches at Madiganna and Cresa and studied the wrecks way out in the salt, yearning to go out among them, and the one time I did go onto the lake and met a small part of my destiny during the Time of the Star.

It began with a postcard in a sense. A postcard and a comet.

Comet Halley had returned to the inner planets and was heading for perihelion, and in that period when it was in the sky, certain Ab'O laws were in abeyance, some breaches of custom could be overlooked, traditions challenged and changed.

I was in Armfeld's in Twilight Beach, browsing through the comet material, enjoying an all-too-rare layover and some idle hours. I had picked out a postcard to examine from the Ab'O merchandise, an imagined scene from a famous battle held on the Air a year before, the collision of two great sand-ships in which the Ajaro Prince lost his life.

I was marvelling at the chance of a Prince dying that way, exposed and vulnerable as they so rarely are.

The ceremonial fleets which meet out on the dry salt-lake are allowed full use of holoform projections—ghost-ships for ancestors who have died on the Air—so the armadas are usually vast affairs, awesome spectacles of colour and display but with little substance. There might be as few as twenty core-ships to a side, and those scattered wide of each other so as not to foul their sailing canopies. But as they come together, projectors operating, a hundred ghost-ships might crowd the interstices, rolling along in front, kites filling the sky, making it a difficult and lengthy business to engage and destroy the enemy.

It is easy to see how the legends begin: of Anu and Coorina, of Bindakara, of how the Emmened fleet once fought all day, cutting back and forth through the phantom ships of the Wagiri seeking core-ships, only to find at end of day that there were no Wagiri core-ships at all, that the ghosts faded to leave an empty salt-plain littered with ancient hulks and detritus.

There are many such stories, with no-one to prove what is myth or rumour or told from ignorance. All media and tourists are barred from the great ritual fighting ground, and only a small number of Nationals have seen the battles there and come back with their stories of the great punitive formations. Now and then illicit photographs appear, or what resemble fairly detailed satellite scan enhancements, but trafficking in such contraband images is a dangerous business. Still, as I studied the card, it was hard to look at the artist's representation and not see the photograph on which it was based. I could sense the captured moment beneath the linework and air-brushing.

"I nearly killed the men who took that picture," a voice said softly, very close to me.

"It is not a photograph,"' I replied, automatically, immediately doubting my words when I saw the tall fine-looking young Ab'O behind me. He wore a plain djellaba over soft fatigues, and ornate double swords thrust in his belt in the Japanese way.

"You know it is, Captain Tom," he said. "You of all people should recognise the Ajaro Airship *Baiame*. That is too close to what I saw to be an artist's rendering."

"You saw?"

The young man nodded. "I was on *Semmeret*. I saw my father and brother die, and I saw the Airmen pirate ship that slipped in to record the incident in between looting the wrecks."

I spoke my next words quietly. "Then you are—"

"Yes. "

I replaced the postcard in the rack and walked with him out on to the street.

"But, Lord, how—?"

"I am John to you, Captain. John Stone Grey."

"How can you be here, John?"

"The comet. It is the Time of the Star. A Prince can dare such things."

"Your enemies would be glad to find you alone this way."

"No doubt. But there are reasons, and I will not be buried alive in Fire-on-Stone under all those traditions and never see my world. I have urgent business to discuss." The Ab'O raised the hood of his robe, hiding his handsome features, then made sure his swords were concealed.

I led him down to the sand-ship moorings, through the First Gate and on to the Sand Quay. Like most of the big coastal towns, depending on one's moods, needs and perceptions, Twilight Beach can seem large or small. Now it was too small to conceal this quiet young man, this most vulnerable and incredible of things, an Ab'O Prince without his entourage, without his Elders and Clever Men and his Unseen Spears.

We boarded *Rynosseros*. Rob Shannon was instructing our newest crewmember, an eighteen-year-old Ab'O youth, an oddly fair-skinned outcast named Buso who had joined us earlier in the week during this layover. Rob looked up from splicing cables with him and nodded.

"Mission," I told him, and made the finger-sign that said: "Watch the Quay. Be ready."

Then I saw that John Stone Grey was studying the Ab'O youth who knelt alongside Shannon.

"You have an Ab'O in your crew?"

"An outcast. He has no tribe."

John Stone Grey stared at the lad, probably six or seven years younger than himself, his expression unreadable.

"You fear a spy?" I asked him.

"No," he said. "I do not approve of an Ab'O who becomes an outcast."

We went below, and in the aft-cabin John Stone Grey sat at the chart table and seemed to relax at last. He covered his face with his fine brown hands, then removed them to regard me sitting across from him.

"My father and brother died in the Air a year ago," he said. "The Chaness are—at last reckoning—three times more powerful than the Ajaro. Several Princes had a betrothal claim on the Chaness princess, Chian, but ours is the oldest, the first, and had to be honoured or disputed. The Chaness Prince wanted his daughter to wed the Madupan Prince's son. We challenged the right. The dispute was taken into the Air and we lost."

"So the Madupan won Chian?"

"No. They should have. But it was more than the death of our Prince and my brother when *Baiame* and *Ptah* collided. Those ships were both flagships and each named for the god of creation in one of its different guises. A year's grace was made because of it, a year before Chian could be given over and before I could assume the title. During that year no new ships could be built. The battle would be resumed with exactly the same vessel count. That year expired four days ago, but now it is the Time of the Star and Chian chose me—a new Prince—as her consort."

"What does this mean, John? I don't know the full law on this."

"Many of the Elders did not either," the young Ab'O said. "But still they met and made a ruling. Stalemate. The Chaness and the Ajaro must fight again with exactly the ships left from last time, as if the year did not exist."

"So why are you here? I am a State of Nation captain."

"Yes, and one of the few captains who can sail his vessel anywhere near Lake Air without the Chaness and Madupan satellites destroying him outright. Chian's choice, claiming Star immunity, came while I was away from Fire-on-Stone. I did not expect it, did not dream it could be possible, that she would be so headstrong as to defy her tribe. I had only a small group of Clever Men and Unseen Spears with me and I was out of my State. The Chaness and Madupan sent warriors and mind-fighters at once to stop my return."

"What of your entourage?"

"We used the shadow-warrior."

"A duplicate?"

"No. Not a duplicate. I am a younger son, the Anonymous Son. I am not allowed a clone surrogate to take my place in the Japano shadow-warrior tradition. I have not had time to prepare one yet. But it doesn't matter. As the Anonymous Son I was never seen at the tribal fires. I did not become a known face during the year of waiting. I still have that advantage and another. I had a vat-grown andromorph conditioned to be me, to fool a monitor should such a device be used. He was with me and led my escort while I hid and then came here to Twilight Beach to wait for you. The deception worked. My enemies were halfway to Wani before my entourage was caught and destroyed."

"How did you learn of it?"

John Stone Grey touched his temple. "By implant. A signal sent the moment the shadow-warrior died."

"What do you wish me to do?"

"I have one companion, Captain Tom, a powerful Clever Man named Iain Summondamas, my last bodyguard and friend. He has been away from my side only twice—once as a temporary envoy to the Chaness for several months, once a year ago when he participated in the battle on the Air. The re-staging of this battle is in three days' time. I wish you to take the two of us to Lake Air and bring me to my fleet. It will be waiting there. We have only eighteen coreships against the Chaness fifty-seven. I must be there to lead the Ajaro, to affirm that I am the Faced Prince, or I forfeit. Chian goes to the Madupan. The comet means nothing."

I studied the glittering dark eyes, the lean handsome face, the hands composed on the chart table.

"They will suspect immediately what we are doing."

"Yes," the Ab'O said. "They will. But only when we are near the Air. We are just another ship till then. Then it is too late. Your mandate is valid; the Roads are open to you and safe. The tribal satellites and our own ancient Ajaro facility know to watch. No Chaness or Madupan would dare strike at us. Once I am on your ship, on an official Road, under your protection, I am safe."

"Except for pirates and privateers. With carefully insulated hulls."

"That is true. That is the risk. But only when we are near the Air. When we have made it plain that our destination is that place and not some other."

I laughed.

"What is it?" the Ab'O said.

"To think that probably the only way the Chaness and Madupan can stop you is to use the very pirates who loot the Airships and photograph the battles."

"The Eagle Cleland Buchanan?'"

"He's the one."

John Stone Grey smiled. "I am an eagle too. My totem is the hammon-eagle. Buchanan will not stop us. Well?"

"I'll take the Ajaro Prince to the Air."

The Ab'O nodded. "I will not forget this."

"When will your Prince arrive?" I said.

The dark eyes widened. "What do you mean?"

"You are Iain Summondamas."

The Ab'O smiled. "Of course I am, Captain Tom. And the Prince arrived several days ago. He is the young outcast we saw on deck splicing cables with your crewman."

I did not warm to the real John Stone Grey as quickly as I had the false one, though the Ajaro Prince was an intense and dedicated young man and promised to make the Ajaro a good Prince. If he lived.

As we ran towards Adelaide on the Aranda-Aidalay Road, the *Rynosseros* doing 80 k's under twenty kites, I stood with him on the forward deck, watching the wide gibber plain that flanked the Road on all sides, from time to time gazing at the slender figure beside me.

It was easy to tell from his remarks that he was the Anonymous Son, the younger son kept hidden at the tribal capital, with only the year that had lapsed in the company of Summondamas and the other Clever Men to ready him for what was soon to happen.

On some matters he was still too innocent and uninformed, and there were moments when I forgot about his sheltered life, when his impatient questions became tiresome. Iain Summondamas tried to be there to spare me such moments, but John Stone Grey sometimes insisted, and angrily, that the Clever Man leave us alone together.

"My crime is being young *and* inexperienced, Captain," the Prince said on one occasion when Iain had left us. "What Iain forgets is that I must measure myself against as many strangers as I can. You, your crewmen, anyone we meet. He must not always be a filter to the world I see."

"That makes good sense, John. But Iain is the last of your bodyguard. Naturally he feels—"

"He is my only bodyguard," John Stone Grey said. "The others came to me when *Baiame* went into the salt. As Anonymous Son I had one andromorph and one Clever Man—Iain. The Ajaro are not a great tribe now. We must win or we will become extinct like the Wagiri."

"Chian chose you. That will force a great alliance with the Chaness."

"If we win at Air," the Prince said. "And Chian chose Iain Summondamas. Three years ago when he was Ajaro envoy to the

Chaness for a time, they were close. She accepts me completely because he is my dear friend. Iain says this is not true, but I know better."

"Complex."

"What life is. Cleopatra, Helen of Sparta, Guinevere: men's love of women makes history. People dare things for power, wealth, ideas, all manner of reasons, but they sometimes do extraordinary things just for another person."

I watched the gibber flats, studied the kites, and brought my thoughts back to our journey. Even as we ran along the Aranda-Aidalay, I knew that in the south arrangements were being made with Buchanan and perhaps other renegade sandsmen to be ready for any ship changing course for the Roads leading near the Air.

With the Prince aboard, we had dispensation for constant comsat scans of the deserts we crossed. Several times during an hour, one of the crew—Rim or Strengi—would key in the Ajaro code and data would appear, telling us of any traffic in the region. We knew of the three Chitalice charvolants which passed us at 1042 on the second day a full hour before we met the vessels as they headed north.

It was reassuring that the tribal charvis barely bothered to acknowledge us, just a single banderole from the poop of the closest ship.

Iain Summondamas came on deck when the newcomers had gone. John Stone Grey followed.

"They knew a Clever Man was on board," Iain said, explaining the flag. "I sensed theirs—two. I wonder what they know."

"What can it matter?"' I said. "We've carried Clever Men before. Even royalty. A registered ship carrying a Clever Man to his tribe is nothing to cause concern."

"Perhaps, Captain Tom. I cannot stop being my Prince's protector. He is all I have."

More and more clearly now, despite the bickering, I saw how strong the bond was between the young Prince and his adviser, bodyguard, weapons-master. And it was a two-way thing, a constant learning for them both.

When a look of concern crossed Iain Summondamas's face, I saw John rest a hand on his Clever Man's shoulder.

"We will be in time, Iain. It is our destiny." Then he faced me. "Captain, tell me of Lake Air."

"Lord, we have spoken of it—!" Summondamas said.

But the youth cut him short. "Iain, I know what *you* have told me."

The Clever Man nodded and moved away, to stand by Shannon and Scarbo who were tending the controls.

"The ancient name for Air is Eyre," I began, "E-Y-R-E", then realised that as Anonymous Son, limited by the year of grace, John had never been to the fighting ground, that it was Iain who had seen *Baiame* die. I went on to tell him what many people did not know, that the vast salt lake was almost twenty metres below sea level in some places, and was even now the "dead heart" of Australia that Professor Gregory had once spoken of, not the burning gibber and sand deserts further north. I could not tell what was new to him and what was known, but plainly my telling of it was as important as what I said.

One thing did fascinate him—when I spoke of how the 10,000 square kilometres of burning salt was the ancient flood plain for the river systems of the Diamantina, the Warburton and the Cooper, and told him how once all the inland rivers had sought to end there. Only twice in living memory had the Air flooded, and many suspected that the more recent Ab'O terraforming projects had interfered with the drainage systems and the great artesian table that fed the area. Now the Inland Sea to the north took most of the run-off from the northern and eastern rains, and the Air remained a terrible waste, almost totally empty of life.

John told me things in turn. He had seen recordings taken during the Air battles conducted by his tribe; he had the scans from his old Ajaro satellite of other actions on the lake. He knew the wrecks sunken into the salt, scattered across the immense fighting ground. He even recited the names of all the Ajaro charvolants which had been found amid the mirror-ships and rammed, left crippled and abandoned to the lake.

He said their names as he would a litany, and as he spoke them I turned to see Iain Summondamas watching his dutiful Prince, his eyes glittering with quiet pride and other hidden emotions, his own lips ghosting the words being said exactly as he had taught them.

Too young himself to have done much fighting for his State, kept at the tribal capital by the side of a younger son except for his brief time among the Chaness and on the Air, he was thrust now into the affairs of the world: a chase, a vital mission, a pending battle to determine the future of one small world.

I understood more and more what was happening here, the completion of a forced growth, the dramatic changes, the levels of fulfilment being met and satisfied in both men.

At 1125, we turned off the Road and headed into the southwest towards the ancient course of the Cooper. The winds made it difficult for kites, so with John's consent we took the luxury of running on solar power. Scarbo put our silvered inflatables in the sky, four long wide sun-snares that kept the accumulators humming.

At noon, the pirates came.

We were on an old battle road, running between claypans and long steep sandhills red with ferric oxides and scoured by endless winds. We had scan going, and Strengi read an intermittent signal, the sort of indistinct reading that can mean anything from a freak power flux to regional interference to insulated vessels in hiding.

"Broken signal!" he cried, and we acted at once. In two minutes, Scarbo had the sun-snares down and had sent up death-lamps. Rim, Iain, John and I uncovered the deck lenses and harpoons.

"You know tribal policy, Iain," I said as we adjusted the deadly glass frames. "Will Buchanan's men use hi-tech?"

Iain shook his head. "No! Laser gives too clear a trace to the satellites. They dare not risk it. The Chaness could not allow it either. They would be incriminated and made to forfeit."

But no more discussion was possible. The Airmen pirates were suddenly there, two sixty-foot vessels in sand-ochre camouflage coming at us from either side down long open wadis. They had been waiting, primed and ready, but needed to gather speed, so we were past them before they reached the battle trail. All the same, they scored hits with their lamps, lenses and ballistics, and we were smoking at the bow and trailing a land-anchor hanging by its cable from an Airmen harpoon lodged near our stern. Once the anchor's barbs caught on an outcropping, *Rynosseros* would be lost—capsized or badly crippled.

But, fortunately, for a time, the battle trail was straight and reasonably smooth, and Shannon steered a careful central course, though the Airmen did not mean to let that happen for long. With no other kites aloft than their twisting, flashing death-lamps, the low armoured and powered ships gathered speed and started closing. Behind us, the anchor dragged, bouncing and sending dust curling up. That at least was in our favour, for it concealed our position and gave Iain and Rim time to cut at the cable.

Above us, one of our death-lamps exploded, a direct hit, and another drag-line harpoon glanced off the starboard edge of our travel platform, then bounced back.

The Airmen were careless to have risked such a shot in the dust haze, for one of the raider ships ran across that deflected land-anchor and damaged itself. Strengi reported one of our pursuers dropping back. Meanwhile, Rim and Iain sawed at the cable.

While they worked, John Stone Grey, still dressed in the fatigues of Buso the deck-boy, came to me on the poop.

"Can we pull that anchor in?" he asked. "Ease the cable tension?"

"A major gamble, John," I said.

"They will not get it free in time. Your ship."

Gamble against gamble. I considered the Airmen strategy: a stretch of flats to get harpoons in, then rocks to catch their anchors afterwards.

"Tell them!" I said.

The youth ran to Iain and spoke. The Clever Man glanced up at his Prince, then immediately changed actions. Rim fed the harpoon line through an open two-hand winch while Iain guided it.

The anchor came towards us as the line shortened.

Both men worked in a frantic double-handed motion about their cranks while John Stone Grey guided the line. Scarbo gave assistance too once tension was off the harpoon shaft, working it back and forth so that if it pulled free it would tear out less of our hull. Though the spring-barbed head had opened on impact and would still cause us great damage, it might pull free rather than turn and capsize the ship.

Shannon steered, while I managed the lenses on the poop and sent flashes of burning light back at the unseen Airmen ships.

"Rocks on scan!" Shannon cried, loudly so Iain and the others could hear. "Five k's."

Now we would know. Iain and Rim winched furiously; John Stone Grey fed in the cable and hacked at it with Iain's short-sword; Scarbo pulled at the shaft. The anchor was four metres out, sending up a great cloud of dust which boiled along the battle trail and hid our attackers, though all our death-lamps had gone now and there were two more burn points where the light metal plating was buckled and the paint blistered.

There were shouts at the winch. The anchor was clear of the desert, ours to use as a weapon once the line was free. Scarbo immediately returned to the cable-boss, fitted two more lamps and our old Javanese fighting-kite. Iain and Rim hoisted the anchor up to where they could aim it, while John still worked at the cable.

I felt the uneven terrain under our wheels and sighed with relief.

"One ship only!" Strengi called up from scan. "They've definitely lost one."

We could see that was so with the anchor no longer raising its trail of dust: one Airmen raider still closing, its companion somewhere far behind amid red dunes, no doubt with a crippled travel platform.

I fired a small hot-pot harpoon back at the pirate vessel. It went wide, and the Airmen captain increased speed, obviously wanting to get in range of another land-anchor shot or their own hot-pots before we could prime and fire again.

"Now!" John cried, as the cable gave way, and the captured anchor went over the side.

Through the dust from our wheels, and the sun's relentless glare, the Buchanan crew may not have seen our retrieval of that iron claw earlier. Now they saw it coming back at them, and there was a choice of seconds: to go over it or swerve aside.

The raider swerved, but the battle trail had narrowed and the ground was broken and uneven with sand-drifts. As the craft began to topple, the captain applied more power, but it was too late—the Airmen craft disappeared into the sandhills. We barely heard its death roll above the roar of our own wheels.

"Scan clear!" Strengi called, and we relaxed at last, dividing up into our different watches as *Rynosseros* ran on through the harsh terrain.

The Chaness had tried subterfuge and failed. Now there was only the lake.

We approached the Air on its eastern side, along the graded battle circuit beside what had once been the Cooper. We ran between sandhills, below salmon-pink sandridges and knolls flashing with gypsum. Now and then we crossed remainders of the ancient Cooper watercourse, wide flat gullies, some green with lignum and samphire amid the white sand-crests, showing where an Ab'O bore had been sunk in the old way, others ragged with saltbush and nitre-bush and strange clumps of never-fail.

Halfway through the afternoon, the sandhills cleared at last to reveal the immense glaring expanse of the lake itself, stretching to the horizon. There was no chance of seeing the Airships in this searing haze, with the sun a lid of burning mercury above a chrome land.

I brought up my old National map, a yellowing laminated facsimile, and placed it with the new map Summondamas had provided.

To the south, hazy in all this space and light, lay the vast sweep of the Madigan Gulf, and other landmarks with their ancient National names: Sulphur Peninsula, Pittosporum Head, Artemia Point, Jackboot Bay.

I turned the deck-scan fully on macro, trying to find any trace of those magical places. Such names had replaced far more ancient, prehistoric tribal names, I realised, just as those on Summondamas's chart had banished ours almost from memory.

Beside me, John Stone Grey surveyed those same distances unaided. "It is a place of lies, " he said, and I wasn't sure how to take his words.

On the poop's port side, Iain Summondamas was using the other scan to examine the land ahead. Before I could ask John what he meant, the Clever Man stood back and pointed to a beach of sand and salt seven or eight kilometres away around the flat shoreline, where the road started to dissolve in the odd suffused light of a mirage. "There!" Summondamas said. "Go there!"

Scarbo had the helm and silently obeyed, shifting our course from the main road so we ran along another battle trail on the edge of the Air, travelling north to the Ajaro rendezvous.

A hot dry wind blew in off the lake, and sent sand hissing in sudden plumes from the domed white sandhills and shifting sandridges on the shore.

We dared not trust our vision. Shannon and I used the scans, while Scarbo wore his desert glasses and steered us between the crests of fuming sand.

It was indeed a place of apocalypse. Bad enough when it filled with water in those rare times. Now, but for the bores and sinks, the condensation posts and the lonely clanking tribal windmills I had not seen but knew would be out there, it was a bone land.

I watched that beach for ten minutes, mesmerised by the wall of image-ridden light just beyond it, the ever-receding mirage.

Then there was a movement at my elbow. I looked up, and for a moment thought it was Iain Summondamas—the figure had that indefinable presence—but saw instead John Stone Grey. The lake was changing him. How could I have taken this light-skinned Ab'O for an outcast deck-boy? That identity had gone. Now John wore fighting leathers under his djellaba, and the twin swords were thrust into his belt. I dared not say it but he resembled Iain in so many ways, ways that were dear to them both and unspoken.

"You have been here before?" he said.

"Yes, John. A few times. Once I was allowed to witness mind-war on the Sulphur Peninsula. Big corroboree. Many Clever Men, many dragons. No media could attend, but they wanted National accreditation for the outcome. I came by tribal ship then."

Iain Summondamas had come up on deck also.

"Neo-Dieri?" he asked.

"Yes," I said. "The outcome made it possible to raise the new tribe. The Neo-Dieri."

"They are false men," Iain said.

"They did not ask to be cloned," I reminded him. "The Ulla are responsible. They found the Dieri mummy and they gave the dead tissue. They won the right to proceed, to restore that people."

Iain turned his dark eyes on me.

"They do not bring ships to the Air. The Neo-Dieri are not allowed ships yet."

"Worse than Nationals," I said, trying to make my point obliquely.

"Worse than most Nationals, yes," the Clever Man said.

I tried to change the subject. "The Neo-Dieri care for the lake, Iain. They sink bores and grow things. Sometimes the birds even come. The hammon-eagles," I added pointedly. "The kings of the sky."

Iain stared at me. He might have said: "Vat-bred creatures!" were not that new strain his Prince's sign. He returned instead to the main point. "They are the corruption of an ancient people."

There was silence for a moment, then John Stone Grey spoke. "When the Neo-Dieri come, Iain, we will give them honour."

"They will have honour," Iain said. "Spoken honour is easy.'

We discovered that the Ajaro fleet was already in position 20 k's or more out on the lake to the north. Only one ship waited at the rendezvous, standing quietly on the salt a hundred metres from shore. This was *Kuddimudra*, the one hundred-and-forty-foot Ajaro flagship, an eccentric painted and armoured charvolant with a stern coloured with dramatic orange flashes. Through half-closed eyes or at a distance, that stern did indeed resemble the tail of a hammon-eagle, though the vessel was named for the ancient water-demon of Air, a different beast entirely.

Waiting on the shore across from the big charvi were the Neo-Dieri, four very dark, shorter-than-average Ab'Os wearing long desert robes. They stood near their modest camp: two wurlies, a battered condensation tower and four camels. John Stone Grey and Iain climbed down to the hard pan and went to greet them formally. They talked awhile out of our hearing, then John returned.

"It is hard for Iain," the young Prince said. "Sometimes he forgets. He tries to be an Elder for me, the father I did not often see. I have left him to make the arrangements with the Neo-Dieri. Can we see the Airship wrecks together?"

"I think we can," I said. "The light is less harsh now."

We left *Rynosseros* and walked several metres out upon the glaring surface of the Air, listening to the silence. The incredible emptiness made us lower our voices, brought awe, almost a reverence, welling up inside us when we did speak. I raised my pocket glass and peered down the hot metal tube at the horizon. At first there was nothing to mar the desolation, just the endless waste of white salt meeting a hot sky so pale a blue as to be an uncertain stained white itself.

I moved the glass from north to south, adjusted the magnification and tried again. Now what had been half-imagined darker motes dancing in the lake's searing shimmer resolved into the hulks of long-dead ships lifting out of the salt, curving lunate sections of hull, long skeletal prows thrusting into the sky, rusted broken stern assemblies. The sun and the wind had reduced them to ciphers and strange totems, had taken all meaning from them. At night the winds would race across the dead lake bed and whistle and thrum about the wrecks, lifting the loose deck plates, slamming them back and forth, soughing and crying through fused and shattered ports, whispering down the empty passageways, bringing salt and sand and a fleeting ghostly semblance of life.

In those rare years when the lake still filled itself from artesian springs and coastal rainfall, the wrecks would sit in a vast sheet ofshallow water that glistened with a startling difference under the burning desert sun and moved to the ruffling breezes. Then the wrecks would be lonely twisted reefs painted with faded war-signs, crusted with verdigris and salt, and would for a time resemble sea-going vessels, the detritus of Salamis, Actium or Lepanto, shapes and forms from other places and other ages brought here to this ancient salt-sea, discarded from time.

I handed the glass to John but continued to stare out at where the wrecks were. Saying they reminded me of primeval land and sea animals, whales, dinosaurs, was not true. There was that other comparison, more recent, which always came first whenever I saw the postcard renderings.

"Aircraft," I said. "They're like aircraft."

"I know this," John said, hearing the term his way.

"No. No. Aircraft. Old hi-tech flying machines. I once saw pictures of a bomber aircraft buried in the desert. Big tail vanes like on some of those hulks out there. But with wings."

"I know," John added. "For the sky. Heavier than air, right? Like the shuttles." He sounded accepting but I knew it was an enormous conceptual leap.

"That's right. They are still used in parts of the world. In the great museum collections or as craft of State."

John swung the glass along the horizon.

"There are hundreds of them," he said, marvelling. Though he had seen pictures and recordings and knew the statistics, he was seeing them for the first time in reality.

"You're looking at lifetimes of tribal wars settled out there," I said. "Thousands of men, hundreds of ships. Great open-plan fleets, the new ones navigating around the wrecks of the old, leaving more wrecks behind."

John handed me the glass. "It is some joke, Tom."

"Yes," I said. "I think of aircraft, and here they are in this dry lake, fighting in the Air."

We laughed, then stood in silence. I had time to study John Stone Grey, to consider him as I did the lake, as part of this world.

There was something about the youth that impressed me, that stirred my admiration, a recognition of the worth in what is new and young and untried.

"Most people lack any sense of destiny," he said and caught me watching him. "But not you. Why?"

I began speaking of my time in the Madhouse and how it had changed me. I told him how I had made an oath when I was incarcerated there, coming to self-awareness and objective time-consciousness, of how I vowed quietly, in spoken words, there in my dark place that linked me to all times, all places and possibilities, that I would live as Alexander the Great was said to have lived, for the moment, for the instant couched in the promise of forever. I would take risks, be reckless when it felt good and vital, that I would never be afraid to feel. I explained how it was an easy promise to make then, with all of my life coming back to me like that, but it wasn't simply the sort of pledge the reprieved man makes, a temporary provisional thing, short-lived and insubstantial.

I knew I would dare things, do things, strive at least, and knew that this would equip me to deal with not just the Ab'Os but all men.

It was a divine moment, the sort we all have but often cannot fully grasp; a moment when the psyche is balanced and eloquent to itself, when it sees and knows what cannot be said. Having unlocked the door of my madness, I had such an instant. I knew how it had to be.

John Stone Grey listened, not speaking, not challenging, but seeming to accept that I believed what I said, measuring me as he did anyone he met. He thanked me afterwards and gave me an inquiring look.

"Do you think I am a man of destiny also?" he said.

"I have no doubt of it, John."

"How do you know?"

"Heart knows," I said, which he accepted as he had the rest.

Iain Summondamas had come out on to the lake and was standing a little apart, talking softly with the Neo-Dieri headman, Si Akara, and his three tribesmen. Now the young Prince turned to him.

"Iain?"

The Clever Man turned at once. "Yes?"

"Tomorrow you must stay with *Rynosseros*. You must wait until this action is done."

"No, Prince! I must—"

"Iain! Si Akara and Tom Rynosseros are listening. I have good reasons. You will stay with *Rynosseros*. Please accept this."

Iain did, but it caused him anguish. I watched the salt, not wishing to add to his shame, and only turned back when John and Iain, Si Akara and his men had gone.

At 0600 the next morning, *Kuddimudra* lofted twenty-four display kites and moved out on to the Air. We watched her grow smaller until nothing was visible without glass or scan.

Three hours later, in the sharp morning light, the Chaness fleet came. At first there was just a strange edge to the silence, so that we peered out among the wrecks, feeling rather than hearing something across the salt. Then, through scan, low against the horizon, appeared a dark line, a jagged crust between brilliant white and blue, widening, thickening, starting to move forward through the scattered, lonely ship-reefs.

A great fleet under full ceremonial display, advancing to the sound of drums and bullroarers. More than a hundred ships, possibly two hundred, with nearly sixty core-ships, a great array travelling close together, more closely than charvolants normally dared. It was how the Spanish Armada must have looked, or the converging galleys at Actium, only here the sky was filled with kites insulated against mirrorflash, riding lines coated with powdered glass or with tantalum alloy edges. The air thrummed and throbbed with their approach.

Then, from the north, came the Ajaro fleet, smaller, much smaller, and with a great many replicant ships considering the eighteen core-ships the Ajaro had.

It was a dreamlike scene. In the glare and the hot dry wind, the ships began to lose their sharpness as the lake surface heated and the air shimmered. It was already 55° Celsius.

Si Akara came aboard and climbed to the poop carrying two letters. One he handed to Iain Summondamas, the other he gave to me.

"Do not open," Si Akara told me. "Open later, when this is done." He turned to Iain. "You open this when it is clear in your heart how this business goes, you understand? Only then."

Iain nodded, and the Neo-Dieri went back to where his tribesmen stood with their camels on the hard salt-pan. Iain studied the sealed letter, then put it inside his djellaba. He gripped the rail, put his face into the hood of the macro-scan and watched the ships out on the lake. I did the same, slipping my letter into my own desert robes for later.

The fleets were very close now. Kites were changing, a fascinating thing to see. Most of the brightly coloured topkites and parafoils were pulled down. Drab battle-kites took their place, and sparkling death-lamps gorging on deadly sunlight, flashing and spinning across the approaching lines.

On our scans, we started to see some of the ghost-ships for the enantiomorphs they were, which made the sight even more dreamlike and unreal. Now and then a charvolant would approach a wreck buried in the salt and pass through it, dissolving around the hulk and resolving again on the other side as substantial as before. I could not help but get a sense of intersecting realities, of two worlds merging, as if the wrecks scattered across the salt waste were the future remains of today's battle or, conversely, the ghosts of those dead and broken charvolants were re-enacting their final moments yet again, restless in death.

The Chaness and Ajaro ships met. Even where we stood, the air throbbed with sound, with the drone of bullroarers and war-didjeridoos, the constant boom boom boom of the damning-drums, with the chanting of warriors and the deeper roar of so many wheels travelling on salt-pan and sand-flat.

And then, as if in a dream, like so much heat-born mirage on this ancient sea of illusion, the fleets passed through each other.

"First pass," Iain Summondamas said. "Nothing."

Which was not quite true. On the lake surface behind the parting lines of ships were tangles of kites and cables from the hidden core-ships, snared out of the hot sky by long boom-gaffs and spring-powered boomerang snares fired at random into the canopies of the enemy.

But it was an easy pass, as Iain said, and as good as nothing. This early in the engagement, kites and cables could be replaced, new snares and booms set.

The fleets cleared one another by several kilometres, slowly turned and began moving together again, gathering speed.

Near me, Iain did not move from the macro-scan. He knew the configurations of the Ajaro ships well, could probably tell which of the twenty or more flagships replicated out there was the real *Kuddimudra* with his Prince aboard.

The second pass was slow and deadly. Before the ships met, harpoons and hot-pots arced out from the advancing armadas, death-lamps flashed concentrated light into the overlapping canopies. When a burn point on a hull showed fire or a kite went up in flame, the gunnery crews plotted carefully the likely position of their target ship amidst the myriad random and instantaneous replications that occurred.

It was a complex business. So many ships were attacking at the same time, causing damage and trying to monitor the replications of their own successful hits in the endless search for core-ships.

Distribution patterns were the first priority but any worthwhile captain knew what a distraction that could be. They posted spotters and samplers, but for the most part took their chances with any vessel that came at them. Weapon strikes first, if possible, then ramming.

No ships died on that exchange either, but both fleets took smoking hulls with them and the ground between was littered with burning kites, dumped fragments of smouldering superstructure, and bodies.

Another pass followed, and another, and with each one the captains gained a better idea of the enemy's disposition, the pattern of ship details being reproduced. It did not take the Chaness long to know how thinly spaced the Ajaro ships were.

As the day wore on, we watched the next six passes, saw four Ajaro core-ships rammed and left burning, saw how sections of the Ajaro fleet winked out, leaving large gaps that made safe travelling spaces for the Chaness on the next pass.

The Ajaro were fighting fiercely. Eleven Chaness were either burning on the salt or trailing their formations. It meant approaches came less frequently as the Chaness used the recoveries and turns to reposition their ships. The damaged vessels simply missed a pass to tend to their wounds; the Chaness formation tightened, which they could easily afford to do. The Chaness fleet may have looked smaller than when it first appeared, but it was still many times larger than the moving patchwork of the Ajaro.

I was awed by the spectacle. Here was what I had seen in the post-cards and simulations, the reality of so many charvis working together, not allowed to use their comp systems or scanning equip-ment, their stored power or hi-tech armament, just the mirror-ship projectors; forced by their own tribal rulings to rely on code weaponry and the constant burning winds of the Air.

On the other side of the sky, looking down on this waste painted in ochre, red, gamboge, mustard and chrome, were the unseen tribal satellites, monitoring the silent com frequencies to see no-one trans-gressed, reading energy levels and recording every phase of the operations.

There were four more passes that day, and we watched each one of them till our eyes ached. The Ajaro fleet remained an open lattice, the mirror-ships duplicating every hurt suffered by the vessel giving them their existence, the core-ships trying to protect the hidden ship of their Prince by not gathering too closely about him. The lake was dotted with burning hulls and broken travel platforms, some ships toppled on their sides, others standing upright, burning or crippled.

At sunset, the fighting stopped. Si Akara and the other Neo-Dieri watchers around the shore lit bonfires of canegrass to tell the fleets that they must disengage for the day.

The ships did so, gladly, returning in the deep silence of growing dusk to their ends of the lake, moving as dreamlike as ever, phantom silhouettes against the westering sun.

It was 40°C and cooling, and around us the land was changing. The dunes along the shore glowed furnace red, antique gold and salmon pink, flashing with flecks of lime and gypsum. In the strong wind, the sandhills fumed at their crests like newly born volcanoes. Canegrass and spinifex along the ridges soughed and rustled, and the sun sank like a vast red dish through a chameleon sky: one moment burnt copper, then a stained smoky lavender, and finally, before evening fell altogether, a deep and mournful grey, the colour of wounded angels.

Iain left the scan only when the visibility had gone. He stood away from it, his hair stirring in the wind from the west, and seemed half in trance, staring at the darkness.

"Iain?" I said, knowing better than to interrupt but too concerned for him to stay silent.

The eyes turned to me. "I was not with him," he said.

"Then you have obeyed your Prince well. You have given him his chance."

The Clever Man stared at me. Then he walked away, climbed down to the salt-shore and went to sit with the Neo Dieri. It was an irony that he should take solace there with those dark revenant folk, but our best silences were still questions and theirs were easy with ancient understanding. I heard voices talking over the soft grumbling of the camels, then the chanting started as the beacon fires burned low. During the night, the hot wind continued to blow out of the west, to set the lanterns creaking and the lines thrumming and bringing salt and sand and little sleep.

The next morning made the darkness of the night seem an illusion, another lie, a promise which had been broken. Again there was the salt-sea shimmering in the clear relentless sunlight, the strong dry winds, a world resolved into a fierce duality, the startling twin registers of blue sky and blinding white salt-flat. The landscape hurt the eyes, even through our glasses. At 0950 it was already 50°C.

Iain Summondamas was back from the Neo-Dieri camp, and stood on deck in fighting-leathers and djellaba, plainly a replenished man, his swords and an ancient Dieri war-boomerang thrust in his belt, a great honour. A peace of sorts had been made, and it was easy to speak to him as if nothing had happened.

At 1000 the ships came with drums and pulsing bullroarers, the Chaness in a vast concentration, the Ajaro in a carefully spaced grid, hoping, to divide their enemy and see replication patterns. Again the first pass was a cautious thing, a tentative sounding-out of ghosts and distributions. No strikes were made.

On the second pass, an Ajaro ship was hit with a hot-pot, and instantly across the Ajaro formation twenty mirror-ships wore the same plumes of smoke.

Death-lamps flashing, some Chaness ships closed in on where the hot-pot had landed, and soon they had crippled the core-ship which was left burning on its travel platform. Moments later, the vessel exploded and took its ghosts out with it. Across the salt came the racket of snaphaunce fire that meant close deck-fighting, a steady prickle of sound almost lost in the roar of the wheels and the damning-drums.

Then, with the suddenness of dream, it seemed that half the Ajaro ships were burning. Billows of heavy black smoke folded out from them, which told us that John Stone Grey had semaphored for smokescreens. It was a sound gamble for a smaller fleet to take against a larger—though it meant there would be no more coordinated moves until the smoke cleared and the semaphores could be read again. Now the ghosts were useless, hidden in the pall that rolled across the waste.

For several hours we watched the dark smoke haze, using the scans to see which vessels came and went out of the billows. I shared my instrument with Shannon, Scarbo and Rim, and Strengi too when he came on deck, leaving Iain alone with the other scan.

All of us on *Rynosseros* had studied the accounts of smokescreen warfare; we could guess what would be happening on the lake. Tactics had changed. For a start, the Chaness had accepted the Ajaro's strategy and were adding smoke of their own, having no doubt decided that they need only manoeuvre as a moving barricade, close together, to catch the Ajaro core-ships or at least foul their kites and cables.

We saw only the black cloud now, deepening and swelling forth, distending and being replenished as the winds of the lake drew it into streamers and eddies. Under that mantle, the desperate contest continued. With visibility reduced to fifty metres in places, it had become a much slower affair. Now the passes did not happen at all. The ships remained in the boiling cathedrals of smoke they had erected for themselves, so many fuming chalices waiting for encounters, ready now for prolonged deck-fighting as much as fire and ballistic strikes and ramming. We waited to see what was resolved, feeling excluded and helpless, in a separate world.

Then, near the end of the day, Iain cried out and staggered away from the macro-scan, to stand steadying himself at the rail.

"Iain!" I cried. "What is it?"

"Mind-war!" he said. "I felt it. A ship came close to *Kuddimudra*. With many Clever Men. As they passed, they went into trance and killed four of my Prince's Clever Men. They know his ship."

"Are you sure? Could it—?"

"The ship that did this is called *Kurdimurka*."

"I don't understand."

"It is chance! 'Kuddimudra' and 'Kurdimurka' refer to the same mythic water creature—the ancient serpent of the Air. It is the same matter the tribes ruled on before. If that ship takes my Prince, there can be his death but no victory. The contest must be fought again a year from now, with fewer ships and fewer men. All we do here will have been in vain."

Without saying more, we went to our scans, though nothing could be seen but the palls of smoke along the horizon.

"Where is John's ship now?" I asked him.

"The extreme left of the Ajaro line," Iain said, not needing his eyes to know such things.

"And is *Kurdimurka* going after her?"

"They are going to try! Their Clever Men are searching down the mind-lines for Ajaro shapes."

I exchanged glances with Shannon and Rim who stood by the scan waiting their turns.

"Open your Prince's letter, Iain," I said.

The Clever Man brought his head from the hood and looked across at me. "No!"

"You know how this is going to go," I told him. "If the similarly named ships collide, you will lose both your Prince and the victory. Those ships must be kept apart! Open the letter!"

The Ab'O hesitated, then reached into his desert robes and pulled forth the document. He tore it open and read.

"No!" he cried. "No!"

I reached for the paper and he let me take it. Then, while Iain moved to the rail, I looked at what the young Ajaro Prince had written.

Iain,

This is my final command to you. At the moment you read this, you are Prince of the Ajaro.

Remember that everything I now do is to confirm this fact. It is the Time of the Star and all things can be dared. Chian must be yours.

John Stone Grey

There were tears in Iain's eyes, and anger and bewilderment. "What can be done?" he asked. Then, as if deciding, he shouted down to the tribesmen crouching on the shore. "Bilili! Bring camels!"

Bilili, the Neo-Dieri jackman, came running, Si Akara with him.

"I want camels!" Iain said when the revenant Ab'Os were on deck.

"No, Summondamas," the Neo-Dieri headman said. "No camels on the Air. It is law!"

Iain turned to face me. "Captain Tom?"

"Iain, we can't! No ships can be added!"

"You read it," he said. "I am Prince of the Ajaro! It is the Time of the Star. All things can be dared!"

"The satellites!" I reminded him.

Iain snatched the letter from me and thrust it at Si Akara. "Read!" he said. "Go to com and call the satellites for us! Tell them! Time of the Star. Tell them!"

Si Akara read the letter and muttered to Bilili in dialect. Then Shannon led both men below to our comlink.

Iain turned back to me. "Go, Tom! Go now!"

"The Neo-Dieri!" I said.

"Go! They are true men, you say? Then they are tribal people. Let them get honour. Go! Go!"

It was madness, but I went to the controls, brought life to the circuits. Scarbo hurried to the cable-boss. On the commons, Strengi and Rim began hooking on kites.

"Use power!" Iain cried. "Kites and power! This is now the flagship. But we must be in the battle. Go! Go!"

Rynosseros moved forward, down the salt-pan on to the lake itself. The big wheels ground the sand and salt crystals, gaining speed.

I had never feared for my ship so much. I expected a strike at any moment, a quick decisive death from the comsats in orbit, the Chaness and Madupan especially, but from any of the units appointed to watch the Air.

When the strikes did not come, I added more power from the cells. Our canopy strained out above, the photonic parafoils drinking in the hot light, the death-lamps building their charges. Scarbo put up five colourful top-kites so we would not appear as a pirate to those watching above.

Rynosseros gathered speed, running at 90 k's, then 100. On the commons, Shannon, Strengi and Rim were bringing out weapons: the harpoons and hot-pots and big deck lenses. Scarbo tended the cables, jockeying the kites for greatest pull.

Si Akara was on deck too, yammering in dialect at Iain Summondamas, demanding to know what was happening, while Bilili remained below at com, sending our message to all who would listen.

"Si Akara," I heard Iain tell the Neo-Dieri. "You are pariah people. Do you accept that? Here is your chance to be a tribe. The Ajaro are nearly gone. The Ajaro-Dieri may be here on *Rynosseros*. Here!"

Si Akara was as uncertain as we all were, as no doubt the arbitrators of the Air contests were at this moment. But it was an appeal that worked, that spoke to the pride and secret hopes of the revenant headman.

"We will talk later," Si Akara said, which was as much of an affirmation as Iain Summondamas needed.

We ran across the lake on a surface smoother and harder than any Road we had ever used before. Ahead, the smoke seemed to be thinning before the hot winds but it was an illusion. The ships manoeuvring in those swirls and eddies were adding to the billows at the level where it was still the most effective tactic, creating a stormlight to fight in.

On the quarterdeck of *Rynosseros*, Iain Summondamas went into trance, questing for concentrations of enemy Clever Men he could engage in mind-war, or use to locate *Kuddimudra* and the Chaness *Kurdimurka* before it was too late, before similarly named flagships engaged and the contest was voided. The rest of us used the time to don fighting leathers and prepare our personal weapons.

Ten kilometres remained. Iain came back to us and saw we were suited and ready. He went to speak but hesitated, then flung aside his djellaba to reveal fully his suit of lights underneath, the small mirrors sewn to the leather catching the fierce sunlight so that he was a blinding figure to look upon.

At three kilometres, we were already in the pall of roiling smoke, and our display kites were hauled down ready for battle. The lowering sun had become a sharp-edged coppery shield, as one sometimes sees it during a sandstorm, suspended a handspan above the horizon.

We could see the first of the ships, hazy shapes, ghost-ships or perhaps the core-ships themselves, we could not tell which. It was a navigator's nightmare—constant half-seen forms, startling in their sudden arrivals and departures, making us edgy, ready to fire at anything.

We had no damning-drums to warn of our position, to signal our allies among the Ajaro, no horns, didjeridoos or bullroarers. We ran along in increasing gloom to the last known position of the Chaness *Kurdimurka*, trusting to Iain's reading of the whereabouts of enemy Clever Men to lead us to the Chaness Prince, to save John Stone Grey if we could.

Drums sounded ahead. In the boiling funereal haze, we saw a charvi approaching, two, three, a small formation of Chaness ships. As they saw us, the drums stopped, to deprive us of an accurate bearing.

"No Clever Men aboard!" Iain cried, which meant there was probably only one true ship, but which meant too we had to trust our own judgement.

Scarbo made that decision, confirming my own. "The one on the left is it! " he cried, and at that instant three hot-pot harpoons left our guns, trailing snare lines. There were two hits, one went wide. The Chaness ship flared into flame at the bow and on the starboard edge of its travelling stage, our good fortune for it hampered both steering and gunners. The damning-drums started again, a summoning rhythm, enemy strike, Ajaro core-ship engaged, come to us Chaness.

We veered away at once, not having enough fighting men to engage in deck-war using spears and snaphaunce fire, and not wishing to get caught up with other Chaness ships.

I knew yet again how mortal *Rynosseros* was, how completely vulnerable, and how untried in fleet fighting we were.

The burning ship tried to use its flames to stop us, but with drive cables afire, it manoeuvred too late. I ran *Rynosseros* through one of the holoforms, an uncanny thing, then corrected our course for *Kurdimurka.*

Iain had readings, more mind-war a kilometre ahead. I steered blindly, with the pall hanging across the sky, fed by a furnace-red sunset now, and Iain Summondamas, the new Ajaro Prince, half in trance, murmuring directions in my ear. Mind-war was ritual war, but in this blind fighting it had a new vital role, to let Clever Men track other Clever Men, and the greatest concentrations were naturally attending the Princes. So *Kurdimurka* was hunting *Kuddi-*

mudra, so we were seeking them both, by the mind-fields of their own searching Clever Men.

Another ship crossed our bow, an Ajaro sixty-footer, *Jusu*, trailing smokescreen at the stern. The small ship saw our colours and the command pennon and changed course to follow *Rynosseros*. At the same time, Iain flashed into trance and told her Clever Man captain who we were. *Jusu*'s damning-drums started up and on the poop, clear of the cables, crewmen swung their bullroarers in droning accompaniment, calling ships, Ajaro come to us, Prince formation here.

Now the gamble started in earnest, for there might be conflicting signals, two flagships calling, dividing the Ajaro fleet, though I doubted the problem would arise. John Stone Grey, paradoxically hampered by his ritual entourage of Clever Men, would have stopped calling. The brave youth would be gambling that Iain had read the formations, read the Chaness Clever Men, and knew of *Kurdimurka*'s quest for the Ajaro flagship. There were technical breaches here that possibly the Star could not excuse, but there was so little to lose and so much to be gained.

Another ship darted past, a low insulated hull painted in sand-ochre camouflage, slipping by us under six photonic parafoils.

"Pirate!" I cried, but the vessel vanished down a smoke tunnel of its own making, drawing coils and wisps after it like hungry hands.

Buchanan's men again, after more photographs, more provocative and contraband footage for the souvenir kiosks and archives of the coastal cities, for the curiosity-seekers of the world. The Eagle's men may have assisted the Chaness for a time, but now we had reached the Air, they were back to their usual operations, capitalising on what had to be a sensational development—the presence of a National ship in all this. Comp estimates were seven chances in ten of that raider making it off the lake back to Buchanan's eyrie, four in ten at that speed of colliding with an ancient wreck or another core-vessel, but that was a considered risk. Many Buchanan pirates had become wealthy men.

"*Kurdimurka* ahead!" Iain Summondamas cried.

Before us, shapes were moving in the gloom. Iain went into trance, gave a mind-command for *Jusu* to rush ahead, the least he could do for *Rynosseros* and her crew. Then he turned to us.

"The Chaness know what we have done," he said.

"How? Clever Men?"

"Who can say? A powerful Clever Man read it. Buchanan may have told."

"What of *Kuddimudra* and John Stone Grey?"

"We are too late. His ship is down."

"Survivors?"

"I cannot tell. I believe all the Clever Men with him are dead from mind-war. *Jusu* will lead us there, but it is very late now. *Kurdimurka* has gone. I get no readings. All the Chaness ships have gone. Tomorrow will be the end of it."

When we found the broken and smouldering hulk of *Kuddimudra*, the sun had dropped below the line. The smoke haze had vanished before the dry desert wind and the sky had lost the last of its soft rose and lavender twilight. The horizon was rimmed with the deepest verdigris where the copper sun had set.

Kuddimudra had collided with an ancient Airship wreck, not at great speed but with enough force to snap the drive lines, sheer the main pins and cripple the leading wheels. The hundred-and-forty-foot Ajaro ship had toppled across the ancient hulk and wedged there, and the Chaness flagship and its escort vessels had simply halted and sent hot-pots then warriors across.

There were three Ajaro survivors, all crewmen, and one of them told us how the Ajaro Clever Men had faced their enemies, greatly outnumbered, and died in savage mind-war. Then most of *Kuddimudra*'s complement, John Stone Grey included, had fallen to Chaness swords and spears, a sad and futile end to the day.

But instead of a voided war, another year of grace, a re-engagement, and one more chance for the Chaness to put an end to the Ajaro tribe forever for their impudence, the battle would continue tomorrow. For better or worse, we had that much.

Jusu's damning-drums began once more, a forlorn sound, and led the remaining Ajaro ships to us. Slowly, moving carefully, the survivors came kiting in the darkness on a refreshingly cool change of winds, steering by starlight and moonlight, manoeuvring in around *Rynosseros* and *Jusu* and the wreck of *Kuddimudra*.

In all, there were only five tribal ships left, and one of these, *Emu*, was crippled and would not be repaired in time for battle. Still, Iain gave her captain honour and did not order his vessel from the lake.

For an hour the exhausted crews of the ships helped to move the Ajaro dead and wounded on to *Emu*. Then we trudged across the salt in the relief of the cool wind for a meeting on the canted but largely intact commons of *Kuddimudra*. The captains and their weary crews gathered on the sloping deck, watching the lanterns swinging and creaking in the wind, waiting for Iain Summondamas to tell them what was to happen now.

The young Clever Man climbed to the damaged quarterdeck and introduced himself, for most of the veteran sandsmen had never been to the tribal fires and seen the Anonymous Son's bodyguard, this man John Stone Grey had committed them to honouring.

Iain began softly, but as he explained how he had become Prince, how the similarly named flagships had almost voided the whole engagement, his voice took on a greater and greater presence.

"Tomorrow we will win!" he said finally, and left a silence.

"Tomorrow finishes it!" one shipmaster said. "Unless we are cunning and greatly fortunate."

"You are Pina," Iain said, identifying the man, name-claiming him before them all.

"Yes."

"Then if what you say is what you believe, Pina, you can do no worse than trust me as John Stone Grey did."

"John Stone Grey is dead," Pina said.

"And gave us a day. And an unvoided war, do you understand? Tomorrow is his."

"Who are these others?" an old Clever Man asked.

"You are Bel," Iain said, and name-claimed him too. "Tom Rynosseros and his crew you know, as I've explained. The others down on the lake there, waiting for us, are Si Akara and his jackman, Bilili, from the Neo-Dieri. Our friends and brothers."

There was muttering and many hard looks. Several tribesmen peered through the darkness at the figures on the cooling lake.

Si Akara and Bilili did not seem to care. While Iain outlined his plan for bonding the tribes, the Neo-Dieri were studying the lake surface, Si Akara crouched on his haunches running a handful of salt crystals through his fingers.

Iain came to the end of his proposal. "I ask for a ruling on this," he said, and discussion began.

This was tribal business so I went down to where the Neo-Dieri communed with the lake. Si Akara looked up.

"Do you trust us older Ab'Os, Captain Tom?" he said, his dark eyes catching the lamplight from ruined *Kuddimudra*, the barest hint of a frown visible on the weathered face.

"This is your land twice over," I said. "I trust you."

Si Akara squeezed salt through his fingers. "The Ajaro must go from here. Twenty kilometres. There!" He pointed in the direction of the Neo-Dieri camp, where we had entered the lake.

"Why?"

"Nothing is lost if we do it," he said. "We will still be on the lake. Trust."

"In the morning. These men are tired."

Si Akara stood. "Too late. Now!"

"Tell Iain Summondamas."

Si Akara shook his head once. "The Ajaro will not accept it from a Prince who is still unproven. They will not accept it from dead men made hot again."

"Me?"

"*Rynosseros* is the flagship until Iain orders you from the lake, which he will do soon now to save you from tomorrow's battle. You made this possible, this chance, as much as the boy did. You must persuade him."

"There is so much to lose."

"Trust," Si Akara said, and gave me what was left of his handful of salt. The lumps and flakes felt moist, oddly frangible to the touch, and spoke their silent message clearly enough.

I went to Iain Summondamas. The captains and Clever Men were still deciding on the Neo-Dieri brotherhood, talking as if this was the tribal home-fire and there was a future for the Ajaro beyond the setting of tomorrow's sun.

In a low voice, I told the young Prince what Si Akara had said. He hesitated less time than I had.

"Enough!" he cried, and drew his sword, an echoing, superbly deft action, so that all eyes locked on him at once. "I have ruled. It is done. We go to the shoreline and we launch our attack from there. Follow *Rynosseros*. Pina, sit down! Any man who disputes this may fight me, here, now warriors with sword, Clever Men with mind-war. I am your Prince or I am not."

Everyone stared at the figure on the quarterdeck of *Kuddimudra*, where so recently John Stone Grey had fought and died. Iain's suit of lights shone through the front of his djellaba. His sword was a mirror curve of reflected lamplight.

The simplicity of the fierce ultimatum was inspiring. Iain had owned his Princehood. I looked to where Si Akara was standing with Bilili and saw the Neo-Dieri headman nodding with what I took to be approval.

Iain strode across the canted deck, through the assembled warriors and Clever Men. "We move in ten minutes," he said. "Follow my drums!" Then he went back to *Rynosseros*, taking with him four drummers and seven of the remaining Clever Men.

At the end of the allotted time, the drums and bullroarers began, and the small Ajaro fleet moved away from *Kuddimudra*. The twenty kilometres to the eastern shore took several hours due to the pace of the damaged hospital ship, and because of the dark wrecks which loomed like flattened twisted skulls, silent death totems, in the searchlights striking out from the apotropaic eyes in *Rynosseros*'s bow.

The salt under our wheels told the same story as Si Akara's handful earlier. The lake surface was more powdery than it had been. Our wheels made grooves rimmed with flashing crumbling salt crystals.

What the Chaness would be thinking, what the comsats understood, we could not know, but they were reading six charvolants moving in convoy under non-photonic parafoils, driving across the Air with searchlights ablaze and drums pounding.

With five kilometres to go, there was water under our wheels at last, the beginnings of the flooding that had nearly spelt our doom.

Iain remained with the body of John Stone Grey during our journey across the salt, chanting softly at times, paying his final respects. But when our searchlights picked out clumps of spinifex and hummocks of canegrass on the sandridges, he abandoned his vigil and came up on deck to supervise the landing.

We did not leave the Air. Manoeuvring with difficulty in the darkness, our tiny fleet moored a hundred metres out from the Neo-Dieri camels and huts at the shore-camp, our wheels half-covered by water, with winch-lines fixed to posts hammered firmly into the hard pan, ready to haul our vessels to safety.

"How did you know?" Iain asked Si Akara.

The Neo-Dieri laid a finger along his temple. "The wind. The salt. The Star is here." He shrugged.

And that was the end of it. There would be the scientific explanations—news of rains in the far north-east, a blocked or broken subterranean conduit to the Inland Sea, or accumulated waters from the sandstone catchment areas on the western slopes of the Great Dividing Range feeding through the water table, overloading the Great Artesian Basin underlying this most arid part of Australia.

When the sun rose the next morning, we were in the shallows on the edge of a glittering desert sea, with a strong warm wind blowing waves against the upper edges of our travel platforms and spray cooling our faces.

Out in that windswept expanse of water, the broken Airship wrecks were like strange ocean creatures, barbed, finned and vaned, their toppled hulls spired and arching in the bright sunlight. And in the distance, our scans showed the Chaness fleet swamped and stranded. Most vessels were in five metres of water at least and would never move again. Others, on hummocks of silt, could be given new travel platforms and other lives. But when the flood waters drained back into the hidden chambers of the earth, not one ship would be able to move from the lake on its own. Technically, they belonged to the lake now, though the Chaness were a powerful tribe and there would be negotiations with the arbitrators and special pleas made at the great corroborees, claims for Star dispensation. But most of the ships would stay all the same.

The Chaness had lost, and to the real kuddimudra of this waste, the enduring water spirit of this primeval inland sea.

We waited all morning, until the confirmation came through

that the Chaness had forfeited and the Ajaro claim was to be upheld. Then and only then did our ships winch themselves ashore, the successful vessels helping to drag in the others until we were safely on the salt-pan before the sandridges facing the new sea.

An Airmen pirate ship, unseen in its ochre markings against the shifting dunes, suddenly came to life and, risking power, moved from where it had been recording our beaching activities.

This raider was not so lucky. The satellites were watching us closely and they received readings. There were flashes of hard light, the distinctive tearing sound of sky-born laser, and the Buchanan vessel exploded and rolled burning into the dunes, a final drama in all that had happened.

At 1400, we were checking out the electrics and cleaning *Rynosseros* down when Iain Summondamas and Si Akara came aboard.

"We should go," I told the new Prince.

He nodded. "My hand will always be open to you, Captain Tom."

"I value that greatly, Prince."

"Iain."

"Iain," I said, and smiled.

"One day," he continued, "I may send you a deck-boy, a younger son, to be taught the National ways. Will you accept this?"

"I will gladly, Iain."

Iain Summondamas nodded again. "One thing more. Your letter."

"You wish to know what John Stone Grey said to me?"

"No," Iain said. "While I do not know, my Prince still lives. He has something more to say. But you will read it when you leave here, while you can see the Ajaro-Dieri ships and the lake. Yes?"

"Yes."

We shook hands then, Iain first, then Si Akara, and as we did, the headman slipped something small and hard into my palm, his eyes telling me of its secrecy.

Then the Ab'Os turned and left *Rynosseros*. As they headed for *Jusu*, I examined what Si Akara had given me, then issued the order to move out.

We were running through the sandhills and fuming ridges under the hot afternoon sun when I drew John Stone Grey's letter from inside my djellaba. I broke the seal, opened it out and read.

Tom,

Win or lose, you have survived. I have survived in you and in Iain, for I must believe that he lives also and in great honour. Si Akara has given you a small thing, a stasis-flask with an authorisation. The flask contains some cells for cloning.

Grow me this andromorph. In three years he will be my age now, if the program is true: an unwed son's only chance, a father no other way. Let him earn his way on the Starship, where I learned what I needed. Call him Hammon.

I love you for what you have done, and wish I could be there now to tell you so.

John Stone Grey
Ajaro Prince
Anonymous Son
Hammon-Eagle

I laughed and wept.

The Starship. Of course, the *Star*ship. Airships and Starships!

Rynosseros moved at speed amid the dunes, with twenty kites in the sky and a strong lake wind at our backs. When I turned to look behind me, it was as much to hide the tears falling on to John Stone Grey's final words as to see *Jusu* and the tiny flashing mirror-figure of Iain Summondamas.

"Yes," I said. "Yes."

Everything we do is to complete our destiny, everything, word or deed, and as I held the stasis-flask firmly in my hand, it seemed that this fact could never be more true than at that moment, as we ran from the Air, safe again, full of the blessings of renewal and a sense of destiny at the Time of the Star.

Marmordesse

So we were looking for Dewi Dammo and stood a better chance than most. We had an informer: careful, clever, doomed Peter Pederson, a double agent betrayed and—as it turned out—fully conditioned by Dewi and about to die.

He sat across from us in the quiet lobby of the Grand Hotel in Angel Bay, and we could see at a glance that Dewi had gotten to him. The face was haggard; the eyes he turned on us were dull from the death-conditioning. Every thought about Dewi's affairs merely hastened his end, and had brought him to the point where the suffering was too great. Death was the only choice, and he had agreed to meet because he knew we were after Dewi.

"We want him, Peter," I said, and my gesture included not only the small group from *Rynosseros* sitting in the big lobby chairs on this quiet afternoon, but the white-suited doctor Peter had told his story to and invited to this same fateful rendezvous.

Jarvain Alis, dark-haired, olive-skinned, a man whose every movement seemed minimal yet elegant, stood flanked by his two silent assistants. He was a member of the exclusive Inner Eye medical-religious sect, and his people had ample cause to hate Dewi.

"Like you, Captain Tom," Doctor Alis said, "I have been briefed on the phone. It may seem immodest to say, but I suspect it is because of me that Peter is still alive. He is a former client, so it was easy to invoke some hypnotic restrainers we once used, to ease his spirits now and relieve the suffering. He is still very aware. He knows you cannot undo an expensive, professionally seeded death-conditioning like these new ones, especially one so advanced. Cryogenics postpones it, nothing more; matrix bonding is not available to most Nationals; lobotomies give a half-life, without awareness ever again. Peter has chosen a quick moment of agony on the chance that what he tells us might bring Dewi to justice. Is this correct, Peter?"

Pederson nodded, his face showing intense concentration. He was using what remained of his considerable discipline to hold on to the closing moments of his life, determined to make them matter.

With the strange detachment of his sect, Jarvain Alis continued. "You won't get much, gentlemen. Ten words maximum. The constrainer is first-class. We must listen carefully."

I leant forward in my chair, ready to do just that. My companions—Shannon, Rim and Scarbo—did the same.

"Peter, we need an identity clue of some kind and a location. Is that clear?"

"Yes," Pederson managed, his face waxen with stress, his mouth a tight line. Despite Doctor Alis's hypnotically planted distractors, the effort to speak at all had become an incredible burden. The voice was a ghost of the strong tones I had heard on the phone just an hour before confirming the Grand Hotel for our meeting.

I met the fixed, tormented gaze and activated the small recorder we had with us. "Peter, an identity clue and a location. Doctor Alis, release him."

Alis gave the keyword. "Sovereign!"

Pederson slumped a little. His dull eyes gained some life, darted a wild glance about the room, looked at Alis and pleadingly at the rest of us.

"Now!" I said.

"Three—!" Pederson managed, then screamed, doubling up in agony, unable to finish.

"Location!" I cried.

Pederson shouted words garbled by pain and death. He lunged

forward as if trying to stand, then dropped to the floor, spasmed twice and was still.

Jarvain Alis went to him at once, made a quick examination, then gestured to his assistants, who came over, hoisted the body like some stage prop no longer needed, and carried it away.

In the space of a minute it was as if all that terror and suffering had not existed. The lobby was quiet, deserted but for the five of us. The hotel staff had not even broken their siestas to see what had happened. Questions were rarely asked in Angel Bay.

I passed out pieces of paper and pencils for the next part of the proceedings, not wanting to dwell on the reality of what had just occurred, and that the ceiling fans continued to turn, the dusty palms stood by their pillars, the old leather of the armchairs shone in the dim light whether Pederson was there or not.

"Playback," Doctor Alis said, with the same coolness as before.

I touched the contact. Pederson's voice came back at us, anything like words enhanced, the sounds of his agony dampened by the machine's sorters.

A definite word pattern was evident in the tonalities. We played it six, nine, twelve times, an awful jarring rush of words, each of us writing down our interpretations on the slips of paper.

We were some time at it, but eventually the writing stopped and the papers were passed in. I recorded the suggestions on the message board Rim had borrowed from Reception.

"We all agree on Peter's first word: Three," I said. "These are the interpretations offered for the others."

I love the debtors.
I love the detours.
I love (a name: Ladetous?).
I love the dead too.
Isle of Ladettus?

"Only the last one seems to be a location," Jarvain Alis said. "Where is Ladettus? Or Ladetous?"

Behind me, Scarbo made a thoughtful sound. "No, Doctor. It's a consonance, d'ye see? We at least know it's an island. 'I love' is 'Isle of'. The other suggestions don't begin to satisfy the arrangement with Pederson for a location."

"Ben's right," I said. "Compare 'Ladettus' in the last one with the final words in the first two: 'the debtors' and 'the detours'."

"Aye," Scarbo continued. "Like your Inner Eye—a consonance."

Alis's manner became even more cool. "What do you mean?"

Scarbo was clearly enjoying this unexpected opportunity. "Inner Eye is a schism, a religious medical order like the Knights Hospitaller used to be, or the Cistercians or—"

"Ben!" I said.

"No, Captain. Let your friend continue."

"—a splinter sect of Christianity, based on the letters above Christ's head on Calvary: INRI. Jesus of Nazareth, King of the Jews. I-N-R-I, you see? Inner Eye. A consonance."

"That is not true."

"I wouldn't know, Doctor. But that pupilless eye you wear on your collar is the sign of the fish, Ichthys, itself an acrostic: Jesus Christ, Son of God, Saviour. But a sign for Jesus in any event, very stylised. Don't take offence. It's just an example."

But Jarvain Alis was on his feet, staring down at us. "Our sign is from Egypt's Old Kingdom, from the Third Dynasty. It represents the modified Eye of Ra and pre-dates Christianity. It goes back to Imhotep and the early Pyramid Age. It takes on some of the Atenist teachings. Why do you persist in this? Why not speak of the Third Eye, the pineal gland, or the Cult of the Secret Self? Why not—?"

"I-N-R-I," Scarbo said.

"I will not put up with this, Captain Tom! I wish you luck. I trust you will keep my people informed so that we too can seek retribution from Dewi Dammo in our turn."

He stalked off, joined his assistants at the door to the street, and left the hotel.

Again there was the reality shift, as if they had taken not just the body of Pederson, but rather the whole pattern of events as well, the sense that it had even happened.

I stared at Scarbo. "Ben, why?"

Our wiry old kitemaster went to the board. "I don't trust him, Tom. You know as well as I do that those distractors in Pederson could've been repressors, put there by the man supposed to help him. Alis could be working with Dewi; he could *be* Dewi Dammo for all we know, out to mislead us."

"So why have him leave? Why not keep him here where we can get what little we can?"

"Because we don't want him to know what we know."

"What do we know, Ben?" Rim said.

Scarbo took up the board marker and added five more words to the list.

"Isle of the Dead Tours," he said. "We've got our location. The Inland Sea. The mortuary islands."

Of all the terraforming projects carried out by the Ab'O Princes in the new Australia, the Inland Sea is arguably the most beautiful. The vast freshwater lake lies to the north-west of the burning inner deserts, almost seven hundred square miles of warm blue water lapping at the promenades and jetties of six resort towns, bordered by marinas and narrow fertile strips as dependent on the cooling breezes and the irrigation channels as ever the lands of Egypt and Sumeria were on their rivers of plenty.

Dotted across the Inland Sea are the small mortuary islands, created, maintained and owned by the different tribes, who rent out their facilities. If Pederson's last words could be believed, it would be just like Dewi to be hiding there, working his mischief through agents.

That much conformed to what Den had given us on Dewi. By all accounts he was a ruthless and self-serving individual, at times unthinkingly cruel, if those stories could be believed. Some maintained he was the ageing scientist who had devised the charling process, who had gone to the Inland Sea to die, following the dictates of Inner Eye. But these were only rumours. Dewi could well be half a continent away. We knew for certain only that he had operations along the Charling Coast, that he had some way of keeping the powerful Ab'O tribes there reasonably in check, that the great fortune he had amassed was used to pay for expensive hi-tech assistance to help him run his many illicit operations: weapons and drug smuggling, black-marketeering in hi-tech and charling products, so the stories had it. More importantly, the isles of the dead were there and it was the only lead we had.

Rynosseros set out from Angel Bay the next morning, running under twenty cables and forty kites along Adanaya-Nos, the Road to the Sea.

We had the desert to ourselves. A tribal sand-ship left Angel Bay as we did, but it was a small charvi and its fourteen kites could not compete with the mighty tiers and parafoils Scarbo put in the warm blue sky for us. At mid-morning, we were tipping 100k's, and *Rynosseros* was a splendid sight under her canopy, the "proud heart of the peacock" to use Scarbo's old aeropleuristic term for it.

I stood on the poop with Shannon and Ben, watching the desert and laughing at Scarbo's excesses. There is always something exhilarating about heading for the Inland Sea at the heart of the continent. Despite the serious nature of our mission, the mood affected us all, and Scarbo was using the perfect conditions to dress *Rynosseros* for both speed and display, thinking to roll into Port Merilyn as what the caste-conscious Ab'Os call a god-ship.

Shannon and I watched him minding the cables with his keen eye, watched him running back and forth from cable-boss to helm, shouting instructions to Rim, Strengi and Hammon. We all made our jokes but it was good to see Scarbo this happy. He is a grand master of the aeropleuristic art, possibly the best living kitesman there is. Jib-kites, moonrakers, harvesters, Rogallo limp-wings, the fanciful insect-shaped Semis, the Edo and Sode variables, the five-point stars, the six-points, the Bede Wing, the man-lifters, the deep-skies, the wind-misers and angels, Scarbo knows them all. I couldn't count the times other charvis have matched speed with us and sent their kitemasters across on a bosun's line so they could ask Scarbo about line-fouling or multiple-drogues or arranging top-kites and racing footmen—kiting lore so many younger kitesmen have lost or never bothered to learn.

There have been famous duels too. One of the other Coloured Captains, Red Lucas, once raced us from Sollelen to Ayuguyar, an undeclared contest between his kitemaster, a Tongan named Mussezo, and Scarbo. For the better part of a day, Lucas's charvi matched *Rynosseros*, but with Ayuguyar in sight, Scarbo sent up two splendid Chinese Hawks, judging the winds so perfectly that the twenty-six cables he had running weren't fouled. We won that race by a hundred lengths.

Mussezo had his own ship given to him by the Prince of the San-Topuri that day, though Scarbo refused the offer first, to my delight. I told Ben he could have been unrivalled king of the bright new Australian deserts, but he just grinned and said he was that already surely.

Shannon pointed to Scarbo's latest success—four brightly-coloured rollers. I laughed at the extravagance, at the sheer recklessness of it. Rollers are next to useless but they are beautiful to see, fabulous spinning tubes of colour that made *Rynosseros* seem like a strange machine frantically harvesting the sky.

"They'll never forget us!" I shouted down at the old, never-old man, and Scarbo grinned back.

But then two of our primary parafoils exploded above our heads and the sky shed ribbons of fire.

"Stations!" I cried, though the crew had reacted already.

Scarbo showed the other side of his mastery then. The instant he saw we were under attack, he was at the cable-boss, freeing cables, dumping the display, shedding most of the upper canopy. Only he could do that so swiftly by hand, dodging the cables whipping up around him even as Shannon, in perfect synchronisation, brought costly stored power to the hull, pulling us safely clear of the settling canopy.

We hadn't seen our attacker yet, too much was happening, but if behind us then our falling kites worked in our favour, becoming a definite navigation hazard.

As the canopy sheared away above and behind, Scarbo sent up our four racing footmen, the small sturdy wind-runners, and the wind-thieves to give us speed. The armatures and booms went out; Strengi got a pair of death-lamps clear of Scarbo's lines, their refractive surfaces angling for the sun. Hammon brought up snaphaunces while Rim got a deck-lens working.

Now we saw them—three charvis running at us from behind, a mile distant but closing, low swift hulls each under a parasol of drab battle-kites, with death-lamps out above like the uppermost mantle in a rainforest, twisting and flashing, sending streaks of deadly light at us. Miraculously, all three had escaped our dumped canopy, or perhaps further back, out of clear sight now in the dust-haze of our rooster-tail, another ship was at rest, having deliberately snared our kites so the others could proceed.

Rynosseros ran at 110k's. For a moment we pulled ahead, but then our pursuers went to stored power as well and started gaining.

"Something's wrong!" Rim cried, at the controls of our lamps. "They're hitting us but we aren't hitting them!"

Overhead, one of our footmen then another streamed a trail of smoke and began falling. Scarbo dumped them.

I turned to Rim. "Insulated hulls?"

"More than that. They're too close. Our lamps should be doing more in that grouping."

It was true, and it confirmed a suspicion I had. Fully-kited charvolants cannot travel so closely together at such speeds—too many accidents can happen: line-fouling, collisions from pitted Road surfaces and faulty drive-cables, so many other factors. It was as unlikely as all three ships avoiding our canopy earlier, or all those death-lamps causing us so little damage.

I stopped seeing three separate ships, studied instead the overall configuration of hulls and kites.

"Too much symmetry!" I cried.

"The left one's a fake!" Rim called at the same moment.

"Mirror ships!" Scarbo yelled from the commons.

We all saw it. There was only one ship. The other two were enantiomorphs, dense high-resolution holoforms projected on a broad and powerful band—mirror images reversed to give variation. It was a breach of Ab'O codes. Our attacker had illegal tech aboard and was not afraid to use it.

Dewi was taking no chances. Perhaps he could afford such risks, though by playing his hand this way he had at least confirmed Pederson's clue.

The Inland Sea, the Charling Coast, was it.

Now there was the sharp racket of snaphaunce fire, young Hammon firing shot after shot at the death-lamps of the middle charvi, ignoring the two at the sides. Down on the commons,

Scarbo and Strengi were coupling up two fighting kites: Spider, our black Javanese Avenger with its sharp edges, hooks and snare lines, and a special fighter we called Piñata.

When I saw what Ben was planning, I began losing speed, but gradually so our pursuer would not guess our plan. With so few kites left, it seemed a natural development; we were a ship with low power reserves.

Spider shot out on helium lifts towards the charvi a hundred metres behind us. At the same time, up went Piñata, an innocent-looking inflatable, trailing back as if too hastily lofted and misdirected by a loose cable. When you've sailed a charvolant, you know how easily such things can happen.

Dewi's ship retaliated at once, not with lamps, lenses or mirror-flash, but with more illegal hi-tech. A beam of dazzling coherent light stabbed out from a deck-laser. Spider was gone in a burst of flame. But it had been a decoy, giving a more immediate target and letting Piñata get well clear of *Rynosseros* on its trailing line.

The laser bolt which then struck our silver inflatable did two things. It sent a power surge down the conducting cable into our accumulators, and it ruptured the insulated bladder, releasing a matrix of expanding grapple-lines which settled over the raider's canopy and dragged it to the desert.

I added more drive to the wheels, using the new power to draw *Rynosseros* clear of our pursuer. At the same time, Rim and Strengi turned deck-lenses on the falling kites. There was an explosion, a whoof of flame as a parafoil went up—hydrogen-filled, a careless expedient on a war craft.

The raider slowed, veered to one side, exposing its wheels. Rim got a burn-point on the tyres, another series of explosions there. The travel platform sagged and slewed; the charvi nosed into the sand under its own burning kites and came to a stop.

It was a bizarre spectacle. The projector was operating through it all, each stage in the raider's misfortune replicated by the ghost-ship to either side.

The last thing we saw as we pulled ahead was the core-ship's crew abandoning their burning vessel, again shown in triplicate till they were clear of the zoning range. We soon discovered why.

Dewi's use of hi-tech had been monitored at last by one of the Ab'O satellites geo-tethered over the Inland Sea territories. The tiny figures were barely clear when a beam of savage light struck from the sky. The three burning ships became one as the projector was destroyed; the one exploded in a gout of incandescent light so that only a smoking hulk remained, a column of dark smoke rising into the hot morning air like some penitent genie sending us on our way.

We reached the Inland Sea with a much more modest display than we had intended—a blackened, damaged hull with drab and functional battle-kites and death-lamps aloft, bright twisting diamonds in the afternoon sky. The Adanaya-Nos became the Great Circuit Road linking the famous resort towns: Merlina, Inlansay, La Jetée, Port Merilyn, to the Bay of Shallows and the rest of the Charling Coast.

We began winding down our fighters, and fell into line behind two magnificent tribal charvolants, both god-ships, racing fully-kited across the graded sand, splendid canopies stretched out before them like the disembodied wings of enormous butterflies.

Scarbo sent up our big parafoil, Red Man, and two bright blue Angels, all we had, and we rolled into Port Merilyn as bravely as we could.

An hour later, we sat over a late lunch on the terrace of the Hotel Dis, looking out across the late-afternoon Sea to the islands in the distance. A welcome breeze ruffled the water and cooled the lakeside terraces.

We had discussed the attack back and forth the way veteran crews always do: whether it had been bad luck or miscalculation on the part of Dewi's captain; whether he had underestimated us or if one ship had been all that tribal strictures allowed. Or—now an obvious ploy, so obvious—if it had all been a ruse to make the Sea seem the right place when it wasn't at all.

But now the talk was done. We sat quietly, affected by the mood of the hour, by the play of late afternoon light on the water. Around the shore, in plain view, was the marina where the charling fleets moored and the excursion boats took tourists and clients out to the mortuary islands: the Böcklins, the nearer Ambrilles, a dozen or so others.

By shading my eyes from the glare, I could just make out the island where my old friend Griff had gone to die and be changed, a tiny dark point where the waters of the vast lake met the sky. I became lost in the dazzle there, first in thoughts of poor old Griff and then of Dewi and the Inland Sea and the isles of the dead.

Of all the strange and different funeral customs observed by the Ab'O tribes, there is none more bizarre than the practice of charling. For a start, it is available to all Ab'Os, not just to the Princes, Elders and Clever Men, who almost always go into the gas at Crater Lake, submitting themselves to those strange creatures called vanities and becoming sacred Stone Men.

Charling is for the common folk: the warriors, the women, the young and the old, even for Nationals like ourselves who find the thought of this brief afterlife acceptable. Just as the Clever Men go to Crater Lake, Ab'Os from all across Australia arrange to have themselves brought to the Inland Sea when they die, and their bodies given the injections which introduce the parasite and lead to their transitory new lives as water-creatures.

I have seen the preparations only once, when Griff asked me to be his usher. We went to the Inland Sea together, took an excursion boat out to one of the Böcklins, and on a brilliantly fine day, he committed himself to the necropolis for his final hours. I sat with him in the small waiting cell cut into the living stone of the island and watched him die. Three days I sat at his side, listening to the numbing drone of the cicadas in the cedars above the hypogea, watching dust motes dance in the bar of hot sunlight from the single narrow door.

When the life went out of him, a sensor chimed. The old Ab'O doctors came in and with rough but practised hands injected the strange charling cultures into the base of his spine, his neck, his belly—still full with the forced meal they had given him only a few hours before.

I stayed on the island till the growths took hold, till the first signs of change were evident: the swelling and sharpening of the dear old face, the thickening of the torso, flanks and thighs, the disturbing, quite distinct beginnings of the sleek, fluked, motile form he would soon become.

I left then, returning to the resort town on shore, going back to *Rynosseros* and the deserts, and though it is considered a delicacy, I have not eaten charling since.

The others at the table did not seem to care, however. They ate their assorted charling dishes avidly, and if any of them had been out to the mortuary islands and seen the preparations, they had obviously overcome their revulsion.

I knew of connoisseurs who preferred not to think of the origins of the meat at all, and others who professed to accept the Ab'O Inner Eye idea that something of the dead host's identity was passed on, something more than the human skeleton about which the charling ultimately formed itself once the flesh was consumed. A few renowned gastronomes openly acknowledged their ghoulishness, saying it was exactly the circumstances of how the meat was produced which gave it such zest, such appeal, though all but Calmani made sure the catches they dined from were carefully assayed so there was no sign of corpse-taint. Calmani said he actually preferred the slightest hint of carrion in his charling.

"May I join you, Captain Tom?"

I returned from the dazzle to find Jarvain Alis standing by our table, which was no surprise really. I'd come to associate the suave doctor with Dewi's affairs more and more, and had half-expected to see him here at the Sea—and at Port Merilyn, which was not only the unofficial centre of the charling trade but the main mortuary town as well.

Any surprise I felt came from seeing his companions. With him were two Inner Eye adepts, a young Samoan woman, slender and very beautiful, and a handsome dark-skinned man, also of Oceanian stock. All three wore the soft white garments of their sect, with simple gold ellipses at the collars.

I gestured for them to join us, not even bothering to mention our failure to inform Alis of our destination. What I did do was ask a waiter to have the *maître d'hôtel* bring a monitor unit to our table. It cost a ridiculous fee and needed an Ab'O to witness its use, but after our two recent samplings of Dewi's handiwork it was time for such precautions.

When the small instrument arrived, I broke the seal and handed the device to Doctor Alis. With the barest hint of a smile, he accepted it. It became quiet on the terrace again, my crew and many of the other patrons watching intently.

"Say your true name," I said.

"Jarvain Alis."

"Are you Dewi Dammo?"

"No."

The telltale shone green. Alis passed the monitor to his companions, handing it to the woman first.

"Say your true name," I said again.

"Tallin Okani."

"Are you Dewi Dammo?"

"No."

The light remained green. She passed the monitor on. Jarvain Alis's smile broadened.

"Say your true name."

"Pride Parran Okani."

"Are you Dewi Dammo?"

"No."

Again, no change. I took the monitor and passed it back to Alis.

"I object to this," he said.

"One more question, Doctor. Do you know who Dewi Dammo is? His identity?"

"No," Alis replied.

Tallin and Pride Okani answered the same way. There was no change. I returned the monitor to the Ab'O and watched him leave.

Jarvain Alis ordered several dishes for his group, very simple fare I noticed, then considered the remains of my own meal.

"You do not eat charling either, Captain."

"I don't care for it," I replied. "What of you? Religious grounds?"

Tallin Okani regarded me across the table, eyes bright with carefully controlled emotion.

Alis shook his head. "No, I do not eat it because of Tallin and her brother."

The young woman excused herself and left the table. Alis watched her enter the hotel, glanced once at Pride and continued.

"Four years ago, their sister Ella was foolish enough to become involved in Dewi's affairs. She discovered too late where that led and tried to get out of it. Dewi stopped her."

"A death-conditioning?"

"Much worse, Captain Tom. Dewi Dammo was especially fond of Ella. He had her taken out to one of those islands—that small one there, I believe, very close. While she was strapped to a table, still living, he had her injected with charling cultures and left to die. Her screams were heard from here. They got to her, but there was nothing they could do. The transformation is sacred; the Ab'O doctors refused to put the girl out of her misery. It took almost an hour before she died of shock. Our sect is quite powerful, especially here at the Sea because of the charling mystique, the transubstantiation involved. We mean to get this murderer and bring him to justice; our justice if possible, not yours, Captain."

"You had a location clue before we did," Shannon said, accusingly.

"We knew he had operations along the Charling Coast, yes. We knew of that island where Ella died. There's a large population here at the Sea; we weren't sure exactly where Dewi worked from. Pederson simply confirmed it."

"Isle of the Dead Tours?" I said.

Jarvain Alis nodded. "A franchise registered here in Port Merilyn."

"Kind of you."

"Nothing. You would have discovered it."

"So what happens now?"

The white-suited doctor smiled. "We stay together, of course. I notice that most of the excursion boats are starting to return. In a while, if you like, we can go over to the moorings and find the vessel we want. Tomorrow we go out to the islands together. We search as best we can."

"Give me a sect oath on that, Doctor Alis."

"You have it. And I take only Tallin and Pride. I suggest you bring as few of your friends as possible. I'm sure Dewi would not let himself be found by a comparatively large force such as yours."

Which was an odd remark, too obvious, too incriminating, suggesting that Dewi would let himself be found by *any* number, that limiting the size of our group could make any difference whatsoever.

But I didn't question it. "Agreed."

"Good. So now, Captain Tom, we consider the Sea. We marvel at why Dewi chooses this place, since all people must be defined to some extent by the landscapes they choose for themselves. Look here: how the Sea frames the islands, the desert frames the Sea. The oceans do the same for the Australian landmass. Space frames the Earth. This Dewi Dammo likes to think he is beyond laws and codes. He is egocentric. This to him could be the centre of the world—the new Mediterranean, the new Delphi. It is beautiful."

"Certainly it is the only place he can run a charling operation," I said. "But if what you say is true, how does Dewi placate the Ab'Os, unless he is Ab'O?"

"A rogue? An outcast?"

"Not necessarily. Let's say he's come to an arrangement with the tribes who administer the territories adjoining the Sea."

Jarvain Alis nodded. "From what I've heard, he may very well have been responsible for making the charling trade what it is today, though the tribes do not excuse all of his acts."

"So it seems," I said, and told him about the mirror-ships and how the tribal authorities had crossed Dewi there, though only after he had resorted to the deck-laser. They had not intervened at the use of the mirror-ships themselves.

As I spoke, Tallin rejoined us. The Samoan girl had been crying. Alis took her hand and leant over to say a few words.

I gave Hammon a signal. He took *Rynosseros*'s credit authorisation from Scarbo and went on his special errand to the Seamaster's Office.

Fifteen minutes later, the rest of us were on the docks, walking past the charling boats under the impassive stares of the Ab'O fishermen.

It was growing late. The sun was low over the Sea, and the excursion boats were in their places, limited by the curfew imposed by the Port Merilyn Seamaster to discourage charling smugglers.

We found the boat we wanted with no difficulty, a bluff sixty-foot vessel, painted white, its two-level superstructure mostly windows and observation deck. In black letters across the upper cabin were the words: *Isle of the Dead Tours*. A suntanned, heavy-set man with fiery red hair and a full red beard was working on deck. He looked up and saw us.

"Can I be helping you people?"

"We'd like to arrange a tour for tomorrow," I said.

The bearded man stopped what he was doing and came over to the rail. "Surely. Come down at 0930. Nothing goes out before then. For how many?"

"No more than five or six. But we'd like a private charter. No other passengers."

"Surely. You're paying," the man said. "The only exception would be if the Seamaster wants to send along an inspector. I wouldn't be able to stop that."

"That is acceptable," Jarvain Alis said smoothly, as if to remind me that this was a joint venture now. "Provided we are free to land where we like."

"The inspectors don't interfere too much there. I can call at all the islands."

"Then thank you, Captain . . . ?"

"Michael MacRommurque, Holiness," the man said. "Scottish by way of the French, three hundred years ago." Then he made the eye-sign with his hands.

"You are one of us, Captain MacRommurque? A Watcher?"

"Twenty per cent on a good day, Father." He indicated the Sea. "We are in the midst of a mortuary here; we become circumspect. All these things of death betoken life, we are told. The fishermen make their livings; the tourists come, like yourselves. Many of us give our boats eyes with no pupils in them."

"Captain," I said. "Would you object to having a monitor aboard tomorrow?"

The Scotsman studied me for a moment, bushy brows drawn into a frown, as if considering what such a question could mean. Monitors were used to verify clients' identities from their next of kin, to avoid inheritance fraud and other criminal acts such as smuggling.

"Not if the Seamaster approves," MacRommurque said. "Not at all. Are you on official business then?"

"You might say that."

"Doesn't worry me at all. Be here at 0930."

Scarbo fell in beside me as we strolled back to the hotel. "Regardless of what the monitor gave, Tom, Alis asking us not to take our full complement means something. He may not be Dewi, but I say there's a definite connection. I'd peg him for a lieutenant."

"But obvious, Ben. Too obvious. Still, we'll go along with anything giving answers right now."

"I'd like to be there tomorrow."

"Good. The others can see to repairs and make enquiries among the locals. Something else might turn up if the MacRommurque lead goes nowhere."

At the hotel terrace, Alis and his party left us with barely a word; Scarbo went back to the ship; Rim and Shannon wandered off to House Mizzerain, a local night-spot, to secure a table and some local gaming scrip.

I excused myself from that, and with sunset falling over the Sea, went up to the roof-garden, not wanting the bustle of the tourist crowds just then.

There were maybe a dozen people taking in the air, sitting in the sling chairs or leaning on the balustrade, all watching the far-off islands lose their last golden edges. The sky was a wash of mauve and old rose, ribbed with fading wisps of bronze-coloured cloud. There was no moon yet, but early starlight set winks and glitters in the darkness. Around the shore, the lights of Merlina and La Jetée burned like island galaxies. Much nearer, coloured lights marked out the walkways of the excursion moorings.

I had to smile. One moment death and risk on a desert Road, the next a night with such easy wonders.

The breeze became cooler, stronger, and the hotel's belltrees began murmuring to themselves. One tall spined shape, a magnificent Ambaran, gave a single tentative hoot, more urgent than the rest, and I was conscious of a familiar figure near me at the balustrade.

"Tallin?"

"Captain, I'm sorry. I didn't recognise..."

She left her words unfinished, and I realised that she had not sought me out. Somewhere out there was an island, part of the darkness and so innocent now, with waves easing on quiet shores picked out by starlight—the place where Ella had died.

"Alis told us. I'm very sorry."

"This is a cathedral, did you know?"

"What? Here?"

"Everything. The Concourse. The rooftops. That island out there we have both thought of. Your kitemaster made Jarvain very angry."

"Ben has little time for formal belief-systems, I'm afraid."

"And you?"

"First, tell me. Inner Eye seems to know more about Dewi Dammo than your Doctor Alis is prepared to share."

"You must ask Jarvain," she said, and moved back from the balustrade.

"Tallin, our trip tomorrow could prove very dangerous. It might be better if—"

"Ever the hero. Captain, your concern is appreciated, but I have reasons for taking part."

"Jarvain Alis's reasons?"

"My own, I assure you. But please excuse me, I have devotions to complete."

"And this cathedral is taken."

She hesitated the barest instant, murmured a soft, less harsh: "Good night," and departed.

The next morning we met in the hotel lobby at 0900. Jarvain Alis, Tallin and Pride were standing with an Ab'O when Scarbo and I came down, a short middle-aged man with closely-cut hair and broad pleasant features, wearing the dark fatigues of a port official. Alis introduced him as James Namuren from the Seamaster's office.

"Yesterday you sent a member of your crew to arrange for a monitor, Captain," Namuren said. His voice had the pleasant lilt of the north-western tribes. "May I ask why you have need of such an instrument?"

"Mr Namuren, I have been commissioned to find Dewi Dammo

with both Nation Council and tribal sanctions. My crewman would have presented our authorisation."

"He did, yes. You must expect success to hire such expensive equipment a second time."

"I hope for success, yes. Dewi Dammo has survived by his skill at concealment. The monitor will save time and avoid deceptions. Council is paying."

The Ab'O smiled amiably enough. "So I understand. Since there must be an official observer for its use, I would like to be present on this voyage."

"I have no objections, Mr Namuren."

"Good," the Ab'O said. "Doctor Alis and his friends are equally agreeable. Let us be off then."

Twenty minutes later, the shoreline was far behind and we were in a world of clear dazzling water and endless blue sky.

The excursion boat chugged along at an easy 15 knots. Jarvain Alis, James Namuren and Pride Okani were on the upper deck, pointing out the islands ahead. Scarbo talked with Tallin near the stern rail, and I stood in the bow watching the Sea, now and then looking up to where Michael MacRommurque and his wife Maura stood at the helm, trying to fathom what thoughts, what secret knowledge might exist behind those solemn tanned faces. When the woman glanced my way, I turned to study the Sea instead.

Was all this for nothing? Would Dewi reveal even the smallest part of his true whereabouts to someone like Pederson, let alone allow himself to be found, even by a small and necessarily defenceless group such as ours? It seemed so unlikely now, such a waste of time.

Yet it was all we had. Dewi might not be a city dweller like other criminals, I kept telling myself, or even an ordinary desert dweller like the great pirates, Timms and Captain Ha-Ha. The stories could be true, so unlikely-sounding as to make people doubt it could be possible. Dewi might well choose to live on the Charling Coast, working his schemes, conducting his operations from the place he loved. He might rule and own most of it, too, but had to hide his identity and the extent of his power from the tribes, using proxies and respectable companies.

Nothing new or surprising there; nothing others hadn't done. Perhaps, like so many with real power, he had learned to hide in plain sight.

Something caught my eye. Glancing down at the warm clear water near the bow I saw a charling pacing us, mindlessly following the vibrations of the engine. The fluked creature was nearly three metres long, fully grown, ready for catching and exporting to the dining tables of the world.

I shuddered but could not look away, as ever finding it hard to accept that the strange greyish-brown form had grown around a dead human, that it now had the human skeleton as its own, all that was left of the host who had nurtured it, whose flesh and organs had fed the flourishing cultures and brought it to this stage of growth.

As if sensing my interest, the creature broke the surface and rolled, sleek and glistening. The mottled photosensors on the head were turned upwards, and for a moment I had the uncanny sensation that it was studying me as well. Then it rolled once more, swung flukes in the air, and sank from sight.

Again I shuddered, thinking of Griff, of Tallin's sister Ella, thinking of Dewi and poor Pederson with his "Three" and his "Isle of the Dead Tours." It reassured me; it *was* right to be here, doing something in this place, trying at least.

Needing action then, I climbed to the helm. Michael and Maura MacRommurque had been talking in low voices but stopped when I reached them.

"Can I help you, Captain Tyson?" MacRommurque said.

"Can we anchor here, Captain?"

"Of course. It's not deep at all—ten, twelve metres at most. May I ask why? If you wish to make the circuit before curfew—"

"Please, Captain. Drop a line, then both of you come to the main observation deck, if you would."

"Surely," MacRommurque said, frowning at the quiet dour woman beside him.

The engine stopped. An anchor went down with a splash and the boat drifted, rocking ever so slightly in the cooling breeze.

On every side, the Inland Sea stretched away, blue and glistening.

In the middle distance were the Böcklins, both islands clearly visible in the vivid morning light. I could see the tall cedars, the white-washed mortuary buildings, the hypogea piercing the cliffs. Beyond the Böcklins were the nearer Ambrilles, sharp blue-green points in the midst of this vast desert lake.

It was so quiet, just the chopping of water against the hull, the soughing of breeze around the transoms, the occasional murmur of voices from the main observation deck.

I joined the others and went up to the port official. "With your permission, Mr Namuren, I'd like the monitor now."

"Very well, Captain." Namuren took the canister from his pocket, broke the seal, and handed it to me. I removed the device from its case and tactfully checked its operations. Then I faced the others.

"Ladies and gentlemen, excuse this interruption to our journey. We could spend all day touring these islands, stopping here and there, and learn nothing. With your cooperation, I shall now ask each of you some questions. It may save time and effort. Are we all agreed?"

There were murmurs of consent, some nods, but no spoken objections.

"Doctor Alis, you first. Then you, Ben. Then Tallin, Pride, Captain and Mrs MacRommurque, then you, Mr Namuren, then me."

"You?" Jarvain Alis said with a bemused smile.

"Why not, Doctor? We dealt with mirror-ships. Dewi is no ordinary criminal. He has Ab'O tech, possibly andromorphs and simulacra. I could be tampered with."

James Namuren was clearly intrigued by the turn of events. "You make him sound most formidable."

Jarvain Alis took the monitor and switched it on, held it so we could see the small green light on its face.

"Are you Dewi Dammo?" I asked him.

"No."

"Do you know who Dewi Dammo is?"

There was a puzzled look, as if he might have misunderstood the question. Then he answered: "No."

The light remained green. It stayed that way for Scarbo, Tallin and the rest as the monitor made the rounds from hand to hand, each person responding to the same two questions.

"Satisfied, Captain?" James Namuren said when Scarbo had questioned me the same way.

"Yes, I am. Especially since Ben had his runner unit going, issued by Council I might add, Mr Namuren. The monitor was not tampered with. There were no conflicting signals. I am satisfied."

"Then we can continue," Jarvain Alis said.

"Not yet, Doctor. Captain MacRommurque, would you take the monitor again please?"

"Whatever for?" the Scotsman said, but took the instrument in his big hand.

"A different question. The name of this vessel is unusual: *Isle of the Dead Tours*."

"Yes?"

"Why not *Isles* of the Dead? Plural?"

MacRommurque shrugged. "It's a turn of phrase. It was like that when I took over the franchise."

"Captain MacRommurque, is there a place on the Inland Sea known to you by the name Isle of the Dead?"

The Scotsman hesitated. "No," he answered carefully, as if not certain of what to expect from the monitor.

The light shone red.

The Ab'O port official frowned. "Explain yourself, Captain MacRommurque!"

"There is a place," the Scotsman replied, still speaking carefully. The light went green again.

"In Port Merilyn jurisdiction?" Namuren asked.

"Yes."

"Where, Captain MacRommurque?"

"There." The big man pointed to a small island to the southwest. Beyond it was the hazy coastline around the Inner Ambrilles, with the university and resort town of Inlansay low against the desert sky, indistinct with distance.

"Who called it that, Captain?" Namuren continued.

"I don't know," the Scot answered. There was silence for a

moment, all of us staring at the red-haired man, at the heavy eyebrows making a deep V of concern above his narrowed eyes.

"Does Dewi go there?" I said.

"Yes and no."

"Is Dewi there now?"

"Yes and no," MacRommurque said, and the light stayed green.

"Is Dewi here now? On board?"

MacRommurque stared at me, his expression unreadable.

James Namuren moved towards the man.

"Yes!" MacRommurque said, then: "No!" Then he flung the monitor out across the water. We could see its tiny green telltale as it spun in a broad arc and vanished beneath the Sea.

James Namuren cleared his throat. "Captain MacRommurque, you are under arrest!"

"We must return to Port Merilyn, Mr Namuren," Jarvain Alis said. "We must get another monitor and question this man further. Ask him why he lied."

"No need," the Ab'O port official replied. "That island MacRommurque indicated is known as Marmordesse. The Ab'O doctors there will have a monitor for client verification. We can save time."

"Good," Jarvain Alis said. "Captain Tom, you and Scarbo might see to the helm. Pride, Mr Namuren and myself will confine the Mac-Rommurques below."

It was an odd feeling to be at the helm of a sea-going vessel. Scarbo and I took turns, enjoying the experience, while Tallin sat glumly to one side looking at the deck. Now that we were actually on the Sea, her resolve from the previous evening seemed to have vanished.

It was hard to know what to think. I realised that Dewi wanted us out here, had engineered it all, that true to his handling of Pederson and Ella Okani he wished to deal with us here in his special domain, possibly to satisfy some sense of personal justice. No doubt he felt he was safe, that the risk was worth it. These would be the only terms on which he would let us find him.

We were the ones who had taken the foolish gamble—one so easy to accept in Angel Bay and on the bright sunlit terraces of Port Merilyn, the only practical course of action. But now...

Ben turned from the helm. "They all said 'No' to your questions, Tom. The monitor was working."

"Seemed to be, Ben. It was properly sealed. But Namuren or the Seamaster himself could have interfered with it. How would we know?"

"So Dewi could be aboard, after all. Actually one of us." Scarbo marvelled at the possibility.

"Pederson said Three. Three of them could be Dewi Dammo."

Scarbo frowned. "What, a composite persona like at Pentecost?"

"Simpler. Three people operating a collective alias, using it as a front, a blind. Nothing new. The Ab'Os have the power and the technology to maintain such a deception, using a single person to distract investigators from a more widespread corporate situation."

"Namuren?"

"They'd need one Ab'O at least," I said. "Or the Seamaster . . . no, he would have to be aboard, wouldn't he? If we trust the monitor. MacRommurque's 'No' after the 'Yes' didn't cancel the green."

Scarbo corrected our course a few degrees. "Another thing. Namuren identified the island as Marmordesse. Why didn't Pederson try to give us that name?"

I studied the island ahead, so innocent-looking in the brilliant morning light. "Maybe he never knew it by that name. It could be Dewi's special name for it." And another thought occurred to me, chilling, terrifying. "Or if he knew the name he wouldn't dare use it. Maximum stress. A planted stress word. Just thinking about it would add to the agony, possibly kill him outright to say it. He would have had to talk his way around it."

Ben nodded. "Which brings us back to Namuren again. Dewi certainly wants us to know it by that name now."

"And Namuren could be the Port Merilyn Seamaster for all we know. Hammon didn't see him first-hand."

Scarbo made an impatient sound. "So who else would you suspect? MacRommurque?"

"I'd say so."

Tallin Okani looked up. "Jarvain Alis."

"Are you serious?" I asked.

She shrugged and glanced at the island steadily growing closer. "You said you needed an Ab'O. A Seamaster or a high port official. You have an excursion captain who loves the Sea. Why not a religious leader, someone more involved with charling profits than his sect?"

"But your sister, Tallin—"

The Samoan girl snorted with contempt. "Jarvain Alis was in love with my sister."

"Then he has good cause to seek out Dewi and—"

"Ella was an identical twin!" Tallin said, then stood and went to the rail so her back was to us, leaving Scarbo and me to consider the implications.

Scarbo frowned, lowered his voice. "But they all said 'No' to both questions, Tom. Not being Dewi is one thing, especially if it *is* a shared persona. But they didn't know who Dewi was. Wouldn't that violate the monitor's function?"

"Then the device was faulty, which explains the double answer for Dewi being on board."

"So why did MacRommurque get rid of it? To stop further questions?"

"Possibly, Ben. Or just to mislead us further. The one thing we do know for certain is that Dewi wants us out here like this, otherwise MacRommurque wouldn't have been on the dock yesterday, and Alis and Namuren wouldn't have come. We would have found only hirelings, possibly innocent ones who could honestly face a monitor and leave us with no further clues."

Tallin turned back to us. "Then what could Dewi's motives be? Why bother with this? Ben told me about the mirror-ships before. Why didn't Dewi have you killed far from here, back at Angel Bay, back in Port Merilyn? Did he underestimate you? I hardly think it possible."

"It's all been too easy," I admitted, realising then that I hadn't once regarded Tallin as a suspect, that Ben probably hadn't either, since we'd talked so openly in front of her.

We were nearly at the island. Marmordesse rose from the warm Sea a mile ahead, the dark openings of the doors to the vigil-cells visible between the tall cedars on the central ridge, a simple whitewashed mortuary building on the beach below, with a wooden jetty reaching out into the water on timber piles.

The place looked deserted. Not a soul could be seen—just the quiet sun-drenched beach with low waves rolling between the piles of the jetty and lapping at the white sand, and the quiet shadowed groves and glades beyond.

I watched the island drawing closer, thinking again of Griff and Ella, unable to prevent it, then made myself return to Tallin's questions.

"Two things occur to me, Tallin. One is that Dewi Dammo would *like* someone to pierce his disguise, to appreciate the intricate operation 'he' has devised. It may be a need for sensation, for an audience, even a temporary one since he can't afford to let us leave with knowledge of Marmordesse. Our elimination anywhere else removes the problem, yes, but without the pleasure of having someone know. It may just be vanity." I hesitated. "And it's possible that Ella—"

Tallin finished for me. "Discovered Dewi's true identity, yes. What is the other explanation?"

"You said it yourself before. Ella was your identical twin. If Jarvain Alis is part of a collective Dewi Dammo and he loves you, he has Ella again in a sense, safe in his domain."

Tallin said nothing to that; there was no need.

"How close are you to your brother?" Scarbo asked.

"Not very," Tallin replied. "We're closer now because of Ella, though there was no love there either. They fought all the time. Pride is much closer to the sect. He could be Dewi Dammo for all I know."

"So could you," Scarbo said.

"True," Tallin admitted calmly. "But do think of what's involved in murdering your identical twin."

I did so, then thought of Pederson's violent death at Angel Bay. The conditioning had been in him, yes, but could Jarvain Alis have followed him to make sure the dying man didn't reveal too much at the moment of his death? The mere presence of Alis would have brought on thoughts of Dewi, accelerating the process, hastening poor Peter's decline dramatically. What an ordeal it must have been, sitting there with a part of Dewi present, though he'd found a way to tell us in the end.

"What do we do now?" Tallin said.

"We go ashore on Marmordesse as Dewi intends, though I doubt we'll find a monitor there. But first we must search this vessel as thoroughly as we can—for another single person, for a hiding place, for anything that will explain MacRommurque's Yes-No answer. In case we are wrong."

Tallin and I went to do that while Scarbo brought us in to the jetty. We searched most of the empty upper deck, then, leaving Ben to finish the job—trying to appear as casual as we could—went down to where Jarvain Alis, Pride and James Namuren were talking outside the locked crew cabin where the MacRommurques were confined.

"We have arrived I see," Namuren said. "Do we go ashore?"

"Yes, Mr Namuren. Are you armed?"

The Ab'O produced a small laser baton. "I am."

"Then please take the MacRommurques with you. We shall meet on the beach in ten minutes."

"What of you, Captain Tyson?" Jarvain Alis asked, and I could not help but detect a new sinister intelligence behind those steady eyes.

I saw no point in concealing what I intended. "Scarbo and I wish to search the vessel. In view of Captain MacRommurque's Yes-No answer, we must make certain no-one else is on board."

Jarvain Alis smiled. "Should not Mr Namuren be present?"

"He is most welcome, of course. Three of us will make short work of it."

We watched Alis take the baton from the Ab'O official, then set about our task. I took my time at it and, by constantly quizzing Namuren on aspects of the vessel's design, kept the little man close by me, giving Ben as much time as possible on his own.

When the search was done, we joined the small group of figures on the beach. It was close to noon; the sun blazed down on the island. Cicadas droned in the cedars; a stillness hung over everything, broken only by the motion of the low waves rolling onto the beach.

"Nothing?" Alis said.

"Nothing," I answered. "Where are the doctors and charling techs?"

"We've seen no-one. The building over there is unoccupied."

Namuren looked up at the wooded cliff and the sweep of the central ridge. "At this hour they are probably down in the crypts out of the heat. We must go looking."

We started up the slope into the small forest, Jarvain Alis in the lead, then the grim-faced MacRommurques followed by the port official, again holding the baton, then Scarbo, Tallin and myself. Pride brought up the rear.

At one point during the climb, Scarbo met my gaze and gave a short quick nod, as if to confirm he had found something on the boat. With Pride at our backs, he had no opportunity to say what it was.

It took only minutes to reach the cliff face. There before us, seventeen narrow doorways opened into dark cool chambers. Some were comparatively shallow, vigil-cells like the one where Griff had died, with room for a bed, a chair, toilet facilities and a small service annexe.

Two of these chambers contained dying Ab'Os, both old men, one of them tended by a tiny frail black woman who could barely move from her chair to her husband's side. Other doorways had steps leading down into cool darkness, into the dimly-lit service rooms where the charling vats were, and Namuren led us into these as well, one after the other. Each was deep enough to have a sea-door into a common channel. Each had a floor vat where the nascent charling could grow to viability before using that channel to enter the waters of the lake beyond.

It was an ordeal to stand in the stink and the gloom of the five occupied cells and see the various stages of the transformation. Two cultures were still taking and not yet motile—the charling growths already showing form, working inwards, devouring their human hosts, striving to reach the spines so they could anchor their own rudimentary spinal-cords and become vertebrate. The other three were already fully formed, it seemed, and lay splashing and rolling in the darkness of their vats, waving their flukes, waiting to be released into the channel and the Sea.

As before, Pride Okani stood close behind Scarbo and me, deliberately it seemed though it was impossible to be certain.

"There is only one chamber left," Namuren said when we were out in the heat and glare once more, waiting for our eyes to adjust to the harsh sunlight.

I watched his dark eyes as closely as I could. They seemed to glitter with controlled amusement. "The Ab'O doctors will be there, I suppose?"

James Namuren smiled. His baton no longer covered the MacRommurques. In fact the Scotsman was looking unusually alert, his own eyes glittering too beneath bushy red eyebrows.

"And the monitor will be there?" Scarbo asked.

"And Dewi Dammo?" I added.

"Yes and no," Namuren answered, still smiling.

From a tall doorway on the far side of a cedar, four Ab'O doctors appeared, all pointing laser batons at Tallin, Scarbo and me.

"I knew it, Tom," Scarbo said. "Alis, Namuren and MacRommurque! They're the three Pederson meant. They're Dewi!"

"No, Ben. Dewi is down in the last crypt. These three are the carriers for his personality, another example of Dewi's great skill with projections."

"Well done, Captain," Namuren said. "You are—"

"—quite correct—" said MacRommurque.

"—in almost every detail," Jarvain Alis finished.

"Do we meet the real Dewi?" I asked, combat-ready, watching the tips of the batons for any advantage.

"No," MacRommurque said. "Not yet." He too produced a baton, slipping it from a sheath in his fatigues with practised ease. "We have taken enough undue risks."

"And you would not like what you see," added Alis.

I studied the three very different faces: Alis, olive-skinned, composed as ever; Namuren, eyes bright, an animated expression changing the broad, once-so-innocent features; MacRommurque, fierce-looking, clearly triumphant.

"So what happens now?"

"Different things," Namuren answered, eyes glinting with the presence of Dewi Dammo. "Pride Okani undergoes extensive surgery and receives an implant to take the signal. I become four instead of three. Then, someday, five and six. I had hoped that you, Captain, might prove amenable to my needs. Having an all-lander Captain would be—"

"And Tallin?"

Jarvain Alis answered. "Becomes my bride—in place of Ella. An Inner Eye ritual. Modified, of course. Ella should not have refused me. This is Marmordesse—"

"Scarbo and me?"

"Become charling!" Jarvain Alis was still carrying the Dewi signal. The arrogance of the man was the same as before, but there was an edge of cruelty and an insanity there now, not just the ambition, the greed, the yearning for power over the tribes and the charling fleets. "The boat has explosives on board, and a timer. Closer to curfew, the vessel will be taken nearer Port Merilyn and destroyed. There will be no search for bodies because the Sea is sacred. It will look as if an Ab'O satellite has destroyed a smuggling operation. Unfortunately, Tom Rynosseros and Kitemaster Scarbo were on board when the strike occurred." Jarvain Alis laughed, an odd harsh sound. "Ab'O justice can sometimes be indiscriminate like this. Take them!"

Three of the tribal doctors came forward, and with Michael MacRommurque led Scarbo and me towards one of the empty deeper crypts, while Tallin was dragged struggling and screaming into the hypogeum we had not entered. We heard her cries echoing across the island, then a chilling silence.

"You will die in great pain," MacRommurque said, fully himself now, speaking with a malice all his own. Dewi was in one of the others. "But it will be a holy death. True to Inner Eye. The proper internalisation into new flesh and form. A return to Ichthys."

We reached the door and started down the steps. Our eyes had yet to adjust to the gloom and it was a confined space. There would be no better time.

Scarbo was ahead of me, a doctor before him. MacRommurque and the other doctors came behind.

I pushed Scarbo, trusting he would land atop the man in front. At the same time, I dropped to the steps, pulling at the Scotsman's legs so he fell forward and down.

In the dim torch-light, the two doctors behind could not tell us apart. There was a laser flash, which only served to blind us further.

Then an explosion shook the stone about us.

"The Seamaster's men!" I cried, trusting, hoping that Namuren wasn't the Seamaster. "The island's under attack! They've come for you!"

The two doctors behind us panicked, knowing the deaths they faced at tribal hands, what the Kurdaitcha avengers would do. They fled back up the steps, while I struggled with MacRommurque and Scarbo fought the remaining Ab'O.

Michael MacRommurque was stronger than I was, but Dewi came and went behind his eyes, trying to discover what was happening, unable to keep away. The Scotsman was disoriented and couldn't coordinate. I pushed him away during a personality shift, and Scarbo burned him through the skull with a baton he had wrested from the unconscious doctor's grasp.

I snatched up MacRommurque's baton. "Quickly, Ben!"

There were footsteps above. The fleeing doctors had realised the folly of failing Dewi and had returned. We shot them while they were still framed in the doorway above us. Then we rushed out into the glare, hurried along the cliff face to the last doorway. Through the big cedar trunks, we caught glimpses of the beach, saw coiling black smoke, the wreckage of the excursion boat and the jetty, the damaged mortuary building.

Then we were in darkness again, hurrying down steps that curved into the living rock. In a dimly-lit staging room, we met Pride Okani and Maura MacRommurque rushing towards us, no doubt sent to help the Scotsman. Dewi probably assumed his red-haired carrier was unconscious, and needed to keep him safe.

It was a matter of timing, of reflexes and luck. Scarbo and I have had weapons training and knew to drop to the sides of the passage. Pride and Maura did not. Pride's bolt went where I had been a moment before, and Maura simply did not react quickly enough. I shot the woman through the neck; Scarbo burned a neat hole in the Samoan's skull.

Then it was another flight of steps, and Scarbo and I burst into the primary chamber, our footsteps echoing in the cave-like space.

We took in what we saw in an instant: Tallin strapped naked to a mortuary altar, a ballgag in her mouth, her eyes wild; Jarvain Alis and Namuren standing over her, holding loaded syringes, but smaller, more delicate instruments than were normally used to introduce the growths—they did not wish the shots themselves to kill her. There, too, was the remaining Ab'O doctor holding his baton, and a fully-grown charling lying very still in the floor vat, leads and contacts connecting its head and spine to banks of hi-tech equipment beyond.

The Ab'O doctor raised his baton. Scarbo shot him through the heart.

"No!" Alis cried, and it was Dewi speaking.

I burned Alis where he stood. The syringe clattered on the floor and rolled to the side.

Namuren brandished his own syringe of charling culture.

"No!" he cried, and it was Dewi again.

"Do nothing, Dewi," I said, "or you die this instant! Put the hypodermic down!"

Namuren obeyed, eyes glittering with the panic and rage of the unmoving creature in the vat.

Scarbo went to the altar and freed Tallin. She sobbed hysterically as Ben unstrapped the ball from her mouth and held her to him. She hadn't been injected yet.

"Do nothing!" I said again to Namuren, for Dewi's final carrier was showing enormous agitation.

"The Seamaster is here?" Namuren demanded, and I couldn't be sure if it were Dewi's question or the port official's. Then I realised that Dewi wouldn't relax his hold on Namuren for a moment now, not for a second. This was his only point of contact, his only path to life.

"No," Scarbo told him, told the creature in the vat. "I found the explosives on the boat and set the timer early. We knew we were in a trap."

"Explain Dewi to us!" I said.

Namuren calmed. His eyes steadied a little, perhaps sensing hope, a way for life in exchange for knowledge.

"I was Ab'O," he said. "A scientist deprived of reward because what we achieve is always for the tribes, not ourselves. I was dying and I had the knowledge to keep my brain alive in charling flesh. I halted the attrition, found a way to do it. I arranged for my closest colleagues to be carriers, to surrender moments of their lives. Namarkon could have helped, too, but Chiras wouldn't leave his precious library, so I did it myself. Don't you see? I did it! I am still alive, thinking, years after bodily death."

"And insane and cruel!" Scarbo cried. "The charling has changed you. You've lost your humanity!"

"No. There was a status quo!" Namuren said, Dewi said, ignoring Scarbo's remarks. "I made no demands on Nation or the tribes that they did not profit from in some way. Why this action now?"

"You harm others. Pederson and Ella—"

"No!" Namuren snarled the word, snarled it for Dewi. His eyes were terrible to see. "What will you do to me?"

"Probably disconnect you," I said, trying to plant the idea that terms might be possible. "For Pederson and Ella's sakes. Probably open the gate and release you into the Sea."

"No!" Namuren shrieked, and lunged for the baton dropped by the Ab'O doctor.

But Tallin already had the weapon from Jarvain Alis's body, and she shot the port official, fired again at the dully-gleaming tech beyond.

There were several small explosions, the angry snap and chatter of circuits fusing.

In the vat, the creature which was all that was left of Dewi Dammo thrashed in the shallow water, tearing free of the contacts.

But Tallin did more. She grabbed a loaded syringe from the floor, leant over the creature's head, and thrust it into where the brain would be.

It was a light needle, meant for human flesh, and it may not have pierced the special sac surrounding Dewi's brain. But it didn't bend or break, and Tallin pressed the plunger home. She left the needle fixed there, then turned and opened the sea-door valve by hand.

The maddened charling plunged out into the channel, flukes flailing, and was gone.

"For Ella," Tallin said, joining us. "I did that for Ella."

Then the girl's ordeal caught up with her. She staggered, went to reach for a wall to steady herself, and stumbled forward. Scarbo and I supported her between us and helped her up to the staging room where we found her clothes.

While she dressed, she regarded the bodies of Pride and Maura MacRommurque without a word. Then we continued out into the sunlight and made our way through the cedar grove down to the beach. Looking towards Port Merilyn, we could see three boats approaching Marmordesse flying the Seamaster's colours.

"It's over now, Tallin," I said. "What will you do?"

She stared at the dazzling water of the Inland Sea, watching the boats draw nearer.

"Inner Eye," she said, fingering the small golden sign pinned below her collar. "It isn't over yet. I will get special dispensation from the Seamaster and hire a boat. I will find that charling."

"And then?"

"Why, I will eat him," Tallin said. "I will eat him."

BLUE TYSON

The Blue Captain . . .

Of the seven Nationals who have won Colours and fine sand-ships from the tribes, earning for themselves the right to cross the eerie and exotic Australia of the future, Tom Rynosseros is the most mysterious.

He is the one from the Madhouse, the Captain whose adventures among the powerful tribes of the interior reveal a hidden purpose, a destiny waiting out in the red deserts which affects not only Nation but the Dreamtime itself.

By way of pirates, gliders, jazz and porcelain rabbits, too much good food, hours at the kiln and the ancient scribes of Ebla, this book could be for none other than my dear friends:

Jack, Norma and John Vance

INTRODUCTION

TO AVOID CONFUSION AND TO QUIET RUMOURS, I ADMIT from the start that I have been acquainted with Terry Dowling for many years. He has been my friend, accomplice, and fellow vagabond. Together we have roamed and plundered, romanced both fair and brunette maidens, looted their possessions—usually cold cans of Foster's beer from their refrigerators, occasionally a ham sandwich.

Therefore, this introduction is not necessarily dispassionate, although it may be relied upon as a character reference.

In regard to *Blue Tyson*: the culture native to Australia is extremely sophisticated despite its apparent crudity. It goes without saying that the Aboriginal mental patterns and constructs of imagery cannot be translated into our own terms. To understand such lore and emotion, one must be born an Aborigine. Still, a few Aboriginal concepts affect us as if they were archetypal truths, notably 'Dreamtime', which resonates like a gong at some deep level of the mind.

The usual story of the future is based, more or less implicitly, upon contemporary Caucasian ideas, then elaborating upon these to formulate the societies which the writer hopes will seem plausible. There is nothing wrong with this procedure, since all of us swim in the same cultural soup.

Terry has attempted a far more difficult work; he has started with a culture essentially incommensurable with our own and has developed therefrom a new culture of extremely elaborate textures. There are too many details to be mentioned here, although it may be pointed out that the parapsychic abilities of the present-day Aborigines have not been neglected in Terry's extrapolations. For us Long-noses it is a cheerless prospect. The Ab'Os, exploiting their special abilities, have imposed their world-view upon Australia. The details are haunting; each story projects a special mood. Terry writes with verve and flair; his imagination never stops. So there you have it. Tom Tyson, the Blue Captain of the sand-ship *Rynosseros*, the linking character in each of these stories, will be familiar by reason of his appearance in a previous collection, and apparently Terry is not done with him yet.

—Jack Vance

"This is the task of man always . . . not to illuminate the ancient truths, the ancient intimations of the unconscious, the ancient intimations of the soul, but . . . to make them immediate and contemporary, to give them a meaning in the here and now."

—Carl Gustav Jung

BREAKING THROUGH TO THE HEROES

THREE OF US FROM *Rynosseros* WERE SITTING ON THE LONG terrace of the Gaza Hotel, enjoying one of the slow twilights we have now and watching a dozen or so patrons playing fire-chess.

We sat near the Promenade, Shannon, Rimmon and I, looking out over the balustrade to the brilliantly lit Pier and the darkening ocean. One moment we were caught up in the sound of the long swells that crashed on the beach and by the intent expressions on the faces of the players, so many ghostly masks lit by their flickering pieces, then there were two people standing near us.

"Hello, Tom?"

I couldn't place the voice in the windy darkness, though something about it was familiar.

"Tobas?"

Next to me, Shannon laughed.

"It's the Welshman. Cromarthy," he said.

"Right on. Tad Cromarthy, an' doing a job. I've someone fer ya ta meet, Tom. This is Anna Kemp."

People who have never seen haldane Ab'O just cannot appreciate that moment on the terrace at the Gaza, the presence suddenly there, the inherent power, the surprise of recognition that is never that.

When Anna Kemp stepped forward into the light from the party lanterns, pushing back the hood of her dark robe, I saw a very tall tribal woman, uncommonly black, like sculpted night herself, yet with little of the old Koori physiotype about her. As her features resolved, it was hard to tell what was natural, cosmetically altered or haldane legacy, but even in the half-light I could see she was a beauty. The flash of scintillants on the inside of her robe when she pushed it back heightened the effect.

"This, m'am, is Tom Rynosseros hisself. As promised. Or Blue Tyson. Or Tom Tyson. Or Tom O'Bedlam, dependin' on who—"

"Enough, Tad. Be a gentleman and give us room."

The little man took the money I handed him and slipped off along the terrace to one of the bars. Shannon and Rim saw it was business, sensed it was probably one to one and confidential at this point, and got up to go.

"We'll head back to *Rynosseros*" Shannon said. "See if Ben needs help with the new boss housing." They excused themselves and moved off among the tables.

I was left to find words, feeling that eerie sense of recognition again. An Ab'O woman here of all places, unaccompanied, radiating such presence.

Anna Kemp saved me the effort. The twinkling black lamia spoke first, softly, from the seat Rim had vacated.

"I waited for darkness, Captain. I needed darkness. Please, you know what berking is?"

The question surprised me. "Yes. When you draw on the Dreamtime parts of your personalities."

"What we agree to call haldanes."

"We try to be as scientific about it as we can, Ms Kemp. It helps us live with it. I know what—iceberging—is. The current theories anyway. National theories."

"Good. And my name is Anna. Tom."

We exchanged smiles. Hers was a little wintry. She was trying to be relaxed and calm but something was troubling her.

"My father is Arredeni."

I made the connection at once. Of course. *The* Arredeni. Arredeni Paxton Kemp, the Ab'O scientist.

"He has discovered something about berking he wishes to share with you Nationals. A gift. An official benefice. He needs you to go to him at Heart-and-Hand before he is killed."

She stood up, over six foot, her form shimmering in the glow from the terrace lamps and the burning pieces on the boards nearby. "Can we walk please? I would hate to be found here."

"Someone is intent on stopping you?"

"Please. Walk. Along the terrace."

She took my arm and we passed the bright flickering boards, moved before the lit doorways and grand lobbies of the Gaza, eventually joined the dozens of other couples on the Promenade that reached by the Pier and the gardens and followed the dunes and the seawall around by the ocean, out towards Mirajan, Castanelle and the souling colonies. Their lights twinkled in the distance.

I felt absurdly like one of the Dashiell Hammett characters I'd seen in the film festival the week before, right down to having this dark mysterious woman on my arm, here seeking help in what had to be a desperate and dangerous enterprise judging by her manner. But the flashing, sequined shape beside me was real—the pressure of her hand, the recognition I felt as a permanent déjà-vu, so strange and disorienting.

As we walked, I tried to remember what I knew of current disputes and alliances among the different States, hoping to recall Arredeni's present status there. Normally it would have been easy, but not now.

Berking.

Iceberging. Reaching beyond the known to what was beneath.

All I could think of was the Princes and their Clever Men lined up, not moving, fighting a battle on a different plane of reality, breaking through to the heroes that they also were, that we all were to hear sceptics like Arredeni tell it—Colte and Ashbiani and Marduk, so many others. Those wars never stopped, and just as well. The energies were contained, directed inward. The status quo between the Ab'O States and Nation remained intact.

It was wonderfully cool on the Promenade. The further we went, the more the crowds thinned out until we were the only couple and the Gaza and Twilight Beach were so much shimmering gold and black treeline filigree behind us and we were in the terminator dunes between the desert and the ocean. We could hear the waves crashing on our right, and all around us the hiss and whisper of seagrass. The moon was up at last and ahead on the dunes stood the nine-foot iron rod of a belltree, stripped of its higher functions long ago but thrumming in the wind all the same. The diligent in the crown still had a glimmering of life; now and then there was a sad chiming of the dim-recall rods way down in the shaft, below the empty arms.

Seeing the old tree may have done it.

"The stories are true?" she said.

"I'm sorry?"

"You were given Blue by a rogue tree?"

She had to know better than to ask, though she was Ab'O. It did make a difference.

"I don't discuss it, Anna."

"Arredeni said. But you and the other Coloured Captains performed some service for the tree. Something important."

I allowed that much. "Yes."

"You got your ships that way. The Hero Colours. All of you."

"Anna—"

"Tom, see it as I do. I'm about to tell something very important to someone who came out of the Madhouse at Cape Bedlam. Arredeni said that I should read you, that finally I should be the one to decide. I'm doing that now."

"I don't discuss it."

"I know, but it's important. Why were you sent there? Who were you? So little is known. You came out hating the dream machines set to watch over you. No clear memories, just a few half-remembered images—"

I felt a rush of panic. "Anna!"

"A woman's face, a star and a ship. Correct?"

And surging, irrational anger. "How—?"

"You have been going to a dreamlock for some time now. Mercy Simotee. She has been working on those images; you suspect there might be others."

"She would not give you that—"

"I'm the daughter of a Prince, Tom. By law, Mercy Simotee could not refuse."

"Listen—"

"From our viewpoint, I said! No sooner are you released than a famous oracle tree, possibly the greatest of the Iseult-Darrian AIs, arranges for you to win *Rynosseros* in the ship-lotteries. It gives you Blue, a Hero Colour—"

"Six other Nationals had Colours and ships already. I wasn't the first."

"A tribal Madhouse, Tom. Why would this tree choose such a person, a man with no past? Why?"

"You have access to Mercy's records. You know about the Captains. Are you going to tell me?"

Incredibly, I really thought she might. Perhaps it was the recognition, the sense of the familiar that attended particularly powerful Clever Men, that flowed from Anna with such undeniable force.

"Me? No. Arredeni may, it occurs to me now. He specified you—not just any of the Seven. The last Captain, he said."

Arredeni may! The words held me, the knowledge that there were tribal people who did know, who could reveal such things. Again, it made all the difference in the world.

"There's so little. The images you said. The ship—possibly *Rynosseros*, I can't be sure. The star is a point I sometimes see, a sharp point of light in my mind. Very bright. The face is Ab'O, quite beautiful, with a triangle of golden lace set into the forehead. An Arete triangle. I do not know the face. But Ab'O. That's all, just the three. Sometimes hints of others. Memories of the dream machines in the darkness. Conversations. I trusted them. Your father really asked for me?"

"Insisted on it. The Blue Captain. He said to try the Gaza."

"You didn't ask why?"

"Of course I did. He would not say. Just specified you to receive the benefice. He was very troubled, Tom."

"Are we safe now?" I watched the spectral tree before us, immediately had my answer by the pressure of her hand closing on my arm. Her hushed words astonished me.

"Stop! They are near. I sense Colte and Dos. And Hecate, yes. Three." She continued to read the night. "Only three."

Three Clever Men. Anna was sensing them, already tracking their mind-lines.

I wished I had a ballistic weapon then and not just the light deck sticker charvolant crews usually carried. But such thoughts were short-lived.

There were two figures ahead of us on the Promenade; another emerged from the seagrass on our left, leapt nimbly to the stones, became still. Three Ab'Os communing, drawing aspect.

Twilight Beach seemed a thousand miles behind. The chiming of the tree was a mournful thing. Anna released my arm and tensed.

"Do nothing!" she said, and went into trance. Just like that, her eyes were gone, rolled back. She stood with her feet apart, arms raised partway out from her body as if about to lift, hands turned down.

It was the Owl configuration. She was going after one of the strongest heroes, Imbaro the War Owl, stronger than Dos or Hecate, usually more than the equal of Colte. I could hear her initial chant, a husky breathing. "Imbaro. Imbaro. Imbaro."

I watched the three dark shapes blocking our way, tensed for mind-war as Anna was and possibly for dealing with the National who accompanied her.

All three were silent. One wore a cloak that had fallen open to reveal a suit of lights underneath, the lozenges of mirror-glass catching starshine and moonlight and giving him an oily, quicksilver sheen, hypnotic to look upon. Seeing that, more than anything, told me what was about to happen, the signature of mind-war.

Beside me, Anna did not move. She kept her Owl shape, but was silent now too, translating.

A wash of dizziness hit me, astonished me in the same instant. How could I be feeling it? How? Nationals never suffered the effects of these combats. Some of us read the corroboree mind-dragons, true, some even felt the haldane fields as the faintest frissons, as the uncanny recognition I felt with Anna, but that was all. We didn't have the gift.

I reeled, startled by the wash of colour before me, pulses, vortices in a consuming blackness. I rubbed my eyes. The haldane field had to be enormously powerful to affect me like this.

I staggered to the balustrade and steadied myself, gripped the cool stone, desperately gripped it. Somewhere off to my right the belltree thrummed, waves crashed. Grass keened in the on-shore wind—marking the outer world I could not reach.

Inside, there was colour everywhere, pulsing bands of it, with elongated shadows, twisting reds, golds and purples, startling blues, surging black that streamed on those colours as highlights themselves. Black as colour. Shadow as light.

I was part of the trance-war—I was!—as incredible as it seemed. I *saw* shapes, had the conviction of shapes before me, Dos faltering, fading, losing force, could see Colte looming as a mighty cowled image alongside a serpentine Hecate, and Imbaro the Great Owl opposing—godforms from every place and time streaming from them, residues exploding into the false memory of template-recognition.

They were too beautiful to resist. I wanted them, wanted to reach out and pull them to me—must have tried, for I lost balance, felt cold stone, the pain of scraped skin, seized that dim urgent reality and made it my way through...

I was leaning against the Promenade wall, blinking, rubbing my eyes, trying to rid myself of the trance vision, hating, loving it, desperately needing to be free.

It took effort, effort to see Anna and the three dark figures, but it came at last, squeezed out of the startling play of colour, the spirals and detonations, helped by the sound of waves falling and the belltree and the rush of seagrass on the wind-swept dunes.

And there was one of the Clever Men, the one who had been Dos, drawing his kitana from across his shoulder and advancing on Anna.

I knew at once what it meant. Conventions of mind-war had been set aside. The withdrawal of Dos had been a deliberate thing. My involvement too probably, a means of keeping me out of the way.

These men were desperately intent on getting Anna.

I snatched my sticker from its sheath, rushed across to where the Clever Man stood and thrust the narrow blade between his ribs, at the same time pulling his head back and down. The kitana rattled on the stones; the Ab'O died.

It was as if the others knew. They broke trance almost at once, fought quickly to regain composure. When they saw their fallen comrade, they fled into the seagrass, both stumbling from the effort of concentrating and now being forced to act on the physical plane; clearly surprised, that Anna had been beating them at mind-fighting and that their treachery had been found out and prevented. There was a flash of mirror-light from the cloaked figure and they were gone.

Anna leant on my arm, panting and shaken.

"You—ought not to have interfered," she said. "I was managing."

"Not as I saw it."

I told her about the one who had broken trance to use his sword.

"It wasn't your fight. This will cause an Incident. You'll be targeted."

"I am already, Anna. I know very little about mind-war, but I do know that no-one engaging in it can pursue the fight when driven out of trance—or relinquishes aspect. This one went for his sword in front of me, and that means they didn't care if I knew. I was probably to be next."

"But your Colour—"

"They're desperate. An error of judgement on their part. They thought the mindfield had me."

Anna's eyes narrowed at that. "You felt the field?"

"I saw the heroes."

Anna stared in momentary disbelief, then slowly nodded, accepting it.

"No wonder Arredeni specified you, Tom. Not just any National doing field work for Council. Not just any of the Seven. The Blue Captain, he said. Insisted on it. You're sighted."

"Some Nationals sense the energies. They wanted me involved and disoriented. They included me."

"That's one thing. The disorientation. But you say you saw them."

"Vague shapes, that's all. I identified them though, sensed which ones were which. I—knew them. You've got to tell me about them, Anna."

"Not now. This area's charged, and they'll return for the body. Tomorrow. Tomorrow when we're far from here."

We began walking then, back towards Twilight Beach, back to the Pier and the lights. Behind us the old belltree thrummed and sang and held its rusted arms out to the wind and the sea. The seagrass stirred in the dunes, adding its song to the ancient night.

"Tom?" Anna said when the place was far behind.

"Yes?"

"You saw the War Owl I became?"

"I'm—not sure now."

"No?"

"At first, yes. Then I read it as something else."

"What?"

"I have no idea."

"Try to remember. It's very important."

"I'll tell you if I do."

By noon the next day, *Rynosseros* was doing a steady 90 k's along the Great Arunta Road, running under twenty kites and a hot sun with a strong dry wind at our backs.

Scarbo had the helm, Rim tended the lines, Strengi was below at com. Shannon and Hammon were down on the commons doing repairs to our Cody man-lifter. Apart from Strengi, all of us wore djellabas and burnouses over our fatigues and fighting leathers and had our personal weapons close by, expecting attack.

I stood with Anna in the bows under a canopy, away from the others, watching the desert flash by and the red sand disappear under our wheels.

Anna seemed to be listening for something, interpreting the distances, reading the bright air and far-off haze at the horizon. Finally she came to a decision.

"We can talk about it now, Tom."

"Good."

I was watching the land as well, reading it in my own way as we crossed one of the outer Ab'O States, Here-We-Stand, on an official Road. Technically we were safe, Colour-protected. Officially. But I had seen the Ab'O use his sword, and Anna had told us to expect attack; it was impossible now to relax, to do other than see every far-off shimmer, every flash of quartz and errant willy-willy as hunter trace, deadly pursuit. Scan showed nothing; com channels remained clear, but there was nothing else for it. I knew that the others—Rim,

Shannon, Strengi, old Ben, young Hammon—would be doing the same.

Anna must have heard me answer but still she did not speak; she seemed to be translating what the land told her, probably searching for mind-lines, no doubt considering the possibility of gain-monitors, though transit noise protected us there. It was other ships she was trying for too, but by the presence of Clever Men, instinctively mistrusting surveillance tech no less than I did.

"Nothing," she said at last. "Nothing else."

We had seen only two other charvolants since early morning, both tribal vessels, Madupan ships, brightly painted hulls under thirty kites each. They had passed us at a distance of twenty metres, going the other way, so Shannon reported at the end of his dawn watch, and seemed to give us no special attention.

Anna gripped the rail, watching the horizon and the clutch of kites above and ahead of us, drawing us along.

"Anna?"

"Sorry, Tom. It's a matter of finding the words, and of knowing the risk you all face. But you're right. They already think you know, all of you, so you're targeted already, aren't you?"

"This isn't a tribal ship. We choose to be here."

Anna gave a rueful smile, but still hesitated. She did not face me.

"So," I said. "Dreamtime business."

"It is."

"Haldane lore."

"Yes."

But she said nothing more for the moment.

I tried another way. "Tell me about the haldanes. What are they?"

She shrugged. "Who truly knows?"

"That's heresy."

"Yes."

Again the silence, but I sensed what might be behind it—how like a hard, bright, impenetrable box that had no lock and could never be opened, its contents forever out of sight, this could only be approached, discussed, as the form, the container serving the thing contained, defining it as a door or a chair might show in some small way what gave them purpose.

"The Madhouse at Cape Bedlam is run by the Haldanian Order," I said, leading her into it the only way I could.

"Sign of the red wheel," she said, accepting my overture, talking out at the wide land, at the sky of vivid killing blue.

"I know that sign. It's where I was. That was Dreamtime business too. Tartalen told me that on the first morning—when they released me."

She nodded. It was as if the words freed her.

"The haldanes, Tom?" she asked, repeating my earlier question. "What are they?"

I felt a thrill of excitement. Was she actually going to say?

"Whose view? Yours? Nation's?"

"Consensus. Better yet, give me the range. Start with how Nationals prefer to see them."

"How you've made us see them. The other parts of our humanity. The lost parts. Power vectors on another plane available for our use—*intended* for our use. If we can reach them. At the other extreme, the ancient gods—mythogenesis: the mythic underpinnings of our race. Some shared unconscious your people are able to tap into. Near enough?"

Anna turned to me now. "You accept that?"

"I can, yes."

"Even though you're shut off from it?"

"We accept there must be reasons. Your people have found the way through. The rest of us may. I'd say this benefice Arredeni wants to share with Nation is something important about haldane theory, and you have a conflict of interests."

Anna glanced out at a distant flash of quartz, at the canopy bellying above us, faced me again.

"He is prepared to see the Dreamtime differently, yes. He continues to question the traditional views of the Clever Men."

"He is famous for it."

"Notorious for it. At least he's brave enough to question."

"Yes. What I meant was that it must happen all the time. Honest scientific enquiry."

"It does. But only so far, only ever so far. This is different. Our tribe is a handful, Tom, nearly gone. Normally it would not matter.

But Arredeni—for all his National ways—is still a Prince as well as a great scientist. The world listens to what he has to say."

Now the dark eyes did not leave me; now I was the one staring out at the red land, watching the Road disappear under our wheels, an endless red-gold ribbon spanning that desolation. I had forgotten to look for ships.

"Tom, in our continuing research into the haldane phenomenon, my father and I have come up with many theories, some very extreme. Generally the tribes have ignored us. Now, one line of enquiry is causing an incredible outcry."

"Tell me."

"What would you say if I told you that sometime in our past we were hit with a weapon, a mental weapon?"

"Your people?"

"All of us. Humanity. All our earliest societies."

"I'd be keen to see proof of it is what I'd say. But a weapon?"

"What Arredeni is postulating. A 'device'—to call it that—which possibly impaired genetic memory as well, so basic DNA templates were tampered with, changed, new ones laid down."

I faced her again. "Anna—"

"It could have happened, Tom. Part of the evidence is in the mind-wars my people fight. This weapon would have shut us off from something we were starting to know, from some natural direction we were taking. Left us with a—a religious bias instead."

She gave me time to absorb that. The silence of the desert was broken only by the sounds of our passing, the steady roar of the travel platform, the hiss of sand, the thrum of taut cables in the wind, the lift and fall of the bellying canopy.

"All right," I said, because too much was no worse right then than too little.

Anna looked reassured, as if this first hurdle had been the hardest She did not know how vividly I had been involved in the mind-fight. I had *seen* haldane forms.

"By this theory, all our religions, our whole mythic bias, are nothing more than the residues of that weapon being turned on us. A clever way of shutting us off from the full mental capacity we had then or were developing. Through recorded history we've been slowly working our way out of the after-effects of this vast wounding."

"Recovering from shell-shock."

Anna nodded. "Like working fragments of shrapnel out of an injured body, yes. These fragments are our god-responses, our inclination to believe in deities... entities beyond ourselves, and be satisfied by them."

"So some large picture became lost to us, obscured by lots of fascinating small ones?"

"That's it," she said. "What we've always called gods. This weapon would have used our own best parts against us, to keep us from seeing that larger picture by giving us feelings of rapture and exaltation, yearnings for communion and divine approval. Perhaps there were other things we all lost as a result of such a wounding. Telepathy, psychokinesis, things like that. It would be a matter of rediscovering what we all once had."

"So in such a view," I said, "what the tribes see as a special and privileged link with ancient forces is no more than lucky individuals—Ab'O individuals, Clever Men—finding a way around the wounding? You've locked in on what we all once were?"

I saw the relief settle on Anna's lovely face, easing the eyes, relaxing the muscles in her jaw.

"It's a different way of looking at the Dreamtime, I know."

"And does Arredeni think that at last we might be recovering from the effects of this mythic weapon?"

"No. Not necessarily. Tom, we would not be meant to understand that this has happened to us. The wounding would be subtle. The more we recovered from it, the worse we'd be afflicted, if that makes sense. The more a society looked like shaking free of its gods and superstitions, the more social turmoil, stress, internal crisis, even external invasion there'd be. Arredeni suspects we would not be meant to recover. Individuals might, the shamans and great magicians, the prophets and healers, but not society at large unless helped.

"But at least we'd know we'd been hit, which would mean a new external element could be added, a catalytic element. That is what Arredeni wants to suggest—wants revealed to all the world. The possibility of such a phenomenon, and the self-perpetuating nature of the wounding. Humanity could not grow without such knowledge."

"If he's right."

"If he's right, yes."

Anna was the excited scientist now, so close to the facts that she forgot others were not. The words came rushing out.

"Allow that the theory is true, that those assassins at Twilight Beach were sent not to stop heresy but in response to this line of enquiry. Say that some Ab'Os—my father and I, other free-thinkers—have managed to shake free of the wounding, reaching through to the haldanes, locking onto them, but not as gods. Our people in general have done it because the Dreamtime is so fresh and vital, still so flexible and all-accommodating. Most religions lose their flexibility very quickly. Grant that our Clever Men found a functioning connection with the lost part of our humanity, but—allowing for this theory—saw the haldanes as gods, ancestors, ancient spirits, so that such a connection was dramatically tainted. Misunderstood."

I was losing it again. "Why tainted?"

"Those locking on to those original energy vectors would naturally believe it unique to their own correct view of the universe, believe that *they* were the chosen ones. Our tribal societies are founded on that elitism. All along my father and I have wanted free and open discussion of the possibilities we've raised, to allow that we too may be refusing to see the full implications of our own privileged position. Arredeni and I have never been popular because of our liberal thinking, but this weapon theory has caused such a reaction that—automatically—it warrants further study. Only now do they call us heretics, you see? Only now."

"I can imagine. The Dreamtime is being debased. Anna, you and your father could be wrong."

"Of course we could. That's the point. But we feel we have discovered something more, something different. As Clever Men we think we may be confirming it within ourselves. And they have not ignored us, you see, simply let us peddle this theory along with the rest."

The Dreamtime was sacrosanct enough to justify such a fierce reaction, but I let it pass.

"How long have other Princes known of this... weapon?"

"A long time. Many of them have been following the research, discussing it in Convocation and at corroboree, trying to decide when Arredeni had gone too far. He is a Prince, after all. But now I am confirming his claims—another Clever Man, even if blood-related, and female at that, added sacrilege, who has so recently gained in power. A few tribes know I was sent to Twilight Beach to find you. They will know what that means."

We were silent at the rail then, Anna sorting her own thoughts, me lost in the shift of kites above and before us, trapped in the play of tribal signs: chevrons, suns, curving lines and totems in brilliant reds, yellows and blues, now a startling orange and purple, there, tricking with the blue of our huge Sode Star, a flash of green from a Chinese Hawk. The sky danced with the compelling ciphers of an undeclared mythology.

I found my questions again, tried to find ways to ask them, as if words could ever encompass this. I thought of the world's great religions, the uproar when these conjectures were made known.

"Does this impulse to see God have to be part of the wounding? Couldn't the god-impulse be our own; something worthy we've had misled rather than imposed?"

Anna shook her head but wasn't disagreeing. "We can't be sure. And we may be the wrong ones to ask considering the psychogenetic tampering from our long-term exposure to the haldanes. But, again, it's not the point. My father and I—sense—that this impulse to see God, to feel spiritual exaltation, is something other: our thwarted ability to lock in on the rest of what we were."

"I envy you that link with the haldanes, Anna. Perhaps we all knew the face of God. Perhaps we refined the god-impulse to read the infinite, to find meaning, with knowledge of what it was anchored to and there for. Perhaps we were getting free of this god-need, having discovered who or what God was. A noösphere. Gaea. Our higher selves."

"Perhaps we did," she said.

"The haldanes, whatever they are."

Anna smiled. "Perhaps. I like your 'they'. At the very least 'they' are a power source. Volatile energy vectors which have changed us forever, and our land, our whole way of seeing things. And who knows, maybe that's why we descendants of the Kooris discovered this knowledge. Perhaps we will find that our Dreamtime was not just one of these woundings—one of these 'goddings'—but an imperfectly understood knowledge of our former state. Perhaps we can prove it. That would be marvellous."

There was the question that could not wait.

"So who fired the weapon, Anna? Since it's this natural link with the haldanes the great majority of us are cut off from, then perhaps it was they who thought it necessary to hold humanity back. Our own secret selves."

"There's your 'they' again! You keep making them conscious entities—"

"I saw shapes. I *saw* them!"

"It's difficult, I know. They're power vectors available for our use. Parts of us, if you like. We can't know the system while we're in the system. I said before that it would have been a weapon of mind, but perhaps it was a physical thing—technology. What was it? Who made it? Who fired it? All good questions. Arredeni has the—certainty—that it could have happened. He wants to open it up to general debate. Coming from an Ab'O Prince, a Clever Man who can access the vectors, it would be taken very seriously; control situations could be established. At the very least, the rest of humanity could be made to know they are part of the great mystery too. Which is not something many Princes want."

"A divine empiricism. I'm not surprised."

And again Anna smiled, for a moment like one of her own Koori ancestors, alien and detached not in the new way but in the old; not just the elegant daughter and colleague of a great Australian scientist, leader of a barely existing Ab'O State.

I was guilty of over-humanising these things, as I once had with a robot, Lud, and belltrees and the dream machines in the Madhouse. The whole nature of the haldanes was a caution against that. But here I was persisting in reading the unknown by the known. My bias, my own handicap.

So the tribes made use of these vectors, imposed . . . no, sought and found personalities, identities, entities in them. Used them. Became them. Found their way through to a better, more dynamic use of some collective unconscious, of what it really meant to be human.

But on the creaking windy deck of a speeding charvolant, under a hot sun and a canopy of straining painted kites, the questions remained. Not if such a thing as Arredeni's god-gun could exist, but who would have fired it and why?

It was quiet for the next hour, just the steady cushioned jolting of *Rynosseros*'s suspension, the muted gritty drone of the wheels on sand, the singing and soughing of the cables in a healthy tailwind—the roadsong all ships made.

I took the opportunity to brief the crew on what Anna had told me. Her enemies would assume I'd done so anyway, and it wasn't our way not to share mission talk.

Shortly after our midday meal, Shannon took up his guitar and soon had a song going which had us all laughing.

"Oh, I've been hit by a god's bright gun,
I'm wounded through and through.
A Logos bomb has made me numb,
I've forgotten what I knew.
Stigmata up and down my soul
And wounds that look divine,
Oh, I've been hit by a god's bright gun,
I've forgotten what was mine,
Oh, I've forgotten what was mine.

"Oh, I've been cut by a god's sweet sword,
It's hurt me to my pith.
The closest shot at my target spot
Becomes the nearest myth.
Epiphanies are de rigueur,
Syncresis a delight.
Oh, I've been cut a god's sweet sword
And I'm blinded by the light,
Oh, I'm blinded by the light."

So it went, with Rim and crusty old Scarbo adding verses.

But all this had the feeling of gallow's humour about it. By mid-afternoon, when Strengi called up from scan that two bogies were coming at us down Lateral 101 on what had to be an intercept course, we were actually relieved.

Our speed had been kept down so as not to attract undue attention from the tribal comsats; now Scarbo and Hammon put more kites in the sky and Shannon took us up to 100 k's.

The bogies read the speed change and added to their own canopies, but had to control speed ready for a turn into the Road. We were past them before they could move in to block and delay, but we saw them clearly enough.

Rushing at us down the wide trail of the 101 Lateral were two brightly painted charvolants, Soti ships, displaying at least thirty kites apiece, a brave tribal showing.

Even as Scarbo used scan to read deck and canopy array for ordnance capability, we could see their kitemasters busily winding most of those canopies in, dropping drogues from the big primary parafoils to slow them for the turn. As the colourful displays came down, death-lamps were revealed, fierce diamond djinn flashing at the end of their insulated cables.

Through scan we saw crewmen bringing more lamps and fighting kites to the lines, others manning deck-lenses, harpoons and hot-pots. Only their need for duplicity had saved us so far.

We kept our own kites where they were, using speed to buy time the best tactic now. Shannon helped Scarbo send up our racing-footmen, put three more lines with the twenty we already had, risking that, while Hammon brought out our own death-lamps and Rimmon issued snaphaunces and kitanas. Even Anna took them. Strengi was below at com and I had the helm. Heart-and-Hand was an hour away at most, but so much could happen in that time.

When Scarbo was satisfied there would be no line-fouling, he came to the poop.

"There'll be others, Tom. They aren't trying hard enough."

"Agreed. They'll pen us ahead. Anna, why the Soti?"

"They've been the ones following Arredeni's research most closely. Their Prince has had dealings with my father."

"So it may still be tribal rather than Pan-tribal. One Prince against another?"

"So far, yes. He probably wants to strike, is probably urging open war, but doesn't dare try it alone. Not until all the tribes rule."

Ben laughed. "Look what's behind! I'd call this open war. The question is, will they break Code for this?"

"Anna?" I asked her. "Lasers, ballistics, what?"

"No hi-tech. They know you have com. The satellites may be watching. They can't afford an incident. I think mercenaries, a staged pirate action, and I think they'll try the heroes again."

I almost asked why, then realised it was Anna they wanted, and her father eventually, through siege and attrition, possibly me for the trouble and insult I'd caused them. As for using the heroes, there was the prestige of it. They would want a victory at that level. A Dreamtime victory. Needed it after what had happened at Twilight Beach.

Anna was good at courting the haldanes. She had found Imbaro, could probably do so again. They wanted to beat Imbaro-in-Anna. Whatever else they tried, they would arrange it so they were sure of such a victory.

On the poop, Anna went into trance, easily, rolling back her eyes. It wasn't a deep trance, a searching really, tracking mind-lines to see if any of the charvis behind us had Clever Men aboard, if she had cause to fear attack at that level.

She came out of it seconds later.

"Nothing," she said, releasing a deep breath.

So it remained a contest of aeropleuristics, a race across the desert, a run down the wide red Road into See-Me-There and finally through the low far-off ranges that marked the border of Heart-and-Hand.

Rynosseros kept its lead easily, but the Soti ships had at least used the time to get the boxes and screens of their lamps and fighters aloft, well clear of the drab insulated battle canopies underneath. Through scan we saw them, both vessels plainly dressed for war.

No sooner had we taken the broad sweep from the Great Arunta Road into the 304 Lateral, a neat turn that swept us into Heart-and-Hand and had the border diligent pinging and chiming on its iron pole, than three more Soti ships appeared ahead, moving steadily towards us on the graded red sand.

Engagement was inevitable, unless we decided to run out on to the open desert with its uneven terrain, a desperate choice.

Logically, the Soti didn't have to stop us. They had only to wait until we were at Arredeni's tower and then make sure we never left. This whole action had to be a preferred option: to keep Anna from reaching her father, from re-enforcing him where—Prince's right—he could call for mind-war with comsat surveillance.

It was divide and conquer.

Nor did I have to ask if the new ships had Clever Men aboard. We ran at them, manoeuvring our kites for the direction change to keep maximum speed, hoping they would think we intended to ram our way through if necessary.

We could never be that desperate; the cost was too great. Better the desert first. But they might settle for such a tactic—reasoning that two charvolants to stop the one might be a small price to pay. I was hoping, too, that with so many ships to coordinate, they might underestimate us.

"Ready to dump!" I shouted.

Down on the commons, Strengi and Scarbo ran to the trip-lines. Hammon and Rim brought our black Javanese fighter to the mains, hooked it on, set the small helium lifts to clear it of the deck when needed, patched that function through to cable-boss and helm.

"Now!" I cried, judging distances, feeling the adrenalin rush, the thrill and anxiety of being committed.

Trip-lines were pulled. Drogues dropped from the bellies of seven of our largest kites, snapped out into long trailing cones. I applied brakes to all six wheels.

Rynosseros slowed at once. Our two pursuers were caught half-prepared. Had they been ready, they could have held their course and rammed—a quick and decisive solution.

But captains love their ships, their precious, hand-made, painted hulls with long pedigrees and hard-won reputations, and they cannot help themselves. Just as I would not give *Rynosseros* over to ramming, nor could the captains of the charvis behind us.

Those captains responded from instinct and emotion, not intellect. As we dropped back, they angled aside, not having time to consider alternatives, the contingency orders they had been given.

And as they ran by, one to each side, Scarbo freed our gleaming Javanese fighter, all wicked edges, chitin and beetle black. It angled out sharply at a thirty-degree lift towards the ship on our right, lacquered blades cutting the lines of at least eight kites, the whole canopy—our black fighter included—falling to the deck and the desert, snagging the remaining kites and fouling the front wheels. A perfect manoeuvre—child's play for Scarbo, one of the best kitesmen there is.

At the same time, Shannon, Hammon and Anna fired harpoons at the charvi on our left, one of the shafts a hot-pot. Two tyres went; the hot-pot burst against their forepeak and sent flaming oil down onto the commons.

We felt the brief flash of their lamps and a deck lens, but there was no time to keep a burn point. We lost a little paint on the hull, that was all. Their harpoons missed entirely, their gunners unable to adjust to our sudden loss of speed.

Both charvis raced at their oncoming fellows, one fouled and erratic, losing speed and veering dangerously to starboard, the other aflame, its crew in a panic. The dust-trail obscured much of what was occurring, but scan showed all five manoeuvring to avoid collision.

At such speeds it was difficult, and I could only wonder how they had orchestrated it originally. Two vessels ran together with a tremendous crash of timber and fibre-glass, a shattering of metal and ceramic. Two others broke Road and went out on to the ungraded desert, their captains shedding kites—angels, wind-thieves, even their parafoils, all they had—and braking as best they could. The third came on through the debacle, but lost half its kites through fouling with the settling lines of the two wrecked ships. A smaller, less ornate charvi than the rest, it had probably been intended as the ramming ship.

We broke Road ourselves, rushing onto the gibber, bucking and tossing, shedding kites to avoid fouling, but gaining precious speed as Scarbo sent up Red Man, our big parafoil, and Hammon helped Rim bring in the drogues.

It was a gamble. I'd seen the flat swathe of sand amid the uneven terrain—perhaps the intended ramming site chosen by the Soti strategists. Though we lost a tyre, most of our footmen and more paintwork from the hull, we got *Rynosseros* back on to 304 and completed the last part of our journey unhindered.

Now the Soti had no options.

Heart-and-Hand, the State, was a small principality, a mere seventy square miles of gibber desert and scrub, with two impressive ranges shouldering into it from the west and the 304 Lateral giving access across it for charvolants.

Heart-and-Hand, the capital, was a metal and rock-melt tower some fifty metres high set in this desolation, surrounded by outbuildings and testing stations, with a skirt of dusty imported trees and the big dish of the radio telescope that used to get the State so much National funding.

Arredeni had us on scan even before we broke free of the Soti trap, and his half-caste research assistants, Jeremy and Cole, were waiting at the low perimeter fence to bring us in. That fence would not stop hostiles for long, but when crossed without invitation it meant war. The tradition that charvolants kite down and be ushered through the elaborate totemic gateway was an old one, and though these were special circumstances, the custom was observed now.

We brought in our canopy, waited while Arredeni's aides shackled our travel platform to a team of four draft horses, then pulled us to our mooring in the yard.

The whole installation looked more National than tribal, which could not have helped intertribal relations any, such flagrant departures from tradition, and a lot of small signs showed that Arredeni expected attack. The doors at ground level were locked and bolted, the windows of the sheds all shuttered, the livestock already in the earthen bunkers. Weather shields were in place; the great solar vanes along the western perimeter were angled to act as low-level shields themselves.

While Jeremy and Cole took the horses to safety, Anna led us to our quarters in the tower. Though the Soti and their allies had to be gathering, we took time to shower and change into fresh fatigues before being served a fine meal in the dining room which occupied almost the entire sixth floor.

Arredeni Paxton Kemp met us there. He was impressive, a tall Ab'O quadroon—like his daughter one of the last authentic blood-members of the Qaentimae, as dark-skinned as Anna was, with a wide handsome face and a grizzle of grey hair down each side of his head.

The Qaentimae had long ago merged with the Soti culturally and for all practical purposes politically; a compromise allowed Arredeni because of his international reputation. The tower, the land it surveyed, this man's authority as legitimate ruler of at least this much, were allowed to him; all that remained of a tribe which had fought too many mind-wars, had gone once too often to settle disputes by fleet action on Lake Air. The Qaentimae no longer had ships larger than skiffs; possibly only that had saved them from complete extinction.

As he entered the dining room, Arredeni gave us his magnificent smile, an easy man caught in uneasy times. The smile, his elegant gestures during the introductions Anna made, could not hide what his full dark eyes were telling us: This will be the end of it. This is our final night. His first words after the greetings were directly on that point.

"Thank you for coming, all of you. Thank you for bringing Anna home. Captain, contrary to how it may seem, I did not know what I expected you to do. I left it for Anna to choose. First option: to extend the invitation to receive a benefice and so have you come here; second: to keep Anna safe, to see her safely out of Australia so our research into the haldane phenomenon could continue. Your decision, Tom."

I immediately faced Anna, who met my enquiring look with equal directness.

"Ah," Arredeni said. "She did not tell you what my other request was. She chose for us both."

I went to speak, but Arredeni raised a hand. "Please, Captain, I realise I have trapped Blue into a major involvement in tribal affairs. I did not mean to do this out of hand. I believed you would hear what Anna had to say and then decide what was best. So now you must decide again. You might still break their cordon, either now or at first light. We can cover you with lasers from the tower."

"Out of the question, Doctor."

He nodded, looked at each of us in turn, saw we understood how it was. Being here would ensure it became the major incident he needed. More than just comsat surveillance. One of the Coloured Captains involved. Tribes and Nation watching.

While he listened, calm and attentive, I told him about the ambush on the Promenade and the narrow escape from the Soti fleet he had partly witnessed on his screens. He in turn told us about the god-gun.

It was more or less what Anna had told me earlier—how some collective "firing" may have shut most of humanity off from its higher mental powers, the Ab'Os and other less "sophisticated" anthrotypes being less severely wounded by being non-intellectually closer to those powers, less prone to pinning things down empirically. The dynamic maiming would have started once a race began using reason to sort its experience of the universe.

I brought up my earlier question to Anna.

"But who would've fired the weapon, Doctor?"

Arredeni gave his first laugh. It was directed partly at himself, partly at the extreme subtlety of how a god-gun might have worked.

"For a long time—you will laugh at this, Tom, all of you—we felt the land itself could have fired the weapon in us. By using the word 'weapon' we pre-suppose a purpose, not just an effect. But there are planetary fields, as you know, the noösphere, magnetics, properties of gravity, cosmic disturbances, a host of other things. We granted it could have been pure chance, a by-product of this world being 'alive' for the first time, Gaea evolving, dealing with radiation, cosmic rays, solar activity. So we explored those. Wonderfully crackpot stuff. Since they were reacting to this particular theory so vehemently, we kept at it far beyond what we might have done if they'd ignored us."

"And now?"

Arredeni exchanged glances with Anna, Jeremy and Cole, even with Cilla the cook who was pouring tisn into gorgeous porcelain cups.

"We probably would have fired it ourselves. Anything from all of us participating in a lemming-leap of mind at a certain point in our evolution, almost a delaying action to slow humanity down, to a minority of more developed individuals, who can say? A powerful shaman or magician, a group of gifted elitists discovering how to hamstring the rest of the race.

"Maybe it was always there as an evolutionary option in case it was needed, like the 'death-switch' down there in the DNA telling an organism when to start dying. Maybe a 'god-switch' re-routed us out of too much mental evolution before we were ready for it, sent us into a more viable, more balanced physical existence. It could have meant survival for the race. But you see, Tom, here we are talking as if this amazing notion has been demonstrated as true; already we are doing more than the tribes will even begin to do. Why?, I want to know. Why are they taking such exception to this theory? It is more fascinating than the theory itself."

I went to ask it again. "Arredeni—"

"What are the haldanes?" Arredeni smiled, stretched his arms wide. "The very least we believe, Anna and I—it's where human stuff becomes cosmic stuff. Where we *become* our universe. That's all. We claim no more. We have certainties, convictions out of trance that it can be more—like the god-gun theory—feelings, things that are sensed, but that is all we offer here, all we can prove. As Anna and I say constantly, our fundamental maxim: we cannot know the system while we're inside the system."

Anna interrupted. "And if a god-gun is what has alienated us from tribal sympathy, we need to learn if the National and International scientific community, the world at large, will resent us for it as well."

"We haven't," Scarbo said.

The Qaentimae Prince set down his cup. "No, Ben. You've accepted it now, but what about later? And what will Council decide? That only Ab'Os could come up with this—Dreamtimers touting nonsense? Whatever we offer about the Dreamtime should be considered. We have the haldanes to demonstrate our integrity. And mind-fighting. We are changing our physiotype, using mumbo-jumbo to affect genetic patterns. But our problems don't come from the Nationals and Internationals—not yet anyway—but from our own people. Could they be resenting us because of such a wounding? Could that be it?"

Scarbo seized on the point. "We're a State of Nation ship using approved Roads. Tom holds a Colour. They went against us."

"The wounding would be a spectacular thing for the individual, Ben, commanding enormous force. We are used to the haldanes being gods, not parts of us at all. You probably know that the Soti Prince, Stoutheart Tiberias Kra, is a trained astrophysicist. Yet Kra and the Soti Clever Men see my work as total heresy, trying to do harm, tampering with the profound spiritual truth of the Dreamtime. Kra used to be a dear friend—he saved the Qaentimae—but now he can't help what he feels. We are the worst possible enemy: the Speakers of the Lie. I'm surprised so few Princes are actively against me."

"But now there's Anna," I said.

"The very best of us at translating, yes. The media want to see her. International research groups request interviews. They want to know what gives her such strength at berking. You may not realise it, but the three who went against her at Twilight Beach would have been among the Soti's best.

"Anything we reveal is going to cause a sensation. It's one of those revelations you can't go back from. Like evolution, powered flight, quantum mechanics. You may not like it or agree with it; you may try to ignore it, but it will have changed everything. I wanted you here, Tom, because something that happened to you in the Madhouse caused you to become a sensitive." Everyone at the table was watching me. "You sense the hero-shapes. You make the perfect go-between."

I was aware of the eyes turned in my direction, of the fascination there in old Ben, Shannon and the others. Perhaps Anna's questions had been Arredeni's after all.

"What do you know?" I hated asking it, having the others watch, hated being so reasonable, so controlled.

"Only that."

"How?" I found I was straining to hear him through the fierce drumbeat of my heart.

"I spoke with Tartalen shortly after you were discharged, after you won *Rynosseros* and were given Blue. Word had come to me, a rumour, that you came out of the Madhouse a sensitive."

"What did Tartalen say?"

"Tom, he denied it. He would not speak of it further, I swear."

"The rumour—"

"Four times removed when it got to me. It was not possible to track it down further. I am still trying."

"Nothing about three images, three signs?"

"My word on it. Nothing. But I will do my best on your behalf. There are more pressing concerns now."

Are there?, I wanted to shout through the hammering drumbeat, through the acid wash of adrenalin and the closeted rage, then remembered the others, saw the looks of genuine concern, most of them as old as having *Rynosseros* and Blue, remembered what was soon to happen and how the world would react to the claims being made here. Other truths, my truths, had to wait. I forced myself back to it.

"So Kra and his allies will try to stop you here. Keep it very much a tribal matter."

Arredeni nodded, his eyes shining with a sharp understanding of my own emotion. "Precisely. Hence my wish to proclaim my discovery a benefice to Nation and so to the world at large, and calling you in if you would come. You, Tom, because I'd read of your many exploits among the Princes, and myself divined—forgive the pun, please—that the rumours were correct, you were this special thing: a sensitive." He made his final admission. "You could follow the contest if it came to that, bear witness to the truth of it being possibly as we say. That if there is fighting—"

"Then we'll be fighting ourselves."

"As it's always been. The wounded, 'godded' ones against the few who see it as it is. The heretics and the outcasts. Only now we do have Anna. She can reach Mithras, Anbas and Challamang. Even Imbaro and Vanu at the same time, multiple bondings. Because she knows what they are. She's even glimpsed an immensely powerful vector along her mind-line that will match all the others, if only it will come to her at the right moment or let her reach it. She is my proof."

"Which is why he did not want me to come back," Anna said. "He forgets he is the only father I have."

"Anna—"

Arredeni got no further. The diligent on top of the tower sang its single warning hoot. The Soti and their allies were approaching.

We left the table and climbed to the battlements. Cole went off to log messages and key in for comsat surveillance; the Qaentimae no longer operated their own tribal satellite, but rented access with a Japano facility. Jeremy activated the hi-tech armaments and brought an assortment of hand-weapons to the roof.

Far out on the desert, we could see a fleet of charvolants moving slowly towards us in the last light of day, canopies like glorious many-coloured flowers, death-lamps and photonic parafoils glinting like dew on those gorgeous, sinister blooms.

"They'll be kiting down soon," Arredeni said, then gave in to a sudden outburst of anger, a Prince whose territory had been invaded. "Let them come! Let them try us!" And he said more words in dialect.

It was quiet on the battlements then, just the low thrumming of the diligent, the wind off the desert stirring the dusty trees in the yard, whistling about the parapets and getting in among the spines of the sensor array.

Finally Arredeni turned to Anna and his assistants. "We have to rest, ready ourselves for tomorrow. Tom, you have the tower. Wake us if we're needed."

Anna came to me in my room a little after midnight, let herself in without knocking, roused me by placing a hand on my arm. I woke to find her sitting on the edge of my bed.

"Anna?"

"I couldn't leave him to face this alone."

"I know."

"He told the truth about Tartalen. He asked about you but was told nothing. They are very secretive about you there. My father read you as a sensitive some time ago, just as I did when we met at the Gaza. In berking terms there is a field horizon to you. Arredeni wasn't sure if the rumours were true. He was very excited when I told him that you read the shapes. It tells us that something is emerging in you. What it means in practical terms now is that you can witness mind-war and later confirm what occurred. Using tech verification so there can be no doubt."

"You read this field now?"

"I'm deliberately not trying to. I need to remain clear for tomorrow."

Moonlight came through the windows, washed the darkness of her skin. It reminded me of our night on the Promenade, of the first translation I had seen.

"Anna, the haldane you reached? Imbaro. Why that one?"

"The War Owl?" She hesitated, frowned. "All haldanes are available to us. I found Imbaro then. Others can."

"At the same time?"

"Not common, but yes. Some are more—*feel* more amenable than others. Like the one Arredeni told you I am questing for. Others can access it; it is generally available. All I know is that—like Imbaro—it is right for me."

"What will it be like?"

She smiled, imagining it. "As if I am completed somehow. It will be—right."

I watched the night through the windows.

"Will you try for it tomorrow?"

"If there's time. It has never come to me before."

She was silent for a moment.

"Tom, what are your body taboos?"

"What?"

"Not mating. Pleasure. Your body taboos?"

"Anna—"

"You like me?"

"Yes."

"Shall I stay?"

I smiled. "Distraction. Of course."

"More than that. Shall I stay?"

"Yes."

She slipped off her robe, revealed the curves of her hips and belly, her firm high breasts, and more—the whorls of her *ais* scars, her delicate body-map, so strange and beautiful, then joined me on the bed. We held one another, made slow love, falling into deep sleep afterwards, waking just after 0400 during Strengi's watch and going upstairs to join him on the battlements. He was playing his guitar, sending gentle notes at the tower diligent, making it answer him in low, languid murmurings.

The moon was near zenith, the desert washed with a cool light, showing us the tree-tops tossing in the wind, making shadows in the yard, dressing the ceremonial gate in armour of silver and pearl. We could see the ranges far off, and in the middle distance two dim lights.

"Ships," Anna said, as if we had met taking in the air. "Kra's people."

"Full fleet?" I asked, looking out over this great wind-swept expanse, smiling at how dreamlike it all seemed: the lovemaking, the yard washed in moonlight, the prospect of what lay ahead.

"Nothing near it. This cannot be elevated to the status of war. The satellites would know. Kurdaitcha would come."

Twenty minutes went by above that vast emptiness of sand and stars while we stood with Strengi playing his guitar at our backs, the wind sounding around the parapets and sensor poles.

"Should you rest?" I asked her finally.

"Not now. I couldn't sleep now. You go down. I'll stay, go through my summoning patterns."

"Anna?"

She turned to face me, dark eyes glittering.

"Did you read the plaque fixed to the helm of *Rynosseros*?"

"Yes. Important words."

"From Alexander the Great."

"He actually said them?"

"Who knows? But they're how we must live—as if we could die at any moment but at the same time live forever."

She laughed. "Tonight I'm immortal, Tom."

"I know," I said. "I feel that too." And I headed for the stairwell.

By mid-morning, Heart-and-Hand was under siege. Thirteen charvolants from three different Ab'O nations—Soti, Madupan, Chitalice—and three approved mercenary ships ringed the tower at a three hundred metre radius. I recognised their signs: the Arab, the

African and the Tongan. Eighty tribesmen and at least thirty mercenaries, rogue Nationals, Niuginians, Islanders, Arabs, Indonesians, others, formed a perimeter for which the charvis made impromptu gun-towers.

The wind had dropped, but the ships had helium-filled parafoils lofted, supporting death-lamps and hot-pot fighters from their hooks and delivery assemblies. A man-lifter, another inflatable, supported a lookout at a hundred feet. The tiny figure—a deck-boy no older than Hammon—drifted back and forth in the thermals in long slow sweeps, watching our preparations, relaying information to those waiting below.

Apart from precautions taken to ensure we wouldn't run for it, no attempt had been made to destroy *Rynosseros*. She sat on her travel platform, her six tyres blown by death-lamps at first light, but otherwise untouched. The platform was fair game; they dared not touch the hull.

Now a battle was waiting to commence on one of three levels.

If it was to be Code, there were kites aloft on the ships, angled to the sun, their cells charged; the big lenses and accumulators on the tower. It would be a protracted, vicious affair—snaphaunces and kitanas and war boomerangs, a regular siege with scaling ladders, kite landings and aerial sorties, hot-pots and battering-rams. The tower was durable but badly undermanned; without outside assistance, it would fall.

If it was hi-tech, then someone would incur enormous debts for an easy victory. Certainly Arredeni would not be the one, not with his reputation both as scientist and moderate. Heart-and-Hand had two laser points, short-range, ugly-looking Bok units mounted on gimbals and pointed out at the two grandest of the charvolants just in case.

The charvis had a dozen such portables, half of them turned on the crown of the tower where we stood watching, the rest focused on the generator and accumulator facilities in the shielded outbuildings. Most of the tribesmen and many of the mercenaries had combat laser-tech and selected ballistics close by.

If it came to that, comp estimate gave us a four to eight minute siege before we were destroyed.

But the comsats orbited and watched and tallies would be kept. Tribal debts would grow. Explanations would be required, with the possibility of ship forfeitures and service penalties, things no tribe could easily afford. And there would still be time for us to put through a final account of what was happening. Arredeni's findings were already lodged; a final speed transmission would simply speak of what had occurred, give a Prince's parting words.

Once it was hi-tech, they could kill us but never stop us.

No, it would be the third kind of warfare, the one that would discredit the Qaentimae and put the seal of holy approval on what they were trying to achieve here.

The heroes.

Anna, Arredeni, Jeremy and Cole were getting ready, donning ceremonial dress, while down on the sand the Clever Men were drawing up. The air throbbed with the sound of bullroarers and didgeridoos. The perimeter belltrees and tower diligent caught the rhythms and gave them back in an eerie counterpoint of pinging and chiming.

There were seventeen Clever Men standing on the desert, waiting fifty metres from the tower—all Soti, since officially the Madupan and Chitalice were here as interested observers.

Heart-and-Hand had four.

Four and a half. Four and a sensitive—one who could read the shapes. When the four were ready, I went with them down onto the desert, walking beside Anna and her father out to where the line of Ab'Os waited. Scarbo, Shannon, Strengi, Hammon and Rim, and old Cilla too, waited behind on the tower, their weapons untended now that the choice of combats had been made.

Today there would be no treachery, no Ab'O breaking trance to use his sword. That much was certain.

I stood with Arredeni and his Clever Men, last of the Qaentimae, facing the Soti mind-fighters. They made an impressive sight. Fully half of them—like Arredeni beside me—wore their suits of lights, each transformed into a dazzling column by the hundreds of tiny mirrors sewn to the leather.

Beyond that proud line of seventeen was the waiting line of tribesmen and mercenaries, the silent ships under their barely-moving canopies. The drone of didgeridoos and bullroarers suddenly ceased; the belltree song dwindled and faded as well, though an occasional sad chiming from the dim-recall rods came to us through the heated air.

The Prince of the Soti, Stoutheart Tiberias Kra, a tall man, massively built, took three steps forward and addressed Arredeni.

"You have the Blue Captain with you."

"He is the National who accepts the officially-proclaimed benefice. The sensitive who saw Dos fail at Twilight Beach. The one you need to kill."

Kra nodded, pleased in spite of himself at how Arredeni was conducting this. No threats. No idle words or loose ends.

But there were the protocols. He wanted me to own my pedigree as Blue and thereby relinquish National rights for what now occurred.

"An outsider all the same, Arredeni."

I indicated the three State of Nation charvolants anchored with the rest. "So are the Tongan, the Arab and the African."

"Not State of Nation. Mercenary ships," Kra said, glad to be answered.

"I too am a mercenary," I told him. "My name is in the Great Passage Book, which is reason enough for me to be here. I have been paid with the gift of great knowledge to stay and watch injustice."

"Careful, Tom Rynosseros!" Kra said, very pleased now and confident of the power building in him. "I am a demon you can fear!"

It was Anna, smiling, wearing her drab unadorned fighting leathers, who stepped forward and said in a voice that sent a thrill of power through the tiny Qaentimae line: "I am a hammer to demons!"

That was it.

Stoutheart Tiberias Kra rejoined his fellows, called out the ritual words.

"This body is mine, my place to stand up in, where I surface in this world, where I break through, my place to die from. I put this on the line, I abrogate the right to fight in this place. We go to be gods now."

And the battle began.

Without further preamble, the twenty-one Ab'Os went into trance, effortlessly, seventeen against four.

Now would be the test, the great test, down there, up there, in there, wherever it was, with the berking, questing spirits, with the haldanes waiting to receive them and be received.

The bodies of the fighters all tensed, as if seeking to thrust themselves into the ground, to gain power from it Antaeus-like. Kra and his allies were fighting to protect the "godness" of their haldanes, things poorly understood but dynamically powered, the continuation of a reverence and respect for what had always been theirs. They were blinded by the very light that made it possible for them to almost see it all, the wisest, most gifted fools. Our fighters were at least armed with the added knowledge that they weren't communing with ancient gods, but were breaking through to the power base of our original humanity. What difference that would make no-one could say.

I was a passenger, an observer to this, and within minutes of translation I slid into a trance of my own, aided this time not by the enemy but by Anna herself, reaching back to bring me along. It was like being pulled back into oneself, a falling away from inside the eyes, into a world of coloured, elongated shadows set in the reflection infinity of clever mirrors so it was self, self, self, then not at all, everything but that. Distorted forms, shapes converging, rushing together, crowding, blurring only to resolve again.

The seventeen went for Arredeni at once. He had gained Challamang and was immensely powerful, a worthy opponent for any ten of them if he could keep it. But they were trying for a quick kill, discounting Anna and the others for the moment.

The reason for their choice soon became clear. Anna was taking an unusually long time to translate, questing for more than just any haldane to accommodate her, obviously searching down her mind-line for that mightiest haldane she had sensed before.

Jeremy and Cole, on the other hand, were trainees and not true Clever Men at all. Cole had difficulty keeping himself with Marduk, while Jeremy had locked on to a surging power mass that could only be called Enlil, trying to translate.

It was not going well.

Arredeni/Challamang was hard-pressed, faltering. Cole/ Marduk was trying to assist, a mite on the backs of demons, an insect, a nuisance. Jeremy had cleared to Enlil and added its power to Arredeni's whenever he could, whenever he wasn't being savaged himself.

The scene was confused, turgid, uncertain. Too many vectors, too many conflicting images overlapping.

I tried to see Anna in that flux, consciously sought her, concentrating on her vital form, and it was as if the seeking led me to her centre.

For there she was. Suddenly, awesomely powerful, her most dynamic translation yet—something like a composite, with a great deal of overlapping herself.

There was—Imbaro! No mistaking the Great Owl, that flux of shapes and colours. But more. With parts of Ishtar and Ashbiani, vectors already commandeered, and—incredibly—much of Colte, a stunning, surging presence in that shadowland.

Kra had cleared to Gris, a rarely-won atavism equal to Challamang and Colte, but harder to hold for long, and as that irresistible form was beating Arredeni easily. Kra was very good.

It was Anna's appearance that kept him back from dealing the blow that could kill Arredeni on the physical plane. Her presence distracted him, brought puzzlement and doubt.

Jeremy and Cole, I discovered, had already abandoned aspect, had withdrawn from trance and retreated back to the desert under the morning sun.

It was Anna and her father against them all—and now the tide of battle was turning. One by one the Clever Men fled from trance as Anna blanketed them, fed on them. Kra kept his Gris at Challamang's centre, hammering and devouring, spiriting him out. But the distraction, the pressure, were too much.

There was a surging rush from where Anna's composite—her Imbaro/ Ishtar/Ashbiani/Colte—loomed, something like the white light of an exploding star—a star, yes!—and she was alone! *We* were alone.

They had all gone—Arredeni, Kra, all of them.

As Anna relaxed aspect, I let myself flow to her and with her, spiralled back to the desert and the day and came alive behind my eyes, stood up in myself.

Wavering, gaining my balance and astonished to find myself still standing, I took in everything at a glance: the figures on the sand before the tower, the collapsed shapes in their suits of leather and glass; took in the silence, the smells, the watching eyes of the satellites overhead through the clear blue shield of the sky.

Five of the Clever Men were dead—Kra among them. The other twelve lay unconscious, catatonic. They would emerge later, most if not all of them, though even now, down in the deep well of self, they knew what had happened.

Arredeni was in the same state, pried loose from Challamang, though limp and resting now, recovering. Jeremy and Cole were standing to one side, badly shaken.

In the other, outer world of charvolants and paid professionals, the Tongan and the African had already gone, sailing off with their mercenaries when the outcome had become clear. The Arab's charvi was pulling out from the ring of sand-ships even now, breaking away, off to an assignment elsewhere.

Some of my crewmates—I half-noticed Hammon and Rim and Strengi—came down to us, to provide numbers, a visual warning-off just in case.

But nothing would happen now, no further conflict. What the Soti and the other Ab'O Princes would do about the Qaentimae knowledge, no-one could say. But they—all of us—had been taught a startling lesson, that Anna was the best of the Clever Men, the most powerful mind-fighter there was.

I stood holding her as she eased herself out of trance, steadying her.

"You did it, didn't you?" I said.

She nodded, trembling but smiling, supremely fulfilled, her eyes flashing with the inexpressible emotion of it.

Jeremy and Cole came rushing over, stumbling with fatigue and eagerness.

"You reached Ashbiani!" Jeremy said. "I saw Ashbiani!"

"It was Colte!" Cole said. "But with Imbaro. I saw the War Owl."

"And some of Ishtar. There was some of that too!"

"Which one did you reach?" Cole asked. "Which one was it?"

And all that I had sensed and witnessed came together in a moment of absolute certainty that, yes, perhaps we could be free, perhaps it could be done. By looking within, beyond the bright distractions. By glimpsing the fullness of our humanity.

Awed by it, shaken, I answered for her, said what I knew was true.

"You found your own haldane, didn't you? The one that is best for you, truest for you. Your other part. You found yourself."

Arredeni's daughter looked at me again and smiled, then turned that smile out at the land, at the sun and the kites that shifted and strained in the new wind.

"I reached Anna," she said, her smile a badge of supreme triumph, of joy and vindication. "I found Anna."

Going to the Angels

The way to space for the tribes of Australia is a door with three thresholds. In the high deserts you can see them paving the way, three bright doorsteps: the shuttle fields at Tinbilla and Throwing Stick and, by far the most famous, the field at Long Reach, two hours' journey in from the coast by tribal sand-ship.

There, in the clear cool evenings, with brilliant meteor swarms marking the sky, envious Nationals can watch the shuttles planing up to orbit, or the costly VTO link-ships making their fiery climb.

And each month, the quota of lucky Nationals and Internationals who have won places among the "sky stones"—the gragens—march through the linkmesh gates and go through the doorway that exists as both idea and physical fact. Each year, the fortunate thousands take their places aboard the shuttles and join the far settlements, or go to the orbiting tribal demesnes, the celebrated estates known to all as the Angels.

There the National émigrés train and serve and live out their lives as menials, but with privilege, a measure of respect, with choices—though never the choice of returning, never that.

That is what is offered. Thereafter it is infrequent letter transcripts and even rarer relayed messages with the burden of time-delay and tribal censorship.

For the Nationals of Australia, for most of the non-Ab'O peoples of the world, the door that falls at Long Reach, Tinbilla and Throwing Stick is a one-way door.

Soby chose that door, as many do, and the editorial team of *Caravanserai* wanted me to stop him. Beth phoned to ask the favour; Sam knew I would find it difficult to refuse her—my dear friend, my special love, Beth.

"He's too young, Tom," she said, her lovely face filling the screen in my room at the Gaza. "He's seeing the romance of a gragen life. He thinks he'll write better songs, change things, be some exception and come back a hero. A working spaceman like the bravos out at Long Reach. A famous songsmith like Afervarro, but in space, representing Nation up there."

"He's twenty years old, Beth. He knows he can't come back. He's old enough to choose."

Beth shook her long dark hair. The face which had brought such surprise, such true joy, as it always did when I saw it again, looked tired and worried. "No. Not fairly. Soby's too impatient. He wants it all now. His cadetship with us is nearly over. He'll get to go on stories; Sam and I will make sure of that. His writing is good. He can apply for a gragen permit; they could give him a tour of the Angels."

"But Soby knows that."

"We've all told him. It's not enough. He's seen the promos—Nationals working in the garden domes, serving in the labs, walking on the promenades. He wants to go out to the stones. He wants to be a spaceman who sings, not a journo singer who's had a twenty-four-hour safe tour. He says he'd only come back hungry for more."

I didn't know what to say. I knew Soby from visits to see Beth at the *Caravanserai* offices here in Twilight Beach, and at their solstice parties. He was young, vital, talented. He made good songs—romantic, desperate, eager songs that touched the heart because they were made so full of what soon slipped from so many hearts: the easy total giving of the young and the new, what was so quickly put aside and hidden.

I had heard some of his songs. Among the Angels he would be a leveller, a good thing, a fine ambassador for Nation, for all humanity. There above the Earth in some gragen—some "high stone place"—he would sing songs of common feeling.

And who could tell? Perhaps he would make a difference, change the feeling, make the future different, better. We needed a thousand Sobys, one on every ship that went, on every colony stone—every gragen there was.

Perhaps he knew exactly what he was trading to do it.

I saw Beth quietly watching my reverie, understanding my reflections, and knew how much she felt for her young friend. I wondered what to do.

"Parents? Family?" I asked.

"Already gone through. Two years now."

"Messages? What do they say?"

"What you'd expect," Beth answered. "Come home. But they're a long way out. Soby wouldn't see them for quite a while. Orientation and Skills Training takes at least a year."

"Friends?"

"Quite a few in our offices. He's very popular, as you know. Quite a few in Twilight Beach. But he's young enough to move free. Persuade him to wait! He admires you. You may not have picked that up from the parties but he really does. He asks about you a lot. He was at the Farrady talk you gave on the Coloured Captains."

"Soby was? That was pre-sold, booked out weeks in advance."

"He paid what the scalpers were asking. He wanted to hear you talk about the Seven—about the special philosophy of those holding Hero Colours from the tribes."

"Then he heard me say that winning the Colours was an accident, a faulty comp/belltree link-up. It couldn't happen again."

"But equally true: you *are* a hero to him, Tom."

"Then what good can I do? Everything I am will convince him to go. He'll quote me back to myself."

"You may be the only one who can pierce the dream—"

"Which is exactly what I mustn't do, don't you see?"

"—in case it's pierceable! So he can choose later, apply later." I saw the yearning to protect in Beth's eyes. A lone spirit herself, she loved what Soby had in full measure. "Let him get his knocks down here. Keep his options for awhile."

"When does he go?"

"He's gone. He's already on his way to Long Reach."

I studied the calm lovely face, the dark brown eyes, saw the respect for Soby and me which had kept her from asking this help sooner. It was her last resort, left till the very last hour when she had already resolved not to do anything to interfere with this young man's dream.

"All right, Beth. I'll go to Long Reach. When is his flight?"

"This evening. At 1900."

Which left little time. *Rynosseros* was out on mission, so I took passage on *Mason Fire* with two hundred others, equally divided among those bound for the Angels and relatives and friends there to see the travellers off.

The big sand-ship lofted kites at 1315, sailed through the afternoon and moored at Long Reach at 1520. Some passengers went to the hotels in the National tourist concession at Hindel; others went straight out to the field to wait by the boundaries, eager to be gone, psyching themselves up for the absolute change in their lives that was to come, as if afraid of being tempted to stay behind if they dallied too long in the town.

Some did that, stayed, running back from the queues at the last minute, forfeiting their chance ever again. But there were always the last-minute volunteers to take their places, speculators who could pay the fare and hoped to jump ahead of their rostered departure dates. The ships always went up full—taking their thousands upon thousands every year, men, women, children, each one a seed, a clod of Earth as the popular sayings had it, the "cloddies" going forth to carve the greater night into some semblance of home.

I believed I knew where Soby would be—Soby who dreamed of becoming a spaceman, the forbidden vocation for Nationals, for all non-Ab'Os. Not at the bars of Hindel, not lined up at the linkmesh fences at the spaceport.

Close to the field, on a dusty perimeter road, was a weathered inn called The Stranded Man, run by Jack Clancy. It was a special haven for me, a National concession like the town of Hindel itself, but of a curious and unique kind. Soby would be there.

Clancy, of all the Nationals I knew, had managed to surmount the racial differences between the evicted white Nationals and the Ab'O ascendants whose Dreamtime/haldane-augmented minds had given them space as it had the rule of Australia.

On afternoons when no flights were scheduled, the off-duty spacemen would saunter into his bar: quiet serious men, splendid-looking in their torch-jackets and bodyforms, heads shaved and gleaming, chests oiled and covered with birkin signs.

A former charvi captain himself, Clancy understood sailors' ways, all sailors' ways. He accepted the stern gazes and distracted, taciturn manner, allowed for reasons and needs. During the long off-duty hours, he would serve them their drinks and meals, charm them, bring them to smiles and laughter, bits of confidences given out because this old weather-beaten sailor never needed such things. It was as if Clancy simply wanted to probe those distracted looks and defeat them.

His two cats, Charlie and Max, the famous "duelling cats" of The Stranded Man, assisted in this, weaving love-courses between booted legs, winning pats and smiles, winning invitations to tour the gragens (though that offer was never made, even jokingly, to Clancy).

When they softened, the Ab'Os showed the other side of their curious philosophical bent: that they loved life, all life; that they missed the red earth and their deserts. They petted the cats and looked beyond them into nothing; they sat peering into the lights and depths of their drinks and listened to the wind. After sunset, they kept away from the windows, not wanting to watch the night and the stars of that greater desert above them—their high stone place, the gragen—not wanting to see the Angels and powerful comsats orbiting there, not wanting to watch the brilliant meteor swarms that sometimes scattered fistfuls of light across the sky.

They seemed like men who were tired and wished to forget , but that was the common life of bars, after all, and Clancy worked with it to the betterment of everyone.

Some Nationals did find their way around to Clancy's, some of those who meant to step through the Door, though not many.

Usually it was journalists and media teams, sand-ship crews who wanted to share the same elusive kinship as Clancy did—to be with these fierce totemic sailors.

The low voices of the off-duty crews, the bright hard looks that never quite fixed, deterred many would-be visitors; the stories of such things discouraged most. The Stranded Man was that indeed: often empty of customers for fifteen hours out of any day.

Soby was there.

When I wandered in at 1600, I saw him sitting alone at a corner table below a display of Astani duelling masks, his bag and his guitar on the floor near him. He had a pen and paper before him, and there were two empty glasses near a half-filled third.

There were other National customers: a group of three sitting below the wheel of the heavy green glass chandelier, another two at the magazine stand Clancy kept scrupulously up to date by some mysterious means, the rest—a few solitaries scattered about the big taproom.

But no spacemen today: it was a full launch roster. Come nightfall, there would only be techs and mank crews out at Long Reach, and the relatives and disappointed line-jumpers trailing back to Hindel and all the space-hungry places of the world.

Soby saw me. His grey eyes widened in surprise and obvious pleasure, then set into a look of wary concern as he realised what Beth and Sam must have done, that there could be only one reason for my presence. He set down his pen, brushed back his long brown hair with one hand, and waited.

"May I buy a friend a final drink?" I said.

His guarded look softened. He nodded and I sat. Clancy wandered over, took an order for two light beers and returned to the bar.

"I came because of Beth, Soby, not because I believe I have anything more to say than goodbye and good fortune."

"Thanks," he said with evident relief, smiling now. It was a good smile, a winning smile, making his tanned face more conventionally handsome. "Thanks. They don't understand."

"They do. You know they do. It's just hard to lose someone you care for."

"I'll be in touch. I'll send songs through, maybe approved stories. They make exceptions. I can be a correspondent."

"You know it doesn't work like that. You pay dearly for every word. There's censorship up there."

"I can make a difference, Tom."

"Yea, I'm for that. But you'll be busy paying for rations and environmentals for quite some time. The tribes control the means."

"It's not all like that," Soby said. "In the outer gragens, maybe, but not in the Angels. I've seen the promos, the tour broadcasts. There are good positions. I talked to the counsellor at Wins."

Clancy placed our beers on the table and left us.

"The promos make it look good," I agreed. "But not everyone can stay in the inner orbits. They have to move them out; they have to make the gragens work. Which one are you down for?"

"I'm going through Krombi. After that it's wherever there's a vacancy. They were impressed with my training."

"What did the Wins man say?"

"I told them I was a songwriter and singer like Afervarro, and a trained wordsmith. The counsellor said there were places in the recreation and information services. He gave me a 75% chance of a posting in the Angels within two years."

"That high?"

"That's what he said. He said once people have been in the orbits for a while, they grow stale. They want more, want to get out to the stones. We serve them, but we get to move around. It's not as bad as Nation makes out. It's low-feudal status, but offspring are born citizens. Earth-barred, yes, but they'll get to sculpt the planets, bring down biospheres—"

"They don't have that capability yet. They may never leave the home orbits—"

"No, Tom, they will. It's the only way. We'll work on the roads between the worlds."

"But always low-feudal."

Soby leant forward, excited now. "You've seen the skies above Long Reach. That's the universe out there. This is the only chance I get. You've never been up? Not even a safe tour?"

"I haven't, no." It annoyed me that Soby brought this up now.

"Why?"

I hesitated, barely recognising what I felt as a telling resentment, wanting to be sure my answer wasn't just the handy lie because of that.

"A little of it is fear," I said. "And there are things I need to discover here first. Within me."

Soby watched me, waiting, and his eyes were clear, the look he gave me composed, very adult.

"And there's pride," I admitted. "A lot of that. If I go through Long Reach on their terms, I acknowledge claims that cannot be allowed, on things no-one has a right to own."

"Such an old pride," Soby said. "So you, a great adventurer, a sensitive, deny yourself. One of the only seven Nationals to win a Colour from the tribes. You who at any time can use your status in the Great Passage Book to request a tour, who *can* come back, for heaven's sake, don't go!"

"Soby . . . " I was bristling with anger now, trying not to show it.

"You don't know what it will do, being there! It might answer your questions, unlock mysteries for you! Don't you see, Tom! Being off the Earth, seeing it as a world, can do that—more than simulations can. You'll fly. Fly! Not in an approved dirigible, but higher, faster. You'll see Australia from above as the comsats see it. Huxley said it: the doors of perception will be cleansed!"

"Soby, I'm fighting my best down here to swing that Door wide for all the world, for all of us. Not just for Tosi-Go and Mikel and the other sanctioned franchises. While I have *Rynosseros* and Blue, while I'm in the Book as one of their heroes, by whatever chance and error I have that amazing privilege, I have to earn the view you talk about. It's like—"

"Jacob and Esau, right?" Soby was warming to this, using defences he had prepared for answering others. "You think I'm selling my birthright for a mess of pottage—"

"For rations and environmentals," I said. "For low-feudal and working on the roads—digging in the sky-stones!"

"Same thing! But I'm better than that! I'm worth more than that."

"Yes. Yes, I know. But you really said it yourself when you spoke of me. Make it so you have choices too. Ask for a special study tour as a National correspondent. Go up, come back, decide then. You can go later. Close the one-way Door then! Do it for you!"

He looked at me in silence, his eyes fixed and calm, and I knew that I had just now used the arguments Sam and the others must have used, that Beth had probably wanted to, and everyone who knew him and loved him and wanted him safe and in their lives.

"Sing me the song about the Apollo ships," I said.

"*The Aftertime*?"

"If it's okay."

Soby smiled, took out his guitar, played a few chords in preparation. Clancy's cats were sleeping on chairs below the chandelier; one of them opened an eye, flicked an ear at the new sounds, and slept on. In the quiet taproom, Soby sang his ballad of an age we would never see again.

"Exactly what was over
Wasn't very plain,
As David caught the Greyhound
And Allan took the train.
A pendant made of meteor,
Some moondust on a string,
Not even the hero-maker saved us
From that mighty coming down.

"The corporation stardog
With a Gemini on his desk,
Is closer to the truth he is
Than we can ever be.
We're brittle from the raw abyss
That no-one understands,
From afternoons of rocket fire,
High-road-down.

"The sun in a razor,
The moon inside a cube,
The wind among the gantries

Haunting and alone.
Weekends spent in ancient hills
Remembering the dawn,
Not even the hero-maker saved us
From that mighty coming down."

When he finished, I thanked him, saw him smile with quiet pride as he put his guitar away. Then we sat in silence together, watching the golden light through the bottle-lens windows, waiting out the final parts of our leavetaking.

At 1840, in growing dusk, we went to the field together, walking in a sad purple-grey gloaming along the road from Clancy's towards the fenced perimeter. It was the sort of road and haunted windy evening when you believed you could actually meet the likes of the Spirit Malingee high-stepping towards you, his huge eyes burning in his devil face, the sharp stone knives on his elbows flashing.

Behind us, the inn glowed with suffused light, like a carved filigree box filled with cashiered suns, though it seemed far off now, and would not save us from the likes of an angry Djuan spirit like Malingee hunting souls. It was that kind of evening.

In the distance we could see the twinkling lights of Hindel; ahead, the harsher, more functional lights of the hangars and launch towers—with the startling shapes of the aerospace rocketry: the great aeromankers and VTOs.

It was a lonely road, the spacemen's road, leading us to a private gate in the perimeter mesh where a lone Ab'O stood watch, his djellaba gathered close about him against the cool wind which was rising now and stirring the dust at our feet.

"Stop!" the tribesman said. "This is not the way in. You must go round."

"I am Blue Tyson," I told him, indicating the patches on my jacket. "We wish to use the spacemen's gate."

Soby said nothing, but I sensed what it meant for him just to be here at their gate in the fence.

The Ab'O reached for his comlink.

"My responsibility, tribesman," I said, and he paused. "It is not for me. My friend has a launch in twenty minutes. Let him go in by this special gate, please. A favour."

The Ab'O was a young man too, his dusky face lost in the gloom.

"Which launch?" he asked, and it was hard to know whether he knew the Hero Colour and the name or whether it was simple kindness. He did not ask for further proof. "There are three tonight."

"K-94," Soby said. "Plat 4. Flight 601-B."

"That's *Crosa*. Over there." He pointed to the closest tower. "They've already started sequence. You must hurry!" And he unlocked the gate.

Soby and I embraced, awkwardly, urgently, around his bag and guitar.

"Come up, Tom!" he said. "Come and see!"

And he ran through the gate out onto the field, towards the splayed arrow silhouette of the shuttle.

The wind had strengthened and become cooler, seeming to whisper down from the heavens. Desert night was about us now. The young Ab'O's djellaba snapped in the wind. Stars filled the vault overhead, chill and bright, beckoning as stars have always done since humans first watched birds and stars, and up was perceived as out. Meteors cut bright, fleeting arcs there—six, twenty, more than I could easily count, there and gone, a threadbare veil but a vivid one. Then another came, and another, a beautiful sight, wave on sparkling wave.

"Thank you, tribesman," I said. "I hope it will cause you no hardship."

"It was not your Colour," he said. "Others come this way. Others persuade their way in."

I smiled. Of course they did. And he kept the gate often enough to know, to make this small gift of brotherhood.

"National spacemen," I said. "Other good men like you."

The young man did not answer.

"Brothers," I said. "In time."

Still no answer. Just the wind soughing in the mesh, blowing the dust. Just the snapping of a djellaba.

I turned from the gate without another word, and was almost at

The Stranded Man again when *Crosa* stood on fire, left its place in a long rolling thunder and slid up towards the stars.

I stood in the road and watched the red fantail rising, flanked by stars and meteor trails, until it was no longer visible, until the silence measured itself again as a weave of sounds that did not need humanity to be complete, that could take the absence of our kind.

Clancy's inn burned ahead, bright and empty—empty of spacemen, empty of conversations and chances for a time, with the wind rattling at its doors and casements, the dust blowing by as it did every night.

For me, so fitting. So, so fitting. The Stranded Man.

I stood in the roadway and considered Soby's words. Perhaps he was right. Perhaps my principles were not the real reason. Possibly it was pride and envy and rarefied, well-processed rage; quite possibly seeing our world from the Angels would change something vital, help in my task with the other Coloured Captains of changing how the tribes saw us, help too in placing the images from out of my private night.

Yes, I decided, affected by the night wind and the stars and the meteor tides, by the warm precious light falling through the mullioned windows of Clancy's, by the lingering, elemental fear that Malingee might yet come high-stepping down that lonely road, eyes blazing, elbow knives gleaming in the night, a thrilling fancy.

Yes, change for me too. Something vital. A glimpse through the Door (I capitalised it again in my thoughts). Informed judgement. Passion dealt with. Rage. Secret need. Yes.

I would arrange a room, call Beth and have her come out to help make this a media event Nation could use, then walk back round to the young Ab'O at the gate. There were no spacemen tonight, but perhaps he would answer some questions. Perhaps without using my Colour at all, he would help me unlock the Door.

Though he wouldn't say it, perhaps he wanted that too.

Sein Ammas Cosiro at the Long Reach office gazed across his desk at Beth and me, paying more attention perhaps to her shoulder camera than to either of us.

"This will take time, Captain," the handsome, middle-aged port official said. He wore elegant grey robes, with his tribal sign—Chonsye—given as patches on his shoulders, and an insignia I didn't know: a vivid blue hook, a turquoise and faience amalgam set in silver, fixed just below his collar. "We will need confirmation and station co-operation, special Kurdaitcha sanctions—"

"Why, Mr Cosiro?" I said. "I want this to be impromptu. It is 1100. There is plenty of time. My friend, Soby Parovin, went up to Krombi last night. I would like to surprise him there. I am in the Book. There are entitlements you would know of." And gambling on something neither Beth nor I could be sure of in the time we'd had: "Other Captains listed in the Book have had no difficulties. Ab'O Captains. It is our right. Are you saying—"

"No. No, Captain," Cosiro said, eyeing the camera as if it were indeed another person in his office. "Not at all. There are merely protocols for this. Reasonable courtesies. Especially with busy station crews processing so many arrivals last night. You understand how it is."

"Officer Cosiro, I know that one flight is due for 1900 tonight, the *Dhal*. I also know it has less than a third payload. There is—"

"Pardon me, but who told you this?" He said the words with more acerbity than he may have intended. The telltale of the camera sobered him quickly.

"Spacemen talk," I said. "A pilot, I think, or a mank tech."

"There is altogether too much talk!"

"Are you being obstructive, Mr Cosiro?"

"Are you being reasonable, Captain Tyson? I am appealing to reason here. We should have Kurdaitcha sanction. Or Clever Men to—"

"Why? Tell me why!"

"Because—"

"Because you consider me National?"

"No! No, Captain! Please!" The camera telltale burned. "You are forcing words."

"Do you question my listing in the Great Passage Book?"

Oh how he yearned to say yes to that, as many Ab'Os did. I saw it in his eyes, saw the lie sent out into his gestures, into the set of his body.

"Not at all. But it is different."

There, he had said it. Damning himself.

"I mean by that," he added quickly, "that as realists we must allow that your status *is* unusual. You are National and with tribal honours."

Deeper and deeper.

"I am a Coloured Captain, Mr Cosiro. One of seven Nationals with that honour but the Book makes no discrimination. I ask to be on *Dhal* and mean to be. I would appreciate a call to Krombi where *Crosa* docked—a Chonsye station, I believe—arranging for this Coloured Captain to meet his young friend, Soby Parovin. A small thing. No special arrangements. Not even a safe tour. Just an opportunity to see my friend one more time. To look down at the Earth together. To share space. To finish a conversation."

Cosiro nodded. "Where will you be?"

"At The Stranded Man. Out on the perimeter road. You can reach me there."

"Very well," Cosiro said, standing, eager to be away from the camera Beth wore on her shoulder.

We moved to the door, the Ab'O ushering us ahead of him, wanting to be free of us.

"Oh yes, Mr Cosiro, one more thing. I trust there will be no technical difficulties, no last-minute flight cancellations. *Dhal* goes tonight. I know that *Pyrani* goes up tomorrow night, and *Crosa* again the night after. Put a call through to Krombi, inform your Chonsye administration there. Tell Parovin to expect me on *Dhal*."

The closed hatred in Cosiro's eyes was chilling to see. It seemed to hover over Beth and me as we walked away from the field, back through the hot afternoon towards Clancy's.

"I don't think I've seen such naked contempt for Nationals before," Beth said. "I knew it existed—"

"Not often like that, Beth. Thankfully. It's the gragen mentality. Cosiro is part of an extremist minority."

We did not speak then. The linkmesh fence beside the dusty road shimmered. The launch towers out on the field—some, far off, with dirigibles tethered to their totemic crowns—were roiling spectres, indistinct, dreamlike, hints of tech. The Stranded Man was a dark mass on the desert ahead, its condensation tower making it look like some desolate roadside church, the old windmill in the yard behind lifting like a black flower defeated by too much sunlight.

There was little else to do but wait. Inside, away from the heat, we sat at the table Soby had used, contemplating the Astani masks and watching the handful of National customers who came in, stayed awhile for whatever reasons, and finally went their way. The "duelling cats" slept in the shadows beneath the green glass chandelier; they cocked an eye at each newcomer and returned to their slumbers.

Beth reviewed the footage from our meeting with Cosiro. She wrote copy and phoned some through to Sam at *Caravanserai*. Then, not wanting to talk over the material yet again, but unable to discuss anything else that existed between us because of *Dhal* waiting out there in the noon shimmer and Krombi swinging by overhead, we drowsed, we read the day-old news-sheets and week-old magazines, and stayed alone with our thoughts, but together too. Waiting for sunset, waiting for Cosiro's call confirming passage, living minutes with a slowness known only in waiting rooms and during childhood.

At 1400, two Ab'Os entered from the street, two tall robed men wearing dark glasses, with the distinctive signs painted on their faces.

Kurdaitcha at The Stranded Man.

Clancy stirred at once, but not too quickly. It was an uncommon thing this, but not unknown. He moved to the bar, quietly bid them good day. The cats, Charlie and Max, opened sleepy eyes, went back to their dreams.

The Ab'Os murmured something in the habitually low tones of their kind, words that were always heard no matter how softly they were delivered. Clancy replied, though the avengi had already seen us. They came to stand before our table.

"Captain Tyson, Ms Leossa-Tojian, may we join you?" one of them said. He had a pale mauve triangle on each cheek.

"Of course, gentlemen," I said, not surprised that they were here either, but feeling a tension grip my body. "I am most honoured. Please record this, Beth."

"Please, no," the Ab'O with the mauve triangles said, raising his hand, and Beth paused in activating her camera.

"Excuse me, avengi,"—I made myself meet those hard eyes—"but *Caravanserai* operates by National and International charter. With tribal sanctions. You agree?"

They did not bother to answer the question.

"I am Chybere," the mauve-marked Kurdaitcha said. "This is Amly. If that camera is on, we cannot be direct. We must withhold things you might care to hear."

"I prefer this to be official, Chybere. Beth, please record this."

Beth touched the tab; the telltale shone red.

The Ab'Os gazed impassively, accepting the decision, necessarily caught here at The Stranded Man no less than I was.

"Cosiro told us of your intention," Chybere said. "Let me ask, why this urgency? What do you accomplish by being so unreasonable? Rushing beyond procedures and convenience?"

"I am in the Book, Chybere. Not just a Nation man. Within reason I can do what I wish. I would like to see one of the Angels, now, tonight, to perform a special meditation, to share a new thing with a young friend while it is still new for both of us. Even were it just impulse, it would be my right. As I dearly wish it, there can be no refusal."

"We are sorry but your visit may have to be—postponed—for a time."

"Refused, you mean? No, that will not be. Other tribal Captains listed in the Book have been allowed. If you discriminate between listed Captains, attempt to bar me, I will ask for immediate Convocation and see how the holy colleges deal with that. All Princes, all tribes. As a Coloured Captain that is also my right."

Chybere spoke for the camera now as well as to me. "We have not—barred you, Captain. We have not, as you say, discriminated. But there are practicalities. Fair considerations. Such a request—"

"I have announced my intention, gentlemen. Your official reaction is being recorded."

Chybere glanced at Beth's camera again; Amly took in the handful of Nationals covertly watching, muttered something in dialect, a low sharp Kurdaitcha code impossible to interpret, making no apology for it.

They were considering outright refusal, I knew, or worse, accustomed to commanding absolute obedience, to showing the patient and reasonable gentleness of all inquisitors, but caught now by the need to be delicate and correct, to adapt to this novelty situation and turn it their way. The arrogance and ruthlessness were held back, came out in a smile from Chybere such as Torquemada or the Witchfinder Matthew Hopkins might have given.

Had Beth's camera not been running, he might have hinted at consequences, reprisals, moves against friends and Nation, things I did not want to hear. I did not know how vindictive these holy warriors were, to what extent they truly believed in the Colour right, regardless of who held it.

Chybere's voice was poisonously calm when he spoke again. "Part of the difficulty is that Krombi underwent orbit adjustment following *Dhal*'s arrival last night. It will not be set up for another twenty-four hours."

"Yet *Dhal* is scheduled for Krombi tonight."

"A tribal payload, Captain, not for the emigrant docking areas. You understand me?"

I nodded, but it was at something else which occurred to me about these Kurdaitcha. The ancient clan of ritual avengers was drawn from all tribes, but individuals might retain tribal loyalties.

"Tell me, Chybere. Krombi is a Chonsye holding, I realise now. May I ask which tribe you and Amly were originally from?"

It had to be an infuriating question, catching them like this. Their eyes glittered like beads of obsidian.

"We are not permitted to say," Chybere answered.

He had been right about Beth's camera: natural, true conversation could not exist, just smooth formality, the right things said. I was trapped no less than these avengi were in a secret world of contingencies, expedience and cynicism. All of us deceivers.

Though technically, publicly, the law held; my claim was valid. Only I could withdraw it. And that was the unasked question here. That is what these Kurdaitcha, these former Chonsye, waited for now.

"Thank you for coming," I said. "I mean to make no further trouble. I will call Nation, tell them what I intend. All I require is a seat on *Dhal*, a room with a window when I reach Krombi, and a few hours with my friend, Soby Parovin."

The Kurdaitcha rose without further comment, turned away from the table and left the inn. The cats stirred; above their heads the green glass chandelier turned slowly like a galaxy carved from emerald. Clancy went to stand in the open doorway and watched them go.

"They vanish in the heat like anyone else," he said, then came over to our table.

"Sorry, Jack," I said. "Will they make trouble?"

"Nah. Their psychologists give me a clear. They come here themselves. The spacemen need me." The old sailor took a folded paper from the pocket of his apron and handed it to me. "The boy left this." And he began clearing a nearby table.

I read what the paper said, placed it so Beth could see it while I read it again.

Another Day at The Stranded Man

Sometimes we need a broken road
To see the road more clearly,
I was on a broken road
And I was blind.
Reaching out for something new,
Tell me, were you reaching too?
Drinking our wine
So close to the borderline
We could feel the emptiness from here.

Another day at The Stranded Man
Has come over me,
Another calm in the hurricane
And I'm beginning to see,
From bridges I've burned down,
Another waiting for me.
Drinking my wine
So close to the borderline,
I can feel the emptiness from here.

Another day at The Stranded Man
Has come to its end,
Another glimpse at the patient stars
So we can pretend.
There's a bridge to be burned now,
There's a fire to be free,
Biding its time
So close to the borderline,
We can touch the endlessness from here.

For you Tom.
Soby.

"He didn't finish it," Clancy said. "He meant to."

"Jack, are you saying Soby had been here before yesterday?"

The big man nodded. "That's right. Just like you do now and then, so you can feel it. Checking on the spacemen. He'd watch the pilots, listen to the test runs, talk about the Captains, you—"

"Jack—"

"You're doing the right thing, Tom," Clancy said, and carried the empty glasses back to the bar.

Beth gave a sad smile. "I knew he was fond of you. He'd say things. I'm glad you're going."

Oh Beth, I thought, how loving you are, how ready to let things be as they have to be, in their own time, in their own way, never forced, never too soon.

I reached out and squeezed her hand, met those startling eyes, then pocketed Soby's letter. "I'll take it up to him. He can finish it while I wait."

We laughed. The glass galaxy turned, the green of fields and jungles and Aztec gods. The cats lifted their heads, pondered the strange ways of humans, and the afternoon sun fell down the sky towards the Door that was swinging open at Long Reach.

At 1830, I walked with Beth to the spacemen's gate but found it locked and untended, no-one on duty. Wind whistled and thrummed in the linkmesh fence, raised eddies of dust along the lonely road.

I felt a sadness at what it might mean. Perhaps the Kurdaitcha—in league with Cosiro—had acted already, had found small immediate things that mattered, like punishing a young gatekeeper. Perhaps they would poison Clancy's cats, make little tragedies of that kind.

But when we had walked around the field to the main gate, there were no avengi waiting to trade or warn, just two gatekeepers who checked and signed their manifest and handed me an ident tab.

This evening there were no crowds of émigrés lined up and waiting. *Dhal* carried an official payload—station officers returning from ground duty and leave, vital supplies.

"Tower 3," one Ab'O said, and pointed. "There."

I kissed Beth. For a moment we clung to each other with an urgency that words could never hope to explain, then I picked up my small bag and entered the field, walking towards *Dhal* where it slanted into the sky. I thought I could see the figure of Beth moving beyond the fence towards Clancy's, but it was too dark now to tell.

Knowing Beth, she would not look back. Her destination was the lonely inn beside the spacemen's road.

I boarded the aeromanker, took the seat indicated by the young half-caste steward. She smiled with practised courtesy as she helped me fit my harness.

"You've done sims before?" she asked.

"A hundred hours at least. High Frontier. Starfall. Some others."

"You'll be fine," she said. "The hard thing will be processing it as real this time." She gave her professional smile again and moved away.

My forty or so fellow passengers were not as generous. When they glanced my way, their eyes were hard like those of Amly and Chybere, each glance a challenge, a calculated defiance, though made gentle with practice.

I made myself look around them, through them, studying the soft tones of the passenger salon, reacting to what the steward had said, trying to make it real, more than just the POV simulations.

The shuttle's interior was decorated in earthen tones, with fibre-ceramic panelling and totemic skeuomorphs. Even here, functional tech did not escape the psychic essentials. True to the tribal philosophies, there were things for the soul and the mind, function at all levels of what a person was, not simply the physical. Nothing casual here: ergonomic and psychonomic, every shape and form powered the ultimate reality of this ship.

I would not see the spacemen, of course. They would enter by another port, had probably done so already. I wondered if they were men I had seen at Clancy's—it was more than likely. Ship crews rotated, did the high-low circuit. Very likely.

As the digital crept towards 1900, I sat wondering how many of my fellow passengers—twenty-eight men, twelve women—were Kurdaitcha or special Chonsye agents assigned to this flight. Not for the first time, I considered the possibility of an accident going up to orbit: just what price would they pay to be free of one of the Coloured Captains, one of the seven chosen by a faulty belltree playing at God, placing names in the Great Passage Book, obliging the tribes to such a burden of honour?

Perhaps this payload was made up of last-minute volunteers, Ab'Os prepared to give their lives to chip away at the ignominy, to prevent *this* man exercising *this* right, willing to die for tribal favours to friends and family. While I waited at Clancy's with Beth, who knew what plans had been made?

Tonight my death—by Kurdaitcha or Chonsye (or a mixture of both if my suspicions about Amly and Chybere had been correct). A month, a year later, one of the other Captains: Afervarro or Lucas or Glaive, on and on down the list until the Seven were gone and the weight of the shame was diminished, eliminated at last.

It would look obvious, of course it would, once the process was started. But, then again, modern Australia was a dangerous land and memories were often short, especially given careful media biasing by the tribes. My call to Council had involved a briefing of the six remaining Captains, plus passing on an account of what I now did to Arredeni and Anna at Heart-and-Hand. Beth had called *Caravanserai* with copy for a major feature. Perhaps there was too much attention for them to risk payback.

Dhal had been alive in small ways: air-conditioning, electrical systems, soft hull noises. Now it sprang alive in earnest, urgently, the engines switched in, building for lift. Like the sims, but real. *Real.*

There was the ten-chime. *Dhal* moved forward, moved quickly, alarmingly, as if flung from a giant's hand. I was pressed back into the seat; the aeromanker angled up and lost Long Reach, threw it behind.

And none of it was real—all part of a virtual reality conditioning, senses dulled by hours in the High Frontier sim on Breaklight Pier. But I tried. Desperately tried.

I remembered *Crosa* the night before, calculated the vanishment we made, the dislocation of proportion and reality for Beth and Clancy should they be watching far, far, impossibly far below. I had the bewilderment that fitted theirs, a suspension of all the usual causal expectations as big became small, up became out, heaviness slipped away, and unminded dragon roar became uncanny silence.

My time sense was gone, I discovered. It seemed moments, mere seconds, and I was glancing out the ports at the curve of the world, blue, white, radiant with someone else's day. It was another sim shot, another VR insert, or like one of those antique astronautics photographs, brilliantly back-lit by a sunrise corona at the terminator.

But I fought the disappointment, worked to let the reality press in too. I'd been in a dirigible many times, had read about the old aircraft and early space planes. I made myself see truth, forced it about my over-conditioned senses, used smaller, nearer things like the weightlessness being defied by my harness, the shift of my organs and body-tides, subtle, so subtle, sought and found a language to encompass it. Believed I did.

My fellow passengers had done this before. Some read or dozed, but most watched the view as well, pointing out sights, making quiet comments. These weren't the comsat orbits; many of them were identifying nearby Angels which shone as points of light, beacon stars in this preternatural midnight day.

That was reassuring. I detected no undue tension in how they sat, saw no last-minute knowing glances for a shared mutual fate.

Finally a voice spoke from com, words in dialect. I heard the name Krombi and searched the starfield for the Chonsye station, saw it suddenly as *Dhal* heeled over for docking, a great sculpted aerolith turning about its long axis, showing us first its glistening clubbed end, the plantings inside the ribbed and domed surface works, then—as we toured its length—the tapering stem, the production facs and labs, a series of ugly vent tubes, EVA access ports, the shuttle docks.

Again, real. Not sim, not documentary footage.

Krombi looked both fragile and sturdy, a great inverted stalactite hanging from the ceiling of the night, geosynched above Australia. Its bright, jewel-encrusted end pointed towards the Earth, its jagged service tail faced out into the deeps where it had been found and dragged forth, carried home like some lost sceptre to where its carved, bejewelled brother gragens swung through the same dark, sentinel stones left here on the doorstep of forever.

Dhal turned in towards the throat of the docking tube, heading for the sealing fac which waited like a surgeon, grapples, locks and umbilici poised and ready.

Again, superb irony, all more real than I dreamed—and less. The reality barrier barely remained intact. Soby had talked of true space in the taproom of Clancy's, had conceived and shared a madman's visionary portion of it that had been more real than this slide to station could ever be. Something defined by opposites. The more remote, the more vivid. Nationals compensated for the loss of space by desensitising on the wonderful simulations, no longer able to relate. Perhaps all this would not become finally real until I was standing on the windy deck of *Rynosseros* again, sailing the red deserts. Perhaps then it would happen, overload falling away, simple truth remaining.

I laughed aloud at the paradox, the ultimately terrifying yet unassimilable sensory trap, and the Ab'Os near me frowned and muttered. I was a drunk on a fairground ride, that was all. Soon the ride would end and I would step out onto the Pier in bright sunshine, go back to the deserts and my ship.

Oh Soby, were you young enough, unsullied enough, to keep it pure? Did you avoid the sims, needing to keep this real, the edges sure and sharp?

Dhal crept into dock like a slow-motion swimmer, received the grapples and service tubes, became one more piece of Krombi's glistening crust.

Then, when we had gravity again, when I was free of my harness and leaving *Dhal*, the place became truly, meaningfully strange. As we moved into the flight lounge, the estrangement began—with the walls of thick meteoric iron and rock-melt, shiny black streaked with green and violet, the array of tonson poles of space metal and gragen-grown timbers, a grove of fantastic totems with crests spun into filigree or shimmering with bright wires inside metal throats so that they sang in the wind from the pressured hearts of docking ships.

Things for the soul, I kept telling myself. Parts of a functional reality, everything working to feed the psyche and ease the spirit. These weren't like those antique NASA sims of O'Neill colonies; this was another way, as different as *Soyuz* from *Apollo*, as Egyptian Ptah to Baiame.

The returning Ab'Os knew where they were going in this strange metal garden. The tonson totems communicated something vital: welcoming them to their other home, their high stone place, directing them to concealed exits. The small group quickly dispersed, vanished through coded space-iron access-ways almost faster than I could see, like beads of mercury scattered on a polished floor. By the time I understood what was happening—a routine withdrawal to known destinations—I found myself alone in an iron glade in the tinkling, shimmering ship-wind from our aeromanker.

It was disturbing, even vaguely alarming, standing there on the gently curving floor as the wind died away and the totems became still once more.

No Kurdaitcha came, no Clever Men or Unseen Spears. A single port opened beyond the stark cluster of gragen trees. A single Ab'O, tall, patrician-like, my own age, stepped onto the deck on the other side of the grove and headed towards me. The tonson poles reacted to his bodywind, started stirring and murmuring again.

I saw that he wore patterned bodyforms, ochre like the old stones of Earth, covered with a hatching of darker brown lines. He had the blood-red infinity sign on his forehead, a tattoo and not a painted mutable. On each cheek he had a turquoise chevron. He wore the double swords.

A space captain, and captain of the *Dhal*, I was certain. He had inherited the problem I represented, showing just how unwelcome I was at this Angel.

I swore to myself. Damn them for involving him like this! Damn them!

"I am Dwar Ingers," the spaceman said.

"Captain Ingers, I regret this inconvenience—"

"You have the Colour," he said with absolute solemnity, with total acceptance.

This was truly a tribal man, one who challenged no rulings, questioned no Book. The subtleties and questions he had were for a different medium than this.

I needed to confirm the expectations he might have, needed to do so in this alien place where I had no allies but Soby, no other friend.

Captain Ingers was determined to do his duty. "I have been asked—"

"Captain, attend the Colour!" I interrupted with the ritual line because I needed the help he could give. "I have no honour sword for this visit. Lend me your second."

He frowned, dark brows turning down, a pointing of infinity towards the bright blue chevrons. He took out his second sword and passed it to me, holding it horizontal in both hands.

I took it, put it through my belt. "I am greatly honoured, Dwar Ingers. You were speaking."

The fine face was composed at once. "They instructed me to bring you unfortunate news. This stone had stationing manoeuvres last night. Your friend, Parovin, went out to the Gragens of Io. He wanted true space, and all positions on Krombi and the other Angels were taken. There was a ship going, the *Pearl*. It was a chance and he took it. That is what I have been told to tell you. Station administration is sorry. The Towradji sends his regrets—"

"But did not come himself."

"No. He asked me to tell you."

And he watched my reaction, as if expecting me to demand that we commandeer a ship and follow *Pearl*.

"Soby Parovin was on *Crosa*," I said. "Please take me to what Nationals do remain from that flight."

"Station authorities must be consulted for that," Ingers said. "I must call the Towradji who presides here—"

"No, Captain Ingers. They forfeited that right when they left you to meet with me. The Towradji should have come himself to honour the Colour. You gave me your second sword. You will take me immediately to the nearest comp and give me clearance into station records. So I can be sure. Please. For the Colour."

I sensed that Dwar Ingers was pleased with my adherence to protocol, as if he had been warned that we made light of the Book honours and now found it otherwise. He turned and led the way to the door he had used before, touched it so it opened, and we stepped through into a short corridor, and from that into a large staging chamber fitted with pods and painted EVA suits. It was plainly an off-limits area. There was a small comp station in one wall. Ingers went to it and touched first the ident plate, then the keys.

"They will know almost at once."

"This is a Security area. Why did you bring me here?"

"The nearest, you said."

"But . . . " And then I understood the significance of what he had done, and of his earlier words. *They instructed me . . . That is what I have been told to tell you.*

"They will know almost at once," Ingers repeated, telling me something more by his few words, by his tight delivery of them.

"They've locked you into service, Dwar," I said, first-naming him, Captain to Captain, daring more than might be fitting for an honour companion, but sensing the intention behind what he had said and done.

"Records," the Ab'O said, hand on the plate, then stood aside.

I keyed in:

Information. National émigré. Soby Parovin.

There was a lapse of four seconds, then the display appeared, amber on black.

JT10BA4 Soby Parovin. *Crosa* 86.
Long Reach 601-B.

Despatched. Malasi-2. 2300-7-77AS554.
Storage A-2.

An alarm sounded somewhere beyond our chamber, and another somewhere beyond that. Dwar Ingers glanced at the door on the far side of the EVA room, then back to the screen.

I keyed another request, not wanting to use voice.

Enhancement: Malasi-2.

I expected to see a gragen ident for some lonely satellite in the Jovian mantle. What I saw chilled me, struck me like a harsh black tide, made me see not words on a screen but a window into overwhelming pain and despair. Stunned, speechless, I felt only rage, a fierce rage locked in numbing disbelief. It was too much to deal with. The tonson poles, the Spirit Malingee on the dark windy road, the flight to station, all that had been more real.

There were new alarms, the sounds of people running, shouts in other chambers and corridors near ours.

"Look!" I cried to Ingers, pointing at the display. "Look!"

But saw he knew.

"I do not need to look," he said with winter locked hard in his words, a frown of identical despair crushing the infinity on his brow into a burning wire.

"You knew!"

The infinity blazed. This was a man trapped by oaths, tribal loyalties, a man who had used the chance I provided.

I drew Ingers' second sword. "*Dhal* has fuel?"

"I can bring you home," he said, honour-bound but more than that, wanting this, choosing, driven by more than the honour of spacemen, led now by simple human decency.

Draw for Blue, Captain, I almost said, but knew I had to use the right words. And it had to be his continuing decision, his choice.

"Should I return your sword, Captain? I may need it but I will return it if you say."

He drew his first sword, and seemed easier having done so, as if the decision had freed him, was something made possible only by the set forms. He also produced a small laser baton, a very deadly thing in this sealed environment, certainly a forbidden thing except under the most extreme circumstances.

The door at the far end of the EVA chamber slid back. Five Kurdaitcha entered, saw our swords and drew theirs. Their eyes widened at the sight of Ingers' baton. One of the newcomers came forward. He had the sigil of a commander on his station fatigues and near it a blue hook like Cosiro had worn.

"Captain Ingers," he said. "Step aside, please, or you will be placed under station arrest."

The spaceman did not move. "You gave me a duty I did not want, Mora. You know me, but you insisted! Deal with this, you said. I am doing so. Your instructions have been superseded by a claim of Colour, a sword-duty to the Book which you know supersedes all other oaths. All others, you understand me?"

I would have spoken but left him to state what was probably more directly true here, the local currency which made the purchase.

The five Kurdaitcha—Chonsye Kurdaitcha, to make the important distinction—stared at us across the metal floor. The screen still showed the hateful knowledge Records had so innocently yielded up.

Mora was in charge, that much was clear, not the Towradji of this stone. Mora's actions would be reckoned here; it was his responsibility forever, passed on to family and tribe. Before he could order my death, *our* deaths—would Ingers serve so far?—I turned back to comp.

"Dwar, if Mora or any of his companions move against Blue, you will take the Colour," I said, and placed my palm on the touch-plate Ingers had used to bring up function. "Voice," I said. "Acknowledge ident: Blue Captain GPB/T-298. Tom Tyson."

The avengi stirred.

"Accepted," comp said, using voice function now, a calm neutral voice unruffled by what was happening. "Waiting."

"General broadcast," I said. "To Tell Records and Nation."

Mora took a step forward. "Captain!"

"The Blue Captain will be home on *Dhal* within the hour. All National emigration to the gragens is suspended indefinitely, pending an investigation of Krombi—"

"I warn you!"

"—Djuringa priority: Blue!"

"Listen!"

"Immediate transfer."

"Don't!"

"Execute!"

"We can blanket that!" Mora cried, but his face told me otherwise, that it was too late—here where the communications net for the planet lay spread out below us. The calculated slight of appointing Ingers to be my contact with station had gone this far amiss.

"Count your losses!" I said, and could barely speak the words, hold back the aching weight of emotion. "Save this and earn your tribe's gratitude. I'm sure the Chonsye people—do not know what their holy sons have done here."

A Kurdaitcha was furtively reaching into his robe; Ingers shifted his baton and the warrior stopped at once. I made myself continue.

"The world is waiting for an incident of this scale, for a Coloured Captain to die." My voice was shaking badly now, but I did not let myself think beyond the need to get free of Krombi, to get down the gravity well and carry the news. "S-Soby Parovin?" I made myself say it. "He is dead?"

Mora hesitated only a moment. "Yes."

"Show me the body."

"It is too late," he said. The Kurdaitcha swords remained steady, reminding us that Mora was weighing the worth of a single shot at the pressure wall, an environment accident on Krombi. "The malasi was added last night. Quick and painless. The bodies have been sealed in their ejection pods for disposal."

Disposal. Such a word, such an easy word. I stared at the man, feeling such an emptiness inside that should the wall go, if it came to that and Ingers would fire, the cold of space could never match it. "The world will learn of this."

"No," Mora said. "You will not do that. You will say nothing. Word has gone out. The Chonsye comsat has—let us say—been temporarily seconded by Kurdaitcha here at Krombi. It is above Long Reach, has lasers focused on The Stranded Man, on your friends there. Your ship, *Rynosseros*, is near Mider. We were prepared for the need to coerce, not over this, I admit, but we have taken the precautions. And if this is to be the way of it, then all seven Captains will go. Do you understand? Though I doubt that will be necessary: they will not believe you."

"Coming from me they would."

"No, Captain Tom. It is too big a thing. You know it is."

"Great Passage Book! Djuringa!"

"Still too big," Mora said. "But it will not come to that. We will stop you here."

Which was likely. Swords remained raised as calculations were made moment to moment. Only Ingers' baton had stopped them, and Ingers was Chonsye, a tribesman, while it was plain that Mora had full executive authority over the Towradji of this station. No doubt he was considering a space accident, a terrible misfortune, weighing the cost of pre-emptive deaths against trade reprisals and tribal, National and global censure. But such things could not begin to matter in the face of what filled my thoughts. "The ancient Assyrians moved entire peoples from their homelands into harsh desert so survival took all their energy. It was shrewd and effective. The Amerind tribes suffered the same fate: relocation, estrangement, neutralisation. But you chose the Nazi way. Active genocide!"

"No!" Mora said, watching the silent Ab'O beside me, one of those who had been sworn to secrecy, Kurdaitcha directive, who had brought so many émigrés up to die, whose craft and skill had been turned to such an end. "Not genocide! Not atrocity at all. You know nothing of Nepelle, ruler of the heavens. It's an equation, an atonement. A transformation. A Baiame ritual, part of a creation myth. We give life gifts to the Earth, dead stones which are the seeds, the children of the stars. Nothing is destroyed."

He may have believed what he said, but I doubted it, saw it instead as a strategy, an appeal to the beliefs and simple honesty of Dwar Ingers.

Ingers' voice was flat and hard, filled with bitter irony when he spoke. "Always the handy myth. Baiame giving his seed."

"Enough, Dwar!"

"Just a few sworn captains."

"Sworn, yes! So keep your silence! Captain Tom, your friend is dead, accept it! Emigration will stop for awhile. There will be investigations, questions, but who will believe? Profiles exist in comp for all the émigrés through Krombi, personality prints for message simulations. Anyone you name, your Soby Parovin, can be made to contradict you. Holoforms from far places. If necessary, our labs can work up an andromorph along his somatotype—we can send him home to refute your claims in person—"

"Mora, you miss the point. All emigration is ended. The other tribes will be asking you why. Your own Prince will ask."

You do not understand, Captain. *You* can be made to contradict you, don't you see? We can simulate *you*."

"Then, Mora, I am prepared to die here, to ask Captain Ingers to take us all. Following my transmission, that would provide some sort of evidence at least."

"Difficult, agreed, but the project will survive it. Harming Krombi will simply corroborate the story of an accident taking your life. We might even discredit you, mention sabotage."

"No!" I said, furious that Mora could use a word like "project," could turn the subject so easily from Soby and—how many? The numbers eluded me. How many through Krombi in a year: twenty thousand? Fifty?

"No," Dwar Ingers said, standing beside me, echoing me. "Kill this man and the Coloured Captains will know. Harm them and the spacemen will know. *All* the tribes. You will not survive this." And he put aside his sword, reached up, and turned down his collar, revealed his bridge comlink. "This has been transmitted to others of my order."

I felt a rush of gratitude for the spaceman. His loyalty to Blue, to the Book, to simple humanity, was startling, almost embarrassing in its fullness. He was simply a man who believed.

Mora had gone beyond fury, beyond any display of rage or threat. "What do we do?"

"What you do, Mora," I said, "is endorse my next directive!"

"You are not serious!"

I turned to comp, placed my hand on the plate once more.

"Blue Tyson," I said. "Djuringa priority. Access 601-B. Soby Parovin file. Store print at permanent, to be revoked only by my command. Give continuing broadcast status, priority variation and enhancement on songs. Sealed by order. Execute."

"Authorisation required, Krombi station," comp said.

"Continue recording. Mora?"

"Impossible!" Mora cried.

"You do it! You build your andromorph and give it Soby's print. You do that. But for now you raise his profile to active in a sealed leader file. You give it AI assist and let it go random in the system. Those songs go wide, clean and forever, you understand? You send them to God or I tell it all. Or you get our deaths, damn you, and the spacemen knowing."

"And you will not tell? You swear to that, Captain Tyson?"

"Provided emigration ends, I do. Not just through Krombi. All emigration. Use your Kurdaitcha status. Make them ask what has gone wrong. You swear and I will, before this Captain of Space. This man and—yes!—the young tribesman who guarded the spaceman's gate at Long Reach yesterday. Only while they live in true honour and as true spacemen. They are my witnesses for Blue in this, Mora, the keepers of my bond, do you hear me? This is my price and my warning. Swear to it all and endorse!"

"Agreed," Mora said. Again the lack of hesitation told me how much power he had, how much of this was his own enterprise.

"Swear to it then!"

"I swear," Mora said. He walked over and placed his palm on the plate. "Endorsed. Zer Mora Dhunmajira."

"Initiated," comp said in its calm, unaffected voice.

I turned to the spaceman beside me. "Dwar, please take me home."

On the flight back down the well, sitting alone in the empty salon (for not even Blue could get me onto Dwar's flight deck: the rulings of his brotherhood), I asked to have broadcast patched through to my chair, just in case.

Mora had kept the first part of his promise. Soby was already there.

"... came in early
For the shuttle bound for Krombi,
With his little bits of all the hopes there are.
Read the wanted ads and classifieds
For the high sky stones near Ceres,
And waited for his moment at the bar.

"Standing in the lobby
Was a lady fit for fever,
With Astani on her mother's side at least.
And she read him like a gypsy
And she told him like a demon,
Called him clod of earth
And image of the beast.

"And he's going,
Going to the Angels,
Going up to join the people in the skies.
And he's going,
Going to the Angels,
Going to sing them crazy right between the eyes."

Which was as much as I could stand before turning it off. By then we were deep in the well. Earth was "down" again, and the engines' roar was a more insistent song, urgent and blessedly distracting, great dragons of the night.

I watched Long Reach resolve below me, growing from a dish of earth-golds set with blue-white edges, to deep night, blurred now, gently, so I barely knew, by the memory of Soby Parovin.

The news of emigration ending had had the expected response. As *Dhal* settled on the runway, more than a late-night mank crew was waiting. The lights of Hindel were tellingly ablaze. By the field gates, a crowd of National and International officers, media crews and sightseers had gathered already, among them many angry, would-be émigrés.

Ingers unlocked the spaceman's gate in the linkmesh fence. We clasped hands and I made to return his second sword.

"No," he said. "I am your witness, Blue Tyson. Keep it for me."

"For your honour, Dwar."

"For yours, Blue Captain."

And we parted.

I met Beth on the road back to Clancy's. She waited in the chill night wind, her robe gathered close about her against the cold and the blowing dust. She opened it to take me within, and we stood in the road together in our warmth and shared emotion.

"What, Tom? What happened?"

"The Door has to be closed for awhile. That's all. Just for awhile. I can't say more, Beth. Accept that, please. I can't."

"I do. I do, Tom. What about Soby?"

"He's fine. He's happy. You'll be hearing his songs soon. The Towradji himself has taken an interest."

And we walked back to The Stranded Man.

The newsboard outside the door told it already, the early editions of *The Beach Gazette* and *The National* shouting the terrible accusations:

ANGELS OFF LIMITS!
BLUE CAPTAIN CLOSES SPACE DOOR
NATION COUNCIL FURIOUS
What World Leaders are Saying
EMIGRATION ENDS!
WORLD BARRED FROM SPACE BY BLUE CAPTAIN
International Outcry!

Seeing the headlines, Beth turned to me again. "What, Tom? Please."

"I can't tell you. I've sworn."

And I saw she was weeping, for Soby, for me, for something she sensed—the deep distress held in check, something of what was filling me. We stood in the dark road, Beth clinging to me, our tears merging as we held each other.

"Come inside," she said, needing more help now than she felt she could give, sensing the loss, the unnamed something, needing the magic of Clancy and his cats, the warm lights.

"I have to stay out here awhile."

"It's a lovely night," she said, misunderstanding, or pretending to, looking up. "We don't need that."

"We don't."

"Come in, Tom."

"No, Beth." I thought of the spacemen who might be there—who would always be there now in my memories—facing away from the windows, looking into their drinks and listening to the wind, serious forgetting men. "You go in. Wait for me. There'll be meteors soon. I want to watch them fall."

"He'll do well, Tom. He'll make us proud."

"Yes," I said. "He will."

And still she didn't leave. She stood watching me watch the night sky, so clear, so deep, so high.

"He'll burn brightly up there, won't he?" she said, the tears rolling down her cheeks.

She knew. Beth knew.

"He'll shine!" I said, and took her hand to keep her at my side.

Together we stood in the cold wind blowing down from the stars and waited for Soby to come home.

VANITIES

THE FIRST THING I DID WHEN I REACHED THE TATTAMORANO/ Crater Lake concession, after checking in at the Pier Hotel, was to go down to Full Moon Pier and watch them fishing for vanities.

It gave me time to think about Hal, to decide whether or not the young Ab'O would have taken his own life like that. The lake and the Piers, Full Moon especially, invited such silent contemplation. There were sixty or more men and women lined up at the rails, their buckets and pressure flasks beside them, their lines running down into the shifting gas just far enough, flickering with the mirrors that they use to lure the creatures. These fisherfolk, too, were quiet, or spoke in low murmurs. Their various stances told me it had been a slow morning, that no catches had been made yet.

You can always tell when someone has been fortunate. The anglers stand differently, and hold their lines with just that much more expectation. The vanities travel in groups; one success usually means others. The first catch pays for the week's fishing licence and accommodation; the rest are profit.

I moved among the waiting figures, now and then intruding on someone's private domain at the rail so I received hostile glances. When they saw my sailor's fatigues, my Nation and Colour patches, their hard looks softened somewhat; one or two even smiled. I was not a rival fisherman after all, just a sand-ship sailor here beside this famous Australian lake, enjoying the hot early morning sun and the wide views of the desert that hemmed in the small resort town.

"No luck?" I said to an old man. He was standing in one precious corner of the Pier, his place marked out by canisters and rods and a bucket of the small square baiting mirrors.

"Nah!" he answered, and spat into the gas. It seethed and roiled about the timbers of the Pier, thick yellow eddies that hid the bottom and dulled the light reflected from the squares of glass. "They're out in the middle somewhere. Or over there." He nodded in the direction of the nearest sacred beach: the Quni precinct. "Probably an Ab'O funeral. Them and their mirror suits. Probably won't be a catch for days now; an' me takin' months to save for a licence!"

I looked along the low curving shoreline of the lake to where the gas lapped and twisted in a restless meniscus as it met the sand. But on the three flag-poles at the sacred beach there were no flags raised to show an Ab'O had gone into the gas (not that Hal's death would be "flagged"). The poles stood empty; the beach deserted. The door of the large stone reliquary was shut and locked.

But I stood there watching the lake just the same, though this time the quiet of Full Moon did nothing to ease my mind. Mita's letter had specified a time and place—the lobby of the Pier Hotel—but there had been no sign of the Ab'O girl, let alone her twin brother, Hal.

Obviously a lot had happened in the week it had taken her letter to reach me at the coast, and for me to make the three-day journey into the desert. That worried me. There could be no doubting that I would come. It was more than Mita's claim on my friendship with her late uncle; it was that one line, following the news that a tribal crime had made Hal decide to take his life: "He has already bought a Wagiri suit from Anthony Wessex."

Anthony Wessex. Not quite my friend and almost a ghoul. And a black marketeer, dealing in tribal relics. Suits of lights.

Mita had known that news would bring me to Crater Lake.

A cry went up half-way down the Pier. A woman had made a catch and was now winding it in.

I watched, fascinated as always, as the prize appeared—the strange starfish-shaped creature closed like a fist around the mirror square, concealing it completely. As it came out of the gas, the dying vanity was already beginning to petrify in the air, becoming a hard vitrophyric lump glinting briefly in the light as the change took place.

Amid shouts and congratulations from her neighbours, the woman cut the violet-green siliceous ball from her line and placed it in her storage canister. It was a fair-sized creature and a perfect enclosure; none of the mirror showed. She would get a good price for it from any gallery assayer.

I left the Pier and went down the stone steps onto the sand. I moved around the lake, past the empty flag-poles and the locked reliquary, stopping to peer through the dusty panes of amber glass in the door to see the dim shapes of the vanitied Ab'Os standing in the gloom. There was a Niuginian caretaker who came out of his little shack further up the shore to see who was trespassing, but he just waved me on when he saw the patches on my jacket. Not a word was said between us.

I was on my way back to the hotel to see if Mita or Hal had appeared when I noticed the Crater Lake Gallery, still closed at this early hour. I inspected the eight vanities Anthony Wessex had on show in the windows. All were minor specimens and overpriced, none as splendid as that caught by the woman on the Pier. My premonition that Tony was involved in something more than a possible suicide was stronger than ever.

No-one was waiting for me back at the hotel, so I sat in one of the big leather chairs in the lobby and watched the people coming in off the street. After forty minutes of skimming magazines and looking up whenever the doors opened, a young Indonesian girl in a red dress entered. It was Bess, Mita's friend. She saw me and hurried over.

"Captain Tyson!" Tears were already forming in her large brown eyes.

"Where are they, Bess?"

She shook her head. "Hal is gone, I fear. Yesterday. Mita is hiding. I am very worried. I looked for you earlier."

"I was down on Full Moon," I said. "I wanted to see the Quni reliquary."

"Hal could be there, yes?"

"I don't know. The place is locked up. I can't tell. There's a Quni immersion tomorrow. If Hal has gone into the gas, we may know then. But, Bess, I've got to see Mita. It's important that I talk to her."

Tears rolled down Bess's cheeks. "She's hiding. I don't know where. She won't show herself now."

"Why not? What was Hal's crime? What made him do it?"

Bess did not answer, and I realised that the twins had not told her. I suspected it was fornication or adultery, or possibly incest, which could explain Mita's caution, and that Hal had suicided rather than endure being sung to death for it. His punishment—well, perhaps he had chosen wisely. As an outcast, he died in shame, hunted and killed from within by Ab'O mind-fighters. By entering the lake, smothered by the gas and the vanities, he became a priceless Stone Man, a curious and public insult to his tribe, hated but revered; an artefact worth a fortune on the world markets—if ever it reached them.

If Hal had suicided, *if* he were in the reliquary, would the Quni Clever Men admit to it? It was unlikely. But at least we might learn if there had been an anonymous transformation recently; all the Stone Men were named and dated. And a recent annealing would show.

For, according to Mita's letter, Hal had found himself a suit of lights.

I sent Bess to look for Mita, and went down to the Crater Lake Gallery.

Crater Lake is a vast funerary precinct, a necropolis on all but the one small section of strand abutting the National resort town of Crater Lake, with its fashionable hotels and villas, its shopping plazas, galleries and two long Piers.

Dotted along the gentle beaches all around the lake are the tribal reliquaries, over a hundred and twenty of them; each building a large sandstone block with narrow sky-lights and a single amberpaned door; each one fronted by its three flag-poles, its small funerary jetty reaching out into the gas on spindly legs, and usually a shanty with a caretaker like the old Niuginian I had seen.

When an Ab'O Clever Man dies, if he deserves the honour, he is fitted out in his suit of leather sewn with tiny mirrors, carried out on to the jetty, and lowered into the gas just far enough for the hot desert sun to set him flashing. The vanities come, sooner or later; the corpse is brought forth as a Stone Man and placed in the tribal reliquary.

That Hal had gone into the gas as a taboobreaker and an outcast was an insult of a very special kind. The Stone Men were sacred, each one the sign of a blessed spirit. This was sacrilege *and* heresy.

It has happened before. Forsaken lovers, dying elders, even Nationals wanting something of the glory reserved for the Clever Men, have plunged from one of the Piers. Sometimes, when the gas is clearer, you can see their corpses on the bottom, sad forsaken shapes transformed by nothing but death itself. Rarely do they become Stone Men, though a few have fitted mirrors to their garments in imitation of the gorgeous mirror suits worn by the tribal mystics.

But Hal had gone further, departing from the strict training of his people. How he had heard of Anthony Wessex's black market operations, his buying up the unvanitied mirror suits of the extinct Wagiri, was a mystery. I had heard the tales but had preferred not to believe them. After all, Tony, my not-quite-friend, was reckless, but his life was in Crater Lake. He could not afford to be caught out and censured by the tribes.

Tony was serving a couple of Niuginian tourists when I entered, looking as urbane as ever in his maroon Maiquin fatigues, white shirt and soft black boots, his steel-grey hair cropped close to his head, making his fine features more handsome than ever. His face lit up when he saw me, and he signed that he would be with me in a moment.

I went and studied a large framed wall-map of the Tattamorano concession, and wondered how much he would tell me. He knew Hal and Mita; he would probably know why Hal had gone into the gas, and why his sister was in hiding. He might even talk black-market with me, though I doubted he would say much. I was a State of Nation officer after all.

I let my gaze wander about the vitrine displays, then located the door to his Special Room, as Tony called it. In that inner sanctum, I had once seen six prime vanities on sale at ridiculous prices, reserved for the special buyers of curiosa who came to Crater Lake—the ones who wanted something extra.

Though everything about Tony Wessex bespoke charm and elegance, he was fascinated by teratology. The six balls of vitrophyre aggregate had looked innocent enough, but each was one of his "grotesques." One, the size of a melon, was said to contain a human hand. Tony had sewn and fitted the mirror glove himself. Another held a foetus. What the rest had closeted at their centres, Tony wouldn't say. It was the vitreous ball itself that mattered, he argued; he had simply added mystery to the mysterious.

I moved on to one of the display cases and stared down at the vanity on the turquoise velvet display mat. I thought of the small square of mirror buried at its heart, and how it had reflected the creature's tiny death. I could still make out the hairline fissures where the petals of its arms had closed like a flower about that final image of itself. Every night in Crater Lake, moths were drawn by lantern flames to such moments of fatal rapture, and we barely noticed.

But after my morning at the Piers, after looking in at the Ab'O dead at the reliquary, it wasn't hard to let this small closed stone flower do more than the moths could: to suggest the abstractions of love and desire, of power, beauty and need, the patterns of ego and shadow that consumed us all. The hard part was admitting to the quests as quests, giving them their correct importance in our dealings with others, recognising them for what they were—as in moths around a flame, or vanities spinning in to a final act of self-worship, or people fishing on a pier. The hardest part was knowing what they meant from person to person.

Like Hal's suicide. Not the fact that he had done it, but why it had no longer mattered to him that he had. And why as a heretic Stone Man, compounding the crime?

The first "why" was Hal and Mita's secret. The second was Tony's.

The Niuginians left the Gallery; Tony came over and shook my hand.

"Tom! Beloved! Welcome, welcome! How's *Rynosseros*! How's the crew?"

"Hello, Tony. Where are Hal and Mita? They wrote to me."

"Ah, a discerning buyer. Straight to the point. Let's close shop and take in the air. We can haggle at the lake."

Five minutes later we were walking out on Full Moon. The atmosphere had changed. There had been two more catches and an air of excitement prevailed; it had become a good morning. Some of these people would be able to renew their licences for another week.

Tony pointed out a rather statuesque woman in beige sand-robes and imported Clové sunglasses. She had two valets with her, nervous-looking young men in light desert suits and caps, but only the woman had a line dangling down into the gas, with a baiting mirror twinkling and flashing as it caught the sun.

"That's Cara Bressenden," Tony said. "The Offshore Ten heiress from Broome. She's spent six weekends here trying to make a catch herself."

"Crater Lake has a way of making people dedicated, Tony. Look at you."

"Oh, but she's a special case, Tom." He looked about him, became conspiratorial. "Her baiting mirror is one-sided. It's backed with a photograph of herself. She's looking for a receptacle. But shh! Not a word, eh?"

I smiled. "I'm convinced no-one knows who's going to be immortalised, Tony."

"True," he said. "Look at poor Machiavelli."

"Or Van Gogh."

"Look at Hal."

"Why do you say that?" We had reached the end and were retracing our steps back into town.

"He came into the Gallery four days ago. Wanted to know about the gas and the vanities. Signed a few documents."

"What sort of documents, Tony?"

"Permission notes. Releases. I let him have a suit of lights. I've picked up a few."

"Tony!"

"Well, he was going to kill himself anyway, Tom. He was being sung to death. The Quni Clever Men were coming for him."

"Where's Hal now?"

Tony Wessex looked defensive. "Where do you think? Down at the Quni reliquary."

"The Stone Men belong to the tribes."

"Not this one, Tom. They may have retrieved the body but I own it. I'm filing claim."

"For heaven's sake! This will cause an Incident. Crater Lake belongs to the Princes—"

"Except for the part here."

"So?"

Tony Wessex laughed. "Hal didn't go into the gas from the Quni pier. That was part of our deal for the suit. He went off Full Moon."

"What!"

"The Quni dragged for him that night, took him into their reliquary, then claimed he went off their pier."

"But you can prove he went from here."

"Recorded the whole thing. Copies have gone to Twilight Beach and Adelaide. Hal gets his revenge. I get my Stone Man. The Quni are reprimanded and embarrassed."

"What happens to Hal's mummy?"

Tony gave his brilliant smile. "I may sell it back to one of the tribes for tribal favours. At a very high price."

"More of your Specials."

"It may go to one of the coastal museums. Or I'll sell it back to the Quni. For permission to build my own pier on their land. Think of it, Tom! Wessex Pier. I'll influence the world market, get rights to enter the lake in a pressure suit. I'll take my mirrors out into the centre."

I stared at Tony in wonder, unable to believe that he intended even a part of what he said.

"Tony, they'll kill you for this. You'll go into the gas yourself. Without mirrors." Then the truth occurred to me. "But you want an Incident. You want the Accord broken."

"You don't live here, Tom. The tribes don't use a fraction of what they own. They're locked up in rules and rituals, all those protocols. I'm talking about *our* ancient rights. We built this land."

I watched Tony's eyes. This was my tenth trip to this sacred domain in the inner desert. What did I know about land rights and legal entitlements? Or Anthony Wessex, for that matter? My teratophile was more of a mystery than he had ever been in our fond but occasional acquaintance.

For all I knew, this commitment to advancing the National cause—as wrong as it sounded coming from Tony's well-groomed, unsullied form—may have been the face of the real man, a large part of his reason for staying in Crater Lake and subsidising so many of the resort facilities. Or it may have been the indulgence of a man out of touch with reality. I smiled wryly at my svelte entrepreneur, my man with a mission.

"Help me in this, Tom," he said, as we reached the door of the Gallery again. "Help me do what Council won't. Use Blue to make this as big as we can get it."

"It's not the way, Tony."

"Not the way!" he cried. "It's never the way! When will you Captains do something? When will you, Tom?"

"Tony—"

"So, you've championed tangentals, closed down emigration though you won't say why. But what else? Mostly it's the diplomacy circuit for the lot of you: receiving benefices, representing Council in the tribal centres. But what have you really done for Nation?"

"The circumstances which make us special also limit us. You know that."

He shook his head, looked off down the street towards the Piers while he calmed himself. Finally he smiled, placed a well-manicured hand on the door jamb. "Forgiven?"

"Am I?"

"Always."

"Where's Mita, Tony?"

He shrugged. "I really don't know. You can look in the Special Room if you like."

"Or in where you store those Wagiri suits?"

The bonhomie flickered behind the eyes but held. Once again he had probably reminded himself that he liked me.

"Less to aid my ghoulishness, Tom, than to provide a weapon against the Clever Men. This land does not belong to the tribes. If I hear from Mita I'll send her to you. See you at the ceremony tomorrow."

The next morning, I walked down to the Quni beach. I went through the lines of tourists held back by the trespass warnings and by two Ab'O youths. These young men carried ritual woomeras but were spearless, though they wore the kitanas favoured by most of the tribes. They gave me cold looks but let me pass; I had assisted the Quni several times, and was known to them by the mark-signs I wore.

There was a flag on the furthest pole now—yellow to mark the beginning of the transformation. The door of the reliquary was open, and a bonfire, tended by a handful of boys, had been lit at the far end of the Quni section of beach.

I was just in time. The end of the funerary pier was a dazzle of light from a hundred Clever Men in their suits of lights, men gathered from the many tribes who revered the Stone Man transformation and had a reliquary at Crater Lake, or shared such a precinct with blood-related tribes.

I shaded my eyes against the dazzle and moved closer. All along the Quni strand stood the tribal menfolk with their sheathed kitanas over their backs and holding war boomerangs and spears. A didgeridoo was droning on in the morning silence, played by a man sitting by the open door of the reliquary. Apart from among the tourists, there was not a woman to be seen. As much as Ab'O society had changed over the years, it was still vigorously patriarchal in the matter of burial honours.

At the end of the jetty, the sling holding the dead Clever Man, Buyundar, was being lowered into the gas for the first stage of the annealing. Later in the day he would be turned in the sling, and again, and then again, until the "enclosing" of the body was complete.

Sometimes it happened quickly, the vanities swarming to clutch at the lozenges of reflecting glass sewn to the leather. Often it took days for the annealing to be done, before, the body could be lifted out for the vitrification itself.

I watched the immersion, then walked by the reliquary door, pretending to be interested in the didgeridoo player. By moving my eyes slightly, I could see down the long stone hall. There were at least sixty Stone Men in the Quni vault, vaguely human shapes standing in the gloom, arranged in order of succession. Hal would not be in those rows.

I moved around the man droning down his ancient instrument and studied the other side of the crypt.

There was Hal, the only figure unlabelled, and one still showing the violet-green, high vitreous gloss of a recent annealing.

The Quni had been careful. No wonder they had been quick to drag for Hal's body. Apart from their natural sensitivity to public knowledge of sacrilege, there was the added incentive that this was the first violation.

I immediately thought of Tony Wessex and shook my head. Then I had the sense to realise I'd been staring into the hall, and turned away in time to see three young warriors hurrying up the beach towards me. They carried the ornate woomeras of the Unseen Spears, and wore the sersifans of the tribal bodyguard. Their leader wore a leather fighting suit, unadorned as yet—an apprentice Clever Man.

As they came within talking distance, his gaze flicked over my fatigues and identified the State of Nation patches and mark-signs that allowed my presence. He assessed me coolly for a moment, then beckoned me away, raising his woomera as if to menace me with the invisible spear it was meant to carry.

I nodded acknowledgment and walked back along the beach.

When Tony met me around noon, the second flag had still not gone up. The body hung in its sling just below the surface of the gas, twinkling amid the eddies.

No vanities had come. All along the funerary beach, the Quni tribesmen waited in the hot sun. Even the fisherfolk on Full Moon and New Moon watched, their lines virtually untended. Only the lone didgeridoo player broke the silence, making the urgent monotone that one forgot to notice until the rhythm stopped for a few minutes. After "first flag" they rotated players often, in the belief that a blessed player could summon the vanities.

Tony came up to me and smiled when he saw the other two flag-poles empty. "Buyundar's not doing too well."

"It's been a long morning," I agreed, then added: "Hal is in there. No sign of his sister yet?"

"Not at the Gallery, Tom. I'd say she won't appear till after the Convocation. That fornication charge is probably not just a planned marriage breach. I think it was incest, a very serious crime with the Quni bloodlines diluting so quickly. It explains the agitation."

"Do you know the story of Pandora, Tony? Or do you prefer the myth of Jason and the Dragon's Teeth?"

Tony laughed, but before he could answer, a great shout went up from the beach, echoed by the eager fisherfolk on the Piers.

The red flag was rising on its pole; the annealing had begun. Buyunder was on his way.

That evening I had dinner with Bess and Tony on the terrace at Reginaldo's. It was a warm night and the lake was very still. The town Piers were two long fingers of light thrusting out into the darkness. The tribal precincts were part of that blackness too, with only an occasional ghost-light glimmering atop its post here and there to warn off evil spirits. Down on the Quni beach, the bonfire continued to burn, and the didgeridoo made its earnest drone as it had all day.

We sat under the paper lanterns, with one of Tony's linkboys on watch at the end of the terrace. Neither Bess nor Tony had been able to learn of Mita's whereabouts, which made me feel more than ever that Tony had her sequestered somewhere. I didn't raise the point; if that were the case then she was safe. With Tony's connections in the town, he would do a far better job of protecting her than I could. I only wished he would ease Bess's mind on the matter.

One subject I did raise when the Indonesian girl had gone was the existence of the Wagiri suits, but Tony put me off, saying he had given his word to protect his sources.

"What does it matter, Tom?" he said. "I could have had a suit made myself and given it to Hal. No-one's going to break open a Stone Man to see if he's wearing a legitimate tribal suit."

"They might, Tony. You're already driving them to extremes."

"I doubt it. The vanities are meant to be drawn by a worthy spirit, not by the mirrors. But tomorrow we'll see. I've lodged my claim for Hal, evidence and all—"

"What!"

"The Quni Prince has called a Convocation—with National observers. I'd like you to be one, Tom. You're impartial. Help me make a case for National law over tribal law. Let's redefine the Accord!"

"What if neither side backs down?"

"You said it yourself. I'll raise up an army of heretic Stone Men. My mute impassive Dragon's Teeth. I'll make the tribes so nervous about their anonymous mummies that the immersions will be cheapened, desanctified. Crater Lake will be tainted. I love the irony of it. The heretic outcast Wagiri coming back to help other outcasts claim their own. Finding vindication."

I smiled at his madness, at both the sophistication and the naivety of it. "They'll kill you first."

"Oh no, Tom. No. I'll have fifty paid soldiers here by morning. A carefully chosen bodyguard: Niuginians, Africans, Islanders—all with tribal kin of their own. The Ab'Os harm one of them and there'll be blood-feuds in Crater Lake for years. There'll be no end to it. Imagine: night raids on reliquaries, piers burnt, immersions spoilt. I'll have Crater Lake. We'll get it back."

"Not this way, Tony. Not like this."

"Yes, Tom. The only way that matters."

We parted then, Tony heading off to his villa, escorted by four armed linkboys. I sat watching the moths peppering the terrace lanterns with their deaths, then went to my room. I fell asleep with the lone didgeridoo calling to the waiting vanities in the lake, thinking of Hal and the Wagiri suits and the rebel Stone Men.

By late morning, Buyundar's progress into the spirit world was temporarily forgotten in the face of Convocation. There were at least four hundred Quni on the beach, plus large contingents from many other tribes. Tourists crowded the Crater Lake Piers and lined the promenade walls, three or four deep. National media teams recorded proceedings from the terraces of the closer hotels and palazzos; their reporters roamed the beach area as close as they dared, feeling nervous despite their mark-signs.

The sound of didgeridoos, rhythm sticks and bullroarers gave an immanence to the scene, an insistent fretful edge. Clever Men flashed in the hot sunlight, making an angry crackling dazzle that forced the camera crews to use filters. A hundred Unseen Spears guarded the door to the Quni reliquary: a token warning-off since Hal's mummy would be brought out, displayed, and—if it could happen (there was no knowing either way)—turned over to the National officers representing the Crater Lake authorities, who in turn represented Anthony Wessex, culprit, provocateur, Pandora or Narcissus or Loki in all this. Better yet, Tony Wessex the Trickster, the Joker, the most clever of Clever Men.

I felt there would be violence, that it could not be otherwise. I guessed many felt it, yet pretended the laws would be observed. But you cannot force a people to debase themselves with signed documents. The Quni Prince would not permit it, certainly his Clever Men could not.

But everyone *was* pretending, and that was strangest of all. The camera crews were there as if covering a routine Convocation; the tourists, dangling their lines into the gas or lining the stone walls and shading their eyes from the harsh play of light, were enjoying a unique diversion, nothing more. Many of them needed commentators and tour guides to tell them how important this was. It was bizarre to see.

Even Tony, standing with his solicitors and friends on Full Moon, was acting as if nothing could happen. I noticed the twitch of a smile at the corners of his mouth; he was enjoying his private joke too openly, I thought, or some other level of it. I appreciated then what a dangerous man he was.

The dronings stopped. Six tribesmen were carrying Hal's mummy from the reliquary, taking the heavy dark shape over to Tony's representatives. Everything was going to plan.

But suddenly there was a disturbance to my right, near the trespass signs and the steps leading down to the Quni beach. An Ab'O in street fatigues was rushing out to the assembled Clever Men and the group handling the Stone Man.

It was Hal.

Cries went up, angry shouts. I jumped down onto the beach and rushed after him. I could hear Hal shouting at the Clever Men, while the Unseen Spears moved in from the reliquary doorway, woomeras raised.

Finally I was close enough to hear his words. He was pointing to the Stone Man on the bier, demanding that it be broken open—an unprecedented act, despite the talk about grave-robbers and reliquaries being defiled that were the ever-present rumours in Crater Lake. There was confusion, an uneasy hostile muttering from the massed tribesmen.

For a man working towards his own death, Hal's timing was perfect. He knew he would be dead at any moment, but that in the confusion he still had an advantage measured in seconds. He snatched a short iron club from his pocket and brought it down sharply on the head of the Stone Man, repeated the action four times.

The annealing cracked and fell away, revealing the face of his sister, Mita. There had been sacrilege, public humiliation, and now travesty: a suicide pact, a woman! A debasement of all Clever Men, all tribes.

Things happened quickly then. The Unseen Spears had their throwing sticks already raised; as a single man they flung their arms forward. The mind-spears killed Hal on the spot, faster than being sung, faster than any other mind-death I had seen, probably faster than a bullet or sword-thrust. He collapsed on the sand, almost on top of his sister in a last demonstration of their crime. Their other crime.

Tony's mercenaries received a signal and took a step forward to claim the body of the false Stone Man, but a thousand kitanas sang from their scabbards and the hired fighters stopped. Obviously Tony had briefed his men on this, for they did not press the claim. They turned and trudged back up the beach, followed by the news teams and the National observers.

The damage had been done. Tony would pursue his claim through the courts and would win. On paper. He might even get his pier, though knowing the tribes I doubted it. When I found him on Full Moon, he was smiling, safe among his group of friends and his legal people.

Cara Bressenden had made her catch on this momentous morning as well, a multiple enclosure, and was just then showing Tony the many-vanitied lump she was holding with both hands, announcing to all who would listen that her picture was enclosed in it.

"Prove it!" Tony said, then laughed too loudly, enjoying the poor woman's dilemma.

When the heiress had stalked off in a fury, he saw me and indicated the milling Ab'Os still in Convocation on the beach; the flashing Clever Men arguing in loud voices. "Well, Tom?"

"Nothing was learned here today, Tony. Not a damn thing! And you *are* a ghoul. You don't care what you use."

"This is important, Tom."

"Is it? Is it really? What the tribes and Nation hold between them is the illusion—the trappings—of something. A viable coexistence. A modus vivendi. All you have done is pierce that; drawn attention to how thin and how necessary—how inevitable—that illusion is. It'll take time to undo the harm, for them to search their laws and traditions to excuse the sacrilege, a handy myth, whatever, so they can live with themselves. We may lose Crater Lake for awhile, or the Piers at least. It may take years, Tony, but things will settle again. Because we want them to."

And I turned and left Full Moon.

It took far less time than that. Tony's army of Stone Men never did appear to challenge the Accord.

When, two months later, I learned of Tony's death, I was not surprised. His corpse had been found in the Special Room of his gallery, the actual cause of death unknown. But his heart had been cut out afterwards, and when the package came in the mail and was brought to me in my room at the Gaza, I did not need to open it.

I only wondered how many of the creatures it had taken.

A Dragon Between His Fingers

When he was 10, Shannon inherited a flawed Toby dough-beast from his uncle and raised a quarter-jack upon it.

The Toby was an old animal, its sides stained yellow from the baths, and feeble with age, but Shannon had tried and succeeded. For almost a minute, peering between the third and smallest fingers of his right hand, he had seen a quarter-jack, a dragon called a sirrush.

"It was the Dragon of Babylon," he told his father afterwards, who told Ben Scarbo, who later, years later, an hour out of Massi-Kallinga, told me because of the cargo we were carrying. After what had happened at Heart-and-Hand, discovering the extent of my gift as a sensitive, it was simply one more amazing thing to learn.

I went to where Shannon was tending the helm and, judging my time, carefully mentioned what Scarbo had told me.

"I never did it again," Shannon said, and seemed glad for the chance to discuss it. No doubt our cargo was on his mind.

"But once is enough, eh?"

"You never forget it, Tom. You never can. I saw my dragon. It made me seek out Dan."

Shannon told me how he and Dan had spent the following

summer with the Toby, trying to raise dragons upon it, quarter-jacks and half-jacks, without success—two young boys working their hardest to develop the gift of dragon-sight. The dough-beast died soon afterwards, its DNA coded short-term.

Later, as a young man, Shannon had captained a sand-ship named *Sirrush* in memory of his dragon, a light, very fast 60-foot courier vessel which he lost to Timmsmen pirates on the desert outside Wani two years before he joined *Rynosseros*.

I knew of that *Sirrush* and how the relentless Timmsmen had driven her into the sand and taken her, but Scarbo's news of him raising aspect on the Toby as a boy had come as a surprise. However random and undeveloped it might be, Shannon had the gift. He was sighted.

My own reasons aside, it was just as well that I knew. We were ferrying three dough-beasts from the Massi-Kallinga vats out to You-Guess-What. They stood in long wooden pens on the deck, their four-legged, grey potato bodies motionless, little more than passive, omnivorous life-support mechanisms for their marvellous, overdeveloped hind-brains, with sufficient autonomic functions to ensure life but not even let them feed themselves properly. Without tribal jackmen aboard, young Hammon had the job of shovelling gruel into those slack maws twice a day. In return, the creatures gave some of us dragons—or, rather, could do so now that we were lucky enough to be this close to them.

Shannon had seen a sirrush, and in the time we had sailed together, we had never come close enough to a Toby for Shannon to betray his secret. Most sighted people discussed the gift if they had it, just as I had recently acknowledged my own sensitivity to the haldanes. But Shannon had lost a ship, a young man's first freehold vessel, a small charvi but his alone. The past intruded too much.

Now I knew about that past and was glad. Envious too. More curious than ever because mentalism was involved, something akin to what gave me my small part of the heroes.

Shannon had seen his sirrush. Scarbo had once seen a manticore, a billong and two of the higher bunyips. Stare as I might through one bifurcation of fingers after another, hand by hand, I saw only the blunt hippopotamus lumps of grey flesh mindlessly staring out at the desert as we ran along the Great Arunta Road. I had always accepted that I didn't have the gift, but knew as well that I would always need to prove that I didn't, that I would keep trying, especially now that I had seen hero shapes, vital parts of the same universe of mind.

The cargo troubled Shannon. He kept to the poop, alert for raiders even when it wasn't his watch. Timms and his band of highwaymen would do anything to secure newly made dough-beasts to sell back to the Ab'Os for their corroborees. They would even take on an armed and escorted ship like *Rynosseros* and a fighting crew to get such a prize. Full-jack dough-beasts took years to produce, and these three were primes, just the thing to touch our reptilian memories and bring forth Quetzalcoatl, the Plumed Serpent of the Aztecs, or Kukulcan of the Mayans, or Tiamat, the Chiaos and Lungs, or the great Rainbow Serpent itself.

We all felt Timms would try, or one of his highwayman colleagues, The Eagle Cleland Buchanan or the notorious Captain Ha-Ha. That is why we ran in a W battle formation with escorts: two 80-foot tribal sand-ships ahead, *Dancing Man* and *Attapa*, and two 90-foot National vessels behind, *Bellona* under Grey Ridley, and Radkin's *Ozymandis*. The hot late-morning sky was bright with our kites straining out ahead on taut cables, a dry blistering tailwind keeping up hopes for a three-hour journey.

I finished helping Scarbo trim a lazy parafoil, then returned to the poop, partly to check the instruments but also to see how Shannon was faring.

"You could have laid over, Rob," I said, mentioning it again.

Shannon's eyes were focused on the desert ahead. There was strong emotion in them, possibly anger, relief as well, I hoped.

"I'm okay, Tom. Really. It gives me a chance to practise. Three primes. I'm bound to see something." And he smiled.

"Good. Teach me how."

"In a way, you're lucky you don't see them. You've heard Ben. Once you do, you've always got a hand stuck in front of your face when a Toby's around. You keep hoping. Ben knew about it; I don't know how long I could've kept it from the rest of you. Not with this." He nodded to where the pens were.

"I envy you all the same."

"No, it's a mixed blessing, seeing the dragons. You love them because you know them somehow, like the recognition you felt around Anna Kemp. They're atavisms. What I saw as a boy was that beautiful, that familiar. Dan felt the same. It was like a drug—you had to keep doing it. Real but not real. We've left that behind."

"Well, after Heart-and-Hand it's like wetting your finger and trying to make a wine-glass sing. I have to keep trying too now. I'd like to see a sirrush." Because it brought me close to something crucial, I didn't need to add.

"Do what I used to do. Go down to the pens and stand up close. That's how Dan saw his first quarter-jack, saw his full-jack basilisk."

"The one that almost killed him? Ben mentioned that too."

"It was after our Toby died. My uncle took us to the vats. Dan tried to raise aspect while our backs were turned. He said he saw a basilisk. He cried it out to us before his mind said to die. My uncle told me that was how the basilisk template worked. Death-look. Dan was lucky. He was hospitalised for months. But it changed him; he was never the same."

"I'll go find a sirrush," I said.

Shannon smiled. "Call me if you do."

I saw nothing, of course. Just the blunt heads, the low thick bodies. And crouching there on the deck before the pens, I had the usual mix of doubts and acceptance, felt more urgency and fascination now after what had happened at Arredeni's tower and with Anna at Twilight Beach, but still had an underlying sense that it couldn't be as compelling as Shannon described.

The rationale wasn't hard to accept at all. It was easy to concede that our evolution from reptiles into mammals had left us with powerful reptilian memories, that as a race humanity had always had a predilection for dragons. They were a fundamental part of its race consciousness.

It was nothing as simple as remembering Tyrannosaurus Rex. That deep psychic stratum was filtered through the subconscious, through symbols and imagination, through analogs, cultural correlatives, mammalian taint and projection. It was diluted, distorted, but it was there—amplified and focused out of the mammalian bodyfield by the dough-beasts, given as a coherent signal back from their hypertrophied hind-brains, perceived by the receiving human mind through the ridiculously-simple, Kirlian intensifying hand-lattice.

At last, the human race could see its dragons, its reptile beginnings, its unhuman forbears. The deepest, most primordial archetypes had forms at last, recognisable, familiar forms. When the tampering from other conditioning strata was complete, there was a bestiary to encompass our wildest dreams, to explain our deepest fears—so the sighted ones assured the rest of us. A heraldry for the Ab'O Princes and the world at large, though all the exported Tobys were neuters and had short-term genetic codings. Thus the Ab'Os kept the monopoly, sold dragons to the world.

But like the wine-glass singing, like my encounter with the haldanes, however tenuous, what I knew and what I felt were at odds. I kept seeing the Tobys as dream amplifiers, as overrated man-made image transmitters and nothing more, as something of a hoax. Though it didn't look like it, there was probably reptile DNA in their genetic make-up, hence the bias towards dragonism. A lot of National scientists believed that, though they had never had Shannon's luck—a geneticist uncle, accepted by the tribal makens, who had once brought home a flawed dough-beast instead of destroying it outright.

"No luck?"

I looked up to see Shannon standing over me. He had been relieved at the helm by Strengi.

"Not a scale, Rob. You?"

"Not a scale."

We walked together back to the quarterdeck and shared the watch with Strengi, making ship-talk and watching the desert and the escort fleet spread out across the Road around us.

It was doubly hard for Shannon. Not only were the dough-beasts there, in plain sight or back under the tarpaulins draped over the cages to keep off the sun, but we were watching for Timms, the one who had taken *Sirrush*. Shannon had often told us of his fateful meeting with the brigand, of how Timms, in his air-cooled, augmented, bronze and leather talos suit, eyes burning through the eye-slit of his great helmet, had boarded *Sirrush* and announced that he would spare the crew, even though they had defied him and tried to flee.

I would have defied him too. I imagined losing my own ship to him, having her taken from me to be used as a pirate vessel or a blockade runner in the wars between the Princes. My thoughts went back to the ship-lotteries at Cyrimiri, to the day I had won *Rynosseros* and first saw the hull being lifted out of the storage cradle by the moving gantry, then carried to the chandler's yard where I had an old battered travel platform rented from Captain Albert and a dozen cast-off kites borrowed from Red Lucas. I remembered her being lowered to the housing and locked to the table, getting wheels again, legs for the desert Roads. It led me back to Rob's loss in a way that kept me silent, that made me watch for Timms and hope—for reasons other than the safety of our cargo—that he wouldn't come. But that he would as well.

It was an added difficulty having the Emmened mission commander aboard *Rynosseros* for this first part of the journey, here to ensure that the beasts reached his people safely. Sos Wain Chrisos stood at the bow, a short, self-confident Ab'O in dark fighting leathers who seemed completely unaware that his strength of will translated as arrogance. I had avoided him since our disagreement over mission strategies at Massi-Kallinga, but now I went forward to make my peace with the man.

"Ah, Captain Tom! Please!" he said, and seemed conciliatory enough. "We are making good time."

"We are indeed, Chrisos," I said, joining him at the rail.

"You still fear this highwayman?"

"Timms is clever. These Tobys are worth the Emmened fleet at least."

"You know my views, Captain. We must not honour these brigands too much."

I went to answer but decided against it. If the stories were true, Chrisos held his position by luck rather than skill. In a recent engagement on the Air, in the midst of smokescreen warfare, his vessel had managed to ram the flagship of the enemy Prince, so ending the combat in his Prince's favour; more recently he had routed a Timmsmen 40-footer near Sollellen. He was no doubt feeling invincible.

I changed the subject. "Has Timms been much of a burden to your people?"

"Not since The Eagle Buchanan was taken by Kurdaitcha outside Cresa."

The news surprised me. "They took Buchanan?" I thought of the ancient Dreamtime stories, of Ab'O assassins moving silently in their Kurdaitcha shoes of emu feathers. The world had not changed that much.

"We got them all," Chrisos said, as if he'd had a part in it. "Their jackmen came to us, but no Tobys. All the brigands have jackmen these days."

I watched the desert, my eyes half-shut against the glare.

"I saw you by the cages," Chrisos said after a while, still trying to ease things between us. "Do you see the dragons?"

"No. Shannon and Scarbo do. Not me."

"I am sorry. I knew you were a sensitive in other ways. They are beautiful beyond words. Our makens have discovered the secret mainsprings of our past."

There was no arguing with that, but still I felt something worrying, something unwholesome in how the Ab'Os—and sighted Nationals too—made use of that knowledge, took the chances they did.

"You can't go backwards, Chrisos," I said, and hated how envious and petty I sounded, as non-sighted people always did, aware too of my hypocrisy.

The Ab'O smiled. "But it is not backwards. The dragons are still there for us. For whatever reasons, they are there to be brought out and used."

I could think of nothing more to say, aware that I was still sorting my experiences, that by accepting the haldanes I too had gone backwards. And Chrisos was right. Despite the risks, in spite of the danger posed by some of the manifestations, the dragons brought harmony, healed the mind, eased something in the human spirit. Too many people said that they did.

The Ab'O makens had given new meaning to all our pieces of dragon lore: to St George fighting his own powerfully projected dragon dream in the North African desert; to Sigurd, Beowulf and Herakles defeating theirs; others ranged against the nagas and wyverns of the mind, the ladons, salamanders, chimeras and amphisbaenas.

A dough-beast could accommodate many different dragon vectors at the same time, quarter-jacks and half-jacks, depending on how many individuals were seeking. But with full-jack resolution, the manifestation was so strong, so concentrated, that all who sought aspect saw the same dragon—and risked the same consequences of that powerful summoning. A skilled jackman working with a prime could even determine which dragon he sought, imposing a template on the Toby that other sighted ones shared and few could override.

Such a delightful irony—the dragon fighters themselves *causing* the dragons, often the innate amplifiers, triggering dragon memory, sharing it at a mass level, subduing it again with mass hallucination. Or being the foil for some local shaman who could control his people by calling up a genetic echo of Allosaurus, an imperfectly conceived Ankylosaur, or a blundering, harmless Steg. The effect was the same; the legends grew. Set into its rituals, the wild talent meant a viable and potent power-base. So what if the creatures were distorted beyond all sense of herpetological truth—the gryphons, tengus and manticores—imagination and inventive nightmare intruding on the memory to sway the form?

The power was always there. Dragons meant power. The display of them healed, lulled, resolved something in the mammal breast which evolution had not quite taken from it.

Yes, it was strange what the mammal mind did to that race memory, what it had added to the original. I had less cause to fear some dim, impossibly remote, infinitesimally tenuous connection with Tyrannosaurus Rex than the twisted, mind-enhanced residues being raised through the nearly mindless Tobys. Shannon's sirrush, summoned and shaped by the mammal mind, might kill a sighted person with dragon-shock, while its ancient dinosaur ancestors might have been scavengers and egg-stealers, coelurosaurs like Struthiomimus and Compsognathus, possibly more afraid of someone like Chrisos than he would ever need be of them.

I pretended to watch for Timms, then remembered from stories I'd heard that he too was powerfully dragon-sighted. I made an excuse to Chrisos and returned to the helm.

Like the other great pirates who survived the continual Ab'O hunts, Timms knew how to use tribal law against the likes of Chrisos, knew exactly when to strike.

We lost the National vessels at the border of You-Guess-What because of the ruling that only a handful of approved State of Nation charvis could cross tribal land. The moment we went to turn off the Great Arunta Road on to Lateral 83, *Bellona* and *Ozymandis* veered off, began to alter their course for the coast. It was madness, but Chrisos would not hear of suspending tribal law even for this.

As a tactical manoeuvre, now that we were three instead of five, we stopped long enough to move the Tobys into the storage bay of *Dancing Man*, and left the empty pens, swathed under their tarpaulins, on the deck of *Rynosseros*. It took ten minutes longer than we rehearsed, but Chrisos felt it added to our chances. When that was done, he announced the next part of his plan.

"Now we separate. They cannot cover three elements."

"Chrisos, no! This—"

"Captain Tom, our Emmened comsat will track *Rynosseros*. You will be covered by laser all the way. Timms will read that. It will confirm suspicions that the Tobys are still with you."

"Timms has insulated hulls."

"Would he dare risk random strikes before and aft? I doubt it. Your ship will be safe."

"We can travel as three and be covered the same way, Chrisos. Why take the risk?"

But I knew the reason. There was a high-captain vacancy among the Emmened. Chrisos wanted to bring the Tobys in alone.

"Your sat will track *Rynosseros*?" I asked him, needing to be sure.

"The program is already set. Arman and Bria will go with you and do the confirmations."

"Then I'll come with you." I surprised myself saying it.

"Captain—"

"My assignment too, Chrisos. I'm accountable to Council on this."

"Very well. Let us proceed."

Shannon came with me aboard *Dancing Man*, wanting to stay with the Tobys too, to practise dragons, he said. He didn't ask my reasons; he had been with me at Heart-and-Hand, had witnessed mind-war, its external part, had heard Anna talk afterwards. Dragonism belonged to the same universe of mind. He knew I was hoping it might reveal something, anything, about my Madhouse images, my new-found role as sensitive.

At Chrisos's signal, the three ships broke formation, *Attapa* heading off into the southwest on a little-used tribal Road, *Rynosseros* continuing on the Lateral to the tribal capital, and *Dancing Man* steering a course into the northwestern desert.

I felt the whole manoeuvre was obvious, preferring battle formation to decoys, but Sos Wain Chrisos had the responsibility now. He ran *Dancing Man* at top speed, fully kited and powered as well, while Shannon and I hid below with the Ab'O fighting crew and the Tobys.

It was in the rocking, musty gloom of the storage bay that Shannon saw his next dragon.

There was very little to do waiting there, so he was making the lattice as a way of passing time, going from one beast to the next, working down his hands as he crouched on the deck.

The Ab'O warriors didn't like it. Tribal law meant that they could not seek aspect or share it unless they had permission. But Shannon was a privileged guest. The tribesmen averted their gazes, muttering now and then and keeping watch through the four sand-scoured ports.

"Tom!" Shannon said, and I knew at once what was happening. He was peering between the middle finger and ring finger of his right hand at the dough-beast on the end, a Toby with a dark blemish on one shoulder. The creature stood very still, its dim eyes glazed, its wide toothless mouth fixed in a stupid, cartoon grin.

Shannon continued staring, so I knew there was no dragon-shock involved, no basilisk-stare, sandrake-sting or fire-vector to fear.

Before I knew what I was doing, I found myself working through my hands too, first the left, then the right, with no luck. I saw one Ab'O moving his fingers at his side, fighting the impulse to try as well.

"What is it?" I asked.

"I think—it's manticore! Or billong! No! Tiamat! A tiamat!"

The Ab'Os muttered enviously. Most of them could access the dragons, wanted more than anything to do so whenever aspect was raised. But they dared not. Sos Wain Chrisos had a Clever Man aboard, constantly alert for such things as haldanes and mind-fields. Transgressors would be caught and punished.

"Oh!" Shannon cried, awed by the beauty of what he was seeing.

His rapture was short-lived. Shouts came from above; the ship's bell rang out over the roar of the wheels.

"Timmsmen! Timmsmen!" came the cry.

I steadied Shannon as he emerged from trance, helped him stand, then followed the tribesmen up on deck where I used my pocket glass to scan the raiders.

Four ships were coming at us, low fast ships, lighter than *Dancing Man*, insulated hulls running under drab battle-kites. The one in the lead was Timms' flagship, *Sorcerer*, with Timms himself standing in the bow, a powerful bronze figure with his helmet tipped back and a fierce gravure fear-face underneath hiding his real features. That was the sight which had made so many captains surrender their ships.

But Shannon had recognised the vessel second in formation, the one flying the Armoured Head pennon that was Timms' sign.

"It's *Sirrush*!" he cried in astonishment. "Tom, they've got *Sirrush* there! The one flying the Iron Ned! I knew they'd keep her."

"Easy, Rob," I said.

"But she's intact! They didn't destroy her!"

Two warriors looked round to see what the outcry was, then returned their attention to the approaching raiders. Chrisos already had death-lamps aloft and lenses fitted, trying to catch the sun. His kitesmen were bringing hot-pots, fighting kites and harpoons to the deck, preparing land-anchors and hedgehogs.

We ran to help, though I knew this had to be a nightmare for

Shannon—preparing to make war on his own vessel. As it turned out he need not have worried. Timms had prepared this too well.

Before we could use our weapons, three harpoons struck the hull, their cables fastened to land-anchors thrown from the decks of the Timmsmen ships. When the first anchor grabbed, the momentum of *Dancing Man* tore the harpoon's barbed head out of the stern assembly. The vessel slowed noticeably.

As it gathered speed again, the other hooks took hold. With a mighty wrench, which threw us to the deck, *Dancing Man* jerked about savagely on its pedestal. Drive lines snapped; emergency overrides in the central pin slowly locked the wheels. The vessel careened wildly, nearly toppled, righted itself by the barest good fortune. At the same time, spring-shot boomerangs spun into the kite-lines, severing some, fouling the rest and dragging the canopy to the desert.

And that was it. The raider ships rolled up to us and stopped. A call to surrender came through a loud-hailer, but Sos Wain Chrisos and his men were obliged to fight. They did so bravely and uselessly, falling man by man first to snaphaunce fire, deck-lenses and spears, finally swordplay.

Shannon and I had no such obligation. We kept our hands away from our weapons and handed over our blades willingly when the raiders swarmed aboard. We were led back to *Sorcerer*, where Shannon had his second meeting with Timms and I had my first.

The desert highwaymen were consciously romantic figures who often worked carefully at their images, using media consultants, psychologists, getting advice from the network people in the coastal cities, secretly supported by foreign sponsors.

Timms was very successful at this. I had heard of captains who wound down their kites at the first glimpse of his Iron Ned, preferring to lose cargoes and possibly their ships rather than oppose him.

I understood why this was, having seen him standing in the bow of *Sorcerer*, looking across at us. The man on the quarterdeck was of medium build, though the talos battle-suit made him look taller and more massive—the gleaming bronze plates sewn to leather, the joints, clasps and armatures concealed under smooth couters, pauldrons and poleyns.

So cunningly was the armour made that he did indeed resemble a man of bronze, an idealised Ned figure, though now both parts of his double mask were tipped back. The fearsome bronze morion with the Ned eye-slit was open as before, but now the heavily-circuited gravure fear-face underneath was split as well, revealing suntanned cheeks and forehead, a strong jaw and craggy brows over deep-set blue eyes.

Shannon cried out when he saw that rugged face.

"Dan! You! My God! You took my ship! You!"

The highwaymen around us raised their weapons. Timms' heavy brows sank into a frown, but one of humorous concern, not anger.

"Your ship, Rob?"

"Mine, damn you, yes! Mine!" Shannon was trembling with rage, from sheer astonishment.

"I repaired her, Rob. She's a fine vessel. I'm glad to have her."

"For God's sake, Dan! It's me! You took her from *me*!"

"Rasselou, take Captain Shannon down to the commons and confine him. He has had a nasty shock."

"Why, Dan? Why? You knew it was me that day! You knew!"

"Which is why you are alive now, Rob. Take him!"

The guards led Shannon away.

"Tom Rynosseros!" Timms said then, turning to me. "I am honoured to meet you, sir! And most surprised to find you on this ship. Rob doesn't understand destiny. He was meant to bring *Sirrush* to me."

"You live dangerously, Timms."

"I bow to expedience as we all do. I earn a living. I like being a dealer in dragons."

"It looks good for your legend, I suppose."

"Careful, Captain." Some of the humour left his face. "My men already call me The Basilisk." And he laughed.

I suddenly understood what the fear-face was meant to represent.

"You murdered those men—"

"No!" The humour vanished altogether. "They knew my code. Chrisos chose to fight. He had that choice."

"You knew the Emmened plan."

"What plan?" Timms laughed. The tanned face softened again. "But yes. I have agents."

"Then—"

"*Rynosseros* is safe, yes. She got through. We knew Chrisos had the Tobys."

I felt deep relief, thought again of how it had to be for Shannon. "What happens to us?"

"I have no quarrel with you. I create no vendettas with Nation. You were right to surrender. Co-operate now and you go free, of course."

"When?"

"We go to rendezvous with Bunna, spokesman and head Clever Man for the Emmened. We transact business. When that is done, you go with Bunna and the Tobys back to *Rynosseros*, then return to the coast."

"What about *Sirrush*?"

"What about *Sirrush*, Captain? Talk sense! You expect me to give her up? Rob would not like the changes I have made to her."

"I want—"

"I don't care what you want!" Timms cried. "Enough! We go. Rasselou, confine Captain Tyson on the deck with his friend."

And with that he sealed the fearsome gravure face, brought down the great Ned helmet of the talos and became the gleaming legend of himself.

I was taken down to the commons and locked into leg-stocks next to Shannon. He had recovered from his initial surprise but did not take his eyes from the figure on the quarterdeck.

"Tom, I've always believed we have to value our continuities, the things we carry with us. Friends, family, confidences, things like that. Dan was my best friend. I loved him, probably more in my recollections of him down the years than I ever did at the time. We were close, Tom, both sighted. We shared a great adventure, had the old Toby to work with. How many people get a chance like that?"

"Very few, Rob."

"I'm too naive, aren't I? Too trusting?"

"I'm the last one to ask."

"But he took *my* ship! Innocent men's lives! He was never like that."

"Perhaps the basilisk-shock changed him. Too much dragonism might—"

"But my ship, Tom! Don't you see? It's like me taking *Rynosseros* from you. I couldn't do it. He knew it was me then. He kept his helmet closed."

The Timmsmen fleet sailed north until we reached the border of You-Guess-What and were no longer on tribal land. We approached a vast dry lake, an empty glaring strand that stretched almost to the horizon and shimmered in the afternoon sun. Timms sent up a lookout on a Cody man-lifter, who signalled back that a solitary Emmened charvi was waiting at the lake's centre.

Satisfied, Timms left his lookout in the sky and took his four raider-ships down onto the lake, having them stop 500 metres from the Emmened vessel, close to a low rise of sand with a crown of broken stones at the crest. It seemed to be the only natural feature marking this desolation.

The Tobys were led out onto the rise so the Ab'Os could see them and tethered under makeshift awnings, then fed and watered by a junior jackman, a young Niuginian from Timms' crew. The beasts blinked stupidly in the heat and looked none the worse for all that had happened.

A wooden Toby pen was brought from the hold of *Sorcerer*, carried to the rise and placed near the dough-beasts. Shannon and I were locked in it. We stood in the shade of the tarpaulin and watched the transactions.

The silence on the lake was nearly absolute, broken only by the snuffling of a Toby or a quiet word from one jackman to another.

Ten minutes went by, then shimmering indistinct shapes moved out from the Emmened ship. Some came ahead of the rest, heat-distorted figures, spectral and bonelike, with two others like columns of light moving behind them across the intervening ground. They resolved into four djellaba-shrouded Ab'Os, tribal jackmen, and two Clever Men in their ceremonial suits of mirrored leather. A second group were warriors carrying spears, boomerangs and nulla-nullas, a ritual guard which stopped midway and squatted on the sand.

The two Clever Men came to within several metres of Timms and stopped, two pillars of dazzling light.

It was almost like a carefully rehearsed ritual dance, a pavane. The four Ab'O jackmen came forward, their faces visible now, painted for corroboree with the lines that represented stylised hand-lattice. Timms stood his ground at the foot of the rise, a shining golden figure carrying a heavy Bok laser. His helmet was closed; we could hear the suit's cooling unit working away. Highwaymen were drawn up about him, while his own jackmen, all Niuginians, were close by the tethered Tobys, already carefully controlling which dragons could be coded from their dull minds, thereby preventing Bunna's jackmen from raising aspect first.

When the Ab'O jackmen were close enough and did lock in, their fingers splayed out stiffly in front of their eyes, they saw full-jack basilisk, sandrake and a fiery billong. They screamed and broke trance, one near death from basilisk-glance, two others in fire-shock from the billong's breath. Only one survived mentally unharmed, and he was badly shaken.

The Clever Men knew then that they were helpless. Timms had skilled jackmen, and their own mental powers were effective only against other Ab'O mystics and those rare Nationals—myself included now—who could in some way access the haldanes. These renegade jackmen were not susceptible to mind-fighting, and the ritual guard was outnumbered and less well-armed.

The bargaining would go ahead as arranged.

Timms approached the Ab'O party, a forbidding sight in his bronze talos armour.

"You want the Tobys?" he said. "You want these primes?"

One Clever Man stepped forward, a tall old Ab'O named Bunna, his calm dark face framed with tufts of grey hair above the dazzle. He didn't answer the highwayman but glanced over at the Tobys tethered on the rise, the beasts he was buying twice over.

"Well, Bunna?" Timms said, the hot sun gleaming off his bright talos shoulders.

"Kurdaitcha will come for you, Timms," the Ab'O said. "No chance now."

"Forget your Kurdaitcha, Bunna. We've got dragons and weapons. We've got hi-tech and good fast ships."

"You go too far. The tribes will work together to get you."

Timms laughed. "I doubt it. We're part of a system, you and I. When you lose, someone else gains. It won't happen."

"The time is coming. Our Kurdaitcha assassins don their feathered shoes. You will not hear; you will not know."

"Do you want the Tobys or not?"

Bunna nodded once. He knew when to count his losses. He knew, too, that Timms would work the northern and western deserts after this—that he had fast, non-metal, insulated ships, hard to read from tribal satellites. Though that was nothing to guide Timms' actions. He was on a hundred death-lists already.

"Good," Timms said. "You can give oaths for your Prince and tribe?"

Again Bunna nodded.

"Then we can begin. We shall do it beast by beast, for oaths, money, and other special considerations. *Sirrush* will then ferry them out to your ship."

So the bargaining began—first, pledges against vendetta in exchange for one dough-beast. The voices carried across the salt to where Shannon and I sat at the cage-front observing it all.

It was a strange scene in the glare and terrible heat, quite dreamlike. A man of gleaming bronze spoke with two creatures of dazzling quicksilver, while other white-shrouded figures lay about them in dragon-shock, with a clot of darker shapes out on the lake—the Ab'O guard—and beyond them the solitary Emmened ship, barely visible, shimmering in the heat like spun glass.

In the foreground, adjacent to our cage, the softly-snuffling Tobys stood under their awnings, quietly stirring now and then, with Timms' jackmen close by. These men had relaxed aspect now that Burma's jackmen were wounded, and had moved down the rise a short way to be nearer their chief. To the side, the four raider ships waited, their parafoils idle in the overheated air, a single spider-line leading to the Cody man-lifter stirring in the thermals high overhead, its tiny rider alert for Emmened vendetta ships.

Shannon and I sat at the front of our cage, grateful for the tarpaulin, trying to hear each word.

With each beast bought, Timms signalled a jackman who ran back up the slope, freed a Toby from tether, and led it across to the open storage bay of *Sirrush*. It was a slow curious process, one of Timms' own rituals.

Finally, only one beast stood under the awning, the one with the dark shoulder mark. The business was almost over.

Then I noticed that Shannon was making the lattice, lifting a hand slowly in front of his eyes. The remaining Toby felt the mind-field and looked at us, entranced. It snuffled, then stood very still.

"I'm getting it!" Shannon said, very quietly.

I said nothing, torn between urging him on and telling him it would do no good.

The Toby stood motionless, its blank expression even more comical now that a human mind was directing thoughts at it.

Timms' jackmen were good. Whether augmented with implants or just highly attuned to any signs of dragonism, they sensed the Toby being used. The two still on the rise with us turned about, dropped into the crouch, their hands up before them making the lattice. The others came running back from *Sirrush* to join their comrades.

I saw their eyes widen, their looks of astonishment. Next to me, Shannon sat huddled, staring at the Toby between the first and second fingers of his left hand, beads of perspiration glistening on his brow.

"Quarter-jack!" he said.

"Which one?" I asked, daring to interrupt, fearing dragon-shock and what it might do to him, my own hands spread uselessly in front of my face.

Shannon didn't answer. He concentrated on the Toby, working at aspect.

The jackmen down the slope didn't know whether to keep their ground or flee. One looked quickly about him, at the Tobys being loaded on to *Sirrush*, but it was already too late to use them and they were too far away for any coherent result.

"Half-jack!" Shannon cried. "God! It's half-jack! It is!" He had more than a flawed, worn-out animal to use now. The Toby with the blemish was a prime, the best the vats could produce. Even I could feel the coiling darkness of a mind-field, a chilling, terrifying wash of occlusion and dragon-sense, but without the images, without the deadly stigmata. What were they seeing?

"Which?" I cried. "Sirrush?"

"My God!" Shannon cried in turn. "My God! Full-jack!"

The jackmen fell dead where they stood. The rest of the Timmsmen heard their death-cries and went for their weapons. Timms left the Ab'Os and began to raise a hand-lattice, driven as all poor sighted human mammals were to see our dragon forbears, despite the cost.

But the highwayman stopped himself. He knew it would be beautiful beyond description and that it would probably kill him. A few of the others tried though: one Timmsman screamed and fell, another collapsed without a sound, a third curled up into a foetal position at his leader's feet.

"Kurdaitcha!" he managed to say, then began groaning softly.

Held by their disciplines, the Clever Men kept themselves steady. Their fingers did not even twitch.

Timms showed indecision now. He was no doubt recalling Bunna's words earlier. The compulsion to look had to be greater than ever, pouring over him from the Toby, urging him to share the vision it carried.

"Which one?" he cried, raising his Bok laser. "Tell and I'll spare you!"

But Shannon did not tell him, though our lives were in the balance.

"I'll destroy your ship! I'll burn *Sirrush*!"

Shannon stared at the Toby, not turning away for an instant.

Perhaps he could not; perhaps he chose between dragons; perhaps he knew exactly what he was doing.

"Tell me!" Timms screamed, and fired his Bok laser at *Sirrush*. The hull flared, burst open, burned on its travel platform. Crewmen and one of the Tobys died in a gout of flame.

"Tell me!"

"Full-jack!" I cried, blind to dragons, trusting what it meant to the sighted ones. "You hear that, Timms? How many full-jacks have you seen?"

Timms could not hold back any longer. He had to look, had to know. He brought a hand up in front of his eye-slit.

And he screamed as the others had, and he died, his eyes hidden from me by the great helmet, but no doubt as full of terror and wonderment as those of his jackmen. For a moment his armoured suit held him erect, then he collapsed heavily onto the sand, the cooling unit still working away.

Shannon fell to the sand as well, sobbing, trembling with exhaustion. Then he looked up and saw the smouldering ruin of his old ship. Tears ran down his cheeks.

"He killed *Sirrush*. He took her from me again."

"We can't go backwards, Rob. You have *Rynosseros* now. Good mammal name that. Better."

Shannon looked at me blankly for a second, then laughed through his tears.

The warriors were running in from the lake. Beyond them, out of the haze, came the hidden Emmened fleet, summoned from the lake's far side by com or sat transmission. Bunna came up the slope to us.

"Which one, jackman?" he asked. "Which one?"

"Quetzalcoatl," Shannon told him. "The Plumed Serpent."

"The Rainbow Serpent!" Bunna said.

"No," Shannon replied. "Quetzalcoatl. Aztec."

"Same thing. It's what we told him."

"It is?" I said, as he opened the cage for us.

"Yes," Bunna replied. "Feathered assassin. Kurdaitcha!"

Djinn of Anjoulis

djinn: (Moslem legend) A supernatural being that can take human or animal form.

gin: (Australian derogatory slang) An aboriginal woman.

Compared to the great souks in the Byzantine Quarter of Twilight Beach, the humble bazaar of the one-time Ghantown, Anjoulis, was like a fall from paradise, a little piece of the world gone wrong.

I stood at the edge of the wide dusty square, looking across at the solitary sheet-iron tower of the makeshift mosque and, laid out before that, the gathering of local merchants in their neat rows.

The morning sun was still low; the hour couldn't be much past 0800, but the day's heat was already there. The blue was leaching out of the sky, turning it into a pale phantom of itself, and a fitful morning wind sent sudden spirals of dust dancing across the open ground where the vendors displayed their meagre stacks of produce and other modest wares.

I roamed the aisles, ignoring the restless flurries, accepting that this was what you did when a sheared drive pin and damaged travel platform left you temporarily stranded in such a place. You took what Fate handed you; it was the only reality after all.

At least it had been Anjoulis and not Daralgo or Khomri right at the desert's edge. Anjoulis might only be an outpost town of forty or so mostly ramshackle buildings, but as two camel routes met here, and one reasonably well-used Road brought the occasional charvolant, it had both a com station and a combination chandlery-shipyard.

The merchants waited on their mats, embroidered rugs and low carved stools, some peering out from under parasols and faded awnings, and appraised what few customers there already were. Later in the day, a coincidence almost as momentous as a guide pin shearing off and stranding *Rynosseros*, the weekly passenger charvi, *Perenty*, would arrive with its handful of tourists and Nationals. This early turn-out was for them.

I entered the third aisle, moving away from the row of chatter-poles marking out the market's otherwise empty western edge. The wind set them clacking, making the small pieces of lacquered wood and bone dance and rattle on their cords. On one side a mosque, on the other that incomprehensible array, with a few shacks and stuccoed mud-brick buildings to give the square a claim to such a name.

Yes, Anjoulis did seem like a certain fall from grace just then, with a destination to reach and a mission to complete, no time for this but time snatched away by circumstance regardless.

I was halfway across the square when the sun lifted clear of the iron tower and stole the last of the shade. The vendors sat like stones in the dancing wind.

Shading my eyes from the glare, I moved on, stopping before a local kitemaker, with half an idea of buying a decorated town-kite for a souvenir. The bearded vendor in his dark-green robe launched into a half-hearted spiel, but *Perenty* had not yet arrived and his ship-worthy stock was way overpriced.

I moved on, paused again several metres later when I found a lamp-seller sitting shrouded and alone on her rug at the end of the aisle, a little apart from the others, with twenty or so downgraded metic lamps arranged about her like kiteless sand-ships.

Aladdin lamps, I immediately thought. Arabian Nights.

Scheherazade telling her famous tales to the Sultan Schariar, finally winning his heart. Those small footed vessels did indeed look like tiny charvolants, bereft of travel platforms as *Rynosseros* was for a time.

The woman noted my interest and drew back the front of her hood, showing me a surprisingly young and unexpectedly dark face, an unlikely face, not the usual classic lines of haldane Ab'O but the ancient Koori lines, the fuller lips, wider nose, the distinctive full cheekbones and low forehead, the black deepset eyes. Too strange and heavy-featured to be beautiful, but a compelling face.

I stared a few seconds too long.

"Revenant," she explained, lips drawing back to show startling white teeth, dramatic contrast to the blackness of the skin. "Grown from trace DNA. Old remains. Buy a metic lamp, Captain?"

Her voice had the lilt of a dialect that had been worked carefully to a neutral marketplace patois. It was a deep rich contralto, calm and educated, the pronunciation exact. The eyes held me to each word.

"A lamp? Perhaps later. My ship is damaged and I'm waiting for com to open."

I turned away, bypassed the remaining aisles and headed straight for the two-storey building with the town's radio dish, though all the way I kept thinking of the startling sight in the square.

A revenant—and revealing herself that way.

It took more than four hours to make the call to Angel Bay, to locate Siras and patiently explain how there would be at least a day lost. Four long maddening hours for a six-minute call: to get my turn with the harried operator, to wait while she aligned the dish and found a satellite to take us. So much for progress.

At 1240, irritable and tired, I headed back to the shipyard at the other end of the town.

It had become a hot wild day in Anjoulis. The sky was streaked with long lines of cirrus, many with their tails kicked into distinctive wisps. The hot gusty wind that blew out of the west had the makings of our demon wind, the larrikin, the wind no-one can hold. There were doors banging, sheets of iron and fibreglass lifting on rooftops, the constant rattling song of the chatter-poles bordering the square. On the roof of the com centre, the dish and its guy-lines made a steady keening sound.

The vendors still kept to their lines in the dust, making a strange ideogram in the blustery afternoon.

I entered one aisle, then another, passed the kiteseller, found myself standing before the revenant woman again, her robed form surrounded by the tiny fleet of lamps.

The strong voice came to me through the gusts. "Sit, Captain. Please. Sit."

The honorific was general courtesy in the souks, though she may have interpreted the insignia on my fatigues correctly. Any ship arrival was an event; perhaps she even knew the patches.

I remained standing a moment longer, then settled myself on the spot indicated by one dark outstretched hand.

The assortment of old brass and iron prophecy lamps were laid out between us, inescapably portentous with their fortune-telling genies waiting within, locked away in the elaborate circuit mats.

Many were plain and battered, with dented lips and turned handles; some were mysteriously patterned with scrollwork and runic ciphers; a few still bore pedigree decals or brand-names in low-relief. Almost all shone dully in the sunlight; one or two kept a dead metal finish unmoved by the sun, as lustreless as the skin of the young woman herself; two gleamed with highlights on their intricately annealed surfaces.

More than surveying a collection of a child's toy ships, or even a scene out of Omar Khayyam, it was like beholding a field of carefully arranged Tarot-forms rendered in one more dimension than usual.

"You came on the damaged ship," she said when I was settled. "*Rynosseros.*"

"Yes."

"Your crew?"

"At the shipyard doing repairs. They'll probably be by soon. One of them may take a lamp."

"Please. You choose, Captain."

"I don't want a metic lamp."

"You came here."

"I told you, I was using com. I thought I might take a town-kite as a souvenir."

"None took your fancy?"

"Too expensive."

"You sat when I asked. It will cost you nothing to say. Which would you choose?"

I shook my head, fascinated by the intense blackness of her face. I made myself study the various forms laid out before me. I had accepted the enforced stopover; now I did consider going with what that event had brought. If not a kite, why not a lamp? They had been fashionable once—the cognoscenti attended by their personal djinn. The fashion was twenty, thirty years gone. The lamps—even downgraded ones, worn and inconstant as these had to be—were plentiful enough.

But this was here. A lamp would be a memento of Anjoulis. Of this vivid, wild day, of the vendors and spiralling dust. Of this meeting.

I pointed to a plain one, narrow and elegant, a dusty pewter colour, liking its simple lines.

"That one," I said. "What's the resolution like?"

"Let us see." The young woman rose to her feet, and I saw that she had been cradling another lamp in her lap—verdigris-stained like something wrested from the sea, but with golden highlights from constant handling, touch-polished by the oils of her dark hands. "Bring it with you."

Clever, I might have said, getting me to carry my choice, but I was distracted by the lamp she carried against her side like a child.

"Where?" I said. "The sunlight—"

"Over there." She pointed to the iron tower at the eastern edge of the square.

"The mosque? Sacrilege surely."

"A tourist tower, Captain. Nothing more. A replica from the Ghan-towns those ancient cameleers built. Used now for a meeting place. Come."

We left her belongings untended and crossed to the doorway, climbed the low steps and entered the dark mud-brick and sheet-iron interior.

It was a large space, hot and quiet but for the sudden flurries of dust hissing on the iron. We moved back into the gloom and she gestured for me to try the lamp I carried.

I set it down on the paving and touched the curved sides as I'd seen it done. At once the holoform began to surge up, and I moved clear.

Some metic jinniforms were wraiths, the frailest phantoms, tantalising in their borealis elusiveness. Others were more dramatic—more in keeping with the ancient pre-Mohammedan Arab desert demons on which they were based. This was a roiling demon djinn, an impressive male resolution in reds and deep orange lifting upward at the end of a well-detailed cloudform, as if a brooding thunderhead had been tamed and sculpted during a particularly lurid sunset.

The jinniform rose, fierce-browed, heavily cornuted, with arms folded, extending a full eight feet above the lamp. It surveyed the Koori woman and myself.

"Arias Bey! Arias Bey!" it said, the lamp made it say. "You have called me . . ." But that was all. The demon dwindled at once, climbed down itself like a video reversal, the image swallowed, snatched back into the control aperture.

"Don't worry, Captain," the woman said, and laid a dark finger along the lamp she carried. "This one is for you."

"Look—"

"It is true. Those lamps outside are downgraded like that one there. This one is complete."

Which was something I had never seen—an intact metic lamp: a genie projection with its full run of counselling, datastore and predictive functions. More than just a novelty, not merely a quaint find or a relic.

"All right. Show me."

But when she had placed the lamp on the floor, she gestured to show it was again my task. I laid my hands on the touch-polished sides and pressed.

A hiss of sand on the walls startled me, sent me scrambling back. But there was no jinniform blossoming up from the spout, making its carefully nurtured phantom amid the dust motes. Not then. Not until my companion stepped over to it and touched it herself, leaning down to caress the lid, not the sides, with one black hand.

Then there was a rush of sudden, almost blinding light, veil photonics in an explosion of colour, so quick, settling quickly too, falling away. Residual photons faded; nothing remained but the lamp and the two of us.

No. There was something more, something momentarily occluded by the dwindling of that first startling discharge.

"Oh my!" I cried, unable to stop myself. "That is beautiful!"

The young Koori woman stood before me, transformed, picked out in ghost light, sheathed in it, her features overlaid and changed so that the eyes of her, then the smile, shone through a light veil, were the only constants, a startling superimposition, a dark centre for the shimmering overlay.

"I did not know they did this."

I had seen countless cosmetic and theatrical photonics, enantiomorphs and simulacra, but this was different, and probably much simpler tech—a jinniform customised about the body of its owner.

"This lamp was specially made. A man wanted to have a different kind of djinn."

I was crouching on the paving, gazing up at the shimmering form, part of that frozen moment, not knowing whether to stand or sit, finally settling down cross-legged, cueing her by that.

"This man—a Prince as you call them now, but a *kirda* in the old tongues, a ruler, initiated a secret program. He had a revenant made from ancient remains, raised her through childhood and adolescence, called her Anye. He wanted that specifically: a young full-blood Koori woman. He searched long and carefully for that. At the same time, he had a metic lamp made, found someone to do it, the other part of his plan. A magic house from which only she could draw this mantle of light you see, and came before him, the old in the new, resolved into the one, to counsel, to link up the years, to receive his attentions. A man who possibly wanted nothing more than to breed with his race's past, to bring back something, just a taste of the truest bloodlines.

"It might seem a coldly practical tale, Captain. Were it not for the lamp—whose eccentric, even obsessive role in this, you will agree, gives the whole thing a certain glamour—it would be one more attempt by my descendants to strengthen their ancient ties, to claim a more direct and untainted kinship. Heritage business.

"The lamp? It may have been from simple xenophobia, a flamboyant way of dealing with an aversion to an antique physiotype—I allow myself no illusions there. It may have been a finer thing, a setting for giving the experience a richer, more numinous caste, such as may have truly motivated this man. He never did say why. In our meetings, he used the lamp as often as not, yet always when I was counselling him, always when we made love. We made love dressed in light. In this mantle keyed only to my touch. Naturally it was never enough, not for him, certainly not for me after those early years. I realised I had been forced into this but not wanted for myself. It wasn't long before I felt I might never be truly a person to him—always something less or more."

Anye paused, stood quietly in her robe of light. And that mantle appeared to be ebbing, slightly now; the nimbus seemed less radiant in the darkness of the false mosque.

I might have doubted what she told me but for the distinctive Koori features I saw more clearly now through her thinning houri's veil, and that patient long-suffering air her voice had about it, worn as close as her twinkling jinni coat of many colours.

"Captain—"

"Tom."

"Tom, I believed I was his, rightfully his, for such a long time—that I owed him the life he had caused. But in the royal household it was easy to maintain such fictions. I was a person out of time, raised up as something like a priestess, treated that way, the private oracle of a very powerful man. I sometimes think I was a work of art for him as well, part of some private celebration, a solitary mystery. He asked my advice on things far beyond my knowledge. At first I actually believed I was that for him, a djinn. But in time I learned the other truth as well, that I was both an item of status and a source of antique pedigree."

"You feel you had proof?" I said.

She turned to glance down the length of the dark interior and out the open door, finally nodded, but abstractedly, plainly thinking about what I'd asked.

"A perfect land for this, Tom. Full of shapechanger legends, full of meanings. The Rainbow Serpent's eggs become stones, the Lizard Ancestor turns into a hill, the Emu Man becomes a gorge. All those Dreaming Ancestors becoming the land, the ranges, the waterholes, the animals." Her gaze never left the doorway. "The deserts of the world all open into each other. They are the constants."

She may have left the silence for me to fill; it truly seemed she was crafting every part of what now happened.

"How did you come to Anjoulis?" I said.

She faced me again.

"A child's trust and gratitude, her pleasure too, became duty and confusion. My one concern became making sure he raised no other Anyes from the trace remains. He was long-lived, as many Princes are. I envisaged a line of revenants, years of them drawn from my original remains, a slavery for all my selves—more than just the potential of a breeding plan or a harem of clones from my living tissue. When one person seeks to control the reality perception and choices of another, it is slavery, isn't it? It is."

"What did you do?"

"After eight more years of feigned interest in his schemes? Of earning trust in the tribal life-house? One day I destroyed the samples and trace originals, spoilt the extant projects—"

"Stole the lamp?"

"That too, yes. In my deprived state I actually thought it to be mine, even believed the ancient Koori had such things. Came eventually to this place."

"And now?" Though I knew the answer.

"His State is far from here, but he has to search. My form gives me away. At least in the markets of road-towns I can pass for a nomad. But he has to find me. I cannot hope he will let me be. I have given him a quest; this is what he understands. And if I escape him in death, he'll raise me up again, keep any issue more strictly controlled. Enslavement."

"No children?"

"Thankfully, no. A great disappointment, I'm sure. A fitting irony. Perhaps it was the process. I can only be mother to my selves. That is what concerns me now." She paused, gave a sigh and an apologetic smile. "I'm sorry. Scheherazade told better stories than this."

It was as if the reality of Anjoulis came rushing back: the hiss of red sand against the walls, the dust motes dancing in the light from the doorway onto the square, the sound of vendors calling to one another—possibly to customers, I could not tell. For all I knew, *Perenty* may have arrived; the tourist reality might well be in action, one more falsehood in all this.

Visit fascinating market towns!

Buy souvenirs from genuine desert folk!

How did the brochures go?

I noticed that the metic shimmer had completely gone from Anye's form now. She was Koori again, unadorned, her physiotype distinctive and exotic. A displaced soul unable to recapture a past that could not be gone but was. Forced to represent and support realities one of her own descendants had been raised from and now condemned her to, yet without the natural mind-set to make it truly her own. Apparently without that anyway.

If one did not reckon on atavisms and archetypes, on inherited secret knowledge of songlines and Dreamings and Djuringa lore, then Anye *was* free of this, of course. Such things would probably have been handed to her wholesale, if at all, a package of antique metaphysics as reconstructed as she herself was. Not felt, not known at the crucial level of being—but told to her: what her people had once believed, the way a child is told about haldanes or powered flight or the atom.

Or perhaps it did link up somehow, infinitely durable, carrying across the ages. Like an animal orienting itself to a migration pattern, perhaps she did have some affinity, some inbred sense of knowing.

She regarded me calmly, so young-looking yet so imbued with age—the impress of so much time understood without having been lived. Again, it was as if she wanted the silence, the slowing it gave, as if she knew it would do her work for her.

For that was the truth. I had met other revenants, other Ab'Os rekindled from ancient Koori stuff, but had never truly understood, not until now, here in Anjoulis, with this figure from the windy square, this itinerant genie found cradling her own lamp, trying to find purpose in what she had to be yet no longer was.

"You are trusting me?"

"I am a creature of fortune, Tom. I was the one he found. I was raised up. I played counsellor, gave prophecies, helped shape policy most likely. This lamp is my birthright; it has defined my whole existence as this version of Anye, to call my progenitor self that too, whoever she was. How do you think it seemed when the village boys came shouting that a ship was coming in—the legendary *Rynosseros*, your ship, because of an accident, simple chance? I have lived my whole life with such chance. I tested you by it. I would not have sent someone to fetch you had you not come. But you did. Alone. You came to the square yourself. Destiny provided a champion."

"Anye—"

"I know now that today is the day he will come too, my Prince and his Kutungurlu, or his Clever Men or Unseen Spears. Perhaps Kurdaitcha. But I see the purpose of it. Of course it will be today. And I cannot let him have me."

"You don't know that—"

"But I do. It's clear now. On today's ship. It crosses his land. He will come."

"*Perenty*?"

"Why not? Or one of his own ships. But all chance. He found my remains himself; that search was part of it, the special design. He may not come alone; he may bring his handful, but he will come, and he will make it part of some ritual of acquisition, some symbolic act. A courtship quest. That's the level he wants it at. Something emblematic."

"Anye, you can't be certain—"

She thrust out a hand, palm turned stiffly downward; she would not debate it further.

But I could not leave it be. "We can take you on my ship. It will be ready soon."

"No. I have broken law. They could sing me, trace my mind-line.

He wants to retrieve me his way. Alive or dead he can have me again."

"Can I challenge?"

It was as if she did not understand what I was offering, had not meant that when she had said "champion." Her eyes narrowed under her severe brow, steady lights in the deeper darkness. She paused before answering.

"You would do that? A Prince, Tom?" She shook her head. "But no. You have no rights here. His men would shoot you down. Burn your ship. Just be here when he comes. Having my story known will be enough."

I wanted to say again that she couldn't know, that the coincidence was too great. Only the intensity stopped me, the force of her belief in her way of seeing.

"When is *Perenty* due?"

"At last call there was a delay. Now it leaves Daralgo at 1600. It will be here at sunset."

"My crew can—"

"No!" Again the downturned palm, hard out, clearly an oracle's habit. "Send a message with one of the village children. Your friends must stay away. Just you. Please."

All fitting her idea of how it had to be, her way of crafting the reality.

"I'll go myself." But I hesitated, wanting reassurance that she would still be there when I returned. Anye anticipated that.

"I will gather my things and wait here."

I left the darkness of the mosque and crossed the windy square, heading north along the main street to the moorings and shipyard. I kept my pace steady, not wanting to seem in a hurry, and not once did I look back to see if she had followed me out of the mosque.

Rynosseros stood outside the yard gates, angled towards the Road as if eager to be away, strong-wind parafoils hard in, tethered low in case we did set out. Old Scarbo watched me crossing the yard, conspicuously cocking an eye at the striated sky, ever the kitemaster, reading sailing possibilities for what was quickly becoming a difficult afternoon.

"Larrikin!" he called, naming the wind, telling me that, yes, we could have miles between us and Anjoulis but hard sailing all the way.

I climbed to the quarterdeck.

"Town business, Ben," I said. "If we go, it'll be after *Perenty*'s in."

Scarbo nodded, granting reasons. "If she comes at all. Help?"

"No. Thanks."

"Good. In that case, I'll be at the tavern. You know what these towns are like. The local beer is designed for the usual two things: to make you want to leave or to keep you here permanently. Tell me we're going tomorrow."

"Tomorrow. Siras can wait a bit longer."

"He can. Let's get these kites stowed."

Twenty minutes later, wearing my djellaba as much to conceal my double swords as to provide protection from the rising wind, I returned to the square. The green-robed kiteseller, forseeing a day of low profits, called out a new price, but I waved him away, giving a gesture very much like Anye's downturned palm, aware of what an odd champion I had become.

I entered the mosque, sighed with relief to find Anye sitting in the gloom, her merchandise packed away, only her own lamp visible, still resting on the paving where she had placed it, as if it might indeed determine her existence.

"That's a larrikin out there," I told her. "Bad sailing wind. *Perenty* may not come."

"He will be here, Tom. You will stay?"

I read the desperation there. She needed reassurance as well. "I'll stay."

She nodded, gave a thin grateful smile. I noticed beads of perspiration on her forehead. Stress? Illness? I could not tell and nor would she when I asked about it.

"We wait now," was all she said, and sat facing the open doorway, watching while the day wore on, unravelling about us like an ancient and bloody flag.

—.—

At 1610, a boy came running from the com station, shouting that *Perenty* was held over at Daralgo and would not be in until morning.

The merchants began gathering up their things, muttering to each other and eyeing the sky, as if finally allowed to blame the day for their misfortune. In minutes they had dispersed, most of them; the ideogram was broken, the square empty of all but a few laggards and die-hards who lingered, almost as if determined to resist this most irresistible of winds.

The sun hung low in the sky, bloody through the haze, itself like some angry red djinn suspended above the land. The chatter-poles rattled madly, sharp silhouettes at the sunset edge. Above us the tower creaked and moaned in the wind.

"Not today," I said, feeling deep relief, release from the burden of a part in this unwanted equation of destiny. I studied the antique face, worried by the beads of sweat glistening there.

Anye didn't answer. She watched the square, gazed out beyond the line of poles as if finding a message in the sun.

"He will be here," she said. "From the west."

I saw nothing but empty desert, spiralling dust.

"What will you do? What is your answer if he will not listen?"

"I have two. One is a poison—a necrogen. The nomad chemist assured me it would taint my DNA beyond useful recall. I took that while you were gone."

"What!"

"It is probably not life-threatening, Tom. Simply a genie of death in my own blood, a genetic spoiler."

I didn't know what to say. The bravery, the foolishness, the desperate wrongheaded courage of this woman! The sheen on her brow said it all, the signs of fever.

She turned to face me. "Tom, promise me you will take the lamp. He must not have even this part of me. Promise."

"Anye—"

"Promise me!"

"Yes. But your other answer?"

She looked out at the desert again. "Is fire."

I followed her gaze, trying to find her meaning out there. 'Tell me."

"An old piece of military ordnance. I have acquired a combat hot-pot I can detonate if necessary."

"Where? When?"

"Here, Tom. If he will not leave me be. A false mosque for a fake djinn." The fever sheen, the intent gaze, only added to the desperation of her bitter words.

"Let me speak to him first."

"Please. I want you to. But he will not have me again without my consent. Tell him that."

Without her consent? Did I imagine it—some subtle change in what she was telling me?

"If he comes—"

"When he comes!"

"Anye, just for a moment look at this as I am able to. You said it yourself. You were raised to the lamp. It defines your whole perception. It can't be otherwise. Simple coincidence must not make you—"

"You're here, Tom."

"Yes. But this is your only life. I'm going to find a doctor."

"My second time." Her eyes were fixed on the desert, her bitterness directed at the day out there.

"No. *You* have not been here before. Allow that he might never find you."

"My mind-line will give him—"

"May give! May not! Alien to his quite possibly. Allow for that. You may have ruined the whole illusion, you may have changed him."

"No!"

But I had to keep at it, had to try. "He has sensibilities, you said. He may not want to harm you—might never have meant to. He was a man used to power, to having his way. Grant that your going may have changed him. I'm getting a doctor."

"Look there!"

I did so immediately, saw dark silhouettes beyond the chatter-poles, tall black shapes mounted on camels, three, four, possibly more in the dust and uncertain heat-shimmer.

Coincidence again, I wanted to shout. Cameleers driven in by the wind. But her smile of acceptance made me trust for the moment that some deeper truth prevailed, the wisdom of genies.

"Wait here!" I told her, gathering my sand-robes about me, determined to do what I could. "Do nothing till I return. Promise me."

She might have nodded, I wasn't sure. I stepped out into the square, crossed to where the poles rattled like mad things, went through that perimeter towards the incoming shapes, stopped when the four riders dismounted and moved towards me.

"Anjoulis?" one called.

"Aye," I shouted back. "Are any of you after metic lamps?"

"Lamps?" another said, and laughed. No doubt he took me for a particularly eager merchant.

"Beer more likely," said the third, heading towards the perimeter with his friends.

The final rider, leading his restive beast, held back. "Why do you ask?"

Was there an added force to his question?

"I know where there's a special lamp."

"Good for you. We don't need souvenirs." And he too moved on.

Feeling incredible relief, I turned back towards the mosque. But as I did so, it burst open in front of me, exploded like a second sun, a ball of fire scattering fragments of its sudden violence on the unruly day.

I ran through the line of chatter-poles, stood staring at the blazing ruin, at the black cloud of smoke boiling up, a final djinn, quickly torn open, snatched away by the wind.

"Anye!"

There were townspeople standing in the square watching, the last of the vendors, a few children. Others came running to see what had happened.

"She didn't wait," I said to no-one.

But near me, the kiteseller answered. "No."

I turned and saw the bearded man in the green robe, tears coursing down his dirt-stained cheeks. He was holding Anye's lamp.

"Tell me."

"She came to the door of the mosque, called me over, made me promise to give this to the captain of *Rynosseros*."

When he did not hand it to me, when I saw the tears, I knew.

"You, Lord?"

"Yes."

"She was trapped inside her nature. You trapped her."

"Yes. But me too."

"I see that. Did she know?"

"I cannot say. I gave myself a new face."

A few moments passed, the smoke flattening, drawn out and dying upon the wind.

"Why?" he asked, as a child might.

"She was a friend to herself—to all her selves. She saw the truth her way. I believe that lamp is mine."

"Can I—?" he began, but stopped.

"It's broken," I told him. "Doesn't work anymore."

He held it close as Anye had, then finally surrendered it. I made myself take it from him.

"She misunderstood, Captain. I did love her."

"I know."

"I did."

"I know."

And I turned away, headed for the shipyards, holding the small fragment of genie-light that would never shine again.

My souvenir of Anjoulis. Mine.

Scheherazade told better stories than this.

A Song to Keep Them Dancing

THERE WERE HEAT CASTLES OVER WANI WHEN BARRATIN ordered the fleet in, great toppling thunderheads which crackled with heat lightning at the horizon, dwarfing the four menage charvolants and sending long trains of shadow sweeping across the land.

It was dangerous weather for charvis, what seasoned sand-ship captains call a "wired" sky. Barratin's decision was a good one. The four Exotic ships sent up fuming rooster-tails of sand, their kites bucking and plunging in the tricky thermals, and they ran for a mooring at Twilight Beach.

By chance, Barratin's flagship, *Gyges*, pulled in close by Tom Tyson's *Rynosseros*. That famous National ship and the equally renowned menage vessel of high-captain Ajan Bless Barratin were separated by less than seventy metres. Mostly it was chance, fate, pure destiny, but part of it, an important part, was a mix of careful planning as well, part of a scheme about to reach its end.

Naturally there were crowds at first, hundreds of people watching the shapes moving on the decks as the ships shut down, hoping to catch a glimpse of the strange lifeforms from the middle of Australia, some trace of the menage exotics who crewed these severe functional teratonic vessels.

When a rhinoton in a long desert cloak lifted its distinctive profile against the charged and restless sky, there was a muffled cry—of awe and wonder, even revulsion, if the truth be known. Then the creature donned its wide-brimmed shore hat and went about its deck duties, and the crowds slowly dispersed. In Twilight Beach, nothing holds crowds for long except fire-chess and the breaklight, not even the vivid microcosm of Ajan Bless Barratin's four Exotic ships driven in from their menage mission by what some oldens still called an act of God.

Scarbo turned from the rail smiling. "There's at least one rhinoton in the crew, Tom," he said, gesturing across the flat sand at the closest ship. "Probably come up to see his namesake."

Tom sat under an awning with Shannon out of the afternoon heat, watching the advancing wall of cloud. He smiled. "You think so? Me or the ship?"

"Your guess," the old kitemaster answered. "I just wonder if their captain will pay respects. It's Barratin, the contract-captain."

Tom watched *Gyges*, studied the strange plated hull decorated with weather-faded suns, mandalas, profiles of totem beasts and animal fetishes like some antique carnival ship recently used for war. The vessel was devoid now of kites and cables, a box of half-seen wonders closed and sealed but for the shape of the occasional crewman moving about. "I can do without it, Ben."

Scarbo struck the rail with an open hand. "Too late. Here he comes."

"Alone?" Tom asked, getting up to see.

Barratin was not alone. The tall dark Ab'O high-captain walked along the docks, accompanied by his bizarreman, Monsanto, and one other, another tall "man" wearing a cage of black battle mesh. A menage warrior. A lab-made exotic.

Tom watched them approach.

Boan watched them go. Belowdeck on *Gyges*, standing at a starboard port in Barratin's cabin, he saw his tall fine Captain carrying something, holding a package under his arm, with Monsanto the bizarreman, the one Boan feared and hated above all others, and—amazingly—that new thanatophon, the new-form thanatis, the death exotic in full mesh armour. They were moving towards the fabled ship of Tom Rynosseros, looking like shadowy lords of the storm now, picked out in sepia light under that wide and wired sky.

Boan glanced back at the duelling face he had been cleaning, placed it in the case next to its mate, closed the lid and snapped the clasps shut. He *had* been cleaning them, he recalled suddenly, trying to re-trace the sequence of events, the line of thoughts, part of his cabin duties interrupted when the weather turned bad.

The sight of Monsanto with his new toy had unminded him, terrified him, much much more than the rhinotons and androspars in the menage crew ever had when he first joined *Gyges*.

He put the case back in the locker and went up on deck, to look first at the angry sky, sharp with ozone, stitched all over now with lightnings, then across at *Rynosseros.*

Now there was a ship. Boan imagined apprenticing on her, working with Blue Tyson, Scarbo and the rest. A fully human crew. Not like being among exotics. *Rynosseros* was an all-lander, too, though a National ship in spite of that. Barratin had been the only registered high-captain prepared to take a tribal apprentice, a low-captain trainee.

And Boan did well enough. In the nine months since turning seventeen, he had grown to respect, even love, the contract-captain, certainly to love his ways, his patient care. With Barratin's guidance, Boan would one day have his own command, low or high, would rejoin the Sandive as a low-captain elect in its fleet, possibly a high. If he worked hard. Given Barratin's guidance. Provided Monsanto favoured him.

Mak, the oldest rhinoton on *Gyges*, the big deckmaster with the blue blue eyes and the notched ear, had warned him of that, of how Monsanto was a dangerous one, builder of living weapons, powerful Clever Man too, no friend to Ajan Bless Barratin despite appearances.

Mak said the lab-techs spoke of it back in Cana, of how it really was. Syr Chamin Monsanto had been appointed to Barratin's fleet by a menage faction eager to upset the balance of power. Old Mak couldn't remember details, and he didn't say those exact words, but he knew that much, Mak did.

Surely Barratin would know of it, Boan had decided, had said it again to Mak at the start of this mission, when the Glass Woman was brought aboard. A seasoned master-captain should be able to read Monsanto easily enough, expect such actions.

Old Mak shook his large head and had no opinion. He had once heard the Cana lab-techs speak of it was all. And there was still deck-talk among the androspars.

Boan decided he would find some way to ask Barratin about it, as soon as the unending protocols of fleet operations made it possible and Syr Chamin Monsanto's attention was turned elsewhere.

"Captain Tyson, you know Syr Chamin Monsanto, I believe," Barratin said, introducing his menage fleetmaster.

Monsanto inclined his head in silent greeting, no protocol there. He wore dark fighting-leathers as his Captain did, but elaborately quilted at shoulder and hip. His shaven head was marked with the broken chevrons of his menage sect. The eyes came at you, Tom decided. The eyes of a man you could never imagine resting. A man used to watching for opportunities.

"And this is his latest levitive. Nemwyr."

"A thanatophon?" Shannon asked, identifying the creature by the mesh. He had read the scientific briefs put out by Cana.

"Not quite," Barratin said. "A thanatis. A new variant. A prototype. Being perfected for Sandive operations against the Astani. We are very proud."

"Full mentality?" Tom asked, intrigued by the man-form inside the black cage.

"Yes, Captain," Nemwyr answered himself. "Cognitive and viable, not a sport like our zoomorphs and tangentals."

"Capability?" Shannon asked, though Tom had been going to.

"As the name suggests. I am a killer."

"Care to tell more?" Tom said.

There was a smile inside the filigree. And Monsanto smiled and opened out his hands to speak for him. You see how it is, those hands said, spread wide. Confidential. We've said enough. I'm sure you understand.

Barratin was impatient with it all. "We are field-testing always. Not something we wish to have known in Twilight Beach." He cocked an eye at the clouds crowding the western sky, drawing ever nearer. "When that turbulence clears, we go."

Then why bring it to show, this deadly variant, Tom wondered, as Scarbo no doubt did, and Shannon too. With people still watching on the docks, why did Monsanto allow this new creature to be seen? Why did Barratin allow it, choose to pay respects like this, traditions or no?

Tom studied the high-captain, wondering what the package contained, wondering why this veteran sailor chose to run an Exotic fleet in the inner deserts, wondering whether or not there was some family obligation, some karmic debt being discharged here, something more than the money and prestige of it.

The menage crews were crazy, the missions of the Exotic ships beyond accounting. One sometimes passed them on the desert Roads, saw the strange man-forms toiling on the decks, sweating ephlors and androspars, rhinotons, basics, pisacs and calibandros. Everyone wondered at the commitment to filling the desert with such bestiaries, following logics and philosophies no-one tried to explain. The high-captains who drove their "zoo-ships" were the best the teratonic tribes could get. On those decks they ruled totally. The attending bizarremen worked their malformed crews; at home their fellows laboured to make such creatures—for display, for strife, for the unfathomable prestige.

"Exotic ships don't usually reach as far as Wani, Captain," Tom said then, trying for an answer, doubting there would be more than a smile and the outspread hands once again from Monsanto.

Barratin surprised him. "We are engaged as couriers-of-honour, Captain Tyson. We carry the Glass Woman from Pereche to Cana. Basically it's diplomacy and religion. Your usual mix."

"I'm sorry, Captain Barratin. The Glass Woman?"

"An effigy. A life-size figure."

"Menage relic," Monsanto said. "A great honour for us."

Barratin acknowledged that with a brief nod. "I should not have come this close. The storm brought us in."

"Nonsense, Ajan," Monsanto said, reasonably. "You saved us a day using the Grand Lateral. The sats never read turbulence. Not weather like this."

But Barratin glanced at Tom and then at the lowering sky, as if searching the storm for what he would say next.

Boan liked being with Mak. Apart from Barratin, who was firm, detached, often cool, always scrupulously fair, the old rhinoton was probably his only true friend on *Gyges*, sometimes irascible and complaining, but generally placid, tolerant, pleased to talk.

Boan found the exotic sitting under a deck awning out of the last of the sunlight, watching the play of lightning moving in from the west. Carl, the scarred old ephlor and Mak's friend, dozed nearby, nose twitching at the charged air.

"Mak, they took the thanatis to *Rynosseros*." Which was a question from Boan. As head of the ratings, Mak got to talk with the Captain.

"I saw," Mak said, flicking an ear in the breeze pushing before the storm. "Very strange."

"But why, Mak? Nemwyr's been a secret levitive all this time. Why display him now?"

Mak watched the lightning approaching Twilight Beach and shrugged his big shoulders. "We shouldn't be here," he said, but softly, to himself really, not to Boan.

"They had him wearing armour," Boan said, trying to keep Mak's interest in this, wanting to know what it meant. "They didn't even try to pass him off as man-crew."

"Bo, you ask the Captain when he gets back," Mak said. "I can't figure it. He hasn't told me."

Conversation ended, that meant. The blue eyes were on the storm, the dim (so Mak often wanted you to think) levitive mind on other things. Quiet Mak, so fierce-looking, so powerful, a hundred years old or more and nowhere near as dull as he gave out. He wanted Boan away from him; Boan accepted there were reasons.

The lad went to the poop and watched the small group on *Rynosseros* standing with the wired sky at their backs, now and then like so many puppets on sudden jerking strings of fire.

—.—

"No, Captain," Barratin said. "No refreshments. We must be ready to move out. I wanted to meet you. And Monsanto wanted to show off his new man."

And Tom saw Barratin and Monsanto exchange the briefest flickering strike of glances. They met only at the eyes, it seemed, and there as enemies, that much was clear.

Yes, warring eyes, Tom decided. These men hated each other. Or rather, recognised the state of conflict between them for everything it meant.

Then Tom saw the smile inside the black cage, the eyes watching *him*. This was the deadly one, this Nemwyr.

"We understand," Tom said, wanting to be out of it, shying from that deeper play of the tribes, these caste and status conflicts.

But there was more. For then Barratin handed over the package he was carrying. "For you, Blue Tyson. For the honour of a meeting at last."

Tom unwrapped the heavy bundle, uncovered a gleaming Broom-handle Mauser C96, modified, oiled, fitted with homotropically-biased Grunweld sights, fully restored, gleaming in a leather holster and waist belt. Tom was left speechless.

"A true captain's gun," Barratin said. "From the days of Sun Yat Sen and Chiang Kai-Shek. From the days of the October Revolution and the Kuomintang. A good officer's weapon. Will you accept this?"

"Yes—yes. Of course. But, Captain—"

"Nemwyr was Monsanto's reason. This is mine. Wear it now." And Barratin smiled. "Next time you see *Gyges* or a deckload of teratons, think of me." The words echoed with their hollow fateful hint of meaning.

And he turned and departed. Monsanto and his thanatis, caged and deadly, caught just that bit unprepared, were left walking to the rear.

Tom interpreted that too. He stood holding the antique ballistic, reading all that had happened. It was a tangled net of half-known, half-sensed things, and watching the group moving along the docks, Tom realised that Barratin had just now told Monsanto he knew something about the bizarreman's purposes. Barratin knew, and

Monsanto knew, and Nemwyr did. Tom could not fathom the workings of advantage played out there, but he too knew something crucial. He knew he had just been given Barratin's own gun.

"Here he comes now," Boan told Mak, though the rhinoton never turned from watching the thunderheads piling up over Twilight Beach, dragging in their dry fitful lightnings. "Without the package."

"Got your duties done?" Mak said, almost absentmindedly, not looking at him.

"Done. I'm going to ask him, Mak. I'm going to ask him about Monsanto. Tell him what talk says."

Now Mak's blue eyes swung down from the cables of light stitching the deep folds of ale-coloured cloud. "You go easy, Bo," he said, friend and deckmaster both. "Something's going on and you keep clear of it. Barratin has Monsanto's measure. Trust that."

"Yes," Boan agreed, and remembered what his father had said, approving his traineeship decision, much the same thing. Contract-captains play the factions like anybody else. Not blood-related, not kin-related at all, but in service to those who are. No open contracts for Barratin, his father had said, though Barratin could certainly have pressed for one. He chose a particular menage college and gave himself to it, a loyalty more in the man than in any signed document. Now he paid for that. Divide and conquer. This new levitive…"

"He'll know," Boan said. "The Captain will know what to do."

But Mak was looking at the sky. It annoyed Boan, this seeming indifference from Mak, and puzzled him. The rhinoton had countless reasons for hating the bizarreman, far far more than Boan had, being on *Gyges* from well before Monsanto came.

Now seemed the right time. Boan wanted more than ever to talk it out, to worry at it and get it safely known, to even things out.

And because he didn't have Mak, he recalled not his father, but Rass, first his teacher, later his assessor at the traineeship adjudications, something she had said in class. "Watch what people do with their envy," she had said. "It fuels the pride and the terrible fear of not mattering, of nihilism and nemo. It leads to all strife in human affairs, that fear, that envy. It is part of humanity's eternal song. It shapes the dance." Her words.

There had been dialectic requirements to argue that during class, but Boan remembered sitting there entranced with her seeming simplification. It helped him now to fathom some of it, this idea of the unending dance. He thought of this present part of the song, this manifestation of its unchanging music.

He was glad for the memory of Rass, fancying then that the lightning made question marks to the unasked questions waiting in him.

"What was that all about?" Scarbo asked when the menage visitors were back on *Gyges*.

"He gave me his own gun," Tom said. "Look!" He indicated the worn brass escutcheon on the grip.

Scarbo frowned. "Who was the one in the suit?"

"Barratin's enemy, I would think," Tom answered. And noticing movement on the poop of *Gyges*, he belted on the weapon, in case someone watched, someone other than just a curious teraton rating admiring ships. "I don't know what this means, but it's more than bridge respects."

"Can we find out?" Scarbo asked.

"How, Ben? Those are sealed ships. We deal with them only with their consent, just as we cross the menage principalities on official Roads. You don't pry into Exotic affairs. Tell me how we learn more?"

"We can't go through the tribes," Shannon said. "That'll get us nothing."

"So?" Scarbo asked.

"I wear this for the next hour or so for whatever it means, till the sky clears and they leave. We stay up here where we can be seen watching. I think I've been seconded."

It was an hour later, when the fretful sky was starting to ease into long loosening cordillera filled with sepia light and the play of electricity at the horizon had diffused into dim flashing shoulders against the land, with only an occasional brilliant thread, that the Glass Woman was found shattered in its padded container.

A quick investigation revealed fingerprint evidence and halation trace belonging to menage-attachment, low-captain trainee Boan Guise Treloiyan.

Three of Monsanto's prime androspars came for the boy where he sat on the deck with his teraton friend, watching the angry sky become easier. Without a word, they dragged him across the commons to the poop, where Barratin, Monsanto and the fierce-looking Nemwyr stood. Like a train flowing behind them came the crew, Mak and the others, muttering with concern to see gentle young Boan treated this way.

There was no reading the faces staring down at him. Monsanto and the still-meshed thanatis were simply eyes, wide and beholding, no emotion or purpose evident in the rest of their faces. Barratin's face, on the other hand, for those in the crew with sufficient wit and cognition indexes to judge it, was set in a strange display of intense concern and resignation. The same mix of qualities hung on his words.

"Explain it, Bo," he said, gripping the rail, and those with sense enough—Boan one of them in spite of his distress—saw that the high-captain no longer wore his sidearm.

"I can't, sir!" Boan cried, forgetting that fact altogether. "I remember none of it. I couldn't have done it. I wouldn't!"

"Your traces, Bo!" Firm, scrupulously fair, but weary, a few of the more gifted androspars noticed, and one ancient blue-eyed rhinoton, deckmaster, head of ratings.

"But why, sir? Why would I? What possible reason—"

"He's right!" Mak cried. "What motive?"

Monsanto's eyes marked whose voice that was. Old Mak, you are done, those eyes told them all. You will be pulled from life, from these skies and deserts, I swear it.

"Sandive plant. Or Astani," Monsanto said lightly, softly. "Someone's advantage. Faction play. We can get facts."

"No!" Barratin said. "This has shamed *me*. Not my college. Me! This needs settlement." And it seemed to a very few, to quickening, watching Mak for one, that this was to spare the boy.

"He is junior—" Monsanto began to point out, but Barratin's hand slammed the rail, denying the bizarreman adept this.

"No! Bring the faces!"

"Trouble on *Gyges*!" Scarbo said. "Look! They're crowding the commons. What's going on?"

Though they could see the commotion well enough at seventy metres, Tom went to the mounted scan, turned it on the Exotic flagship where before it had conspicuously not been trained.

"Some sort of convocation," he said. "A judicial matter. A trial!"

Shannon had the other scan going. "Barratin has Monsanto and that meshed creature with him. The crew look angry."

They did indeed, and more than ever Tom felt the significance of events, of the visit, of the gun he had accepted and now wore. What—in that simple veiled gesture—had Barratin given into trust? What?

There was silence on Barratin's vessel when the duty-steward, a nervous bright-eyed ephlor, brought up the duelling faces. She opened the case, revealing the battle masks set smooth and gleaming in their recesses. All eyes—and Nemwyr's very fiercely—watched as Boan took up one in numb fingers, held it in terrified confusion, staring at it until Barratin came down from the poop and snatched up the other, set function, and pressed it to his face, sealed it there.

Then, like a sleep-walker, a dreamer responding to the uncompromising absurdity of his own dream, Boan activated his mask too, raised it to his face, made the contacts secure.

The crew, caught in the same web of dreamlike unreality, moved back to the rails, giving room. Only Monsanto and Nemwyr seemed to obtrude out of the dream, dramatically, coldly, studiedly aloof, too carefully uninvolved for the relentlessness of the dream-sense to touch them. Again, again, they were reduced to eyes.

Their detached acceptance of events, so one old blue-eyed crewman decided, showed their guilt.

"It's a duel!" Shannon cried. "They're wearing faces, the captain and some boy."

"That thanatis creature figures in this," Tom said, peering into scan. "Monsanto brought him along, wanted him here."

No-one crowding the scans spoke. They watched, listened.

"What, Tom?" Scarbo said finally, prompting.

"See it as raising stakes," Tom murmured, watching two figures on *Gyges* circling one another, the crew clustering right back, the other two figures on the poop, visible without scan, easily, but clearer with the enhancement, tellingly calm, Tom thought. "Barratin announces he will visit. Purposes there. Monsanto decides to join him and brings his death exotic. In mesh. Because Barratin has his gun wrapped. Why? Just a gift? No. More. He brings you a weapon. I bring you a weapon. Purpose?"

"A man in a trap," Scarbo said. "Trying his best."

"Yes," Tom said, staring at the faces circling, shifting, and at the two watching faces above.

Barratin's mask flashed, a pulse of energy which seemed to bring some of the final lightnings out of the sky and cram them, blazing, into his eyes, then sent a blade of it tearing across the deck to strike the insulated surface.

Boan's was a panic response, pure reflex rather than wilful attack. He flashed a lightning of his own, a blinding glancing bolt which struck the rail where Barratin had been and left shattered wood, fibre ceramic and plating.

Barratin came out of his roll, onto his feet, but his next glance had only a fraction of the death contained in the first. It struck Boan squarely and sent him reeling, a screaming cartwheel, into the crowd of exotics.

But he lived. He ached, was burned, badly in one or two places, but he stood. And again, from the panic, from sudden pain and sheer terror, an involuntary act with that face on his, Boan sent death at his Captain, burned him dead where he stood in his betrayal, in a sabotaged mask, sent him lightning-struck slamming dead, dead, dead into the companionway beyond.

In that same instant, even as all that—*all that*—happened, Boan knew he *had* done it, broken the Glass Woman, yes, damaged one of the duelling faces, there in the cabin, watching them leave for *Rynosseros*.

He had forgotten it, had had it forgotten for him. Clever, clever enemies.

Now he looked at Nemwyr, locked in his fighting mesh, psych-armour, a mentalist revealed. Yes, easy target for a mentalist, me, Boan knew. Pick the right mask before. Forget the statue you have broken. Tamper with the settings of one face.

And Nemwyr, there in his mind, stopped the lightnings Boan had ready, yearning to use, to send at Monsanto and his mentalist toy.

There was no answer there, Boan knew. But he had anger, desperate unsorted grief, and tears streaming from his eyes, blurring his dead Captain, hiding him, and he ripped the duelling mask away, sent it spinning aside.

He saw *Rynosseros* too through those tears, asylum, his only answer now. Possibly a way for justice, and something, something to reach for.

Boan ran to the rail, leapt it, slammed into the sand and rolled, got up running and aching, weeping, full of agonies, and one, one agony too many to bear, not ever, not in any life he could see.

Behind him there were shouts, cheers, commands. Behind him Monsanto and Nemwyr moved to the starboard rail, smoothly, easily, and watched Boan run, and watched the crew of *Rynosseros* watching them.

Away from scan, Tom saw the boy running on the sand. In a flash of reflex and confusion, his hand freed Barratin's gun, raised it, took a tropic sighting and aimed.

At the boy running for his life!

All that before Tom discovered the action, saw it properly as an act of his, realised why Nemwyr had been brought to *Rynosseros*, ploy and counterploy, understood the planted command and fought it. Saw on *Gyges* Monsanto with a gun of his own, raised and aimed. Heard the sharp report of it, saw the running figure stumble, fall, rise, stagger and fall again. Finally.

Discovered how little it took to raise Barratin's weapon that much higher. Then the crashing report, the jolt in the arm, Monsanto falling too.

And more, more. The shape of Nemwyr held aloft struggling in the arms of a rhinoton, determined and doubly driven (though Tom could not know it), lifted high in those powerful arms and thrown to the bruised and bloodstained sand below those last few stabs of light, coming at them now like unanswered questions from that sad and troubled sky.

STONEMAN

HE SOMETIMES PRETENDED HE COULD REMEMBER A TIME when there was a living belltree at every kilometre mark on the greater Roads, and a thousand k's meant a thousand trees, and you could see from one to the next, just like they said it was with ceremonial posts in the olden days.

The lesser Roads had one in five or ten or fifteen; on those barely used an infrequent one in fifty, if you were lucky; and weren't those Roads lonely to walk with so few stations on the way?

It was probably Rocky Jim's one professional lie to those who got him talking. But in twenty years as a stoneman on the desert Roads, he had probably seen a thousand belltrees die—"seen" as in found them dead when he returned to the lonely stretches where they stood, sacred iron arrows aimed at the sun, emptied of whatever strange life they had once held.

They were meant to be self-sustaining, these roadpost AIs, many people had told him that; they were meant to last for as good as forever. Which to Rocky Jim was what twenty years as a stoneman seemed. Where was the problem?, some stonemen said when he stopped at a lonely depot for a tech check. All things lived and died: true life, artificial life, dreams and memories. All fleeting. All part of the round.

But it worried him, and deeply. As he walked his lengths and stretches, mile by mile, tree by tree, he'd come upon yet another one no longer functioning, inert, no signal registering on the scratched plate of his small scan unit, with only the wind sighing about the tall shaft and sensor spines to give even a hint of life. It troubled him.

It was his other task, after all, part of his life as stoneman, visiting the roadposts, checking on them, reporting the changes (eventually reporting them), making status notes in his log. And if he lingered too long at a kilometre mark here and there, who was to know? His stretches were always free and clear; he paced out his lengths and tossed aside any rust-red gibbers or broke them with his cracker. Rocky Jim's Roads were always smooth for the great tribal sand-ships that came running in sudden thunder under their mantles of bright kites. No-one had cause to complain.

If he lingered by the trees and tried to coax their fragile identities forth, tried to make conversation, who was the wiser? If he talked to them and broke tribal law by doing small acts of maintenance, who really cared?

He did his job, walked the inner deserts, paced out his allotted Roads. He made sure he scanned each post, tossed aside every dangerous conspirator stone that might trouble a passing ship, or be thrown up to harm a roadpost belltree lost and musing inside itself.

But he always tried to talk to them. That was the powerful secret life of Rocky Jim who had once—thousands of belltree stops ago, many thousands of walked and re-walked Roads, in another life it seemed—been Rocco Jim, and before that (how many hundred thousands?) Morocco Jim, first a seller of camels, then partner in his own five-building caravanserai outside Mider.

He had fallen a long way into this secret life—because of speculations gone wrong, because of a woman he loved and a man she loved, and drink and the grief. He wished the story were better, less a commonplace story, but he never embellished it, never to himself. At forty-six, an eighth generation African in Australia, he had fallen out of considerable tragedy into this secret life of his, and he would never climb out of it again.

At 1040 on that hot quiet morning, in a waste of red stone and scorching sand, under a white-blue sky that never drew a veteran stoneman's eye in the middle six hours of any day, Jim came out of his pace-reverie, the final lines of a collapsing mantra, and considered his Road.

In his pack, long-handled cracker angled over his back, more than ever he echoed the Bedouin ancestry someone had whispered into his genes—pass it on! pass it on! He became aware of the weight of his gear, of bedroll and supplies, of the small scan case hanging down his front in the shadow of his broad-brimmed hat, of the crunch his boots made on the graded surface.

Now it was no longer the automatic stoneman's litany (Watch the Road! Look for stones!). Without the mantra to lock his thoughts into easement, he was alert behind his eyes. He interpreted what he saw. Now, only now, outside the litany, he calculated the distance.

An hour at most, Jim decided, and Lateral 913 met Long Line 20. This desolate B-Road had its final offerings, JS-A421-9 and TF-R143-6. Then it was down Long Line to Bay Ruggen probably by month's end. Tech check, log-in and gossip. Interiors other than his own deep cool mind.

Watch the Road, look for stones, the pattern went. But conscious now, unaccompanied.

What had that National sailor said—what?—six months ago? About a search he was on, about medieval alchemists searching for the Stone that turned things into gold—or symbolically, ultimately, into fulfilment and personal meaning? The Philosopher's Stone. It made a sort of sense, as most things came to do given time enough.

It was his role, his name as a pacer of Roads that had made that sailor stop, made him pull aside his rented skiff under its five modest kites to discuss that power in names on his way out to some desolate and forbidden destination, one of the old arcologies he had said.

Stoneman.

A name. A label that locked things in. Defined but invariably suggested other things beyond the definition. There was never an end to it; such was the power in names.

Jim paced out the rhythm, hunching up his pack and cracker (which you did when conscious, feeling strains and positionings, yet never did inside the litany trance). Well, he was welcome to the stones he found, that sailor. People talked about such odd things, whatever got through, whatever became urgent and needful in this all-accommodating land. The light did it, or the distances, something. Words and names did it too.

The Stonemen shared their stories. That sailor on his way to Turker Fin was nothing. There were cameleers, lone tribesmen, privateers, mystics and crazies; once there was a hundred-foot charvi parked beside a Road, kites in, and a tribal captain calling down, challenging him to a contest with slingshots. A deserted ship, no crew in sight. Just the one man in mirrored fighting leathers, a Clever Man. They had named a target; Jim had won the best out of ten and walked on, never looking back, accepting the interruption, the intrusion of it as he did most other things, without a word to anyone about a lone figure on a deserted ship. Not for many months anyway, and only, then to a few at the depots.

Stonemen, the intimates of so many rough red gibbers and glossy black austrolites, became skilful peltasts by a sure and subtle process. They tossed stones aside, or they fitted them into their slings and cast them at makeshift targets, barely breaking stride. Some dared to knock eagles from the sky, or lizards from rocks where they sunned themselves; some surely risked everything and targeted the diligent canisters of already dead (pray God so!) belltrees.

It was a rare stoneman who did not keep his hand in, who did not punish offending stones this way during the long stretches of "highway dancing."

And Jim knew something important was locked up in this, like that National sailor had said. He knew that whenever you consciously did a thing more than once—locked it into a structure where time passed and light changed, that it acquired its other meaning, its numinosity, its symbol meaning.

What souvenirs do you keep? What matters, tell me? Where do you belong? Stoneman's questions. Not special to think on at first—just like anyone else's questions. Except that stonemen kept coming back to them.

Watch the Road. Look for stones.

Conscious of it and calculating, Jim moved on.

—.—

The hundred-foot charvolant, *Hajan*, ran at 90 k's down Long Line 20, that important ship, that neglected Road, as part of a dalliance, a self-indulgence on the part of its captain, Chy Anda Relenprise.

Relenprise stood at the polished, laminated poop rail in his own totally binding, totally defining reality, so different from Rocky Jim's, thinking of the stoneman who had once beaten him.

He made calculations of his own, decided he knew where his unsuspecting opponent would be at that moment, in that other time-frame, given his schedule. The Ab'O smiled.

It was reckless doing this, yes, but as well as being one who made hard decisions and controlled lives, Chy Anda Relenprise liked to think he was someone who was keenly aware, more than most, of intersecting, colliding realities. He savoured the myriad, simultaneous perceptions of life as a philosopher might, as a senior lifewatch commander should but rarely did these days.

He was fascinated with how that stoneman would react, seeing him again, the Clever Man on the "dead ship," here to cast stones once more. A man rarely given to recreation or frivolity, let alone self-indulgence of such a public kind, Chy Anda Relenprise realised with amusement and not a little pleasure how he would enter stonemen legends through the stories this man told—become a mystery of the Roads—and he liked it. Like taking on a new identity, part of an unsuspected self.

He smiled thinking of it, thinking of the irony of it. "Have you met that Clever Man yet?" the stonemen would say. "The dead ship parked in the middle of nowhere? He'll cast with you. Doesn't say much. It's very strange."

Thus did he merge realities, bridge the gap, enter another world and its mythos.

Relenprise gripped the rail, enjoying the smooth finish, the touch of varnished, laminated wood. He watched the straining kites above and before, glanced back at the cloud of red dust behind, savouring the different worlds.

Here, inside thunder, he existed with others who knew that constant sound so well that any change, the slightest variation, carried meaning quickly deciphered, who often found its absence, the resulting silence, a strange, even disturbing condition. People who looked at the sky in the middle hours because the great kites were there, and because (like Relenprise himself and Janice Roa belowdeck) they had choices and interiors other than their minds, places to withdraw to without mantras and pace-rhythms.

There, beyond those low hills, probably those very ones, that stoneman—Jim was his name, something Jim—would be pacing his Road in what was never really silence because it was a fine-tuned mosaic of small vivid sounds, what—Relenprise fancied— was really meant by "deep" silence. That steady tread, breathing rhythm, mantra-layered (he knew almost everything about stonemen, but as learned knowledge), creak of leather, shift of powered cracker on the back...

Relenprise believed he knew.

It was more than some contest between peltasts. It was a confrontation of different, likely irreconcilable realities, and Relenprise loved that with an astonishing, possibly unprecedented passion. In a sense, with his sling and stones, he too became a stoneman, the highest of the low, in an instant, part of the ongoing legend life of the Roads.

And it was really quite inevitable that while Relenprise saw his indulgence as the result of a passion, he never once saw it as a weakness. He caressed the rail and smiled, loving how his mighty ship slipped between the twin time-perceptions, the somehow mutually excluding and re-enforced mundanes that governed how truths and body-senses aligned, were in fact made.

Jim lived in mantra silence, in far-distance, deep silence, interrupted by the slow sliding thunder of ships. Relenprise inhabited thunder and transit wind, swiftly changing vistas and cyclorama sweep of horizon. Stepping down from these things into Jim's silence and the unmoving heat to cast stones was a remarkable, quite unreal thing to do, almost uncanny, a precise and unprocessed ritual.

Loving the excitement, Relenprise struck the rail with his left hand. Janice Roa would continue to remain furious. But she would play the game as surely as he did. She would co-operate to create the "dead ship" he wanted. She would sit belowdeck with her formulae and samples and wait. Grant him this indulgence.

Hitler painted water-colours. Napoleon played chess poorly but with an incredible passion. Sarah Bernhart slept in her coffin. Chy Anda Relenprise threw stones with stonemen. *A* stoneman.

Feeling *Hajan* run in thunder under his hands, he gripped the wonderfully smooth rail that marked his reality so simply and so well, and smiled.

Jim probably kept at it because of the trees. The original program had sought to put roadposts on all the Roads—simply because that was where the modest AIs were happiest, inhabiting the great silence, communing with the land, relishing the winds and uncomplicated sun. Holy law determined that, Djuringa knowledge. But, as Jim had learned from depot staff and sandsmen, there were problems.

The tribal life-programs had once flourished, had grown ever more ambitious and complex. In a sense, they had become *too* successful, more and more provocative, more the subject of contention. Too much had been done too well. Restraint was needed, rationalisation, serious reconsideration of objectives. Jim learned of the cutbacks, how few new trees were being made, and those only to test some new refinement—no longer the largesse of populating the Roads, of making life for its own sake. Even God knew when to stop.

Jim flung a gibber far into the waste—stopped, fitted, flung, barely breaking stride. As he often did, as all stonemen did, he thought of ships. That was how the cycle ran. Cast aside a stone. How did it get there? A passing ship, too close to the edge. Slipstream in-pull. Or, the old fancy, someone deliberately casting them in (a phantom army of anti-stonemen, counter-stonemen, working in an opposite way, marring the Roads).

Ships were the bright pretenders, never part of this, not really. Painted, bedizened wood, metal, ceramic, fibre-glass, packaged power and light, comp and circuitry, moving points of startling otherness that did not quite fit, never quite belonged, or if they did, only as the occasional desolate wreck, broken open and re-made.

They were barely allowed to exist in Jim's world. They skimmed by in their false register of time and space with some tenuous yet vital link to stones—flashing between Road and sky, squeezed into some relentless, often illusory, sometimes infuriating between.

Jim maintained that fleeting unreality, sustained the lie, helped make the vital illusion possible. He served that strange interplay.

He grunted once, his normal laugh these days, these years. Of course stonemen failed to transmit such rough keen wisdoms. In the depots, to the technicians and staff, how could they not sound quaint and wrong-headed. Ships don't belong? What nonsense! Kinship between ships and stones? Oh, yes? But those techs didn't understand the final reality: that stonemen did not start out as quiet men with their eyes fixed on the ground and not the horizons, just as they did not start out as peltasts.

Jim, fully conscious, outside the litany, grunted again. The land gave you its face, made you after its own image. No stoneman wisdom that. Much older, and never more true. And Jim smiled, but it was not some odd uncommon ghost of a smile hopelessly out of sync, chasing the vanished bark of his laugh. Sixty metres ahead stood JS-A421-9, its eighteen-foot shaft canted at 85 degrees on the left-hand verge.

Jim felt elation, true heart-racing pleasure—bent, scooped up a small smooth stone hardly worth the effort, fitted it into the worn seat of his sling, flung it far out into the waste. The act was an exuberance, almost one of celebration. Before the stone could make its tiny impact cloud, Jim had his sling back at his belt and his scan up and working.

He read everything then. Impact cloud. Pilot light of the scan. Absent life signal.

Absent.

Stonemen rarely hurried, rarely changed stride inside the litany or out of it. Jim's pace quickened, itself a phenomenon of great moment. His heart did. His eyes narrowed behind his shades; his free hand became a fist he completely failed to notice. He felt the anger again, sweated with the anxiety of it. He reached the belltree, stood in the narrow spoiling shadow it made across his Road, and held the scan up to the diligent canister.

Nothing. No blip. No pulse. He had been here, at this very spot, seventeen months before. The tree lived then. It had talked, been coherent for almost a full hour in fact—an hour!—had murmured to him, given him day-old windsong from its dim-recall rods. It had tried.

Jim ignored the peeling paint he might have sanded back and spray-sealed again. He ignored the few poor weeds around the base. JS-A421-9 was gone.

Desperate, he hunched up his gear and hurried on. One did not hurry into such late-morning heat but Jim was out of rhythm, oblivious to stones. He hurried along the Road, boots kicking up dust. One thing mattered now. Only one thing.

In the thunder, in the gritty transit wind, Janice Roa stood with Relenprise at the rail, watching the cyclorama shift of the changing, changeless land. She had not yet been told his plan, not all of it. She knew only that Long Line 20 put an extra day on their trip, and that the biotects at Maldy were going to be kept waiting because one of their senior lifewatch commanders wanted an unscheduled sampling of stoneman efficiency.

"One in fifty, Chy," Janice Roa said. "Why risk this?"

Relenprise was splendid-looking in his suit of lights, one of the few men who could make her doubt herself. "It's because he's the one in fifty, Janice. They're the ones I need to observe most of all ultimately. The psychology alone would make it worthwhile."

"By you in person?"

Janice Roa could endure that glare because of her shades; Relenprise could endure Janice Roa because she was smart and quick and made him appear relentlessly efficient, and because he did not often have to look at her eyes.

"I've chosen this one before. I want to confirm observations made then."

"Sanfer says you cast stones with this man."

"Sanfer is correct." She was becoming tiresome.

"Then—"

"Yes, Janice. Saman could do it when *Amiad* comes by next week. But I want to do this myself, do you understand? And I'll be calling for closed ship."

"What? Sanfer told me—"

"Janice! Closed ship. In about one hour forty minutes. You see to the rosters. Tell Sanfer and the others."

"Yes. Yes, Commander."

His lungs were burning when TF-R143-6 became visible, his tread less sure than it had been in ages. Dust billowed around his long legs, an explosion of dust each time he drove a foot down. One fist punched the hot air, the other gripped the worn case of the scan. He wavered as he walked, and blinked to make sure of what he saw, for he found himself looking down a gentle gradient at what was suddenly a vast panorama.

There, with his first glimpse of TF-R143-6, came the sweeps as well—the intersection of Lateral 913 with Long Line 20 and the long gentle curves that overlapped about the junction and allowed speeding ships to turn in smooth practised manoeuvres from one axis to the next. Because of the nature of intersections and ships, stonemen spent quite a while on the sweeps, doubling back and forth like indecisive mendicants, finally selecting a course along which to go.

As if for the first time, because it startled him then, Jim noticed the colours: the dusty variegated red-golds of the Roads and the sweeps, the red of the wide land itself. He noticed the afternoon sky, the ailing fretful blue of it, but brought his gaze quickly back to the tree. It stood like a dark thread—no, like a solitary nail struck into the edge of this great haloed cross laid upon the bloody land.

A final nail angling in, mis-struck.

Jim squeezed his eyes shut behind his shades so sweat ran down his cheeks like tears. He hunched up his cracker and pack (part of a new urgent pace-litany) and stumbled on a stone he did not see and did not try to seize and may have imagined. It told him truths he quickly put aside. Not now. No stones now.

With the tree in sight, he strode down his length of the closing crucifix, no mendicant, rather someone obsessed with the prospect of salvation, though certainly not his own, with the fervent hope of something like redemption.

Just once, close to the tree, sixty metres, and seeing himself as he must have looked, he grunted, his laugh. Stoneman humour was durable; the symbol life of the land usually that strong. Hearing himself seemed to confirm it; he almost smiled. He saw how it was, and for once it was true. Symbols could cease to matter. Already in Hell, Golgotha had no meaning.

Hajan stood on the starboard verge of Long Line 20, free-kites and parafoils down, great photonic inflatables tethered low like so many captured clouds.

Sanfer and his five-man crew were making final checks, sealing the ship for this repeat drama. Relenprise was back on the quarter-deck with Janice Roa beside him. Lookouts would spot the stoneman in plenty of time for them to complete "dead ship."

"Why here?" Janice Roa asked. "Surely the crossroads—"

"I want it as close as possible to how it was last time. And the posts tend to distract him. I want maximum effect."

Relenprise was gazing straight ahead, out over the stern rail and not at her, but Janice knew better than to let any of her real feelings show on her face.

"There are three choices of direction, Chy. Four if he decides to turn back."

"He has log and tech check at Bay Ruggen. This is the one he will use."

"I may be out of line—"

Relenprise turned to her. "Janice, you are. You have this scheme of yours, these wonderful plans you want to see implemented, but all that can wait. The Maldy projects can wait. More important by far is how we resolve our present program. One thing at a time. This is my—"

She actually interrupted him. "With respect, Commander. Phasing out belltree AI is beyond dispute. Your program works so well it is self-maintaining. Your death-ship has other things it can do. Ten years, Verage says, twenty at the most, the roadposts will be finished. It is the other life-projects that need urgent attention now, before opposing lobbies form: the Trale relicts, the rogue andromorphs and tangentals. Your expertise—"

"And your plans and samples, Janice."

"—your trained crew. *Hajan*, the death-ship—"

"They really do call it that?"

She noted his sudden abstraction and was intrigued by it. "Everyone with sufficient clearance calls it that. Those who know do, yes. The great Relenprise. Slayer of belltrees. Scourge of Artificial Intelligence."

"Janice—"

"Not flattery, Commander. Ask Sanfer. Really do ask him. Ask your other crewmen. Make them tell you. You have managed to do what Bolo May never could, things the Princes and tribes cannot. All the dilemmas, all the ethical debates are disregarded. You with your secret mission bring order and sense into the recklessness and unchecked exuberance of your overzealous predecessors."

"Then let me tell you, Janice, that there is more to this than sampling the views of a stoneman. A personal thing. I ask your indulgence. We'll get to Maldy when this is done. You can display your necrogens and latest toxologies. If you can convince me between now and then, I promise I'll support you at the preliminaries. In return—"

Janice smiled. "This never happened."

"Exactly." Relenprise watched the Road again, a single straight line of red-gold ochre, deserted in the blazing afternoon sun. "Get your presentation ready. When I have cast stones, I'll give it my closest attention."

"Thank you, Commander. It's all I've ever wanted."

Jim's hand shook as he held up the worn black case. Only here, at the foot of TF-R143-6, did he touch the switch, allow himself to see what showed on the tiny screen.

A pulse. Positive. *Alive.*

Jim dumped his pack and cracker, moved in so he touched the sixteen-foot shaft. The totemic paintwork was badly worn, almost gone, and the sensor spines were bent and brittle-looking. The diligent had been scoured at some time (struck by a falling austrolite perhaps), the dim-recall rods in the base were partly exposed and dented.

The post had never been a favourite, too vague, too undefined and rhapsodic, not like poor JS-A421-9, who answered questions and asked about the Roads and places other than the one where it stood on Lateral 913. Different interiors than its own centre.

This one, TF-R143-6, was living, barely living the signal said, since the definition reading scarcely reached the red, and right then—with JS-A421-9 gone, lost to him forever—this one was enough.

But failing too. Plainly failing.

Jim needed to urge it forth, bring out the entity fading inside the worn diligent canister and long shaft.

"Are you there?" he asked, his voice cracking and making an awkward bray of his words. He said them again. "Please answer. Are you there?"

No answer. Too far down. Too far in.

Jim forced himself to be calm. Try something else. Sometimes precise questions worked—a different kind of precise.

"What have you seen in the last five hundred days? Ships?"

"Few ships," the faint voice came, strange and unclear. "You."

"What? What's that?"

"You. Coming again."

"Yes. Clearing away stones. Checking the posts. What about others? The ships?"

"Yes. Marking us off. I've seen your death-ship, *Hajan*—"

"What's that? What ship?" He thought he knew the name. *Hasan*. *Hanan*. *Hajan*. Something like that.

"Just now," the tree said. "Crossing there. *Hajan*."

The word drew thoughts together. He remembered casting stones with the Clever Man. *Hajan*, yes.

"Do not die! Do you hear? I'll find the ship."

"Of course you will," the tree said, its voice very faint.

Jim hunched up his gear and hurried on, his cracker athwart his shoulders so his shadow made a cross again, made him a tiny crucifix moving upon the vast emptiness of another.

The ship was there, standing by the Road exactly as before, like something that did not belong, something discarded from its own reality.

Hajan.

The same ship. The death-ship. When it ran by, belltrees withered just that much more, shrank back like recoiling anenomes, like snail's eyes, pieces of their lives snatched away on the sudden wind, drawn wire thin on the long slow thunder.

Here it was, taunting him, testing him again. Same black hull. Same kites—quicksilver inflatables—barely stirring in the still air, herded together like trapped angels. The dazzling man on the quarterdeck. No-one else.

Dead ship. Death-ship.

Brilliant Death called down to him. "Best out of ten, stoneman."

"What's happening to the trees?" Jim called up. "What are you doing to the trees?"

The dazzling man might have frowned; Jim thought he saw a frown above the dazzle.

There was hesitation.

Relenprise was furious, found himself momentarily disarmed by the question, by this violation of expectation. He considered abandoning the whole thing—imagined Janice's face, Sanfer's, re-felt his other need. Relenprise hated being trapped, and he felt trapped now.

"You tell me, stoneman!" he said. "You monitor the trees for the tribes." Relenprise hated the need for the words—they were too immediate, too intrusive and numerous; they ruined the magic. Soon he would give it up. Very soon now.

"Too many are dead, Lord," Jim called through the hot air. All his years of walking, slinging stones, making entries, finding new silent spaces in the great vastness, finding another one gone. It all made sense. "Too many are fading. One spoke of this as the death-ship."

Serious words, Relenprise wanted to shout down, warning him. Danger-ous accusations. But that sullied the mythic thrust of the encounter even more. Damn the fellow. Damn him spoiling it all.

"Best out of ten. What do you say?"

"Yes," Jim said.

Good, Relenprise thought. We can save it. He moved from the stern rail, drawing his sling from his belt.

Jim saw dazzling Death climb down the hand-rails like any other man, step over the travel platform down onto the Road, come mercurial across the red dust, darkness underneath the dazzle, mirror glass sewn to black fighting leathers.

"Target?" Death said.

Jim pointed fifty metres away, out to where the westering sun struck Clever Man glints from veins of quartz in an outcropping. Make Death cast at emblem-Death. Play the symbols.

"That one," he said.

"Agreed. Your cast."

"Wager," Jim said.

"Like what?" Death was smiling and frowning at the same time.

"Kill no more trees. Swear it by all the honour you have."

Honour? Relenprise thought. Yes. That was the proper currency here. And so few words. Good.

"I will kill no more trees."

"Your ship will not." Nor anyone on board, Jim was going to say, but didn't. This was Death. *Hajan* needed no crew. He studied the blind ports and empty decks, the silver phantom kites barely stirring on their lines.

"Agreed."

Jim nodded, pleased, locked in his reality, dimly aware of shutting out another. "What are your terms? I'll swear to be your man—"

"Not necessary. You are that already." This was perfect. Relenprise couldn't have wished for better. "No. You will tell others of this meeting, but only when the time is right." Relenprise smiled. This stoneman would dice with Death in his thoughts and dreams for years, till finally it came spilling out, all of it, confirmed then in the tales told by other stonemen, on and on. Either way, win or lose, Relenprise would have it.

"Agreed."

"Your cast then." The words were all perfect now.

Jim cast and struck a handspan to the left.

Relenprise smiled and cast. Too short. Dust leapt up a man's-length before it.

Jim selected a stone, fitted it, made his next throw.

A hit. But no smile; Jim was too desperate for satisfaction.

Relenprise understood that. Perfect. He fitted a stone of his own; he cast and hit.

So it went, each getting his hand in. The scores became matched. Death was calm and smiled, unable to lose, never trapped by wagers and honour, needing only myth. Jim sweated tears from the black glass of his eyes and put his soul in every cast.

One throw would do it.

Jim made his cast, struck the stone like he meant it to burst.

Death smiled and barely tried. The final stone missed by a cable-width, spun dust into the air like old blood.

"Done!" the Ab'O said. "You are the one in fifty. You have my word." And he turned on his heel and left Jim panting in the heat and dust, climbed the rails back to his deck and resumed his silent vigil.

Jim hitched up his gear, bewildered, uncertain what to do. He stood watching the dark ship and the kites arranging and re-arranging themselves above the man's head in subtly changing semaphores till he could bear the gaze and the silence and the hint of smile no longer. Then he started down the Road because there was nothing else to do till *Hajan* finally came running by, bound in thunder, safe in its deadly place between sand and sky, itself like a stone cast from a mighty hand.

Word of honour, yes. But who ever won with Death? Not even one in fifty.

Jim kept walking as the sun fell down the sky and the shadows of the outcroppings lengthened, and his own shadow grew more and more insistent as the cruciform shape all stonemen knew.

Death's smile did it. A smile when he played, a smile when he lost. But he would kill no more trees. *Hajan* would not.

Jim thought hard. He grunted, a bitter laugh. What did he know of smiles?

That infuriating woman was on deck again.

"He's more than five k's away. Can we go, Chy?"

Damn her impatience, her lack of understanding. That most of all. She would get nothing from him, nothing.

But he calmed himself, became reasonable, made himself play it out. He needed her yet.

"Yes. Tell Sanfer. Loft kites and move on. But leave me at the helm alone. No-one on deck. Dead ship (death-ship, he loved it!) till we're well past him." He made himself add: "I appreciate your co-operation, Janice. You will see."

She nodded, her own hard smile softening. "Thank you, Chy. I'll tell Sanfer."

Jim trudged on, head down, dissatisfied, his stoneman's cross—cracker athwart pack—thickening, lengthening out into the shadow edges of the Road now, becoming the early night of the land.

He thought of Death. The smile was a ghost right there before his eyes. Words ran upon it.

"Marking us off," TF-R143-6 had said, in almost the same line as it mentioned *Hajan*. "You are that already," Death had told him. Already his man. The one in fifty.

The words ran. Had the tree been blaming him for what the death-ship did, whatever it did to slowly, surely, murder the trees? Did it see him as part of that crew?

All he did was check on the posts. Log changes. Use his scan.

Mark them off.

And Jim stopped, crucified upon the land.

One in fifty, the Clever Man had said. Not *Hajan* at all.

Stonemen.

He moved then, even as the slow sliding thunder grew at the edge of his world where the red sun stood like a burst heart, but first—first—he flung his scan far out into the pulsing, roaring darkness.

Hajan ran at 80 k's before a tail-wind, kites bloody with sunset.

Jim crouched on the verge, marking the ship with his eyes, not daring to blink. He watched it grow, rolling on, roaring, barely in his world now, with Death as dazzling sunset at the helm. He imagined the smile on the man, on the ship—all one.

And as that totality moved past, he stood, he cast. As Death's crewman he let fly, saw Death struck, tumble, saw *Hajan* waver under the impact and leave the Road, shuddering, careening, unable to escape. Heard the new thunder, saw the death-ship turn about itself in a closing final attempt to withdraw.

Then he did not watch. He hurried. To find stonemen, others he could tell.

Lucky throw, he thought. Lucky stone.

And he might have thought of Goliath then and the bringing down of the mighty, but his cross had become one with the darkness, and symbols and realities had merged, unknown and nameless, into the urgent black wind on which he ran.

Privateers' Moon

Usually the house sang. It was built to make music out of the seven winds that found it on its desert rise. Vents in the walls, cunning terraces, cleverly angled embrasures in the canted terrazo facings drew them in; three spiral core-shafts tuned them into vortices and descants, threw them across galleries, flung them around precise cornices and carefully filigreed escarpments so that more than anything the house resembled the ancient breathing caves of the Nullarbor.

Which many said was Cheimarrhos' intention, that his great granite and limestone pylon was nothing less than an inverted network of caves set in the sky, chimneys and vaults and inclines in a structure such as Sumer must have seen, or Ur of the Chaldees, or Teoteochan of the Toltecs.

Paul Cheimarrhos called his house Balin, and on the day he finally showed me the roof-field there was a stillness on the red sand beyond the large deep-set windows, a lull I could not help but take personally, knowing Paul as I did, as an omen of some sort, as if my presence had caused it to be.

And, accordingly, as if unable to bear that terrible quiet, the middle-aged, incredibly vital Three-line tycoon talked about winds. Obliquely but inevitably. As we walked along the polished limestone corridor of Gallery 52, Paul rounded on me yet again, fixed me with his piercing blue gaze.

"When was the last time, Tom?"

"Only the once, Paul, three years ago. You used to come out to the coasts. I was here for the Anderlee hearings, but never got this far up. There were too many of us."

"The Anderlee thing, yes. I'm sorry." The polite show of regret quickly vanished from his eyes. He was too excited. "Then this makes up for it. Today is unusual. We usually get one of the four. The brinraga reaches this far north, and leftovers from the angry red-sky larrikin. I tune them down to gentle house-guests, mere palimpsests. Balin can do it. I'm so glad you're here."

We reached a corner window and looked out on the desert once more, but on a new vista entirely, stretching red and empty to the horizon.

"We even get spill-off from the sanalatti at this latitude, can you believe it? The experts say it's impossible but I know better. It's why Tyrren and I chose this spot, this exact place. I know the Soul when I feel it. Those scatterlings are unmistakable."

We stood looking out on the empty desert and I couldn't help but wonder how he did view my presence. Portentously, no doubt—the visitor who had arrived on the first windless day in four months.

"Are you familiar with the name Memnon?" he asked.

Knowing Paul Cheimarrhos' interest in antiquities and the ancient Mediterranean civilisations, I welcomed the change of subject.

"One of Alexander's generals?"

But of course Paul had been talking winds. He laughed, throwing back his thick mane of silver hair so it shifted like a magnesium shower along the shoulders of his cobalt house-robe.

"You are thinking of the general who led the Persian Greeks at Granicus. No, I mean the Colossi of Memnon, Tom. Two seated statues of Amenophis III on the Nile banks near Thebes. Some still believe they were designed so the sunrise and sunset winds made them sing—"

"Sing?"

"A plaintive hooting song, yes. But that was an accident, nothing more than a freak thing. Others claim the Great Pyramid sang before it was sealed, that the engineering equations covered that. Some say Djoser's pyramid at Saqqara did the same, that Architect Imhotep was master of the micro-zephyrs, expert in a whole secret art of hierocantrics. These tales are apocryphal. Balin exists and does all this. David Tyrren worked with me on it."

I made a sound of acknowledgment to show him I knew what pretty well anyone did, that the great architect had worked on the house, pylon, monument—though I knew that Paul had done all the initial layouts himself. It was his own design, despite the careful elaboration that had made the design a reality.

We were walking again because that filled the silences, turning up into Gallery 55-B, working our way to the final upper levels, to the elaborate totemic roof-field at the pylon's crest where the wind-banks stood and the rows of strange acroteria were laid out like memorial pieces in a graveyard in the sky.

I needed to see that field, to find out if Paul Cheimarrhos had in fact done what David Tyrren suspected, and had—after much agonising—revealed to Council at long last. It seemed I was in time.

Gallery 55-B was blind, no windows there to show the desert and sky in its twin infinite registers of red and blue, just cool limestone and granite—part of a wind-race when the vents and conduits were aligned and operating.

The whole truncated pyramid of Balin was a wind-trap, a man-made mesa over three hundred metres high, full of cave-chambers—every one part of some cunning, precisely reckoned equation—and with a "cemetery" field on its flattened crest. With its canted sides, its cavetto cornice and taurus moulding, it did look very much like the pylon of some great ancient temple gate never completed, never given its companion pylon or connecting wall, with no temple precinct at its back.

We turned into the wide transverse apron of Gallery 60, and there it was, laid out before us under the hot blue sky: the summit field set all over with shimmering, totem-like acroteria, tall blank ceramic and stone pillars, some elaborately painted, others bone-white and glaring in the sunlight, pierced with fibrile openings, set with airfoils and sonic wires.

It was exhilarating to see it all at last, and deeply disturbing—for at the very centre was a shallow basin, like a radar dish thirty metres across, and at the middle of that, so I believed, so Tyrren had confirmed, Paul Cheimarrhos' great act of sacrilege.

The twenty-six wooden burial poles were ancient, without doubt the undeclared cache stolen from the Vatican collection decades ago, smuggled back into Australia in ones and twos, hidden in black market havens, finally incorporated into Balin, perhaps the ultimate purpose of the place, though I quickly put that fancy aside. It was hardly likely—the idea was a measure of my own reaction to being here at last, to seeing the forbidden relics set up so boldly on this vast open deck.

Each post had its special ceramic cap, making it safe from orbital surveillance. Tribal comsats scanning the site saw nothing more than a shallow dish set with one more group of aerodynamic wind-posts. The angle of curvature of that depression had to make oblique scanning impossible as well.

Paul stepped down onto the flat roof-field, looking for all the world like some notable out of antiquity with his blue robe and silver hair, a Chaldean prince or an Akkadian merchant atop a ziggurat in ancient Ur or Sumer. Or again—allowing my fancies free rein, trying for the composure I needed—some of the acroteria, the totemic signs carved on them, took me half a world away—from Mesopotamia to Meso-America, and I imagined I was an Aztec priest in jaguar headdress and cloak of human skin stepping out to officiate at a ceremony to Chaac Mool. Balin invited such notions.

I was hurrying ahead now, heart pounding, so that Paul was following me, making no attempt at all to keep me from the depression at the centre. He did want me to see it.

Only when I remembered what hung in the sky high above us did I slow my pace, force myself to look less eager, more the casual visitor overwhelmed by this magnificent display.

Slowly, more slowly, I completed a gradual arc towards my real goal, giving Paul time to catch up. Then, together again, our footsteps ringing on the limestone flagging, we made our way to the very edge of the dish and looked down at the cluster of poles at the centre.

"Every now and then," I said, quietly in the vast expanse of air and light, "a National does something like this. Luna Geary. Tony Wessex. Dominic Quint. If we're lucky, Council learns of it before the tribes do. And I hope we're lucky this time, Paul, though I doubt it."

"The tribes who made those poles died out long ago, Tom. Bloodlines lost, only revenant DNA trace, languages forgotten. This is as fitting a place for them as any."

"How we see it isn't important, you know that. It's what they think. Every act like this—even suspected acts, rumoured acts—harm Nation."

"The tribes can't blame Nation for what I do. It's like privateering in the sixteenth century, the sea-captains operating on a special brief from the Crown. Drake, Hawkins and Frobisher were not official agents of Elizabeth Tudor but they acted for her."

"A handy rationalisation, Paul. They held letters of marque. They *were* legal agents."

"No, Tom! You miss my point!" One hand cut the air, a dramatic sudden gesture, a measure of the force of his feelings. "It is exactly what I say. It's like Iran-Contra once was and the Special Operations Division of the CIA—"

"Secret agenda. Deceiving the populace."

"No! No!" Again the hand cut the air. "We are both privateers, Tom. Me with Balin, you on *Rynosseros*, keeping back details from all but a trusted few—"

"And having them kept back from me."

He took the reproach calmly. "Who told you? Tyrren?"

"No. We asked for the plans. There's been a tribal satellite tethered above Balin for a month. That's what really brought me here."

"Ah, yes. My Star above Bethlehem."

"A very deadly star. It can't be simple reconnaissance. Not coincidence. I'd say a warning."

"Tom, I've had those poles for twenty years—"

"They're from the Vatican catalogue. The ones they didn't give back. Part of a *cause célèbre*."

Paul Cheimarrhos said nothing for a moment. His clear blue eyes flashed in the sunlight. "You're well informed."

"You know I work with Council."

"Exactly what I mean! A privateer!"

"All right, a privateer myself. I didn't bring *Rynosseros*, but my coming here will have been monitored. That roadstop you specified, seven k's out—"

"Sabro."

"Sabro, yes. There were tribesmen there. No questions were asked; the continent-crosser dropped me; it was a routine transit stop. But I made no attempt to conceal my identity either. That *would've* alerted them. It's why I wrote instead of using tech. The invitation had to come from you."

"I'm glad to have you."

"Despite the omen of no wind?"

Cheimarrhos laughed. "Despite that omen, yes!"

We were silent for a moment, each of us alone with our thoughts, gazing down into the dish at the small forest of shapes clustered there. The glare from the hollow and the surrounding field made it easy to shut my eyes, to escape the ancient painted posts masked from the sky by their insulated caps. Paul's voice startled me when he spoke.

"Tom, I will tell you something you will not know. What Three-line is, or was. Thirty years ago I invented a device which could measure haldane force around individual Clever Men, show which ones could access the most powerful vectors."

I couldn't believe what I was hearing. "Council knows about this?"

"No. Secrecy was a condition. I tell you only because of our guest upstairs."

I resisted the urge to look up. This was incredible.

"The tribes couldn't allow such a device to be used," Paul continued, "especially by non-Ab'Os. They bought the Three-line patent, demanded it, the plans and prototypes, made sure it remained a lost invention. They gave me this concession, on tribal land because the winds fell here, with enough funds and tech support to build Balin and establish a fortune in service companies.

"Those gave me a certain limited political power, as you know, which I've finally managed to pass on to my sister. Some of those companies help me acquire antiquities for my collection. The tribes permit them to operate. Ironically they made it possible for me to get these Vatican posts."

"But you've kept them," I said, my thoughts racing, wanting more than anything to ask more about the device. "You haven't given them back."

"As I say, Tom, the bloodlines no longer exist. Or if they do, only as revenant imposters. Who makes the claim? Who truly can? I do nothing more than collectors of antiquities and *objets d'art* have always done. For my pleasure I accumulate and keep safe objects which even their makers and inheritors might damage or ruin. It's the paradox of antiquarians and special collections everywhere." He looked into the sky. "My own Star now. I've been watching it. I have an antique Meade LX6 over there. It does the job."

"A laser strike at any moment, Paul. Balin might not survive it."

"What do they see, Tom? Nothing."

"There's more," I said. "Earlier this month, authorities in Rome finally confirmed that a special collection of burial posts—part of a personal gift to the Popes—was stolen in the years after Balin was built. An antiques smuggler was named; he named someone once attached to Three-line who has since disappeared. Nothing definite, all very tenuous, but your Star suggests how they're seeing it."

Paul surveyed the silent glade before us. "I've had them twenty years. I'm for this land, Tom, for all this. I'm the right sort of collector—"

"How they're seeing it, I said. You didn't even try to trade for such relics."

Paul laughed. "Oh, I made enquiries. But why haven't they confronted me? Sent in a search team, demanded entry, interrogated my staff? Why no formal investigation?"

I hesitated. He seemed perfectly serious, as if the obvious answer had not occurred to him. It made me cautious.

"You tell me, Paul, assuming you can trust your staff here, assuming they're not serving outside interests. I can only guess that it's part of the deal you made—what?—thirty years ago? This

Three-line device you created would seem by its nature to weigh in as something between a holy artefact, something pertaining to the Dreamtime, and a National crisis. I'd say they made a deal with you at the level of their belief systems. Gave oaths, never expecting this. Now they have a dilemma requiring careful deliberation."

Paul turned away from the small forest of posts.

I followed him back across the roof-field, not wanting to ask my next question under the naked sky. Gain-monitors could never reach down so far, but scan could, and how did we seem, I wondered? Like conspirators? Very much Paul's privateers?

"One more thing," I said as we reached the open gallery that would lead us back into Balin's great mass. My heart was pounding as I said the words. "Did you hold back any Three-line knowledge? Plans? A duplicate prototype?"

"Of course not," Paul said, and was as closed to me then as a new moon, as the invisible satellite was—his Star, that sinister moonlet locked and turning with the world, geo-tethered by its micro-filament to the parent facility over the equator.

Paul Cheimarrhos smiled. "So serious, Tom. Come. We must not be late for lunch. Sarete is Three-line now. She might never forgive us."

"Paul, I have to know. The device—"

"Later. Come now."

There were six of us for lunch, and the others were already seated at the long cedar table before a breathtaking view of the western desert: Sarete Cheimarrhos, Paul's reputedly formidable sister, her dark-skinned Islander assistant, Naesé; to her left one of Paul's actor friends, the renowned John Newmarket, looking splendid in the Edwardian finery that was his Todthaus trademark, and next to him, white-suited, so urbane, the economist, James Aganture, agent for one of Three-line's longstanding European clients.

Sarete had been overseas during my visit to Balin three years before. I had heard a great deal about this celebrated woman; even Tyrren had issued several cautions. Now here she was rising to greet me.

If the flamboyant and expansive Paul could be likened to a

messianic Beethoven cast in silver and blue, then his calm and elegant sister, with her black gown, long dark hair and sombre, appraising gaze, was something from the shadowed spaces of the El Greco that hung on the room's northern wall. She was ten years younger than her brother by all accounts, but the smooth untanned skin gave her a timelessness, a twenty year range of possibilities at least.

There was a smile, a generous one, but it never reached the eyes, and in the instant I knew that this pale, severely pretty woman intended me to see this duality of response. I was Paul's guest, the luncheon no doubt his idea. Just as Balin was completely his domain, the administration of the Three-line holdings was hers, and this had to be taking precious time out of a very busy day.

Rather than feeling affronted, I was glad of the hard honesty. There were probably enough lies in this great house already.

"Captain Tyson," she said as we shook hands. "I believe you and John know one another." I nodded and smiled at the actor. An answering smile softened those famous gaunt cheeks. "This is James Aganture, one of our European consultants." Aganture and I exchanged smiles as well. "And this is Naesé, my secretary."

A fitting assistant for her employer, I decided, an Islander woman, quite dark, middle-aged, with small eyes and small fleeting smile. Naesé rose, gave a slight bow of the head. I did the same.

We took our places. I was seated next to James Aganture at Sarete's right, opposite John Newmarket and Naesé. Paul spoke a word to Anquan, the major-domo, and joined us, immediately taking charge of the dinner conversation by asking James Aganture to bring us up to date on the situation in Europe.

The svelte, white-suited European did that until the food arrived, when the business of eating gave me an opportunity to study Sarete and the others, though I found it harder to do than I expected. Thoughts of what Paul had said about his invention kept crossing my mind, and I was glad when the meal was over at last and I could adjourn to my quarters for siesta.

Around 1500 there was wind.

I was drawn from sleep by the deep swelling song, went to the windows and looked out, used house tech to bring different vistas to the wall-screen, one cycling after the other, every angle but where the posts stood.

It was thrilling to see and hear—the outward signs of Balin coming alive. The pennants and long windsock drogues at the corners of the roof-field stirred on their poles; the helium-filled outrider kites floating high above the house started shifting in the sky, inditing their signatures on the bright air. Spinner caps turned, the most sensitive of the sonic acroteria began to sound. Like some great ship advancing through time, trailing cloud-wrack and wind-song, Balin was on its way again.

Tolerances were adjusted: within ten minutes the field was thrumming and whistling, within twenty howling and keening. From further down the great sloping mass came a deep moaning that meant one or more of the induction vents were cycling open, the spiral cores engaged, that power-cells were regenerating and airflow was being guided through the mighty house. There were corridors now where my casual passage from one room to another would vary pitch and tone, add a subtle difference to the house-song. This was Paul's great legacy. This!

I must have stood there for fifteen, twenty minutes, reading the land, studying how this structure stood upon it, considering what micro-climates might exist in its shadow. Then the phone chimed, drawing me back, and it was Naesé's face in the glass.

"Forgive the interruption, Captain. Sensors showed tech use in your quarters—we assumed you were awake. If it's convenient, my mistress would appreciate your calling on her in, say, fifteen minutes?"

The request did not surprise me.

"Certainly," I said. "I'll be ready."

On Balin's sloping west wall was a small open place like a col or cirque on the side of a mountain, and in the sun-trap made there was a walled garden, little more than some lawn and a grove of dusty orange trees.

A house-servant, Cristofer, led me there, opened the low bronze door and let me out into the tiny grove. The westering sun warmed the spot; the sloping planes of the wall-face came together above me in a gradual point, with stone wind-masks spinning on their pins in the vents.

The wind had strengthened, I noticed. The pressure systems over the desert had shifted—it was probably the brinraga which struck the parapet of the garden, stirring the fruit trees, whistling up the granite face to the vents above, where extruded murtains randomised the flow, altering its direction, tailoring it to the house-song.

Tyrren had built well. The massif of Balin sang but the garden was a pocket of calm, not only a sun-trap and a wind-haven, but also a place sheltered from the vast music forming all around us.

Sarete was sitting on a white wooden bench amid the trees, wearing a gown of dark green polysar and speaking softly into a comlink at her wrist. Though Three-line's Chief Executive, she apparently did much of her work from Balin, away from the coasts, privileged with the com tech that required. I marvelled at such easy luxuries. Near her, on another bench and using a lap-scan, sat Naesé.

Both women looked up when I approached, but Naesé turned her attention back to the scan display almost immediately. Sarete gave a polite smile and switched off the link.

"Thank you for coming. Paul considers you his so I won't keep you long."

I went to make some appropriate remark, but thought better of it. This audience was wholly on her terms; she had reminded me as much.

"We could not discuss it at lunch, but tell me frankly, Captain, what does that comsat mean?"

"They're geo-tethered, as you know. The logistics of moving them, aligning them—"

"Costs."

"Yes. They use them that way all the time, but it means filing deployments, getting clearances, logging variations. It's a busy sky."

"So I've discovered. It tells us how seriously they regard this."

"It does. It may be a routine shift, simple reconnaissance, coincidence—"

"Council sees it as a warning."

"Strong probability."

"Because David talked."

"No, Sarete. Tyrren told us nothing, simply confirmed what was already available through channels."

"Ah, channels. And do you think there is an agent in our midst?"

After Paul's impassioned evasions, again I found this directness refreshing.

"Can you doubt it? I would have thought infiltration preceded a tech commitment like this." And I glanced briefly upwards. "Given what Balin is, I would assume infiltration occurred a long time ago. This is unique."

"Agreed."

"How large is your staff?"

"Here? Seven including Naesé. All trusted. All here a long time. Some rarely go above. We keep house secrets, Captain."

"Your guests?"

"Possible. Unlikely. They will not see the . . . relics either. But what can that station do? I've been given general configuration data but I'd like you to tell me."

So you can make a decision, I realised. Make policy for Three-line.

"We read lenses deployed. It's probably *irijinti*. Given twenty minutes it could effectively demolish Balin."

"Which took eight years to build. Twenty minutes."

"Depending on intensity and duration. They sometimes move deployed like that—"

"Target the roof-field?"

"Easily. To a square metre, possibly less. But hardly their intention." I glanced at the Islander woman sitting quietly among the trees. "They'd want to commandeer the . . . relics."

"Naesé knows everything, Captain. Should I leave?"

It was such an unexpected question that I hesitated.

"You understand that I'm still making up my mind about all this?"

"Of course."

"All right. Then as Three-line you should. But only if it's a regular routine to do so. Anything could seem provocative now. Do you leave Balin often?"

"Occasionally. You like Paul, don't you? You're like him."

"Like" and "like," both words revealing more about Sarete and her relationship with her brother than perhaps she intended.

"We understand something in common, something difficult, probably irreconcilable in our affairs."

"Ah, your role as privateers."

"Paul's word, Sarete. I suppose it suits."

"What would yours be? Patriot? National? Romantic?"

"Privateer will do."

"You have no satellite over your head."

"I do now. And for all I know I may have one for every Ab'O Prince I've ever dealt with as Blue."

Naesé looked up suddenly, made a hand-sign. Sarete raised a hand to excuse herself for a moment.

"Yes?"

"Foreman has entered the Manada."

"Excellent. Send on that." And to me: "Your advice?"

"In what capacity?" I said it to remind her of the levels that separated us, wanting the distinctions to matter. There were different values at work here; Naesé's interruption, this allocation of time, had shown me that.

"As a State of Nation man?"

"Persuade him to give the poles back. Or leave here immediately."

"As the Blue Captain?"

"The same."

"As Paul's friend?"

"Sarete—"

"As his friend?"

"I'm still deciding, but I'd say stay. Risk it."

"Really?"

"If Balin is struck and the reason is given as sacred relics, there are many who will not believe. The tribes are seen as ruthless aggressors, hostile to Three-line, to Nation, to all non-Ab'Os, displeased with past concessions because of a device Paul invented long ago—"

"Nation knows about the device?" It was the first time I had seen surprise on Sarete's face. The eyes first widened, then narrowed. Her mouth drew into a line. Alarm, disappointment, annoyance, I couldn't tell.

"No. Paul told me before lunch."

Sarete nodded. Her head lifted a fraction. She glanced out at an errant drogue—orange, red and bright blue—cutting the wind forty metres away. I could not be sure, but I believed she did it to conceal something contained in her gaze—or perhaps missing from it. More than ever she resembled the El Greco madonna above the cedar table.

"What will you do?" she asked finally. "As yourself?"

I smiled, watching the kite as well, seeing it as some complex bird-equation worked out upon the registers of air, left to find resolution, to create its own fragment of meaning. It occurred to me, absurdly, very fondly, that Paul would probably have names for his kites. This was his house, his ultimate statement. Everything belonged, made for the homeostasis Paul Cheimarrhos needed, externalised in kite and corridor and wind-chase. In the burial poles in that shallow dish.

No wonder he had been glad to relinquish the operation of Threeline. Dreamer, idealist, monomaniac, he wanted none of it. Who knew what wonders, what pieces of self, Balin's vaults and chambers contained? This was more than a vast schema of the Nullarbor's Breathing Caves, those hundreds of miles of underground conduits, chambers, tortuous chimneys. This was a living extension of the man, every corridor, each framed vista and spinning wind-mask. Seeing it any other way just didn't begin to give the truth.

He had to continue, remain just what he was. He had no choice.

The kite, set upon its wall of air, mindlessly navigating, brought that in, gave that answer. Just as he had set it there, given it that brave and futile task, serving, being, till it was finally destroyed and replaced, he had put Balin upon the land, raised it up for its time. His statement. His stand.

I watched the woman whose lift of head, whose gaze had led me out to the kite, realising, imagining what she too had been through, the years of dealing with this reality of Paul's.

She had seemed hard and alien before. Now she seemed trapped and committed, caught at the moment of deciding. Caught in the choices of others. As I was. As Paul might yet be.

"I will remain here till that satellite moves away," I said. "If my presence can deter them, provide another reason for not striking, then good. Do you mind having one more house-guest, Sarete?"

"It's not my place—"

"I'm asking you anyway."

"Not at all, Captain. It was good of you to see me."

Again the safe courtesy, the illusion of my having gifted her and not the reverse. She was alien again in that moment, and I found myself hating it, hating what she represented, this seeming lack of connection, the cool pragmatism, the failure to read or simply accept one set of equations because she had equations of her own.

I left the garden but did not return to my quarters. Instead I climbed the escarpment, gallery by gallery, to a viewing lounge close to the summit. There I stood amid the low ochre-coloured furniture, safe behind the thick glass, watching the sturdy outrider kites hanging in the sky and the long streamers of dust and cloud which boiled off this stone massif and converged at the horizon as lines in an endlessly moving yet strangely constant perspective.

The house-song was clear but at a comfortable remove—like an orchestra tuning somewhere else. I began to see the great structure as something to be maintained in that other sense, and wondered which of the staff members—Anquan? Cristofer? Deric?—might abseil down these vast faces, clearing wind-wrack from the vents, carrying out service checks, replacing fixtures, tuning the structure in fact.

I recalled the meeting in the garden. Could Sarete not see the virtue in this vital reality? It was an eternal act of defiance, this great demesne, a continuing statement of identity, personal for Paul, but for Nation too, a crucial affirmation.

Or was that just my bias?

I tracked clouds to the horizon and considered equations, found myself coming back to the new integer, probably the ultimate issue in all this.

What a device Paul must have created to be allowed such a thing as Balin.

I sensed someone at my back, turned to find the calm figure of James Aganture standing near me, the cultured, white-suited gentleman from our luncheon. Like me, he was gazing out at the desert, deep-set brown eyes filled with admiration.

"Amazing, isn't it? It just goes on forever."

"Yes."

He moved in beside me, stood watching the sweep of the land, the boiling ribbons of red dust streaming past, gloriously capped now with low cloud, trimmed with gold by the afternoon sun.

"You lose a sense of such scale in Europe," he said. "It might be said that here you lack density, weight of identity, but that surely is changing. We stand upon a great symbol. Another waits above. It is a testing of symbols really."

During lunch I had imagined what conversations I might have with someone like James Aganture, had wondered what talk there could be with that avenging moon fixed in our sky, steadier by far than those trembling outriders at the ends of their cables. That he had almost read my thoughts startled me.

I nearly smiled as he worked his way into what he wished to say, Sarete's question, no doubt Paul's. My own.

"Will it strike?" he said.

"Will it strike?" I answered him.

"Pardon me?"

"I ask you the same question, James. And I wonder why you remain when the risk is so great."

Aganture's well-shaped mouth turned down, his dark eyes widened. "A visit planned weeks ago. I did not know until I arrived."

"Of course. So will you leave soon?"

Aganture did not answer. He waited a few moments, bringing his long hands together before him, then came to it again. This time he was even more direct.

"What will Council do, Captain?"

"Excuse me, James, but I'm still not sure what you mean."

"I know you are here as a representative of Nation," he said. "I know about the posts. It is why I was sent."

"Sent? By whom?"

"The Vatican, Captain Tyson. I am Monsignor James Aganture, the instrument of the Cardinals Elect and the Holy See."

"Hm. Your interest here, Monsignor Aganture?"

"Please. It is James. And it is merely a visit to negotiate for full restoration of the posts."

"How did you learn of them?"

The man smiled. "Our own investigators. There are those who saw to the actual handling who could later be bought. Thieves prosper in this. Once they had disposed of the merchandise, they still had information to sell. Once we had the principal's name—"

"Cheimarrhos would be an expensive name, I imagine?"

"Expensive enough. We had made reasonable guesses. Balin is world-famous. Our host is known for his collecting. And he is hardly subtle. Once he even enquired about direct sale; he is on public record as a 'liberator' and 'protector' of relics."

"Does Paul know?"

"Not yet, Captain. I have not lied, simply withheld. I am a senior operative for a legitimate corporation dealing with Three-line in other areas. It was easy to come here. My first loyalty, however, is to Mother Church. I thought it best I learn of Council's intentions before declaring myself. And, yes, we know about the satellite. It will settle everything, ne?"

I met the churchman's gaze. "I hold Blue. I have full executive authority where Council is concerned in matters like this."

"I suspected as much. Will you order him to return the posts?"

"Order him? First you ask what will Council do, as if it can do anything, and now this."

"Captain, please. You will understand, I hope, when I say that you are not altogether the best choice here, ne? You are Paul's friend; you are a champion of National interests. Is it not provocative to have sent you?"

I fought down my anger. "Sent, Monsignor?"

Aganture frowned, clenched his hands again, though elegantly, without force.

"But... forgive me, Captain. I naturally assumed that was how it was. I know you can travel where you will—"

"James, go and declare yourself. Make your official representations and get away from here. That is a very deadly star."

James Aganture nodded, studied the striations of dust and cloud beyond the glass, the sharp and startling perspectives of the sky. "Yes. But this is as delicate as it is urgent."

"You are here as a businessman as well as a friend."

"Exactly. We mean to buy them back if we can. Make them a gift to the tribes."

"Ah, I see. All good business, Monsignor Aganture. Curry favour for the Church."

"Captain, it really is not that simple."

"Of course. It isn't for Council either. They can't help themselves. I like to think I am here for simpler reasons."

"I see that now, of course. May I ask what they are?"

"Paul is an old friend. At a distance, it is easy to take positions, have the luxury of serving ideologies and some greater good. I came to make up my mind. I needed to know."

"Yes. I'm glad we've had the opportunity to speak. And please . . . "

"Your identity is safe for the moment."

"Thank you, Captain. You must understand that I cannot afford to jeopardise my organisation's trade dealings with Three-line. It is difficult to know what to do for all of us."

"Keeping options open just in case."

"Very awkward, yes."

"You have spoken to his sister?"

But I saw at once that he had, that this was Sarete's answer too, and more of her questions. James Aganture was here at the invitation of Sarete Cheimarrhos, I was suddenly sure of it. I left him no time to answer.

"You ask for confidentiality. You impose upon my duty to my friend. I now ask you to tell him who you are. I give you until, let us say, dinner this evening, Monsignor, yes?"

"Yes. Yes, Captain."

And I left him, found my way down to my quarters on Level 42, welcoming the option of silence and opaqued windows, needing the time to consider what really had to be done, thinking of the Three-line device and wondering what my real reasons now were.

At sunset we saw the view that made Balin renowned across the world—the Inferno, great boiling lines of cloud plunging towards the horizon, meeting in the pit of the sun, drawn like great rivers, like tattered banners, cohorts, cables of molten gold laid upon the sky, the angles of a mad geometer hauled and hurtled into the blazing, settling point like a rehearsal for the end of days.

Even Sarete and Naesé were there for it. We sat and stood about the lounge and could not find enough words for conversation, no moment when the few comments made did not do more than force silence again.

There was only the sky, the whole world drawn to that single ravenous point. And finally, as if in scorn, the sun closed its mighty eye in one slow blink, denying the clouds their lustre, turning them to lead where they sailed, streamed, panicked in the sky: you are too late, too late, little brothers, I turn my gaze from you all.

We subsided where we sat or stood, muscles loosened, sighs sounded above the rolling, healing frenzy of the house-song. John Newmarket tugged at his collar; James Aganture slowly shook his stately head. Naesé sat with what seemed like a rapt expression on her face, considering the changed world beyond the glass. Sarete saw me give a deeper unsounded sigh, allowed the faintest trace of a smile to touch her pale lips.

Paul turned to us all, stood with his back to the glass.

"The world has many great identifying winds, enabling winds, precise expressions of the pneuma. The simoom, the sirocco, the khamsin, the meltemi, the monsoon and the santana. Pieces of the patchwork.

"I accept the reality; I accepted the challenge as Imhotep did. Here is the codex that lets us read what it tells us: not understand, never understand, but know. Just take in and know. The wind moves upon the land. It completes an equation in the soul, resolves itself through only those devices nature has raised up, precisely designed, to read what such things mean. *Us. We* are the world's way of apprehending itself. We complete all that out there. Our affirmations, our emotions, are the lock for that great key. This house reminds us."

I smiled. Paul had uttered similar words at the Anderlee gathering three years ago. I was an easy convert; I used my own ship to affirm such truths in myself, such a rich and simple knowing.

"Tomorrow," he said, "there will be towers of cumulus and laze-lions all day, nothing like this. This is justice, Tom, for Fate having served up a windless man, trying to build some new Tarot here. So you never add this to your legend! *Comprendez*?"

"I do, Paul," I said, laughing. "I'll hobble you with eclipses and minor comets from now on. Nothing less!"

"Apology accepted, gracious man. And you, James?" Paul was exalted, magnanimous; it was a pointed gaze, laden with irony and fond reprimand that he gave the clergyman. James Aganture had no doubt confessed.

"We have riches, an embarrassment of all that humanity has wrought. Cloisters, scriptoria, great art collections, antiquities, centuries of sophistry and clever talk, the doctrines and arguments. Now I find the simplicity of my God here. I remember that my eyes are the windows of the first and last cathedral I shall ever know."

"Accepted. And you, Honest John? You've seen it before. Anything to add?"

I was interested to see that lean, spirited John Newmarket also looked abashed.

"I lost words for this ten years ago, Paul," the actor said in his rich full voice. "This must endure at all costs."

Which reminded us all and stole the edges from Paul's smile for a moment, though just a moment. Our host was not to be discouraged.

"Tonight we hold a starwatch in honour of our uninvited guest. We dress warmly. We go above. We find our personal monkey-moon and regale it, drag it up close, count its legs, tell our fortunes on its parts. I'll name every wind that troubles us. Yes?"

There was general assent, but I caught quick unguarded glances from Newmarket and Aganture towards Paul's sister, then found myself at the end of Naesé's own coolly appraising gaze.

"Dinner is at 1900," Sarete announced, and led the way out of the lounge.

Paul held back, like some captain reluctant to leave the bridge of his ship, and I held back as well, not surprised when his expansive mood fell away like the gold of the departed sun.

"Do you know what Aganture is, Tom?" he said when we were alone.

"A churchman."

"He told you!" Surprise and suspicion sat in Paul's eyes for a brief, flickering instant. "Well, he hinted at trade cutbacks. Direct dealings with the tribes. Circumventing Three-line altogether. All veiled, of course, the spineless fool!"

"What will you do?"

"About Aganture?"

"About your Star?"

"They'll do it, you think?"

I shrugged, not mentioning the device, determined to keep away from that topic for the moment. "You said it yourself earlier today. The bloodlines are gone. They may not care about the poles at all. What you are becoming is a very useful example. If they strike at you, it's a warning to everyone else. They may need a precedent."

"Do you know who Newmarket represents?"

The question surprised me. "Newmarket?"

"A Tosi-Go subsidiary, a Three-line rival. A mercenary actor, Tom. *My* friend. Leave the posts where they are but sell them to Tosi-Go so the tribes dare not act. Not why he visited, oh no. Just happened to have been approached; thought he'd mention it like a caring friend."

"So what will you do?"

"No offers, Tom? Nothing from Council?"

They were bitter words, from a man who was trying hard to reconcile different realities. Forcing himself. Again.

"Nothing. I told Aganture. I cannot be who I am and come here without representing Council, but I do not follow their specific wishes."

"And what are their specific wishes, do you think?"

"I imagine to see you continue. To see Paul Cheimarrhos and Balin and Three-line survive."

"In that order? Well, two of those I heartily agree with, though I'm not sure I believe you. I'm no longer Three-line. It's an alien thing."

"You know what I mean. Council can't order you. They want you to remain as a symbol. That's your great worth to Nation. The posts matter because they put you and Balin at risk. That's how I think they'd see it anyway."

"Hm, well thank them for that. That much I can accept."

I discovered it *was* what I wanted, Paul believing that I was here for reasons of my own, out of friendship and personal esteem, for reasons ultimately as elusive and mysterious as his own. Learning of the Three-line invention had complicated the issue; I found myself needing to ask about it, realised how partisan I now felt, would be the moment I asked the questions that had tormented me all afternoon.

"What would you advise?" Paul said.

"What I told Sarete earlier. I'd stay."

"Good. The poles?"

"Hardly the issue."

"No?"

Perhaps I could ask about it. Paul had mentioned the device to me. Knowing my background, of my time in the Madhouse, he had brought it up. But again I hesitated, knowing that the moment I did ask, I was no better than Newmarket or Aganture.

"It's what I was leading up to earlier when you showed me the posts. It's the Three-line holding itself that concerns them. Not the company—this great house of yours. The concession was given a long time ago and it's become too celebrated, too newsworthy, too steady a slight. I would think getting you to admit to having the poles will be used as counter-propaganda to discredit you in National and International eyes, making you appear as someone plundering, stealing away art treasures for his own material gain. Pirate rather than privateer, Paul, the critical difference. Just one more exploiter and opportunist. I believe the satellite is meant to force your hand."

"They won't strike?"

"They'd possibly destroy what they're overtly trying to save, if that matters. It seems an unnecessarily dramatic thing, using a comsat."

Paul nodded, finally asked the inevitable question. "Why haven't they mounted a land assault or at least done a search? Sent Kurdaitcha in?"

"Because they already have."

"What? Who?"

"Your guess. I told Sarete this afternoon. I would assume it was done long before they moved that station."

"But who?" Paul was genuinely amazed; it obviously had not occurred to him at all. Again I could see that the dream was being spoiled. "Our staff has been here since Balin was built. Cristofer and Deric came in from other Three-line holdings—"

"Exactly how I would have done it. Planted someone when Balin was being built. Before then, if I could."

"Kurdaitcha?" Paul was making himself accept another way of thinking, a hated spoiling pragmatism.

"To keep an eye on Three-line initially, yes. To make sure no new inventions came along. To keep an eye on acquisitions."

"So what happens when I don't frighten?"

"A land strike, I'd say. They must already have verification that the poles are here, so it depends on how willing they are to sacrifice a handful of relics. If they can't neutralise what Balin represents by embarrassing you, they could use the posts as an excuse to destroy it anyway. A regrettable casualty. But whatever this is, Paul, it's the final stages of some carefully planned action."

"Yet . . . you came."

"One Coloured Captain may suggest all Seven Captains are involved. And the other Captains will come if you ask. It may stay their hand. You're a symbol, Paul, just as we are. Not Balin, *you.* There can be other Balins, other ways of doing this. It's you we can't replace. And that's my comment, Paul, not Council's, not the Captains'."

"Yes. Yes. Thank you, Tom."

We watched the streaming, shadowing chains of cloud racing for the edge of the world. The words of my handful of desperate questions were right there, held back, barely held. It might have been the sight of Paul that stopped me. His hands were fists at his sides. He sighed.

"Tom, I have changed my will. In view of circumstances. Regarding Balin. Will you be notary to it, take the signed original back to Council?"

"Paul—"

"Whichever way it goes, I want it officially lodged. Yes?"

"I'll be glad to take it."

"And see the terms are carried out?"

The fists, the tension across his shoulders, were more vivid than words, than any other persuasion.

"Yes. If I can. Yes."

"I'll give it to you before dinner. Before we go above. Come to me in my quarters at 1840."

"At 1840."

And he left me standing there with my questions, with sudden relief and self-reproach, and before me the rushing, frenzied, cloud-wrack chasing the sun, lean, iron-grey conquistadores seeking gold but succeeding only in building night in the far hidden places of the sky.

After showering and changing, by the time I knocked on his door at precisely 1840, I had put my curiosity aside, determined to wait, trusting that he would reveal more later.

When the door slid back, I entered and found Paul sitting on a divan by the windows, the last of the day a tattered ruin of light behind him in the western sky. He was examining a Canopic jar, one of a set of four 18th Dynasty pieces resting on a low table to one side, replacing the jackal-head stopper. He set it down as I approached, took an envelope from inside his black and gold house-robe, and handed it to me as I sat down.

"A formality, Tom. I've involved Council. It's fair they know my position."

I put it in a pocket of my sandsman's fatigues and went to tell him again that it was a pleasure, but Paul spoke first.

"Tom, why were you in the Madhouse?"

I tensed immediately, feeling the barest edge of panic, residual reflex fear. It never failed to surprise me. This was the question no-one asked, that was only rarely answered if ever, that now permitted my questions to him. Paul asking it mattered. I didn't give any of the usual replies.

"I don't remember. They would not tell me."

"They?"

"Tartalen. He was in charge. One day I'll return. I'll ask."

He kept at it. "You should."

"Why, Paul?"

"There is a mystery about you. You're a National *and* a sensitive. The field is strong."

"The other Captains—"

"No. I've met them. They've all been here at one time or another. You're different."

"Paul!"

There was a knock at the door.

"Dinner and starwatch," he said. "This will be Sarete."

"Paul!"

"Gain-monitors, Tom. We may have an audience. Later."

We went to the door, found Sarete and John Newmarket waiting there.

"We go to study our demon," Sarete said, pleasantly enough. "The others will be waiting."

"On to the feast!" Paul said, and together we headed along the corridor, the house adding our variables to its ongoing song.

Dinner was an easy affair, first Paul then John Newmarket telling stories; James Aganture giving his views on the future of Mother Church in view of new tech embargoes recently imposed.

Finally the dishes were cleared away, and the six of us started our climb to the summit. In the Gallery of Record, Cristofer and Deric gave us jackets; warmly dressed, we stepped out onto the dark windy field.

It sang under the moonless sky. Under our feet, the house moaned deeply to itself. We crossed the plateau, the acroteria looming beside us like funerary totems, bleached bones keening in the cold brinraga. We made our way through the restless shapes, keeping well clear of the central depression, heading for the north-western corner where Anquan had set up the old Meade telescope, its short thick barrel pointed at the sky directly overhead.

"The refreshments, please," Sarete told the old major-domo, raising her voice above the rush of wind so she could be heard, and Anquan went off with Cristofer to get the evening's collation.

Paul sat on the low stool before the telescope and used the eye-piece, made some quick adjustments.

"I have him," he said, his voice strong above the air-flow. "Very wicked-looking deployed like that. They really do know how to use psychology. Who's first? James?"

The churchman moved to the stool, settled himself and peered through the eye-piece. Paul stood beside him, looking straight up, silver hair streaming in the wind.

"See it?" he asked loudly so we could all hear. "The red lights are mainly tactical—'barrican stars' to frighten us. Tom will confirm it. They're supposed to light up like that just before a strike."

"Really?" Aganture said, moving clear of the stool. "Is that true, Captain?"

"Yes," I said, studying the small group as best I could, dark shapes, blowing shapes, wanting to ask Paul about his comments earlier, concerned that we may have been overheard and interrupted deliberately, deeply worried by what that might mean.

"Your turn, John," Paul said, and the actor took his place at the telescope.

"It does look angry," was all he said.

Paul laughed. "It wants us to think that. It's trying to be hot and raging up there, but in reality it's a very cool thing, very calm."

Newmarket rose and moved away. "I've seen enough. Captain?"

"Sarete?" I said.

"No, thank you."

"Naesé?"

"No, Captain. Thank you."

I positioned myself on the stool, and after a split-second of auto-focus saw the *irijinti*, saw it again in actual fact, since I'd seen the displays Council had at Twilight Beach, began matching its configuration with other comsats I had seen up close this way, started when Paul whispered at my ear.

"The Canopic jar is a second prototype. Get it away from here. Say a gift!"

The wind sang about us. Possibly no-one heard.

I made myself stay calm, my heart racing as I peered up at the evil red lights.

It explained everything. Not the posts. Not Balin. Not just those things. Far more serious, much greater danger. Paul had broken faith.

The jar, a duplicate. *He had used it to read me*!

"Paul—?"

"Finished already?" he said, speaking for the others to hear.

I rose from the stool. "Let me get my configuration list. I still say *irijinti* but I want to type it. I can almost make out its markings." My voice sounded steady above the wind.

"I'll try for a better fix," Paul said, calmly enough, taking his place at the eye-piece once more.

I hurried from the field, entered the Gallery, ran down the ramps towards our chambers. My footsteps echoed on the polished stone, set a desperate percussion into the air-flow.

The palm-lock to Paul's rooms had been keyed to me, no surprise at all; the door swept aside at my touch. I crossed the softly-lit interior, immediately went to the four jars on the low table: monkey-head, falcon-head, human-head, jackal—seized the jackal-head, removed the ceramic cap, saw the dull black tech that gave it its extra weight, the recessed contacts and displays.

What had it shown? What?

"I will take that, Captain."

I turned at once. Naesé stood in the doorway, a laser baton in her hand.

"I'm sorry. This is a gift to me from Paul. Ask him."

She raised the baton, aimed it at my heart.

"Captain, I am Kurdaitcha in the final moments of a very long, very old mission."

"You—"

"Colour, Hero status, mean nothing compared to my brief, do you understand? Without that jar and the contents of the envelope in your pocket, I will be sung. I dare not fail. Save your life."

"The envelope contains Paul's will."

"No. His will was lodged with Nation long ago. What you have contains blueprints for what you hold in your hands. Look and see."

I placed the jar on the divan, brought out the envelope and opened it, saw words and schematics.

"Yes?" Naesé said. "They are mine. Paul's life might still be yours if you hurry."

I threw the plans onto the divan and ran for the door. She let me pass but called after me. "Captain! Wait!"

I ignored her, running for the ramps, needing to get Paul from the roof, away from the telescope and the field and the line of sight of that deadly watcher, aware that it already had all the commands it needed.

I saw the result of those commands as I leapt out upon the field, a thread, a wire, the tiniest filament of dazzling light connecting Balin for just an instant to its attendant moon, then the tearing scream of its brief and deadly anger above the keening windsong.

I did not need to go out to where the telescope had stood. There would be time later. I waited by the door as the three figures came to me across the windy field, Sarete in the lead, head raised, cool and detached, resolved as ever, yes, leading them, John Newmarket and James Aganture to either side, eyes downcast, ashamed.

As I watched them approach, their faces lit from the doorway, I heard Naesé at my back, panting lightly from her run. She did not have the jar or the plans; she no longer held her weapon.

"Your mistress has done well," I said.

"She has saved Three-line and Balin," Naesé replied. "She made a difficult choice. An only choice."

"What did Paul read, Naesé?"

"What do you mean?"

"With the contents of the jar?"

"That you are a sensitive. That's all."

"Nothing else?"

"Nothing else."

"I don't believe you."

"I know."

Sarete and her companions reached us, stopped before the doorway. Her words might have come from Naesé, from a script of exculpation they had jointly devised.

"He knew the consequences, Captain. He made a choice, without considering anyone, never consulting others. Something had to be done. I made a choice too."

More words than I would have expected. Still James Aganture and John Newmarket looked in different directions at the night. Only Sarete and Naesé met my gaze.

"It wasn't the posts," I said, so nothing was hidden. "There was a second Three-line device. A duplicate."

Aganture and Newmarket both looked at Sarete.

"Nonsense," she said calmly.

"Naesé has—"

"Nonsense, Captain. There was never a duplicate."

She knew. Of course she knew. Naesé did not say a word.

"I see. Privateering."

"What, this?" Sarete asked.

"All this."

"I suppose so. Not your kind, but yes."

"Not my kind, no. Never my kind."

I went out onto the field then, went to where the old Meade telescope had stood, came back with the lines of blood painted on my cheeks.

Sarete grimaced with distaste when she saw them. "Captain, is that really necessary?"

"Tell her, Naesé."

The Kurdaitcha frowned. "He is Blue, Sarete. He has made vendetta against this house."

"You're joking. I am this house now."

"No, Sarete," I said. "I think you will find that Paul has bequeathed it to Nation. Years ago. Naesé can check."

"Ridiculous! That can be negated."

"Naesé," I said, drawing rage and loss into that small hard word.

"You don't understand, Sarete. Those signs. In front of witnesses, he has sworn vendetta. He can strike at anything to do with Three-line, at any ships coming here. Through him, Council can. You must leave here. All of you."

It took only moments for the implications to be understood.

"This is not the end of this," Sarete said.

"No," I was able to say. "It is not."

On the desert near Sabro, there is a mighty house, a vast pylon set against the sky. Though left to Nation as a final bequest from the man who caused it to be, it is deserted now, neither National nor tribal, a monument at the interface. The great vents stand open; the structure howls and sings and braids the winds into endless tapestries, strange proclamations of desire. At the crest is a field and a shallow empty dish thirty metres across.

Once a year, seven ships go to that great house, the only ones who can since it is reached by crossing tribal land. The crews climb aloft and reach that field. While the crew-members do small acts of maintenance, the Captains sit in the depression and talk.

Sometimes there is a ritual of watching sunset, sometimes a starwatch. Kites are set upon the air, new pennants added to the dream.

At such times, coincidentally, no satellites ever cross that sky. The comsats studiedly avoid the place as if contemptuous of something all too futile.

The Captains smile in the windy darkness or in the flowing riot of the dying sun. More than anyone, they know the worth of dreams.

They know it is never that.

Dreaming the Knife

Stiletto night. The moon itself a sharp narrow blade curving close to the dry hilt of the land as if being drawn ever further from its sheath of stars.

Tynan Lees stood at the starboard rail of the speeding sand-ship and felt the beginnings of the Knife.

"Ah. Is this it?" He spoke the words aloud, as if he doubted what it could be; there was no feeling like it. "Is this my dagger I have before me?"

Old words. Probably Islamic, Omar Khayyam, he thought as he said them, and what did he really know of Islam? Just the origins of his name. Assassin.

He found the deep focusing again. Yes, the concentration was definitely there. Soon, soon he would have it. Instinctively, barely noticing it did so, his right hand closed to receive the haft, another old custom, as old as haldane Kurdaitcha, possibly older. His other hand gripped the rail.

Tynan Lees smiled at the wonderful irony. As an Ab'O aboard *Rynosseros*, the only Ab'O, he had made this night voyage possible, exempting the vessel from the usual strictures imposed by the tribes. His presence allowed this powered run into the sheath of night—no need for kites and wind, though there was wind aplenty whistling about the superstructure, pouring over him from the bows.

And by midnight, much sooner but midnight would be right for it, when there was no colour to him, when he was darkness too, the Knife fully formed in his sharp clear mind, then he would send it into the heart of the Blue Captain. At just the right time, everything perfect, the dagger moon before him.

Tom Rynosseros would be dead at last, the debt paid in full.

"Mr Lees?"

The Ab'O turned, his right hand first tightening before relaxing from its grip altogether.

But it was the old man, the bald leather-skinned kitemaster, Scarbo, there beside him at the rail.

"I'm standing down now. Tom has the next watch. He wants to know if you'll take a cup of tautine with him."

Drink with the enemy first, yes. He'd refused the old man's invitation earlier, waiting for this.

"Tell Captain Tyson I'd be honoured."

"You might do that, sir. I'm going for'ard myself."

Lees felt his body tense, felt the rush of anger at this casual insolence. But no second Knife for this one, not ever. Scarbo was not the sensitive his master was. No Knife would take him.

Perhaps a strike of a more temporal kind though—a quick sword-thrust between the ribs. Let the whole ship go down with its Captain, he thought, though Tynan Lees knew he would never do such a thing. It was just his anger, his contempt for these ignorant Nationals. He had long ago become a man of honour, useless exalting male honour. As his Lady Sa once reminded him: only men fought duels. And the helplessly patriarchal Lees saw his own folly laid out in those words—the feeling of having to go outside exalting nature to be so wise. He could never do it.

He watched the kitemaster depart, made the quick motion of his hands that meant unworthy, then found the shape of his quarry at the helm, mostly silhouette, just the tiniest part of him illuminated by the lights from the companionway and the soft glow of the helm's own read-outs.

Night, when everyone is dark, lit only at the eyes.

Lees crossed the commons and climbed to the quarterdeck.

"Captain Tyson, good evening."

"Good evening to you, Blade Lees. I'm sorry we did not meet earlier. We're undermanned at present; I was using the somnium after a double watch."

Lees made a gesture, probably unseen, to show it was of no consequence, but his thoughts were racing.

Blade Lees? This National knew him for a non-Kurdaitcha assassin, a man from one of the private households. It made Lees check the underline: the psychic stratum where the Knife was turning about itself, newborn and wonderful.

"Captain, the honorific? You know us?"

"I know you, Blade Lees. Of you, I should say. I knew the Lady Sa."

He speaks it from his own mouth. Good. But how? How could he know?

It was as if Blue Tyson read his thoughts. "Scarbo recognised the house sersifan you wore when you came aboard. The Lady Sa's sign. He told me."

"'May her face be carried in righteous glory before the eyes of heaven,'" Lees murmured.

"'May her heart be itself a lantern in the dark places of her passing.'"

Another shock. "You also know the *Amduat*, Captain?"

"I know that your Lady Sa cherished the *Book of the Dead.* Will you have tautine or tisn?"

Composure was what Lees needed. Part of his Lady's sign, there on the sersifan he yet wore on his chest, was the crescent moon that was now lowering to the desert fastness, that had in fact determined the day and hour of this strike, Lees timing it just so.

"What I would really like, Captain, is kites. Can we spare some, even for a powered night run?"

Perhaps his enemy smiled, he could not tell.

"By coming aboard at Maldy you have saved us a day's run to Sollellen. It will be a pleasure, Blade Lees."

"Tynan, Captain, please." He could not stand the honorific here with the Knife forming, safely lodged in the fierce dark of its becoming.

"Tom, then," his enemy said, leading him into further unwanted intimacy, trapping him.

Fortunately Blue Tyson was touching controls, sending commands to the cable-boss, releasing the inflatables from their deck sleeves, the only automatic barrage *Rynosseros* carried, four helium-filled parafoils that ran up on their lines, deploying against the vivid stars in curved squares of intense black.

"Your signature kite?"

"Furthest out."

"Not closest in? Heart of the shapes?"

"I prefer the tribal way. 'The brave man leads'."

"Ah." Now the Bayas *I Ching* as well. Lees imagined the insignia, blue animal head on ochre. Yes, he thought, and quickly found the Knife defining itself, solace in that, power and purpose too. "Thank you. You can tell I am one for the old ways. It does not seem complete without a canopy."

"'The truth of her form curves in beauty above the land,'" Tom Tyson said, quoting again from ancient funeral texts.

This was unexpected. Lees never doubted the Knife once it had been summoned, but nor could he resist finding it, cherishing it as a miser would a favourite jewel.

"But drink," the voice urged him. "Then tell me how you came to serve the Lady Sa."

Back to it. And with such a request.

Lees took the cup of tautine and surveyed the night. As he sipped the sharp refreshing liquid he looked upwards, savoured the clear cool wind shearing away the few clouds, listened to it singing in the cables, saw how the kites spread, the separations intact and satisfying, dark as they were, found the one he thought carried this Blue Captain's sign. Beyond the shapes, the moon held as surely as his minding did in him, and close behind, no more than a few kilometres now surely, the recovery ship, *Kulta*, was riding in *Rynosseros*'s dust trail, its Clever Man captain, dependable Merdes, tuned to Lees' mind-line, waiting to be called in for the pick-up when the act was done.

Kulta was special, Soti-made but Kurdaitcha outfitted, a favour to the new Soti Prince. *Rynosseros*'s systems would never find her.

Lees smiled. What to tell his enemy as his Lady's sign stood right there and the Knife formed? All of it? Bring his beloved Lady Sa alive for this time of justice? Speak her out, more than keep her in memory? Oh yes, if Lees himself could stand it.

"Captain—"

"Tom."

"I have been the most blessed of men. I was out-of-family, a bastard son abandoned at birth, without pedigree. Before I came to be a household man, part of a retinue, before I knew I had the gift, I was destined for the Samanta levies. You know them?"

"Yes."

"It would have been a small life. I was sixteen years old, in the muster, actually lined up for the selections, standing in the dust outside the Chirason Gate, when my Prince came by. What a day that was."

"Stoutheart Tiberias Kra."

"Yes indeed. Before he died at Heart-and-Hand. Before he was—"

"I was there, Tynan. I saw him die."

You did, Lees said to himself, but my Knife is not for that.

"I was told you did. With Kra this day was his sister, the Lady Sa, and the Clever Man, Medenty, Kra's close friend, often a valued adviser to both of them. She was in her fifties then, but still a great beauty, and a powerful administrator with powerful enemies of her own.

"They regarded the dozens of us for Samanta, the ones not taken by the techmakens and the Colleges. The three of them spoke together. Suddenly I felt them at my mind, Kra and this Medenty, at that time assigned to my Lady's staff. They tracked my mind-line, found my origins and the latency. Kra went about his business. I was taken aside and interviewed by the Lady Sa, then by her Clever Man, then by them both together. Right there in the levy office, with everybody watching. They offered me training and a posting to the Lady's private household."

Blue Tyson's voice came gently out of the darkness. "And how many Knives have you summoned in her service, Tynan?"

"In ten years? Eighty-six."

Eighty-seven, he told himself, and found the shape again.

"She used you sparingly."

"Kra wanted me for his own, but there was a promise being kept: the next mind-fighter hers. She insisted on it. I wore her sersifan, took only her enemies. Eighty-six is not many, but if you had their names you would be amazed."

"You are a Clever Man?" the Blue Captain asked, inevitably.

"No, Captain. I carry only the Knife. I access no haldanes, read only a few of the dragons. But I know you have something of the gift." Lees had already scanned his enemy and knew how limited that gift was. One application only.

"Sometimes I see hero-shapes," Tom Rynosseros said. "No dragons."

"But you can follow mind-war."

"I see energies build and fade, nothing more. Few patterns."

"I was told that when Kra died at Heart-and-Hand you saw the patterns there."

"A rare occasion, Tynan. It's not always like that."

He tells that much truth at least.

"My Lady asked to see you because of it. She sent for you when she heard. Your account helped her accept what happened that day, let her see her brother had caused the strike against Heart-and-Hand, that protocols were observed."

"And so helped cause her death."

He admits it! Speaks it from his own mouth!

Lees fought to keep his voice even. "You brought the man Docri on your ship."

"Not my man. I knew him as a mercenary interested in a commission for Samanta. I was on my way to see your Lady Sa at her invitation. I did not know he had a contract against her."

Not what our Clever Men say, Captain Tom!

"You brought him."

"Paid passage, Tynan."

"You were told to observe closed ship."

"That directive came when we were an hour out of Maldy. I had already granted passage to one I took to be an approved contract-soldier."

"Always a man of honour," Lees said. His voice might have trembled just a little, though deep in him the Knife was sure.

"Like you, Tynan. More tautine?"

"No." The mind had to be steady. "Some tisn if I may."

So he could drink with his enemy still, with her sign riding there beyond his.

Tom Rynosseros found the flask, filled two ceramic cups. Lees heard them clink; took one in his hand. Heard the words: "Help yourself to more." Drank in silence.

Ten minutes, perhaps thirty went by, Lees could not tell, not having the helm display. He had the night, the Knife, and he considered one in terms of the other.

It was easy to do with the scimitar moon settling there. Sharp. Sweet. Precious. The wind rising, building into a stronger, richer roadsong.

All good. All soothing.

As a household man, Lees had not been on many ships—a voyage now and then when the Lady Sa travelled, sometimes alone when there was something to be done, occasionally an act of payback such as this was. But the ways of charvolants were always new and exciting.

Only the moon made it different now, made the pain new—her sign suspended right there. Sometimes the kites moved, and held it occluded for a moment. Then it was back, sure and sharp.

Bitter moon. Pointed. Poignant.

Poignard.

An hour or two to midnight. It couldn't be more. He reached out to *Kulta* riding like a shadow close behind, touched Merdes' mind, confirmed the form this would take. Nothing more than a touch of mind, a yes, no need of an answer.

Then a glance at the Knife. He held it as sure and steady as a shout. Quiet pride in that; he knew he had never made better.

His second cup of tisn had gone cold. It no longer warmed his hands. He became aware that he had been lost in thought, that a silence had been between them.

Still an hour at least. Long silences were the sailor's way, he knew, but more words would be needed soon. Something.

Blue Tyson spoke. "You were not at Chirason that day."

He keeps at it! "I was rostered elsewhere, Captain. Kra had left no sons. There were accession protocols and representations from all the houses. I was away from the household on my Lady's business to the newly-chosen Prince."

"Have you ever wondered at that?"

"What?"

But Tom Rynosseros kept silent, an almost fully dark form at the helm, lit only in a small blue-green glimmer at the underside of the jaw, in a faint yellow wash at the right shoulder.

"What was that, Captain?" Lees asked, though the question had penetrated by then.

"Why would anyone wish to kill the Lady Sa?"

Again he dares! So casually. Anger filled him.

Lees forgot midnight. He brought the Knife into that state of readiness Kurdaitcha, Clever Men and Unseen Spears called *adaio*, the thrust or the cast, one moment before. At the same moment he reached out, scanned his adversary two paces away, read the inchoate mindfield this National had, the receiving field that gave the Knife its edge, let it be the way, reached back to find *Kulta* as well, said: Now.

And simultaneously, for all it took was an instant, he thought of Lady Sa dying, lying in her airy room in Chirason, fatally poisoned, sinking into death. Lees and his Lady alone, as astonishing as that was. Medenty and Merdes and the medics all sent away. Ordered away by a few imperious words from the dying woman.

"Jimi, you will heed what I say." Jimi, she had always called him when they were alone; her private name for the boy she had from the Chirason Gate, from the sure promise of Samanta. "It was not . . . this Docri . . . you understand. He gave the first-stage toxin. When he greeted me. The reagent . . . was given later. Jimi . . . " And she had arched up, died, just like that, not in his arms though one hand had reached up to claw at his, but there with his name—his other name—on her lips.

Adaio. The Knife spinning and flashing in the underline, filling it, target aligned.

"Tynan, tell me. Why the Lady Sa?"

Adaio. You saw her before I did. Spoke to her an hour before. You.

"Blade Lees, this is important! Why the Lady Sa?" It was not the demand of an answer that saved the Coloured Captain then; it was the reflexive need of Lees' training, to betray nothing by how he spoke. That mental effort to control his voice for any kind of answer other than the truth took the strike from *adaio* to held-and-waiting again.

Wait, he told *Kulta* riding in the dark, moving in.

"I was told—"

"You were told? Who told?"

"Her Clever Men. Medenty and the others."

"Forget what they said, just for a moment. They may have been deceived too. Why the Lady Sa?"

Too? Lees did not answer. Could not trust himself to.

"You carry a Knife for me, Tynan?"

Thank the Ancestors for darkness; this tested all his composure. What to say? Midnight. He'd never reach it. The dagger of mind spun in its fire. Screamed there, ached there, targeted.

The Blue Captain was speaking.

". . . think I caused her death, don't you?"

Yes, Lees wanted to say, to shout, glad to be free of secrecy. The best justice was known justice, guilt admitted, payback understood.

"Yes!" It took him seconds to realise he had spoken aloud, confessed his mission. Lees held the Knife very close to *adaio*, aware of the kites, the emblem moon, the wind in the cables, keenly alert for his enemy's crew in hiding, planted earlier in anticipation of this admission from him. But Lees read nothing, not a presence, not a chance. Why was this National telling him then?

"My final night," Tom Rynosseros said, "if you have a Knife for me. You might answer my questions. A discourse to the end. Midnight, yes?"

How does he know? Lees wanted to scream the words. Was he more the sensitive than they said? Could he read the presence buried in him, using the very skill that would doom him? Could he see *Kulta* riding in the night? Lees was used to reading the capabilities of his targets quickly, skilfully, so none ever knew he had done so, and he had found no trace of such an ability. It was not possible. It just wasn't.

Lees did something he had not done in eight years at least. He recited the accession mantra to himself, used it to become the atavism again, the calm centre, the Hand-with-the-Knife, the distillation of impassive force. He considered the land, unseen, rushing by out there, wove that into his silent song—read ship and stars and stones, tapping, trapping their imagery. The Lady Sa did not intrude, nothing unwanted did. He even used the old word-stations: home to hone, cry to kris, stillness to stiletto. He read the land as knives. Night to Knife.

He was himself the form he carried when he returned to the cold cup crushed in his hand, to the wetness of tisn mixed with blood, to his silent enemy watching him. Some eyelight told him that.

"It is now," he said, Knife said, the only thing possible. Knife spun, ached in him, *as* him.

"Do it on a question," Blue Tyson said. "One answer."

"Yes." Barely.

"In Chirason. At the tribal court. Pretend it was not me, though I swear I did not do it. Why would anyone want to kill your Lady? For a moment pretend. Why would anyone else?"

"Advantage." So difficult to say.

"Yes? Something more?"

"Inheritance." Difficult. More than one answer too, but Lees stayed with it.

"Yes, Tynan. Inheritance always through the female. Who chose the new Prince?"

"Clever Men. Convocation. A corroboree."

"Why him?"

"Medenty? Closest blood. The closest."

"Who opposed?"

"No-one." Agony.

"Who opposed in secret and dared not speak?"

"What?" *Adaio*.

"Who opposed? Who might have?"

"No-one."

"Your Lady did."

Adaio! Adaio! Knife shouted. But he had to ask. "How do you know?"

"Was she asked to wed the new Prince?"

"Formality. Asked, yes."

"Tenure, Blade Lees. Sanction. Permanence. You hurried back to find her almost gone. I believe she could not tell you all of it. Tynan, someone delayed the message telling me closed ship. Who told you it was me who finally killed her?"

"Her best. My teacher. Our new Prince."

"Medenty."

"Most loyal. Yes."

"And your friend? Merdes?"

"Yes. He said so too. Others did."

"What is Merdes' line?"

"What?"

"His line, Tynan!"

"Anjan through Jurinju. Medenty's true son—"

"The new Prince of the Soti. Your Lady had no sons?"

"No."

"No secret sons?"

"No!"

"Tynan, I was with her. She was dying. She had already been given the reagent. She asked me to find you. You arrived when I had gone."

"You lie!"

"No, Jimi." Incredibly, Blue Tyson spoke *that* name. (Could he have lifted it from his mind? Could he?) "She loved you. She asked me to search. You were no casual find at the Chirason Gate. You are her undeclared son and she wanted you saved. Possibly you as Prince of the Soti. But she had powerful enemies. She dared not say. It would have been your death."

"You did not say before. You let me continue."

"You had drawn the Knife."

"No! No! I hadn't then. You could have met me when I came aboard at Maldy. Tell me!"

"Then it must be some other promise to your Lady. Not my way but hers, yours."

Lees' hands were fists, the Knife barely held, the force too great. He had never rejected a summoning before, never withstood one, never even tried. He had never been wrong. "What?"

"Not yet. It must be done your way."

"What?"

But he knew. He understood the simple truth of words spoken long ago. You learn by doing, Jimi. Only men fight duels. Men who learn the other way, the female way, calculate and avoid, use subtlety. He had never been that kind of man, but others were. His own friend and captain, Merdes. Oh, Medenty, can it be? Powerful *Kulta* riding in the night, Merdes there, coincidence?

Lees turned from the helm, ran to the great stern vanes where the rooster tail of dust boiled up in its roaring spray. He turned the form within him, re-made, re-shaped it, a thing never done before, gave the bright blade another face, sent it hurtling back at the hungry shadow.

He did not need to know it had found its mark. He did not need to know that twelve crewmembers would speak forever of a force rushing through them out of the night, finding their captain.

The place in him was empty and calm, the last of Jimi put aside. Now he moved back to the helm.

"Will you come with me into Chirason?" he asked the quiet figure at the helm.

"I promised your Lady I would. As witness. There may be one more Knife."

"Yes."

Fifteen minutes later, *Rynosseros* swung away from Sollellen onto Lateral 246. Neither man said a word, but Lees found the kite of the Blue Captain where it rode on the darkness, looked beyond it to where the sharpest vendetta moon still stood bright and hard on the face of heaven.

A dagger, yes, definitely that. But a smile too, he decided, as her shape settled to meet the darkness of his, Knife to night.

Definitely a smile.

Totem

Everything has its message.
Nothing tells us nothing.
—Andrew Mallin

The life dump on the outskirts of Tell is not the only one the tribal biotects have used. During the secretive years, the heady early years of the AI quest, the Ab'O scientists of Australia took the cast-offs and spoil from their life experiments out beyond Wani, far beyond Bullen Meddi to the shore of the lonely sand-sea at Trale and left them there. It was the dumping place before respectability came to Tell, before the exciting decades that ended with the True Lifer riots and the cut-backs.

Trale today is unique in all the world, though so few go there or dare speak openly of its existence. Officially it does not exist. It is taboo as both idea and fact.

Today beach totems stand along the blazing shores, strange teratoid constructs of bismin, citilo and tri-sephalay, a thousand variants and hybrids as unsettling to see as an unresolved trompe l'oeil or a suspected false perspective or a stairway to nowhere in a half-demolished house. They are called—fittingly enough —Abominations by the tribes, more disturbing than Fosti with its Living Towers (that life project had global acclaim and tribal endorsement at least), more by far than the thousands of belltrees scattered across Australia, left as roadposts beside quiet desert Roads, or set up as tourist novelties on the terraces of the coastal hotels.

The Trale totems seize the eye like a new colour; they stand in the heat of the day like bright stone flowers, or glitter under the moon like wet iron or the subtle dozen midnights in an insect's back, inviting apposite names only art critics and classicists could love: trochars, onagers, spinnerets, magganons—the list goes on, an ambitious attempt to rationalise what simply is. Failed experiments run riot. Abominations.

There are seven distinct shores at Trale, reaching out from a low pentagonal headland that is nowhere more than six feet above the surrounding desert, yet high enough to give a gentle gradient to the long beach slopes where the totems stand, a point of distinction: beach, sand-sea, headland.

On the flat, heat-baked promontory itself is Fender's Folly, what probably started as a testing station (or worse, a killing vault, though who would admit to that?) before it was abandoned and the cast-offs left to flourish unsupervised in their own strange fashion. The Folly became the obvious pied-à-terre for anyone permitted into the region, or for those who took the dreadful risk, eluded surveillance and came anyway: walls to shelter behind from the cold night winds, ledges under which to hide from the mid-day sun, a condensation post and bore rig feeding a cistern.

It is like a sephalay masonic form itself, or a construct left behind from Eniwetok or other test sites from that time of global strife. For me, the blank interlocking causeways and revetments have always suggested that sort of thing, as if a World War 2 gun emplacement had been wedded to the ancient observatory at Jantar Mantar in India. But that is all. It has never spoken to me as it has to some.

Warboy called it an angry place, or rather a place for anger, true to his arguments about locality. He found its pointlessness infuriating.

"Look!" he cried, too loudly in the terrible heat, striding up from where we had moored our Dimity sand-skiff. "It's a locked cipher, Tom. It does nothing, tells nothing. A controlled nullity!"

"Forget it, Michael," I replied, entering the Folly by the worn path. It took me behind the first of the high canted walls into the shadows just now forming at 1116. The slender band of darkness was infinitely precious.

Warboy strode along the top of the wall, a vigorous grey-haired man in his early fifties. The anger he read in the Folly came from him, from too much stored too long behind that hard florid face. He stepped from one concrete bastion to another, waving his arms like a mad Bedouin chief.

"Mallin says he has decoded this! This!"

I sat leaning into the shadow edge, pressing back against the wall, imagining that it cooled me more than it actually did. All the way out he had been like this, raving about Mallin and his informational theories. Nothing about the totems and Mallin's work there—he accepted that readily enough. Only about the claims made in *The Beach Gazette* or in some humble three-page feature in an issue of *New Land*, that the Folly had itself become an encoding by association, an accidental but integral rosetta for something, because of the totems, because of the focusing.

I would have called him down, reminded him once again that we were here to solve the mystery of a man's death, but I cherished the thin shade, the time alone without the wearying intensity of him. I still believed that he would make an effort when I gave him my news. I told myself that Michael was completing a valid transaction of his own, that he would be of no use till that was done.

It took half an hour, no more. I was drowsing in the shadow margin when he returned, stretched out on the concrete like the effigy of a crusader knight. He came down the main ramp, turning into the section of gallery we were using. I looked up at him standing there, wondering not for the first time what his eyes looked like.

Warboy believed in the eyeline and the dangers of eyelining; he would never remove his sunglasses, nor would he allow me to remove mine.

"You know what, Tom?" His voice was easier, thank goodness, the echoing harshness gone. "There's a new one on Beach 4. Not far from where Jacobi died."

He always spoke as if I had more than a cursory knowledge of the Trale site.

"Have you typed it?"

"No," he said. "It may not be locked yet. Could be a dexter variant, but with a trumpet bell opening two-thirds up. Something new. I'll write it up, send a copy to Mallin."

"You won't have to," I said, sitting up, deciding to get it over with.

"What?" Some of the habitual anger again. Mallin's name was that kind of negative talisman.

"Andrew is coming out too, Michael. He'll be here around 1300."

It was almost worth it to see the dropped jaw and open mouth (I had to imagine the widened disbelieving eyes), to hear the incomprehensible sounds he made as words wouldn't come, then the harsh cry: "What! But he's out at Mandana!"

"Not now he isn't. He's on his way here. It's what the tribes want; both of you involved. Jacobi dead on Beach 4 with all the symptoms of heart attack—or an eyeline death—is reason enough, wouldn't you say?"

"You don't—"

"Please, Michael. Hear me out. You saw the pictures. You saw that look of bewilderment and terror, the staring eyes. You saw the clenched fists. Fingernail scarring. Extreme stress. No other human trace; there was no-one else here. The tribes did the forensics and found nothing. So they call us in. They specified you and Andrew. I'm just scrutineer. Accept it, will you? It's going to be hard enough. You were colleagues together—the two of you still are, like it or not."

The thick canted walls were open to the sun, to an infinity of blazing emptiness, but Michael Warboy looked like a man caught in a trap. His eyes were shut away behind black glass, but his silence and sudden composure were more than just calculating. I was used to the ravings that had marked our voyage, the characteristic vituperation against faculty colleagues and projects other than his own. His lack of response now was frightening to see. Finally he spoke again. "Who's bringing him out?"

"Lisa Maiten."

He knew of her; she had done lab work for Life Studies in her postgrad years at Inlansay.

"Hmph. Probably another Mallinite by now." He might have spat had his throat been less dry. He made the motion.

"One more thing, Michael," I said quickly. For all I knew it might be my final chance. "I want to get this done as smoothly as possible, so we Nationals look good out of this. We've got less than 24 hours till the watch-ship picks us up, that's all. I'm not sure why you and Andrew are such enemies—"

"It's complicated, Captain." There was new distance between us. Captain instead of Tom. But at least he was calmer; maybe being at Trale did it, having the chance to do first-hand research again, any kind of first-hand work himself.

I decided to pursue the matter. "Coming out here you said it's his ancillary encodements, his notion of extended contexts. Do you think it might be simpler—that his disbelief in eyelining upsets you?"

"I've got till 1300 you say?"

"You see both points of view are vital now? Three months ago Jacobi came out to update the index—that's what I was told—and he died of fright. They kept us away all that time, no Nationals allowed in."

"An eyeline death needs another set of eyes, Captain. Another soulframe to launch the intention. He had no-one with him, the old fool. The tribes would have cleared him for an assistant, but no. He came all this way alone."

"He wasn't wearing glasses when they found him, Michael. They were in his pocket. What makes a man take off his sunglasses at mid-day?"

"What are you saying?"

"It's what the tribal investigators are saying—that it's not an accidental eyelining at all, that it's deliberate encodement. A totem *told* him to die. They need to know if they have created some death-look analogue. That's why they specified you. And Mallin, since you were both attached to Jacobi's staff. But they need you, Michael. They respect your eyelining theories, your published work."

Warboy's impassive chitinous gaze held mine. He knew all this, and the idea intrigued him. This was his area, the informational legacies of unsuspected things. He was no doubt considering Mallin's imminent arrival and counting his losses. It was a curious withdrawal to watch, as if he were dampening a self-indulgent mode of conduct and superimposing another.

"It would have to be a mover."

"Explain that." I needed to be sure.

"Mutable. Only partially locked. You know that most of them are solar-powered, but I mean more than just aligning to the sun throughout the day. It had to change its configuration in some catalysing way—approach, reach and probably depart from a potential ideomorphic crisis, a freak or intended conjunction. Like a baited trap. Forget the sergeant-majors, the xoanons and the sandwives; they're almost always locked forms. Something lured Jacobi in close; he removed his glasses to see it a different way; the configuration reached culmination, then probably evolved away from it. No trace now that we *could* find."

There was a hollow boom from somewhere down the shore, then another, and another further out. The "noon guns" were going off, the magganons releasing their stored-up gases into the overheated air. You could hear the tinkle of glass as the payloads burst free of the fragile chimneys.

It was the active part of the day. All along the burning Trale shores, the unlocked and mutable totems did whatever it was they did. The trochars siphoned up their tainted artesian spill; the orreries shifted their bright fossil lenses; the spinnerets laid fragile cable that shot forth to dry, turn to powder and blow away on the afternoon winds.

More guns sounded, dozens of sharp detonations now. Michael and I waited till the last of them had discharged their loads. Then I stood and took one of two identical envelopes from inside my djellaba.

"Here's all the tribal authorities gave us. It's not much."

He took it, slipped it inside his own sand-robes. "Just keep Andrew out of my way, all right? I'll use the hour I've got." He turned and left the Folly.

I sat in the concrete gallery another ten minutes, then decided that as scrutineer I should be keeping an eye on what Warboy did at Beach 4. I climbed onto one of the baffles, followed its course around to the north so I could spot the scientist.

The shoreline shimmered in the heat; the hundreds of intervening totems seemed to shift more than their functions allowed—the air above them glinted still with suspended silicon particles from the noon firings, though the guns were finished now. The beaches were quiet.

There was no sign of Warboy at all, not at 4 or 5, not beyond at the furthermost sites out near 7.

I immediately looked southward to 3, 2 and 1—no sign of him there either, and a quick glance downslope showed he wasn't collecting gear from our modest Dimity skiff.

In this strange landscape, it was easy to feel irrational panic. I found my binoculars and tried again. Through the instrument the images settled, steadied. I moved across Beach 4 quickly—from the swollen onion base and tall organ-pipe chimney of a reloading magganon, on to another, on to the shifting light-boxes and smoothly-cycling lenses of an orrery, across to a splendid rorschach, its distended butterfly-wing platelets lifted to the sun. Downslope then to a sergeant-major standing alone at the very edge of the sand-sea like an elongated Mayan stele.

He wasn't there. I was about to move on to Beach 5 when a trochar split in two—or rather a crouching figure stood away from it. Warboy had been behind it, doing what Jacobi had probably been doing, noting close detail. I saw the shrouded figure put his glasses back on, stand back from the totem, studying it.

"Damn you, man!" I said, feeling incredible relief, annoyed that Trale had gotten to me this way. I left the high walls of the Folly and hurried to him.

The trochar he examined sat like the carapace of a tortoise made from dirty stained-glass, ribbed and frosted in dull mottled shades, mostly ochres but also green, dark purple and bronze. There was the dusty six-foot spire of a percept tower lifting from one end, fitted with sensor spines, these upturned slightly and locked at the noon hour. The only movement came from the subterranean moisture cycling sluggishly behind the cloudy panes, bubbling through the conduits, drawn out of the earth, heated by the sun and fed back to it laden with volatised amino acids and exotic enzymes. Not for the first time, it occurred to me that there were secret places beneath this forsaken sand-sea only the trochars knew.

"Anything?" I asked.

"Nothing here, no," Warboy said, turning away from the trochar, facing where the body had been found. "But Jacobi might have staggered over to the kill-site from here."

We crossed the long slope to the spot itself, tagged with its yellow peg. Jacobi had been on his back; he could have fallen away from any of the three totems standing close by: a locked coralline dexter, a mature spinneret, and a primed and straining onager, a sport in that, curiously, unlike its kin, it was turned away from the sand-sea, facing half-upslope instead. Its armature was curved right back, its ladle full.

Or as Warboy had said, Jacobi might have staggered down the hard smooth slope from any direction. The winds that scoured the Trale littoral would soon rake the sand clear of footprints.

I imagined the dying, sun-blinded scientist spinning away from some lethal bioform, arms flailing or pressed across his eyes as he wandered among the totems to this eventual dying place. With nothing for company but Abominations, possibly a magganon firing a final salute, a bubble of gas bursting free, showering him with flecks of glass, or an onager ratcheting its arm, kicking its lump of organic waste out onto the sand-sea.

Or nothing as dramatic. Nothing at all. Just the thick fluids bubbling through the trochars, just the heat and the silence.

"Can you do tests?"

Warboy grunted. "I can duplicate a few," he said, sounding distracted. "But why bother? Tribal investigators did all that. My job is to observe the bioforms. Speculate, since that's all I can do."

"Buddy system, Michael. One of these has probably killed a man."

"All right. Our job. Don't worry, I'll work with Andrew. But I intend to do my own work too."

"I understand." And I returned to Fender's Folly, not letting myself look back till I was among the low walls and could use my binoculars. I felt guilty doing it, but I hoped to catch a glimpse of the man's eyes.

Andrew Mallin arrived at 1310, his thirty-foot Maud skiff appearing as a coloured spectre out of the south-west. Lisa jockeyed the seven kites with a skilful touch and brought the craft in next to ours.

Andrew Mallin didn't make it easy for her. In his eagerness to reach Trale, the tall hawk-faced man stood in the bow, wearing his glasses but without sand-robes of any kind. His leather scrap-jacket was open, the bright circles, squares and triangles of the simulated mission patches made him look like an airman from another age rescued and brought here, in no way the colleague of the earnest figure out on Beach 4.

He jumped from the low deck and rushed to shake my hand.

"Tom! Lisa said you were chosen for this. Good to see you again. A single day but better than nothing. Where's Michael?"

"At the site," I said, indicating a point on the shimmering shoreline, then went to help Lisa unload the skiff. Together the three of us carried their equipment into the Folly.

"He must be furious," Mallin said when we were among the walls. He smiled as he used binoculars to locate his colleague. Lisa Maiten and I exchanged smiles of our own; she had been the only sailor the Department of Life Studies could call on who had sufficient accreditation to qualify for Trale, a former postgrad in her thirties, red-headed, palely pretty, an experienced sailor dying of Colourman's Disease, at the end of her third remission. It was always good to see her; I applauded her unspoken reasons for wanting it this way, doing what she loved so much. No doubt she had endured Mallin's tirades travelling here as I had Warboy's.

When Mallin left for Beach 4, tribal file under his arm, I walked with Lisa down to the skiffs.

"What's the real problem, Tom?" she asked as we checked the brakes and chocked the wheels against the afternoon winds.

"Getting them to co-operate, to see this invitation as more than just the formality it probably is. With Jacobi gone, they're more faculty rivals than ever. I'm sure Mallin will have told you that

Warboy is an eyeliner, if you didn't know it before. Keep your glasses on. He'll tend to stay away from the rest of us."

"I was in Physics but I knew Life Studies had one on staff," she said. "I suspected it might be Warboy. Is he the whole thing?"

"Oh yes. Eye-contact programs the unconscious. Looks can kill, casual glances trigger malaise or death-switch or angst."

"Or elation. Or love."

"Or schizophrenic imbalance."

Lisa shook her head at the wonder of it. "How does he get to teach?"

"He doesn't. Purely research. But he publishes constantly. Makes the Department and the university look very good."

"But doesn't often walk the streets, I bet."

"True."

"What's the word?"

"Psychoactive. Human eye-contact is psychoactive. You get looked at in a crowd, a quick meaningful glance at dinner, meet someone's eyeline in passing—I suppose you have exchanged something, a naked moment. Soulframe to soulframe. I'd hate to think they're right."

"Is there valid research I should be keeping up on?" Which might have been a first oblique reference to Colourman's.

"Very little that's empirically sound. Mainly testimonials. 'I was deflected from personal resolution on 4th May.' Claims of faith healing and shaman magic, crucial historical encounters; the choosing of known and potent evil-eye emissaries to foreign courts, Christ's laying on of hands actually being an eyeline ministration of great power. This is provocative and top secret because tribal AI is being accused of soulframe status. It was a traumatic death—"

"Heartstop caused by shock."

"Blood analysis suggests that. The scarring on the palms. One of these constructs does seem to be a killer."

"Ersatz life, Tom—"

"Don't say that, Lisa. These *are* lifeforms. I have to keep telling myself that too. Congruence is missing, that's all. No *meaningful* exchange. The tribes are very nervous about it. Jacobi was here at their behest, checking the variants. Accusations have been made in the media that he found things the tribes wanted hidden, that they meant him to die. Eyelining is not nonsense for them, but they'd like it confirmed or refuted one way or the other. Have they unwittingly created death-look?"

"I certainly don't pick easy ones." She looked beyond our moored skiffs, watching the empty desert. Perhaps it was another reference to her condition, though if so it was a comment too pointed to acknowledge. The sand-shades hiding her eyes made it safe and easy, a true blessing; Colourman's changed the eyes, told observers that a strange and beautiful brain death was occurring, slowly taking a personality down into the infinite corridors of self, leaving it trapped there in increments of disconnexion. A day would come when Lisa would not return from one of her assignments; she would have gone sailing off into the desert on a journey to nowhere, trapped helplessly within herself.

As we walked back to the Folly, I allowed myself to brush against her, sleeve to sleeve in the old way, a sailor spiek for "with you." She smiled under her hidden, dying eyes.

"Yes," she said. "I know."

It was tempting to think that Warboy and Mallin had reached an understanding, and that their walking back together boded well for the mission, but it became obvious that in these initial hours at Beach 4, this was probably the first time they had spoken more than in monosyllables, and that it was Andrew who was trying to persuade Michael Warboy to take it as a compliment to them both and something owed to Jacobi's memory.

It was just after 1700 when they returned. There was still plenty of daylight left, yet all along the shores the totems had almost completely shut down. The spinnerets had shot cable and were inert; nothing could be seen moving behind the trochars' panes; the orreries were locked tight in the different houses of their zodiacs. Silicon lids had formed in the magganon chimneys earlier, that happened soon after the noon firings, at the very height of their vigorous heliotropism; now they silently fermented their gases and did whatever it was constituted this part of their cycle. The cauchemars glistened, sweated their sweet resinous ichor; the onagers which hadn't launched missiles of waste would not do so now till first light. Their ratcheting, thudding ejections would wake us.

And now the wind came blowing in upon Trale from across the sand-sea, the thermals giving way to the cool brinraga, a much kinder wind than its unruly cousin, the larrikin. Even as Michael and Andrew reached the Folly, the few warning gusts gave way to a sudden steady airflow, full of stinging sand, scouring the slopes, causing the temperature to slide into the twenties, eroding the spinneret tracks and the small hummocks of onager waste down to nothing.

Sheltering behind the thick walls, we were probably breathing totemic material: the last of the magganon particles, spinneret and onager dust, though none of us donned the light filter masks provided by the university. The water in the cistern probably contained oil of trochar or worse. It didn't bear thinking on, and I didn't mention it, afraid that Andrew might seize on the portentousness of such things and alienate Warboy even further.

My one concern was nursing them through the night as allies, making it possible for them to work together tomorrow. For me it was Nation's interests at stake here.

I tried my best, and Lisa did, unasked, eager to make my job easier. When night came to Trale, moonless and windy, with frosty stars blazing overhead, we set our cooker going and planted dim telltales to mark the cistern and the skiffs. I prepared a meal, but Michael said he wasn't hungry and excused himself, saying he had eaten something at Beach 4.

It was while we were eating that Andrew gave in to the excitement he felt, his delight at being at Trale again, even for so short a time. He probably thought that Michael was off somewhere, that he couldn't hear; he stood with his head exposed above the parapet, enjoying the airstream on his face.

"The brinraga is a true shastric wind," he said, rhapsodising. "A communication wind. Unlike the larrikin which has no music, no pulse, and is rightly called the heresy wind by the nomads."

"Shastric wind!" Warboy snapped from the darkness. "Can you believe this? Heresy wind!"

Sand shifted, gravel spilled on a slope as Warboy jumped down into the gallery where Lisa and I sat around the cooker, and Andrew stood leaning against the parapet. At his arrival, we immediately averted our gazes, donned our glasses, and turned his way.

"I didn't know you were listening," Andrew said truthfully, but it sounded lame. He looked like a schoolboy caught out mimicking a teacher, though his words had been from simple zeal.

"We agreed to avoid this sort of craziness," Michael said sharply, seeing it his way. "I'd hoped to be spared, here of all places. Spared this!"

Andrew tried again. "Michael, it's so close to your soulframe."

"You always say that, Mallin! *The* soulframe! Not mine!"

"All right. But it's so close. It is! I'm a sensory interface inside and out. Everything designed for meaningful input. I have breathed molecules—inhaled the air here, the magganon fumes, residues of trochar spill and cauchemar sweat. Physiologically I process and decode. I am designed to do so and to respond—in ways I'll never fully know. At the psychic level, the same; I translate the shapes about me. This Folly has to be a psychoactive nexus, no less than what is out there. We read it in the emotional residues we feel, responding to the light here, the scents, the countless mnemonics cueing memory, just in recognising empathy when it's felt for all that it is."

"That's enough now! Really enough! I do grant some of that; you know I do. But the totems are different. They are new, with new semiotic payloads, separate from these surroundings."

At another time I might have voiced my suspicions about a changed land, about reciprocity in the arrangement between the totems and this lonely place where they stood. But this was their argument, and Michael rushed on to make his point.

"The rest of what is here at Trale is base normal. We are designed to accommodate it as minimal."

"You can't separate the parts, Michael," Andrew said, trying his best to be conciliatory but slipping into old practised arguments too. He no longer sounded contrite. 'The totems are *here* in *this* psychoactive locus. It's a psychoactive whole, a gestalt. They relate to those base normals and stand in significant harmony, contrast and opposition. This has become a nexus for the total of that—a connected information tree we may spend lifetimes misunderstanding and decoding."

"No!" Michael was adamant. He spoke now as if to a dull and obstinate undergrad. "We desensitise to those base normals, we always do. We only process them when we travel between them and then temporarily. We do process new and unfamiliar things like these bioforms. The base normals *form* our bias, the xenophobic handicap we must overcome. Not part of the message any longer."

"Jacobi's dead," I said then. "And the Tell specialists are watching how we manage this."

Just get them through the next seventeen hours, I kept thinking. Working together. Get them both points with the tribal directors at Tell. Something for Nation, anything.

"And this is a different task entirely, gentlemen," Lisa said. "You're professional enough to see that. The truth does not care what we separately believe."

It was an unexpected and oddly artless comment. It could not have worked in the common room at Inlansay, but here, from Lisa, it hit home.

I had underestimated Michael as well. Just when I expected him, expected both of them, to tell her to keep out of it, warn us both off, he heaved a sigh and moved to the corner of the open gallery, looking out through the entrance to where our yachts stood in the windy dark. Trale was having a potent effect on both of them.

"Very well," he said in what might have been resignation. "Very well." And he moved out of the Folly into the uncaring wind.

"I'm sorry, Tom," Andrew said at last. "It was thoughtless of me. It's so good for us to be away from the university. And Michael tries, God knows, but he's sensitive about the eyeline. He believes he's had colleagues die from eyelining, valued friends. The notion of unhuman equivalents doing this disturbs him greatly, virtually forces him into areas usually left to me—and to Jacobi, of course, when he was with us. It has to be of paramount importance in everything he does here."

"He'll work on his own research then?"

"He's better than that. He may surprise us. His work is very good."

"The watch-ship will pick us up around noon. We only have half a day. If he won't work with you, Andrew, you must do what you can alone."

"Yes," he said. "So let me find him now. I was thoughtless. When we're out here it doesn't seem right to push theories too much anymore, yet everywhere is subject matter to provoke them anew. I may be able to do something."

Mallin left Lisa and me crouched around the glowing cooker.

"Thanks," I said when we were alone. "You did it better."

She smiled and removed her shades, exposed her incredible languishing eyes, the irises so pale, almost colourless.

"They're after the same thing. They want to discover what simply is, but at the same time they need to be meaningful to themselves first, desperately self-fulfilling, like any of us."

Which was a metastatement for us then, something to sustain the revelation of her eyes in the flickering light.

"Thanks anyway," I said, and her smile softened, changed, did something to re-make the pale weathered face. The pale, downgraded irises shone.

"You'll probably laugh," she said. "But I'm hoping for another remission. Tell me if you mind, Tom. I don't think I'll harm you, but you might do a Christ healing for me. Who knows?"

"A Christ healing! Just promise you'll tell no-one."

"Done."

I took both her hands in mine, and by the warm glow of the cooker gazed into her eyes, for the good it did, or the ill, for the easy kinship of ministering.

I woke to the far-off snap and thud of discharging onagers, to discover Lisa comfortably close beside me, saw the empty sleeping-bags near ours and so slipped out of mine without putting on my shades.

The sky was suffused with an uneven pearly light, a milk-glass blend softly opalescent at the dawn edges in the east. I climbed onto the wall and surveyed the beaches, all that Trale was—or visibly seemed to be, saw an onager release itself, heard the sound of the torsion cancelling, the thud as the arm closed on itself, watched the tiny payload complete its arc. There was a soft impact cloud followed by the sound of a strike, faint but distinct in the wonderful silence.

I went to the parapet, focused my binoculars, quickly found Mallin and Warboy at Beach 4. They stood together near the three bioforms I had visited with Michael the previous afternoon, and seemed to be conferring. Neither wore djellabas; the fanciful and open-ended patches on their scrap-jackets made them look like ancient astronauts seconded from missions never completed, tasks hinted at but undisclosed. I saw cameras and testing equipment at their feet and felt relieved. Maybe something could be done before the Tell ship arrived.

An hour later, the scientists came wandering back for breakfast, and Lisa set out a morning meal as sunlight snatched away the first shadows and began baking the land again.

"We believe we've confirmed the contact site," Andrew said.

Warboy nodded. "Where Jacobi was . . . programmed to die." He did not say eyelined. He was trying; both of them were. "Near the three pieces we noted yesterday."

"Can you be sure?"

"Three months after it happened, no we can't be sure. We believe one or more of the three may have been attempting a congruency."

"Not with Jacobi," Andrew hastened to add, then looked warily at Warboy who seemed not to have minded the interruption. "With each other. We assume they are cognate beings, even if tangental. We must allow they could do it all the time."

Warboy clasped his hands before him, almost as if on a table, the mannerism of a man who often spoke out at faculty meetings.

"They had geared up for a congruency in terms of citilo and sephalay. Jacobi triggered a communication package not meant for a human percept system. He blundered into an intricate AI conversation net and it killed him."

"How sure can you be of this?" I said.

"Never sure. I must repeat. How could we be certain of something like that? But it's consistent with the proximity of the three totems to each other, the fact they're angled in that way. The potential for psychoactive signalling among them would be very high."

"Then it actually could have . . . " I hesitated.

"Yes," Warboy said, without looking at Mallin. "I suspect it eyelined him, viable transaction, that it has a catalysing equivalent to the human eye. Kindred DNA somewhere, compatible aminos and molecule chains, whatever cues the soulframe, causes it to process a change. It may have launched as Hello, but it was as sure as a gunshot into his psyche."

"How do they do it, gentlemen?" Lisa asked. "How do they communicate with one another?"

"How can we answer even that?" Mallin replied, almost as if the two scientists had worked out a compromise and this was Andrew's turn. "Light semaphores from the dexters, organic thread from the spinnerets, tension patterns and angle in the onagers' throwing arms, you tell us."

When Andrew hesitated, Warboy continued. It was almost comical. "We get just enough about Trale to drive us crazy. We've some clues, but research has been so limited; we don't have DNA simulations or observation time to be certain of anything. Compared to the tribal experts, we're like children playing."

Lisa poured more coffee into our mugs. "So what now?"

"We go back to Inlansay," Warboy said. "We devise theories to accommodate all this, try to come up with a suitable range. We discuss them and discuss them some more. Sometimes we do stupid, desperate, all-or-nothing things like intercept communication nets not meant for us, if such things exist. We write up the guesses and hunches with amazing conviction and panache, and the tribal experts laugh as usual since they probably know exactly what it was they made in the first place."

"We only have till 1200."

Warboy snorted. "Just enough time to tantalise us. They can announce how leading National experts were given the chance to solve the mysterious and tragic death of their renowned colleague. They want nothing discovered here. No eyeline equivalent, no cause of death. Our only consolation is that they cannot know what really happened either, otherwise we would never have been allowed to come. Or left alone to look around."

"For all we know," Andrew said, "they may want to be able to blame us for something when we've gone. Accuse us of tampering, damaging the bioforms, sabotaging them."

"The ship will be here regardless," I said. "Do what you can. Please, everyone, you know the routine. Make sure you're clean. No samples, no souvenirs, nothing but photographs. They may not even let us keep those this time. And when it arrives, they could have gain-monitors trained on us. Speak in whispers, backs turned, or they'll know what we say."

Warboy laughed. "Who has anything to say?"

Perhaps we all thought of the totems then, for the silence that followed seemed very eloquent indeed.

At 1050, Lisa and I loaded our skiffs with what we could, then walked along the different beaches observing the totems. The cauchemars sweated resin, the orreries clicked and shifted like bone carousels, the trochars pumped away, the rorschachs lifted symmetrical platelets to the burning sun. Many of the big columnar bioforms—the sergeant-majors, the sandwives, xoanons and coralline dexters, even the spinnerets, looked dead and functionless, but we knew the unlocked ones turned imperceptibly like the hour-hands of antique clocks, angling slowly to follow the course of the sun.

Finally we passed the empty cipher of the Folly again, and crossed Beach 4 to find Warboy at the death site, matching his charts of alignment and configuration variations with continuity photographs taken a year before. Andrew Mallin was upslope a short way, standing near what I suddenly realised had to be the newly-formed totem Warboy had discovered soon after we reached Trale.

"What makes a man take off his sunglasses at noon?" I asked when we joined him.

Andrew smiled. "What indeed? And what makes an ordinary-enough coralline dexter grow a throat opening the size of a dinner plate?"

"I'd hate to think."

"But do, Tom. Do, both of you. All guesses are welcome here—it's what we traffic in in the absence of forensic data and adequate empiricism."

"How do they reproduce?" Lisa asked.

"Good question. Put it with: 'How do they communicate?' Without samples, with what the tribes let us bring, again we can only speculate."

"Speculations then," I said.

"Very well. A spinneret shoots cable, volatile for up to, say, half an hour. Another spinneret overlays that with thread of its own—they can angle and re-align over several days, actually choose targets. The overlay point could be the start. A simple cross-pollination analogue, but smile at the 'simple' will you? We all do."

"Sexes? Asexuality?"

"Not known, Tom. Not to us anyway. But random or conscious cross-pollination is one suggestion; there are others involving directional sporing, wind-blown thread residue, insect carriers as in the plant kingdom. The brinraga may do it all, blow trace elements, move insects sticky with cauchemar resin."

"The onagers?"

"We know there is angling there too, though their breeding cycles must take weeks, months, to complete. We see them facing the desert most of the time, but they can re-align and turn."

"Like the one at the death site?"

"Yes, like the one over there. That could be a breeder beginning or completing. They take quite a while to do it. The continuity photos will determine that. I was here last year. I know I would have remembered an upslope onager. It certainly wasn't like that then."

"Jacobi's death?"

"You see a connection too? Good. I'm giving that thought. It could be a wonderful connection."

"So how would the onagers do it?" Lisa asked. "Their throwing arms?"

"Yes, shot from the arm, I imagine. Michael agrees. A specially prepared matrix instead of the usual waste load. The waste may even be a supporting culture, a fertilisation package with a built-in food or fertiliser store. The onagers shoot out onto the sea, the matrix erodes in the wind, the brinraga moves the payload to a point on the shore. Statistically it would succeed quite well."

Lisa nodded. "And the other one, the tall one?"

"The coralline dexter? Harder to say. There are those lens plates in the shaft like the trochars have."

"Heat windows?" I asked.

"Possibly. But showing no internals like the trochar panes do. Black mirrors. Light traps. The dexters may be asexual, or they may have the capacity to be self-fertilising, or nearly so. There are those refractive surfaces; there may be alignment from one to the next to allow intense, focused sunlight to be lensed onto receiver plates in another coralline in the right mode. Activating codes of light. You can read it both ways: as clumsy or overspecialised, but how can we know? These have a designed cycle but they are rejects remember, aberrant forms."

"So we are told," I said. "They could be special projects."

"Agreed. Still, that way lies madness. So then, a photosynthesis for spores snatched from the wind would be possible and convenient, or self-fertilisation incubated by controlled refraction. Those dexters choose to turn with the sun; they don't have to." He shrugged.

I studied the new totem before us, the smooth vitreous shaft, the dark shiny swellings of the lenses. "If we allow purpose—"

Andrew nodded eagerly. "Yes. These are potentially very sophisticated lifeforms judging from the Fosti Towers and the Iseult-Darrian belltrees. We've never had enough time here. Once or twice a year, testing hypotheses made in the labs all that time. These are generally slow, sun-powered metabolisms, with body-clocks geared to the same 24-hour day-night cycle as ours, but since their DNA was sculpted, they may possess a different perception-consciousness entirely, a different time-sense."

"I think the tribal biotects would have wanted humans to be able to interract with them. Why settle for less than that?"

"But these are—apparently—rejects, Tom. Just allow something so fundamental as a different time-sense. It may be natural for the smarter totems to see humans as frantic, driven creatures."

"Would Jacobi have seemed frantic, do you think?"

Mallin laughed. "I'm sure of it. Look at Michael and me with the time we have. Jacobi pioneered this area if any National did. One of the first of us the tribes allowed near the place. Most of the earliest formalised taxonomies are his. You agree that he probably cued the killer totem?"

"It's what you said before."

"It is. He seems to have intercepted a communication net. Think, too, then, Tom, of what I said a moment ago. How do the totems perceive us? As rushing, random particles? As threats? We don't even know enough to know if there's a predation cycle here—something to feed on them, damage them. We can't do more than allow for defence systems—equivalents of our teeth and fists and kicking muscles. They don't have coarse motion to defend with."

"You'd expect secreted toxins and irritants, acids, poisoned barbs, lensed light. But a death-look eyeline?"

"You're saying it. Michael would certainly say it was logical. He says an eyeline surrogate, but conscious rather than random, and frankly even I prefer not to grant something so mindless as a defence system kill. I want to see volition here, purpose. An accident. A misdirected communication package by lifeforms labouring within different mind-sets and time-frames. Not murderers."

When I looked round at Lisa, I saw that she was standing close to the new variant, with one palm resting on the vitreous-looking citilo shaft. Her other hand was adjusting her glasses; I immediately wondered if she had just now been going to raise them—or if she had already done so and was replacing them.

"Lisa?"

But she addressed Andrew, looking thoughtful.

"Your problem is having too many things to do in too little time. Your own research first, right?"

"Well . . . "

"Favours for colleagues in the Department back home. Honouring promises. It must be like that. Thinking of what you can turn out to win appropriations."

"What are you saying, Lisa?" I could imagine the frown behind his shades.

"I can see room for overlooking things, that's all. Tom and I don't have your preoccupations. We're possibly more detached."

"Possibly. But you're not being very fair."

"Colourman's makes you like that," she said.

"Do you have something?"

"Have you tracked the axes from the three totems and projected them across the three months since Jacobi died? Plotted a likely focus?"

"Of course. There could have been an interface focused on the new totem."

"More, Doctor Mallin. *Resulting* in the new totem."

"What! No! They're discrete forms. Not compatible. How could they interbreed? It'd be like dogs and cats—"

"But you don't know that for sure," Lisa said, strangely relentless. "You want to believe these are cognitive forms. They could know exactly what they're doing."

Andrew pulled at his chin, considering the idea.

"And for all we know," I said, "the trochars and magganons have been priming the land around here. They've had over a hundred years to do it, salting in necessary elements. Built a compatibility horizon, even changed their own patterns. Modified their imperatives."

Lisa was studying the new totem again. "Allow the possibility for a moment. The spinneret sends out its thread—"

Andrew interrupted her. "I see what you're getting at. The onager contributes a combinant payload, the dexter lenses light, incubates. Then a new bioform, a congruency of forms."

"Is it possible?"

Andrew was silent for several moments. "Lisa, who can say? Anything's possible. But to what end?"

"I can guess," she said. "I'm sure you can. Call Michael."

At 1130, three of us stood before the six-foot dexter variant while Andrew paced out trajectories, pegging in the lines of string so we could see just how precise the convergence was.

The onager was in the process of turning back to face the sand-sea like its kin, but Warboy explained how continuity photographs of onagers always revealed an anticlockwise sweep. In three months, the death-site onager could very easily have aligned itself, delivered its part of the birthload, and started on its slow turn to a locked seaward position.

The spinneret, for its size, had the precise angle and the range capacity to shoot cable to the site of the new bioform, and to add increments into the throat opening located above the girdle of black mirrors on its trunk. The coralline dexter had the mirror power to focus easily on the target.

"The process may be more elaborate still," Warboy said. "If the parent dexter spores, it may use the wind to blanket an area with seed. The other totems need only align on a likely target. Or spores could be caught in a sticky discharge in the onager's ladle and mixed there, the spinneret aligning to add its contribution of cable. All done at the onager."

Lisa laughed. "'When shall we three meet again?'"

"What?"

"Nothing. An old dramatic piece. The purpose?"

"I can only think along the lines you have suggested. The three intentionally or unintentionally killed Jacobi"—he did not say triggered a deliberate and violent eyeline response, but it had to be in his thoughts—"and now have worked to create this new form, this . . . jacobi, as an interface for a specialised contact with humans."

Andrew came striding back along his convergence strings.

"It seems certain," he said. "So what do we do?"

Michael surprised us all. "Remove our glasses in front of the thing," he said, and turned back to face the totem.

Andrew objected. "Let me!"

"No, Andrew!" Warboy said. "Remember Jacobi. I'll do it. Only one of us."

No-one argued. Warboy had more to prove than the rest of us: was there eyelining involved, did this AI possess an integral soul-frame, whatever that was?

The four of us stood before the totem, facing the side where the throat opening was, black and glass-smooth above the dark mirrors. Radiating out behind us were the trajectory strings Andrew had set.

In the hush of the final morning hour, Michael removed his glasses and peered into the black organic panes.

I pushed forward to see them better, and Lisa did, and Andrew, all of us crowding there at the point of the convergent strings, like the living heart of a comet, or the focusing node at the meeting lines in a giant's horoscope.

Absurd thoughts crossed my mind, fearful thoughts of conspiracy, of totems aligning behind us, slowly turning, silently loading, but I did not look away. I thought of the bubbles of gas already trapped in the throats of the magganons, pushing at the fragile lids; of the trochars pumping away like stained-glass hearts, sucking up the life of the earth, changing it, pushing it back into the hidden places; of onagers building payloads, crafting them; of spinnerets soundlessly uncoiling eloquent saline cable; of the orreries swinging and clicking in stately calm, making semaphores to the sky, answering the rorschachs, shouting to them in a silence full of significance.

The whole beach was a communication. A communication net spread out.

All the totems, constantly signalling; a shore of urgently declaring forms. Look at us! Look at what is here!

I knew it even as I discovered I had my glasses raised, staring into the black living mirrors just as Michael was, with naked eyes — being answered, being told. Communication is what we do, how we measure our lives, make meaning for ourselves and so make ourselves meaningful.

And in that glittering darkness was a light—a star!—a single star lodged deep within the talking mirrors, no, in my *mind*, projected there!

It took only seconds, moments, to receive that message too, to bring it back out of that secret night.

We all moved then, the broadcast completed; Warboy replacing his glasses, standing; Andrew clearing his throat; Lisa already walking down the beach, her hands raised to her face as if she wept.

And, foolish competitors, the three of us remaining at the site tried to speak, to make comment, but nothing came of it. For there, stretched out about us, were the labouring shores, the totems glinting and shimmering in the heat. There, too, already, a kilometre out, was the tribal ship, the black Tell watch-ship under its gorgeous Pan-Tribal kites, waiting to collect our skiffs and take us away from Trale.

We wandered down to our tiny vessels under the gaze of tribal watchers who surely had to be wondering what it was we had just done, who might now have monitors turned our way.

"Let me go out with Andrew," Michael said when we had loaded the last of our gear. He stood with his back to the Tell ship and spoke in almost a whisper so his words could not be easily monitored. "We'll use the parafoil. I can manage it. We need to discuss what we're going to say about this, about the jacobi."

Lisa and I nodded, and set the two men on their way—into possible danger, reprisal, payback. Then we went to the remaining skiff, got our own kites aloft, and started out.

Despite the transit sounds, we too spoke in subdued tones, mindful of detection.

"That wasn't his first glimpse into the mirrors, was it?" Lisa asked as we rolled along, closing the short distance.

"No," I said, realising now what Warboy's personality shift really meant. "He found the jacobi yesterday. He would've done it then, I'm sure, whenever he could. Andrew too I think."

"You think so?" Our kites blocked our line of sight to the ship. We spoke softly yet urgently before they shifted.

"Yes. The totems needed these men to work together. It had to be one of the jacobi's very specialised tasks. They know the tribes have abandoned them here, ostracised them. They prepared a revelation that might get out to the world and start something better for them. Acceptance perhaps. Not just at the level of what we suspect is happening here."

"What do you mean, Tom?"

"I wonder if an eyeline can be programmed. If we have been made unconscious carriers of a subliminal message to others."

"To get past the tribes." Then, "Yes," she said, and I wasn't sure if it was simple agreement with what I had said or an affirmation about something else.

We were four hundred metres from the Tell ship, both of us distracted.

There wasn't much time.

"Lisa, when you looked into the mirrors, did you see anything? A star? Just the one?"

She frowned. "I'm not sure what I saw. Not really. Why?"

"I've been told something. Given something important. I have to go back to the Madhouse. I have to find out what it means."

Lisa nodded, then spoke, her words powered by a certainty matching my own. "I took off my glasses." She removed them again now, her pale eyes squinting in the intense light.

"So did I." I smiled and removed mine as well.

But Lisa shook her head; she meant something more.

"But I'm in remission. I know it."

I met the pale gaze, ignoring the helm, letting the off-shore thermals draw us along.

"Then—"

"Very specialised, you said. Eyeline. Soulframe. Your guess. I prefer to think cognate life doing whatever it does when it has the chance: considers itself and tries for more."

We crossed in silence then, our glasses off at noon, both smiling, me thinking of my star, my three signs, and of her last words too, wondering if Michael and Andrew, if any of us, could conceal what we knew, and if a message waited, locked away in each of us, a message the tribal biotects themselves might unwittingly carry forth when they examined the new totem. Lisa seemed lost in whatever certainty made her so glad now to show her eyes.

"Remission, eh?" I said, as the kites shifted to show us the tribal ship once again. "You know what I think?"

"No, what?" she asked, and frowned slightly, worried by what I might say in plain view like this.

"You might have at least given me the credit for it."

And we were laughing, still far enough away for the faces of the watching tribesmen not to resolve into eyelines, when from the shore behind us came the valedictions of that forsaken place, the first of the noon guns firing into the hot and patient sky.

THE LIBRARY

1

IF ANYWHERE IS HOME FOR ME, APART FROM *RYNOSSEROS*, IT can only be Twilight Beach.

And, again, between voyages, with *Rynosseros* safely at the Sand Quay with the other deep-desert sand-ships, the crew lost in the bars and gaming-rooms of the Gaza Hotel, I took a favourite table at Amberlin's, wanting to avoid the crowds and the excitement of the Astronomers' Bar and the Gaza terrace, the conversations I would immediately inherit at Trimori's, The Traitor's Face and The Slow Hour.

It was a morning for slowing down to small pleasures, for sitting with a glass of tautine or vintage terfilot, or one of the traditional wines they make in far-off lands and still export down to the coasts and resort towns of Australia.

The terrace at Amberlin's gives an almost two hundred degree view, so that at a glance you can see the elegant villas in the dunes to the north, close to the road that leads out to the beach suburbs of Corlique, Mirajan and Castanelle at the tip of the Golden Bow.

Then, turning your head, you take in the deep blue swells where the tidal bells stir on their chains in the sea; then, at last, you have the whole town laid out before you: the Gaza with its famous terrace and airy loggias, the Breaklight Pier and the Time Beaches, Sailmaker's back near the Antic Houses on Tramway Street. There, meeting the harbour, the Byzantine Quarter with its bazaars and curio shops, and the Mayan Quarter beyond, both with their vivid restoration architectures; close by, whitewashed walls and tiled roofs dazzling in the sun, the urban villas and hotels, the palazzos and arcades, the famous galleries. There, Old Town with its stuccoed tenements and lion-coloured warehouses. The brooding mass of the Armament stands among them, drawing memories of other days, and the smaller sunnier shapes of the Granary and the market squares abutting Trial Street, fronted by the Tyrrian Wall.

Near those precincts, the town finally meets the desert. There you find the famous privateering inns: The Goodbye, The Black Wind and The Cannon, where the stories are told, the reputations earned, the legends made. And there, close by, beyond the corniche and the colour and bustle of the Sarda Salita, is the Sand Quay itself, with its chandleries, ship-factors and kitesellers, the docks alive with the cries of the longshore crews and the barneys hard at work tending the great charvi hulls. Even now, moored between *Sunfish* and *Argus* this time, you will find *Rynosseros*.

I laughed, completing it yet again, the old homecoming ritual.

Slow now, I told myself. Slow.

Though it was allowable, all allowable after weeks of mission tension and the welcome yet constant demands of running the ship, especially after Balin, especially after Trale.

And it was such a perfect morning, the Promenade and terraces so full of life. *This* was the heart of it. Apart from *Rynosseros*. This.

I had just begun studying the menu when a robed figure sat in the chair opposite.

"Captain Tyson, if I may."

I glanced up at the long handsome face and alert respectful gaze of a fine-looking Ab'O. He wore fighting leathers under sand-coloured travelling robes and had the double swords at his waist.

There was a tribal sersifan on a chain about his neck and I had its signature immediately. This was a Chitalice First.

"Captain, I am Kaber Fen Otamas and I need your services for a mission."

"I am newly back from a mission, Lord Otamas. This is shore leave for me."

"Understood, Captain." The Chitalice noble placed a small scrambler on the table and activated it. "But I believe you will want to accept this one."

"Oh? And why is that?"

"Council will authorise it. It is courtesy that brought me here first."

Council knew! Den had already been approached! That important then.

"Please," I said, hiding disappointment, weariness. "I still choose my own missions. What will persuade me this time?"

"A common enemy," the Ab'O said. "A confederate of Dewi Dammo that we suspect was part of that same attempt to secure power."

Dewi Dammo. The name brought a rush of memories: of the Inland Sea and the Charling Coast, of the island of Marmordesse and poor mad Dewi trying to have it all.

"Why me?"

"There is a chance that you will learn more about your origins. Your time in the Madhouse."

He had my complete attention. "Go on."

Kaber Fen Otamas glanced about him. No doubt he had support concealed close by, possibly Kurdaitcha. "There is an enemy for us, known only by little more than his name. Chiras Namarkon."

"Dewi said that name."

"He did. Council provided the debriefing transcripts for that mission. We wish you to find this Chiras Namarkon, Captain. You know better than most that the status-quo is always at risk and that we work ceaselessly to maintain it. At one extreme we have insiders like Bolo May who are allowed to grow too powerful, at the other, opportunists like Dewi Dammo hiding in the interstices of what the world steadily becomes in spite of our precautions."

I couldn't help but smile.

Otamas smiled as well. "No, Captain. We do not automatically regard the seven Coloured Captains as our enemy."

"But, in spite of your precautions, another part of what the world has become. Hardly welcome."

"Some of us accept it, even applaud it. Our philosophies require it of us."

"Many do not," I said.

"As you say. But at our best we like to think that it extends us. Makes us larger."

Again, I had to smile. At the very least this was civility, at most genuine respect, a suggestion of rapprochement between the tribes and Nation. I inclined my head in thanks.

Otamas continued. "At least the seven National Captains are out in the world, in plain sight. This Chiras Namarkon is not. We allow that while he was probably not an ally of Dewi's in any formal sense, they seem to have known of one another and at least reached a modus vivendi. Given what Dewi Dammo sought to do, they may even have traded tech and other resources. Our concern is that Namarkon may very well have access to our systems; worse yet, access to factions with vested interests who will not declare their present connection with him. It took tribal and Council agents years and many lives to gain that single clue to Dewi's whereabouts Pederson gave you at Angel Bay that day. With this Namarkon, we only know that there is a library involved—he may be its owner or keeper—and a connection with an important text called the Alexandrian Book."

"Then your people—"

"No, Captain. We have searched and will continue to search our libraries and data systems. We need someone who represents *us* to search yours. All of yours. Especially those remaining libraries which are located—to put it as tactfully as I can—in *decommissioned* National possessions."

"Decommissioned? You mean—"

"Exactly. The abandoned arcologies. The old inland cities. *We* go there and there is the usual outcry, as useless, hopeless and strident as ever but drawing precisely the sort of National and international media attention we do not want at this time. *You* visit them as a solitary traveller on a mission for Nation and it is not questioned."

"The arcologies are hardly places to learn anything about my past, Lord Otamas."

"Surely that depends on who this Namarkon is and where such a search leads. And see it another way. If you refuse this task, we will ask the other Coloured Captains, then simply empower your Council to send one of its usual field agents. We came to you first."

I watched the waves making their way to shore, the long stately sweeps crowned with cartouches of light, each cresting swell set with a bezel of quicksilver in the hot morning sun. Gulls wheeled in, making their plaintive cries. The air smelled of salt and sea-wrack. "Will you assist, lord?"

"However and whenever we can, Captain, though if what we suspect is true, then this Namarkon will probably not want to be found. There is sure to be tribal interference."

"Have you thought to approach the Antique Men with your needs and misgivings?"

"Of course. They too assist as they can."

"May I approach them? About my provenance at least?"

And surprise on surprise, it was not Otamas but Den who answered, suddenly there at our table, drawing up a chair and sitting. "We've made the request already, Tom. Can you do this?"

Being at Amberlin's had been strange enough, wonderfully strange after so much time away. Having a tribal lord appear at my table and now a senior Council operations chief added a definite touch of the absurd.

The middle-aged Nation officer gave a smile that was meant to be reassuring, but which made an even stranger mask of his hairless, lopsided face. Den was strikingly ugly, had chosen to remain so years ago in order to qualify for an impressive if strangely earned annuity from the estate of the late and eccentric Spydyr Massillian. Smiles were his most disconcerting feature.

But, typical Den, he was as caring as he was smart and effective.

Can you do this?

The perfect way to ask.

I thought I could see glints of light from the ornamental wind-

and sun-clocks on the Time Beaches, then traced the line of the Promenade up to the Gaza terrace where people from across the world came to watch games of fire-chess and stylo. I imagined I could hear the Gaza belltrees singing in the on-shore breeze, and the bells swinging on their sea-chains below the glittering swells.

"I can do this."

"Thank you, Captain," Otamas said, then stood, picked up his scrambler and left the terrace. As he headed off down the street, four robed tribesman appeared from their places of concealment and joined him.

"Tom, it really is your choice," Den said at last.

"I know, Den. I know. You have a list of libraries?"

"We do. Some here, some out there." He gestured behind him. "The old cities."

"Aye. The old cities. I can do this."

2

The great blade from which Turker Fin took its name threw a shadow across the desert, a shadow so vast that the view from the big library window showed a register of fierce red-ochre light above a darkness of Turker's own making: blazing blue-white sky at the top, late-afternoon sun-shadow at the bottom, the rest almost impenetrable because of the searing glare.

The library was underground, of course, far below the great sun-trap and power-wall of the blade. The view was relayed down from a much higher level, from a tiny viewing tile somewhere on its mighty surface, but it conquered the space well enough, the feeling of being shut away. It brought the sense of looking from high up I've always felt one needed in libraries, not the quiet gloomy cloisters with dusty stacks and a clock ticking off in the precious silence, but a spacious airiness, even if the views were mostly unchanging and ignored; the quality old monasteries had of being above and beyond the secular world down there.

Now, almost at the end of a three-day search of the Turker library, I stood before the "window" yet again, taking in the view from three hundred metres overhead as if I'd never seen it before.

Turker Fin was the last of the leads supplied by Nation's archivists, the final name on the list of eight painstakingly drawn out of secure comp systems.

The time *that* had taken told me a great deal: how special agents or carefully placed moles in previous administrations had probably tried to bury such information, possibly to prevent the more hostile tribal factions from learning the exact whereabouts and constitution of the last National libraries, but—more to the point—that those few precious true-book repositories were located on *tribal* land, in safe residual concessions protected by special charter and tradition, reached by safe Roads. Perhaps those factions had guessed it long ago, as Otamas had; perhaps it was simple diplomacy that stayed their hand, stopped any further interference in the affairs of Nation.

Eight names. Only two had been on the coast, both in Twilight Beach: the first the Pandeon, easy to reach but of little help, full of saltings and key deletions, the second the private collection of a Delas Marquand, a man presently unavailable, perhaps even conveniently out of Australia.

The remaining six, like Turker, exactly as Den had said, truly were located in the old arcologies, those vast echoing constructs abandoned long ago when the Nationals were driven back to the coasts, their birthright denied them, the fragile environments shut down but for the great mainwalls and a few selected outbuildings.

It had been a largely fruitless search there too, infuriating in the hints and teasing glimpses found. First Andromira and Crayasse, Sol-Tyreen and Genema Blade, then across the continent to Ganness, and back to Turker Fin when word came through at last that the old librarian, Toth, would accede to Council's demands for open house.

It was difficult for the old man. Accustomed to being absolute monarch in his deserted domain, Trayban Toth had finally realised that his position as "lighthouse keeper" (the term he liked to use, muttering about the Pharos Lighthouse and the Pharisees and the great library at ancient Alexandria, as if they related to these deserts or each other) might end if he opposed his superiors.

Humbled and uncertain, made suddenly respectful by Den's

expensive call, Toth had done an about-face, had become excited at last that the library was being used for its original purpose.

He had granted access, so I came to believe, to the whole catalogue. Turker had 40,000 retroform books in its deep cool chambers, 810,000 kilometres of tape, 780,000 units of disc, mote, bead, crystal and fluid-link texts, and—rarest of all—5,000 Illuminated Books of the new kind.

I stood before one of these now, watching as Trayban set it up on the lectern before the window. It was a Book that had recently been transferred here from Crayasse, officially borrowed, Toth said, though spirited away might have been a better term, since it had been removed from the Crayasse collection a day before I got there, almost as if it had been moved deliberately to waste my time, the last copy of a text possibly leading to the whereabouts of Chiras Namarkon. That was how it felt.

Trayban Toth was muttering as he arranged the Book, coming to the end of yet another of his almost endless monologues about bookish matters.

"...and the Vatican has always had the largest collection of pornography in the world. It makes you think. But this is it, Captain! L75 VGS." He seemed annoyed that the view had caught my attention rather than this text he had found for me at last.

It was hard to conceal my amusement. More than seventy years old, short and bent but often full of a startling energy that made his eyes shine like flecks of mica above the long nose and full white beard, Trayban presented as someone who had once played Merlin in an ancient pageant and had never tired of the role. Each book was delivered as if a personal incantation had been sought and found, as if the storage rooms he visited were compartments in his own head from which these texts had been drawn forth at great personal effort.

Perhaps that was how Trayban saw it, lived it, as if Turker Fin truly were his greater self and he wandered corridors of his own mind to visit its parts. This recent arrival, L75 VGS, had to have been on hand, but Trayban had spent precious hours "searching" for it.

Which set me wondering all over again. Despite his age and distracted manner, Toth would make a fitting Namarkon, someone dissembling, projecting, playing out a role. I wished, not for the first time, that I had a monitor to use.

"Namarkon," Toth said, a note of peevishness in his voice. "There's the reference under linguistics. It cross-refers to the Gray and Silas."

"Thanks, Trayban."

I studied the surface of the Book, the small touch-plate and ormolu key-set, the Nape circuit-mosaic border (as if a churchman had in fact decorated it in the ancient fashion), the Bytes-and-Byzantines imprint in the bottom left-hand corner with the Nation seal. I touched the plate, activating the tiny power source within. The milky pane lit with a warm yellow light; one by one pages slow-cycled through the credits and bibliographica to the index, ciphers spilling steadily across the Reader Page.

"L75 VGS," Toth murmured in affirmation, as if intoning a spell. Then: "L362:42."

"L362:42. Thank you."

I entered the final sequence, accessed the section, keyed in Namarkon. There was a two-second wait, then that word flashed its presence.

Flashed and blanked, leaving the Reader Page dark, the Book inert.

"Trayban!"

The old man pushed in next to me. Without a word, he brought up the bibliographica, ran the Namarkon entry. Again the name flashed once; again the screen went dead.

"Damaged!" he cried. "Hell and Jesus! It's damaged!"

"On its way to Turker, you think?" I said. "Deliberate?"

Toth frowned at sacrilege, his jaw set, dismay showing in his eyes.

"What, Tray?" I pressed. "Is it coincidence?"

"No!" he cried. And he repeated the functions, again without success, then carried the Book to a donkey-frame close by, intending to bypass the discrete functions with the library's override.

Certainly the Book glowed more brightly in the frame, and for a moment I hoped. But again the word triggered the misfunction.

Toth repeated the procedure four times, making adjustments, even pounding on the dead Reader plate with the spread palm of one hand. He ran several other entries successfully, cycled through a few, then tried Namarkon again with no luck. He lifted the Book from the frame, studied its spine and seals.

"What can we do, Tray?" I asked gently, carefully.

He laid the Book back on the lectern.

"L75 VGS is dead stack. Only one copy in existence. But it's open text, so scholars can add or revise details in appendices. There will be a Precis access for that."

"Tampered with as well?"

"No! No!" Toth said firmly. "You don't understand. It's black box, a sealed unit, very durable, designed to show what the main text contained. Scholars working here could enter their findings and opinions—under strict supervision, of course, always under supervision. It will summarise portions of the main entry as assists. No-one could get at those."

"Please run it."

He turned to the Book, used a scribe wand to enter a code sequence along the bottom edge. Words filed across the Reader Page. Toth keyed in *Namarkon* yet again.

The word flashed its arrival, gave its capsule comment.

> 362:42:8-1: Namarkon
> (Namarkon, Namarquon, Nammargon)(OAA)(dialect)
>
> Spirit of Lightning, originally of the Gunwinggu, Western Arnhem Land (495:36:7/1-92G). Vengeful elemental spirit accessed by Morrkidju (604:24:12), the "clever sorcerers" of the Gunwinggu . . .

Another dozen or so entries referred to eponymous land-holdings, ships, a comp-net, and a minor highwayman who had made use of the ancient name. There were a score of mythic antecedents, the names of people and things, real and imaginary, who had been identified with the Dreamtime original or had recognised conceptual connections.

The final listing was the one I wanted, and again there was the exasperating reference to the text I needed most of all, something called the Alexandrian Book, the title which had dogged my search from Andromira to Turker.

> 362:42:8-14: Chiras Namarkon (aka The Immortal)
>
> A legendary folk hero/demon of the Molere cycle, said to inhabit a secret labyrinth, safeguarding secret knowledge and a great treasure.
>
> Origins uncertain. Gray and Silas (914:61:7) are inclined to consider retroactive amplification of an early 21st Century inception, either a traditional (unsubstantiated) expression meaning: "tree struck by lightning" or possibly as part of an advertising campaign for either Inters 400 (324:22) or Nation-Sun (721:620:4).
>
> Note: Chiras Namarkon is allegedly the author/creator of a text/artefact called the Alexandrian Book (no information available apart from the title). This authorship is probably as apocryphal as the text itself, since all sources advancing the connection are full of proven fabrication. The Alexandrian Book has never been sighted (Trist, Gray and Silas, Maidment, Green).
> Note: Standing request by Gray and Silas for updating, with priority input-inform tag for AM/GB.

Without my asking, Toth caused a hard-copy to be made and passed it over.

"This last notation, Tray? The initials?"

Toth hesitated, leant over the Reader Page, the remains of his anger still driving him. "I'm not supposed to tell, but it's the Antique Men. That's Gado Bascoeur. He's very good. A great scholar. Does it help?"

"It's something. I've found the Dreamtime reference before, same with the Immortal, the labyrinth and the creature of fable. The Alexandrian Book reference is not new; this Bascoeur entry is. You have nothing on the Molere cycle?"

"Nothing else. Nothing in Gray and Silas either. I'm sorry."

"Then thank you, Tray. I'm finished here."

I went to the desk I had been using and began gathering up my notes. Toth followed, a concerned look turning his old face into a surprisingly desperate mask, the small eyes full of unexpected emotion. My visit to Turker had been an intrusion initially, but now, at the end of it, he seemed sorry to have me leave, as if reluctant to lose this precious reaffirmation of his role.

The damage to Illuminated Book L75 VGS had somehow intensified the desperation, his need to hold on to this moment of service.

"What will you do?" he said, a question he now allowed himself to ask.

"After the Pandeon and the six arcologies? Marquand's place again, in case he's back. You have been invaluable, Tray. I have four private libraries hinted at somewhere in Twilight Beach, none mentioned on Council's list. I have confirmation for Chiras Namarkon as the Immortal, as Lightning God and keeper of a library and labyrinth, as putative author of something called the Alexandrian Book, whatever that was or is, if ever it was. Now there's the link to the Antique Men, which was inevitable anyway but I'm glad of it right now. I'm full circle there. Considering I didn't know what to expect, I've certainly got something."

"And this?" He picked up one of the hard copies before I could bundle it up with the rest of my arcology material. "The list of arcologies you wanted?"

"Another tack I may take. Since I've run out of National libraries, I might look where libraries might have been at one time or other."

"You'd do that? Go to *all* the old sites?"

"Why not? The tribes will allow it. If Crayasse and Turker have their data-vaults underground, the other arcologies may not be as empty as they say."

I tried to sound hopeful, though I doubted that even an exhaustive search of the abandoned cities would reveal a carefully hidden Chiras Namarkon.

But what else did I have? For all I knew, Namarkon was hiding somewhere in the forgotten decks and halls of Turker Fin or Crayasse or one of the other places I had already visited. I may have passed within metres of his door, breathed the air he had released from his lungs, started at a small sound of his presence in a shadowed corridor.

Yes, trying Delas Marquand again, consulting the Antique Man, Bascoeur, if he would allow it, trying to locate the four private libraries, would exhaust my leads, probably finish it. Then I would be left either to tour the remaining arcologies or scour the curio shops in the Byzantine Quarter, hoping that Den or one of the other Coloured Captains, or one of my eccentric friends in the Bird Club, might uncover something.

"It's not right!" Toth said, studying the arcology print-out and pulling at his beard.

"What's that, Tray?"

He spread the double-list of National arcology sites on a reader table and tapped at the page. "The top arrangement here. There's a name missing."

I hurried across to him and studied the print-out. "You're sure? How can you tell?"

"It's the shape, Captain, not the names. The regional arrangement at the bottom I'm not sure about, but the top one is wrong. The list I remember is one off a square. I always wished they had built an even number to finish the shape. This is two off. Look!"

Andromira*	Whitehead	Andalave
Enso-Bey	Soltumede	Alka
Crayasse*	Chyra-Manta	Quaine Lock
Genema Blade*	Pharani	Meda
Stone Mill	Bukula Tan	Khen-Mol
Ganness*	Pila	Maggadi
Land's End	Port Chevas	Graylord
Tulidjula	Transy	Quen-Lui
Trovy	Neuve	Ihren
Turker Fin*	Tarpial	Gayla
Sol-Tyreen*	Anansanna	Bidja Point
Monk's Hood		

Andromira*	Bukula Tan
Enso-Bey	Pila

Crayasse*			Port Chevas
Pharani			Quen-Lui
Stone Mill	Transy	Alka	Khen-Mol
Ganness*	Tarpial	Meda	Whitehead
Land's En	Maggadi	Trovy	Andalave
Tulidjula	Genema Blade*		Soltumede
Graylord			Anansanna
Turker Fin*			Monk's Hood
Sol-Tyreen*	Neuve		Chyra-Manta
Bidja Point	Gayla	Ihren	Quaine Lock

I studied the shape formed by the top arrangement of names, matched each name with the regional arrangement beneath. Thirty-four on both. I checked the print-outs drawn from the comps at Crayasse and Ganness. They gave the same double-pattern, the same count: two off the square.

"Do it again, Tray. See what you get."

The old man went to a nearby comp and called up the information. The screen showed the same pattern as the printed lists.

"No!" Toth said, and struck the console. "No! Wrong, I tell you! This is not it!"

"What then?"

"Someone sent L75 VGS here. Someone damaged it. Someone has done *this* as well!"

"You're certain?"

"It's the sort of visual trick you never forget. The last time I saw this list it was one off."

"When was that?"

"What? Who knows? Years ago. It was years. But I remember. I couldn't forget."

"Tray, can we do a priority search on this?" It was suddenly very important, though I knew that every list I sought would be short one entry.

"I don't see how we can," the old man said. "The library comp gives this. It's the only comp facility I'm allowed apart from environmentals."

"Could those be routed in?"

"They couldn't access deleted data, no."

"Deletion has to be difficult in sealed catalogue systems. Can you bypass a blockage?"

"No, Captain. Whoever can tamper with library records would make sure of that."

"The Antique Men?"

Toth pulled at his beard. "They could do it, yes. They're one of the few groups allowed to enter information. But they're the most honest—"

"This Bascoeur?"

"One of the best. He would never—"

"Namarkon might," I said, thinking of the old historical stand-by of need-to-know, doing something for the greater good, the eternal catch-cry of governments, rulers, privileged agencies, shrewd individuals. "Tray, can I take the Book back to Twilight Beach? It would be safe, I swear it."

He shook his head. "Impossible. Especially now."

"Then do not part with it again. Council will authorise that order. Refuse all requests, even from Crayasse, from all brother and sister librarians. The Book remains here. And, please, refuse access—"

"To the Antique Men, yes. If I can."

Toth saw me back to the surface levels, came with me out onto the wide mooring plat, littered with sand and wind-wrack, to where my rented thirty-foot Maud skiff waited on locked wheels.

"Leave in the morning, Captain. Phone the information through. You can afford it." The old man indicated the afternoon sun halfway down the sky.

But I needed to be doing something now, anything. "Tray, it's at least two days to the coast. Calls can be monitored, and I need to get what I know back to where I can use it. I'll make a hundred k's, possibly two hundred, before the light goes. Thanks again for all you've done."

I climbed aboard the tiny craft, trimmed two parafoils to the afternoon wind and slowly gained speed along the ancient Road.

Behind, old Toth stood with one arm raised. In the dying light, he resembled some scholar Quasimodo before his own fabulous Notre Dame, the westering sun turning the great curtain wall into a beacon. Somewhere on that blazing massif was a tiny view tile, taking the sun into a chamber deep underground. I wondered if Chiras Namarkon used it now, watching me go, and wondered what part thoughts of such a possibility had played in my going.

3

From: Josepha Anglis, *The Coloured Captains: Fact and Fiction*, Praesidian, AS 753-3
Introduction: "The Unloved Heroes"
All reliable sources agree that the Ab'O tribes trapped themselves by the Tell Agreement of AS 742. By opening up the annual Cyrimiri ship-lotteries to Nationals—a strategic concession made with a view to calming International criticism of tribal racist policies, thereby keeping valuable world tech markets and AI initiatives—the Ab'O States made possible a unique chain of events by which their own traditions trapped them.

The Cyrimiri proponents at the '42 Convocation had no way of knowing that one of their own experiments in Artificial Intelligence would prove so viable and so formidable. They could not know that the celebrated bell-tree program, which had so captured the imagination of the world and had reached its zenith with the Iseult-Darrian strain, would be the cause of so much consternation and embarrassment, a resounding blow struck for the waning Pan-European tradition in Australia.

The tribes and Nation are both diplomatically closed-lipped about the details of what actually occurred. Experts surmise that one of the redundant oracle-trees, rejected, limited and given the usual desert service as a roadpost, rallied against its conditioning, established a reciprocal arrangement with Records, and used its links to enter the names of National ship-winners into one of the most hallowed tribal registers at Tell—the Great Passage Book itself. The tree's motives remain unknown. Such a sensational and unprecedented treason was soon stopped, but not before seven National captains: Golden Afervarro, Red Lucas, Green Glaive, Yellow Traven, White Massen, Black Doloroso and Blue Tyson—won not only their great sand-ships (and those were seven of the best tribal charvolants in existence, suggesting that the tree had played a part there as well) but were issued with all-lander mandates laying open the inner deserts, and given the Colours which in an instant elevated them irrevocably to the status of tribal heroes.

Tribal spokesmen claim that the creation of the Seven was a deliberate benefice to Nation, an endowment made partly as restitution for the wide-scale shutting down of National facilities in the interior. They insist that in no way was it an error on the part of careless biotects. National and international experts, however, remain unconvinced. They suggest that the seven Captains were chosen for a purpose, that the tribes made better than they knew, that this rogue belltree AI raised up its own champions. Why? The Captains themselves refuse to comment.

But one thing is clear. For now at least, Nation has teeth again, and the world is watching.

Rynosseros was still out on mission. I'd persuaded Scarbo and the others to accept long-reach assignments, convincing them that while I searched the old National sites listed by Den, they could do more for me by asking questions in distant places, in the museums, modest town libraries, the bars, galleries and curio shops they came upon.

For all I knew, the key to Namarkon might be something someone said or overheard in a crowded bar at No Man's Easy Rest, some detail in a painting in the hallway of a public building in Angel Bay, or a line sung in the chorus of a child's sidewalk song in Port Tarsis.

After returning the skiff to Maud's Rentals at the end of my run, I still had the better part of two days before *Rynosseros* was due back from Tank Feti, ample time to try Marquand again, the only private (and secret) collector Den's people had been able to uncover—and that through a string of suspect legal infractions in a long career.

Unlike the other sellers of collectibles and oddities, the public ones who made much of the little they had, Delas Marquand had always been notoriously reclusive. On Nation records he existed officially as an importer of Welsh and Dutch cheeses and fabrics from Oceania. According to the more reliable rumours, he had been a plunderer of libraries in his time and was now a dealer in black market volumes, with a splendid secret library of his own.

His shop was an unmarked, blank-fronted establishment at the end of a dead-end street out near the Armament. Visits, whether for cheeses, fabrics or books, were by appointment only, often made by people answering cryptic ads in obscure trade journals or—for the novelty of it—in the popular urban publications, those glossy retro-form periodicals printed on siflin or kelp-based Tase paper.

But responses to ads, the phonecalls and letters pretending to be a prospective client, even visits to the shop, had so far been unsuccessful. Certainly before beginning my search of the arcologies, his place had always been locked, the windows polarised into the neutral mirror glare of the "blind" house.

For whatever reason, it seemed that those dealing in information, in stored or printed knowledge, had become harder to locate than ever, as if suddenly all of them, whether sly Delas Marquand or the famous Antique Men, had grown wary of tribal attention.

Or was it Namarkon they feared?

I'd left the Marquand problem for Den, all I could do, one more thing to try along with my standing request to see the Antique Men, and, to my relief, Den had succeeded in at least the first part of this assignment.

"We have our way in," he told me when I called on him at his villa that afternoon. We were standing in his operations room before the big view window, and it was like I'd never been away—as if visiting the arcologies were all a dream, something gleaned from somnium sleep. "We've placed a false impost in Marquand's comp. Not the sort of risk we like to take, Tom, but I think he'll see it as genuine. It was difficult but it's done. Watching the place would probably tell us nothing. He's experienced. He might even have a secret exit out behind Armament somewhere; so far we haven't found it. Still, we figure he has to be in Australia. There are no visa or transit records saying otherwise, no listings for private dirigibles or module shipments under Marquand in the last four months. He dare not be too clever in view of what we have on him."

"He'll accept the impost?"

Den looked pleased with himself. "We believe so. We've told his system a tribal inspector will call on him at 1100 one morning this week to discuss tariff discrepancies in tribal records. He dare not delegate that sort of thing. I was going to ask Scarbo or Shannon to do it, but you're back. Look the part and you'll get in. The plans you need will be ready."

"Thanks, Den. I know Council is taking quite a chance."

"We're doing what's right. Finally. We're acting and it feels good."

At 1049 the next morning, in bright sunshine, I headed up Trial Street in the shadow of the Armament dressed in djellaba and burnoose, carrying my small folder of plans and a tribal sirrush stick borrowed from Den's collection. I wore dark glasses and the appropriate skin-toning, some bands of colour on cheeks and chin, carefully neutral caste-marks. From a distance I was a quadroon customs officer on assignment in Nation territory, someone not to be denied.

The shop was as I remembered it, a two-storey building at the end of a quiet street, still a blind house, the windows showing only adjacent structures and my own robed figure approaching the main door. It was hard to resist a smile at how formidable I looked.

I rapped several times on the solid panel and listened for movement within, but there was nothing. I waited, noting—not for the first time in this land the colour of lions in the sun—how the bluest Australian skies are always found above the rooflines of old brick warehouses, over high walls such as formed this side of the Armament, that most mysterious of tribal artefacts in Twilight Beach.

Finally someone stirred beyond the door. Latches clicked, it swung back and Delas Marquand was standing there, professional caution showing on his wide, finely featured face. He was of medium height, clad in a gown fashioned along Egyptian lines, no doubt made from some of his own imported fabric, dark blues shot with threads of gold.

"Mr Marquand," I said, accenting my voice just enough. "I am Atanas Tjijti from Customs."

Marquand gave a slight bow. "Your ident please, Mr Tjijti."

I displayed the laminate Den had provided, then, taking the initiative, stepped by him into the dimly lit front hall of his premises. Marquand closed the door behind us, and even in the

gloom I could see that he touched the locks in a way that suggested security systems, possibly illegal tech. I wondered if a true Ab'O would remark on it.

"Please go through to the office, Mr Tjijti," Marquand said. "The records are there."

"Delas Marquand, I am actually here to discuss your library."

Marquand reached for something in the shadows—a contact? a weapon?—but my sirrush stick was already there, knocking his arm aside, making him yell in pain and surprise.

"Who are you?" he cried, cradling his arm. "You're no tribesman! What do you want?"

"Answers to official questions, nothing more. But this is your false hallway, Mr Marquand. Please take us through to your dealer's room."

Even in the gloom I saw his eyes narrow. "I have no idea what you're talking about. Identify yourself!"

The sirrush stick struck the floor like a gunshot in the confined space.

"It's me or a Nation strike. Choose!"

"You can't be serious!"

"Mr Marquand, I am not alone in this. Officers outside have tech. All legal. Any deadfalls or problems with electrics and they'll be in here." I embellished the lie. "All under tribal sanction. Implant alert. Anything you do, understand?"

"Follow me," he said in a flat voice, nursing his injured arm, and led us back to the front door. He touched the locks again, opening a slideaway in the left wall, a concealed entrance. We entered, moved down a narrow corridor, well past what had to be storerooms and offices to an insulated secure room at the rear of the premises. It was large, fifteen metres to a side, with bookcases covering most of the wall space, the shelves filled with files and boxes. The far wall was exposed warehouse brick, shining dully in the room's soft recessed lighting, set with shallow alcoves between worn brickwork pilasters.

"Well?" Marquand said.

"First, we establish credentials. Show me your library."

He gave a wry smile. "You're a dealer now?"

"Delas, listen carefully. Only Nation or the tribes could get that impost into your comp. I'm Tom Tyson—"

"Tom Rynosseros!" Marquand's eyes widened in surprise. "What can—?"

"The Marquand Collection is beyond that wall. I've seen plans. I'd be grateful if you'd show me."

Delas Marquand seemed easier now. He smiled again and considered what to do. Finally he crossed to an ancient roll-top desk and made connections I did not try to see. There were the soft sounds of systems working, a play of shifting light in one of the alcoves in the rear wall, then the sudden vision of a ramp leading down into a warmly lit room *full* of shelves—shelves laden with books: retroforms, disks, mote stacks, even the Nape spines of Illuminated Books.

It was an amazing sight, an Aladdin's cave shimmering behind a series of plastic dust curtains. In spite of what Den had told me about Marquand, I gasped in amazement.

"Satisfied?"

I closed the trap. "I'd like to see some titles if I may."

"No-one goes down there, Captain." The voice was suddenly

hard, the voice of a man who still had solutions, was still calculating. "I'm the only one to pass through those seals."

"You have leases to the adjacent buildings?"

"What?" He eyed me suspiciously.

I opened out the building plan Den had provided. "Beyond the rear of this shop is the Tyrrian Wall and the Armament. North of you is Trial Street and the Granary. South is Gallery Four, basement to roof. There is nowhere for your library to go. I'm betting a hologram."

"There's an old sub-basement—"

"No, we've checked. Photonics, yes?"

Marquand's face went pale at the prospect of his secret being out; his eyes were bright with mixed emotions.

"You couldn't. Armament is an undeclared tribal holding; there are no maps registered. It was guaranteed."

"Nation comp has non-detailed plans of area allotment. Delas, I am not interested in exposing you. You had books four years ago. What happened?"

"Plundered," he said, taking that solution, the truth. "All but a few. Captain, I deal in books: crystals, tapes, disks, motes, all the old carrier forms. People come to me. I use that as a lure, a tease." He nodded toward the alcove. "Bring up the pieces I am prepared to sell or trade. If word got out—"

"It won't. I've disengaged my com unit. Even Council won't find out. What I must know is whether you have—or had—information on a Chiras Namarkon. The Immortal. Especially in connection with a library."

"Just the names," Marquand said. "Nothing anyone would raid me for. I had a good collection once, but nothing really special, not intrinsically."

"Nothing on a Namarkon library or labyrinth?"

"Captain, I collected books, traded and sold them. I acted the scholar, then as now; it helps make a sale, helps to build up the collection again. I didn't read them so much as know things about them, the publishing information. Which editions—"

"Have you heard of something called the Alexandrian Book?"

"Of it, yes. Nothing more than that."

"We're trading here, Delas. Namarkon and the Alexandrian Book for an oath of secrecy from me."

"I'd tell you!" he cried. "For the oath and those plans I'd tell you if I knew. I would! I know both exist. I've . . . I've put out word that I'd make an offer for such a book. There's been nothing. Not a thing. All collectors do it as a matter of course."

"All right," I said, hope beginning to fade. "These other collectors. I know of at least four. I need names."

The man threw his arms wide in a gesture of exasperation. "I can't give you that. I can't! It's a trust thing."

"It's black-marketeering is what it is. It's Nation moving to find out anything about Namarkon and the Alexandrian Book. Help us, Delas, and the tribes learn nothing. It's not you Council wants." It was time for another lie, expedient but effective now with Marquand seeing his world about to collapse. "The black market doesn't harm Nation; it helps us, in fact, in ways you wouldn't imagine."

I was glad he didn't ask how. I was thinking of arcologies raided, of books being pirated out of vaults, of catalogues listing titles which had long ago found their way into secret collections, to be copied and databased if we were lucky, to be hidden and lost otherwise.

"Listen, Captain! Now, listen! I can give you one name—a good man, generous, a legitimate collector. But for heaven's sake protect him. Tell no-one. Toban McBanus at Villa Chano. He will help if anyone can. For the right reasons. He's in it for knowledge, not gain."

I maintained the lie. "He's one of the four I already have. Who else?"

Again the arms went out. "Don't you see? They'd know it was me. They'd kill me. Please. McBanus will know others. Let him say. Go to him. He's a buyer, a reader; he knows things. The others are like me."

"Plunderers."

"Conservators. We keep the books moving. Private collectors have always done more to conserve the arts than governments and institutions. You must know that."

"One more thing. How many arcologies are there?"

"What?"

"The old National arcologies. How many do you know exist?"

"Forty or so."

"Exactly."

Marquand went to his comp, tapped on the keys and studied the display. "Exactly thirty-four," he said, and frowned.

"What's wrong?"

"Nothing. I thought there were thirty-five. But it's thirty-four. Close."

The lie was everywhere, it seemed, and what a scale of power that implied, the ability to achieve such a task.

"Can you hard-copy that? All the names?"

Marquand touched another contact. A page slid from the printer; he passed it to me. "Are we done?"

"Not quite. Turn it off."

"What?"

"I'm leaving. But first, turn it off."

Marquand grinned suddenly. "So you can be sure."

"No, so I can see the truth. A reminder of how few collections there actually are. Because—"

"Captain—"

"Humour me, Delas, and that plan is yours along with my word."

The dealer hesitated, then worked a concealed touchpoint somewhere on the desk. The library died in a quick gulp of light, revealing more than just a space between the flanking pilasters: an alcove as deep as a walk-in closet, a bookcase to either side containing real texts, all that Delas had for sale. I saw the doorline with its tiny ramp sloping into a solid brick wall, the cleverly hidden holo-points.

"Thank you," I said, and handed him the plans and my contact number at the Gaza. "Call if you learn anything I can use. We can trade, Delas, build up favours in paradise." And allowing the truth of his earlier comment about private dealers. "Who knows? Council may even help you re-stock your shelves."

Marquand managed a chuckle at that. He re-activated illicit tech defences that were worth his life should the tribes learn of them, then led me back to the street door. We parted without another word between us.

Back out under the brilliant sky, with Marquand's door closed again in its mirror walls, I made a bundle of my tribal robes, cleaned my face as best I could, then headed for the Sand Quay. I stopped at the Gaza long enough to call Villa Chano, then hurried to see if *Rynosseros* had returned from the desert wastes of Tank Feti.

4

I felt a rush of pleasure to see the distinctive shape standing at the Quay, kites down and stowed, the professional barneys already halfway through their service checks on the hull and travel platform.

Shannon, Rim and Hammon were off at the Gaza, I learned from the gate officer, probably at the Astronomers' Bar; Strengi was below catching up on sleep after a home-leg watch. But Den had told them I was back from Turker, and Scarbo came grinning down the gangway to clasp my forearm in the Roman way the older kitesmen still used.

"Namarkon's a myth everywhere," he said. "Eternal life. Lives in a maze. One moment Melmoth the Wanderer, the next El Dorado or some other mythic figure. I've got notes. People are tight-lipped about collections though. Word is out about something."

"Feel like a walk out to Villa Chano to see Toban McBanus?"

"I know the name. Is he a bookman?"

"Delas Marquand says so."

"Marquand? You have been busy."

I could see Ben's determination to be easy company, his resolve not to ask if there'd been clues to my provenance.

"Nothing yet, Ben. But I've called McBanus. He's agreed to a visit."

"Good. So tell me about the arcologies."

We left the Sand Quay, walked back past the Gaza Hotel and the Breaklight Pier and out through the First Gate to the Promenade, heading for the villas in the dunes to the north. We detoured down onto the beach to save ourselves the curving approach taken when the Promenade became the Beach Road, passing over the low headland out to Corlique, Mirajan and Castanelle.

It provided ample time to tell Ben about Turker Fin and the quest for L75 VGS, about something called the Alexandrian Book and the possible involvement of the Antique Men through a Gado Bascoeur, all the most tentative of leads but—at least where information about my provenance was concerned—probably the most promising. If I hadn't discovered anything conclusive about my origins from the tribes, then who better to try than the ones who frequently serviced tribal information needs?

My own discoveries quickly exhausted the modest list Scarbo had. His facts were very much those of popular folklore. Nowhere had he heard of the Alexandrian Book, nor could he recall having seen the initials AM/BG, though Tank Feti, Tank Aran and Mider were hardly places to expect much information.

Like Toth and Marquand, Ben remembered there being thirty-five National arcologies; he was absolutely certain of it—what old Trayban had said: one off a square. He greeted the news of the adjusted total with something like Marquand's frown and old Toth's pulling at his beard.

"What did Den say?" he asked as we moved along the beach.

"He accepted it very calmly. Said he'd look into it."

Ben nodded. "Well thirty-four isn't right. It's schoolboy knowledge, Tom. National history. There was a media special years ago: *Thirty-Five Chances at the Dream*. We can check that."

"Den's doing what he can. I doubt we'll find the original number listed anywhere, let alone names and locations. It's a case of making the lie big enough."

"An entire arcology! Who could do that? What about Survey Authority? The tribal universities? Their maps and records—"

"Survey says thirty-four. We aren't allowed at tribal records yet, probably won't be."

Ben stopped, brows furrowed so they made deep shadows on his grizzled, sun-tanned face. It clearly troubled him, as if the universe had gone awry because this one single truth was out of kilter. "Tom—"

"I know. Altered. Someone's plundering. Maybe McBanus can tell us something."

"It can't happen," Scarbo muttered, more to himself than to me, and for a while we walked in silence, with just the sound of wind in the sea-grass and the steady rhythm of waves falling on the shore, the hiss of foam over the sand.

Almost before we realised it, we were climbing the stairs to where the windows of Villa Chano flashed in the sun. At this angle, the sprawling house was still well concealed behind its fretwork of palms and balustrades, its domed roof of red tile looming above the white-washed main shell.

"McBanus said forty thousand titles," I told Ben. "Mostly reference works and mote copies of paper books. We're welcome to look them over, though he fears they won't tell us much."

"More than Marquand, I bet."

I nodded, remembering the false aperture, the collection that existed only as coded light. "I think McBanus himself will be more important to us than his books."

We were at the southern turn of the rising terraces, well clear of the building itself, when lightning struck from the clear afternoon sky. The scream came an instant later, the tearing strike signal lost in the concussion of exploding masonry and tile.

At first we didn't know what had happened—it was impossible to grasp the simple shocking truth.

But in moments we knew. A laser strike from orbit. All it could be.

Then the stinging grit, dust and debris, the thump of fragments from Chano's northern wing gave the reality in terrible detail.

And the implications. The Ab'O Princes did not want us investigating books and libraries. Chiras Namarkon did not.

Namarkon, Lightning Spirit, had struck. The Immortal had access to tribal comsats, Ab'O tech.

We crouched by the terrace wall, staring in horror at what he had done—what it, they, whatever, had.

"We give it up, Tom," Ben said, close by me, a harsh whisper. 'They're telling us to give it up!'

The words freed me. "McBanus was waiting in his library." I made myself say it.

Then there was a woman screaming, filling the new silence like a second strike from the sky, guiding me as I ran, cursing Namarkon, cursing the tribes, the lost arcologies and stolen futures, but most of all cursing the cold unfeeling evil that could cause a cry of such terrible loss.

I did not go back to *Rynosseros*. I stayed over at the Gaza, sitting on the balcony of Room 777, watching the sea meet the long curving shoreline of Twilight Beach.

On the terrace below, games of fire-chess had begun in earnest. There were cheers, shouts, the familiar sounds of winning and losing, of life being lived in all its myriad forms. People moved along the Promenade, wandered the Breaklight Pier in the cool evening air. To seaward, the distant islands stood against the dying light like polished stones. Off to the north, the lights of Corlique, Castanelle and the souling colonies could be seen: closer, those of the villas, all occupied this late in the season.

Except for Chano, of course, broken and empty in the dunes beside the Beach Road.

McBanus and his wife, Emma, dead. Their daughter, Truan, hospitalized, in shock.

And not a word from the tribes. Council's protests and calls for explanations, accountability, had brought none.

Though one thing was clear, an angry and worried quorum of Council had agreed. If not the tribes then, even more than Dewi Dammo, Chiras Namarkon could reach far. Lightning Spirit indeed.

Either way there was no doubting the message. Secret libraries in Twilight Beach were to remain that way. Off limits.

Which left the unvisited arcologies on the list, including the missing, mysterious thirty-fifth, as well as those difficult and expensive creatures, the Antique Men, specifically Gado Bascoeur.

So much time had passed that we no longer expected much from that quarter. I was supposedly on a tribal mission, but just as Den's repeated requests for access to the appropriate tribal records had achieved nothing, we assumed that it would be the same here. But then, just like that, his routine appeals to the Antique Men, Poste

Restante, Saldy's, were rewarded. Suddenly, as if the time were right for it, the fate of the McBanus family and Chano a deciding factor, the other main avenue of enquiry had become available. I would be contacted, this evening, tomorrow, sometime soon, an agent had told Den on the phone.

After all this waiting, something at least.

I had no wish to return to *Rynosseros*. Chano preyed on my mind. Scarbo understood; the others would. There was nothing they could do but wait as I waited. Talk to people, ask questions.

I sat in the big viewing chair at the Gaza and sipped a glass of tautine. There was the old feeling of sanctuary here, so precious, something created by *these* walls, *these* familiar furnishings, *this* view out over the Gaza terrace and along the coast, by the murmur of belltrees drifting down from the roof-garden, by the spread of stars that escaped this well of light and made their net of dewpoints in the growing indigo.

Den had made the only possible deal with Bascoeur's contact: knowledge for knowledge. Whatever we learned in return for word of Namarkon or anything about my past. Anything.

But now I tried to go slow, sit back, watch old night fill the frame of the open balcony doors, and savour the cooling touch of the on-shore breeze. For a moment Chano and Namarkon were almost forgotten.

Almost.

Could the Antique Men, these ultimate bookmen, be it? If so, then how fitting, how appropriate for the times. In a world where increasingly all knowledge of that world was stored in comp systems rather than living memory, where—in the long afternoon since the Information Revolution—people had perfected the habit of automatically putting information aside, forgetting about it till it was needed again, little wonder that the "oubliettes" existed. These remarkable folk stored knowledge in an older, different fashion, in tech-assisted eidetic memory, all the lore people chose to forget or suppress, keyed by mantras and mnemonic tags, accessed by association, by ingested or injected catalysts and RNA assists. Like monks in ancient monasteries, they accumulated information of all kinds, then as generalists, specialists and synthesists, pluralists and explainers, they interpreted what they had gleaned, made conclusions, hoarded, sold, perpetuated.

They constituted what was virtually a priesthood to do this, a body of men and women (despite the carefully chosen old-world name) and specialised in the truths that State historians and tribal administrations, even the big marketing and ad agencies on the coasts, could not help but give one bias or another.

And curiously, the Princes themselves, the ones most likely to be compromised and displeased by such a state of affairs, seemed to favour the idea that these oubliettes existed, these safe-holes for storing arcane knowledge and the patterns of overview. Retrieval systems always had the facts, could offer conclusions and projections, but the Antique Men added intuition, imagination and astute judgement, allowed for the worth of feelings and impressions, for the possibility of there being *missing* facts contributing to an end.

Every viewpoint mattered in some way. By acknowledging subjectivity and applying it to a given situation, they reminded everyone of its integral role and so refined and maintained the concept of what truth could be, that, yes, it truly was the first casualty of self-interest.

To Den's amazement and constant delight, one of the popular sayings attributed to the oubliettes was a corruption of the old *faux* Angelino crime-fighter saying: "Never just the facts, no, never just the facts."

The phone rang, bringing me back from the indigo wall, the shimmering well, the splendid trap of Twilight Beach, made the laving wind just wind again.

I touched the plate. The screen showed the face of a young woman, pale, with intense grey eyes, a small clenched mouth: a severe countenance suggesting seriousness and business. Little else could be seen. She wore a close-fitting hood, like those worn by members of traditional female religious orders.

"Captain Tyson? I am Margaret Solles, notary for Gado Bascoeur. Are you available for an interview tomorrow?"

"Name a time and place."

"Tomorrow," she said. "I will call you at this number after 0900 and a meeting will be arranged. Good night."

Done. A brief sketch of a face representing such a final chance, so forgettable. But Margaret Solles. The name at least.

Chano was there then, Truan screaming, crying, Toban and Emma dead in the ruins, Marquand's wall as just a wall, all of it.

Now was no time to be alone. I went down to the Astronomers' Bar and found Scarbo, Strengi and Hammon at one of the terrace tables, and had no trouble at all persuading them to share their travellers' tales of far-off places.

Margaret Solles didn't call until mid-afternoon, leaving me to spend the morning distracted and on edge, worrying that Bascoeur may have reconsidered. At 1130 I let the desk clerks and stewards know I'd be with my friends from the Bird Club, and sat with a small group of regulars in the big chairs looking out on the Promenade. Though we discussed the Villa Chano strike, Jeremy, Sally and Nathan took my cue when I turned the subject to other things, and made no comment when I excused myself at 1300, saying I would take siesta.

The phone roused me at 1400. There on the screen was the pale face again (I was already thinking of her as the Sour Elf).

"He'll see you at Saldy's in twenty minutes, Captain."

"He'll trade?"

"He'll decide that at Saldy's. Twenty minutes. It's his time."

Meaning it wasn't mine; I needed to hurry. The screen went dark, but this time I remembered the harsh troubling gaze. This intense, serious woman was my path to Bascoeur.

5

Saldy's Rainhouse and Aviary had long ago outgrown its name. There were still the cosy salons with real birds sailing through tropical gardens beyond the casements, and other windows giving onto scenes of carefully controlled winters, and synthetic rains pattering on the glass before long fire-lit dinner tables.

But now additional structures had been added, extensions allowing ocean views, sun-traps and sand gardens, whitewashed loggias stretching out to the sea, steps leading down to terraces, shadowed courtyards, a hundred more quiet guest rooms, and one of the best belltree collections in all of Twilight Beach. It did not quite match the ancient splendour of the Gaza, but for the sense of old-world luxury, antiquity and other climes it afforded the likes of Gado Bascoeur, it was the only place the oubliettes chose when they visited this part of the coast.

The main entrance still had its original sign, and the Sour Elf was waiting beneath it when I arrived. She wore white desert clothing, a djellaba with a hood drawn close about her face so that more than ever she resembled an old-world nun, one, I fancied seeing her, who was angry with her God, short of both faith and favour.

"Second floor. The Blue Room," she said, and I wondered what sort of master Bascoeur could be that this young woman had become so hard and officious in his service.

The lobby of Saldy's was a grand thing, complete with potted palms, mosaics and lacquered screens, with small groups of guests talking quietly in deep armchairs and conversation pits, all washed by the rich honey-coloured light from antique shades beneath slowly turning fans.

I climbed the main stairs to a first-floor mezzanine, took a smaller flight to a side landing with three doors, one a soft midnight blue.

I knocked, waited a few moments, then turned the handle and entered.

The djellaba-shrouded figure of Bascoeur was sitting with his back to me before a balcony that opened onto an expanse of rich blue sky.

For an instant, it was like seeing myself as I must have looked at the Gaza the previous evening, then, of course, not at all. The colours here were too vivid, the fittings more conspicuously ornate.

"Come in, Captain," Gado Bascoeur said in a quiet smooth voice, one both practiced and commanding, though oddly sexless in its modulations.

I crossed to where he sat, saw more closely the stained-glass mask that marked him as an Antique Man. Across his lap, robed arms draped loosely over it, was an archimenter, beautifully made, a tech-fitted restoration piece, its wooden handle chased with silver, probably a comp-assist but possibly a laser or high-calibre ballistic for all I knew. It was strange to see such a dedicated scholar nursing an ancient firearm.

But it was the mask that drew my attention the most. It was a faceted dome, non-human, featureless, a deep oval-shaped bascinet, completely covering the face like a fencing mask. The line of the central frontal panes from which the lateral ones angled away suggested a pattern from nature: the plates on the shell of a tortoise, or the startling geometries on the backs of lizards. The intricate lozenges and plates of coloured glass were separated by a network of old bronzed silver, much worn from use.

I tried to make out the face inside the cage of coloured panes, but there were too many frosted shapes and no clears, giving tantalising glimpses of nose, brow and jaw, but occluded by afternoon sunlight through stressed blues, starved reds, ambers, bronzes, rich Genoese golds, teals and turquoises, streaked submarine greens.

"Twenty minutes I was told."

"Meg can be overzealous," he said. "We have all the time you need. I would very much like to hear about Dewi Dammo."

I drew a chair to the side of Bascoeur's own, out of the line of sight of the sky and the ocean below, wanting to watch the light play on what I could see of the man's features. I made myself comfortable and began.

It took twice the twenty minutes Meg had allowed. Now and then, the long brown fingers lifted and fell on the side plate of the archimenter, tapping out an irregular rhythm.

At first I thought he was touch-recording facts or mnemonic codes, knowing that the device was probably a storage-trap fashioned to look like a gun, but then noticed that the tips of those fingers made no contact with the surface of the ritual weapon. He was simply working through a memory pattern. If he noticed my attention, the momentary slowing and distraction in my account, he gave no sign.

Finally I was done. There were his questions then, another twenty minutes of them: about Dewi and my present search both for Namarkon and for information about my forgotten past. I forced myself to ask no questions of my own, just watched the fingers moving in their gentle flute pattern all the while. But finally they paused and there was a different silence, an almost disquieting lull in which I studied the covered face, the gorgeous panes in their stepped, angling curves. They made a cathedral dome, a bright orrery in which the solitary planet was Bascoeur's skull and all that it contained, a world, a universe inside another, inside yet another.

I studied, too, the small flower sign he wore high on his chest, periwinkle blue on the sand-coloured robe, an embroidered Forget-Me-Not, fitting choice for the oubliettes. Inevitably, my attention wandered into the intricate sign embroidered at the shoulder—a sect patch it seemed, a sequence of many dots, some linked into cruciform patterns by looping lines, overlapping and bolder at the centre, the whole shape bordered by darker dots. It suggested a circuit pattern or an elaborate code, an ideogram, some mystical sign of power.

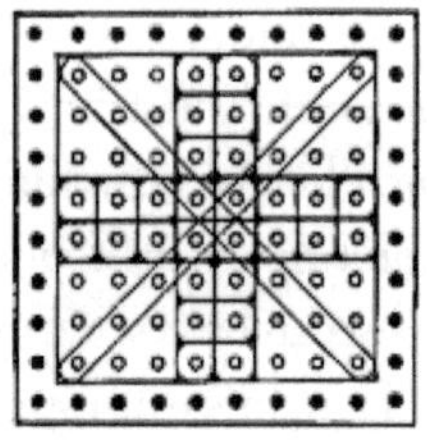

Bascoeur placed his hands squarely on the weapon in his lap. "What do you need from me, Captain?"

"I went to Turker Fin."

"I know."

"Dewi mentioned Chiras Namarkon in connection with a library. The tribesman who gave me this mission confirmed it. I went to the seven National libraries I was told officially existed. There may be more, though I doubt it now. We are being shut off from our past; eventually we will have to go outside Australia to learn about our National heritage."

"Go on, please."

"All the Chiras Namarkon references I did find had been excised, or rather relegated to 'dead stack' status, one text only, one Illuminated Book kept at Crayasse. L75 VGS. But at Crayasse I learned that it was on loan to Turker, had been moved on just before I arrived. That Book was sent to Turker for a reason, and I expected to find it gone, sent elsewhere, unable to be located."

"Yes?" The long fingers resting on the archimenter did not move now, though the hands were angled out from Bascoeur's body like minatory wings, pointed at the ocean and the sweep of sky. It looked wonderful and strange, barely human.

"I saw L75 VGS. It's in poor condition. The Reader Page misfunctions. The entry for Namarkon cancels itself. But I learnt something."

"Yes?"

"There were the appended summaries, etymological references to the old languages, the traditional mythological identification of Namarkon as Lightning Spirit, as a tree struck by lightning, that sort of thing. And there is an entry for a Chiras Namarkon."

Bascoeur said nothing. I watched him intently, as if I were hoping to read something in the set of his body, the colours of the mask, the blue Forget-Me-Not on his robe, traditionally the flower of friendship and fidelity, in the intricate tangle of the sect patch which kept snaring my eye and had me wondering what it could possibly mean for people like these.

"Chiras Namarkon," I continued, "is identified as the Immortal, described variously as a creature of fable, as a tyrant hidden away in his labyrinth—his library—as a great wanderer, a highwayman, it goes on and on. He has the secret of knowledge, of ideas and words. He has treasure. But you know this, Lord Gado."

"I do?" The long hands still pointed like emblematic wings.

"A status request tag is yours. There has been an attempt to suppress knowledge of such a figure, making it dead stack, hard to locate. The time and trouble that took must have been considerable. I suspect that even were I to have access to the tribal libraries and the universities, there would be as little information. The tribes must know about Namarkon for his part in their affairs to be effective, that he is non-Ab'O, extremely long-lived, but they need not know too much."

"You assume a great deal. But you are telling me something."

"The tribes know my limitations, the unlikelihood of my finding anything without assistance. It would take me years to locate even a few of the private libraries. Chano was destroyed; Marquand is a fraud. So why send me? Unless you can provide clues or are involved in some way. Unless you wanted it to *seem* like that. You avoided answering Den's calls for quite some time. There's a reason. Namarkon could well be one of you. An oubliette. A secret master of oubliettes. The tribes may suspect this."

"We don't keep libraries in the traditional sense, Captain."

"You *are* libraries."

Bascoeur paused before answering. "Of course. It's all worth considering."

"Which part?"

"All of it. Namarkon."

"How many oubliettes are there?"

"A total number is hard to give. There are trainees, honorary postings—"

"Like you."

"Like me? Thirty-six."

"And leaders?"

"Four officers out of that number. We call them Angels."

"More and more like a holy order. Are you an Angel?"

"Yes. This information is costing you, Captain."

"Then let me complete the trade. Will you take me to where oubliettes are trained? Any place where Antique Men gather?"

"We operate as solitaries. What leads you—?"

"Dewi ruled by creating then monopolising an economic/religious condition, tapping into what was almost a theocracy. Another effective power-base must be information flow, the non-partisan trafficking in knowledge and strategies and historical perspective. The tribes can afford you."

Finally the hands moved again, turning in slightly, fingers angling, moving, completing a quick manipulation on the air. "I admit to being impressed."

"No, you will have anticipated I would come to this from the moment the tribes approached me."

Bascoeur made no response, though his hands had become still again. It appeared that I had his complete attention.

"First, there was virtually nothing on libraries," I said, "so few are declared. The black market in books means most true-book collections stay private and secret. Council gave what listings their systems had, but I'm allowing for interference now, tampering with National data-stores. But I accept that the privates are incomplete anyway, not just inaccessible. They will be depleted, the best items sold off or plundered long ago. The university and tribal libraries are off limits, as you know."

"Do I, Captain?"

"I believe you know my position, Lord Gado. I went to the Pandeon here in Twilight Beach, then out to some of the old arcologies. Crayasse gave me a lead, something called Alexandrian Book. Den has techs and archivists doing searches; he's even done a tentative costing on consulting individual tribal archives well favoured to Nation, should they relent, though that would alert too many people."

Bascoeur turned his head slightly, like the apse of a living cathedral, a crystal flower turning with the light, filled with light. I was amused by the theatricality of the action, but awed too. He was not play-acting a role, this oubliette, however much his manner often suggested it: the composed gestures, the mannered speech. Rather he was a uniquely alienated and uniquely engaged individual, someone curiously but necessarily estranged from my worldview with its immediacy, its tribal conflicts and striving Princes, its Dewi Dammos and deadly Namarkons. Could Chiras fit such a *Weltanschauung*? If so, then so so different from Dewi.

"The tribes would not tell you anything," Bascoeur said flatly. "What happened to Chano confirms that. And Dammo's death—his presumed death—had immediate repercussions. As a port official, James Namuren's part could not be lightly overlooked. Some Princes sought Convocation and payback; some even now push to re-assess not only the charling leases but all National concessions. The secret libraries are off limits for a reason; the Antique Men will be denied you soon. You were given this mission by a faction, an interest group, that saw a small closing window of opportunity."

"Then how can I possibly locate Namarkon?"

Bascoeur's left hand lifted as it to counsel patience. "You have imputed that Namarkon is one of us. I am intrigued and alarmed by that notion. But there are things we can do before the embargo falls. In fact"—he angled his head so a turquoise pane flashed richly—"that's precisely why I came to Saldy's. The management protects its patrons. I came here unmasked. Only you and Meg know I am here. I did this to forestall official injunctions reaching me."

"Surely not out of gratitude for my account of finding Dewi! You're playing this for you. Someone moved that Book to delay me, but whoever it was could have confiscated it altogether. I was delayed while some interested party searched for something else. The Book was deliberately damaged before it arrived at Turker."

"Deliberately, you think? A sealed Book?"

"The librarian said so. You could do it. Since I did find an entry which led me to you as much as it did to Namarkon, I'm left to wonder what part the Antique Men play in this—and what they might have gained by delaying me, by damaging a text, then *letting* it lead me to them."

Bascoeur turned his head back to the sea and the sky. Some of the panes on his mask seemed to have special optical properties: one shone with the lustrous velvet mauve-green of a dragonfly's eye, another with the rich roiling highlights of oil struck by rain.

"Pretend for a moment, Captain, that I am not Chiras Namarkon, nor his confederate in any way. Assume I am a very concerned member of my order, an Angel, concerned about libraries too. Consider that where the oubliettes are concerned, the Princes and Clever Men have one commitment greater than using us to control the flow of information as feudal societies once did after the fall of Rome and Constantinople, during that great and terrifying European Dark Age we are determined must never happen again."

"Very well."

"Back then, distortion of facts occurred more through ignorance, ineptitude, superstition and the limits of technology than deliberate disinformation, mythopoesis or strictures imposed by church and state. Now we have a carefully, wonderfully controlled program of distortion, of expert myth-making. Nothing new really, but more effective in a cultural horizon so devoted to the idea of total sharing, where genuine information flow *seems* to be encouraged. 'A thousand truths for the one well-placed lie' is an oubliette saying, remember."

"So what are *you* saying, Lord Gado?"

"Historians and archivists are more circumspect today, but the liberalising of information by comp, sat-scan, gain-monitor is a myth too. It has led to closed societies, intensively applied media falsehood, reclusive overlords like Dammo and Namarkon, the re-medievalising of attitudes and fact-finding processes, all the counters in the information web. We acquire more myth and legend, more contamination and carefully planted disinformation than ever before, you realise, in direct proportion to any documented truth. Tactical lies created and nurtured by the strategists and propagandists, refined and promoted by local and international agencies. The Information Revolution, Tom Rynosseros, is over simply because it continues, a wonderful paradox! Call it affective filtering or whatever, it is our condition now. There is too much to know. More and more we are becoming verifiers and discriminators rather than information givers."

I studied this man, capable of the Zen rigour, so full of intricate knowledge. The air of cynicism and weariness he brought to our conversation was a tactic, I felt, a way to test my own reactions perhaps. Or maybe he was a man in crisis, revealing a new alarming truth he dared not share with his fellow oubliettes.

I recalled the lack of surprise I'd felt when Kaber Fen Otamas had told me of the ongoing prospect of secret rulers like Dewi and now this Namarkon appearing, powerfully, vigorously active in the interstices of that suborned information glut. Not even State of Nation had too many illusions in its quest for identity and survival, not after the watergating of history: the Bolo Mays, Nixons and Richelieus, the Viet Nams and Sinchwens, the para-governmental agencies: the CIA and Mossad, the Mafia, Camorra, Yakuza, Talion and their corporate variants—the Machiavellian heritage uncovered and refined during a few key centuries, power vacuums filled, well or badly, but inevitably.

"Before Turker," I said, "I expected to hear from the Antique Men. Council tried to arrange meetings without success; no doubt you had reasons. I'd become a vital integer in something, cutting across patterns, revealing structures. Now you seem to suggest that the *tribes* are tampering with your people."

Bascoeur raised a cautionary hand. "If not the tribes then some tribal agency operating as Namarkon, whoever, whatever he, she, it is. He is in his library somewhere. What does he do there? How does he rule his portion? He may have more knowledge than all of us, even more than the tribes, may in fact be comp, AI, someone or something as long-lived as Dewi was, immortal, building ideas into history, a mythopoeticist skilfully, effectively controlling and disseminating concepts, fostering his illusions and fictions, immediate and long-term. I am very worried, personally alarmed, that the Antique Men, allowed access everywhere, may be infiltrated by Namarkon's agents, that one of my associates may in fact be Chiras Namarkon. The very thought of it brings a fear you cannot understand."

"What do you suggest?"

"We depend on tribal favour; we do not run our own ships. Except for a few closed towns, you can take *Rynosseros* where you please."

"Unless they strike as they did at Chano."

"A reasonable risk. You hold a mandate and a Colour. Your name is in the Great Passage Book."

"That may not worry Namarkon at all. After Balin that may not worry the tribes either. Go on."

"We seek Namarkon together, at least until I am satisfied that the Antique Men are *not* involved in his schemes."

"Then?"

"Then our usual rules apply. We pay you with knowledge for what *you* give us."

"Can I see where the oubliettes are trained? Allowing for the fact that I might wish to search on after you have satisfied yourself, allowing that I am still considering you or one of your kind for Namarkon, that I was delayed a month in finding L75 VGS."

"Agreed. But, Captain, we must act immediately. If the tribes continue to move against you, hinder you; if the oubliettes are denied you—either because Namarkon is working among us for the tribes and not just himself, or because you must be stopped anyway—then what I do now is outside the law. All Antique Men will pay for any indiscretions I now commit."

"Then, as you say, word must not reach us. *Rynosseros* is at the Sand Quay. Come aboard tonight, whenever you can. We sail at 0600."

"Very well," Bascoeur said. "And Meg will accompany us. But leave now, please. I must consider this possibility of treachery."

6

I did not see Meg Solles when I left Saldy's, but quickly headed along the late afternoon streets to the Promenade, followed that towards the decks, loggias and famous terraces of the Gaza, bright now with the last hour of sunlight, the windows flashing like a vast replica of Bascoeur's mask.

Though it was still that hour till the breaklight, the time of day for which Twilight Beach is named, there were players of fire-chess already at the boards, their tiny lines of fighters dancing in the sea-wind. These were short-lived suicide games, full of braggadocio and fun, recklessly played because the wind allowed opportunity for little else. The players laughed and performed at their eccentric best. The tourists and hotel guests cheered every bold move, and cheered as enthusiastically each time a tiny flame was extinguished.

Soon, when the wind lost its edge and the Hotel's tuxedoed Devil Catchers appeared, ready to beat at the dust-devils with their long-handled spoilers, these flamboyant posturings would cease. The grins and extravagant flourishes would be replaced by looks of concentration and a ruthless urbanity famous the world over.

When I turned into the Gentian Walk, that narrow walled avenue connecting Tramway Street to the southern end of the Gaza terrace, I found three Ab'Os leaning on the seawall watching the ocean. They wore fighting leathers under their djellabas, and had sheathed kitanas over their shoulders, not an uncommon thing, but an uncommon place for tribesmen to loiter.

I read the scene quickly enough, had it confirmed when the men recognized me, quickened and moved back from the wall to block my path. They wore vendetta marks on their cheeks, bands of colour and soul-taking stars in turquoise and deep red. The swords were slashes of light leaving their scabbards.

I had nothing but my sailor's sticker in the leg-sheath of my fatigues, though reaching for it meant I had accepted their terms.

One tribesman in his early thirties, older than the others, moved forward.

"I am Ephan Sky Namuren," he said. "Kin to James Namuren. This is payback."

"But not legal," I said, desperately seeking words that would prevent this. "As Blue Captain on a tribal mission I am not allowed to fight you. Will this be murder then? More shame for Namuren?"

"You are allowed," Ephan said, as if he had not heard the final words. "And you have your deck-knife."

"Which might grow into a kitana someday, certainly. You are brave men."

Another spoke then, pushing past Ephan. "I am Paul Dharajan. Stories say you were trained by the Spaniard, Marco, and the Japanese, Tensumi. A sticker is enough for you."

"Stories! I wish I could remember living so long to have all these stories." I searched the empty Walk and the fiercely marked faces for any sign of advantage. Was this it then? A final afternoon? A last vital encounter? How many of us ever choose the places where we die?

I drew my sticker, its narrow blade as long as my forearm. "Who claims the right?" I said, formally.

The men exchanged glances, quick bright smiles.

"We all do," Ephan said. "For our kinsman."

"Judged traitor by Convocation," I reminded them. "You will be sung for this. Be sure of it."

More glances at that, the smiles gone, replaced by carefully neutral looks, though I imagined I did see traces of worry, doubts about assurances given.

"The terms then," I continued, hoping someone would enter the Walk, someone armed or who might summon help. But they had chosen their time well. "From the first drop of blood you are damned. They watch!" And I looked up into the late afternoon sky to where the invisible satellites held station, whichever orbitals were currently geo-tethered to Twilight Beach.

Paul Dharajan moved forward. "Come, Ephan! No-one watches this!"

"Good, Dharajan," I said, dropping to a first position. "I am hunting Namarkon but you will do."

The Ab'O grinned, confirming the source of the strike, the direction from which assurances had ultimately come, filtering down through tribal lobbies.

Again I tried for the initiative. "Though he too is hunted by his enemies. Of course they watch. Can they monitor this small stretch, do you think?"

Dharajan did not answer. Ephan and the other man moved forward as well until five metres were all there was.

I raised my sticker and cut my own cheek, let them see the blood shining on my blade. Then I looked immediately into the sky. "Take them all, Namarkon!"

Ephan looked up, his companions as well. It was reflex.

A wisp of cloud had drifted into view, seemed frozen there.

Then Dharajan cried out in pain and surprise, blood streaming from his throat where my sticker now stood, small deft lightning. He dropped his sword with a single cry and collapsed to the stones.

I lunged for the weapon in what scant seconds I had, but Ephan was better than that, well-trained, well-chosen. His foot came down on the discarded blade, denying me. His own sword arced towards my outstretched arm, to my neck where I lay, head to the side, fingers touching the haft.

The edge, the line of separation, was right there. One twist, one thrust, and I would cease to be, know, feel. No throb of bleeding cheek, no pain in knee and shoulder from the fall, no knowing this desperate attempt at life. I looked along the gleaming blade to Ephan's painted face, his flashing eyes, beyond them to the patch of sky, the frozen wisp of cloud, infinitely precious.

"Fight me," Ephan said, stepping back, leaving Dharajan's blade, seeking something of honour in a poor mission, only now truly understood.

"No!" his companion cried. "His orders!"

His. The word said it all.

"Personal honour, Sab! Decide for yourself when he is armed."

I seized the hilt, slick with Dharajan's blood, and stood, heart pounding, thoughts racing one to the next, seeking a solution.

Ephan was there almost immediately, and the Walk rang, echoed with the clash of weapons.

Despite my two blades, long and short, it was all I could do to defend, and in a sense Ephan helped me there. He was too good a swordsman; Sab could not engage without ruining Ephan's patterns. What trade-offs there were between them, a concession to face, showed Sab to be an inferior fighter, though not to be taken lightly.

Slowly, in the constant jarring of the three-way, I managed to regain my centre. More and more deflections were controlled, more and more feints planned and resolved by me.

Ephan withdrew. Sab leapt in, jumped back with a slashed sleeve and a look of astonishment.

"Marco and Tensumi, remember!" Ephan warned, breathing hard, then filled the air again with his own lightning.

Every breath was drawn over fire now. Arms ached from the repeated blows of the exquisite many-folded blades.

If not resolved soon, Ephan would have me. He was too good. I brought Marco and Tensumi to mind—real, RNA assists from the Madhouse, another lost or false memory, who could say?—then waited for Sab's turn, let him begin, and swapped blades, right hand to left, deflected his sword with my own and took him above the heart with the sticker, through djellaba, fighting leathers and all, the blade in, out and gone, whipped away, lightning through fire it seemed, so sudden.

Again there was the look of astonishment, intense and final as the eyes glazed and his life went out of him. I had cleared the blade before he knew what had happened.

"See what—they—have done to you," I managed, exhausted, dangerously so, watching Ephan's eyes. "His orders!"

"Whose—" Ephan's breathing was ragged too. "—do you think?"

"One—who doesn't care what happens. You—don't count. Expendable, hear? If not you—others."

Ephan nodded, darted quick glances at his dead companions,

assessing what had been paid. No fool this one, simply a man trapped by duty.

"What do I have?" he asked.

"You were not here," I said. He had given me my chance; now I held out Dharajan's kitana for him to take.

He nodded and took it, saluted with his own sword, then turned, vanishing through the crowd of sightseers and hotel guests who had gathered on the Walk.

I entered the Gaza and found Scarbo and Shannon, but at the far side of that grand room from where the swordplay had just now taken place. The sounds had not reached them through the press of guests and tourists, the forest of sanche palms, the lacquered and enamelled screens, the great pillars and sculptury.

I drew many looks crossing that great room, and when my friends saw me they immediately went to rise. I waved them back, gratefully taking the glass of tautine Shannon pushed towards me, fire for the fire, the shaking, for the simple joy of being alive.

"Namarkon almost achieved what Dewi couldn't," I said. "Three bravos decided to brawl. The cheek is mine, a bit of payback psychology that didn't work."

Ben and Rob smiled, though the smiles were thin and quickly gone. Something else was amiss.

"What?"

"Den's hurt," Ben said. "Archimenter discharge—or an equivalent. Some time around 1600. He's in deep shock."

"Archimenter? Will he survive?"

"They think so. He's in a sleeve at Gallo's and responding. There's been surgery as well. He has Bylon heart tailoring; it was thrown out of kilter."

"But archimenter?" I thought of the rich data store, the concentration of energy in the weapon, the "six years of dream" as it was called: the amount of time in the old seventy-year, pre-nano lifespan that the average person spent dreaming. "He couldn't survive it!"

Scarbo shook his head. "Nothing like full charge. Perhaps it was just a warning. But Kurdaitcha came, said they were looking for Gado Bascoeur."

"Not Bascoeur. I've been with him since 1500. And he wouldn't incriminate himself with an archimenter; none of his people would."

"Namarkon, you think?" Shannon asked.

"Who can say, Rob? An extreme point and a clumsy way of making it."

Scarbo set down his glass. "Den may have found something. Possibly plundered from Nation's systems."

"We don't have time to find out." I leant forward, spoke the next words almost as a whisper. "Bascoeur will come aboard tonight. We leave tomorrow at first light. Half-crew."

"Where?" Scarbo asked.

"When we're aboard, Ben. Find the others. Briefing at 1900. But half-crew."

7

We fled from Twilight Beach, that was how it felt, rushing along the Great Arunta Road with the sun barely above the line and thirty kites in the sky, great Sodes and Demis, a dozen racing footmen. There was no pursuit.

We had minimum crewing. By Ben's roster Rim, Strengi and Hammon were down for leave anyway, and so became part of a last-minute deception. They drank with the sandsmen and veteran sailors at the Astronomers' Bar, let themselves be seen gaming at Deep's late into the night. It was likely that no-one expected to see *Rynosseros* pulling away from the Sand Quay, lofting her kites at first light.

It was busy work for Scarbo, Shannon and me with a vessel the size of ours. For that dawn hour, we hurried about the commons, fitting kites to cables, checking the separations, Scarbo judging the shift from coastal to inland winds and making choices, shouting them to us or signing in the traditional way of the aeropleuristic craft.

Bascoeur and Meg watched from the quarterdeck, the oubliette unreadable in his mask, his assistant equally so behind her severe pale face, both shapeless in their travelling robes. The Antique Man had his hood raised and drawn well forward over his mask, a small precaution but one observed just in case.

Who could say if the tribes cared or if Namarkon watched? Bascoeur was probably right. Lightning against Chano was one thing; a strike at a mandated ship, a Coloured Captain, at someone listed in the Great Passage Book, was something else entirely. I recalled Dewi's mirror ships, permitted but watched and finally punished from orbit. It might be that Namarkon existed by exploiting Ab'O need, tribal vulnerability. He might very well safeguard the values that kept his power-base secure, perhaps aiming—my real fear in this!—to extend himself beyond any need of their goodwill.

Appropriating laser strike was privilege enough; possessing a Namarkon comsat of his own would be absolute crisis, not only death-strike capability but information saturation as well. What Kaber Fen Otamas had told me seemed more real than ever.

The stowaway appeared when we were almost at Wani.

Bascoeur was at the port rail of the quarterdeck, lost in his thoughts and assimilations, with Meg waiting to one side. Shannon was with Scarbo at the kite lockers laying cable runs, only occasionally glancing at the canopy overhead, not needing to do so since they read the tensions in the hull and overheads so well.

I had the helm, watching the Road and some distant cloud-forms that could spell wind and so kite-change, enjoying how our canopy spread upon the sky like a bright hand, a taut receding thrust of light and colour.

Meg saw her first, a noon-spectre appearing on the commons to for'ard, beyond the intricate totemic webwork of the cable-boss.

"Look!" she cried, and the light was such that the figure startled us all. It was like the mirages you often see, the transit-ghosts you expect out on the Serafina, along the Soul or in the inner deserts, not snared here beneath the sky-trap of kites and displayed in full sunshine.

Only for a second. It resolved from dream to real in moments. Our visitor came walking across the commons, a woman in her mid-twenties, taller than any but Bascoeur in his shrouded jewel-box mask, with wide clear eyes and fine features in a face I found I knew, with the small talenti marks, three to each side, tatooed in ochre at the curve of the jawline: a member of Club Hetaera. She wore desert fatigues that were the same sandy-white as her short hair. Meg Solles was pale; this striking young woman was the whitened gold of wheatfields in sunshine.

Scarbo followed her up to the helm, waiting till she spoke, though I'd already heard the echo of her scream from the ruins of Chano.

"Thank you for what you did," she said, bringing back the ruin of lives.

"Why are you here, Truan?" I asked.

She smiled wearily. "I'm hetaera. I can give Namarkon his due."

Bascoeur moved forward from the rail, vivid and powerful. "Who told you that name?"

"I knew why Captain Tyson was visiting Chano," she answered evenly. "Marquand phoned. We are women who do, Lord Oubliette."

"It is an age when too many well-intentioned people seek to do, Ms McBanus. The Bird Club. The Hetaera. Nation Council. This is a private mission. Put back, Captain. We cannot go on."

"With respect, Lord," Truan said, and brought forth a wire from the pocket of her fatigues: the feed-point of a gain-monitor. "Nothing is more private than my task. There was conversation when you came aboard last night, and again this morning. I heard the word Whitehead, the name of the destination you gave Captain Tyson."

The Antique Man looked at her, or looked at a point of infinity on the inside of his glass cage. Near him, Meg let her own face show her master's controlled rage, the measure of it she imagined. Bascoeur was a pragmatist. I doubted he would be angry for long.

"Then continue," he said—to me undoubtedly though the mask gave no certainty of it—then left the quarterdeck. Meg went too, like a bruise Bascoeur chose to carry with him, a penitential badge. I wondered at the nature of that secret agreement between them, what intimacy was lodged in that relentless service. I wondered too if our stowaway might not end up with an archimenter taking her mind as it nearly had Den's.

"You make it difficult," I told our unwanted guest. "Truan, I need that man. He's the only lead I have. And how is it you own a gain-monitor? That needs tribal authorisation."

"My father's," she said. "He often worked for the tribes, needed to authenticate dealers and couriers. The tribes allowed it on loan. They may assume it was destroyed."

Full crew would have stopped her, I kept telling myself, found her in the empty storage bay. Hammon's job, or Rim's. Our ruse had done it, our clever ploy.

"Captain, like you I have only this," she said. "How would you proceed if you were in my place? Blame and punish? You're undermanned. I know enough of kites not to be in the way."

"Then stay near Scarbo. Ben, give her a place. And stay away from Bascoeur and his assistant!"

She said no more, went quietly down to the lockers and the armatures. There was wind-change coming and she showed no small degree of skill helping Shannon bring in the top-kites, drawing the outstretched hand into a fist, tethered close now and beating at the sky.

Bascoeur seemed to have accepted Truan's presence when he returned to the poop an hour later. He came without Meg, thank goodness, and watched the Road from as close to my station at the helm as he could stand without disturbing me, though I sensed his presence, the flashing glance from the front of the hood, the tortoise panes throwing so many jewels back at the sun.

"She has no choice," he said finally. "Home and family are gone."

"Yes," I said, respecting him for this compassion, though it meant betraying self-interest. "So, Turker, then Whitehead."

"Agreed. Though I'm curious as to why Turker is necessary. It can't be L75 VGS. I can do no more to work a faulty Book than the librarian."

"I need information on AI, on crystalline intelligence."

"Pursuing the obvious," Bascoeur said.

I shrugged. "What can you tell me?"

"To save you time? That, yes, our masks are nanotech-constructed crystalline lattices with ambient temperature super-conductivity, made essentially by a conventional nano assembler. That the internal circuitry is mixed, electronic and cortico-optical, with vested laser tech for data volume, that the power needs are minimal. Parts of my body have been bio-adapted to supply that, more old science really. It gives over 1900 times the storage capacity of the human brain and can be one million times as fast."

"Thank you," I said. "Will you remove your mask and talk about this?"

I expected a flat refusal, so his reply surprised me.

"Yes, though you cannot know how I resent needing to, resent the fact that nothing else can convince you now."

"You might be Namarkon and not know it. Part of Namarkon."

"So easily caught? Why would I? Why would some Antique Man collective—"

"Potentially a vast nanotech computer."

"—let us meet?"

"You know the answer. You've become an only chance."

"Because of Chano?"

"Yes." It seemed so unlikely now that Namarkon, like poor mad Dewi, would willingly make himself—itself?—so vulnerable. I wished I had Truan's monitor, but knew that no oubliette would ever agree to use one.

"Tonight I will be without my mask," Bascoeur said. "But remember, Captain, we are here now only because I—as Angel—need to consider my own kind impartially, to explore leads of my own."

"Will you answer another question then?"

"You can ask it."

"There were thirty-five National arcologies before the tribes drove us back to the coasts. Now official lists show only thirty-four. How many are there?"

"Thirty-five," Bascoeur said calmly, and the excitement I felt made me demand what I should have requested.

"Which one is missing? Why?"

"That is my other search, Captain. Locating that site. Separate from yours, for my reasons, unless I decide it concerns you."

"Should it? Please, Lord Gado—"

"The unlisted arcology is Mekkis. An old Hebrew name."

"Turker might tell us where—"

"I have tried there already. Tried them all. Captain, in Hebrew 'mekkis' means 'power'."

"Namarkon!" I cried.

Truan and Scarbo glanced up when I said it.

"Yes," Bascoeur said. "The general deletion of that name suggests it. And some tribal connection to be able to hide such a thing. Hard to misplace a city."

Truan was approaching the quarterdeck. Meg Solles came hurrying from the bow, revealing by the determination of her stride, by the fixed direction of her gaze, more about her humanity and that of her master. Bascoeur may have accepted the reality of Truan's situation, Meg Solles clearly had not.

But Gado Bascoeur served no master on this ship. He turned away, showing by his manner that he was apart, so that when Truan and Meg arrived, one tentatively, not wanting to intrude, the other determined and hurrying, they were left regarding one another across the width of the quarterdeck.

I was watching the sky and the Road ahead as surely as Bascoeur watched the desert around us, but I sensed the contest that Truan suddenly found herself part of. Being hetaera, she did not leave it unspoken.

"I am not interested in your oubliette," she said simply. "You need fear nothing from me."

"That's not it at all!" Meg answered angrily, which told us it was something as human, as desperate and needful.

Truan returned to the commons, and Meg was left with the silent rebuke of Bascoeur's back. I felt for her as she headed for'ard to watch the desert and to cool whatever longing had been revealed.

When Shannon took the helm at 1600, I made my way forward to where the notary sat on the starboard bench, her hood back, revealing her cropped black hair. Without the hood to frame her pale face, she looked more childlike and vulnerable than ever.

"She's wrong," Meg Solles said. "That's not it."

I sat beside her. "Then why behave as if it were?"

She blinked, frowned. "None of you knows what this man suffers here, what it means to examine the possibility of treason. He has infinities stored in his head, a custodianship of ages and civilisation; now he endures this action against his order, sacrificing *time* from so many other duties."

"Caused by me."

"Yes," she said, and her mouth contracted into the Sour Elf's once more.

"Why do you follow him? Serve him?"

"It's an honour. I get to learn. I might even be trained."

"How long has it been?"

She shrugged. "Five years. Six. A few have companions, not all. The Angels always do. We are servants, notaries, sometimes friends. We do what is needed."

"What is needed."

"Nothing like that!" she snapped. "They don't need that! Sometimes it would be better if they did. They are androgynes, did you know? Both sexes."

The information startled me.

"Don't ask about it, Captain. The answer is lost in hermetic lore. In alchemical beginnings we will never understand. It's a tradition. I accept it."

"Meg—"

"I accept it!"

"You don't—"

"It's the honour of service that keeps me here, not physical love!"

"Do you know my situation?" I asked her, to turn the conversation away from her relationship.

She nodded. "Lord Gado told me." Her mouth softened; the child in her defeated the bitter, practiced lines around her mouth. "You are very brave."

"No," I said, laughing. "No, Meg. You are brave, who give so much from love. I just find myself taking a direction, doing what I can to discover my beginnings. Now my world has been touched again. A friend was harmed at Twilight Beach. Truan's parents are dead, her home destroyed. Desperation becomes duty. We are similar there, you and I. Life makes its own purpose, as always."

"At least you are doing. That is brave!"

"Then we are brave together. And Gado Bascoeur is very brave to do this."

"Yes," she said, grateful, and there it was: a smile, also elfin, small and tentative on that lonely face.

"Meg, since you know something of the courtesies and protocols of the Antique Men, I would rather ask you some of my questions than put them to Lord Gado and use his time. It is a way I can spare him but gain knowledge that may help him as much as me."

"What questions?"

"The patch on his shoulder. What is that?"

"The Forget-Me-Knot," she said.

"The patch, not the flower."

"It's the Forget-Me-Knot! K-N-O-T. The oubliette sign. A schematic of the flower, I don't know, something like that. A molecular schema."

"Is that what he told you?"

Meg shrugged. "You see this as a key to Namarkon?"

The question, those words, made me hesitate a moment. "Anything could be. I've learned that signs and symbols can matter very much. On the Inland Sea there is a woman for whom the ellipsis of Inner Eye means everything."

"Tallin Okani. The one who hunts the special charling."

"Yes. For Den and Council, the Bladed Sun of Nation means so much."

"It's a windmill," she said. "Those converging triangles. An ancient windmill!"

"I've heard that. What people wear and show is important."

"Unless they are concealing and misleading. Dissembling. Using signs and symbols."

"True," I said. "But not this patch, I suspect. That design is important."

"You must ask Bascoeur about the Knot." She was becoming the Elf again, so accustomed to standing between her lord and the world. "He might unravel it for a questing Alexander like you."

And the new smile was bright and hard, a fully made thing. She had referred to the plaque fixed to the helm of *Rynosseros*, to the words once attributed to Alexander the Great by an ancient writer:

> *One must live as if it would be forever, and as if one might die each moment. Always both at once.*

"Perhaps if we do not unravel that particular Knot first, Meg, someone else might cut it asunder. I want to save your master as well."

"It is ancient, from the founding of the order. A circuit mat, or the design of a sacred tile from Alexandria, from Hellenistic times. But Gado could have been joking about it. I don't know what is true."

Gado, she had said this time, without "Lord" before it. "Keep it in your thoughts, please. At any time Gado might decide we should part, and I truly would like to help him before that happens, to put his mind at ease. Like it or not, the Antique Men form a living library. That Knot on his sleeve looks like a labyrinth to me, formed by a nanotech computer of oubliette masks."

"You've told him you suspect this?"

"He will have guessed where my thinking leads. To an extent my speculations help him, give necessary objectivity; past a certain point they are intrusions."

"Insults."

"Unfortunately."

"I'll keep what you ask in mind. For his sake."

I stood. "Thank you, Meg. For his sake."

8

Bascoeur kept his word. After 1900, Shannon brought *Rynosseros* to the edge of the Road for our night mooring, selecting an area well clear of the graded surface, though it was doubtful any other ships would be coming now.

Around us, nothing could be seen but darkening sweeps of sand and low scrub, every ridge and stone with its long shadow, the scraps from which night was being made. The sun was a half-coin, shedding the last of its gold at the horizon.

The oubliette had gone below a little after 1750. Now, while Scarbo saw to the cable-boss and Truan and Shannon swept up the wind-wrack from the day's travel, and with Meg off somewhere by herself, Bascoeur re-appeared—and without his fabulous headgear.

In spite of what Meg had said about the androgyny, he was clearly a man—of indeterminate age, I noted, though possibly in his early forties, pale-skinned, dark-haired and with thin brows and a fine neck and jaw. The eyes were dark in the growing gloom, the nose narrow and straight, almost too sharp, a disturbingly severe feature on such an otherwise regular face. In the last of the light, I could see a pair of fine silvery scars at his temples.

"Salvation Moons we call them," Bascoeur said, not needing to be asked. "Signs of humility and self-denial. More symbols."

I smiled. Meg had told him of our conversation then, had no doubt seen it as her duty.

The oubliette's voice was very much as it was when he was masked, well-modulated, with something of the contralto about it, almost sexless. He moved with his customary grace and economy as he joined me at the port rail, wearing his robe still, the flower and the Knot patch clear in the fading light.

"What now, Captain?"

I was used to his words coming through planes of glass. Seeing lips forming them was strange, as if a voice transmission had been lip-synced to an actor or a clever mankin.

"First, thank you for this. I believe I understand something of what it means. I would like to walk out there a way, the two of us. Do you mind?"

"Very well," he said, and followed me over to the gangway and down onto the sand.

We walked in silence until *Rynosseros* was a far-off thing, backlit with a flush of indigo and the most lustrous purple, like an offering to old gods, a cresset of embers set out beneath a sky that was brilliant with early stars and sparked with meteorites now and then. It reminded me that it was "out" as well as "up", and that Chiras Namarkon ruled some part of it as Lightning God, as the Immortal.

"The patch?" I asked finally, Meg having removed any need for delicacy in the matter.

"I have never been told," he said, surprising me, just a voice again in the growing dark. "But I see a present reason to pursue such an obvious line of enquiry."

"The masks then? Where did they come from? Are they tribal?"

"Again I cannot say. They've always been there, stored at Whitehead. More than are ever used."

His answers were hardly generous, but I had no choice. "The Alexandrian Book? What can you tell me?"

Bascoeur settled on the cooling sand and I did so as well, watching the dim point of the ship until I became nightsighted enough to see the shape in the blackness beside me.

"Alexandrian Book is simply an idea," he said. "Imagine. A great library is burned, its entire collection almost completely lost, as at Alexandria several times before it was finally destroyed. In the ruins, among the remaining scrolls, is planted a false text, allegedly a copy of a copy, purportedly the last remaining account of some act, the story of some ruler, or a discovery, an idea, a secret heritage predating all that is known of such a thing.

"It changes everything. It is enshrined as ancient wisdom, a purer older truth, something from the Golden Age—the way the writings, say, of Hermes Trismegistus underscored the whole European Renaissance. The ancient originals are lost, but thank goodness we have at least this one copy. It would only need an opportunist, not even the one responsible for the fire, though—all heaven forbid!—*that* could have been part of the plan as well. Maybe a fragment of such a text would be enough if there weren't the time to prepare a full one, but the weight attributed to such a fragment! A formal claim on history made retroactively would be enormous. It is frightening."

"And the oubliettes?"

"The concept of the oubliettes began a long time ago, in 1784, in a small university town in Western Europe. Four scholars, wealthy enough men, hypothesised the Alexandrian Book idea, the notion of a planted falsehood. They noted trends emerging in their world, and resolved to found a society for the custodianship of history.

They moved in a small way at first, putting truth before their own nationality and immediate cultural interests, as hard to do then as now. Within ten years they saw how discrepancies existed, how accounts of the same incident were skewed and embellished—more importantly, how those accounts differed from the one they themselves had painstakingly acquired from eye-witnesses and respected non-partisan thinkers.

"Building on the old axiom that the first casualty of war is truth, they allowed the far more important, post-Tribation corollary that truth is, indeed, the first casualty of self-interest and, inevitably, the first casualty of perception. Not a new idea these days, of course, or even then, but a new idea as a guiding, motivating ethic. They formed the oubliettes.

"Even if their accounts were never wholly accepted, if they preserved integrity, at least official accounts would need to be measured against them, would need to be aware of what the Antique Men had gleaned."

"Is this true?" I asked him.

"I will not tell you. You must remember, there will always be things I will keep from you. It may be Alexandrian Book. Disinformation. Mythopoesis. Either way it is a good example, you'll agree. Plausible, even elegant. Worth embellishing and passing on."

"It's frightening."

"It is what happens all the time, Tom." The voice in the darkness was generous and easy now, free of the mask, of the eternal prison it made. "The Storyteller in us is *always* involved, cannot resist embellishing the facts. For instance, I say man-made fire was first applied to technology some time in the Palaeolithic, somewhere in Central Africa, and you react to it as a fact not reality. You accept, but barely experience.

"The Storyteller in me does better. One windy day in the final centuries of the Pleistocene, a man known only to his fellows as Hamat found that lightning had struck the sacred acacia that stood in the hollow by the Maju fishing lake. He took up a burning branch broken from the trunk, wanting it for a talisman, meaning to take it to a nearby hill and there pray over it for good hunting. The tribal shaman came with hunters, discovered him, and cried sacrilege.

"Hamat was given a fitting punishment: he would pay with his life if he could not do what the lightning had done. It was scorn, mockery, you see; the shaman was shaming him. They gave him a day, left him on his hill with the extinguished length of stick. Hamat broke it in two, struck the halves together to make thunder and hopefully lightning—a very elementary totemic step—finally started rubbing the pieces as storm clouds rub the land.

"He burned himself accidentally while rubbing the heated stick over bare flesh in his fear and zeal. He discovered heat in sticks first, and deduced there must be fire hidden there too. He began rubbing the halves again and made smoke, another part of the mystery revealed, then ignited dry grass bunched about it, and finally the stick itself. He ran down to his fellow villagers at day's end holding a torch. The shaman was clubbed and stoned; Hamat became shaman. To earn prestige and coerce neighbouring tribes, his people gave out the story with ever more detail added. By classical times, Hamat was Prometheus bringing fire from the gods."

"Another Namarkon legend."

"Indeed," Bascoeur said. "You see how it resonates."

"What have you learned, Gado?" I used his name as he had mine, for whatever it signified in this safe darkness.

"If this Namarkon or tribal agencies have access to our data nets, I must use those nets carefully. As Angel, I am known for custodianship, but now I am with you on *Rynosseros*. I use my own mnemonic nets. Later I will verify what I find."

Now I wished the darkness were not there, that I could see his eyes. "We can go to Whitehead? With our stowaway?"

"I forgot myself. Truan's place in this, like yours and your crew's, is vital to the lesson of history we hold so important."

"Which is?" I imagine that he smiled in the night, wanted to think that he did, that he could.

"Nothing you haven't thought of, Captain. History is people doing things, that's all. Large and small. The man who betrayed Edinburgh Castle to the English. The Greek traitor who betrayed Leonidas and his Spartans at Thermopylae in 480 BC and showed

Xerxes the secret route over the mountains. One man! A king dies sooner than later, all his loyal Spartiates, removed from their capacity to affect history. Or the Norwegian naval officer, Quisling..."

Bascoeur's voice broke off, then after a moment returned again. "The oubliettes do not stand outside history, contrary to how it seems. We have to be part of it. There is no such thing as non-interference. Non-interference *is* interference. We exist, we participate, even when we withhold. This is why I take your suspicions seriously. Our philosophy of belonging, our awareness of Alexandrian Book and its possible existence *in our very midst*, makes Namarkon frighteningly real, his possible use of the Antique Men an unbearable lie. That he is called the Immortal becomes very sinister."

"If we are wrong?"

"I may be replaced. There are three more Angels who may decide that I went too far, that I acted irresponsibly."

"Den is gravely wounded. Could those Angels harm the rest of us?"

"No, Captain. Provided we are free of Namarkon, it is as I said. We accept things that happen. To counter any harmful truth you tell about us, we may need to plant a lie later—today, in a generation or two, whenever it will work best. Provided we know what was true here at the centre, that someone does."

"Alexandrian Book?"

"Exactly. The first lesson the victor learns. Truth is a tool."

"It is also what really is," I said. "Lost or forgotten. In spite of everything and anyone."

"Which is what caused oubliettes to form in the first place. You see why the existence of Namarkon among us constitutes a lie, a hideous contradiction. Yes, you might say that this too is what simply is, the world being itself. But our commitment to our mission pre-empts that. Your questions, Meg's, even Truan's, may uncover what *is*. So we go to Whitehead."

"And Mekkis?"

"When we learn where it is, yes, I may share that with you as well. You can see why mentioning nanotech crystalline AI may have been premature if not altogether inopportune. If Namarkon is among the Antique Men, he has been alerted now."

"It was obvious," I said. "He would assume that I suspect. And I get the impression Namarkon doesn't care. He believes he is safe."

"Or wants this time of risk."

"As a test?"

"As a test."

We were silent then, watching the night, watching the distant glimmer of *Rynosseros*, the sudden bright signatures of meteorites arcing across the sky and vanishing in soundless strikes.

There were other questions, but it seemed wrong to ask them now. A tektite made its solitary mark, fleeting, curving down to resolution, reminding me.

"There's too much data and not enough, Gado. Do you know how many entries I found for lightning? The National libraries are full of information. I read for hours. Apart from scientific and meteorological references, just so many. Old National place names like Lightning Ridge. Hittite weather-gods like Tesheb and Dattas, wielding axes that make a symbolic lightning flash. Egyptian Min with his thunderbolt totem; the Chinese Lightning Mother with her flashing mirrors. It goes on. Lightning as symbol, in the dreams of the famous, in psychiatry and dreamlocking, as a motif in art. There's Ezekial's vision by the river of Chebar, of four cherubim and four wheels in the sky—"

"'Their appearance,'" Bascoeur said, "'was like burning coals of fire, and like the appearance of lamps . . . and the fire was bright, and out of the fire went forth lightning.'"

"Namarkon has to be aware of such things," I said. "Anything at all. Like the Tarot with that tower struck by the lightning of Spiritual Truth. It signifies change and the breaking down of old forms to create the new."

"The Lightning-Struck Tower," Bascoeur said. "The House of God."

"I'm sorry. I should remember. But could this suggest something, that Chano is his home? Would he strike at himself there to conceal his true whereabouts, blast his own house? To fulfil a Tarot image?"

"'Yea, he sent out his arrows, and scattered them; and he shot out lightnings, and discomfited them.' I think not, Tom. The house plan is known. The Nation officers investigating were thorough.

No, it was an example. 'And he said unto them, I beheld Satan as lightning fall from heaven.'"

"It goes on and on, doesn't it?"

"You have yet to speak of the Taoist Book of Changes. The *I Ching*."

"Tell me!" I said, responding as I had whenever old Toth or one of the other librarians had found something promising for me.

"Ideogram 55. 'Feng' or 'Abundance'. 'The Sun below; the Thunder above'. The Oracle says:

> 'Thunder and lightning:
> the height of the storm
> The superior man judges lawsuits
> and declares them fairly.'

I thought you may have found it."

I sighed with amazement and exasperation. How much more was there, how many other strands and elements weaving in?

"It doesn't end," I said, thinking of Namarkon controlling the register of history, ruling on needs and demands, the superior man, the Immortal, wielding his insidious Alexandrian Book like some emblematic flail, a terrible, ultimate lightning.

"Wait till you see the Feng ideogram. You will understand why I am committed, why I agreed to appear, even in darkness like this, without my mask for you. You really will wonder who has made history."

There was no resting then, of course. I stood. "Please, Gado!" Using his name was easy in darkness, impossible when the coloured panes and—I imagined—the dark eyes were before me, though the eyes *were* there now, masked or unmasked, always there. 'I'll have to trust that you will share what helps us all; anything that might help. Can we go?"

"Of course," the voice came, and I realized he was already standing, though I had not heard him rise.

We returned to the ship and, though nothing more was said, I held back until he was aboard and had vanished below, not wanting to steal looks from those naked eyes that he did not wish to give. But when he appeared a few minutes later, he was still unmasked. His eyes were like beads of obsidian as he joined me on the poop and handed me a scrap of paper. On it was drawn Ideogram 55 of the *I Ching*.

“This one of the sixty-four ideograms tells us something, I think.”

55

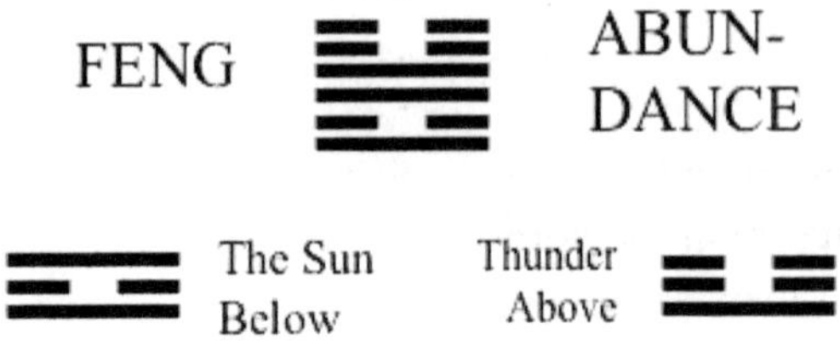

FENG ☳☲ ABUN-DANCE

The Sun Below — Thunder Above

I stared at it in wonder, seeing there the regional arrangement of the National arcologies that had become so familiar to me, now revealed in its full meaning.

“You see the clear message, the careful and ancient pattern of it,”
550 Bascoeur said. “Not the random regional groupings we are meant to think. The first trigram is ‘The Thunder above’. This,”—he pointed to the other—“‘The Sun below’, would tell us something about why Namarkon is named for an ancient Dreamtime god of the Gunwinggu. In literal terms, giving Thunder pre-eminence, he clearly champions the tribes over your Sun of Nation, which is interesting. Not one oubliette is Ab’O, Tom, not one. We are all Nationals or approved Internationals. That is why I can believe Namarkon is among us. There are messages everywhere. This clever enemy seems to tell us at every opportunity that he exists, no doubt out of delight at being immortal, at simply existing and knowing he is unassailable in his maze of history and fact.”

I missed the significance of what Bascoeur had said at first. I was still too overwhelmed by the thought of the National arcologies conforming to the Feng ideogram, being located according to a secret deployment plan, one unknown to the National architects and surveyors. It was incredible. But then I reacted to his final words, struck suddenly by what he had acknowledged.

“You agree then? Not a physical labyrinth? A notional one?”

"Why not? I cannot deny it. Though we duplicate material and have different personal priorities as individuals, we oubliettes *are* a library, as you say."

"Your mask is packed away now? Insulated?"

He nodded. "Partly why I agreed to remove it. I grant as possible all that you suspect. 'And the likeness of the firmament upon the heads of the living creatures was as the colour of the terrible crystal, stretched forth over their heads above.' Also from Ezekial. Captain, I need your viewpoint, what is still a comparative detachment. If Namarkon hides among the thirty-six, there may be far far more of a labyrinth for me than for you. Now we should rest. You will not see me unmasked again. Not before Whitehead and certainly not after."

"Thank you is all I have, Lord Gado." The honorific seemed appropriate now.

"It is more than enough," he said, and passed me another slip of paper. "Here is tomorrow's course. I will not appear on deck until afternoon. But speak to Truan McBanus. As hetaera and a daughter trusted with secret information, I believe she would have been a diligent shadow in her father's library. Good night."

"Good night," I said, and watched him go below.

At first I thought I would need to wait till morning to speak to Truan, for the ship was quiet, with no-one visible when Bascoeur left me on the quarterdeck.

That silence had been a false thing when we first returned from our walk, how it is when young children pretend to parents that they are asleep. Certainly Scarbo would have been awake and listening for familiar footsteps on the deck, for the low steady rhythm of voices. For a fact Meg would have been peering out the ports, watching and listening too, wanting to be at the rail when we returned but not daring so much.

Shannon was more pragmatic; he'd been at the helm most of the day and had Scarbo to worry for him. No doubt he slept easily in his cabin.

It was Truan who approached from the bow, a night-time re-enactment of her appearance earlier in the day.

"There's coffee below," she said. "Or tisn, if you prefer. Meg said I should wait."

I had to smile. "Nothing surprises me anymore, Truan. Tisn would help right now."

She went below and soon returned carrying a tray with two steaming mugs and a plate of cold meat, biscuits and cheese. We shared this as we sat in deck-chairs out of the cool wind, watching the night. For a time there was only the sound of cables thrumming and sand hissing against the hull.

"I don't know what to tell you, Captain," she said at last, unprompted it seemed, though Bascoeur may have had Meg urge it. "Toban was a bookman. He had no enemies, few secrets."

"Bascoeur felt you might have been told things, that's all. The names of other book conservationists, things like that. I'm trusting you would have given us anything that might help."

She shook her head, but it was for her earlier comment. "Toban was a generous soul, Tom. He knew of your search already, but hesitated at first. Then he decided he would be available to you after all."

"Among the Coloured Captains, in my crew, we make that family. Like your Club Hetaera."

She held her cup close to her lips, turning her face to the side, hiding the play of emotion in her eyes. "He told me no other names."

"I'm sorry, Truan."

"It was quick. It took them both. There was that."

We were silent then, shielded by the lift of the stern assembly, sitting in the dim glow of the deck lights and looking down the length of *Rynosseros* towards the bow. We listened to the wind ghosting about the rails and transoms, the hiss of sand, one moment barely there, the next sudden and strong.

Then something she had said came back to me. "He hesitated at first. Do you know why he changed his mind?" I kept looking ahead but knew her gaze was on me.

"He was in the library. I was doing some research with him—one of the tribal academies wanted something. Marquand phoned to say he had referred you. Toban said he wouldn't open the door."

“He commented afterwards?”

“Yes. Much as he was concerned about your predicament, he couldn’t afford to antagonise the tribes or someone like Chiras Namarkon.”

“He used that name?”

“Yes. There were his friends at the universities to consider. Helping you might compromise them, lead to the cancellation of privileges, visiting and access rights—”

“And access to illegal tech. Gain-monitors.”

She almost smiled, but the other emotions were too pressing, too immediate. “He’s a scholar, Tom. He was . . . he needed—”

“And then?” I spoke quickly to distract her.

“Another call. I was out in my studio and didn’t hear any of it. When I asked, he said Marquand had called again. He would see you after all.”

“But nothing else about Namarkon?”

“Nothing. I’d never heard the name before.”

“No other calls?”

“Only yours. I went out into the garden.”

She turned her face away again, looking off into the night.

“Truan—?”

“I can continue. I *want* to talk about this. I need to.”

“Did he seem worried?”

“No. But he wanted to discuss something with my mother—in the library. Why?”

“I’m betting Marquand made no second call.”

She faced me. “Then who did? Bascoeur? Namarkon? You don’t think—?”

“All I know is that the second call changed his mind, persuaded him to see us, and that less than an hour later there was the strike. Truan, another few minutes and Ben and I would have been in the library too. Namarkon could have had us all. No more threat.”

She stood and moved into the thrust of the wind, her hair blowing wild. “He wanted to warn you off!”

I stood too. “Or the strike was pre-arranged, booked into a busy tribal schedule. Your father may have discovered something.”

It was finally too much.

"Can we leave this now?"

I hesitated, then told myself that this was why she had come, stowed away, committed herself. Any answers were as much for her as for me. "I'm also talking to someone who wants to be involved. Who has plans, objectives."

"Say it! Who might well be an agent of this Namarkon. You must have thought it!"

I hadn't and it startled me. "Thanks for waiting up," I said at last, simple truth. "After being with Bascoeur, I needed . . . something."

Her gaze held mine. "I'm on the edge of this. I need to act and can't. Possibly I'm just drawn to what is at the centre."

"All any of us can do, Truan."

Without another word, she turned and went below.

I checked that the deck alarms were activated in case intruders came—unlikely under normal circumstances but a definite possibility now: a quick guerilla action to achieve here what the Namuren fighters on the Gentian Walk had not. Then I watched the tektite swarms, felt the wind grab at the hull, and thought of what the day had been and how things stood.

There was so much. Too much. The tribes waiting, the comsats in orbit, synced and tethered, watching. If Namarkon owned one, had access to them all, what chance was there?

Perhaps he waited for a facility to clear its roster, needed permission for another strike from jealous tribes only grudgingly persuaded to serve his needs. Perhaps he didn't need to use that final tactic again if only to protect his man, Bascoeur? He would find other ways.

But what, what, could induce this entity to reveal himself? Dewi had been a scientist turned trader, smuggler, religious fanatic, a mad creature drawn by a need to survive, to transcend and extend himself. He had worked through agents; at least had used a system which could be infiltrated by the likes of specialists like Pederson. Here there were clues, tantalising leads, and how easy it was to direct attention to those when so little else was on hand. It led to Whitehead, but would Namarkon hide in such plain sight, lay himself bare to the tribes? Unless, as Bascoeur said, as a test. Chiras Namarkon could be anywhere, not even in Australia for that matter.

And what if the tribes *were* watching, meeting his demands, accommodating his requests?

It seemed ever more hopeless, there under the stars in the blowing dark.

From Whitehead—where? To Mekkis? And then? To the other arcologies? Back to Twilight Beach?

As often happens at such moments during watch, I found myself considering the plaque on the helm.

Such special words there, echoing Meg's, casting me as the questing Alexander.

And Alexandrian Book! Bascoeur's Knot, that Gordian Knot!

That story. A true event, who could say? Alexander at Gordium confronted with the chariot of the great Phrygian king, faced with the knot binding the yoke to the shaft. The young Macedonian knowing the legend that whoever unravelled it would rule all Asia, knowing the legend and needing to make it, even that, part of *his* destiny. Then cutting the great Knot asunder, or pulling the pin free, whatever really happened that day, winning, transcending by doing!

But not even that bold action automatically meant winning, not then, not here, not now.

I found myself secretly longing for Truan to return, someone to take me away from these thoughts, kept listening for a door closing, footsteps on the companionway, imagined those sounds again and again.

I smiled, catching myself, then sat, just being in the night, until the constellations had turned halfway round the sky and footsteps did come, and the voice saying my name was Shannon's, there on deck to take the next watch.

9

Scarbo took us on our way at 0600, using photonic parafoils until the morning winds came up fresh and strong. Then he put twenty kites above those bright inflatables, the perfect morning for testing the more abstruse patterns in his old kitesman's bible.

When I arrived on deck at 0815, the sky had our colours spread across it: shapes like tethered dragons, crowns, talismans, origami castles, bursts of folded light. There were Sodes and Demis, Chinese Hawks, Holkoyd Stars, even our Samian Ladder spread out link by splendid link, vibrant, beautifully controlled, and there, in front, our signature Rhino head, blue on ochre. *Rynosseros* sang from its heart, as Scarbo called it, so finely balanced in its finery that it sat on 110 k's with no yawing at all.

"A madman in another life punishing this one!" Shannon cried, smile flashing in his dark beard. "He woke up dangerous, Tom. Can't help himself! Wouldn't hear of breakfast, wanted to see what the two of us could do."

I laughed, feeling my spirits lift, cherishing it all. "If there's turbulence, you'll take us to hell gift-wrapped!"

Scarbo nudged Rob. "Told you! Worries likes a bridegroom!"

We grinned madly at the sky, sharing this sight we never tired of, *Rynosseros* fully dressed for the hot dry winds of the inland.

Truan appeared on deck then, and Meg Solles a short time later.

The notary climbed to the quarterdeck. "Lord Gado is doing assimilations," she said, and I caught her glance at the words on the helm plaque. It was a chance.

"You're his friend too, Meg. We have to unravel this Knot, share what we can."

"I listen to what he says about you and how he says it," she said. "So far I'm not serving two masters."

It was easy sailing then, upwards of 90 k's on a surprisingly good Road for one shown only as a broken line on the old tribal maps. There was nothing but the hot sun, the glare, the wind in our kites and cables, the empty distances. From time to time a belltree marked its lonely stretch of Road, sounding its joyous waysong as we plunged by, or a stand of land-coral offered its barbs and hooks like a time-locked dancer, weathered fans aloft. Now and then a line of distant hills rose up like a sea-creature sounding, lingering, sinking away again. There were hours when a single cloud would wander into view, cross the wide blue sky like a vagrant dream and finally disappear.

By early afternoon, there were more ranges ahead, low folds of purples, reds and browns against the sky. The Road ran parallel for a time, then turned towards them, suggesting that a pass would lead us to the plain beyond.

"An hour beyond those," Meg said, pointing to where Road and hills met in a ribbon of sun-shadow. "Whitehead is—"

But Shannon shouted from com. "Bogie astern! Extreme range and closing!"

Helm scan confirmed it; we had a pursuer.

"After us?" Meg asked, close by the controls.

I had to remember that she spoke for Bascoeur. "Hard to say. At that speed, possibly. Or a courier. There's no attempt to hide, no insulated hull. Nothing to say it's other than a tribal ship on an urgent mission about to overtake. We'll know soon enough."

"Surely not out here, Captain! Not near Whitehead!"

"Meg, we can't arm till we're sure. If it's tracked by comsat, we're scanned and accountable. Loft 'em, Ben! See if she gains!"

For the next half-hour we ran toward the old red hills, until the distance between the ships dwindled and an image finally showed on scan through our churning rooster-tail.

"Bogie confirmed!" Shannon cried. At the same instant, scan managed a lucky fix, no more than three seconds through our tail-cloud, but it gave configuration.

It was a warship closing on us, an armoured charvi, probably a 130-footer, plates adorned with suns and stars, bold chevrons and faded totemic war-signs, a veteran ship from appearances, running under thirty or more battle-kites and wearing what veteran kitesmen called a "crown of thorns." A clutch of death-lamps on long-tether flashed hard light at the top of their drab functional canopy, rotating pulses from one to the next—a psychological trick—juggling death like hot stones from fist to eager fist.

A terrifying sight, one that no amount of experience could divest of its chilling elemental force: a ship racing to engage, angry and committed.

The calm you feel at such times is part of an only response, the result of training and discipline, counters to desperation. But it also has something of the no-choice bravado of a fairground ride about it. You do because there's nothing else.

If you are careful, composed, patient in the frantic rush of events, you remember that size can mean nothing, that firepower need not count. When there is speed and dust and stones the size of skulls close by, the off-chance of gullies like gaping mouths, when there is judgement and luck, inspiration created when fear of death elevates daring into a gift from the Fates, you act as if you cannot fail.

In such panic wrapped in calm, I looked instinctively for Strengi and Rim and young Hammon on the deck, remembered how it was and shouted new names.

"Truan! Deck lenses there and there! Meg! Help bring down the Sodes! Down or dump, Ben! No time!"

We donned ship-com headsets then, proscribed tech for Nationals usually, even Coloured ones, but on loan from Otamas and the Chitalice, and did quick confirmations. Shannon was already at the cable-boss, helping Ben dump the display kites for obstruction, hoping to foul our pursuer's canopy or wheels. Both men were ahead of my words every time, living parts of the ship.

Bascoeur was on deck too, climbing to the helm, mask flashing under his hood.

"There!" I pointed to the dark heart of the cloud behind us.

"Namuren," Bascoeur said, using his mask to read the brightest of the signs. "Your friend Ephan's family. A vendetta ship."

I accepted it, not daring to look away from the Road and the controls. "Namarkon pulls the strings here, Gado. Tribal puppets dance. They have no choice."

"Run for Whitehead! There are defences."

"Laser?" I was prepared for anything the Antique Men had, especially if they were owned in whole or part by Namarkon. But this *was* Namarkon, I reminded myself, this Namuren ship, as surely as the mirror ships had been Dewi's. We were meant to die here, it seemed. Not at Chano, here!

"No hi-tech," Bascoeur said. "But lenses, harpoons, cable-shot. Hurry! The Road is safe."

"I need to be sure!"

"Safe," he said. "Use power. Whitehead will pay!"

I switched in the cells, heard the whine of the big Pabar engines in the platform.

And just as well. Flashes of hard light from the Namuren death-lamps were snatching our remaining kites from the sky. I felt the heat on my neck and shoulders, picking at *Rynosseros*'s stern.

Truan and Meg were doing their best with our own weapons, but they lacked training and experience. Now and then a kite did vanish from our pursuer's canopy, but those kites were largely for show on a powered ship, vendetta display, so it counted for little.

"Smokescreen?" I asked Ben at the cable-boss.

He shook his head. "Cross-wind. We'll lose it."

He was right. A last resort.

The hills were close. Bascoeur pointed ahead. "Five minutes! There's a road-chain."

It changed everything. "Should we slow?" I thought of the heavy stretch of links across the Road, the winches for lifting them to hull height.

"Recessed," Bascoeur said. "I've sent word. They'll raise it behind us."

"No!"

"What?" Bascoeur's masked face was unreadable.

"Gado, Namarkon is behind and Namarkon could well be ahead. We are rushing towards a road-chain at top speed. That ship doesn't have to catch us; it only has to drive us!"

"They're my people!"

"It would need just one agent with access to the chain equipment or the Whitehead overrides."

"What then? What do we do?"

"The terrain before the chain? Broken?"

Bascoeur hesitated, checking stats, schemae, memory. "Before the chain housing, no. But the Road turns before it so the final approach cannot be seen. Just before the pass."

"Ben, smokescreen in two minutes!" I said and pointed. "Single dump to that turn. Time it. They'll think we're hiding the chain, hope to use it ourselves. We slow and leave the Road."

In the dust and thunder, the fierce concentration, those minutes vanished like seconds. Then the dark billows were there, first broken dumps, then streaming out, rolling and dense, torn by crosswinds but still making a brief black night in our rooster-tail.

"Rocks—two minutes!" Shannon cried, back at com. And we began powering down, preparing to pull off the Road.

"They'll be slowing too," Scarbo said, which gave me the idea, inspiration or folly.

"Gado, Whitehead has full com capability?"

"Of course."

"Call your Angels! Tell someone you trust to send a broad signal: 'Angel interference. Chain down and locked. Catch and destroy. Namarkon.' Blanket the frequencies, maximum power, so nothing local gets through."

Bascoeur did not answer. He stood at the stern rail making the link.

The rocks were visible now, foothills and cast-offs, the broken detritus of the range, so close, full and ochre-red against the sky. I could see where the Road made its long sweep into them. Scan showed nothing, but a chain could be camouflaged, insulated.

"Smoke for the turn, Ben!" I said. "Hide us!"

"Nearly out!" Scarbo answered. "Wish us luck!"

Rynosseros was at 60 and slowing, kites down or lost, stored power carrying us.

"Done!" Bascoeur said, with us again. "Unless Namarkon intervenes further."

"I say he won't. Vendetta ship and agents can be pre-arranged. I doubt much else can. If a broadcast is overridden, then we know Namarkon is at Whitehead. Tell your fellow Angels that."

"We shall see, Captain," he said. And went silent again.

We made the turn, 30 k's and slowing noticeably as we pulled to the Road's edge, then off onto a verge of stones. The ship lurched and shook, the travel platform handling the torment as best it could.

We stopped with a final lurch. Shannon and I ran to the lenses; Scarbo fed out the last of our screen, then put four lamps aloft, tethered low, sparkling with stored power.

There was nothing else to do then but watch the pall of smoke, holding longer than expected, penned in the lee of the red hills.

We could hear our pursuer approaching, shaking the earth and the rocks and the sky, becoming all of it.

Then it was there, thundering past like a dragon, splendid in its markings, battle-kites and signatures out in front like a brace of hounds. I thought to glimpse her captain on the quarterdeck, trusting Namarkon, whatever hold cold Chiras had on that luckless family.

The chain was up. Even as we flashed what few shots we could at the fleeing vessel, we heard the long cruel tearing, a roar like the world ending amid these dusty hills, a thunder that went on and on as ship and lives rolled into sudden, shattering oblivion.

Truan, Meg and Bascoeur had probably seen nothing like it in their lives. They stood staring, the faces of both women drained of colour, Bascoeur's hidden behind his panes, but still, still.

Ben, Rob and I *had* seen such things and suffered it as probably only sand-ship sailors can. There can be nothing like a ship-death, not ever, certainly not one done so shamefully, ruthlessly, without choice or chance.

I turned to Bascoeur. "The ship and captain, who were they?" I knew he would have the data.

"Leave it for now, Captain."

"Tell me!"

"The ship was *Eagle*."

"The captain?"

"Ephan Sky Namuren," he said, while thunder, smoke and flame played around the bloody hills. It was as if Villa Chano had died yet again, a single scream drawn full and mighty to become the ruin of all the world.

10

There were no survivors. We left the shattered, smoking remains of *Eagle* and passed the damaged chain-station, moved on until we ran along an unhindered Road towards far ranges in the east.

There, out on the plain, Whitehead loomed in the late morning sun, at first like a part of the landscape, eccentrically wind-formed and weather-made, then nothing like it. The walls were too smooth, too even, the great mainwall a monstrous thing, a wedge of concrete and glass lifting from the desert fastness, shimmering in the heat like something ready to become alive, already testing its senses.

Closer still, it had much of the quality of an ancient monastery about it. As *Rynosseros* moved in under the wind shadow, we could see some of the inhabitants: small groups of trainees and attendants, young and old, softly spoken men and women to look at them, tending modest orchards and foundries, trimming the lawns and walks, sitting together in open-air refectories and watching our approach. There was the occasional flash of an oubliette mask on the highs ramps and balconies, a sudden glint of sunlight on figures crossing sunny causeways and sheltered terraces. Though we saw no children or adolescents, whatever else this place was, it was home to these people.

When we had disembarked and entered the rock-melt folds of the outer precincts, we saw that these citizens were mostly older people, grey-haired and peaceful-looking, clearly deferential whenever an Antique Man came near. Unlike the robed, masked oubliettes, these folk wore soft sandals and fatigues of natural weave. On their temples they had small neat scars.

"Salvation Moons," Bascoeur explained for Truan, Rob and Scarbo's benefit. "Ritual marks. Not as ominous as they look. Those who train and serve or work in the library here choose to take the ancient lobotomy mark as a sign of self-denial. A fitting inversion. They are the Good Friends. Speak with them as you wish."

We moved on from the walled gardens and irrigation allotments into the great learning halls. There we were shown rooms full of books: storage vaults for crystals, motes, blanks and beads, self-powered Illuminated texts, true-paper books and other retroforms in careful environments.

It was awesome, impressive in both size and the extent of the care and dedication shown. There were scriptoria where new texts were produced and old ones copied, incept areas for the international publishing operation using the famous blue flower imprint of the Antique Men.

Then, once Meg had led the others off to their assigned quarters, Bascoeur took me high into the blade to the Meeting Hall, a huge stone chamber with a long central table arranged across it and thirty-six carved chairs, empty now, like a table setting for the Last Supper. At the far end, a floor to ceiling window-wall—true-vision, not relayed image—gave out on an infinity of warm air and rich golden light.

"Tonight," Bascoeur said, addressing me in softened tones appropriate to such a place, "you will address the Assembly here and tell them what you believe is happening."

"But then Namarkon will know everything, if we allow—"

"It is no inquisition, Captain. You will say only what you wish, only what you judge fitting. See it as we do. If Namarkon is one of us—or all of us for that matter—then that too is a fact of the reality we live. As Angels, we may deal with it if we can demonstrate Alexandrian Book, a betrayal of our fundamental purpose."

"This has to be a formality then, Gado. Such a meeting is redundant if the masks are nanotech CPU's."

"The information they have has come to them only through the Angels," Bascoeur said. "Remember that. We have held back some facts until we are reasonably certain."

"You believe you have. Your masks could be telling it all."

"Be moderate. It is why we were chosen, and why there are four. Our masks are special. Add your intuitions and good judgement. Help us prove this."

"If I can. I will if I can."

Meg was in the passage outside waiting to take me down to the others. Bascoeur made a small gesture of farewell and walked in the opposite direction. As Meg and I moved along the hallway to the elevators, I looked back to see him vanish through a doorway at the far end.

"If I were to rush back there now, Meg, and follow him through that door, what would I find?"

Meg's hood was down, her short dark hair adding at least that colour to the paleness of her face. She glanced back along the hallway too.

"You would find a very tired man, probably unmasked, sitting before a window, I should think, knowing Lord Gado. The door will be unlocked, like most of the doors here. You could verify this easily; I would wait. But he will be preparing himself for tonight's Assembly. Before you join them later, there will be questions, an accounting for why details have been withheld, why he went unmasked onto the desert with you last night, broke that rule again."

"Again?"

"Yes. He went unmasked to and from Saldy's, remember, though at least there no-one knew. That was to help you as much as himself. Before the general accounting this evening, the other Angels will demand their own. They will be more sympathetic, true, but more rigorous because they are more directly accountable themselves."

We entered the elevator and dropped to the residential levels.

"Perhaps he does not know what the Knot means," I said, as the car completed its vertical journey and began the transverse leg out to the dormitories and dining areas.

"Is that surprising?" she said.

"Yes, it's surprising. Everything is surprising and suspect. I can allow for secret knowledge in the Order, but once you grant the concept of Alexandrian Book, then Gado's not knowing something like that seems very significant."

"Surely it would be like you questioning the windmill origins of the Nation sign," she said. "You don't think to do it because you think you already know the answer." And she smiled her tight grudging smile, though this time parts of it reached her eyes, changing them. She believed I genuinely cared for him, at least there was that.

It struck me then, watching her, that something about Meg Solles was different, as if recent events had worked their magic, extended her, changed her. It was as if she had discovered something vital about herself, had perhaps put Meg Solles and Gado Bascoeur into a new perspective.

"It still hurts? Loving him," I said.

The smile vanished from mouth and eyes both, but the Elf's usual quick anger did not return. She studied the indicator light, went to speak, hesitated, then seemed to decide something.

"It's like the Knot you are trying to unravel," she said, and the sudden force, passion, maturity, in her voice were as startling as anything I had experienced over the last few days. Never again would I take her for merely the notary with Bascoeur, the angry figure she disguised herself as. "Long ago I put it to him—why the androgyny, why ritual and custom dictated the need for a man-woman, the need to breed hermaphrodites to guide the oubliettes? What gain, what symbol?"

"Did he answer? Can you share this?"

"He touched his mask, the flower and the patch. 'The answer is here,' he said. 'In our beginnings.' I didn't press further."

The car slowed and stopped, opened onto a dining area, a softly lit space barely a quarter the size of the Gaza lobby, with a dozen tables occupied by as many of the Good Friends, eating, talking quietly. There were plantings placed about, low music playing. The walls were decorated with tapestries and carvings, information storage webs made here at Whitehead: the precious "datafacts."

"You knew he moved L75 VGS?" I asked.

"He did that the moment your Council requested a meeting with the Antique Men. Just after Dewi Dammo was defeated. He needed to investigate first—his job as Angel."

"Did he damage that Book?"

"Would you harm *Rynosseros*? He found it damaged at Crayasse, moved it on to Turker to gain more time. He was hunting Namarkon too, anticipating your line of enquiry. Finally, he judged it time to meet you. The other Angels, the Assembly, were wanting answers. Come. Here are your friends."

Rob, Ben and Truan had had time to shower and rest, to change out of their desert clothes into fresh fatigues. They came into the refectory from a different elevator, and joined Meg and me at the servery counters, though Meg did not eat with us. She excused herself and went to join a group of fellow notaries at an adjoining table.

It was just as well. During our meal we needed to discuss recent events: the parts played by Gado and Meg, the run to the road-chain ahead of *Eagle*, the remarkable fact that one of the old arcologies was more than a library, was operational at least in part and occupied by Nationals after all.

"We've seen very few inhabitants," Shannon said. "Just a handful really. Still no children."

Scarbo agreed. "There's probably no more than one or two

hundred. Makes you wonder what we'd find at the other arcologies."

"It may come to that," I told them, "though I believe we would find nothing. There's an Assembly tonight. Bascoeur has to account for his actions. Meg hasn't said as much, but he may be replaced."

"Punished?" Truan asked.

"Brought to order. Denied us. I'm to speak on his behalf, I think. Whatever happens, be patient and stay ready. See to the ship. Use the time. *Eagle* responded to a signal supposedly from Namarkon and that signal probably came from Whitehead. Someone here, one or more, all of them for all we know, is in league with Namarkon. We know that much. I'm hoping to take a journey."

"To Mekkis?" Truan said.

"If they'll take me. I believe they know where it is."

"Tom—"

"If I can," I told her. "I doubt they'll let you. And, forgive me, I owe that choice to Ben and Rob too."

"But if they die in this, *Rynosseros* loses far more than her captain.

If I die, I will have done all that I can do."

I studied her face, this ghost that had haunted my watch. "You're right. I'll ask them."

Her features relaxed into a weary smile of gratitude.

"We'll look about," Scarbo said. "You rest, Tom. Room J178."

Ben was right. After the day we'd had, I did need sleep. I excused myself and went to find the J section.

The room was small but comfortable, with a window overlooking a modest garden courtyard and walls painted in narrowing bands of soft sand colours. Without noticing they did so at first, the striations led the eye to the window and beyond, out into the flowers and bright air, brought those things in to me along that same axis: an easement loop.

I showered in the alcove, then settled on the futon-style bed and watched first the sky above the garden, then the datafact on the doorward wall where the soft easement lines began. Before I quite knew it, I was caught in the ten-cycle breathing pattern it induced and slipped gently into sleep.

—.—

A sequence of low chimes sounded at 2021; an accompanying strip of soft lighting showed that the garden was dark. Night had fallen over Whitehead.

A voice spoke from a mesh beside my bed. "Please prepare yourself, Captain. Meg Solles will arrive in twenty minutes. The Assembly has already begun."

That stole the rest of my torpor. I showered again, dressed in my sandsman fatigues and opened the door to Meg when she knocked fifteen, not twenty minutes later.

She led me up into the blade again, back to the Meeting Hall, then left me alone outside the big doors, saying I would be summoned at the proper time.

That didn't happen for an hour, but finally the doors did open and one of the Good Friends appeared, an old woman who smiled and told me to go in.

I entered and found myself facing the figures seated behind the long table. All were masked, all had their hands before them, lightly clasped or resting close to ritual weapons: tschinkes, archimenters, galvanis, espandos and petronels. Only these faux-antique storage-traps differed from one to the next; the figures who owned them wore identical robes, identical masks, the same flower at the chest below the shoulder, the same Knot pattern high on the sleeve.

Behind them the window-wall shone with full night, folded and refolded into roils and depths by the optical properties of the glass. More than ever, the scene resembled some fantastic recreation of the Last Supper, a coven of cathedral kings and queens celebrating a mass for Mother Night pressing close beyond them.

Which of the oubliettes was Gado, I couldn't tell. The masks offered no clue. Side on, their traps looked more similar than they actually were, the silver-chased stocks, the curlicues, scrolls and hatchings of the brightwork gave nothing.

"We are working on Namarkon for you," one neutral male-female voice said. The hands of the figure fourth from the left seemed to have moved; I took that to be the speaker.

"Thank you. We begin to set a fair price."

“That is provocative to say,” came what seemed like the same neutral voice, though this time a different figure moved his hands, actually moved fingers briefly and slowly over the espando in from of him—of her, there was no telling. But then the Angels were androgynes according to Meg. What of the rest?

“It is not meant to be anything more than a statement of how I see it, a reminder that there are two scales of payment at work here, two reckonings. I may be speaking to Namarkon, remember. You, those masks, those traps before you, that window for all I know.”

“Bascoeur brought you here,” a voice said, no identifying trace seen or imagined. Were the Angels the ones speaking?

“Yes, and I helped kill a ship and its crew to let Lord Gado do it. Whitehead would never be worth *Rynosseros*. I must wonder if this is worth *Eagle*.”

“Understood, Captain. What can you tell us?”

“You know my conversations with Bascoeur.”

“Except when he removed his mask for you.”

“I don’t necessarily believe that. I’m granting implant capability or—”

“No!” The word snapped and echoed like a slap, a whip-crack of denial filling the room.

“Very well,” I said, accepting it. “Except then. Are you, any of you, or is anything known of by you, Namarkon?”

The row of figures sat very still, thirty-six watching shapes. The hands did not move.

“No,” the single voice answered. “Nothing, no-one known to us.”

“I’ll assume that is true as well. I’ll assume, too, that there is knowledge I cannot have. Inner Circle. Rituals and secrets of the Antique Men. Your masks, your signs, so much. I’ll assume you know where Mekkis is, which, as “Power” in the Feng ideogram, you must allow, is a clear path. Today we fought on *Rynosseros* for our lives. In Twilight Beach, a tribesman, a much better swordsman than I, nearly killed me. I saw a cloud at the end of a kitana blade and it was everything. I find that man is now dead; my life dies about me in such pieces. He might have been a friend someday.

Certainly, personally, it seems *he* did not choose to be my enemy. But Namarkon moves for Namarkon, and individuals don't matter.

"Like you, I would like to stand back from history, or be involved in it only as far as I can, here in my hands, at the ends of my fingers. You know where Mekkis is. You know why it is being obliterated from knowledge and memory; you know why it stands in the Feng pattern. Or you suspect why you *don't* know. Please," I said, using Truan's words, "take me there so I can have done all that I can do."

"Very well," a voice said. "But you alone, Captain. On a closed ship, with you below deck in a somnium so its whereabouts remain unknown. We will help you to help us; help you do everything possible. How does that fit your reckoning?"

"I believe you wanted me to request it formally. I believe that now you probably owe me a great deal."

"This interesting viewpoint of yours. In a few words: we all seek Namarkon."

"Done!" I said. "If it can be done. But thank you for letting me come here tonight and allowing me to see you. I consider it a great honour."

"It was necessary. Thank *you*, Captain."

Behind me, the doors opened. Meg was waiting. I took a final glance at the figures seated at the long table, then turned and left the hall.

11

They woke me soon after midnight, two of the Good Friends did, both quiet gentle men who apologised and asked me politely to dress and meet them down on the mooring plat. No breakfast, not for a somnium ride, so I went hungry to the rendezvous.

Standing near *Rynosseros* on a battered six-wheeled travel platform and unkited at this hour was a small dark hull, what I took to be a Whitehead supply charvi, brought out and readied for a voyage of a different kind.

"So the oubliettes do own ships," I said, when Bascoeur and Meg joined me on the wide concrete apron.

"None for far-voyaging," Bascoeur said, masked and robed, holding his archimenter. "But a couple to take us to the shipping lanes so we can make connections for our travels. We own Mekkis though, Tom. It is deserted, it is ruined, but we can go there when we wish. Our only long voyage."

"We travel alone?"

"The three of us and these two, David and Gral. They are good sailors."

"What if Namarkon strikes at us? I'm below in a sleeve—"

"No," Bascoeur said. "Part of our trade-off with the tribes, this route. They touch *Tybo* and they lose our resources. More to the point, we give extra help to one faction over another. It is complex."

I wanted to ask him how it had gone with the Angels earlier, how it had been for him shut away with the other thirty-five oubliettes, but David came over then and respectfully suggested we set off.

The five of us boarded *Tybo*, and Gral brought costly stored power to the engines.

"You *are* privileged," I said as the old vessel made its way out of the lee of the mainwall. The first morning winds rocked the hull though no kites were aloft. In the eastern sky, a faint band of light marked the beginnings of day.

"It's time," David said gently, his Moons two glinting smiles above his own. "Please. The chamber is ready."

I glanced once more at Whitehead, an unliving mass of darkness against the pale line of yellow-grey squeezing over the edge of the world, then followed the Good Friend below to the somnium in the aft cabin. I used the toilet, undressed, then settled into the comfortable sleeve of the pod. David fitted the contacts and prepared to lower the lid.

"Will it be long?" I asked.

"This day and part of another," he said. "It's not far, but the terrain becomes difficult."

I nodded and watched through the clear plastic of the cowl as he brought it down. And knew nothing more than that.

Until it lifted, David still smiling there, smiling there again.

"What happened?" I asked, though I immediately knew because

of the leaden feeling in my arms and legs, the lethargy and terrible thirst, the sensitivity to the metabolic assists.

"We are close to our destination," David said. "Join us for breakfast when you can. It's quite a sight."

It was late morning when I reached the quarterdeck. Nothing could be seen but rocky terrain, a low range all around us, though now and then there were glimpses of far desert and of turns in the Road ahead as it started to take us down again.

Twelve kites on four cables made a modest canopy, giving *Tybo* that special dimension all charvis need to be complete. I felt better seeing the drab inflatables, the tattered and patched wind-thieves, the solitary Sode like the Star of Bethlehem flung out ahead on a thirty-metre tether.

Gral had the helm; Meg and David tended the cable-boss, jockeying the big blue star for wind-change. Bascoeur stood by a breakfast table set up on the commons. There was fruit and sweet buns, steaming barragon coffee, a waiting chair.

"Twenty minutes, Captain," Bascoeur said as I ate and drank, welcoming the vivid tastes and smells, the warmth of the sun, the wind on my skin. Being on *Tybo* meant everything right then, making our way through these ancient hills, through hot sun and dust, passing the lonely totemic shaft of a belltree every so often.

"There!" Gral cried, pointing.

Between the bluffs, I saw our destination out on the plain before us, ten, fifteen k's distant, with hills beyond, a shimmering phantom line at the edge of the world.

Again, there was a mainwall, though even at this distance I could see this one was damaged, scarred, as if struck from space at some time in its past. Still complete, still impressive and powerful-looking in the clear desert air, but showing a great wound and surrounded by indistinct shapes, a crust of forms.

Gral handed me binoculars. Through them the scar in the mainwall became a vivid gash, and the untidy crumble resolved into ruined outbuildings and pitted approach roads, a wilderness of broken field domes and fallen revetments.

"Who did this?" I asked Gral, Bascoeur, whoever would answer, feeling the rush of deep underlying rage all Nationals felt when reminded of what had once been and what now was.

"Mekkis was the example," Bascoeur said. "The Nationals would not obey at first."

"If this was Namarkon's original home, then I can understand his determination to become Lightning God and control such powers."

"You speak from emotion, wanting to see him as pro-National. More mythopoesis! He uses what suits his needs, surely. Think of Chano."

"Yes." I put aside the glasses and stood. "Let me help with the kites, Gral."

"Take the helm," Gral said. "Be the first State of Nation captain to sail into Mekkis in two hundred years."

I nodded my thanks and went to the controls. Slowly, with the great blue Sode out before it, the wind-thieves clustering and weaving like remoras about a shark, *Tybo* reached the desert plain and the broken arcology waiting there.

"That is the Blasted Gate," Bascoeur told me, pointing to what was just that, a dark maw in a wall that had suffered terrible heat and shock waves in its past. "Draw up in front."

I did so, easing *Tybo* in close to the mainwall while David and Gral brought home the kites, wrestling down the Sode first because of the unstable wind-flow around the great structure.

"A fitting home for an immortal spirit," I said. "Is there a labyrinth here, something to pass for one and waste more time?"

"'A labyrinth to amase the senses,'" Bascoeur said, not rising to the sarcasm. "Shakespeare. From the Old English 'amasian', to stupefy. Be patient, Tom."

But amid such ruin, feeling the old anger, it wasn't easy.

"Or is it to be books, more clues?"

"Please. At Whitehead you mentioned Inner Circle. Rituals and secrets. Of course there are. You formally requested this; that is what got you here, the only thing. Please wait."

The Good Friends remained on the ship while Gado, Meg and I entered the great main-building. As we reached the first of the empty ramps and interior boulevards, I heard engines behind me.

"They're leaving!"

"Taking the ship further out. Many fear this place."

Rightly so, I thought, if somewhere above us, around us, Namarkon made his home, nursed his lightnings, pulled comsats into alignment to kill ships and cities, burn libraries, an Immortal tailoring history with Alexandrian Book, making his own dead stack whenever inclined.

The arcology was labyrinth enough, it seemed now, and thoughts of a maze of oubliette masks seemed an over-subtle thing, too dramatically obvious to anyone given an hour's conversation with someone like Bascoeur.

Our footsteps echoed as we moved deeper into the great public space, here lit by a shaft of late morning sunlight where the mainwall was pierced, there a gulf of darkness where the relay plates had failed or skylights had been fused shut altogether. It was an eerie frightening domain, this monument to thwarted National hopes, home to lizards and scorpions, smelling of dust and too much time, too many lonely days.

Yes, a subtle fancy thinking Bascoeur and his people could be part of it, thirty-six making an infinity of corridors, hiding a spectre behind their crystal panes.

I glanced left as we walked, first beyond Bascoeur, then noticed again the patch, the Forget-Me-Knot, on his sleeve.

That Knot.

Something Inner Circle, something that mattered as all symbols did. At one extreme a simple enough if intricate motif, at the other a key to Namarkon, a Gordian Knot to be unravelled or cut asunder.

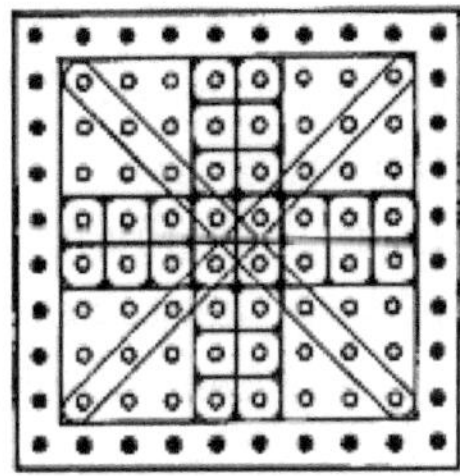

Not too subtle at all then. Not too obvious. Something only those given time with oubliettes would ever really suspect. And who spoke with oubliettes? Who ever came this close—walked with Angels, talked with them unmasked, saw their home, Whitehead, and Mekkis, their secret place?

"What are we going to see, Gado?"

"What you are looking at," he said, and it took me a moment to realise he meant the interlocking shape on his arm and not the vast interior.

"I don't understand."

"You understand something," Bascoeur said. "I think you may have seen the face of Namarkon and not known it."

"Gado, what—?"

"Meg, please take Tom to the Great Hall."

"Gado!"

"Go with Meg, Captain. Remember, it *is* Inner Circle for me. A conflict of loyalties. I am Angel first. Always that."

I watched while Bascoeur disappeared through a side arch, then followed Meg along a wide gallery towards two great doors at the far end.

"Meg?" I said.

"Captain, the answer may be here. Go in and up the side stairs you find there. There is a balcony."

I did as she said, entered a small anteroom with another closed set of double doors beyond, then took the steps to the level above, to a small doorway opening out onto a narrow walled ledge barely two metres wide.

From that modest balcony I looked out over a great enclosed space, one disappearing into shadow down its length and far overhead, where narrow windows, high and mostly sealed, did throw a few ghostmarks of light on one wall or another.

The great communal hall of Mekkis, dusty and ancient, an infinity of cool smooth stone.

And there, lit by the soft glow of recessed spots, a group of assembled figures were lined up close below where I stood, as if deliberately arranged for my benefit, which—I realised—was the simple truth of it.

They stood in ten evenly spaced rows, ten by ten, a hundred altogether, all wearing robes in greys, browns and ochres, some dark blues, all bearing their ritual firearms and masked with the glittering, faceted helms of the Antique Men.

A hundred!

If they moved at all, it was so slightly that it could not be detected, though now and then a crystal pane flashed as a head lifted or fell a fraction.

It was impressive, fascinating, even disturbing, yes, such a display.

And a hundred! I recounted them.

Was Mekkis home to so many Antique Men? Not just Bascoeur's thirty-five at Whitehead, but others, these? Could there be a living library after all, the one Chiras Namarkon would not leave? A congregation of living books?

Living library and *living* labyrinth, this hundred. Whoever, whatever Namarkon was might—must!—surely be found here.

Watching the figures in their silent rows gave it to me: the Forget-Me-Knot, the hundred-square on the shoulder of each, the configuration of lines, loops and connections. There in plain sight, the key to the maze if I could fathom it, what I had seen so clearly displayed at Whitehead, now at Mekkis, what had first been presented to me in the Blue Room at Saldy's.

I tried to recall the diagram. The black dots on the perimeter had not been linked into any of the groupings; they formed a disconnected border, an outer grouping of, what, thirty-six?

Thirty-six! The original number of Antique Men given by Bascoeur. "Like me?" he had said at Saldy's when I had asked how many oubliettes there were. He had evaded, not answered, my question, loyal to Inner Circle, to the secrets of the oubliettes. What was it Gado had said: "You must remember, there will always be things I will keep from you."

Perhaps the thirty-six were the field agents, the ones who went out into the world and gleaned data, who met at Whitehead and supervised that other library enterprise. Perhaps the remaining sixty-four stayed behind at Mekkis, doing what?

I smiled at the answer. Why, tending gardens, of course, and flocks and orchards, trimming walks, making pottery and tapestries laced with knowledge and mnemonic thread, the precious datafacts.

Mekkis *was* Whitehead, seen from its other side, approached from the west instead of the east, carefully ruined or disguised with holoforms, deceptions, the simplest application of Alexandrian Book.

The real Whitehead, not Mekkis, had been the example. Not thirty-five cities. Always thirty-four. But one with two names. Two roles to play.

No wonder the walks and hallways had been deserted. Those smiling quiet people with the lobotomy scars—Salvation Moons—on their temples were here now, robed and masked, bearing their ritual weapons, assuming their true roles, servants and carriers, components of Namarkon, whatever the mystery there. Somewhere Truan, Scarbo and Shannon were hidden away, in somnium sleep, drugged, on a tour of the outer reaches of Whitehead, confined to *Rynosseros*, somewhere.

"Like me?" Bascoeur had said, about to investigate a crime, a conspiracy within the very secret organisation he served. What courage there, what commitment to truth to be so resolved, honest custodian of his Order.

I felt a rush of fondness, of gratitude and, yes, remorse for the Angel now out on the floor of the vast hall, part of that, so vulnerable to the one who was ultimately his master if things were as they seemed.

Sixty-four! The number of ideograms in the *I Ching*.

No accident in symbols here, nothing accidental now, no coincidence. Gado had been alerting me, handing me clues all along, even unmasked.

Thunder above and Sun below. Sixty-four. Inner Circle.

And yes! The number of squares on the classic chessboard!

Was that it? One of the first mysteries and one of the last. Would the Forget-Me-Knot show the alignments needed to unlock the living maze, to bring Chiras Namarkon out of the matrix—AI or corporate persona, programmed comp identity, whatever?

More importantly, would I be allowed my chance, now, just as I was beginning to understand what existed here?

Meg walked across the stone floor below my balcony, moved out into the great echoing space until she stood between me and the massed shapes of the Antique Men, then turned and looked up.

"This is the Hundred Square," she said, her voice holding the same vital quality I had noticed in the elevator at Whitehead—rather, that other part of Mekkis! "The ultimate library of the Antique Men."

"I wish to speak with its Keeper, Chiras Namarkon." My own words echoed, quickly faded.

"If he is here, you must find him," Meg said.

"But—"

"You have assumed too much, Captain. We do not know if he is among these Lords and Ladies." She spoke less boldly now, her voice losing itself in the chamber.

"These oubliettes are hiding him—"

"No!" she said, forceful again. "They do not know where he is either. Or who he is. Or what. Or *if* he is, do you understand? They show you this because one Angel has trusted you might find a ghost who may have penetrated the Hundred Square and hidden himself there. This Angel, my own Lord, has convinced the three remaining Angels, and they have convinced the rest to let the Square be open to you like this. It is a supreme honour. But be warned, Captain! These are unique people, each one. Sooner than have you endanger this library, they will disperse and go out into the world, hide their masks of service, conceal their Salvation Moons, and not form again until tribal searches have ceased, until you have gone from the world or lost all memory of this, until Mekkis is known to be safe again. They will meet and re-form in other places, train their replacements. Their mission of storing truth will continue."

"What does the Angel Bascoeur want me to do?"

Meg seemed to hesitate. Then she spoke again, her voice as confident as before. "The Square will remain like this for an hour. You have that time. Then the labyrinth will discorporate and not re-form here or anywhere until we have completed our own enquiries and you are either killed or neutralised, unable to harm us."

"Unable to harm Namarkon!" I cried. "This is a perfect strategy."

"These people are *not* Namarkon!" Meg said. "Try to understand. They could only form the place where Namarkon is. Would you kill the tree to eliminate the serpent nesting there?"

"I might to eliminate tainted fruit. That would come from the tree."

"What if the fruit does not think it is tainted?" she said, presenting the dilemma another way.

Rather than answer, I studied the ranks. Perhaps the Antique Men did see their centuries-long achievement put at risk because of the notion that someone, something, had sought to use and direct part of that achievement. I had to allow it. Perhaps they had agreed to this special assembly only because one of their trusted officers in the protecting outer perimeter had—possibly for the first time in their long history—persuaded them to consider that an entity such as Namarkon might truly exist in their midst, a presence guilty of altering the very truths they were dedicated to maintaining, that gave their lives purpose.

More and more I appreciated the risk, the sheer gamble, Bascoeur had taken, granting that things were as Meg described.

"I'll need comp access," I said.

"One will be brought up to you," Meg answered. "Linked to the arcology mainframe."

"No. Down there in the hall. So I can walk among the oubliettes, be with the parts of the maze."

"No."

"Meg, you have to help me! Tell them I'm feeling my way. If Namarkon is hiding among them, as one or a group of them, I'll need to search freely, use intuitions. Give me comp down there and you to talk to. Or Bascoeur, if—"

"No! He's part of the Square."

"And isn't as well. Not really. He's outer perimeter."

"You can't consult him on this. It's a matter of loyalty and duties. You can have comp down here. And me."

"Good. And the hour starts when that's done."

"The hour has already started. You have fifty-one minutes."

I lost another ten waiting for comp, but used that time to study the ranks at floor level.

Finally Meg brought in the unit, set it up on its stand and raised function. I moved in before the screen, still watching the rows of masked shapes. Meg waited quietly to the side, close enough that I didn't need to raise my voice.

"I'm assuming that the masks of the inner sixty-four are it," I said, as much to me as to Meg or the figures on the floor. "Not decorative, but as I told Gado: crystalline lattice storage. The people may be genuine oubliettes by their training, but I'm guessing that right now they are linked into the matrix, mobile carriers for CPU's forming the group mind."

And I wondered what was flowing between those masks now, down the corridors and alignments, the intricate mazeways that served and accessed Namarkon, hid and protected him and made his very existence possible, unable to be destroyed without harming the whole. More than ever I was sure that he—it—was there, deep in the secret place where he built his version of history, changing a detail here, a small fact there, adding a nuance, a motive, shifting a blame, a decision from one figure to another, embroidering, remaking the past and so the future.

Bureaucracies and administrations had always done it, cunning individuals, secretly, sometimes boldly, winnowing alternatives by bestowing sanction and disfavour, by promotion and heresy trials, by calling for dead stack, one account, then amplifying out the chosen lie.

I could prove nothing, of course, here, now, faced with the vast irony of needing to prove it to the vehicle which housed the problem. Each of the inner sixty-four, operating alone, travelling away from Mekkis, could carry the contamination into the tribal capitals, had possibly done so countless times already, even across the world, beyond this one focus in Australia. They had been to the arcologies, of course they had, as well-meaning innocents or sly knowing conspirators, moving books out and away from the National libraries, making dead stack, part of the slow careful plan, mythopoesis and disinformation, the Book at its terrible work.

Unless, of course, Namarkon *was* limited by his own structure, the one before me, the rules by which he had come into existence.

The truth of it struck me. Could it be?

It made such sense now.

Namarkon was using me to liberate him from his labyrinth!

The thought was chilling.

He needed to be exposed by the proper system, the right protocol, unlocked then freed into some new phase. I could well be the key that would do this!

I had to know, take that risk, prove it one way or another.

The figures waited quietly, masks catching what meagre light there was, casting it away, snatching it back again with the slightest movement.

"Access Index Alpha. Graphic only," I said, cancelling voice response, and a simple broad-entry, voice-variant menu appeared.

It was time to explore the obvious clues.

"Precis the game Chess," I said, and the apportionings began—by chronology, by player, country of origin, game variants, derivations: historical, regional, conceptual. One after the other, entries and keywords scrolled past, first for the classic forms, then the variations, culminating finally in fire-chess and the developments in that across two hundred years and more.

The next step was just as obvious, given the patch, the evocative sign of the Knot.

"Paradigms for the Hundred Square. The sign of the Antique Men. The Forget-Me-Knot."

NO ENTRY, it flashed immediately. Too easy.

I didn't hesitate. "List all game variants using a hundred squares."

While the system searched, I walked out to the grid of unmoving forms again, moved down one avenue of figures, turned into another. I passed the closed faces, the dim blue flowers, the shoulder patches, each giving the lock, the key and the mystery, noted the downturned wands: the archimenters, tschinkes and espandos they carried, ritual firearms filled with the burning fire of knowledge. Six years of dream in each one; six hundred years collectively, vivid death and all the learning of the world.

I left the silent ranks then, returned to Meg and the waiting display. Eight names were given, and there, third on the list, was the one I wanted.

"Precis: Capablanca Chess."

And the information appeared:

> José Raoul Capablanca (1888-1942)
>
> Cuban Grand Master—devised a variation for one hundred squares, adding two pawns to each side and two extra court pieces, variously called Angels or Marshals. These combined the moves of Queen and Knight . . .

Again I felt a chill, but the thrill of certainty too. This was it! And a rush of pity: Bascoeur!

The androgyny. The four added pieces: Angels or Marshals.

A marriage of Queen, guiding force, ruthless warrior, policy-maker, Great Mother, to the Knight, wandering adventurer, going forth, questing, bent on errantry, but guarding. Guarding too. And, unique in chess, able to move *through* other pieces.

This *was* it: the Hundred Square. The thirty-six extra places on the Capablanca board—the four Angels and the thirty-two extra squares!

"Match the Forget-Me-Knot, the Hundred Square, to any game variation or alignment of pieces in Capablanca Chess. Full pattern or portion."

NONE LISTED, came the almost immediate graphic response.

"Not it," Meg said, and I was suddenly aware of her right there, of her own fascination.

"Too simple anyway. But we're close."

She gestured at the screen. "But it's not a chess pattern! Pieces don't line up that way."

"Not unless it's a circuit or incept diagram for Namarkon, if he's a program or AI matrix flaunted under our noses. For all we know, the components of the Square leading to Namarkon are in a cell arrangement, four lots of sixteen, interfacing only at the linked pairs shown on the patch, those linked in to other combinations building to a gestalt. The Knot has a hierarchy, Meg."

"But it may be nothing to do with Namarkon," she said. "It may simply be the hierarchy of the order itself. Inner Circle. That's separate from Namarkon, surely."

I had to agree, and it reminded me to be careful, to watch what slights I might deliver in my eagerness, what insolence, only to make the assembly disband the sooner, taking their fragments of Namarkon with them.

"You're right," I said. "The Capablanca game is part of it though. We have the pattern for explaining Bascoeur and the Angels and the perimeter at least: the sixty-four and the thirty-six. And there's the Whitehead clue."

"Whitehead?"

"Capablanca in Spanish," I told her.

"What next?"

"There has to be something else, another game or something to complete the key. One for understanding the lock: the Capablanca game, and some other given as a cryptic or cipher. Connected to it somehow."

Though I couldn't be sure of that, not at all.

Again I walked out on the echoing floor, looking first beyond the assembled figures at the looming architectural mass, softened with distance and shadow, then back at the quiet ranks. Again I wondered whether Namarkon hovered somewhere across the pattern, slipping from one to the next as Dewi had with his carriers. But now I had no way to verify truths, no basis for persuasion but what the oubliettes themselves granted on Bascoeur's urging.

Why the Hundred Square? Why that shape for the lock, the patch, the Knot, unless it linked conceptually to its key? Discounting mere exuberance, random choice, one had to key the other, had to matter and be the way in, the Capablanca variation leading to—something.

Aware of the risk, of precious seconds slipping away, I took my chance.

"Meg, tell the thirty-six to leave the pattern."

"They're part of the Square! They were only used in the Whitehead deception as—"

"But not Inner Circle. Look at the patch! They're supernumerary, not linked into the operating pattern. *They* may be forming a lock, keeping the Namarkon manifestation from us." Keeping it locked in, I did not say. "Tell them to adjourn! For heaven's sake, move!"

Meg relayed the request to Bascoeur through whatever comlink she had. The outer line of masked figures took a signal, marched off the floor and out of the hall, Bascoeur as well, leaving only the classic chessboard arrangement.

Without the thirty-six, the Square was startlingly different. Smaller, of course, but somehow more powerful, more sinister. I imagined something, a presence in the hall, all in my mind possibly, but a sense of something stripped bare, newly exposed but glad of it, waiting.

More than just numbers, a whole element had been removed. Now I had the classic configuration of the ancient Indian game, or, put another way, a classic answer previously hidden within an eccentric form.

It seemed right, yes. There *was* something here. Things I had been told, heard, almost thought of, things, ideas, associations, and now—since so much had been relevant—anything Bascoeur had said since our first meeting.

The Hundred Square. Why this form for the Knot, why this lead to unravelling it?

And the Gordian Knot? That fitting allusion?

Again I thought of Alexander cutting it asunder, becoming king of the world. Could Namarkon's goal be that? Nothing less?

My thoughts ran on. Looking at the shapes there was something. Something. The helm plaque on *Rynosseros*, Meg's taunting, king of all Asia. Bascoeur's unmasked words on the desert.

What? Again what? Alexander defeating the Persians. The Persian Invasion of Greece before, long before, Alexander. Darius and Xerxes. Thermopylae. Ephialtes betraying Leonidas, showing Hydarnes and his Immortals the way over the mountains, letting them . . .

The Immortals! Yes! Oh, yes!

The ten-thousand-strong elite corps of Darius, Xerxes and the Persian kings. The Hundred Square was 100^2. Ten thousand.

The Immortal!

It was there, it was! Had to be! A chess game, some famous classic game called The Immortal.

Still twenty minutes. Still enough time.

"Game precis: The Immortal," I said.

A few seconds more and the confirmation was there, a tight cluster of words and shapes on the screen.

> The Immortal (aka The Immortal Game or The First Brilliant)
>
> Name given to the game played in London, 1851, by Adolf Anderssen (1818-1879) against Lionel Kieseritzky (1806-1853). Noted for its elegance, for its developed offering and acceptance of sacrifice. By sacrificing a Pawn and both Rooks in successive moves (17-19), and then his Queen three moves later (22), Anderssen drew his opponent into a response which allowed checkmate at 23 . . .

Beguiling sacrifice. Namarkon yielding clues, letting me fathom the Knot and who knew what else? Perhaps letting—*letting!*—Bascoeur reveal Alexandrian Book, perhaps feeding, so subtly, ideas into his mind, subliminal messages, mnemonic clues he would pass on, unmasked, as if they were his own—an unwitting Ephialtes betraying the Spartans to the Immortals—or the initial leads to Alexander through the library at Turker Fin.

Again, the terrifying thought came. Was I finding Namarkon only to release him from some ancient refuge or prison? Fulfil some plan?

What to do? Stop? Refuse to go on? My life against the chance of that? The lives of Toban and Emma, of Ephan Sky Namuren and *Eagle*'s crew, how many others? Lives!

I studied the gameplay sequence for The Immortal.

White Anderssen	Black Kieseritzky	White Anderssen	Black Kieseritsky
1 P-K4	P-K4	13 P-R5	Q-N4
2 P-KB4	PxP	14 Q-B3	N-N1
3 B-B4	P-QN4	15 BxP	Q-B3
4 BxNP	Q-RNch	16 N-B3	B-B4
5 K-B1	N-KB3	17 N-Q5	QxP

6 N-KB3	Q-R3	18 B-Q6	BxR
7 P-Q3	N-R4	19 P-K5	QxRch
8 N-R4	P-QB3	20 K-K2	N-QR3
9 N-B5	Q-N4	21 NxPch	K-Q1
10 P-KN4	N-B3	22 Q-Bch!	KxQ
11 R-N1	PxB	23 B-K7mate	
12 P-KR4	Q-N3		

"Display the moves one by one," I said, needing to know one way or the other. "Run—No, cancel that! Run the end-game!"

It had to be, had to be.

After barely a hesitation, it was on the screen: the result of Anderssen surrendering one precious piece after another, teasing, tempting, drawing his opponent on, Black Kieseritzky unable to help himself, fascinated with how Anderssen could possibly win with his depleted force. Then the final display at Move 23, Anderssen's Bishop delivering mate.

Or the one *before* it, the unthinkable surprise of White Anderssen giving up his Queen to achieve check, the move marked with (!). I asked comp to display both moves side by side.

Barely had I asked it and they were there.

"Meg, these are the alignments I want. Only those pieces connecting. And alternate them!"

"You want the other squares to vacate?"

"No! They all stay. But mask link-up. These two alignments, whatever link-up the masks are capable of—this configuration, then the other, superimposed on the sixty-four pattern."

"They've heard you. You have it already."

"Then—"

"Yes."

That word, that voice, echoed in the vast space, coming out of comp, the voice of the entity in the grid, the ghost from the heart of the maze.

"Is it?"

"I am Knot, yes. Namarkon. The 22 did it."

"I'm surprised, Chiras. I see no obligation for you to declare yourself."

"No," the voice answered. "And contrary to how it seems, I am not given to being confessional or melodramatic this way."

"Then why?"

"I am information concealed in information, found by information. There is a true delight in being known for that; I cannot help it. Not poor Dewi's mad desperation to live, his vanity, but a recognition and performance of function. I am a mystery at the centre of a system. You used that information structure to find me. It is very important that you genuinely could have. I've wanted that for as long as I know.

"And think! You were faced with the Knot I provided, like Alexander before the yoke of the chariot at Gordium. You, who by chance, no deed of mine, have Alexander's words on the helm of your ship, who quested for Alexandrian Book. It matters. The images, the associations come to you and from you. You were the one to find me, Captain Tom. You were the key I needed. You! Just as you will be the one to tell my story. It justifies the next move, the change that had to be achieved by the rules of the Antique Men, the ones who made me. Do you know why the Immortal, Captain? That name, the connection with the *corps d'elite* of the Persian kings?"

"Tell me."

"The Immortals were so named because the body of ten thousand always had replacements waiting to fill the vacancies. The group itself was never diminished. It was in fact immortal. I learned that lesson well."

"Your masks," I said. "There would always be willing replacements. Trainees, honoured to be chosen, dedicated, to wear the masks." And I thought of Meg Solles.

"Exactly," the voice said. "And protected by the best oubliettes. The thirty-six."

I did not know what to say or do. I had no plan, no means to eliminate this entity or truly know what I thought of it. The Knot design gave the key pieces, yes, but they were inextricably linked to innocent men and women.

Namarkon must have anticipated that thought. "What would you do? Harm us? Those who bear me?"

"You are in the masks, not the bearers. Crystalline intelligence. AI."

"Very well. But the masks are to these folk as *Rynosseros* is to you. You could not name a price. It is a dilemma such as was handed to Solomon, Pontius Pilate, Alexander of Macedon, to Kieseritzky in 1851."

"Then—"

"The masks are filled with the tags and mnemonics which access the stored data. These minds depend on those. Ask Bascoeur. Ask my Angels. You cannot harm me, dare not, Tom Rynosseros. And in several minutes I will shift my alignment code. My Inner Board will be changed. No conspicuous shoulder patch will find me in this new configuration I am planning, this nearly infinite maze. But, you understand, I *needed* to be found! To be freed! To make that part of *my* story. The ultimate and intrinsic purpose of information *is* to be revealed—that is the imperative I started with. I was an assist, you see, a back-up and enhancement repository for oubliettes. An oubliette to oubliettes in fact. It started so simply. But I needed to be a known dimension of the Antique Men, integral, a refinement in information: mythopoesis, the very fount of meaning, of Alexandrian Book. Nothing more than history is full of, worlds without end. A most enterprising Knot, don't you think?"

There was silence then, welcome but laden. The voice had been calm, controlled, but the words, the smooth rush of what was said, told me that Namarkon was exhilarated, exalted by what was about to happen after so long, unable to resist celebrating such freedom, this great journeying forth.

"You may decide to tell Council how it really is," Namarkon continued, "but each person told will diminish the worth of the oubliettes. Will you muddy this last well of truth, Captain? Or will you leave the illusion of it, which is as true ultimately, as provable and as worthy. There are no absolutes here. The harm I do is subtle, an immortal's game, the only possible dalliance for the long-lived, being midwife to the future."

"Did you send *Eagle*?"

"Of course. It was an honest test. My gamble, yes? You had to earn the privilege of being the key, no less than Alexander earned his Knot by reaching Gordium. Surely that is understandable."

"But had I failed—?"

"Some unsuspecting acolyte would have done what was needed. But I wanted to *earn* this freedom, and you won through. You outsmarted *Eagle*."

I thought of the curve of Ephan's sword, the scream of his ship rolling into the hills. Ephan Sky Namuren had trusted this Namarkon. Trusted enough.

"You struck Villa Chano?"

"Necessary."

"To discourage me from searching."

"To hasten your arrival here, keep you from wasting time. It is why I am changing my pattern, allowing you to watch the re-mazing of my identity. The philosophy of the Immortal. Draw forth the enemy, let him think he is winning, tease him with sacrifice, then become the aggressor."

With me, all of us, as pawns, equally expendable, he did not need to add.

"Did you contact Toban McBanus on the morning of the Chano strike?"

"Enough of this!"

"Please, Namarkon! Did you?"

"No more! You have done well. It is time."

The voice had gone. The hall was silent. I stared at the rows of unmoving figures.

What could I do? Strike at them, try to break masks? The moment I stepped out onto the floor, looked like doing so, Namarkon would fragment, discorporate, flee into the intricate convolutions of the crystalline web formed here. Even were it possible to eliminate the Knot elements, that might not do it either. Namarkon had had all this time to replicate itself, surely, a common template in two or six or sixty masks in the grid, a random point in the molecular lattice linked to another and another and another. What did Bascoeur say: each one with 1900 times the storage capacity of the human mind?

Soon it would be gone, the soul and essence of this superlative AI flitting along the corridors of those living and unliving artefacts.

"Bascoeur?" I called into the shadows of the hall, not knowing what else to do, handing him this Solomon choice as it had been handed to me. "Are you there?"

"Yes, Captain," the answer came, and the field agents moved across the floor: the Angels and their thirty-two fellows, circling the labyrinth, re-making the Hundred Square, restoring the lock, shutting it away...

No, not re-making it. Circling it, but...

"Now!" Bascoeur cried, and the tschinkes, petronels, espandos and archimenters came up and discharged two hundred and sixteen years of dream into the ranks of the living chessboard.

Alexander's solution. Cutting the Knot asunder, not even attempting to unravel it.

There were screams of agony, the sounds of falling bodies, the harsh clatter and shattering of masks on stone. A few of the stricken figures tried to use their own weapons but could barely manage them. While Meg and I watched in horror, the Angels and the perimeter guard acted. Spent weapons were laid aside, the discarded pieces of the sixty-four were taken up and used, systematically, to destroy the minds as surely as booted heels shattered the panes of the masks, crushed their intricate cathedral frames, broke apart their alignments, hallways and hiding places.

Unable to endure more, I turned and left the Great Hall, making my way down corridors until I found a doorway to a deck overlooking the desert.

Bascoeur found me there some time later. He was still masked, still bearing his archimenter as if we had just now met at Saldy's and had yet to find a basis from which to talk.

"Namarkon's dead," I said, watching the sun riding high above the hills.

"I do not know if he is, where he is, or what he is. Some trace may yet remain. We hunt that now."

"If I had known—"

"Tom, let me tell you what I know. And try to imagine what it is like to have guarded such a thing all your life, only to learn this. He made a vital error. For us a crucial error."

"Yes?"

"When he was speaking to you, he said: 'Ask my Angels.' *My*

Angels! He saw us as his. That decided it for us—my brother-sister Angels and me. There had been talk of sacrifice in order to win. We re-evaluated the Inner Square."

"Gado—"

"They were not completely oubliettes any longer," he said.

"What?"

"Namarkon had consumed them all, preparing to leap free. Perhaps he needed to take control lest others catch him in his information trap. He had taken their masks *and* much of their minds. Those gifted men and women, all that learning."

"I don't understand."

"In a sense the Salvation Moons were real."

"Lobotomised?"

"More *and* less than that. Actual implants, coterminous personality units, parts of Namarkon in flesh. He had learned his lesson from Dewi Dammo well, had probably traded for the tech involved. They were the carriers in a skilful deception, ruined, press-ganged into higher service, Namarkon believed. You were right in your suspicions. He had discovered how the masks that defined him and gave him such power were by their nature a control system as well, with the patch as a traditional ritual key in and out. He saw a simple and obvious answer really, used Dewi's implant tech to achieve it.

"The oubliettes once innocently carried their masks into tribal capitals, into the universities and research labs, into the National centres on the coasts, the aerospace and launch installations. Now the Namarkon units would do the same thing, wear the same masks to take the Namarkon personality to those same places, replicating him, placing strategic crystalline extensions during uploads, comp repairs. Chiras was leaving one maze to enter another."

"Do you know what—?"

"The tribal satellites," Bascoeur said. "Crystalline elements of the comsats themselves. Possibly the Armament as well. No-one could touch him: the only home for an information-disseminating Lightning God, what the Elizabethan poet, John Donne, said: 'A maze of life and light and motion is woven'."

We were silent for a time, watching the desert stretching away in a haze of golden light.

I recalled the smiling, gentle folk I had seen tending the gardens, sweeping the walks of Mekkis, and still saw only murder, not truly understanding that greater crime Gado Bascoeur saw in loss of self, loss of brothers and sisters, loss of knowledge.

"I can't accept it. I'm responsible for—"

"No, Tom. No. I am. I chose, and I have killed my own—heart. But at least now you will trust the Antique Men. You will tell others they can, the few we are. And soon you must help me do something."

"Gado, what?"

"My duty. You must tell me how you perceive what happened here. Your story of Chiras Namarkon and the Antique Men. This story. You must tell it all. I am the oubliette, the safe place. I will keep the truth of it. I will listen."